CW00554801

Everything Changes But You

JENNIFER JOYCE

Copyright © 2020 Jennifer Joyce

All rights reserved.

For Chris, Rianne and Isobel.

ABOUT THE AUTHOR

Jennifer Joyce is a writer of romantic comedies. She's been scribbling down bits of stories for as long as she can remember, graduating from a pen to a typewriter and then an electronic typewriter. And she felt like the bee's knees typing on THAT. She now writes her books on a laptop (which has a proper delete button and everything).

Jennifer lives in Oldham, Greater Manchester with her husband Chris and their two daughters, Rianne and Isobel, plus their Jack Russell Luna.

Find out more about Jennifer and her books or subscribe to her newsletter at jenniferjoycewrites.co.uk. You can also find her on social media:

Twitter/Instagram: @writer_jenn

Facebook: facebook.com/jenniferjoycewrites

ALSO BY JENNIFER JOYCE

The Accidental Life Swap
The Single Mums' Picnic Club
The Wedding That Changed Everything
A Beginner's Guide To Saying I Do
The Little Bed & Breakfast by the Sea
The Little Teashop of Broken Hearts
The Wedding Date
The Mince Pie Mix-Up
A Beginner's Guide To Salad
A Beginner's Guide To Christmas
(short story)

ACKNOWLEDGMENTS

Massive thanks to my family for all your support.
An extra big thank you to my mum for the
typewriters so I could write my own stories
growing up – first the manual and then the wonder
that was the electronic typewriter.

Biggest thank you to my husband, Chris and our
daughters, Rianne and Isobel.

Thank you to Ruth Durbridge for editing Everything
Changes But You.

Finally, thank you to you, the reader. I hope you
enjoy Ally's story.

ONE

'Well? What do you think?'

Ally arranged herself in the doorway in what she hoped was a sexy pose; right arm raised above her head and grasping the frame, left hand planted on her hip, glossy lips pouting. Her husband lifted his head away from the television, his eyes following gradually, leaving it until the very last second before they snapped away from the screen. The real test of how she looked would now occur. A brief glance accompanied by some sort of mumbled response would mean she looked okay at best.

'Wow, babe. Are you sure you're only going over to The Farthing for karaoke with the girls?'

His eyes were still on her, the film almost forgotten. This was a very good sign. A very good sign indeed.

'Yes, I'm sure. Why?' Ally pushed her lips back into a pout while blinking slowly from under her long fringe.

Gavin laughed. Amusement had not been the response she'd been hoping for as she'd slipped into her new emerald green dress and her trusty, sky-scraper-but-broken-in heels. She'd blown her hair straight – although it was already starting to curl again – and plucked out the couple of grey hairs that glinted at her in the mirror. She was wearing more make-up than usual in an attempt to cover up the crow's feet she was convinced had embedded themselves into her flesh overnight.

'Are you fishing for compliments?'

Of course she was fishing for compliments! 'No, don't be daft,' Ally tittered unconvincingly as she undraped herself from the doorway and perched on the edge of the sofa where Gavin was watching *The Terminator*. Again. Ally didn't know why he bothered to watch it any more. Surely he knew the words off by heart by now, and it wasn't like it was a repeat-worthy film like *Dirty Dancing*.

'I can't believe you're watching this again.'

'*The Terminator* is a classic. It deserves to be watched again and again so you can appreciate the brilliance.' Gavin's attention was now back on the television, his forearms resting on his knees as he attempted to sit as close to the action as possible.

'And it has nothing at all to do with your childhood crush on Sarah Connor?'

Gavin gave a shrug, eyes still glued to the

2

television. 'I'm a hot-blooded man, Ally.'

'And don't I know it.' Ally slipped off the arm of the sofa, landing on Gavin's lap. Gavin's interest in Arnie waned as he kissed his wife, all thoughts of saving the world from the machines vanishing as he found the zip on the side of the new dress.

'Whoa there, mister. Some of us are going out, you know.' Ally pulled away, tugging the zip back into place.

'You can be five minutes late, can't you?'

'Five whole minutes? Has my birthday arrived a day early?' Ally giggled as she hopped off Gavin's lap and straightened her dress.

'Tease.'

'Jared and Paul will be here any minute. You don't want them to catch us at it, do you?' Gavin wasn't that fussed, to be honest. His mates could wait on the doorstep all night for all he cared. Jared and Paul would understand. 'Besides, you'll have something to look forward to later.'

'Really?'

Ally bent over to kiss Gavin on the lips, purposefully flashing her cleavage as she did so. 'Really. And you know how frisky I get when I'm drunk.'

Gavin reached for his wallet and handed Ally a couple of notes. 'Have a few drinks on me.'

Ally swatted Gavin but she grabbed the money anyway. 'What are you planning on doing with the boys tonight?'

'Beer, pizza, poker. The usual.' Tuesdays were

set in stone. Ally would meet up with the girls for karaoke and a gossip while Gavin invited the boys round to slob out.

'Well, have fun.' Ally grabbed her handbag, making sure she had her purse (with Gavin's extra money nestled safely inside), her mobile and lip gloss. 'I'll see you and your little friend later.'

Ally winked at Gavin while he covered his crotch. 'Hey, less of the little. You'll offend him.'

'I'll make it up to him later, don't worry.' Ally gave Gavin one last kiss and skipped away before he could haul her off to the bedroom. Sarah Connor would have to do for now.

Ally closed the front door behind her softly, smoothing her dress down once more before setting off for the pub. Their first home together had been a poky little flat with peeling wallpaper and a dodgy boiler, but Ally and Gavin had made the decision to upgrade a year ago. The terraced house on MacMillan Road was almost as tiny as the flat but it had a little yard at the back and, more importantly, it was four doors down from their local pub. Despite Ally's proximity to The Farthing, she was still the last of her group to arrive, but the karaoke machine was still being set up, so at least she wasn't *too* late.

'Here she is!' Ally's sister stood up, one hand holding her glass of wine, the other pointing at Ally as she headed towards their table. 'The almost-birthday-girl. Say ta-ra to your twenties!'

'Oh, God. Don't remind me.' Ally slumped into her seat and dropped her head into her hands. 'How can I be *thirty* already? It only feels like yesterday that I was at school.'

'You wish it was only yesterday. You're practically an old woman now. You'll be drawing your pension in no time.'

'Cheeky cow.' Ally glared at her sister. Freya was only eleven months younger than Ally so she wasn't so sprightly herself. 'But, as a pensioner, I can't afford to buy my own drinks any more, so you'll have to provide me with alcohol, being a young whippersnapper and everything.'

'Whippersnapper? God, you *are* old.' Freya shook her head at her sister, oozing sorrow. 'I'll go and get another bottle of wine. You missed the first.'

Freya tottered to the bar while Ally's best friend, Francine, gave her hand a squeeze. 'You're not that old, chick. I'll be forty in a couple of years. Now *that's* ancient.'

'You're right. I'm a spring chicken compared to you.'

Francine nudged Ally but she was smiling. 'Wait until you have kids. *Then* you'll feel old. I live for our karaoke nights. It's the only freedom I get. How sad is that?'

'Then we'd better enjoy ourselves, hadn't we?' Ally searched the bar for Freya, wondering where her wine was. She was parched, but it seemed Freya was too busy flirting with the young barman to provide the much-needed alcohol to her elders. 'So what are we singing tonight?'

'Like you have to ask?' Francine sang 'Mustang Sally' every week, without fail. It wasn't a Karaoke Tuesday without The Commitments.

'I can't decide between a bit of Adele or something retro.' Dee, the fourth member of their group, tilted her head to one side as she weighed up her options.

'What's the retro option?' Ally asked.

'Eternal Flame?'

Ally and Francine sucked in their breath before nodding vigorously. Retro it was.

'Look what I managed to wrangle.' Freya returned to the table, waving a bottle of wine in each hand. 'Two for the price of one. *And* I've got a date for Friday. He's pretty cute, isn't he?'

Four heads swivelled around to the barman, who gave a little wave.

'He is cute but isn't he a bit young?' Ally wasn't convinced he was legally allowed behind the bar.

'Is he even old enough to be in here without a responsible adult?' Honestly, he looked like he could be a classmate of Francine's twelve-year-old daughter.

'He's twenty-one.'

Ally and Francine gaped at Freya while Dee gave an appreciative nod. 'Go, Freya. The young ones are the best.'

'Are they?' Ally wouldn't know. She'd been with Gavin since they were fifteen – although they'd had

a bit of a break when Ally went away to university –
so she'd never experienced the younger man.

'God, yeah.' Dee nodded with vigour. 'Think of
all that energy they've got.'

Ally would rather not. Gavin had enough energy
for her. Besides, he'd got past the spotty back
stage and Ally wasn't willing to go back to *that*.

'I'll stick to my Gavin, thanks.'

'And what if *Jason* offered it to you on a plate?'
Freya hopped onto the table, toppling a glass over
with her bum in the process, but luckily it was
empty. 'What if he came in here, right now, and
asked you to ravish him?' She patted her thighs and
threw back her head. 'Hop on board, Ally. I've got
to have you right now.'

Ally scoffed. 'Jason would never say that.' If
only! 'And I'd have to decline anyway because I
love my husband and would never cheat on him.'

'Not even with the gorgeous Jason? But you've
had a crush on him for ages.'

'It's only a silly little work crush. I wouldn't
actually do anything about it.'

'*I'd* give it some serious thought.' Francine's
confession made Ally's eyes widen. She'd been
married far longer than Ally *and* she had three kids.
'What? He's gorgeous. Imagine grabbing hold of
that arse.'

The table erupted into giggles and the wine was
poured. This was what Ally enjoyed most about
their karaoke nights. It was great to get up on the
little stage and throw herself into her chosen song,

imagining she was Mariah Carey – which she most definitely was not – but it was spending time with the girls that she savoured, gossiping and sharing secrets, no matter how silly.

A sudden squeal filled the pub as Keith Barry, karaoke extraordinaire, plugged the microphone into his machine. Keith Barry was fat and balding, but thought he was some sort of love god and had a tendency to wear shiny gold shirts and fistfuls of sovereign rings.

'Now, now ladies. There's no rush. I'm here all night.' Keith Barry rasped into his microphone, out of breath and oozing sweat from lugging the equipment from his van. 'Form an orderly queue if you'd like to have a go with Uncle Keith. But don't tell the missus.' He winked and laughed at his own 'joke'. Nobody else joined in, but that didn't stop our Keith. 'My equipment's up and ready for action. So come on ladies, get stuck in, you randy mares.' Chortle chortle.

'Uncle Keith?' Dee shuddered. 'He's like the dirty perverted uncle you only ever see at family weddings who gets pissed and presses his hard on into your hip after forcing you to dance.' She took in the tableful of creased brows. 'Is that just me then?'

'Er, yeah.' Freya shuffled away from her best friend. They'd been friends since nursery but that was the first time that little confession had slipped out.

'Oh, chick.' Francine reached across the table to

squeeze poor Dee's hand. 'I'd avoid him from now on if I were you.'

'I'd chop his balls off.' Freya caught her best friend's eye and they burst out laughing. If Freya had her way, every man within the Greater Manchester area would have his testicles hacked off. Even Lovely Paul, once Freya's boyfriend of eighteen months and now a good friend of Gavin's, would be a eunuch for some crime or other in Freya's mind.

'Hey, what's going on over here then, ladies?' Their laughter caught the attention of Keith Barry, who was leaning in closer, one bushy eyebrow raised. 'Come on, share the joke. We like ladies to share, don't we?' He shouted across to the twenty-one-year-old barman, who smiled good-naturedly before ducking down and busying himself with the dishwasher.

Ally leaned in towards her friends, her voice hushed as she spoke out of the corner of her mouth. 'Is that supposed to have sexual connotations?'

Dee gave a shrug – like she knew what 'connotations' meant. 'Who cares? I call group song!' Without waiting for an answer, she grasped her friends by the hand, shoving two towards the stage and the slobbering Keith Barry before returning for the third.

'Four at once, eh?' Keith Barry looked as though all his Christmases had come at once. Freya imagined sharpening her bollock-hacking scissors.

They sang 'Like a Virgin', with Freya gyrating against Dee in a very non-virginal manner. Under normal circumstances Ally would have been mortified, but sod it. She was turning thirty tomorrow. *Thirty.* She was going to enjoy herself tonight, no matter what. Even Francine, the most reserved of the group, got into it, shimmying out of her shrug before whipping it off, lassoing it around her head and chucking it out into the crowd. Ally felt alive as she bounced around while waving her arms and belting out the number until her lungs ached. She wanted to bottle this feeling, to relive it over and over again.

'Fantastic, ladies. Fantastic.' Keith Barry applauded as the song came to an end. He whipped a polka-dotted handkerchief from his pocket and mopped his brow. 'What are you going to sing next? "Patricia the Stripper"?' He gave them a seedy wink, which sobered Ally enough to dodge the karaoke host as he lunged at them. Poor Dee wasn't quick enough and Keith's sweaty hands gripped her in a too-tight hug. 'Let's have a round of applause for these ladies. Weren't they great?'

The group returned to their table, draining their glasses and refilling them to the brim. This karaoke business was thirsty work.

'So, what are we singing next?' Freya asked before they'd even caught their breath back. 'Shall I grab the book?'

Keith Barry and his equipment were long gone by

the time Ally and co were turfed out of The Farthing, clinging to one another and giving an encore of 'Like a Virgin', which was still the highlight of their evening. Francine had given her usual performance of 'Mustang Sally', with Keith taking the shine off the experience by making vulgar gestures throughout, and though Dee's 'Eternal Flame' had been beautiful, it couldn't beat the fun they'd had as a quartet.

'We've got to get up for work in the morning.' Francine groaned as they stumbled along the pavement towards Ally's house.

'Drinking this much was a bad idea.' Ally could already feel the onset of a hangover.

'Are you kidding? Drinking this much was the best idea we've ever had.' Freya broke away from the group, throwing her arms up to the dark sky. 'I feel fantastic. I don't even want to go home yet. Shall we go into town?'

'No,' Ally and Francine chorused while Dee hissed that she would *love* to go into town. She wanted to dance and flirt and drink some more.

'Don't forget we're not as young as you two. I've got three kids to get ready for school in the morning.' Feeling a chill, Francine went to pull her shrug back into place but she was no longer wearing it. 'And Ally's thirty now, remember.'

'Hey, I'm still twenty-nine.' Ally peered at Francine's wrist as she tapped her watch. It was after midnight. 'Shit. I'm *thirty*.'

She wanted to cry, right there in the street, and

11

it wasn't only because she'd had too much to drink. How could she be thirty so soon? Thirty was old, ancient, decrepit and she didn't want to be those things. She wanted to be young, youthful, *virginal*. Alright, maybe virginal was pushing it. She did quite like sex. But she didn't want to be *thirty*.

'Sorry, chick.' Francine patted her on the arm, which only made her feel worse. Francine *knew*. She'd been there, washed and ironed the T-shirt. She'd passed Go and everything, and she knew it was all downhill from here. *That's* why Francine was being sympathetic.

'Do you think people will mistake us for mother and daughter when we're out in public now?'

Freya thought she was being amusing, but she was not. 'Eleven months, Freya.'

'Eleven glorious months of youth.' Freya caught the thunderous look on her sister's face and that, coupled with the amount of alcohol Ally had consumed, made her reconsider the string of jibes she'd pre-prepared weeks in advance. 'I'll stop now, I swear. And we've walked past your house.'

The four staggered back towards Ally's house and fell inside, shushing each other with over-exaggerated fingers to their lips. A taxi was called and another bottle of wine opened for the wait. Ally crept up the stairs once the others had left and slipped off her dress, neither bothering to change into pyjamas nor remove her make-up before climbing into the warm bed.

'Good night?' Gavin was a comfort, anchoring

her to the bed as her fuzzy head made Ally feel like she was floating up to the ceiling.

'Brilliant night. I'm a little bit pissed.'

Gavin laughed. 'A little bit?' Ally nodded in the dark. 'Too pissed to remember your earlier promise?'

'God, no.' Ally somehow managed to climb astride her husband without damaging anything vital, but struggled when it came to locating the box of condoms from the drawer beside the bed.

'Why don't we forget about them?' Gavin suggested.

Ally continued to rummage in the drawer, her fingers slow and clumsy. '*Did* we forget to buy some?'

'No, I mean why don't we stop using them?'

Oh. Ally's fingers stopped their search and instead slammed the drawer shut. 'Not this again. Please.' She was too drunk and knackered for this old argument. They'd moved into the slightly bigger house a year ago, and ever since then Gavin had been desperate to fill it to the brim with babies.

'It's got to happen sometime, Ally. You're thirty now.' Like she needed reminding! 'You've been saying we should wait for ages now, but how long do you want to wait? Until it's too late?'

'I'm thirty, Gavin, not sixty.'

'But I want us to have a family. Don't you?'

Ally didn't answer as she slid back under the covers, her back against Gavin's chest. She wasn't nearly ready for babies. And she wasn't sure she ever would be.

TWO

Oh, God. Ally was in the clutches of a hangover before she'd even opened her eyes, her head throbbing on the pillow, her gut churning and threatening to spill at the slightest movement. Her eyelids refused to lift but that was fine by Ally. She didn't want to open her eyes anyway. A whimper escaped her dry lips as it dawned on her what day it was.

It was her birthday.

'Oh no.' The words were barely distinguishable as they bubbled from her lips. She reached out for Gavin, needing the comfort of his familiar skin against her own, but the bed was empty. 'Gavin?' She prised her eyes open and eased herself into a sitting position. Her head felt like concrete, heavy and solid as she attempted to keep it upright.

The bedroom was empty and she knew Gavin wasn't in the shower as he was the world's loudest cleanser, the shower radio blaring almost as loudly as Gavin's singing. Ally was sure even the volume of the gushing water was raised when Gavin stepped under the stream.

But there was no sound emitting from the bathroom. The rumpled sheets beside Ally were still warm so he hadn't been gone that long. Ally squinted at the clock and groaned when she realised her alarm would be yelling at her any minute now. Gavin must have sneaked off to work early in a huff after their row last night.

Well, stuff him. If he wanted to sulk, let him sulk. It was her birthday and she should be enjoying the day, being pampered and having her mind taken off the fact that she was another year closer to receiving her free bus pass, not worrying about stupid quarrels.

Ally's throbbing brain sighed with relief as she sank back down into the pillow, closing her scratchy eyes to make the most of the final two minutes before she had to punch her alarm.

'Happy birthday, darling.'

Ally lifted one eyelid and, in spite of her lethargic muscles, managed to smile up at her husband.

'What are you doing?'

Gavin glanced down at the breakfast tray in his hands and then at his wife. 'Breakfast in bed.' What else could he be doing with a tray of tea and toast? 'I'm sorry about last night. I don't mean to go on at you, but we're in our thirties now. We need to start thinking about this kind of thing.'

Ally's smile drooped into a scowl. 'What is this? Breakfast in bed or a lecture? I don't want to think about babies. I don't want to think about anything right now. I've got a raging hangover and want to die.'

'You never want to think about babies, hangover or not.' Gavin dumped the breakfast tray on the bed and Ally had to leap to steady it before the tea sloshed onto the covers. The sudden action caused her to retch but nothing came up. Closing her eyes, she took deep breaths to calm the nausea, and when she opened them again, the room was empty. The front door slammed shut a moment later, followed by the piercing squeal of her alarm and the noise of both made Ally wince in pain.

Why did she need a baby when she was already married to the biggest, sulkiest baby of all?

Ally was not in the mood for the bus ride to work, with every sharp turn and sudden stop making her want to chuck up her breakfast. The air was stuffy, the seats cramped and there was a kid in a buggy kicking hell out of the side of the bus. The metallic thump, thump, thump was driving her crazy, so it was a relief to finally emerge into the fresh air, away from the noise and chatter. Westerly's Coach Tours was a short walk from the bus stop, but it was nowhere near enough to clear her head before she limped into the building.

'You look how I feel.' Francine flashed a tiny

smile of solidarity from behind her reception desk as Ally threw herself into one of the plush blue chairs in the waiting area. 'We had way too much to drink last night.' Ally nodded, unable to speak as her mouth was dry and fuzzy. 'It didn't help that Maisie was up three times during the night.'

'Three times?' Horror forced Ally's voice into action. 'Isn't she six? I thought they slept through after a few months.'

'Ha! That's what they'd have you believe. Charlotte didn't sleep through until she was nineteen months. But even when they do start sleeping through, anything can keep them awake. It was nightmares for Maisie last night, poor chick.'

'Doesn't Mike ever get up with them?'

Francine spluttered. 'You must be joking. That man could sleep through an earthquake. Or pretend to, at least. But I do get a lie-in every other week when he takes the girls over to his mum's for a couple of hours. It's a blessing she hates me, really.'

A lie-in *every other week?* That was barbaric. Why would anybody want to put themselves through such hell?

'I think I'd better be getting up to the office.' Ally heaved herself out of her chair and began her trek up the old spiral staircase. The building was a former bank, but while it was beautiful and Ally loved the remaining original features, she would prefer the use of a lift, especially on days like these when each step felt like her skull was being rattled.

'Oh, I almost forgot. Happy birthday!'

Ally continued up the stairs, pretending she hadn't heard her friend. She was struggling to deal with this horrendous hangover without adding her birthday woes to the mix.

Ally worked in the HR department of Westerly's, located at the front of the building on the first floor. Sunlight streamed through the large windows, which was usually delightful but today was a menace. Being early spring, the sunlight was weak, but it was still enough to send searing pain through Ally's already aching head.

'You look like shit.'

Ally wandered over to the windows and began closing the blinds. 'Thanks, Jason. It's good to know I look as bad as I feel.'

'Are you okay?'

'Hangover.'

'Ah.' Jason gave a slow nod of his head, a smile lighting up his face. Ally looked away. She couldn't stomach her manager's handsome face, not today. She couldn't bear to see him in his charcoal suit, tailored to perfection and hinting at the amazing body Ally could only imagine was underneath. Watching the gorgeous Jason was usually the only thing that got her through each working day, but it was too much today.

'Jesus, you look like *shit*.' Ally's colleague strode into the room wearing a tiny black skirt and a silky red blouse. Ally counted the buttons that were actually fastened – three – before averting her gaze. Of all the things Ally didn't want to see that morning, Kelly's black lacy bra was in the top three.

'Thank you, Kelly. It has been noted already.'

'Ooh, touchy or what?' Kelly sauntered over to her desk, wincing as she pulled out her chair. Ally noticed the bandage, which was probably wider than her skirt, wrapped around Kelly's wrist. Ally imagined she'd sprained it during some sort of sexual activity and the thought had her reaching for the metal waste paper bin, just in case she had to hurl. Kelly Fox was young and beautiful, with shiny blonde hair cut into a severe bob with a short, sharp fringe. She frolicked about the office in next to nothing, flashing her ridiculously long legs and perky tits, bringing with her tales of rowdy, drunken nights. Even outside there was no hiding from Ms Fox as she drove around in a flashy sports car, music blaring.

'What's happened here?' Jason had crossed the office and was holding Kelly's hand in his, stroking a finger along the bandage. Ally would sprain her wrist too if it meant Jason would hold her hand with such tenderness, but then Ally wasn't enjoying a supposedly secret fling with the gorgeous Jason.

Kelly Fox was a lucky, lucky woman.

'Oh that. It's nothing, really. I was out with Martine last night and we got *really* wasted.'

For a change, Ally thought, her mouth filling with bitterness. Kelly was always getting wasted and this Martine girl featured in most of her drunken antics.

'We were dancing on a podium and, daft cow that I am, I fell off. It hurt like hell but it was so funny.'

Yes, hilarious. Ally fell about laughing every time she came close to breaking a bone too.

Ally placed the waste paper bin on the floor and nudged it back under her desk. 'If you were so wasted, why do you look...' Ally wanted to say fresh-faced and beautiful, but she couldn't bring herself to compliment Kelly. 'Normal?'

Kelly's damaged hand was still in Jason's, so she placed the other to her chest. 'Oh, sweetie. That's because I'm still young. When I'm pushing forty, I'm sure I'll look like shit too.'

Pushing forty? *Pushing forty?* 'I am nowhere near forty, thank you very much.'

Kelly's eyebrows arched in mock surprise and right then, hangover or not, Ally wanted to stride across the office and slap her youthful face. Kelly was twenty-two – practically a *child* still – and Ally now hated that most about the girl.

'Now, now, ladies. I'm sure we've got more important things to be getting on with than having a catfight.' Jason released Kelly's hand and backed away before making his way towards his internal office at the end of the room. Kelly arranged herself neatly on her chair before leaning across the desk, resting her cheek on her good hand.

'Was that true back then? Are you really not nearly forty?'

Ally jabbed at her computer's power button,

pretending she couldn't hear Kelly's words or feel her poison seeping into her pores. She busied herself with her in-tray and clearing out her email's inbox, but she couldn't concentrate as she worried about Gavin and their rows. They had a great marriage and rarely argued over anything more serious than who had used the last of the loo roll without replacing it, but this baby thing was starting to eat away at them.

'I've got a pile of filing to do. I'm going down to the basement.' Kelly didn't usually inform Ally of her whereabouts, despite Ally being of a slightly higher rank, but she always made it known, quite loudly, when she was going to the filing room. The filing room was down in the basement and only HR had access to the key, meaning it was the perfect rendezvous for Kelly and Jason. They thought they were being clever and discreet, but Ally knew exactly what was going on. Why else would Kelly disappear with a pile of papers to be filed and return with the exact same number of sheets?

Ally counted down from ten, muttering under her breath. '…five, four, three, two, one.'

'I just need to go and see Malcolm about next week's meeting.' Right on cue, Jason strode out of his office. Ally picked up her phone and dialled down to reception.

'Jason's on his way down,' she told Francine.

'Yes, I see him.' Francine lowered her voice as the man himself obviously came into view. 'And yes, he's gone down to the basement. Funny,

22

Kelly's already down there.'

'That *is* funny and it's also taking the piss. Do they think I'm going to sit here and work while they skive off? Two can play at that game.'

Ally hung up the phone, already reaching for her post-its and scribbling a note, sticking it to Jason's door before trudging down the stairs.

'If they ask, you saw me heading out towards the depot,' Ally told Francine as she slipped on her jacket.

Francine gave Ally the thumbs up. 'Will do, chick. Where are you really going?'

'To see Gavin.'

THREE

Ally had never learned to drive so it was fortunate that Westerly's and her father's garage, where Gavin worked, were only minutes apart. Gavin would usually drop Ally off in the mornings – sulking days aside – and pick her up in the evenings, depending on his workload. Ally wandered across Westerly's car park and out through the gates, but instead of crossing over to the depot, she continued down the road. She smelled the familiar fumes as she approached the garage and was immediately taken back to her childhood, to the summer holidays she spent with Freya and Gavin, messing about with old, rusty bits of engines that her father had passed on to them. Ally hadn't been really that interested in the inner workings of cars, but Gavin and Freya were fascinated, so she'd tagged along.

Music blared between the clanging and squeals

within the garage as the mechanics worked away. Ally didn't know how they could bear the deafening sounds all day, and she was almost grateful she only had Kelly to put up with in her office. She took a tentative step onto the oily concrete, making her way to the rickety desk in the dark corner that constituted the office area. Papers and dirty cups littered the desk and lever arch files were left open, further papers peeking out of the plastic covers. Ally's father had never been very good at the admin side of the business. He could transform a heap of junk on three wheels into a dazzling, purring motor but had yet to master a sustainable filing system. Ally couldn't help grabbing a handful of loose papers and finding a home for them.

'I wouldn't bother if I were you.' Freya had spotted her sister and was making her way across the assault course of engine parts and tools, wiping her greasy hands on her overalls as she went. 'They'll be a mess again within five minutes.'

Ally finished the job anyway. 'Is Gavin here?'

'He's out on a job. Shouldn't be too long though. Do you want a brew while you wait?'

Ally pulled the rickety chair out from underneath the desk and perched on it while Freya put the kettle on. Bob had expected his son to follow in his mechanic footsteps, but Ally's brother wasn't interested in cars, apart from their ability to get him from A to B, and it was his daughter who inherited the engine-loving gene. Ally had thought her sister just wanted to be like Charlene from

Neighbours and the novelty would pass, but she'd become an apprentice after leaving school and the novelty still had its shine thirteen years later.

'How can you stand this noise?' Ally asked as she took the chipped mug from Freya. Her head felt like it was splitting in two.

Freya shrugged as she blew on her own mug of coffee. 'You get used to it.'

'Even with a hangover?'

'I guess so. Plus, I've taken some pretty heavy duty painkillers I had left from my accident last year. They seem to be working pretty well.'

'You're supposed to dispose of those at the chemist or something. And should you be working with machinery after taking them?'

Freya patted Ally on the shoulder. 'Ever the sensible big sister.'

'Not that sensible, drinking so much during the week. I feel like I'm dying.'

'It's not that bad, surely?' Gavin asked. Ally looked up to see him standing in the gaping mouth of the garage doorway and her stomach turned in on itself, which was ridiculous. She shouldn't feel nervous about seeing Gavin. He was her husband.

'It is. Can I use it as an excuse for my grumpiness this morning?'

'It depends. What can I use as an excuse for being an arsehole?' A smile twitched at Gavin's lips and Ally knew she'd been forgiven.

'There is no excuse for you being an arsehole,' Freya told Gavin. 'I'm afraid it's just who you are.'

Freya backed away as Ally and Gavin glared at her.

'Shall we go and get a coffee?' Gavin suggested and Ally agreed, dumping her almost-full mug on the desk.

Ally and Gavin often met up for lunch at Diner 360, a café around the corner from the garage. It was small and a little bit grubby but it meant they got to snatch a few more minutes with each other. Gavin ordered his usual of spam on toast with lashings of brown sauce – the thought of which turned Ally's stomach that day – while Ally settled for a vanilla slice and a strong cup of coffee.

'I just don't understand what you're waiting for, Ally. We've been together for years, practically since we were kids, and we have the house now.'

'Maybe that's it.' Ally picked at her cake but couldn't bring herself to put any of it in her mouth. She'd lost her appetite as soon as the baby conversation had started up again. 'We've been together since we were kids. We haven't *lived*, not really. We work, we come home, we go to work again. Karaoke and poker on Tuesdays, pint and a kebab on Fridays. We go to your mum and dad's every Saturday evening, mine every Sunday afternoon.'

'So you're bored with me. Again.'

Ally and Gavin had been together since they were fifteen, but there had been a brief period when they split up while Ally was away at university. It had been Ally's decision to end their relationship just weeks into her course, not because she didn't love Gavin – he was her first love and her best friend – but because they were both so young and she couldn't hack the long distance thing.

'It wasn't like that. I wasn't *bored* with you.' Ally brushed the cake crumbs from her fingers and folded her arms across her chest. 'Besides, you got over me pretty quickly.' Ally clenched her jaw and blinked away the sting of tears, determined not to cry over it. It had been twelve years but jealousy still burned when she thought about Helena. Ally had been on a few dates in between studying but never anything serious, so she was shocked to arrive home for Christmas and discover Gavin had a new girlfriend. An actual *girlfriend*. She'd only been gone a matter of months but there he was, looking cosy and loved up with *her*.

'You know I wasn't over you.' Gavin reached for Ally's hand but she snatched it away. 'I ended it with Helena as soon as you came home for the summer and told me you'd made a huge mistake. I still loved you, Ally, you know that.'

Ally did know that, and she loved him too. So why was she getting itchy feet again?

'I just need a bit more excitement in my life. I don't want to end up like Francine, tied down to the kids. She has one night out a week, you know. One lousy night.'

'It's better than nothing,' Gavin pointed out but it only fuelled Ally's argument.

'Exactly! I don't want to settle for "better than

nothing". I want to be free to *live*.'

'So are you saying you never want to have kids?'

Ally thought carefully before answering. It probably was what she was saying, but she couldn't tell Gavin that, not when he was so desperate to start a family. So she decided her best option was to lie.

'No, I'm not saying that. I'm saying I just need a bit more time to be me first.'

Ally stopped off at the reception desk when she returned to work. Her hangover, coupled with the stress of yet another baby conversation, was making her head pound.

'Do you have any paracetamol on you?'

Francine grabbed her handbag and produced a blister pack of paracetamol. Of course she had some – it was highly likely that Francine carried a whole first aid kit in her handbag, just in case. Ally took a couple of pills before going up to the office where she found a card and a stale-looking bun from the canteen.

'Why didn't you tell us it was your birthday?' Jason asked as she tore at the envelope. 'The woman on reception told us.'

'It wasn't something I wanted reminding of, but thanks.' She held up the card and the bun before returning them to her desk.

'We should go out after work for a celebratory drink.' Ally's mood picked up at Jason's suggestion, but it plummeted again as he turned to Kelly.

'What do you think? Are you in?'

'I suppose I could squeeze you into my busy social life.' Kelly fluttered her eyelashes at Jason before turning to smile sweetly at Ally. 'So, the big four-o, is it?'

Ally decided to ignore Kelly. It was usually the best option. 'I'll just have to let Gavin know. He's supposed to be picking me up and taking me over to my parents'. We're having a birthday tea.'

Kelly doubled over, clutching her stomach and banging her good hand on the desk as she roared with laughter. 'A birthday tea? How old are you? Forty or *four*?'

'I am *not* forty,' Ally snapped. She took a cleansing breath and turned to Jason. 'But, yes, I'd love to go for a quick drink tonight.'

Ally dragged Francine along with her that evening, reassuring her it would only be a quick drink to say happy birthday. Francine stayed for one very brief and non-alcoholic drink before she dashed away to pick the children up from the childminder. Ally, being child-free, decided it was her duty to stay for another. And another, until she'd lost count and was feeling rather tipsy.

'We should do this more often, you know. We never go out as a team, do we? And we are a team. Me and you.' Ally placed a hand on Jason's chest. It felt rock hard beneath her fingers. 'And her, I suppose.'

As though on cue, Kelly arrived with another round of drinks. Ally didn't care that she couldn't remember how many drinks she'd put away in such a short space of time. It didn't really matter. The most important thing was she was having fun. She was *living* for a change. She wasn't going home to put the tea on. She wasn't slouched on the sofa, wasting her life on soaps and mediocre crime dramas.

'Is she pissed already?' Kelly asked Jason as Ally stumbled over her own feet.

'No, lady. I am not pissed. Not even a little bit.' Ally looked Kelly up and down – she really was stunning, the bitch – and spluttered when she spotted the glass of orange juice in her dainty fingers. She'd been drinking orange juice all evening. 'We know *you're* not pissed. And you say I act like a four-year-old. You're not pregnant, are you?' Ally gasped and looked at Jason. The thought made her feel depressed, the sparkle of the vodka and cokes she'd been sinking vanishing in an instant. She didn't want babies with Jason – she didn't want Jason herself, not seriously – but she didn't want him procreating with *her*.

'No, I'm not pregnant. I just don't feel the need to get wasted night after night. Unlike some people not so very far away.'

'Ha!' Kelly was wasted practically every night of the week and was constantly regaling Jason with her tales of debauchery. Ally was about to point this out when her phone began to ring.

'Where are you?' Gavin asked her once she'd moved to a quiet corner of the pub, knocking a low

31

barstool over in the process.

'I'm at the pub. I told you.' Ally rubbed at her calf. That was going to bruise, she was sure.

'You said you were going for a quick drink. It's nearly seven.'

'So?'

'So we're all waiting for you.'

Ally removed her phone from her ear and stuck her tongue out at it. Did Gavin have to be such an old woman? Couldn't he be more like Jason? Fun and free and non-whingey?

'And I'll be there.'

'Do you want me to come and pick you up?'

That's all Ally needed — Gavin charging into the pub and embarrassing her. 'No, it's okay. I've already ordered a taxi. It's on its way.' It wasn't a lie, not a proper one. Ally was planning on phoning for a taxi and probably would have done so already had Gavin not interrupted her.

'Okay, we'll see you soon then.'

'Yep. See you soon.' Ally ended the call and slipped the phone back into her handbag before addressing her work colleagues. 'Is it my round?

FOUR

It took another phone call from Gavin before Ally prised herself from the pub, staggering towards the waiting taxi and the worried looking driver.

'Are you sure you won't come into town with us?' Jason asked as he emerged from the pub behind her with Kelly dangling off his arm.

'She can't. She's going to her little tea party, remember.' Ally wondered whether twisting Kelly's sprained wrist would be too cruel under the circumstances. 'Or was it a teddy bears picnic?'

Not cruel in the slightest. 'It's a birthday tea, actually.'

Kelly pressed her lips together as she nodded sagely. 'Of course it is. We hope you have a good time.' She winked at Jason. 'We will, won't we, babe?'

Ally hung back as Jason and Kelly wandered over to a second waiting taxi and stuck two fingers up at the couple's back. It wasn't mature, but then she didn't *want* to be mature.

'Alright, love?' The taxi driver tapped the notice warning of a clean-up charge as Ally crawled into the car.

No, she wasn't alright. Time was hurtling away and there was nothing she could do about it. But she wasn't going to be sick, which was all the driver cared about. 'Fine, thanks.' She slammed the door shut and gave her parents' address before texting Grumpy Gavin, letting him know she was definitely on her way this time. Her fingers felt sluggish and fat so it took the entire journey to compose the text, but she sent it anyway, despite now being outside the house. It seemed like a waste of her efforts otherwise.

'Look at the state of you. A quick drink you said.' Gavin had rushed outside, which was handy as Ally didn't think her legs were in working order any more. 'Thanks, mate. Keep the change.' He paid the driver before helping Ally into the house where she was greeted by her entire family, plus a gaudy banner tacked above the fireplace. What was happy about birthdays anyway?

'Happy birthday, little sis.' Jared stepped towards Ally to give her a hug while his girlfriend, who had never witnessed a sloshed Ally, remained where she was and gave a tense little wave.

'How much have you had to drink? Or are you still pissed from last night?' Freya asked.

Ally was suddenly starting to feel a bit sick and

slumped onto the sofa. Jimmy, the youngest Williams sister and baby of the family, scooted over to the other end of the sofa. 'You're not going to throw up, are you?'

'No.' Ally held her head in her hands, not entirely sure that was true. Her stomach swilled with alcohol and too little food.

'We've already eaten,' her mum said. 'But I've left yours in the oven. Would you like me to bring it in for you?' Ally shook her head. She couldn't think of anything worse than putting food in her mouth, sure she'd see it moments later, covering her shoes. 'I'll bring the cake through then. Turn the lights off, Bob.'

Oh God, no. Not candles. Ally could almost hear Kelly pissing herself laughing at the childishness of it all. Kelly was out having a jolly time with the gorgeous Jason while Ally was having a tea party like a toddler. Why couldn't Ally have a life more like Kelly's? One with excitement and thrilling tales of debauchery? Kelly was young, free and single with spare cash flowing out of her ears by the looks of things. She had a fantastic life with a flashy car and, more than likely, an amazing apartment to match. She wasn't holed up in a tiny terraced house, being pressured into filling it with kids before her ovaries shrivelled to dust.

Linda sang as she brought the cake into the sitting room, encouraging the others to join in too. The room filled with the joyous voices of Ally's family. Now she really did feel sick.

The cake was one of her mother's own creations; a vanilla sponge filled with raspberry buttercream and jam, and topped with yet more buttercream and delicate sugar paste roses. Five candles flickered from the centre. Ally guessed thirty candles wouldn't fit on the cake and was glad. Seeing the physical reminder of her lost youth would only increase her nausea.

'Make a wish then,' Linda insisted as she stood before Ally, the candles still blazing.

Did she have to? What would Kelly think if she could see Ally now?

'Come on, Ally. I'm dying for a slice of Mum's cake.' Jared rubbed his hands together and Ally knew she couldn't deprive her brother of cake. No matter how humiliating this was, she knew her mum's baking was divine.

'Fine.' Ally closed her eyes and took a deep breath. *I wish I had a life like Kelly's*. She let out a puff of air, extinguishing two of the candles. Trying again, the remaining candles were blown out and Ally slumped back against the sofa, job done.

'I take it everyone's having a slice?' Linda asked as Bob switched the lights back on.

'Can I take mine upstairs? I've got to finish my English coursework.'

Freya gaped at her sister. Jimmy was such a swot. 'Don't be a party pooper. You can do your homework later.'

'It needs to be in by the end of the week and I've got loads to do.' Jimmy pushed herself off the sofa, ignoring Freya's mocking face. *She* wasn't going to end up working in their dad's grotty old garage. She was going to work hard and get into university, like Ally had.

Ally watched as a hazy Jimmy left with her cake, a pile of books tucked under her arm. The room began to take on a fluid form, undulating in waves before her eyes. The past two days of drinking had caught up with her and Ally feared she was about to pass out.

'Are you okay? Do you want me to take you home?' Gavin appeared at her side, but while Ally could hear him perfectly, he was nothing but a mass of blotchy colours. She'd felt tipsy earlier, but she must have had more to drink than she'd thought. She couldn't remember ever having felt this bad, not even during freshers week at university when she couldn't even recollect her own name.

'Jeez, how bad is she?' Freya asked as Gavin helped Ally off the sofa only for her legs to buckle beneath her.

'I think I'm going to have to carry her to the car. Can you get the door for me?'

Ally felt her body being lifted into the air but she couldn't feel Gavin's hands beneath her. She was floating through the air, her eyes now closed against the swimming room. There were voices around her, but she could no longer distinguish who the voices belonged to and all the words blended into one mass of sound.

'Thanks for having us over but I'm going to take Ally home now. Look at the state of her. I'll be having words with you tomorrow, young lady. Is she even awake any more? I have no idea. Here, take some cake with you. I'll wrap a couple of pieces up. Thanks, Linda. I'm sorry about this. It's not your fault, love. Freya, can you take this to the car for Gavin? Wait a minute. What for? I'm taking a photo. This is going on Facebook. Freya! Don't you dare. Too late. Right, I'm ready.'

Ally floated out of the house after a series of goodbyes and she was placed in the front seat of the car, tethered down by the seat belt.

'You're not really putting that on Facebook, are you? It's on there already. She'll kill you. I know but it'll be worth it.' The voices tailed off with only a muffled sound in their place and then Ally was flying again. There was the occasional muffled sound, which Ally guessed was Gavin talking to her, but she couldn't pick out any of the words. It was like trying to have a conversation underwater.

Ally continued to fly, and the muffled sounds grew quieter and quieter until there was no sound at all. Panicked, Ally tried to open her eyes but they were welded shut, and then it didn't matter as a comforting blanket of darkness enveloped her and everything was still.

FIVE

Ally sensed that something was wrong a split second before her eyes fluttered open. She froze. Her hands were stretched above her head, grazing a wrought iron headboard she didn't own. Her eyelids unpeeled themselves slowly and painfully, revealing a strange bedroom. Unlike her own bedroom with its soft chocolate and beige tones, brightened with splashes of blue, this bedroom was stark white, from the walls to the furniture and bedspread. It felt cold and uninviting, and Ally didn't want to be there. But, worse, she had no idea *why* she was there. Or even where 'there' was.

She thought back over the previous day. Her birthday had started off bleak with the latest in a long line of baby rows but had improved when she'd stopped off at the pub after work, celebrating with Jason and Kelly. Beyond that, Ally couldn't remember. Her head ached as she tried to push past the fuzz that constituted her memory of the previous evening. She'd been to the pub, drinking more than she'd planned to because she was having such a fantastic time. It had been great to let go a bit and have fun, to throw her old, boring routine out of the window. It would have been even better if Kelly hadn't been there with her sour jibes, but Ally had done her best to ignore her, pretending she was alone with the gorgeous Jason. She'd even attempted to flirt a little with him.

Oh God. Nothing had happened between them, had it? She remembered putting her palms against his chest and feeling woozy when she felt how toned he was. He obviously worked out and she could only imagine how delicious he was beneath his shirt.

But *did* she have to imagine now? Had she continued to flirt with him? Had he taken her home?

Ally scrambled into a sitting position and searched for clues as to her whereabouts and the owner of the bed she was lying in. A bed that she was lying *naked* in. Thankfully the bed was void of any other occupants and didn't appear to have been slept in by anybody but herself, but she listened for signs of life as she took in the room. It was quite a bare room, but it was clearly a feminine one with a silk, floral robe hanging from the back of the door, make-up cluttering the dressing table and a pair of ridiculously high stilettos were strewn on the fluffy white rug. Ally very much doubted that this bedroom belonged to Jason.

Slipping from beneath the covers, Ally shoved her arms into the robe and tightened it around her waist before she eased the door open and listened for signs of life once more. There were none so she took a tentative step out into the hall. The oak floor was cold on her bare feet as she padded along to the next room, which was an empty bathroom. She moved on, creeping along the corridor, noting where the front door was in case she needed to make a swift getaway, before opening the next door. She stepped into a large open plan living area with a pair of red leather sofas and a huge television in front of her, and a dining table and kitchen beyond. This room appeared to be empty too but, not wanting to take any chances, Ally was careful as she moved fully into the room. Her caution was forgotten as a yelp left her lips. Clamping a hand over her gaping mouth, she moved towards the huge portrait hung above the fireplace. The huge portrait depicting a naked Ally, her modesty almost covered by a red silk scarf. A fat, pink nipple escaped from the gauzy material for all to see, and Ally couldn't take her eyes off it.

Who had painted *that*? And when, because Ally had never sat for any painting, never mind a smutty one.

Reaching up on her tiptoes, she wrenched the

painting down from the wall and propped it up, facing the wall. She didn't know which mucky bastard had painted that monstrosity, but they weren't keeping it.

Checking the room for further 'art', Ally was confused to discover a framed photo of herself and another woman on a side table. The women were laughing, arms slung around one another's shoulders and were clearly on holiday, judging from the sparkling sea behind them.

What the hell was going on? Ally had never seen this woman before, had certainly never holidayed with her. Was she the owner of this apartment and the disgusting painting? Had she somehow got her mitts on a photo of Ally and photoshopped it onto her holiday snap?

Still alert for sounds of the owner, Ally began rummaging around for clues, finding a wallet of yet more holiday photos of her and the strange woman and, worryingly, a passport in Ally's maiden name. There were also unpaid bills and bank statements in Ally's maiden name, addressed to a city centre apartment. 18 Marley House, Palmerston Avenue. Was that the apartment she was standing in? It must have been.

This was freaky. What was she doing there? And why had somebody forged documents in her name? And then there were the photos and the painting. Was she even there by choice?

Ally flew to the front door and was relieved to find a set of keys on a little side table. With shaking hands, she slotted the key into the lock and – thank God – it turned. Locking it again and putting on the chain in case whoever lived there returned, Ally sprinted back to the bedroom to throw on some clothes so she could get the hell out of there.

Ally had been unable to find the previous day's clothes in either the bedroom or bathroom and shuddered as she imagined the creepy photo woman taking them as keepsakes. Forced to borrow an outfit from the wardrobe, it transpired Creepy Photo Woman was quite slutty. But with little choice, Ally slipped on an extremely short – and tight – black skirt and a white blouse. Luckily Creepy Photo Woman's clothes fit, even down to her bras and shoes. Perhaps she had bought them specifically for Ally.

Weirdo.

As soon as she was dressed, Ally pelted out of the apartment, grabbing a handbag from the little table in the hall on her way out. The least Creepy Photo Woman could do was provide her with the bus fare to get home. Ally should have felt guilty as she rifled through the handbag a safe distance away from the apartment block, but fear and shock had quashed such an emotion. Besides, Creepy Photo Woman had stolen her identity, she *deserved* it.

Inside the bag was a driver's licence in Ally's maiden name, along with credit cards and a mobile phone. Clutching the phone, Ally dialled Gavin's number and almost wept with relief when it was answered. She didn't know what to tell Gavin about her overnight disappearance because she didn't have a clue how she'd ended up in that crazy apartment. Should she tell him about Creepy Photo Woman? Yes, of course she should. She should also tell the police.

'Gavin?' Ally was confused as she realised the voice on the other end was not her husband. Perhaps he was at work already and one of the other mechanics had picked up.

'Sorry, love. You've got the wrong number.'

'This isn't Gavin's phone?'

'I'm afraid not.'

'Sorry.' Ally ended the call and dialled Gavin's number again, more carefully this time. Her hands were shaking so much from her ordeal, it was no wonder she'd misdialled.

'It's me again, love. Wrong number.' Ally reeled off Gavin's number. 'That's the one.'

'Oh. Sorry.' Ally hung up with a shake of her head. Her brain had turned to mush in all the drama and confusion. She was sure that was Gavin's number. She'd try the landline instead and hope that Gavin hadn't set off for work yet.

This time an elderly lady answered. Definitely not Gavin then.

This was the strangest day ever.

A bus trundling its way towards her caught Ally's attention, so forgetting the phone for a moment, she pelted towards the bus stop, praying there was enough change in Creepy Photo Woman's purse for her fare.

Sinking into a seat, Ally rifled through the bag once more. There were four credit cards, a bank card, several garish lipsticks, a crusty mascara, and a handful of condoms in various colours and flavours. Everything was in Ally's maiden name, which didn't help her figure out who she'd stayed with that night. Too late, she realised she should have pocketed the bills and bank statements as evidence and she'd forgotten about the painting. She should have taken it or at least put her foot through it.

The bus stopped at the station in town, and Ally hopped off and caught another that would take her to the office. Once there she'd feel safer and then she could try and contact Gavin again as well as report the incident to the police. Her hands were still shaking as she made her way into Westerly's and collapsed against the reception desk, thankful to see her best friend. Francine was a proper grown up. She'd know what to do.

'You'll never guess what happened to me this morning.'

'I'm not sure I want to know.' Francine barely glanced up from the magazine she was flicking through as she answered.

'It was awful, Francine. I woke up in this strange bed with no idea where I was or whose bed I was in.'

'Why am I not surprised?'

Ally reeled back in shock at Francine's tone. Instead of sounding concerned about her best friend's welfare, Francine sounded bored. She was still flicking through the magazine, not giving the slightest shit about Ally's ordeal.

'I'm very busy. I don't have time for your nonsense.'

Ally stepped away from the reception desk. Why was Francine being so nasty towards her? Francine didn't *do* nasty. She clucked like a mother hen. She was soothing and understanding and, if all that failed to cheer Ally up, she always had a lollipop lurking in her handbag.

'I don't think you understand. There were photos in the apartment. Of me.'

'Mucky photos, no doubt.'

'Well, the photos weren't mucky but the painting was.'

'Hmm.' Francine chuckled at something she'd just read.

'Don't you care?'

Francine let out a long sigh, finishing her sentence before lifting her eyes towards Ally. 'Like I told you, I'm very busy.'

'Reading a magazine? Francine, I think I may have been *kidnapped*.'

'And yet here you are.' Francine's eyes dropped back down to the magazine. Ally lingered for a moment, hoping Francine would crack a smile and tell her this whole morning had been an elaborate joke. When Francine continued to ignore her, humming as she read her magazine, Ally retreated to the ladies to freshen up. She'd been in such a rush to leave the freaky apartment, she hadn't washed her face – or even had a wee.

Ally jumped back as she pushed open the door and came face to face with Kelly.

'I didn't know anybody was in here,' Ally said. Kelly jumped too. Kelly was also clutching her chest in shock and a frown began to creep onto her face. When Ally stepped forward, Kelly did too.

Except it wasn't Kelly at all. Ally was standing in front of the mirror and, on closer inspection, she could see that it was *her* image she was seeing. Her long, brown curls had been butchered into a jaw-length bob, her fringe chopped to rest a good inch above her eyebrows and she needed sunglasses to counter the glare from the shiny blonde she now sported. How had she not noticed before now? Not noticing the colour was one thing, but the length? She was used to heavy hair and a fringe flopping into her eyes, not *this*.

Ally took another step forward and clutched the sink as she peered at her new image. How had this been done to her without her knowledge?

'Look at me!' Ally tore out of the ladies, striding towards Francine while clutching her hair. My God, it was silky. It must have been chemically straightened or something, and Ally couldn't help admiring its smoothness. But it was *wrong*. Very, very wrong.

'What's the matter? Have you got a split end?'

Ally gaped at her best friend. What the hell had got into Francine? 'I'm *blonde*.'

'Well done.' Francine clapped her hands together and adopted a sickly baby voice. 'You've finally mastered colours. Tomorrow we'll tackle numbers.'

'Why are you being like this?' Tears pooled in Ally's eyes. She was having the weirdest, shittiest of mornings and she needed Francine to be, well, Francine. Not this cold, sarcastic version.

'I'm trying to work. Which is what you should be doing instead of bugging me. Are you really that bored?'

No, Ally wasn't bored. She was confused and terrified and hadn't a clue what was happening to her. She needed to be comforted and reassured, not be the subject of sarcasm and derision.

She needed Gavin.

SIX

Leaving Francine to her magazine, Ally ran up the spiral staircase and up to the HR office in her eagerness to speak to Gavin. There was obviously a glitch with Creepy Photo Woman's phone so she would ring Gavin from her desk. The thought of hearing her husband's voice lifted the weight of dread from Ally's body, but it came crashing back down again when she caught sight of Kelly. And this time it wasn't a mirror image looking back at her.

'Your hair.' Ally paused in the doorway of the office, her finger rising to point at Kelly's brown locks. Did they have a bet to swap hairstyles last night?

'I know, it's crap and mousey but there's no need to point. It's your fault it's like this.'

So they *had* swapped hairstyles. How much had she had to drink last night? She really couldn't remember anything other than flirting with Jason in the pub. What happened after that was a mystery.

'I loved my blonde hair.' Kelly narrowed her eyes at Ally. 'Before you stole it. I could hardly keep it when you turned up with the exact same style, could I?'

Turned up with the same style? So they hadn't agreed on a swap last night then. Did that mean Kelly carried a bottle of hair dye around with her on the off-chance that somebody had copied her hairstyle? But that couldn't be it either because Kelly wouldn't have had enough time to dye her hair between Ally arriving at work and now. And it was just a tad absurd, even for Kelly.

Seriously, what was going on?

'How long have I had blonde hair?' Ally tried to sound casual when all she wanted to do was leap across Kelly's desk and grasp her by the shoulders, giving them a shake as she demanded answers.

Kelly gave a shrug. 'I don't know. A month?'

A month? But that couldn't be. It just couldn't.

Ally's knees felt weak and she knew if she didn't sit down, she'd fall down – and pretty swiftly – so she scurried across the office and sank into her chair. Something seriously weird was going on. She'd woken up in a creepy apartment with beautiful but strange hair – which she'd apparently had for a month – and Francine was being off with her.

She'd been drugged. The night of her birthday.

Her drinks must have been laced with something and she'd been living in a dream-like state ever since. Somewhere along the way she had changed hairstyles, befriended Creepy Photo Woman and majorly pissed off Francine, and only now were the drugs wearing off.

It was the only explanation.

With trembling hands – either through fear or a side effect of the drugs – Ally picked up her phone and *very carefully* dialled Gavin's number. The same bloke from earlier answered, only he sounded a bit pissed off this time, and the same elderly lady answered the landline.

Okay, drugs didn't change people's phone numbers. Ally was about to dial the number of her dad's garage but changed her mind at the last second. Maybe that phone number had changed too. She would go and see Gavin in person. And then probably cry an awful lot.

With the excuse of visiting an employee at the depot, Ally slipped out of Westerly's and hurried round to the garage, relieved by the familiar sounds and smells as she rounded the corner. At least the building was still there. She'd half expected to turn the corner and find a florist's in place of the garage. It had been that kind of morning.

Ally had never been happier to take a lungful of fumes as she stepped into the garage, scanning the space for her husband. Oliver was working on a car at the far end of the garage and Freya was perched on the rickety old desk in the corner of the room, scanning a printed document. She couldn't see Gavin anywhere but that wasn't unusual. He could have been out on a job or perhaps he was out looking for her. She had no idea whether she'd been home or not during the last drugged-up month – perhaps the police were looking for her too. Gavin could be worried sick and he couldn't contact her because Ally had no idea where her phone was. She only had Creepy Photo Woman's possessions.

'Jesus, what are you doing here?' Freya dropped the document on the desk, her eyebrows shooting up her forehead as she stepped closer to Ally, genuinely shocked to see her sister. So she *had* been missing from home. Poor Gavin.

'Aren't you afraid the grease will ruin your hair or something?' Freya stopped in front of Ally, folding her arms across her chest and narrowing her eyes ever so slightly. Ally touched her hair and suddenly she *was* concerned that the greasy garage would ruin her hair. Somebody had obviously gone to a lot of trouble to make her hair look this fabulous and she didn't want the effects to wear off too quickly.

But no, her hair wasn't important. She was back! Ally waited for the shock to drain from her sister's face, to feel Freya's arms around her and hear her weep with relief. Ally was home! She was safe. And her hair looked *so good*.

But Freya's face remained like stone and her arms remained folded across her chest. 'If you're looking for Dad, he's not here. And he's skint, so don't bother asking for a loan.'

Ally hadn't been planning on asking for a loan. Why would she?

'Aren't you happy to see me?' Jeez, Ally wasn't asking for bunting and cake (even if she had been missing for at least a month) but would it hurt to crack a smile?

'Should I be?'

'Yes! I've been gone for a month.' But wait, if she'd been at work during that month, surely she hadn't actually been missing at all. The police wouldn't have had to look very far to find her. Maybe she'd simply buggered off with Creepy Photo Woman (and hadn't been kidnapped as she'd first suspected. She didn't look under duress in the photos. Or even the nude painting, come to think of it).

'Did you find some sap to take you away to the Caribbean again?'

'No.' Or maybe she had. Ally wasn't sure. Could the holiday snaps have been taken in the Caribbean? Ally had never been further than the Costa del Sol, so she wouldn't know. 'Can I sit down for a minute?' Ally's knees felt weak again.

'Do what you want. You always do.' Freya stalked away while Ally slumped onto the chair by the desk, more confused now than she had been when she'd assumed she'd been taken against her will. Why was everyone being so horrible to her, and why couldn't she remember the past month?

She needed tea, sweet and comforting, while she waited for Gavin. He may not have the answers Ally needed, but he had a strong pair of arms that always made her feel safe. She put the kettle on and made her tea along with coffee for Freya and Oliver.

'Blimey, I didn't realise you knew what the kettle was for,' Freya said as she took the cup from Ally. 'But if you're looking for money from me, you've got no chance.'

'What is your obsession with money?' Ally had never borrowed money from her sister and wasn't about to start now.

Freya spluttered. '*My* obsession with money? Are you having a laugh?'

'Do I look like I'm laughing?' Ally had had enough. 'I woke up in a strange apartment this morning and have no idea how I got there. Everyone is being nasty to me and I think I was *drugged*. So no, I'm not really in a jovial mood.'

Freya rolled her eyes. She actually *rolled her eyes*, as though Ally's trauma meant nothing. 'It sounds like a normal day in your world.'

'It does *not* sound normal at all.'

'One-night stand, check.' Freya held up a finger, keeping a visual tally of Ally's misdemeanours. 'You pissing people off, check. Drugs, check. Yep, sounds like your life to me.'

'That does *not* sound like my life. Not even a

tiny bit. I have *never* had a one-night stand.' Unless you counted Travis Brown at university but, as Ally had been too ashamed to tell a soul about that, she didn't regard it as a real event. 'I've smoked weed twice and hated it, so that hardly makes me a user, and I've done nothing to piss people off.'

Freya tilted her head to one side, observing her sister for a moment. Her face softened and Ally's lip began to tremble as she envisioned Freya giving her a well-deserved hug. 'Do you really believe all that crap you've just spouted?'

'It isn't crap.' Apart from the one-night stand bit.

'It isn't true.'

'It *is*.' Apart from the one-night stand bit. 'I don't know what's going on, Freya. I need help.' A tear escaped, trickling down her cheek but Ally swiped it away with her hand. 'Where's Gavin? I want Gavin.'

Freya's face was no longer like stone as she watched another tear make its way down her sister's cheek. She wanted to reach out to Ally but couldn't quite bring herself to do so. 'Who's Gavin?'

SEVEN

'Gavin. My husband.' What was wrong with everyone today? Perhaps it hadn't been Ally who had been drugged but everyone around her.

'Husband?' Freya's eyes widened and she placed a hand over her cavernous mouth. 'You got married? Shit, Mum is going to flip. Of all the stupid things you've done over the years...' Freya shook her head, unable to compute what her sister was telling her. 'When? Is Gavin the Caribbean guy?'

'There is no Caribbean guy.' Not that Ally was aware of, but anything was possible right now, she supposed. 'It's *Gavin*. You know, the man I've been married to for five years?'

'*Five years*?' Freya's mouth gaped wider. Ally could see a filling at the back of her mouth. 'Fucking hell, Alana. *Five years*. Why didn't you tell us?'

'You were there!' Ally threw up her hands,

56

curling them into fists. Frustration was making her want to throttle her sister. 'You were my maid of honour. You hated the dress because you said it made your arse look big.' Which it had. She could have been smuggling a wide-screen TV back there. Ally had lied, of course. It had been too late to start the whole process again by then, finding a dress and having it fitted. 'You had too much to drink and copped off with the guitarist in the wedding band.' Five years down the line and Ally still shuddered at the memory. The guitarist had been extremely hairy. Think Michael J Fox as Teen Wolf.

Freya closed her eyes, pressing her lips together until they disappeared. 'You promised, Alana. No more drugs, you said. What have you taken?'

'I don't know. I didn't take them by choice. Somebody must have spiked my drink.'

Freya threw back her head and barked out a laugh. 'Come off it. Stop with the excuses. You do this every time and we're sick of it. We're *sick of it*, Alana.'

'Stop calling me Alana.' Ally folded her arms across her chest, a scowl on her face.

'It's your name, isn't it? Or have you changed it by deed poll on the sly too?'

Yes, it was her name but nobody actually called her Alana. Unless she was in trouble.

'Look, why don't you go home and sleep off the drugs?' Freya started to guide Ally towards the exit, washing her hands of her sister. She had work to do and they'd been through this kind of shit too many times in the past for Freya to care any more.

Yes, Ally would go home and sleep. Maybe everything would be back to normal when she woke up again, or perhaps Gavin would be there. She hurried for the bus, willing it to go faster and cursing the selfish passengers who dared to stop it to either board or disembark. Finally, they reached her stop and she flew off the bus and hurtled down her street. It was only when she reached the house that she realised she didn't have a key in Creepy Photo Woman's handbag, so she hammered on the door, praying Gavin would be in.

But it wasn't Gavin who answered. It was a little old lady peering at her through the slightest crack in the door.

'Who are you?' Ally thought about barging into the house, but the old lady looked like she would crumble at the slightest touch, so she remained on the doorstep.

'I beg your pardon? I think you may have got the wrong house, dear.'

'I don't think so. This is my house. Where's Gavin?'

'I don't know who you're talking about. I live here with my Rupert. There is no Gavin.'

Why did people keep saying that? There *was* a Gavin and he was Ally's husband.

The next door along opened and a young woman appeared, a thumb-sucking child on her hip. Ally knew Eve Simon and was well acquainted with the howls of the podgy Drew at various times during the night. Even the sound of an inconsolable Drew wailing through the walls hadn't been enough to put Gavin off procreating.

'Are you alright, Maud?' Eve ignored Ally and turned instead to the old woman. The old woman – Maud – widened the crack in the door a little, her eyes crinkling as she smiled at Eve and Drew.

'I'm fine, dear, but I think this young lady here is a little confused. She's looking for somebody called Gavin.'

'Gavin?' Eve tilted her head for a moment before shaking it. 'I don't know anybody called Gavin, but I haven't lived here that long.'

Eve had lived next door to Ally for six months. She was a lovely girl who kept mostly to herself. It was the wailing kid Ally had a problem with.

'You do know Gavin. He lives here.' Ally jabbed a finger at the house. *Her* house. 'I live here too.'

'I'm afraid you're mistaken, dear.' Maud closed the gap ever so slightly. 'This is my house. Do you think you've got the wrong street? Which street are you looking for?'

'MacMillan Road. I'm looking for *this* street and *this* house.' Ally turned to her neighbour. 'Eve, you know me. You know Gavin. He fixed the leak under your sink last week.'

Eve took a step back, shielding the child – from what, Ally wasn't sure. 'I don't know who you are and I don't know anybody called Gavin. I think you should go or I'll call the police.'

Good! Call the police, because if Eve didn't, Ally would. There was an old woman in her house and as sweet as Maud appeared, she was still trespassing.

'I mean it, I'll phone the police.' Eve shifted the child and reached into the pocket of her jeans, pulling out her mobile. 'Go back inside, Maud. And lock the door.'

Ally took a step back. Perhaps talking to the police wasn't such a good idea after all. Something weird was going on but she wasn't sure how to explain it to them without appearing completely cuckoo. Would they listen? Or would they shove her straight into a padded cell?

Ally wasn't willing to take the chance. 'Fine. I'll go.' For now. She'd be back to claim her house as soon as she figured out what was going on.

Two doors closed but Eve appeared at the window of her sitting room, watching as Ally wandered away. She found herself outside The Farthing, staring up at the familiar façade. It felt like only a couple of days ago that she'd been inside, happily singing karaoke with her friends, but how long had it really been? It wasn't simply Ally's appearance that had altered; her entire life was skewed with her friend and sister turning on her, plus Gavin's disappearance. Where was he and why couldn't Freya remember him? None of it made sense and trying to figure it all out was making her head hurt. She needed to sit down and think rationally. She needed somebody to take charge, to give her a hug and tell her everything would be okay. Other than Gavin, there was only one other person who would fit the bill.

She had to find her mum.

EIGHT

Ally tried to keep it together as she made her way to her parents' house, knowing that collapsing in a heap and wailing – however tempting that may be – would be a one-way ticket to the nearest loony bin. Aware she was muttering to herself, Ally clamped her mouth together and forced a smile at the elderly couple who had twisted in their seat to gawp at her. Ally had wanted to jump in a taxi, but there hadn't been enough cash in Creepy Photo Woman's purse, so she'd been forced to catch the bus instead.

While, earlier, Ally had been convinced it was drugs that had caused her life meltdown, other ideas were starting to swirl in her mind. Had she been hit on the head last night? Had she got so bladdered in the pub with Jason and Kelly that she'd fallen over and smacked her head on the edge of a table and was now suffering from some sort of weird concussion? Or had she stumbled into the road, perhaps on her way home, and been knocked down by a car? Was she now lying in a coma while her mind played out this weird scenario, *Life On Mars*-style?

Yes! That was it. That *had* to be it. She remembered leaving the pub now, her head definitely not smashed in, and watched as Jason and Kelly climbed into a taxi without her. So she hadn't gone home with Jason, which was a relief, no matter how delicious he was. She'd left the pub and then… Nope, nothing. She couldn't remember anything beyond that, but it was entirely possible she had been in an accident and was now lying in a hospital bed with her family gathered around her.

'I'm alright, Gavin. I'll wake up. I promise.'

The elderly couple stiffened before leaping out of their seats and shuffling further down the bus, as far away from the crazy lady as their arthritic legs could carry them.

Loony bin, Ally. No more talking to yourself. Ally didn't know how long she'd be in the coma and she didn't want to spend that time in a straitjacket.

Hopping off the bus, she felt calmer now she knew she wasn't cracking up, but all her composure vanished as soon as she saw her mum and fell into her arms, sobbing.

'Hey, hey, come on, love. Come inside. Whatever it is, we'll sort it out.' Linda ushered Ally into the house, settling her on the sofa before putting the kettle on. Ally dried her eyes on the tissue her mum had provided, giving her nose a good blow. Seeing her mum had opened the floodgates for all her fear and anguish to surge out at once. She felt secure with her mum and knew nothing bad could happen to her now.

'Here we go.' Linda breezed into the sitting room and set the cups of coffee on the side. 'How are you feeling now?'

'Better.' Still scared witless but her mum would know what to do.

'Good.' Linda crossed the room and fished in her handbag for her purse. 'How much do you need? I don't have a great deal on me. Thirty will have to do.' She thrust the notes at her daughter but Ally shook her head.

'I don't want your money.'

'Then what do you want?' Linda perched on the arm of the sofa, the money still in her hand.

'I want you to help me make sense of my life.'

Linda chuckled to herself as she slotted the money back into her purse. 'I'm afraid I can't help with that.' Linda had given up trying to guide her daughter a long time ago. Harsh as it sounded, it was a lost cause. Her daughter was on a mission of self-destruction, and there was nothing Linda – or anybody else – could do to stop it. They'd tried everything in the past but Linda had eventually learned that she was powerless when it came to her eldest daughter.

'You don't understand, Mum. I woke up this morning and I had no idea where I was.' Linda held in a sigh. She'd heard this a million times before. Would her daughter never learn? Didn't she realise how much danger she was putting herself in? 'I was in this weird apartment and there were photos of me and documents in my name.' Should she mention that the documents were in her maiden name? Freya hadn't known who Gavin was but perhaps her mum would. 'Do you remember Gavin Richmond?'

'Carolyn and Doug's son? Used to live across the road?'

'Yes!' Ally leapt out of her seat and clapped her hands together. Finally someone remembered her husband. He hadn't vanished off the face of the earth.

'What about him? He wasn't involved in your shenanigans last night, was he?' The corners of Linda's lips turned down. 'He always seemed like such a nice boy.'

'No, he wasn't involved last night. I went out with a couple of people from work.' A memory popped into Ally's head. She was in the pub, talking to Gavin on the phone and she was annoyed with him. 'At least I don't think he was involved.' Ally paused to think about it, to try to stretch the memory a little further. As she did so, her mum's phone shrilled into life and Linda headed out into the hall to answer it. When she returned, she grabbed her handbag and slung it over her shoulder.

'I have to go out. Your sister's been in another

fight at school, so I have to go and have a chat with the head.'

Ally's gut tightened at the thought of going back out into the strange world again. She felt safe inside her mum's sitting room, wrapped in a bubble of love and happy childhood memories. She'd grown up in this house. She'd forged a friendship with Gavin on this very street. Nothing could harm her here.

'Do you think I could stay here for a bit? Until you get back?'

Linda paused, closing her eyes as she contemplated the request. She didn't feel entirely comfortable leaving her daughter in the house, but then she'd already turned down the offer of money, so maybe she'd be okay.

'Fine. I shouldn't be too long.'

Ally's gut tightened again as her mother left the house and she took a few deep breaths, reminding herself that she was safe now, but she was still agitated and took to pacing the sitting room floor. She was on her fourth lap when she realised her wedding photo was missing. It usually hung on the wall above the sofa, sandwiched between her graduation photo and her Year Eleven school photo. The graduation and school photos were there, although there was something off about them. Ally took a closer look and then it hit her what the difference was. In these photos, she appeared to be plastered in make-up. In the school photo, her foundation was so thick and orange, she resembled an Oompa Loompa.

'It's a shame about the wedding photo.'

The voice behind Ally made her jump and she wheeled around to see a tall young woman wearing an old fashioned floor-length nightgown with a lace trim. Her skin was unearthly in its paleness but she had bright blue eyes, ruddy cheeks and ruby lips, which were stretched into a smile as she observed Ally from the middle of the sitting room. Her strawberry blonde hair was twisted into a thick plait that reached the base of her spine.

'It was a lovely photo, wasn't it? You looked radiant and you couldn't even see Freya's fat arse from that angle.'

Ally took a step back, not realising she was stepping away from the sitting room door and therefore trapping herself in a corner of the room.

'I'm sorry I'm late. I was supposed to speak to you first thing this morning but I got caught up with a spoiled brat who'd wished to be a mermaid.' The girl's cheeks turned a shade deeper as she giggled. 'She's currently sitting on a rock being circled by sharks.'

'Sharks?' The word was strangled as it left Ally's mouth. What was this girl going on about? Where had she come from and what did she want? She was the strangest kind of burglar Ally had ever seen but, funnily, this wasn't the strangest thing that had happened that day.

'Don't worry. They can't reach her on the rock.

A bit of fear will do the little madam some good.'

Who was this girl?

'Sorry.' She shook her head and stepped forward, extending a hand. 'I haven't introduced myself, have I? I'm Clementine.'

Ally ignored the hand, not wanting to touch her. 'Clementine? Your name is Clementine?'

Clementine's pale eyebrows knitted together but she still looked pretty even when she scowled. 'Yes, it is. Why? What's your name?'

'Ally.'

Clementine gave a tinkling giggle. 'That's what you think.'

'What's that supposed to mean?'

Clementine grabbed her plait and played with the loose ends. 'It was Gavin who started calling you Ally, wasn't it? After your favourite TV show at the time?' *Ally McBeal.* Ally had been obsessed with it and she'd made Gavin and Freya sit with her while she watched the episodes again and again. Gavin had shortened Alana to Ally as a tribute to her love of the program and eventually everybody else did too. 'But you and Gavin have never been together. You've never even been friends. In fact, poor Gavin was never on your radar.'

'What are you talking about?' Cold dread washed over Ally. On the one hand she was glad this girl knew who Gavin was, but on the other she didn't like what she was saying, how she was rewriting their history.

'Sorry. I'm not explaining myself very well, am I?'

Clementine dropped her plait and it swished back behind her. 'I'm fairly new to the job. In fact, Mermaid Girl was my first client.' Client? 'You made a wish. You wished your life was like Kelly's.' Clementine threw her dainty arms in the air. 'Tah da! Now it is.'

NINE

Ally watched Clementine carefully, on the lookout for twitching lips or any other sign that she was taking the piss. Because surely she was.

'I made a wish?'

Clementine tilted her head to one side, causing her plait to swish to the front. 'You don't remember? It was in this house. Here, in this very room, in fact.'

The cake! Ally remembered now. She'd somehow made it to the birthday tea – head and body intact – and her mother had produced a cake. With candles.

'That's right.' Clementine picked up on the not-so-subtle look of panic as Ally recalled the previous evening, her eyes stretching to giant orbs of horror.

'Were they...' Ally paused and lowered her voice, leaning in towards Clementine so she could be heard. '*Magic* candles?'

Clementine threw back her head and laughed. Gone was the demure tinkle and in its place was a booming belly laugh. 'Magic candles?' Clementine wiped tears of mirth from under her eyes. 'Magic candles? Don't be absurd.'

Ally was standing in front of some sort of angelic being who was telling her that her entire life had been turned on its head after a birthday wish. But yeah, the idea of magic candles was absurd.

'Then what? Are you a guardian angel?'

'Sort of.'

Ally narrowed her eyes. 'You don't have wings.'

'What?' Clementine turned to try and see behind her and ended up doing a pirouette on the sitting room rug. 'Dammit, I've left them behind again.'

Ally's eyes were now nothing more than slits on her face. 'Are you toying with me?' Clementine gave a shrug of her dainty shoulders. 'Can I have my old life back now?'

'No.'

'No?'

Clementine gave a slow shake of her head. 'All wishes are final. It's in the contract.'

'What contract? I didn't sign any contract.' There was hope! Clementine couldn't force her to live this life without her consent! But wait, Clementine's tinkle of a laugh was back.

'I'm just messing with you, Petal. There is no contract.'

Oh. 'So I'm stuck with this life then?'

'I'm afraid so. But hey, look on the bright side.'
There was a bright side? 'It's what you wanted.'

'Well, no. Not really. I wanted a bit of
excitement in my life. I wanted to go out on
adventures with my friends and tell amusing stories
the next day in the office. I wanted to live a little
before I was coerced into giving up my life and
womb. I didn't want to be hated by my friends and
family. I didn't want to lose my husband.'

'Not even for Jason?' Clementine's slight body
quivered. 'He is *delicious* by the way. I can see why
you were jealous of Kelly.'

'I was not jealous.'

'Really? You could have fooled me.' Clementine
muttered the words under her breath but Ally still
caught them. 'Anyway, there's no need to be
jealous now, is there?'

Ally allowed her body to drop onto the sofa, a
huge sigh heaving out of her body as she slumped
against the cushions. There had to be a way out of
this mess. Her whole life couldn't be eradicated
and replaced with this nightmare after a silly little
wish.

'Are you sure I can't go back?'

'Absolutely certain, Petal.' Clementine joined
Ally on the sofa and gave her knee a pat, but it
offered little comfort under the circumstances.

'Never?'

Clementine gasped as she jumped back up to
her feet, her cheeks burning bright on her
porcelain skin. 'Cripes! Mermaid Girl has *fallen in*

the ruddy sea.' Her long, slender fingers rested on her bottom lip as she paced the sitting room. 'This is not good. This is not good at all.' She ceased pacing and turned to Ally. 'I have to go. But don't worry, I'll be back.'

'When?' Ally asked but the sort-of guardian angel had vanished, leaving no trace that she'd ever been there at all.

Ally remained on the sofa, head in hands, as she tried to work out what was going on. She had made a wish, she remembered that clearly now. She hadn't been in an accident and she hadn't – thank God – gone home with somebody who wasn't her husband. But could that mean that her life had been magically erased and replaced with another? It wasn't possible and yet her life *had* changed. She was no longer married to Gavin (or anybody else. She had no ring) and her family thought she was a flaky, drug-using money grabber.

And then there was the flashy apartment she'd awoken in that morning. She hadn't been kidnapped or drugged and her identity hadn't been stolen. That was *her* apartment. She lived there now. She was friends with the woman in the photos instead of Francine and – eww – *she'd* commissioned the mucky painting.

This was crazy. She was either dreaming the whole thing or she was insane. Angels don't appear unless you're the Virgin Mary or completely cracked. And Ally was no virgin.

But what could she do? As far as Ally could see, she had no choice but to wait until she either woke up or became sane again. While she waited, Ally had a rummage in 'her' handbag, tossing aside car keys, tampons, a million lipsticks and located the mobile. She was hoping to find Gavin's number stored in the phonebook, but although there were many, *many* male names listed, none were named Gavin. Scrolling through the messages, she saw an awful lot of vacuous conversations with a woman named Martine, along with messages from Jason.

Hey, babe. Meet at mine tonight?

You look hot today. And I can see your nipples through your blouse. Good work.

I missed you last night. Are you playing hard to get? Tease.

I'll get rid of Kelly and then we'll be alone and you can suck my—

Ally yelped and dropped the phone as though it were burning her hands. It appeared she and Jason were enjoying a bit of a fling. Of course they were! Kelly had been seeing Jason on the sly and so now Ally was. Ally felt a tiny thrill for a split second as she imagined herself getting hot and sweaty with her manager. Perhaps in his office. With his hands *all over her*.

No. Ally shook her head. As attracted to Jason as she was, she could never cheat on Gavin.

But she wasn't married to Gavin in 'this' life.

No!

Ally leapt off the sofa, scooped up the phone and

the pile of discarded belongings and shoved them into her handbag. She loved Gavin, whether she'd made a stupid life-altering wish or not, and he was out there somewhere. Ally hooked her handbag onto her shoulder and left her parents' house, moving towards the bus stop with purpose. If she could find Gavin, everything would be alright. He'd remember their life together, she was sure of it.

TEN

It was almost lunchtime by the time Ally made it back to Westerly's. She gave a cheery wave and said hello to Francine out of habit, but the gesture wasn't returned. Francine was usually so warm and friendly, but Kelly – and now Ally – wasn't and the pair had obviously clashed. From her family's response to her, Ally could imagine she'd been vile to Francine in the past and had earned her scorn.

Dropping her gaze to the floor, Ally headed up to her office and was glad when she saw that Kelly's desk was empty and Jason was engrossed in a phone call in his own office. She switched on her computer, drumming her fingers impatiently as she waited for it to load up. She was going to do a bit of detective work online and locate her husband.

'I didn't think you were coming in today.' Ally jumped at the voice behind her but froze as a pair of hands slid across her shoulders and warm lips nuzzled her neck. The hands slid down to her chest and the sudden pain of a nipple-tweaking brought Ally back to life. She whirled around in her chair, swinging her hand to meet Jason's chops.

'What do you think you're doing?' She leapt out of her chair while Jason nursed his cheek with both hands.

'Ow! For God's sake, Alana. I'm sorry I crept up on you but there was no need for that.'

There was every need, Ally thought, her fingers clenching into fists by her sides as she readied herself for battle. She wasn't a piece of meat to be manhandled at will. She was a married woman!

Except she wasn't. She was no longer Ally Richmond. She was Alana Williams, who happened to be having a hot affair with the gorgeous Jason.

'I'm sorry, Jason. You scared me. Are you alright?'

Jason removed his hands and gave his jaw a wriggle, wincing a little. 'I'll live, I suppose.' He gave a lopsided grin. 'But only if you kiss it better.'

Oh God. She'd have melted at those words a couple of days ago, but right now they brought with them a bucket of icy water which rained down on her and removed all lustful thoughts and temptations.

'Look, Jason. We need to have a bit of a chat. About this.' Ally moved a hand between them. 'What we're doing isn't working for me. It isn't appropriate and it certainly isn't professional.'

Jason snorted. 'Since when were you

professional?'

Ally folded her arms across her chest, covering her still tingling nipples. 'Since now.'

'It's a bit late for that, don't you think? You weren't very professional when you were perched on the edge of my desk with your skirt up to your waist and your knickers in my pocket.' Jason smirked at her. 'I still have them, by the way.'

He could keep them as far as Ally was concerned. She'd seen inside her new underwear drawer and knew there wouldn't be much to them anyway.

'What's gotten into you? I thought we were having a bit of fun.' Jason hooked Ally's waist with his hand and pulled her towards him but Ally batted him away. 'Jesus, Alana. Is it that time of the month or something?'

Ally rolled her eyes. 'Yes, Jason, that's it. That's the only possible reason I could have for not dropping my knickers at your request, isn't it?'

Jason was about to reply but he swallowed his words when Kelly tottered into the office.

'Ah, there you are, Alana. I thought you'd gone part time.'

'I was at the depot.' Ally sat back down as Jason backed away and sauntered into his office.

'Hmm, of course you were.' Kelly sat down at her desk and flicked her hair over her shoulder. The longer style suited her and she still looked stunning, even with the so-called mousey hair. 'You had a phone call from Greta earlier, by the way.'

Greta was the managing director's PA. 'She's arranged a meeting with you and Malcolm on Monday morning. Ten thirty, I think it was.'

'Why do I need a meeting with Malcolm?'

Kelly sneered at Ally. 'What am I? Your secretary?' Her face brightened. 'Ooh, maybe you're getting sacked.' She crossed her fingers on both hands and held them up in the air. 'We can only hope.'

Ally didn't have time to snipe back and forth with Kelly. She had better things to do. Like finding her husband. She turned her attention to the computer, using the rest of the day to scour the internet. Scooby Doo and the gang would have nothing on her detective skills.

It was a struggle to find the apartment again that evening. She hadn't paid much attention to directions and landmarks as she'd fled that morning, but, had she known she'd be returning, Ally would have left a trail, Hansel and Gretel style. She had a vague idea of where to get off the bus, but then she was lost in the maze of houses, apartment blocks and off-licences, and it didn't occur to her to use her fancy new phone until she had blisters upon blisters on her feet.

Alana's phone gave her the directions to Marley House and the apartment that had evoked such fear that morning. Ignoring the painting – which was still propped up against the wall, the offending image facing the wall – she investigated the apartment at a more leisurely pace than she had earlier. Her internet searches hadn't brought up anything useful that afternoon. It appeared Gavin wasn't a member of Facebook or any other social network, and Google didn't have a clue who he was either, so it looked like Ally was stuck with this life for the time being.

The apartment was lovely, now that Ally wasn't fleeing it with her life in peril. It was minimalist and tidied to within an inch of its life, but the cupboards and fridge were practically bare, apart from bottle upon bottle of alcohol. Ally could whip up a number of cocktails but she couldn't manage a basic meal. Not that she could face food at the moment, but having the option would have been nice.

Having scoured the entire apartment, Ally returned to the sitting room and slumped on one of the sofas. So this was it then. Her home until she could locate Gavin and somehow convince the old lady to hop it from their house. Ally would rather have stayed with her mum and dad until this all blew over, but she wasn't sure what sort of response she would get if she asked. If they did allow her to stay under their roof, Ally imagined they'd nail everything down so she couldn't pawn it for drugs.

It really was a lovely place, this apartment of hers. There was a floor to ceiling window making up a whole wall of the living area and a small balcony off the kitchen, which overlooked a well-maintained public garden beneath. The kitchen was small but modern with red high-gloss cabinets and chrome appliances and it was illuminated by millions of spotlights. A breakfast bar with red barstools separated the kitchen from the sitting room, but Ally didn't imagine much eating occurred there, judging from the paltry supplies.

Ally would have been in awe under normal circumstances, but all she wanted to do was crawl into her own bed in her slightly messy terraced house and snuggle up with Gavin. It was so frustrating knowing he was out there somewhere but not knowing where. University blip aside, Ally and Gavin had been inseparable since they were thirteen and Ally missed him. He wasn't just her husband, he was her best friend too and Ally's chest tightened at the thought of never seeing him again. What if she never found him? What if he'd moved away and was now sunning it in Australia?

Ally slid further down the cool leather sofa. Her old sofa was ancient and lumpy, bought second hand when she and Gavin had moved into their little flat, but it was familiar and strangely cosy whereas this new sofa was cold and unwelcoming. There was no furry blanket – whose origin was unknown to both Ally and Gavin – slung over the back, ready to pull over a weary body, and the television, though gigantic, was at the wrong angle. She couldn't curl up and watch *A Beginner's Guide To You* on a Thursday evening or watch *You've Got Mail* on DVD – if Alana even owned it –without getting a crick in her neck. It was all wrong.

Ally heaved herself off the sofa and trudged through to the bathroom where she switched on the shower before tugging off the clothes that belonged to 'Alana' and not her. She still didn't feel any better when she emerged, particularly when she discovered she no longer possessed a pair of comfy pyjamas. Alana owned flirty baby doll nighties and slutty corsets with matching knickers rather than soft, stretchy bed wear. Even after a thorough search, Ally discovered she didn't own anything remotely comfortable, such as a pair of leggings and a T-shirt. Ally settled on the least sheer baby doll and matching lace shorts, feeling severely overdressed (or rather *underdressed*) considering she was in the apartment alone.

Ensuring the bolt and chain were in place on the front door, Ally grabbed 'her' phone and took it through to the bedroom. It wasn't yet half past seven but Ally slipped under the cool sheets of her new bed and switched off the lamp.

A text came through as she closed her eyes and her heart leapt into action. Maybe it was Gavin! Disappointment floored Ally when she realised it was from 'Martine', asking where she was. Shoving the phone onto the bedside table, Ally clamped her eyes shut and hoped that everything would be back to normal when she woke.

ELEVEN

Her eyes popped open early the next morning, but disappointment washed over Ally as she realised she was in the same bed, still in the fantasy land and the fancy apartment. She felt as though she hadn't slept at all, which was fairly accurate considering the number of times she'd been disturbed by 'Martine's' text messages. Ally didn't know the woman but she wanted to slap her.

8:35pm: *Seriously babe. Where are you? There's a dragon fruit vodka martini here with your name on it! x*

8:45pm: *The cocktail is no more. Sorry x*

9:20pm: *Babe? x*

10:37pm: *Callum's here. He wants to know when you'll be here x*

10:39pm: *Are you coming or not? x*

10:56pm: *Are you with J? x*

11:47pm: *You are missing a FAB night, babe x*

12:16am: *Oops. I just sort of copped off with Callum. You don't mind, do you? x*

2:19am: *In a taxi. To Callum's!!! Let me know if it's not cool, yeah? x*

Ally had switched her phone off after that, afraid she'd receive a running commentary on Callum's performance if she didn't.

Dragging herself out of bed, Ally wrapped a robe around her shivering body, covering the ridiculous nightwear, en route to the kitchen where she found a rock hard loaf of bread. After checking for mould, Ally popped a couple of slices into the pristine toaster but ate it dry as there didn't appear to be the luxury of margarine in the fridge. She was obviously expected to survive on vodka and wine from now on.

Dressing would be a challenge, unless she decided to moonlight as a stripper, so Ally put on yesterday's short black skirt (which was the longest Alana owned) and teamed it with a red silk blouse. The blouse required an extra button in Ally's opinion, but it was the best she could conjure from Alana's wardrobe.

The bus ride to work took three times as long now she was in the city centre, which meant she arrived late, sweaty and grumpy, but she still managed a smile in Francine's direction and a hearty 'good morning'. Francine grunted in response so Ally hurried past and climbed the stairs up to the office. Kelly raised her eyebrows as she lifted her wrist to consult an imaginary watch.

'Alright, I'm late. Is that a problem?'

'Apparently not, if you're shagging the boss,' Kelly muttered before smiling sweetly at Ally. 'Of course not. It's not like I have to pick up the slack while you're not here, is it?'

Ally's phone beeped and caught her attention as she was about to deliver a witty response, so she wandered to her desk while reading the message. It was Jason, asking to see her in the pub that evening. When she looked up, Jason was watching her from his office. She shook her head before deleting the message. Whether she was dreaming or insane, she wouldn't even consider cheating on Gavin. She couldn't believe she'd ever had a schoolgirl crush on Jason. Having been separated from Gavin for a day, she already missed him terribly. Going to sleep without him and waking alone had felt so alien and wasn't something Ally wanted to repeat. With renewed determination, Ally switched on her computer and continued her search for her husband.

After a whole day of searching, widening the net to include Gavin's friends and family, Ally failed to unearth anything. There were no mentions of Gavin at all. Not a sausage. Ally wanted to keep going, to stay at her desk all night if she had to, but it was already growing dark and the others were packing up around her.

'What's up with you? You're usually the first out of here.' Kelly was standing by her desk, her computer already shut down and her handbag hooked onto her arm. 'Expecting a rendezvous with lover boy?' Kelly cocked an eyebrow in Jason's direction. 'You've no shame, have you?'

'There's nothing going on with me and Jason.' Not any more. Jason still had the red mark on his cheek to prove it.

'And I'm Mother Teresa.' Kelly hitched her handbag further up her arm so it rested in the crook of her elbow and wriggled her fingers towards their manager's office. 'Night, Jason.'

'Goodnight, Kelly. Have a nice evening.' Jason paused in his doorway until Kelly had fluttered out of the room. 'Can we talk?'

Ally closed her eyes for a couple of seconds, attempting to summon energy and inspiration from somewhere. She hadn't had this sort of 'talk' for many years. In fact, the last had been with Gavin as she explained her inability to conduct a long distance relationship. Gavin had been gutted, she could see it on his face and she'd felt his pain too. It had been a stupid decision in hindsight, but she'd been young and foolish and hadn't realised what she'd be giving up. Some things never changed.

'There isn't much to say, Jason. Whatever we had is over.'

'But why?' Jason crouched in front of Ally, taking her limp hands in his. Ally looked away, concentrating on a floppy houseplant by the door instead of Jason's pleading gaze. 'I know I was a dickhead earlier with the whole sex-on-the-desk thing. It was nothing but stupid bravado. I'm sorry.'

'Don't be.' Ally's eyes bore into the plant as her cheeks burned. 'But you should know I'm not that woman any more. I've changed. For the better, I hope.'

'What do you mean?'

Ally snatched her hands away and shut down her computer, still not meeting Jason's eye. 'I mean I'm no longer into quickies on desks. My knickers will be staying firmly in place from now on.'

'But that doesn't mean we have to stop seeing each other. We can slow it down if you want. Go on proper dates and everything.'

'No, Jason. I'm sorry but I can't.' Ally leapt up from her seat, grabbing her bag and jacket in one fluid motion before fleeing from the office, leaving Jason crouching by her desk. She pounded down the stairs as quickly as she could in Alana's ridiculous shoes. She considered stopping by Francine's desk to say goodnight, but the frosty look her presence generated from her former friend sent her on her way.

Two long bus rides and almost two hours later, Ally finally trudged into Marley House, jabbing a finger at the button for the lift. Even if she had the energy for the stairs, the unsuitable shoes wouldn't have allowed it. She was looking forward to kicking them off and sinking into the sofa as soon as she stepped into the apartment.

'You're late. Where have you been?'

Ally yelped and took a step back, colliding with

the little table in the hall and knocking its contents to the floor. Her calf throbbed from the contact and she imagined there would be a bruise by the morning.

'Of course I'm late. You've stuck me out here, miles away from work. My first bus was late, which meant I missed the second and had to wait half an hour for the next one.'

Clementine waggled a finger at Ally. '*I* didn't stick you here, Petal. It was your wish that brought you here, remember?' How could Ally forget? 'And anyway, why are you bothering with the bus when you've got a car. A sexy car at that.' Clementine gave a wiggle while running her hands down her cotton nightdress.

'I don't have a car.' Ally bent down to right the table and returned the framed photo of her on yet another holiday with the mystery woman. Martine, perhaps? A scented candle had rolled down the hallway and a rainbow of glass pebbles had scattered on the floor.

'You do have a car, down in the car park. You have the keys in your handbag.'

Ally did recall a set of car keys actually, but they were useless. 'I can't drive.'

Clementine gave a tut. 'Ally may not have been able to drive, but *Alana* can. Do you think she'd lower herself and use public transport? Gosh, no. This girl is all about luxury.'

Ally scooped up the rest of the glass pebbles and dumped them in their decorative bowl. She wasn't really interested in Alana's life. It was her own life she was bothered about and how to get it back.

'I'm glad you're here. I need to ask you about Gavin.' Ally hung up her jacket and moved through to the sitting room where she disposed of the deadly shoes. 'Does he actually exist? Because I've looked everywhere online for him and I can't find a thing. Did I somehow wish him away?'

'Oh, Petal, that's quite some ego you've got going on there, isn't it?' Clementine chuckled to herself and gave Ally's head a fond pat. 'Gavin *can* exist without you, you know. And he does.'

Ally's body deflated as she let out a huge sigh and crumpled onto the sofa. Thank Christ for that! 'Where is he then?'

'I can't tell you. It isn't part of my job description and I'm *pretty* sure it's forbidden.' Clementine gave a shrug. 'There are so many ruddy rules, it's hard to keep up sometimes.'

'Fine. I'll find him myself.' Somehow. Ally hadn't had much success so far but she couldn't give up. 'While you're here, can I ask you a few questions?'

'Sure.' Clementine melted onto the matching sofa with grace and flashed Ally a sugary smile. 'Nice painting, by the way. I'm thinking of sitting for one myself. What do you think?' Clementine draped herself across the sofa and pouted at Ally, whose eyes shot from the sort-of guardian angel to the space where she'd shoved the nude painting. The space was empty but the painting –

unfortunately – remained and was now sitting proudly on the wall above the fireplace once more. Ally jumped off the sofa and whipped it down. She was going to burn the bloody thing.

'Sorry, I thought you hadn't got round to hanging it yet.' Clementine, now sitting demurely again, bit her bottom lip. 'I was only trying to be helpful.' Ally may have believed her had a giggle not bubbled from her mouth. Clementine covered her lips too late. 'Anyway, you had some questions for me?'

'Yes.' Ally dumped the painting behind the sofa. 'The first one is about Kelly.'

'Such a beautiful girl, isn't she?'

'On the outside, yes.' Ally slumped back onto the sofa. 'But what I wanted to know was why she still hates me. If we're so similar now, why aren't we friends?' Ally wanted to gag at the thought.

'Kelly strikes me as the kind of person who doesn't have many girlfriends.'

'Because she's so nasty?'

Clementine gave a shrug.

'Not part of your job description?'

'Nope, I'm just not a mind reader.'

Ally and Clementine eyed one another for a moment. Clementine arched an eyebrow so pale it was barely visible while Ally narrowed her eyes.

'Can you take this seriously please?' Didn't the overgrown fairy realise this was Ally's life she was messing with?

'I'm taking this very seriously, believe me. I'm

already on a "final warning".' Clementine made quotation marks with delicate fingers. 'Apparently it's against the rules to allow a client to be "attacked" by sharks.' She gave a tsk and shook her head. 'They were only babies and they barely nicked the girl. Honestly.' Clementine rolled her eyes. 'So, any more questions?'

Ally had plenty, but first she had to clarify that this was real, that she wasn't suffering from a head trauma or in need of psychiatric help.

'Completely real, Petal.' Clementine said it like it was a good thing.

'And I'm not going home? To my real home with Gavin?' Clementine shook her head. 'So there isn't a time limit? I don't have to live this life for a few days to learn my lesson and then go home?'

'And what lesson would that be?'

Ally's heart began to race. This was it. She'd cracked it! She was here to learn a lesson and once she could prove she had, she could go home. Leaning forward towards Clementine, her words came out in a rush. 'That I'm an ungrateful cow who doesn't appreciate what she's got. I had a wonderful husband who loved me and I took him for granted. I lusted after another man – although I never took that seriously, to be fair. I had supportive friends and family but I didn't think they were exciting enough. But they were! I had a perfect life and I want to go back to it. There's no place like home!' Ally leapt to her feet and squeezed her eyes shut. 'There's no place like home, there's no place like home, there's no place like home.'

She opened her eyes, her breath rushing out, her shoulders slumping in exhaustion.

'Do you think you're Dorothy or something?'

Ally was still standing in the flash apartment, Clementine barely able to keep a straight face as she looked up at her.

'There's no time limit. This is it.' Clementine spread her arms wide. 'Your new life. So you'd better get used to it.'

'And you couldn't have just said that before I went off on one and made a fool of myself?'

Clementine giggled. 'Where would the fun in that be?'

Clementine was no angel. She was the devil himself. Or herself. 'Can I not make another wish? Wish for my old life back?'

'I'm afraid not. Although that would make things much simpler, wouldn't it?'

Wouldn't it just? 'Can I tell people about my wish?'

'Of course. We don't restrict your movements and you have complete freedom of speech. We're not the Gestapo, you know. But you may want to give it some serious thought before you tell anybody. It's highly unlikely anyone will believe you and your family already think you're back on the drugs.'

Yes, there was that. Fairy had a point. 'Is it possible for me to find Gavin and make him fall in love with me in this life?'

'That's entirely possible.'

Yes!

Ally's phone beeping interrupted the exchange. It was a text message from Martine, simply saying 'Cocktails?' Ally read the message before discarding it.

'So we can start again and build up our old life together in *this* life?' Ally asked as she shoved her phone back into her handbag, but there was no reply. Clementine had disappeared.

Ally searched the apartment thoroughly. She wouldn't put it past Clementine to start up an impromptu game of hide and seek. But the apartment was empty.

Would she be back again or was Ally on her own now?

TWELVE

Ally had finally managed to convince herself that Clementine wasn't playing a trick on her and hiding in the apartment, about to pop up from behind the sofa and scare the crap out of her, when the intercom buzzed and did the job anyway. With a hand on her overly beating chest, Ally headed to the control panel and asked who it was.

'It's me, babe. Martine.'

Ally groaned. Deep down she'd known this day would come and she would have to meet Alana's friends, but she wasn't ready and, if she was honest, she didn't *want* to meet them. She didn't want any part of this life.

'Hello? Are you going to let me in or what? I'm freezing my tits off out here.'

'Sorry.' Ally hesitated another moment before she pressed the button to allow Martine into the building. Dread rose from her gut and threatened to choke her.

'Get a grip,' she muttered to herself. She'd let the woman in, chat for five minutes – perhaps pluck her own ears off the side of her head so she didn't have to listen to the inane Martine – and then claim she was knackered and wanted to go to bed. Which wasn't stretching the truth too much. All the stress of trying to track down a missing husband was exhausting.

'Babe, where have you been?' Martine asked by way of greeting as she brushed past Ally and wandered through to the kitchen, where she grabbed a bottle of wine from the fridge. She was definitely the woman from the photos but she looked much younger in real life and must have been in her early twenties. Her blonde hair was long and fine, reaching the middle of her back, and she was painfully thin, her caked on make-up contributing to most of her weight.

'You missed an *epic* night, babe.' Martine had pulled a couple of glasses out of the cupboard and was filling them to the brim with wine. 'Chantelle turned up and looked a *state* and then she got off with Fat Ricky. It was *hilarious*.'

It sounded it. Ally could barely contain her mirth.

'So where were you?' Martine sashayed across to the sofas, her wrists jangling with the dozens of multi-coloured bangles that adorned them.

'I was here.'

Martine set the wine on the coffee table and

plonked herself on the sofa. She barely made a dent in the leather. 'Ooh, sounds juicy. Tell me more.' She patted the space beside her and Ally found herself sitting beside the Barbie-alike.

'There's nothing to tell. I had an early night.'

'But with who?' Martine raised her whisker-thin eyebrows. 'Was it Jason? I bet it was, you dirty mare. Or was it Eric from downstairs? He is *divine*.'

'It was nobody. I was here alone.'

Martine spluttered. 'Alone? As in on your own?'

Give the girl a gold star. 'Yes, alone.'

'And you went to bed? On your own?'

'Yep.'

Martine pressed her lips together and wrinkled her brow as she observed Ally. Could she tell she wasn't the same person?

'Well, that's not going to happen tonight, missy.' Martine slapped Ally on the thigh and, although she was tiny, it hurt. 'Go and get changed and we'll go into town. Callum told me about this *amazing* club that we have to check out. He says he might be there tonight.'

Ally tried to say no, but Martine refused to listen and resorted to dragging Ally off the sofa and to her bedroom.

'You bailed on me last night. You're not doing the same tonight. It's *Friday*. You have to come out. You've got five minutes to get changed and if you're not ready, I'll come in and get you dressed myself.'

Ally believed her. Martine was surprisingly

strong for a bag of bones.

Forty-five minutes later, Ally was squeezed into a tacky silver dress – a compromise on the PVC monstrosity Martine had tried to coerce her into – and her face was hidden behind a good four inches of make-up. She felt – and looked – ridiculous.

'Do you think he'll be there?' Martine was checking her hair and make-up in a little compact mirror as the taxi trundled along on its way to the club, touching up her already overly glossed lips.

'Who?'

'Callum.' Martine snapped the mirror shut and dropped it into her tiny handbag. 'You don't mind, do you? About me and Cal? I know you like him, but it just sort of happened, and it isn't like the two of you ever hooked up or anything.'

'It's fine.' Ally didn't even know this Callum dude, so she could hardly take offence that Martine had swooped in and taken him for herself. She was welcome to him.

'Really?' Martine gave a dramatic sigh of relief and threw her skinny arms around Ally. 'You're the best, babe. I quite like him, you know. He's dead fit and he takes my mind off you-know-who.' Ally didn't know who but she kept it zipped. 'Cal said he'd call me but he hasn't yet. That doesn't mean anything though, does it? We only got together last night, and he probably knows we'll meet up tonight. Shall I text him?'

Ally shrugged her shoulders. She didn't have a clue what the rules were when it came to dating any more, or whether there *were* rules these days.

'I'll leave it for now. I don't want to come across as needy. Oh, we're here.'

Ally didn't venture into clubs very often any more. Freya and Dee occasionally dragged her into town but Ally was more at home nestled in a pub with a glass of wine and relaxed conversation. She wasn't relishing the thought of being on her feet all night in Alana's heels and, judging by the queue at the door, it would be quite some time before they actually made it inside. She wished she'd fought her corner more when she'd attempted to grab a jacket on the way out, but Martine had been adamant that she couldn't wear one.

Martine tugged on Ally's arm as she headed towards the back of the queue, which was snaking around the building. 'Where are you going?' Ally pointed to the haphazard row of disgruntled people, shivering in the chilly night. 'Don't be daft, babe.' She laughed and shook her head at her foolish friend as she towed Ally towards the entrance. Two huge guys blocked the doorway, allowing a handful of people inside at their leisure. Ally cringed, picturing the rejection as they attempted to saunter inside, but some sort of voodoo occurred. Martine purred at the doormen, tossing her hair over her shoulder and sticking out her small chest. She giggled, bit her bottom lip and pouted and, miraculously, the big blokes stepped aside and allowed them to step into the club.

'I'll get us some drinks,' Ally offered but Martine

grasped her arm.

'What are you doing? We're not *paying* for drinks. What's up with you lately, Alana?' Not waiting for an answer, Martine stalked towards a group of lads in their early twenties and worked her voodoo until she reappeared with two drinks in hand.

'This is from Philip. He thinks you're cute, bless him.' Martine handed Ally a yellow cocktail filled with crushed ice. It resembled a lemon slush. She took a tentative sip but soon went back for more. It was cool and delicious with a tang of citrus against a syrupy sweetness and a good kick of alcohol. Perhaps it had been worth coming into town after all.

'Have you seen Cal yet?' Martine strained her neck to look in every nook and cranny of the club, and Ally had a nosy round too, though she wouldn't have recognised Callum if he was standing in front of her. 'Where is he? I was sure he'd be here by now.'

'It's still pretty early.' Ally wasn't sure how things worked nowadays – was turning up late still fashionable? But she would have said anything to take the anguished look off Martine's face.

'I guess.' Martine gave a shrug. 'Do I look okay?'

Martine looked like a cheap-rate hooker. 'You look great.'

The club was starting to fill up, so Ally and Martine secured a couple of seats, accepting another round of drinks from poor Philip before

Martine swatted him away. She wasn't interested in holding a conversation with the guy and there were plenty of other saps to supply their drinks for the night. As midnight drew nearer, Martine gave in and sent Callum a text.

'So what's going on with your love life?' Martine sneaked a look at her mobile before slipping it back inside her bag. Callum hadn't replied yet.

'I don't have a love life.' Not until she found Gavin.

'No offence, babe, but that's utter bullshit. There must be someone on the scene. You haven't flirted with anyone tonight, not even the guy who bought the last round and he was *hot*. It's not Jason, is it?'

Ally choked on a rogue shard of ice from her drink. 'No.'

'He's got under your skin, hasn't he?' Martine's mouth drooped as she folded her arms across her chest. 'I knew this would happen. I warned you, didn't I?'

'He hasn't got under my skin, I swear.'

Martine's eyes narrowed, almost disappearing completely beneath the eyeliner. 'Are you sure?'

'Positive.'

'Good, because that isn't part of the plan.'

What plan? Ally didn't get the chance to enquire as Martine leapt out of her seat, eyes now wide and almost popping out of her skull. 'Cal's here. And he's with *Chantelle*.' Giving a strangled roar, Martine stamped her foot. 'That bitch! She's all over him.'

'Are you okay? We could go home.' Ally was already gathering her handbag and draining her drink, her head already halfway onto her pillow. The yellow slush cocktail was delicious, but it was way past her bedtime.

'Are you kidding me? There's plenty more fish and all that. Come on.' Martine grasped Ally's hand and hauled her onto the dance floor where she homed in on the best looking bloke she could see, sliding up and down his thighs like a lap dancer.

Sweet Jesus. Ally could tell the night had only just begun.

It was after 3am by the time Ally stumbled into the apartment, heading straight to bed without bothering to wash or undress. What felt like mere minutes later, Ally was awoken by the buzz of the intercom. With great effort, Ally dragged her pillow over her head as the ignored intercom buzzed again. She had no idea what time it was but she knew it was far too early for a social visit.

After the third buzz, the intercom was abandoned and Ally began to drift off back to sleep, only to be disturbed by hammering on her front door.

'Go away,' Ally growled into her pillow, but whoever was out there was persistent and she was forced to drag her weary body out of bed and into the hallway. She was still wearing the silver dress and her make-up was smeared all over her face, but she was in too much pain to care about appearances.

'Oh, it's you.' Ally should have been relieved to see Martine was still alive and well after she'd gone home with her lap dance partner from the club, but her brain was far too busy thumping its way out of her skull to register any such emotion.

'Good morning to you too. Did I wake you up?' Martine breezed into the apartment looking fresh in a pink floral dress and woollen shrug, her sugary pink handbag in the crook of her elbow. 'Oh dear, you're not a morning person, are you? Do you want to jump in the shower and then we can get going? Our appointment's at ten, so you'll have to hurry.'

'Appointment for what?'

'Blimey, that hangover must be really bad, babe. It's Saturday.' Martine thought that would be enough to jog her memory but was forced to elaborate when she was met by a blank look. 'Sparkle?' Still blank. 'Wake up, Alana, we're going to the salon.'

The salon? No, no, no. Ally had more important things to do than get her nails painted, like finding her husband. 'Actually, I'm really busy today. Could we go another day?'

Martine took a step back and looked as though she'd been slapped across the face. 'We go to Sparkle every Saturday and we're already booked in. *And* you promised we'd go shopping afterwards. It isn't very often I get a whole Saturday off from work and you said we'd make the most of it.'

Shopping did sound like a good idea, judging by the state of Alana's wardrobe. She could buy clothes that actually covered her body and non-stripper underwear. And pyjamas!

'Fine, we'll go to the salon.'

Martine clapped her hands. 'Good. I hate to say this, babe, but your roots are a mess.'

Funny, Martine didn't sound pained as she delivered the news.

Ally showered and dressed in Alana's slutty clothes for the last time before climbing into Martine's Barbie-pink car. They were greeted like long-lost friends at the salon, offered glasses of champagne – which Ally declined due to the fact she already consisted of eighty per cent alcohol after last night – and they didn't have to wait more than five minutes before their treatments began. Ally was treated like a princess as her roots were tended to and she was more than impressed by the customer service. Until it came to paying and then it dawned on her why they had been treated like royalty.

'We do this every week?' Ally asked as she emerged from the salon with an abused credit card. No wonder she was known for going cap in hand to her parents.

'You're acting really weird. But your hair looks fab.' Martine led the way to her car and drove them to a restaurant in town for lunch. Ally could get used to this pampering if it didn't cost so much.

'So, I need your advice,' Martine said as she

speared a tomato.

'Oh?' Ally couldn't imagine what kind of advice she could offer Martine, unless she wanted tips on cotton briefs or quiet nights in.

'You know I have that major crush on you-know-who at work?' Again, Ally didn't know who but she gave an affirmative murmuring sound. 'Well, nothing is working. He isn't picking up on my vibes at all. So that's where you come in. You're the expert at snaring married men. What do I do?'

Ally paused, the piece of chicken sliding off her fork mid-air. The expert at snaring married men? Just what kind of life had she wished for?

THIRTEEN

Ally was itching to carry on her search for Gavin, to actually get out there and find him. Yesterday had been a Gavin-disaster as the salon and shopping trip took up most of the day, and then Martine had insisted on taking Ally for a thank-you drink after pouring out her heart about you-know-who (Ally still didn't know who). The thank-you drink had turned into a bit of a session – Ally feared she was now hooked on yellow slush cocktails – but at least Ally had a comfortable pair of pyjamas to sleep in when she stumbled home, and it had been a relief to pull on a pair of jeans and a top that covered her body properly that morning. Ally was surprised she wasn't suffering from hyperthermia after wearing Alana's flimsy excuses for outfits over the past few days.

The rock-hard bread was now mouldy, so Ally dropped it into the chrome pedal bin and vowed to go shopping the first chance she got. Her appetite was coming back now the shock of waking up in Oz was wearing off, so she'd need to fill the cupboards and fridge. Ally checked the clock on the sitting room wall but she didn't have time to nip to the corner shop for a fresh loaf of bread. Neither did she have time to continue the Gavin hunt as it was Sunday and her family would worry if she didn't show up for their usual family lunch. They were disappointed in Ally enough without her adding to it further, so she grabbed her jacket and handbag and headed for the bus stop.

'Oh.' Linda blinked at her daughter, unable to keep her shock from rippling onto her face. She knew she should be stepping aside and allowing Alana into the house, but her body refused to cooperate. 'It's you. Did you forget something the other day?' Linda hadn't spotted any abandoned items when she'd returned from the school, but then she'd been too busy checking everything of value was still where she'd left it, which, surprisingly, it had been.

'I don't think so.' Ally plastered a smile onto her face, doing her best to ignore the barrier that Linda had clearly thrown up upon seeing her.

'Right.' Linda smiled down at her daughter but it came out in a nervous wobble rather than with love or even friendliness. 'You'd better come through then. Everyone will be surprised to see you.' Linda led the way into the sitting room and forced cheeriness into her voice. 'Look everyone,

Alana's come to see us.'

Ally looked around at her family. Her father was the only one smiling at her, his eyes crinkled at the edges. Freya and Jared were staring at her with open mouths, as though she were a museum exhibition that had suddenly come to life before them. She guessed Alana hadn't made a habit of joining the family for Sunday lunch.

'Would you like to stay for lunch?' Linda asked, false cheer still very much in residence.

'I'd love to. If that's alright.' Ally had never felt like she was intruding on her own family before, but it was quite clear the others didn't think she belonged there. Even her mum floundered at her reply.

'Of course it's okay, love. I'll need to peel a few more potatoes, but it's no problem.'

'I'll give you a hand.'

Linda was jolted by the suggestion and her eyes darted from Ally to the kitchen. 'No, love, you're alright. You sit down.' She probably thought Ally would pocket the silverware and crystal glasses for drugs money – had they actually owned any. 'I'll go and sort it out and put the kettle on. Move over a bit, Freya. Let Alana sit down.'

Ally sandwiched herself between Freya and Jared on the sofa, feeling their gazes burn into her flesh. Rather than inquisitive, their gaze felt harsh and judgemental. Certainly unwelcoming.

'So where's Jimmy then?' Ally guessed their younger sister was upstairs doing her homework, but she had to say something – anything – to break the stifling silence.

'Who?'

Ally's eyes snapped towards her brother's and her stomach plummeted. Jared had no idea who she was talking about. She'd been so preoccupied with fearing she'd eradicated Gavin with her wish that she hadn't even considered the implications on her family. Had she somehow wished her sister away? But no, there she was, her photo grinning down at them from the wall.

'Jemima?' Ally tinkled out a laugh, hoping her guess was correct. 'Our sister?'

Ally had been the one to give Jemima her pet name when she was a toddler, but she suspected Alana had been too busy chasing married men to bother with her baby sister.

'You said Jimmy.'

'No I didn't. I said where's *Jemima*.' Ally rolled her eyes at Jared but he wasn't convinced, especially when Freya backed him up by giving a slight shake of her head. 'Anyway, what does it matter? Where is she? Busy with her homework?'

Freya spluttered. 'Yeah, right. Of course she is. She's upstairs studying really hard.' Freya took a turn at rolling her eyes. 'She hasn't come home yet. She's supposed to be with Shania.'

'Oh, that's nice.' Ally had no idea who Shania was, but she guessed it was far from nice that Jemima was with her by the look on Freya's face.

'Please don't wind your mother up about Jem.'

Bob had leaned forward in his chair and lowered his voice. 'She worries enough as it is.'

'And so she should. That Shania is a right little madam. She's a teen pregnancy waiting to happen.' Bob hissed at Freya to keep her voice down. 'Why should I? You need to do something about our Jem or she'll end up like...' Her voice trailed off but Ally could guess whose direction Jemima was heading in. She was another disappointment for the family in the making.

'We've tried talking to her but she won't listen.'

'Try harder, Dad, before it's too late.' Freya pushed herself off the sofa. 'I'll go and see if Mum needs a hand.'

Ally looked across the room at her father. His face was desolate as he wrung his hands on his lap. He'd already witnessed one child go off the rails and now it seemed his youngest daughter was following the same path.

'I could try talking to her.'

'You?' Jared's face twisted, as though Ally had suggested they send Jimmy – *Jemima* – to ask Katie Price's advice on how to behave.

'We've always been close.' Or at least they had been in their other life. Ally had been fifteen when Jemima surprised the whole family with her presence, but Ally had adored her baby sister from the start and Jemima had latched herself onto Ally, becoming her little shadow.

'*Too* close. That's why she's the way she is,' Jared said.

That did not sound good at all. Ally was only scratching at the surface of her own past behaviour and was already appalled, so she couldn't bring herself to imagine how her shadow had turned out.

'Leave it, Jared. Alana's only trying to help.'

Jared heaved himself up from the sofa and shook his head at their father. 'You've always been too soft on her. It's no wonder she's so messed up.'

Ally shrank back in her seat at her brother's words. She wanted to uncoil and tell him that she wasn't messed up at all, that she had a wonderful life. But from Jared's perspective, she had to agree with his assessment. Her life was no longer wonderful. But it would be, just as soon as she found Gavin.

'Don't talk about your sister like that,' Bob pleaded but Jared had already stalked from the room. Ally gave her dad a smile, grateful that he'd fought her corner.

'I'm going to sort myself out, Dad. I promise.' She couldn't bear to disappoint her family. They'd always been so close and it made her ache to think that they all thought of her with such derision, that they thought she was capable of sleeping around with married men and drowning in a drug problem.

'I know you will, love.' Bob returned the smile and Ally felt the ache recede a little until Bob fished his wallet out of his back pocket. 'Do you need some money to tide you over? I can't give you much but will fifty do? Just don't tell your mum.'

Tears pooled in Ally's eyes but she blinked away

the sting. 'It's okay. Put your money away. I don't need it.'

'No?' Bob's dark bushy eyebrows almost reached his hairline. 'Right. That's grand then.'

'But thanks for the offer. I think I'll go and see if Mum needs some help too.'

Ally found Freya alone in the kitchen, making cups of tea and coffee and singing to herself. It was 'Girls Just Want To Have Fun', the last song Ally had heard her sing at the karaoke the night before her birthday. Ally paused in the doorway to listen, the ache intensifying. She wanted to wrap her arms around Freya and feel the bond they'd always had. There were eleven short months between the girls and they'd been inseparable as children. They'd always been there for each other and Freya had fully supported Ally's decision to end her relationship with Gavin when she went away to university, even though she thought Ally was making a huge mistake. Ally had repaid the favour when Freya had bizarrely broken off her eighteen-month relationship with Lovely Paul, even though it was Freya's best and longest relationship to date.

Ally missed her sister. She missed their easy relationship, their fun but close bond. If Ally needed advice, which she needed by the bucketful right now, she'd go to Freya. But that had changed now. Their bond was no longer there and it felt like Freya was a stranger in her sister's skin.

FOURTEEN

Jimmy – *Jemima* – turned up during the middle of lunch, barging into the dining room while singing along to her iPod. She plucked the earphones out as the family stopped eating to stare at her, Ally more than anyone. What had happened to her little sister? Jemima's gorgeous chocolaty hair had been butchered into messy layers and laced with cheap, yellow highlights, and her pretty face was hidden beneath a thick coating of orange foundation. This was definite Oompa Loompa territory.

Jemima placed a hand on her hip, raising the thin, black pencil lines that stood where her eyebrows should be. 'What's your problem?'

'Where have you been? You were supposed to be home by eleven.'

Jemima sneered at her mother. 'We slept in. What's the big deal? I'm here now and I'm fucking starving.'

Ally's own (real) eyebrows shot up. Of course she swore herself, but she'd never dared to use foul language in front of her parents, not even as an adult. She shrank back in her seat, awaiting the outcome.

'There's a plate in the oven.' Linda gave a barely audible sigh as she rearranged her cutlery and began cutting into her roast beef.

That was it? Ally had been expecting fireworks or a good ticking off at least, but the matter was dropped as Jemima sauntered across the kitchen, returning a moment later with a plate heaped with food. She squeezed between Ally and Bob and started to pick at her food with her fingers.

'So what did you and Shania get up to last night?' Linda asked.

Jemima took in a long, slow lungful of breath, pausing for a second before she puffed it all out in one go. 'We just hung out, okay?'

'No need to get tetchy. I was only asking a simple question.'

'Bullshit. It's never a *simple question*. It starts that way but then it turns into a fucking interrogation.'

'Can you stop swearing please?' Bob finally stepped in, just as Ally was beginning to suspect she was the only one who could hear Jemima's bad language.

'God, Dad. I'm *expressing* myself. Is that not allowed any more?' Jemima flicked her nasty hair over her shoulder and observed the ceiling while her foot tapped beneath the table.

'Not when it means you talking to your mother like that.'

'Leave it, Bob.' Linda gave her husband a tight smile from across the table. She was grateful for his support but she'd learned over the years that it wasn't worth the fuss.

'Yeah, leave it, *Bob*.' Jemima picked up a piece of beef, scrutinising it before curling her lip and dropping it back on the plate and splashing gravy onto the table. 'I'm going out. I said I'd meet up with Toby and Josh.'

'But what about your homework?' Linda asked as Jemima sauntered across the room. 'You promised you'd do it this afternoon if I let you stay over at Shania's.'

'I'll do it later.' Jemima had already vacated the room, the front door slamming shut a second or two later. A hush descended upon the kitchen and everybody seemed frozen in place for a moment before they resumed eating. Ally's food remained untouched in front of her. She couldn't believe what she had witnessed.

'Are you really going to let her get away with that?' She'd been biting her tongue but could no longer keep it to herself. 'How did you let her get so disrespectful?'

Freya dropped her knife and fork as she twisted in her seat to face Ally, a laugh spluttering from her lips. 'How did *we* let her get so disrespectful? Who do you think she learned that behaviour from? Take a good look in the mirror before you go pointing the finger at other people.' She scraped back her chair and rose to her feet. 'I'm sorry, Mum. I can't sit here playing happy families with her.'

'Sit down and finish your lunch, love. Please.' Linda was almost at breaking point. These family lunches were stressful enough, but the strain had gone up a notch with Alana's arrival. Her presence had put everybody on edge because you never knew what you were going to get when she was around. Linda loved her daughter but she didn't like the way she treated people and she wouldn't have other members of the family driven away.

'It's okay. I'll go.' Ally felt like the life was being squeezed out of her from the pressure in her chest, but she managed to stand, albeit on weak legs. It was abundantly clear she hadn't been expected at the house today and, to some extent, wasn't wanted there either. She'd tried to ignore it, to persevere and hope that everybody would realise she'd changed, but apparently it wouldn't be as easy as that. Memories of the past thirty years of selfish and reckless behaviour couldn't be erased over one lunch.

'You don't have to go,' Linda said, but there was relief on her face. The ordeal was almost over.

'I have stuff to do but thanks for having me.' Ally stooped to kiss first her mum on the cheek then her dad. Their surprise at her affection gave her chest another squeeze. She wouldn't be able to breathe at all if she remained there much longer.

Ally had planned to search for Gavin after lunch, to scour his old haunts in the hope of bumping into him, but she was overcome with exhaustion as she shut the front door behind her and headed for the bus stop. She was weary of this life, of missing her friends and family and Gavin. She needed to find her husband, but right then the fight had left her body. She needed to curl up and cry and mourn the life she'd thrown away. She would find Gavin tomorrow, when she was feeling strong again.

Ally prayed that she'd find Gavin soon. She needed to feel his arms around her, to feel safe again. But more than that, she needed to see a familiar face that trusted her.

Ally felt much better by the following morning, having collapsed onto the bed after the disastrous lunch and slept until her alarm clock chirped at her. She'd showered and felt invigorated as she dressed in her new Ally-like clothes. She could sort her life out, she really could. It would take time and determination but she could do it. She wouldn't allow herself to be suffocated by Alana. Today would be the day she found Gavin.

Ally's work was spilling out of her in-tray and threatening to take over the entire desk, but she barely gave it a glance as she began her search for her husband. She would comb his old haunts later, but for now, while she was in the office, she would utilise the internet and the office's phone. A search of local garages threw up a seemingly endless list, but Ally didn't pause to think about it in case it became overwhelming. Instead, she picked up the phone and dialled the first number.

The first three garages didn't have an employee called Gavin, and her phone rang before she could move onto the fourth. Ally snatched up the receiver with a growl, mentally cursing whoever had interrupted her search.

It was Greta, the MD's secretary. 'Alana? Malcolm's waiting for you.'

Malcolm? Why was he – Ally gasped. Their meeting. She'd totally forgotten. 'I'm so sorry. I'll be right there.' She threw the phone down, turned off her computer's monitor to hide her activity and hurried out of HR and along to the MD's office at the end of the corridor. Greta threw her a reproachful look, but she showed Ally through to Malcolm's office without a word.

'So.' Malcolm sat up straight as the door clicked shut, resting his clasped hands on top of the desk. 'You've put in a complaint of sexual harassment.'

'I have?'

'I know this may be very difficult for you, Alana.' Malcolm flashed a smile through his bushy beard and it was an act of such kindness that Ally felt her eyes fill with tears. She'd been met with hostility for the most part over the past few days, so that simple smile brought a lump to her throat. 'Would you like a tissue? A glass of water?'

Ally shook her head and tried to get a grip. 'It's okay. I'm fine.'

Malcolm bobbed his head. 'I know this must be terribly hard for you, but I need you to tell me everything that has happened.' He picked up his pen and pulled a notepad towards him. 'When did it start?'

'When did what start?'

Malcolm looked up from his notepad, pen still poised. 'The harassment. You said Jason Jackson has been making lewd comments and sending you suggestive text messages. Can you remember when that began?'

Nervous laughter fizzed in Ally's stomach but she refused to allow it to roam any further. Jason hadn't been sexually harassing her. Yes, it was more than likely that he'd made lewd comments and Ally had seen the text messages, but it had been mutual. Ally had seen the messages from both Jason and Alana.

Although, when she thought about it, Alana's responses could be viewed as innocent. She thought back over the messages she'd read:

Hey, babe. Meet at mine tonight?
I'm trying to work. Please stop texting me.
Are you playing hard to get? I love it.
And:

You look hot today. And I can see your nipples through your blouse. Good work.
You're my boss. You're not supposed to be saying things like that to me.

But you love it.
Says who?
You, you dirty minx.
You're being very naughty.
Just how you like me.

Could it be that the attention was one-sided and that Alana hadn't been interested? That Jason *was* harassing her? But no, Martine knew about the relationship and there was also the sex-on-the-desk incident. Why would Alana do that if she'd felt she was being harassed by Jason? No, Ally was certain it wasn't one-sided, no matter what Alana was now claiming.

'I think there's been some sort of mistake.'

'Oh?' Malcolm dropped his pen and leaned back in his chair, his head tilting to one side.

'Jason hasn't been sexually harassing me.'

'Then why did you make the complaint?' Malcolm's body was in the exact same position and his tone was still friendly, but something had shifted. Perhaps it was the hardening of his eyes or the stiffness of his lips.

'I don't know.' Which was the truth. Ally had no idea what Alana was playing at.

Malcolm straightened in his chair, folding his arms across his chest. 'You do realise what a serious matter this is, don't you?' Ally nodded, afraid now Malcolm's friendly tone had disappeared. His eyebrows knotted and his cheeks flushed as he leaned towards her on his desk. 'Then why the hell have you made such an accusation?

Do you realise how damaging complaints like these can be?'

'I'm sorry.'

Malcolm's laugh erupted like a baying wolf. 'Sorry? *You're sorry*? You've accused an innocent man and wasted my time and *you're sorry*?'

Shit, she was going to lose her job, wasn't she? She could imagine the smug grin on Kelly's face as she was forced to pack up her stuff and vacate the building. And she'd thought her life was messed up already.

'Get out.' Malcolm's voice was a low growl as he pointed towards his door. Ally did as she was told, leaping out of her chair and scuttling from the room.

This was all getting out of hand. She needed to find Gavin. *Now*.

Ally began her physical search of Gavin straight after work that evening, catching the bus to MacMillan Road. The urge to hammer on 'her' door once more was strong but she managed to quell the feeling and, keeping her head down so she would see neither her old sitting room or Maud and Eve, she scurried past the house to The Farthing. Had it only been a few days since she'd stood on this street, convinced she was losing the plot? It felt like weeks had passed, each day painfully elongated.

The Farthing was open but you wouldn't have guessed it from the lack of customers. A lone old man nursed a pint in one corner of the room while the barman slumped against the bar, his head resting on his hands as he stared into space, emitting little puffs of boredom at intervals. He jumped to attention when the pub door swung open and pounced on Ally.

'A diet coke, please.' Ally took another glance around the pub while the barman sorted her drink but nope, the old man was still the only other customer. 'You don't happen to know a Gavin Richmond, do you? Tallish with dark hair that needs a good cut?' The hair thing had always niggled Ally. He looked better with it closely cropped, but Gavin wasn't that fussed and months would pass between trims until it took on a shaggy quality. Ally would have given anything to run her hands through his unruly mop right now.

The barman shook his head. 'Nah, sorry. Name doesn't sound familiar.'

'He has lovely brown eyes.' Ally was getting desperate now. She was pretty sure the barman didn't go around scrutinising the eye colour of his customers. Not the men's, anyway.

'Sorry.' He placed the drink on the bar, which Ally paid for and carried over to a table in the middle of the room where she would have a perfect view of both the door and the bar.

Ally wasn't sure how much more of this she could take. It wasn't simply missing Gavin. It was *everything*. Being despised by her best friend and mistrusted by her entire family. Peeling away the layers and discovering how deep her vileness in this life went. She somehow had to put things right, and not only with Gavin. She had to convince her family she no longer saw them as her personal piggy bank and show Francine that she wasn't the shallow bitch she thought she was. If it was possible to make Gavin fall in love with her again, it should be possible to change Francine's opinion of her too. It would mean starting their friendship from scratch, but Ally knew it would be worth it.

The diet coke was depleted and the lone man had shuffled off home. It was after seven o'clock and Ally's stomach was rumbling. She should go. The barman didn't know who Gavin was and it didn't look like there would be any other customers anytime soon. Ally would come back tomorrow evening and try again.

Ally gathered her coat and was slipping her arms through it when the door opened and a couple of blokes walked in. Hope surged through Ally's body, heat radiating from her stomach and spreading through her veins, leaving a tingling sensation in its wake. It wasn't Gavin but it *was* Lovely Paul, one of his best friends. Paul would know where Gavin was. Perhaps he would be meeting him here for a couple of pints later. If not, he'd have his phone number at the very least.

'Paul, hi.' Ally bounded over, still shoving her arms into her coat. Lovely Paul – named so because he was the kindest, most gentle and caring man on the planet – looked up at Ally without a hint of recognition. Which was fine. She hadn't expected anything else. Not really.

'Hi.' Paul smiled at her, his eyes squinting slightly as he attempted to place this woman. He didn't have a clue who she was but he was too polite to tell her that.

'Don't worry, I don't think we've met,' Ally said, swallowing the truth. They'd been close once and Ally adored the man. She'd been distraught when Freya ended the relationship after eighteen months and couldn't understand why her sister would let a man like Paul go.

'But I know your friend, Gavin.' Ally was trembling but trying not to let it show. Paul, as lovely as he was, would never pass on Gavin's information if he suspected she was some sort of nut job stalker.

'I'm sorry, who?'

Ally's trembling went up a gear until she was vibrating and practically drilling a hole in the pub's floor. 'Gavin. Gavin Richmond.' She wanted to grab Lovely Paul by the collar and give him a good shake. My husband! I'm looking for my husband!

'I'm sorry, I think you've got the wrong person. I don't know anybody called Gavin.'

Ally slumped onto the nearest stool, her legs too weak to hold her up, and dropped her head into her hands. Of course Lovely Paul didn't know Gavin. They'd met through Freya. Ally had thought she'd cracked it, but now disappointment stung the backs of her eyes. She'd thought she was so close to tracking Gavin down. So close to living happily ever after.

'Are you okay?' Lovely Paul reached out and rested a hand on her shoulder. He crouched down in front of her and attempted to catch her eye through her fingers.

'Yeah, I'm fine. Thank you.' Ally lifted her head and swiped the stray tears of frustration from under her eyes. She'd been so close. *So close*. 'I'm sorry for creating a scene.' Ally leapt from her seat and hurried away from Lovely Paul, leaving all hope of finding Gavin in a heap on the pub's floor.

FIFTEEN

Ally had managed to claw back a little bit of hope by the following morning after a decent meal and a good night's sleep. She'd finally ventured into the supermarket and stocked up the cupboards on the way home from The Farthing, if only to take her mind off the hopelessness of it all. She'd eaten, taken a long soak in the bath (which was a huge, whirlpool type of bath. Possibly the only plus side of this whole affair) and climbed into bed, falling asleep with ease. She dreamed of Gavin and saw his face up so close she could see his love for her radiating from his eyes. That love couldn't disappear. It would all work out if she could find him. She *had* to find him and she would.

'Good morning.' Ally had taken to scurrying past the reception desk and Francine's scowling face, but she forced herself to stop that morning and gave her former best friend her warmest smile, though she didn't hang around to be glowered at. A friendly smile and a 'good morning' was a tiny gesture, but she had to start at the bottom and work her way up.

'What are you looking so chirpy about?' Kelly asked as Ally breezed into the office. 'Run over a kitten on your way to work?'

'No, but I think I clipped your wing mirror.' Ally covered her mouth with her fingers. 'Oopsies.'

'What?' Kelly leapt from her desk and sprinted out of the door despite her six-inch heels, which Ally could hear clattering down the stairs. If she wasn't careful, she'd take a tumble. Where was a banana skin when you needed one?

'What was that all about?' Jason wandered out of his office with a sheaf of papers, which he dumped in Ally's mountainous in-tray.

Ally gave a shrug. 'Just Kelly being Kelly.'

'Do you fancy a coffee?' Ally couldn't meet Jason's eye as he strode towards her, due to both the office quickie revelation and the fact she'd wrongly reported him for sexual misconduct.

'Coffee would be great, thanks.' She began sifting through her in-tray and attempted to make the contents appear smaller by rearranging them in a neater fashion. There was so much to do and some of it was marked as urgent, but Ally had more important things to be getting on with. She opened her saved Google search and, taking advantage of the empty office, resumed her telephone enquiries.

'Idiot!' Kelly burst into the room, gasping for air.

Her legs weren't quite so steady in the crippling heels as she tottered back to her desk. 'There's nothing wrong with my wing mirror and your car isn't anywhere near mine.'

Ally hung up the phone on yet another negative response. 'Oh, that's right. I caught the bus to work. Silly me.'

Kelly narrowed her eyes to slits. It wasn't a good look, even on the gorgeous Kelly. 'You are such a–' She snapped her mouth shut as Jason strode into the office with a tray of coffees.

'Such a what?' Ally asked, but Kelly remained quiet and turned her attention to her computer. She was probably Googling acts of revenge but Ally didn't care. It was peaceful and that was all that mattered. She smiled her thanks as Jason handed her a cup of coffee, waiting until he was safely sat at his own desk before she picked up the phone.

'Hi, I was wondering if you had an employee called Gavin Richmond?' As with all the calls, Ally's stomach fizzed as she awaited the answer from the latest garage.

'Nope, no Gavin Richmond. We've got a Gareth Jones. Do you want him?'

The bubbles in Ally's stomach popped cartoon-style and she slumped a little in her seat. 'No thanks. Bye.' Ally ended the call and dialled the next garage on the list. She was certain she'd be able to find him this way but she'd been hoping it would yield much faster results. Gavin would definitely work in a garage, whether it was in her father's or not. He'd never wanted to do anything but be a mechanic, ever since the first time Bob had let him tinker with an old engine to keep him busy during the summer holidays. He'd loved taking it apart and putting it back together again and had been hooked, spending every spare minute of the summer at the garage.

Ally dropped the phone into its cradle and felt her mouth go dry. No, no, no. Gavin hadn't spent that summer at the garage, had he? Bob had never given him an old engine to tinker with, had never sparked a passion for cars.

What if Gavin had never become hooked on engines? What if he'd chosen a completely different career path in life? If Gavin wasn't a mechanic, this was Ally's strongest lead to finding him gone.

SIXTEEN

The bus was hot and clammy, packed to capacity as people rushed home from work. To their families, Ally thought, shooting daggers at the flop of dark hair in front of her. She bet the owner of that hair was going home to the bosom of his family, to a wife or girlfriend. Ally bet he wasn't about to crack with despair at the thought of spending yet another night alone, long bored with his own company. Lucky bastard.

Ally shuffled towards the front of the bus, clinging onto the rail as the bus made an abrupt but now familiar turn and hissed to a stop. She mumbled her thanks as she stepped out into the cold, buttoning her coat as she ambled along the pavement towards Marley House. The road was long and busy but the apartment block was set back from the road with a tree-lined residents' car park, so you could almost forget you were so close to the city centre.

'There you are!' Martine leapt out of her sugary pink car and clip-clopped her way to Ally. 'Your car's here so I thought you were ignoring me.'

Ally wouldn't do that. She'd already learned it would be pointless when it came to Martine. That was one determined girl.

'I caught the bus to work.'

'Eww, why?' Martine hitched her oversized handbag onto her elbow and fell into step with Ally as she made her way towards the building.

How could Ally explain that she could no longer drive? That she'd never actually had the ability to do so? She couldn't, so she simply ignored the question.

'Coffee?' Ally asked as they stepped out of the lift and headed towards her apartment. She'd planned to kick off her shoes and spend the evening moping about Gavin, but she supposed she had to attempt to be a good host if Martine insisted on joining her.

'Forget coffee. I have wine.' Martine pulled the bottle from her bag along with a square plastic box. 'And sushi.'

'Sushi? Yuck.' Ally couldn't stand the thought of putting raw fish and seaweed into her mouth, but the wine did sound good.

Martine grabbed Ally's arm as she reached to unlock the door. 'But sushi's your favourite food.'

Oh. 'I know but I've gone off it lately.' Ally resumed her unlocking of the door, stooping to pick up a hand-delivered note from the mat as she stepped over the threshold.

'Fair enough. More for me.' Martine bustled past Ally, who had paused in the doorway, heading straight to the kitchen to grab a couple of glasses. She'd poured the wine and was tucking into the sushi by the time Ally wandered in from the hallway.

'You okay, babe?' Ally was still wearing her coat, her handbag still thrown over her shoulder. 'You're shaking.' Ally's hands trembled, rattling the piece of paper she held in her fingers, her eyes re-reading the words over and over again.

'I think I'm in trouble.'

'What are you talking about?' Martine unfolded herself from the sofa and plucked the note from Ally's fingers, her mouth gaping as she read it.

You owe me money. I'll be back. Pay up or else.

'OMG, babe. Who's it from?'

Ally shook her head. 'No idea.' Her eyes were so wide, she feared they were about to pop out of her skull.

Martine flipped the note over. That was it. Eleven measly words. 'It's not signed or anything. Who do you owe money to?' She gasped and bit her lip, her own eyes widening. 'It isn't the Lee brothers, is it? Because Martin's just got out of prison and he's proper mental. Apparently, he bit a guy's nuts off. Or his ear. One of the two.' Martine gave a wave of her hand, jangling a wrist full of sparkly pink bangles. 'It's not them, is it?'

Ally felt sick. 'I really don't know. It could be.' It could be anyone. But whoever it was, they weren't going to go through the legal channels of retrieving their money.

'Babe.' Martine whispered the word, fear swallowing her usual cheerful chatter. 'What are you going to do?'

Ally fought the urge to cry. What *was* she going to do? She'd never owed money to anybody, never mind a body-part-biting maniac. Damn you, Alana!

'I tell you what you need, babe.' Police protection? 'A drink. And something stronger than that.' Martine nodded at the glasses of wine waiting on the coffee table.

'A drink?' Ally could hardly believe her ears. 'Now isn't the time for a celebratory cocktail. This is *serious*.'

'So what are you going to do? Hang around here and wait for the Lee brothers to turn up and batter you with a baseball bat?' Martine clamped her mouth shut as Ally let out a yelp. She placed a hand on Ally's arm and gave it a squeeze. 'That won't happen, I'm sure. I mean, they'll probably *have* a baseball bat, but only to scare you with.'

Ally's legs buckled beneath her, her body wanting to crumple into a heap on the oak floor. This was not what she'd wished for. She'd wanted a bit more excitement, not to be beaten to a pulp by frenzied gangsters.

'Let's get out of here.'

Ally didn't go home that evening. Instead, she blocked out all thoughts of baseball-bat-wielding lunatics with copious amounts of alcohol before crashing at Martine's place. The thought of returning to her apartment filled her with dread, so she made her way straight to work the following morning, wearing the same, now crumpled clothes from the previous day. A fact that didn't go unnoticed at the office.

'Somebody pulled last night,' Kelly sang as Ally passed her desk. Jason, battling with the nearby photocopier, looked up from his task, giving Ally the once-over before turning away with a frown.

'I did not pull. I stayed over at a friend's, that's all.' Ally attempted to keep her head held high as she crossed the office, but failed miserably. She knew what it looked like, but she could hardly confess all to Kelly, could she?

'Oh, a "friend", eh? We believe her, don't we, Jason?'

'Get on with your work, please.' Jason refused to look up as he grabbed his documents and stalked to his office. A 150-mile-an-hour gust of wind couldn't have swiped the smirk from Kelly's face, which remained for the duration of the day. Ally tried to take her mind off her problems by immersing herself in her work, but her mind was never far from Gavin or the Lee brothers.

'What's going on?' It was the end of the day, the sky now a navy blue behind the closed blinds. Kelly had left half an hour ago and yet Ally remained at her desk, fear gluing her to the seat. Jason hovered by his office door, observing Ally from a safe distance.

Ally turned in her seat, planning to plaster on a fake smile and declare that nothing was going on. She was fine. Absolutely fine. Instead, her face crumpled and she burst into tears.

'Here you go.' Jason placed a glass of wine in front of Ally and settled into the opposite seat. They were in The Church, a pub around the corner from Westerly's. It was pretty quiet, with only a couple of other customers, but Ally still felt like a fool with her red-rimmed eyes and runny nose. The length of loo roll Jason had provided her with back in the office was still clutched in her hand, now a soggy, useless mass.

'Are you going to tell me what's wrong now? I mean, you don't have to. Not if you don't want to. But it might help. Or something.'

Ally's face relaxed into a smile. She'd never seen Jason looking so flustered. He must be way beyond his comfort zone, dealing with a sobbing mess of a woman.

'It's nothing, really.'

Jason's eyes dropped to Ally's hands, where she was fiddling with the sodden tissue. She threw it onto the table and picked up her drink, relieved when it didn't tremble within her grasp.

'Come off it, Alana. I know you. You don't do this.' He waved a hand at Ally's blotchy face. 'You don't *cry*. I wasn't even sure you were born with tear ducts.'

Ally found herself smiling again. 'Are you saying I lack emotion?'

Jason shrugged. 'Pretty much.'

That was probably a fair enough observation, judging from Alana's past.

'So, what is it?'

Ally found herself opening up to Jason, spilling everything. Not about the wish, obviously. Jason thinking she was cold and detached was one thing, she didn't want him thinking she was off her box too. She told him about the threatening note and Martine's suggestion that it could be the Lee brothers after her.

'But you don't know it's them?' Ally shook her head. '*Do* you owe them money?'

'I really don't know. I haven't been very good with my finances lately. But whoever it is, they want their money. And fast.'

'Don't you think it'd be a good idea to give it to them?'

Obviously. 'But I don't know who to give it to.'

'And you're not going to find out from here. Come on.' Jason stood up and held out his hand.

'Where are we going?'

'To your place.'

Ally had placed her hand in Jason's, but snatched it away again. 'Are you crazy? I told you the story of Martin Lee, right?' The image of the bollock-biter would haunt her dreams for the foreseeable future.

'I'll be there with you. I won't let anybody hurt you, I promise.'

Ally observed Jason for a moment, undecided whether she should be stepping back inside the lion's den. Jason was solidly built and obviously worked out, but Lee Martin was a nutter. A proper, old-style nutter.

'We'll sort this out. If they turn up, we'll find out how much you owe and arrange payment. There'll be no biting of body parts.' Jason placed a hand over his nether regions. 'I hope.'

'But what if they don't show up until later?'

'Then I'll sleep on the sofa and wait until they do. For however long it takes.'

SEVENTEEN

Although Ally couldn't say she'd slept well that night, it had been reassuring to have Jason's presence in the apartment. They'd stayed up late, watching TV to try to take Ally's mind off the threat, but her mind was constantly alert for any sounds that could indicate someone was on the other side of her flimsy front door, baseball bat in hand. Jason had curled up on the sofa while Ally attempted to sleep, drifting in and out until the sun finally rose again. Ally had never been so keen to jump out of bed and get to work. The day passed far too quickly for Ally's liking and she would have to face her apartment again very soon.

'Give me five more minutes,' Jason called from his office. Kelly had left almost an hour ago, but Ally was happy to stay as long as possible. She felt safe within the office and was dreading going home, whether Jason was there to offer protection or not.

While she waited, Ally scrolled through the list of local garages on her computer. She'd now exhausted the list with no luck. The closest she'd got was a Gavin Hendry, and even Ally couldn't convince herself that he had somehow needed to change his last name by deed pole. She was at a dead end, Gavin-wise.

Ally shut down her computer as Jason locked his office door, following him down to the car park at a snail's pace. She climbed into his car, trying desperately to come up with an excuse for a detour. An emergency stop off at the supermarket? A sudden but imperative need to visit the library to research... something?

'It'll be okay, you know.' Jason gave Ally's arm an encouraging rub. What had given her anxiety away? Her wild, petrified stare? The fact she was grasping her handbag so tightly her knuckles were deathly white?

Maybe they could go to the cinema? It had been *ages* since Ally had been. She'd even watch something explodey or overly gory.

Jason reached across to switch on the radio as his car rumbled into life, hoping the music would somehow soothe Ally during the journey. Of course nothing could soothe Ally at that moment in time, but at least he was trying.

Ally had resorted to praying for a crash as they made their way to the apartment, but they turned onto Palmerston Avenue with the car – and their bodies – perfectly intact. Marley House loomed above them, mocking Ally with its cheery façade, the sun shining off its oversized windows so that it resembled a giant diamond emerging from the lush foliage.

'Planning on camping out in the car?' Jason had already hopped out of the car and was standing above Ally, holding her door open. 'Hand me your keys and I'll bring you a blanket and a pillow down.'

'Funny.' Didn't he realise how terrifying this was for her? There was a maniac after her blood. Jason may have been under the impression that Martin Lee would be reasonable and listen to them before he started trashing the joint, but Ally was not. Hit first, questions later. That's how people like the Lee brothers operated. If they bothered to ask questions at all.

Jason held out a hand and Ally took it, almost crushing his fingers with her intense grip. She didn't let go as they headed into the building and was still clutching his hand as they stepped into the lift. Her grip tightened further as the lift reached her floor and the sound of hammering could be heard.

Thud, thud, thud.

Even before the lift doors opened, Ally knew the hammering was a fist on her front door. An angry fist demanding admittance.

'Stay here.' Jason put a hand out to prevent Ally from leaving the lift. Like she was going to step out there and face Martin Lee!

139

'Wait.' Ally's voice was a low hiss as she reached out to grab Jason's sleeve. 'You're not going out there, are you?'

'We've got to sort this. But get ready to press that button if I come running.' He pointed at the 'G' on the lift's panel before striding out into the corridor.

Thud, thud, thud.

Whoever was out there was not giving up. Ally crept forward a couple of steps, her arm outstretched to press the button to keep the lift doors open, but chickened out of peering around the corner. She leapt back again as Jason appeared. But rather than running for his life, the man was grinning.

'It's okay. Everything's okay.' A laugh popped out of Jason's mouth, which he attempted to cover up with a cough, but the smirk remained in place. 'Really, Alana. Come on. Come and meet your hardened criminal.'

Ally shrank back into the lift, but Jason grabbed hold of her elbow and tugged her out into the corridor, man-handling her towards her apartment. Ahead of them, standing outside her door with their arms folded across their chest was not a toothless, tattooed nut job. It was a short, plump old lady with a greying bun and soft leather sandals.

'You.' The old lady thrust a wrinkled finger at Ally. 'I want my money. *Now.*'

The little old lady – Ellen – sat hunched up on one of the red sofas, arms folded as she glared across the coffee table at Ally. She wore a floral dress with a pastel blue cardigan buttoned over the top and a dainty-looking crucifix around her neck. Ally could hardly believe she'd been frightened of this sweet-looking old lady and had to press her lips together to stop the giggle that was threatening to burst through, more from relief than humour.

'So, how much does Alana owe you then?' Jason placed a cup of tea on the table in front of Ellen before settling himself on Ally's sofa.

Ellen unclasped her patent handbag, removing a little floral notebook. Licking the tip of her index finger, she shuffled through the pages until she found the correct one. 'Forty-nine pounds and sixty-two pence.' At this, a guffaw rumbled from Jason, earning him a cocked eyebrow from Ellen. 'Do you think this is funny, young man? Because I don't. I *worked* for that money. I deserve to be paid.' It turned out that Ellen was Alana's cleaning lady. A cleaning lady who was at the end of her tether. She'd scrubbed and swept and washed and ironed for that lazy madam, and for what? To be fobbed off with 'Can I pay you next week, Mrs Andrews?' and 'It's pay day tomorrow. Can you come back then?' But the worse was 'I just need to pop out to the cash machine. I won't be a minute. Make yourself a cup of tea.' Forty-five minutes she'd waited. Forty-five minutes and the woman never returned. Had never had any intention of returning.

'You sent a threatening note over fifty quid?' The matter was no longer funny. Ally had been *petrified*. Jason had slept on the sofa and everything!

Ellen pulled herself to her full height – which wasn't much, to be honest. 'I did not send a threatening note.'

'No?' Ally reached into her own handbag and pulled out the now-crumpled note. 'You don't find "pay up or else" threatening? Or else what, Mrs Andrews?'

'Or else I won't clean for you any more. I do apologise if you got the wrong end of the stick, dear.' Ellen reached across to pick up her cup of tea and Ally was sure she saw the beginnings of a smirk as she brought it to her lips. 'My daughter says I should ask for interest, but I'm happy to take the amount owed.'

Ally rifled in her handbag for her purse, but there was little more than five pounds in change in there.

'Here.' Jason peeled fifty pounds out of his wallet, which Ellen snatched before stuffing it into her purse and putting an elaborate tick next to Ally's account in her notebook.

'Just so you know, I am no longer your cleaning lady.' Snapping her handbag shut, Ellen rose to her feet and smoothed down the skirt of her dress. 'I hope you understand.'

Jason showed her to the door, almost doubled

over with the exertion of laughing so hard upon his return. Slapping his thigh, he straightened as the laughter died down, only to start again when he saw Ally's face.

'This is not funny.' Ally snatched Ellen's half-empty cup from the coffee table and strode into the kitchen. She couldn't believe she'd been put through so much stress over this. 'And I'll pay you back in the morning.'

'You'd better. Or else.'

EIGHTEEN

Ally kicked off her shoes and dropped onto the sofa, folding her bare feet beneath her while Martine poured two generous glasses of wine and turned on the television. Martine had been relieved to see both Ally and the apartment were unharmed when she'd popped over. She'd been 'so worried about you, babe'. So worried, in fact, that this was the first time Ally had seen or heard from Martine since she'd received the 'threatening' note.

'Oh good, you've recorded them.' Flopping onto the sofa, Martine commandeered the remote and Ally's heart sank as she selected *America's Next Top Model*. It appeared 'she' had put it on series link. Ally had never watched an episode in her life as it wasn't really her kind of thing. She liked watching the soaps and dramas and the odd sitcom. These reality programmes always seemed hollow and pointless to her. But then Ally had never watched one of these programs with Martine, who spent the entire episode commenting on the models. She alternated between overly bitchy and complimentary, and Ally found herself joining in, taking her frustrations out on the poor girls.

'She is the nastiest, vilest person on the planet, but look at those cheekbones.' Martine placed her hands over her rosy cheeks. 'I'd *die* for cheekbones like that.'

'But her lips are a state. She puts Pete Burns to shame.'

'That's true. And my lips are pretty fabulous, don't you think?'

Ally nodded as Martine pouted at her. 'They're gorgeous. I'd snog you if I were a bloke.'

'Aww. Thanks, babe.'

Ally had possibly consumed too much wine. They'd quickly polished off the bottle Martine had arrived with before starting a second from Alana's vast collection.

'Camel toe alert!'

Ally's eyes snapped towards the huge television and she cringed. Nobody wanted to see that, especially when it was almost life-sized.

'Somebody should tell the poor cow.' Ally was mortified on her behalf.

'Are you kidding? It's way more fun this way.'

And, surprisingly, this *was* fun. Ally never thought she'd be able to say that about spending time with Martine.

'Shall I get more wine?'

Ally reached for the bottle and gave it a shake. They'd worked through that quickly. 'We shouldn't. We've got work in the morning.' She caught Martine's eye and they both grinned. 'Go on then. We're going to be hungover anyway. May as well make it worth it.'

'I don't have to worry about looking rough anyway,' Martine said as she weaved her way to the kitchen for another bottle. 'You-know-who won't be in. It's his kid's birthday or something.'

'He has a child?' Ally was horrified. How could Martine go after a man who was not only married but a father too?

Martine pulled a face as she plonked herself back down on the sofa. 'I know. It sucks, doesn't it? Can you imagine if we did get together? I'd be a *stepmother*.' She gave a shudder. 'Gross. *And* we'd never get rid of his wife. She'd always be hanging around, wouldn't she?'

'It's the sacrifice you have to make when you go after married men.' Ally was being sarcastic but Martine gave a sage nod.

'That's true. But he'll be worth it, won't he?'

Ally wouldn't know. She didn't even know the bloke's name. 'So who is he then? And why do you always call him you-know-who?'

'Because you're such a slut.' Martine giggled as she topped up their glasses. 'There is no way I'm telling you who he is. I'm not falling into that trap again.'

'What trap?'

'The one where I tell you I like a guy and you get in there first.'

'Do I do that?' Like Ally had to ask. Of course Alana did that.

'It's like a sport for you, babe. You don't even like them yourself half the time.'

Great. So even her best friend didn't trust her. 'I'm sorry. I won't do it again.'

Martine giggled again. 'Don't think I'm falling for that. If I tell you who he is, you'll go after him.' She shook her head. 'No way. It's my secret.'

'You don't have to tell me who he is but I promise I'll never go after a man you like.' Even if he wasn't married. 'I won't be going after any man. I'm already spoken for. Sort of.'

Martine's mouth drooped. 'Not Jason? I knew it! You've fallen for him.'

'It's not Jason.' Ally was sure she wouldn't have confided in Martine if they weren't on their third bottle of wine but she found herself opening up. 'It's this guy I used to know. We went to school together and were really close. We went our separate ways, but I can't stop thinking about him. I want to find him but I can't. I've tried everything – Facebook, Friends Reunited, places he might work. I even went to our old local pub.'

'Have you tried his mum?'

'His mum?'

Martine nodded. 'She'll know where he is.'

His *mum.* Of course!

'Martine, you're a genius.'

Martine gave her hair a flick. 'I do try, babe.'

Ally sat in the car, carefully placing her feet on the pedals. Clementine said she could drive and so she'd decided to test the theory. Finding Gavin would be much easier and quicker if she could drive, as long as she didn't wrap herself around a lamppost or something.

'Here we go.' With shaking hands, Ally managed to slot the key into the ignition and gave it a twist. The engine rumbled into life and Ally's hand instinctively reached for the gearstick and her eyes lifted to the mirror. Her body was taking over. Her body knew what it was doing, even if her mind didn't.

The car started to glide out of its parking spot. Ally indicated and she was out of the car park, the ride easy and smooth. She joined the rush-hour traffic without freaking out and even reached out to turn on the radio, singing along as she waited in a long line of cars. She was driving! She was actually driving. No longer shaking, she made it to work and rather than being filled with relief that she hadn't maimed anybody en route, she was filled with exhilaration and couldn't wait to get back behind the wheel to give it another go. She had to wait until after work, but finally Ally slid back into her car and headed for Gavin's parents' house. They'd once lived across the road from

Ally's parents but they'd moved to a pretty little village once Gavin left home. It took almost an hour to reach Hartfield Hill but Ally didn't mind as it gave her a chance to play with her new toy.

Ally parked outside Carolyn and Doug's little terraced cottage, marvelling at the ease with which she'd manoeuvred the car into the spot. The couple's car wasn't in sight, so Ally took a moment to calm her nerves and go over her plan. She spotted the car as it turned into the road but she remained seated until the optimum moment, just as Carolyn was emerging from her own vehicle.

'Oh my god, it's Carolyn, isn't it?'

Carolyn shut her car door before turning to Ally. There was a smile on her lips, but a slight frown revealed she didn't recognise Ally.

'I'm Ally Williams. I used to live across the road from you and I went to school with your Gavin.'

'Oh, you're Linda's daughter.' The frown lines softened and her smile widened. 'How is your mum? I haven't seen her in years.'

'She's fine, thank you.'

'Well, tell her I said hello.' Carolyn gave a parting smile before she stepped past Ally and slotted her key into the door. Ally panicked, seeing her chance to find Gavin slipping away.

'How's Gavin?' she blurted as the door swung open.

Carolyn turned towards Ally again. 'He's doing really well. I'll tell him I saw you.'

'Where is he living now?' It sounded desperate

even to Ally's ears, but she had to know. She couldn't allow Carolyn to set foot in that house without finding out where her husband was.

'He's still in Woodgate.' Carolyn twisted around again, her foot now on the doormat.

'But where?' Woodgate was a big place. Carolyn had to be more specific. Like give an actual address.

'Just in Woodgate.' Carolyn practically jumped into the house and slammed the door shut. Ally heard a bolt being slid into place. She'd freaked the woman out, pressed too hard too quickly and now she was no closer to finding Gavin.

Ally knocked on the door, knowing it was probably useless, but she had to try. Carolyn opened the door a crack. 'Please, Carolyn. I just want to talk to him.'

'I'm not giving out personal information about my son. I suggest you leave now.' The door was closed again but Ally refused to move on. She needed to find her husband and Carolyn was the key. She knocked again but there was no answer. She knocked a third time, more insistent this time. This was her one chance to find Gavin. She couldn't give up.

Ally took a step back when there was still no answer, spotting Carolyn at the window. She was peering at Ally through the net curtain, a phone pressed to her ear. She was probably calling Gavin, telling him there was a mad woman on her doorstep.

Good! Maybe Gavin would turn up to see what was going on.

It had started to drizzle so Ally slipped into her car to wait. She didn't care that she was coming across as a stalker. It would be worth it if it meant she could see Gavin again and put everything right.

It started to turn dark as she waited. The rain hammered down on the roof of the car, but at least she was dry and relatively warm. She pulled her coat tighter around her body and leaned her head against the window. A puff of condensation appeared on the glass as she yawned. It was getting late but she would wait as long as it took.

The rain turned to drizzle again and eventually tailed off as Ally's eyes fluttered shut. She drifted off to sleep, only to be woken moments later by tapping at the window. Ally sat up and wiped the drool from her mouth. She *knew* Gavin would come if she waited long enough. Everything was going to be alright.

NINETEEN

It had been a long day but Ally was finally home. She was tired and hungry and no closer to finding her husband. It hadn't been Gavin tapping at the window the previous night, but a short, round policeman who suggested it was time she went home. His ruddy face was half covered by a wide, bushy moustache and his small, piggy eyes were hard and mean-looking as they looked down at her. He didn't look like the sort of chap you argued with, so Ally had admitted defeat and drove back to the apartment. Despite nodding off in the car, she was now wide-awake and only managed an hour or two before her alarm demanded she get up again.

Work had dragged, mainly because Ally was battling fatigue while also giving herself a mental kicking for ruining her one and only chance of finding Gavin. Ally had decided to abandon her telephone enquiries to local garages as she'd trawled through the entire list, and while she'd toyed with the idea of widening the net, she had resigned herself to the fact that Gavin was no longer a mechanic. Carolyn had been her final lead and she'd scared the poor woman, charging at her instead of using a more gentle approach to tease the information out. Carolyn would never trust her enough to pass on Gavin's details now.

With no other leads to work on, Ally had finally tackled her neglected in-tray. It had proved to be a mammoth task and still wasn't complete, but at least a sizeable chunk had been dealt with. By the end of the day, she was both physically and mentally drained.

Flinging her handbag down on the sofa and kicking off her shoes, Ally shoved a frozen pizza in the oven before slinking off to the bathroom. After a quick shower, she changed into a pair of pyjamas and slid her pizza onto a plate. Two bites in, the intercom buzzed into life, which meant only one thing.

Martine.

'Why are you in your pyjamas? It's not even eight o'clock.' Martine pushed past Ally and headed straight to the bedroom where she began rifling through Ally's wardrobe. 'I think the blue dress. You look totally hot in it, babe.'

'Why would I want to look hot?' Ally sat cross-legged on the bed as Martine picked her way through the massive collection of shoes at the bottom of the wardrobe.

'Because we're going out. You look well miserable. You need a few cocktails inside you and a bit of male attention.'

'I don't want cocktails and I really don't want any male attention.'

Martine's spine stiffened and she dropped the pair of heeled boots she'd been considering. Very slowly, she rose from her crouched position and turned to Ally. 'Something strange is going on here. You never want to go out any more, you've gone off sushi and you're wearing the ugliest, baggiest pyjamas I've ever seen on a human being under the age of sixty.' Martine's face twisted as though she were in pain as she sat next to Ally on the bed and took one of her hands. 'Are you pregnant, babe? Because if you are, you're not on your own, you know. I'm here for you and we can sort it out – like that.' She clicked her fingers and attempted a smile through her grimace.

'I'm not pregnant.'

Martine's breath came out in one huge puff as she placed a hand over her chest. 'You really scared me then, babe. That would have really screwed things up with Jason.' She laughed as the tension oozed from her body. 'So that means we can go out, yeah?' She dropped to the floor in front of the wardrobe to resume her shoe scrutiny.

'I'm still not going out. I don't feel like it.'

'Fine.' Martine stood up and slammed the wardrobe shut. 'We'll be boring and stay in then.'

Ally had been hoping she could spend the evening alone, but Martine parked herself on the sofa, helping herself to a slice of pizza and grabbing the remote. Ally didn't have the energy to argue and simply curled herself up on the sofa while Martine flicked through the channels, finally settling on Lindsay Lohan's version of *Freaky Friday*.

Ally almost choked on a mouthful of pizza as she sprang up from her seat. That was it! Of course! In *Freaky Friday,* mother and daughter switch bodies and are forced to live the other's life. Ally now had Kelly's life, so perhaps Kelly had been given Ally's life. *And her husband.*

'Are you alright, babe?' Martine asked as Ally coughed and spluttered.

Ally grinned, her watery eyes dancing. 'I'm great, thanks.' She was feeling fantastic. She knew where to look now. She knew where to find Gavin.

Francine, who arrived at Westerly's at least half an hour before the rest of the office staff, wasn't even behind her desk when Ally bulldozed her way into the building. Now she knew where to find Gavin, she was eager to put her plan into motion. Flinging herself up the stairs, she unlocked Jason's office and grabbed the keys to the basement before flinging herself back down the stairs again. The basement was filled with boxes and filing cabinets that held the entire history of Westerly's, from back in the sixties when Malcolm's father had set up the company to the present day. The personal files of the current employees were kept in the filing cabinet nearest the door so, keeping an eye out for anyone descending the stairs, Ally unlocked it and rifled through the F section until she found what she wanted; Fox, Kelly. She pulled out the manila file and found Kelly's original CV and her address.

Yes!

Scribbling the address down, she shoved the file away and hurried back upstairs. Francine was now seated behind her desk and eyed Ally suspiciously as she emerged from the basement.

'You're here early. What were you doing down there?'

Ally discreetly slipped Kelly's address into her pocket. 'I've had quite a lot of work on lately so I came in early to catch up.'

'You?' Francine's eyes widened, shocked as the question tripped out of her mouth.

'I know.' Ally gave a shrug. 'It's not like me at all but I'm trying to turn over a new leaf. To be a better person.'

'Right.' Francine wasn't convinced. People like Alana Williams didn't change.

'I don't think we got off to the best start, did we? We should start again. Be friendly if not friends. What do you think?'

Francine's shoulders arched, pausing for a moment before they sank again. 'That sounds reasonable.' But she still wasn't convinced, Ally could see that. Her eyes were wary, her face like stone. It would take more than a few pleasantries to win Francine round, but Ally was in this for the long haul.

'Great. Well, I'd better get upstairs. Lots more to do. See you later.' She gave a little wave, which Francine returned with a slight frown.

Ally's first instinct upon finding Kelly's address was to rush over to the house and claim her husband back. But Gavin was more than likely on his way to work – wherever that was – so it would have to wait. She took a few deep breaths as she climbed the spiral staircase, willing some sense of patience to envelop her, but the slip of paper was throbbing in her pocket, desperate for Ally to take action. To distract herself, she threw herself head first into her in-tray and she'd cleared the backlog of work by the end of the day.

'What's got into you today?' Jason asked as she slipped her coat on at exactly five o'clock. 'You've been working away like there's no tomorrow.'

'Isn't that what I'm paid for?'

'I suppose so, yes.' Jason perched on the edge of her desk, settling in for a chat Ally didn't have time for.

'I'm sorry but I've really got to go.'

'Oh, me too,' Kelly piped up from across the office. 'I'm off out tonight.'

She was? 'Who with?' Ally and Gavin usually went out for a few drinks on a Friday night, grabbing a kebab to take home at closing, but maybe Kelly and Gavin did this on a Thursday instead.

'What's it got to do with you?'

'I was only taking an interest. It's called being friendly. You should try it some time.'

'And you should try keeping your nose out of other people's business.' Kelly grabbed her coat and, after saying goodbye to Jason, sashayed out of the office.

Kelly going out could have scuppered Ally's plans. Or they could have made them easier. If Kelly was going out with friends instead of Gavin, that could mean he would be at home. Alone. Which would be perfect.

'Goodnight then.' Jason hopped off her desk and wandered back into his office, snapping Ally's mind back to the present.

'Goodnight, Jason.'

Ally skipped down the stairs, waving goodbye to a still wary Francine as she passed. She had a bit of time to kill before she could head over to Kelly's. She wanted to time it right so that Kelly was out of the house and she could be alone with Gavin. She was sure he would remember their marriage when he saw her again. How could he forget?

TWENTY

Ally held back as long as she could, but it was still quite early as she drove to Kelly's house. She turned into a grotty, rundown estate and had to double-check she had the right address as she pulled up outside a scruffy house with a crumbling garden wall and an overgrown garden filled with crap. Ally could make out an old pram with three wheels, a rusting metal deckchair and an ancient television poking out of the jungle-like grass. The actual house had dirty windows with yellowing net curtains, and the battered front door had a patch of cardboard taped over the cracked windowpane.

Kelly and Gavin lived here?

Ally triple-checked the address before she climbed out of the car, ensuring it was locked before she crept along the pavement and passed through where a gate had once stood. The path down to the house was uneven and littered with broken glass and fag ends. The garden looked in an even worse state up close; it was full of beer cans, empty bottles of spirits and bin liners spilling rubbish.

Could Kelly and Gavin really live here?

She made her way to the door and somehow plucked up the courage to knock. She held her breath but there was no answer. Ally wanted to run back to her car, but she forced herself to try again.

'They're not in, lovey.'

Ally turned towards the next house, where a curvy, middle-aged woman stood on the doorstep. 'I'm looking for Kelly Fox. Does she live here?'

The woman nodded. 'She does, but I saw her leave about twenty minutes ago.'

'And there's nobody else in?'

'Nah.' The woman shook her head again. 'They'll be out for the night now, drinking themselves stupid somewhere.'

'Oh. Right. Thank you.' Ally scurried back to the car, the image of Gavin 'drinking himself stupid' with Kelly playing in her mind. She had to get him back, to rescue him from this lifestyle if nothing else.

It was Saturday morning before Ally had the chance to return to the house. Kelly had been pretty vocal about her plans to get 'trashed' on Friday night and Ally assumed, from what she had gleaned from the neighbour, that Gavin would be joining her. She chose her clothes with care that morning, wanting to appear attractive without stooping to Alana's level. She only had a few items of her own clothing that she'd picked up with Martine, so she teamed a pair of her jeans with one of Alana's less slutty T-shirts. It was so tight she could barely breathe but at least she was covered.

She dried and straightened her hair, which had a definite curl to it now it had been left to its own devices, and applied a little eye shadow, mascara and lip gloss. Her stomach rumbled, but she was too nervous to eat, so she gave the kitchen a miss and headed straight out. Ally held in a sigh as the lift doors slid open in the lobby and she caught sight of Martine outside, her finger jabbing at the intercom while she checked out her reflection in the glass door. She flicked her hair over her shoulder and gave a little wave when she saw Ally.

'You're up! It's a miracle. I thought I was going to have to drag you to Sparkle again.' Martine fell into step with Ally, her feet tripping along in her heels as Ally strode towards her car.

'I'm not going to Sparkle.'

'Why not?'

Martine had stopped halfway across the car park, but Ally kept going, so she had to call over her shoulder. 'I have plans.'

'Doing what?' Martine set off again, hurrying towards Ally before she climbed into her car. 'What's more important than hanging out with your *best friend*? I'm working this afternoon so we won't get to spend any time together until this evening.'

Martine was pouting and batting her eyelashes, but while that tactic may have worked with horny men in clubs, Ally wasn't so easily manipulated. Besides, rescuing her husband from Kelly's clutches was far more important than getting her nails done.

'I'm sorry but I have to go.' Ally slid into her car and set off, catching sight of Martine stamping her foot in her rear view mirror.

She'd been to the house before, but it was still a shock to see the squalor Gavin had been reduced to. They hadn't lived in a palace themselves, and the little flat that had been their first home was a bit grim, but this was something else. Yet more rubbish littered the garden and there appeared to be a puddle of piss inches from the doorstep.

Setting her shoulders back, holding her breath and reminding herself why she was there, Ally stepped over the puddle and rapped on the door. There was no answer but Ally could hear the faint sound of music from within so she tried again. This time the door swung open.

'What?' The woman standing there was clad in a stained dressing gown, her greasy brown hair held back by a scrunchie and her face was pulled into a sneer. The stench of stale beer, cigarettes and something unidentifiable wafted from the doorway.

'Is Gavin in?' Ally was doing her best to breathe

through her mouth – and only when absolutely necessary – but the smell was overpowering.

'Who?' The woman's teeth were a patchwork of yellow, brown and black and a new stench was added to the fog whenever she opened her mouth.

'Gavin Richmond? He lives here.'

'I don't think so.' She folded her arms across her chest, revealing an arm full of tattoos as the sleeves of the tatty dressing gown rode up. 'Never heard of the fella.'

Ally looked around, wondering if she'd made a wrong turning and ended up at the wrong house, but no, this was the address Kelly had given on her CV and she still lived there according to the neighbour.

'What about Kelly? Is she in?'

The woman lifted her chin. 'What do you want with our Kel?'

'I work with her. I'm a friend.' Sort of. Okay, that had been a great fat lie, but it was for the greater good.

'A friend? Since when?' The woman threw back her head and laughed, causing a new wave of the fog to pulse towards Ally. 'She's not here anyway. Buggered off somewhere last night.'

'And she didn't come home?'

'Not that I know of.' The woman stepped aside. 'Would you like to come in and have a gander yourself?'

The fog wafted out, engulfing Ally and making her eyes water. 'No thanks. I'll speak to her on

Monday.'

'Suit yourself.' The door slammed shut, rattling on its hinges and Ally covered her nose and mouth as the movement brought a double strength of smog towards her. She backed away, avoiding the puddle, and scurried to her car. She was opening the door when a voice called out to her.

'Excuse me, lovey. Are you looking for Kelly?' It was the neighbour, standing on her doorstep, her eyes shifting from Ally to the house of horrors. 'You were here the other day, weren't you?' Ally nodded but didn't speak, afraid of a repeat encounter of the one she'd had with the fag-breath woman. 'I thought I recognised the car. Don't get many like that round here. Kelly's in here. They kicked off last night when they ran out of beer.' She thrust a thumb at Kelly's house. 'You're more than welcome to come inside. I'll pop the kettle on, shall I?'

'Thanks, but I should get going.' Ally checked her non-existent watch. 'I'm running a bit late actually. I'll catch Kelly another time.' She jumped into the car and drove away as quickly as possible. She couldn't imagine Kelly living in such a place and with that woman. Had she always lived like that or had Ally's wish somehow altered Kelly's life too? Perhaps Ally had taken over Kelly's life and forced her into this new, unsavoury life.

Ally pulled out of the estate and headed back towards the city centre. It was as she was pulling back into Palmerston Avenue that it occurred to

Ally that she no longer had a lead on Gavin. If he wasn't with Kelly, where the hell was he?

Thoughts of Gavin, Kelly and the vile woman filled Ally's mind for the rest of the day, so when Martine suggested they go into town that evening, she readily agreed. She needed to take her mind off that morning's events, so she allowed Martine to dress her in a tiny skirt and a hot pink top and plaster her face in make-up.

'Are we on the lookout for Callum?' Ally asked as they settled on a blue squishy sofa with yellow slush cocktails in hand.

Martine spluttered. 'God, no. I'm so over him, babe.' That was good, because Ally had only caught a glimpse of him last time and couldn't remember what he looked like. 'Nope, I'm after fresh meat. What about him?' She pointed out a guy on the dance floor who was strutting around in an open silver shirt.

'He looks full of himself.'

'Well, duh. *Look* at him.'

Ally didn't want to. She'd seen enough, thank you very much.

'So how's the Jason thing going anyway? Any update?'

Ally took a sip of her cocktail. It really was delicious. 'Only that I'm not seeing him any more.'

'What?' Martine whipped her head away from Silver Shirt to gawp at Ally. 'You're not seeing him any more? Why?'

'I'm not into him so I ended it.'

Martine stared at Ally, her mouth gaping in an unattractive way, but she was so shocked she didn't care. 'You're not supposed to be *into him*. That was never part of the plan. How are you supposed to prove your sexual harassment case now?'

'You know about that?' Perhaps Martine could explain exactly why she'd made the preposterous claim in the first place.

'I helped you come up with the plan, and it would have worked if you hadn't wimped out.'

'I really have no idea what you're talking about.' Ally no longer had the energy to play along. Her head was already a mess without piling the Jason situation on top.

'I'm talking about this.' Martine reached into Ally's bag and pulled out her phone, tapping at the screen until she'd found the notes she and Ally had made a few weeks ago. She handed the phone to Ally, who was appalled at what she saw.

1. Seduce Jason
2. Gather 'evidence'
3. Make the complaint
4. Apply for Jason's job when he's sacked
5. Celebrate!

'I planned this?' Ally's cocktail began to curdle in her stomach. She hadn't wished for *this*. She wanted to be young and carefree, not a complete bitch who sleeps with men to further their career, shafting a perfectly nice bloke to get what she wants. It was no wonder Francine wanted nothing to do with her and her family didn't trust her. She was a monster.

'*We* planned this, babe. Don't try and take all the credit.'

'I'm not.' Ally didn't want any of the credit at all. She was ashamed of her actions, even if she hadn't been herself when she'd taken them. Everyone thought she was capable of such an act, and they wouldn't be in the least bit surprised if they ever found out. She had to change everyone's opinion of her, to show them that she was no longer the abhorrent creature they thought she was. She'd prove to them all that she had changed.

One way or another, she was getting her life back.

TWENTY-ONE

The coffee in front of Ally had grown cold long ago as she sat in the warm café, watching the raindrops snake their way down the windowpane. Her body was heavy and unwilling to stand up and join the mass of people rushing by outside, hoods up and umbrellas poised as they ran for shelter. A rainbow of coats flew by the window, all merging into one colourful blur until Ally saw it. A blue jacket stood out from the crowd as it zipped by. She jumped out of her seat, knocking the table and sending her abandoned cup flying. Cold coffee pooled on the table but Ally ignored it as she dashed towards the door. The café had suddenly filled with damp bodies and she gave a frustrated howl as she elbowed her way through, the door seeming miles and miles away. She had to get outside *now*.

Suddenly she was through the crush and her body was propelled out of the door. She scanned the deserted street, her head whipping all around her, but he was gone. The rain had stopped, which was lucky as Ally was wearing a flimsy summer dress and bizarrely she'd left her shoes in the café. She was about to retreat back inside when she spotted it; a flash of royal blue in a shop doorway.

'Gavin?' She tore down the long street towards the shop, calling out his name over and over again. It was him, she knew it. She could *feel* it.

'Ally?' He looked confused as he stepped out onto the street. His hood was still up despite the sun now streaming from a cloudless sky. 'It's you, isn't it?'

'Yes, it's me.'

'Where have you been?'

'I can't explain.' Ally really couldn't. Where *had* she been? 'I've missed you so much.'

'I've missed you too.' Gavin lowered his hood as he rushed to meet Ally, scooping her up off the floor. As her bare toes lifted off the ground, Ally was suddenly aware of where she'd been. She recalled the wish, the agonising passing of time as she searched for Gavin. Her utter failure.

'You remember me?' There was surprise in Ally's voice, though she'd hoped deep down that he would.

'Of course I remember you. How could I forget?' Gavin grinned at Ally and her heart beat painfully in her chest. He'd never looked so handsome. 'I love you, Ally.' Gavin lowered Ally to the ground and swept a stray lock of hair away from her face before tilting her chin. Ally closed her eyes as her husband's lips moved ever so slowly towards her own.

Boom! Boom! Boom!

Ally's eyes snapped open. She was no longer in Gavin's arms, nor in a sun-filled street. She was in bed, her hair a nest around her head and drool seeping from the corner of her mouth.

Boom! Boom! Boom!

Ally squinted at the clock and groaned when she saw that it wasn't yet eight o'clock. It was *Saturday*. Why couldn't the girl understand that Saturdays were designed for lie-ins?

'Hang on, I'm coming.' Throwing the covers from her cocooned body, Ally grabbed her robe and shuffled down the corridor, yawning as she swung the door open.

'Morning, babe. I brought coffee.' Martine pushed past Ally's weary body and headed through to the sitting room. Ally followed, her eyes anchored to the take-out cups of coffee now sitting on her table. Why did coffee seem significant? Ah, yes. The dream.

It had only been a sodding dream.

Ally let out a groan as she sank onto the sofa, covering her eyes with her hands. She thought she'd found him at last but nope, she was still here in her showroom apartment with no husband. Weeks had passed with no sign of finding him and Ally was doing her best to ignore the nagging voice that told her she never would.

'You're being a bit dramatic, babe. It's not that early. Drink your coffee, jump in the shower and get dressed. Our appointment's at nine thirty.'

'No.' Ally peeled her hands away from her eyes. 'I told you. I am not going to that salon again.' *Ever* again. Over the past six weeks, she'd had treatments ranging from manicures and pedicures, facials to eyebrow shaping and spray tans, most of which she'd enjoyed. But last week had put her off salons for life.

'Stop being such a baby. You've had a million bikini waxes before.'

Martine had booked her in for the treatment, insisting it must be time for a tidy up, and Ally had stupidly gone along with it.

Big mistake. They'd taken *everything* – including her dignity – and she swore she would never return.

'And look at your roots. No offence, babe, but you look cheap and nasty. Even Chantelle would be ashamed to have hair like that and we both know how skanky she is.'

No offence? How could she not take offence at that? But, thinking about it, the hair didn't look good. While it was once sleek, it was now dry and frizzing midway between straight and curly.

'Fine. I'll go. But I'm only having my hair done. *And only the hair on my head*.'

'Yay!' Martine clapped, sending her ever-present bangles into a flurry, before handing Ally one of the coffees. 'Now get this down you and then get ready.'

Ally had supplemented her sparse wardrobe over the weeks, replacing Alana's swatches of fabric that claimed to be skirts and replaced them with jeans, jogging bottoms and sensible skirts and trousers, swapping the gauzy, low cut tops for T-shirts and smart blouses. She selected a pair of black jogging bottoms and a pink T-shirt, relishing Martine's wide eyes and curled lip as she caught sight of her. This was the new 'Alana' and if Martine wanted to remain friends with her, she would have to get used to it.

Martine swallowed her disgust and led the way out of the apartment. 'We'll go in my car and then I can drop you off before I head to work.' They headed down to the car park and climbed into Martine's bubble-gum car, where Martine turned the music to a deafening level. To save her eardrums, Ally reached over and turned it down a few notches.

'You've turned into such an old woman, do you know that? You'll be having a blue rinse next.' Martine tittered to herself and turned the music up again, ever so slightly. 'Speaking of crap hair, don't you think it's about time you had yours straightened again? I'm sure Andrea could do it today.'

Martine had been dropping hints about Ally's hair as soon as the first kink had appeared, but Ally shook her head. There would be no straightening today or any other day. In fact, Ally wasn't even getting her roots done.

'So I'm booked in with Andrea then?' This was good news for Ally. At least she wasn't booked in with Dena the pubes snatcher.

The girls headed into the salon, going their separate ways for their treatments. Martine let out a squeak and covered her mouth with her hand as she met Ally back in reception after her full body massage.

'What have they done to you?' Martine stamped her foot on the ground and whirled around. 'Andrea! Where is she? *Andrea*?'

'Hey, calm down.' Ally grasped Martine by the arm and tugged her outside. 'I asked for this.'

'You asked for *that*?' Martine wafted her free hand at Ally's head. 'But why, babe? It's so... so... *mousey*. Jason is never going to fancy you like that.'

Ally had asked Andrea to dye her hair back to its original brown – which was chocolaty and not mousey at all. There had been no sightings of Gavin over the past six weeks and Carolyn had threatened to phone the police when Ally attempted to glean information from her again, so a reunion and a return to life as she knew it was not on the cards. But at least Ally now looked like herself again.

'I don't want Jason to fancy me. I've told you a million times I'm not going through with our stupid plan.' Martine was about to protest and point out the plan's so-called brilliance yet again, but Ally held up a hand to silence her. 'Besides, I like my hair like this.'

'Really?' The curled lip was back.

'Yes, really.' Ally ran her fingers through her new-old locks and felt at peace for the first time since her life had switched. She'd been taking baby steps to get her old life back, but this one felt like a giant leap forward.

Ally pretended she didn't spot the wary look pass between her mother and Freya as she stepped into her parents' sitting room the next day. Ally had been visiting her parents for lunch every Sunday, and although she had never asked for money or acted out as she normally did, they were still holding her at arm's length as they waited for the act to slip and the true Alana to return.

Ally averted her gaze and smiled at Bob as she sat next to Jemima on the sofa. 'Hi, Dad.'

'Hello, love. Have you done something with your hair?'

Ally touched her hair, which she was still getting used to again. It seemed she'd grown accustomed to being blonde.

'Eww, what have you done?' Jemima looked up from painting her toenails neon pink and wrinkled her nose.

'Don't be so rude, Jemima. It looks lovely.' Linda looked taken aback that she'd jumped to her oldest daughter's defence. It had been quite a while since she'd been able to. 'I'll go and put the kettle on.'

'I'll give you a hand,' Ally offered. Linda shot a

'help me' glance at Freya, but Ally was already on her way to the kitchen. Linda was so flustered she spilled most of the coffee granules on the worktop as she spooned them into the cups. Ally's chest ached as she realised her mother was nervous around her, and she was forced to swallow the lump in her throat. She attempted to make conversation, but it was stilted and awkward. Speaking to your own mother shouldn't be this difficult.

They rushed through the tea and coffee making and carried the drinks into the sitting room where Jemima was mid-strop, battling with Bob.

'God, you are such an old git. Everyone thinks I'm such a baby, having to be in at ten.'

'Like you ever stick to the rules anyway,' Freya scoffed.

Jemima thumped her arms across her chest. 'I'm staying out until at least eleven. Everyone else does.'

'Not on a school night,' Bob said, which Jemima mimicked in a whiny voice before storming out of the room and stomping her way up the stairs.

'Kids, eh?' Bob grimaced as he took one of the cups from Linda.

'Was I as bad as that?' Ally asked and the whole room spluttered.

'You?' Linda gave a hoot. 'You were far worse.'

Of course she was. Ally, it seemed, had made the mould for bad behaviour. She took her coffee and buried herself in the corner of the sofa. Visiting her family could be such hard work.

'So, what's with the makeover then?' Freya asked. It was weird seeing her sister like this. Ally had been blonde ever since she'd swiped a bottle of dye from the local chemist at the age of thirteen.

'I just felt like a change. In fact, there are going to be a few more changes.' Ally took a deep breath, preparing to admit the embarrassing truth. 'It seems I can't afford the rent on my apartment.' Ally had inherited Alana's finances, which were in a state. Her rent was in arrears, with the landlord now threatening eviction, her credit cards were up to their sky-high limit, and Ally had discovered numerous debts that needed paying off sharpish.

Linda, Bob and Freya exchanged a look. Here we go, they thought. She'd finally cracked and was after money. Surprisingly, it was a relief now that it had happened. They knew how to deal with this Alana and knew where they stood now she was back to normal.

'How much?' It was Bob who voiced the question on all of their minds.

'I don't want your money, Dad. I'm not asking for a hand out. I'm a big girl. I got myself into this mess and I'll get myself out.'

'How?' Linda couldn't bring herself to imagine what her daughter's plans could involve.

'I'm selling my car.' It turned out she owned it outright, a very generous gift from some poor sap. 'I'll pay off as many of my debts as I can and pay the rest in instalments, and I'm going to move somewhere cheaper. So I don't want a penny from you guys. The only help I'd appreciate is a bit of free labour during the move.'

TWENTY-TWO

Ally gave a little wave to Ray on security as she passed his hut and found a space to park. She'd already placed an advertisement in the local newspaper and would miss her car, but it was a necessity if she wanted to dig herself out of Alana's hole of debt. She never wanted to go through the whole Ellen Andrews experience again, especially if it really was the Lee brothers after her next time.

'Morning. How was your weekend?' She stopped by Francine's desk, which she ensured she did each morning and evening, no matter how busy she was. Francine still didn't trust Ally, but who could blame her? Still, she had to keep putting the effort in if she wanted their friendship to be back on track.

'It was okay.' Francine looked up from her magazine and did a double take. 'Your hair.'

Ally couldn't help reaching up to touch it. Being

blonde had been a novelty, but she felt much more comfortable now she was used to the colour again. 'Bit different, isn't it? I fancied a change and decided to go back to my natural colour. It'll be much less hassle not having to straighten it all the time and I won't have to worry about my roots.'

'No, I suppose you won't.' Francine's eyes dropped back to her magazine, her interest in Ally's hair having waned.

'It'll save me a ton of money too.' Ally was clutching at straws, trying to keep the conversation going without appearing frantic. What she really wanted to do was leap up on the desk and cry 'pleeeeease be my friend again', but figured that would nudge her over the desperate border.

'Hmm.' Francine really didn't care that much about the hair. The change had been a surprise but she was over it now.

'Oh, I almost forgot to give you this.' Ally reached into her handbag and pulled out a bright pink envelope, handing it over to a frowning Francine.

'What's this?'

'It's a birthday card. For your Maisie. I didn't know what to get her, so I put a gift card inside.' Ally normally asked Francine what to buy for her daughters' birthdays but had been forced to improvise this time.

Francine eyed the envelope, tracing a finger over the neat letters of her youngest daughter's name on the front. 'How did you know it was her birthday?'

Because I'm your best friend, Ally wanted to say. Because I'm Maisie's godmother and I looked after your older girls while you and Mike went to the hospital to have her. Because I held her when she was less than an hour old and felt the briefest flutter of maternal longing as she gazed up at me with her huge blue eyes.

'We've worked together for years,' she said instead. Francine lowered the card and raised her eyebrows at Ally, still not convinced. 'And I sorted out your maternity leave, remember?'

Francine cleared her throat, not quite sure what to say. She'd always assumed Alana was too self-absorbed to remember little details like birthdays, particularly those of work colleagues' children. Even Francine couldn't recall the birthday of a fellow employee's offspring. 'Well, thank you. That's very kind of you.'

'I hope she has a brilliant day.' Ally, not wanting to push her luck, decided to leave the conversation there. 'I'd better be getting upstairs.'

Ally wrenched herself away from the comfort of her best friend and headed up the spiral staircase. Kelly was already sitting at her desk, plastered in even more make-up than usual in an attempt to cover a black eye. Ally recalled the day she'd visited Kelly's house and met her foul mother while Kelly hid at the neighbour's house. Had her mother done that to Kelly's face? Guilt jabbed at Ally's stomach. She'd put Kelly in this position and though they'd never got on, she wouldn't have intentionally wished this for her.

Despite it being glaringly obvious, Ally decided not to mention the black eye as Kelly had gone to great lengths to try to mask it. Instead, the two women ignored each other's presence, neither in the mood to exchange their usual jibes. Ally switched on her computer and ruffled a few loose sheets from her in-tray but was, in fact, planning on doing a little flat hunting online. She'd already arranged payment plans for the debts and was hoping the sale of the car would pay off a sizeable chunk once it went through, but she still needed to find a new place to live, and her budget for rent was minimal. Martine had offered to rent out her spare bedroom for next to nothing, but while Ally was grateful for the offer and was learning to tolerate Martine, she couldn't imagine actually living with the girl. It would be like a constant slumber party – quite possibly with actual pillow fights – and the alcohol consumption would be through the roof. Neither Ally's mental health nor her liver would survive.

Ally had, however, accepted Martine's offer of using her staff discount at The Housing Warehouse, the home and furniture shop where she worked. The current apartment Ally rented was furnished, so she would have to start from scratch and buy a few basics for her new place.

'Jeez, what happened to your face?' Jason strode into the office and paused in front of Kelly's desk, his face creased with concern.

'Don't worry, it was all my own fault.' Kelly rolled her eyes and winced with the movement. 'I got totally hammered at the weekend and tripped getting out of a cab.'

Kelly giggled while the guilt jabbed at Ally's gut once again. There hadn't been a cab and if anyone had been hammered at the weekend, it was Kelly's mother. Ally was sure of it.

Ally's car was snapped up within a few days of the advertisement appearing, and she found a vacant flat quickly. It was tiny, not much bigger than a bedsit really, but it had a separate bedroom, a small sitting room with a kitchenette at one end and a usable bathroom. And, most importantly, she could afford the rent. The flat sat above an Indian takeaway, which meant the yummy smells wafting through the floorboards would mean she was constantly hungry, but it was a short bus ride from work so Ally signed the contract and began organising the move.

Ally's family helped with the decorating, turning up each evening after work to paint the rooms a drab yellowy beige colour. It wouldn't have been Ally's first choice of colour, but the shade had been heavily reduced and it was better than the patchwork of brown and greyish white that they were covering. The flat's carpets were grubby and emitted the smell of cat piss, but as Ally couldn't afford to replace them at the moment, she'd hired a carpet cleaner, which would have to do for now. She found adequate curtains at a charity shop, along with a floral sofa, which she covered with an old throw Linda had found in the back of a cupboard. She still needed a bed and a wardrobe, so she arranged to meet Martine at The Housing Warehouse to choose them a few days before the move. She'd held a little of the money back from the car sale, which she hoped, with Martine's discount, would cover them.

'How about this one?' Martine threw herself onto a sleigh bed made of Indonesian mahogany and spread her arms wide. 'It's divine.'

'It's also almost eight hundred quid.' Ally moved away and stood in front of a simple divan. 'This is more in my price range.'

Martine reluctantly pulled herself off the bed, wondering how it would look in her own bedroom. She joined Ally by the divan, but took a step back and pulled a face when she took a proper look at it. 'But it's a single.'

'I know. That's why it's perfect.' Ally's new bedroom was minute, so the single bed and a small wardrobe would easily fill it. 'You've seen my bedroom, right? Do you honestly think that will fit?' She pointed at the gorgeous but expensive and extremely wide bed, and Martine was forced to shake her head.

'I suppose not. But it's so pretty, babe.'

'It *is* pretty and maybe one day I'll have a bed like that. But for now, this will have to do. Shall we go and look at wardrobes?'

Martine forgot all about the beautiful sleigh bed at the prospect of further shopping and grabbed Ally by the hand to lead her towards the wardrobe section. She'd spotted a lovely white hardwood wardrobe with ornate feet the other day, and she knew Ally would fall in love with it too.

'Martine.' Ally spoke slowly as they stood in front of the wardrobe. 'It's over a thousand pounds.'

'But it's in the sale. It used to be four hundred quid more. You have to admit that's a bargain.'

'But it's still over a grand. I don't have that much money in my budget.' Ally moved away from the wardrobe and found a basic one that she could actually afford.

'No, babe. Please. It's so ugly.'

It was true that the basic wardrobe was as plain as it could possibly be, but if it fulfilled its role of storing clothes, that would be good enough for Ally.

'Martine, can I have a quick word please?'

Ally's head was inside the wardrobe, making sure the rail was sturdy, so the voice outside was muffled. Even still, she froze, recognising it immediately.

'I'm with a customer. Can it wait?' Martine asked as Ally straightened and swivelled around. She'd been right; the voice belonged to her husband. And this time she wasn't dreaming.

TWENTY-THREE

Ally grasped hold of the wardrobe as her knees threatened to give way. He was there. Gavin was really there, standing in front of her. He looked a bit strange wearing a smart suit, his hair trimmed and tamed for once, but it was definitely him. His name badge said so: Gavin Richmond, Supervisor.

'Come and see me as soon as you've finished,' Gavin instructed Martine before he turned on his heel and marched away. Ally, who had been struggling to control her breath, realised she needed to get a grip. And fast.

'Gavin!' Pushing herself away from the safety of the wardrobe, she raced after Gavin, zig-zagging through the shoppers. Gavin paused and turned around, but Ally couldn't stop the momentum and careered into him.

'Oof! Sorry.' Ally straightened with a wince, placing a tentative hand on her possibly cracked ribs. But who cared about broken bones? She'd found Gavin! 'Hi, it's me. Ally.' *Please remember me, please remember me*, Ally silently pleaded. Gavin cocked his head, a bemused smile on his face. Ally let out a relieved but painful puff of air as his smile widened.

'Alana? Alana Williams?'

Ally nodded. It was technically true, however much she wished otherwise. 'People call me Ally now.' At least they would, eventually. She'd hammered the point enough by now, surely. 'How are you? It must have been ages since we last spoke.'

'Did we ever speak?'

'No, I suppose not.' Clementine *had* said that Gavin had never been on Ally's radar. 'But it's nice to see you again.'

'Yes, you too, but I should be getting back to work now.' Gavin placed a hand on Ally's arm. 'Take care.'

Ally opened her mouth but emitted nothing other than the quietest of squeaks. She had to do something before she lost Gavin again so, giving herself a mental kick up the arse, she called out his name. She didn't have a firm plan in place as Gavin faced her once more, but she had to speak up or risk appearing moronic in a crowded shop.

'I'm moving on Saturday, so I'm having a housewarming party.' Was she? She was now, apparently. 'I'd love it if you could come.' Reaching into her handbag, she grabbed a pen and an old receipt, scribbling her new address on the back before thrusting it at Gavin.

'Oh. Thanks. I'll see what I can do.'

'Great.' Ally clamped her arms by her sides as they itched to throw themselves around her husband. All in good time, arms. All in good time.

'I'd really better be getting on.' Gavin gestured at the vast shop floor behind him.

'Of course. I'll maybe see you on Saturday then.' Ally watched as Gavin walked away, his back straighter than usual and his shoulders thrown back. She was used to seeing him slouched in jeans and T-shirts, or bent over a car engine in greasy overalls, but she wasn't complaining. He looked hot in a suit and it was a look she could definitely get on board with.

'Are you buying a wardrobe or what, babe?' Martine appeared at Ally's side, arms folded across a heavy chest that was desperate to release a deep sigh. 'Some of us have work to do.'

'Yeah, I'm coming now.' There was a spring in Ally's step as she returned to the wardrobe department. She wasn't sure if Gavin would take her up on the housewarming offer, but at least she now knew where to find him.

The commute to work was a nightmare without the comfort and convenience of her car, but Ally knew she'd done the right thing in selling it, and she'd soon be in her new flat and only a short bus ride away. The move was taking place the following day, which meant she only had one more night in the fancy apartment. She'd miss the car, but she wouldn't miss her old home. It may have looked flash, but it was cold and bare and Ally had never felt comfortable there. As tiny as her new place was, at least it would be cosy.

'Good morning.' Ally stopped by Francine's desk as usual, friendly smile in place. She'd had to tone down the brightness of her smiles upon greeting her former friend as the bigger the smile, the more suspicious Francine became.

'Morning.' Francine's reply was mumbled, but at least it was there, which was a start. Ally didn't want to push her luck, so she moved on, heading upstairs but stopping off at the kitchen first to make coffees, which she carried through to the HR office.

'Coffee?' She set the tray down on Kelly's desk and handed her a mug before waving at Jason in his office and indicating the cups. Ally had been consumed by guilt ever since she realised she'd taken over Kelly's life and turfed her into that hellish house, so she'd tried to be extra nice to her colleague to make up for it in a small way.

'I'm having a housewarming party tomorrow if you want to come along,' she said as she picked up her own mug.

Kelly snorted as she dumped her mug on her desk. 'I don't think so. I've got better things to do than hang about with a bunch of losers, getting pissed on cheap wine. I've already got plans.'

'Oh?' Did those plans involve hiding out in her neighbour's house by any chance?

'Yes, I actually have a life. I'm going into town with Martine and a bunch of girls.'

Ally's grip tightened on her mug as it almost slipped from her fingers. Martine had been Kelly's best friend in their former life. And they were *still* friends? Why hadn't Kelly lost Martine along with the rest of her life?

'What's this I hear about a party?' Jason asked before Ally could question Kelly about her friendship with Martine. He grabbed his cup of coffee from the tray and took a sip.

'Alana's having a little housewarming party tomorrow night.' Kelly's answer was laced with a sneer.

'Aren't I invited? I'm offended.'

'You should count yourself lucky.' Kelly grabbed a sheaf of papers and stood up, smoothing down her miniscule skirt with her free hand. 'Please excuse me from this scintillating conversation. I have photocopying to do.'

'I'll do that for you.' Ally snatched the papers before turning to Jason. 'Of course you're invited. I'll write the address down for you later.' She had some making up to do to Jason too after the sexual harassment debacle.

Ally eased her guilt a little by photocopying the papers for Kelly before relieving the girl of the mountain of filing that should have been dealt with months ago. It seemed Kelly wasn't so well acquainted with the filing room now she wasn't knocking off Jason.

'Is there anything else you need doing?' she asked once the task had been completed.

'No.' Kelly placed a protective hand over her in-tray. 'Don't you have work of your own to get on with?'

Ally did have her own work, which had been neglected since she'd found out what she'd done to Kelly. She supposed she should make a dent in her own in-tray for a change, so she left Kelly alone for the remainder of the day. Her in-tray was looking much healthier by the time she switched off her computer and headed home.

'Have a great weekend,' she called to Francine as she passed the reception desk. She didn't expect much in return, so she skidded to a halt when Francine replied.

'You too. Good luck with the move.'

It was the first time Francine had initiated an actual conversation, so Ally seized the opportunity and rushed back towards the desk.

'Speaking of the move, I'm having a housewarming party tomorrow evening. It's nothing fancy, just a few drinks and nibbles, but you're more than welcome to come along.' She held her breath as Francine blinked at her, trying to gauge whether Ally was being sincere or not.

'It would be nice to get out of the house for an hour.' Francine's oldest daughter was turning into a teenager slightly early, her youngest had reverted back to the terrible twos again and the middle girl was vying for some attention for herself. 'If you give me the address, I'll see if I can get away.' She pushed a notepad in Ally's direction, on which she quickly scribbled the address.

'I'll see you tomorrow then.' Ally beamed at Francine and was tempted to jump and click her heels together as she left the building.

For the first time since the stupid wish, Ally was not only awake but dressed and breakfasted by the time Martine buzzed the intercom first thing on Saturday morning. The girl could be such hard work, but Ally had to admit she'd warmed to her over the last few weeks. Yes, Martine was still vain and loose-knickered, but she had been kind during the transition from flash apartment to grotty flat, offering her own spare bedroom and then the staff discount, without which Ally would never have found Gavin. Her stomach filled with butterflies at the thought of her husband, and she wondered whether he would turn up that evening.

So Martine wasn't perfect, but she'd proven to be a good friend when it mattered.

'What the hell are you wearing? No offence, babe, but you look like a bag lady.' Martine breezed into the apartment and perched on the sofa. 'I'll wait while you get changed, but don't be too long.'

'I'm not getting changed.'

Martine blinked eyelashes heavily laden with

mascara as she crossed her arms and cocked her head. 'You cannot go like that.'

Ally looked down at her body. She was wearing a pair of jogging bottoms and a baggy T-shirt, and her hair was finally long enough to scrape back into a ponytail with the aid of a dozen grips. She probably *did* look like a bag lady, actually.

'Martine, I'm moving house. Do you expect me to do that in heels and a full face of make-up?'

'Heels no, but you could certainly use a bit of slap, babe. But I'm not talking about the move.'

'Then what are you talking about?' As far as Ally was aware, moving house and hosting a tiny housewarming party were her main plans for the day.

'I'm talking about Sparkle.' Martine spoke slowly, as though Ally wasn't quite the full shilling.

'Sparkle?'

'Yes, Sparkle. So chop chop. Samantha's expecting you at nine.'

'Samantha?'

Martine closed her eyes for a moment while she took a calming breath. 'Yes, Samantha. You know, the nail technician.' She wiggled her fingers at Ally to demonstrate. 'She did you a lovely French manicure a few weeks ago.'

'I know who Samantha is, but I'm confused *why* I have an appointment with her. I told you I can't afford the treatments any more.' Which was a shame because, hair-tearing-out-of-body aside, she'd enjoyed her time at Sparkle. But while the gaping hole of debt was no longer trying to gobble her up, it was still there and needed to be filled. 'Plus, in case you hadn't noticed, *I'm moving today*.'

'But not until later on this morning, which is why I booked early.' Martine shook her head. Ally could be such hard work at times. 'And it's my treat. Call it a moving in gift.'

'That's sweet, it really is.' A set of pans – since Alana didn't have any – would have been more practical though. 'But I don't think having my nails done an hour before I start lugging furniture is a good idea. Samantha's hard work would be undone within seconds.'

'But you won't be shifting the furniture yourself.' Martine's tone started out confident, but her assurance soon wore off. 'You'll be co-ordinating the move, but you won't be getting your hands dirty, will you? Isn't that why you asked your dad and brother to help?'

'I asked them to help, not do it all while I sit on my arse with a clipboard, shouting out orders.'

'Oh.' A look of pure confusion passed across Martine's face. 'So you're actually going to be, like, *moving* stuff yourself?'

'Yes, that's exactly what I'm going to be doing. You could help too if you're not busy.'

Martine leapt up off the sofa, her eyes wide with panic. 'You know I totally would, babe. I'd love to get stuck in and everything but I can't. Work! I have to work. But I'll see you tonight, yeah? For the party.' Grasping Ally, she gave her two quick pecks on the cheek before she scarpered, almost leaving scorch marks on the hardwood floor in her haste.

Fortunately, Ally's family were much more willing to roll up their sleeves and get stuck in. Bob and Jared arrived in Bob's work van and started to load up Ally's possessions, which didn't amount to much. She'd already donated the majority of Alana's clothes to charity, and the bulk of the furniture would remain in the apartment. Most things would be staying apart from the massive television – another gift, apparently – and the few bits of kitchenware Alana owned, plus Ally's new clothes and bath products. Everything fit into Bob's van in one go, which was both handy and a little bit sad.

'Do you want to say a final goodbye to the place while we put these last bags in the van?' Bob asked but Ally shook her head. She couldn't wait to see the back of the place as it represented everything she hated about her new life.

'Let's go, Dad. Mum and the others will be waiting.'

Linda, Freya, Jared's girlfriend and a reluctant Jemima were waiting at the new flat, so with the seven of them on hand, the job was completed pretty quickly. Once they'd taken delivery of the new bed and wardrobe, the move was complete. The others started to trickle away including Bob, who'd had an emergency call out he could now attend with the move finished, leaving just Ally and

Linda.

'I'll put the kettle on, shall I?' Linda offered. She made the coffees and brought them into the sitting room. Despite the sparse furniture, the space was still cramped.

'You know, I was very surprised when you chose somewhere so small and basic to live.'

'I didn't have much choice in the matter. It was this or a cardboard box.' Ally smiled at her mum to show she was kidding. Almost. 'But, do you know what? I like it. I think I could grow to love this place when I've given it a bit more character.' The new flat reminded Ally of her first home with Gavin. That flat had been tiny too and riddled with damp, but they'd made it work somehow.

'You've done a great job already, love. I didn't know you could manage on a budget.'

Ally gave a shrug as she blew on her coffee. 'It's about time I grew up. I can't keep haemorrhaging money and expecting you and dad to bail me out.'

'I'm so glad to hear you say that.' Linda had heard similar from her daughter's mouth in the past, but she hadn't believed her until now.

TWENTY-FOUR

After making sure everything was unpacked, Ally
ran the vacuum cleaner over the few centimetres
of carpet before heading out to the nearest
supermarket for party supplies, which consisted
mainly of alcohol and a few pre-made canapés. The
guests weren't due to arrive until around seven, so
she had plenty of time to test out her new bath
and prepare herself in case Gavin turned up. She'd
held back one of Alana's outfits, a black halter-neck
dress that, although it hung down to her mid-calf,
had a split in the side that reached to mid-thigh.
Alana had kindly provided a pair of six-inch peep-
toe shoes too, which Ally practised walking around
the flat in. She'd almost mastered a straight line
without twisting her ankle when the doorbell rang.

'Coming!' Kicking off the shoes and carrying
them in her hands, she bolted down the staircase
to the front door, slipping her shoes back on before

she opened it. 'Mum, Dad, come in.'

'We thought we'd come a bit early to see if you needed any help setting up. And we also brought a couple of bottles.' Linda handed the wine over before she and Bob followed a wobbly Ally up the stairs to the flat. 'Oh. Looks like you've sorted everything.'

Ally had bought a few pillar candles, which were lit on the mantelpiece, with cheap tea lights dotted around the flat, creating warmth and sophistication in the drab sitting room. The lone kitchen worktop was filled with nibbles, the fridge was full of wine and the cupboard resembled a cocktail bar, while soft music wafted from the iPod dock.

'Still, I'm glad you're here early. We can have a quiet drink before everyone else gets here.' Ally took their coats, storing them on her bed, before pouring the drinks. With her parents on the two-seater sofa, Ally had to make do with the floor. 'I'd like to thank you both for all the help you've given me in the past.'

'We're your parents. That's our job,' Bob replied but Ally shook her head.

'You've gone beyond parental duty. I know I've been a nightmare. Worse, even. But I can assure you that you don't have to worry about me any more. I've sorted my life out and the new me is here to stay. I'm paying off my debts – *myself* – and I'll never get myself into such a state again. I promise you. You can trust me this time.'

'We do, love. We do.' Linda reached out and

took Ally's hand in hers, giving it a squeeze.

'I won't let you down again, Mum.'

'I'm glad to hear it.'

The doorbell rang, cutting off any further speeches. Again, Ally removed her shoes and scurried down the stairs, hoping it would be Gavin this time.

'Oh. Jason. Hi.'

Jason laughed. 'Don't sound too happy to see me. You'll give me a big head.'

'Sorry. I thought you were someone else, that's all. Come up.' She led the way, slipping off her shoes once more before tackling the stairs. She may as well leave them off until Gavin arrived, otherwise her feet would be crippled with blisters in no time.

'I know how much you love your vodka so I brought you this.' Jason handed over the bottle as they approached the top of the stairs. 'And this. It's just a little gift for your kitchen. You don't have to use it if you don't want to.' Ally tucked the bottle of vodka under her arm as they reached the sitting room and peered inside the gift bag Jason had handed over. Inside was a mini indoor allotment, consisting of a tiny, white shed and fence, which housed a planter for herbs.

'It has everything you need, like soil and seeds and stuff.' Jason pulled a face. 'You think it's lame, don't you?'

'No, I think it's fantastic. Thank you.' Reaching up onto her tiptoes, Ally gave Jason a kiss on the cheek. A throat was cleared behind them. 'Oh, sorry. Mum, Dad, this is Jason, my manager. Jason, these are my parents, Linda and Bob.'

'How lovely to meet you, Jason. Can I get you a drink?' Linda hopped out of her seat and indicated that Ally should follow her into the kitchen. Ally fiddled with her new mini allotment while Linda grabbed a beer from the fridge. 'He's a bit dishy, isn't he?' Linda had to lean in close and whisper as the others were a matter of steps away in the open plan room.

'Who, Jason? I didn't think he was your type, and I'm not sure Dad would approve.'

'I'm not talking about for me and you know it.'

Ally placed the mini allotment on the windowsill overlooking the busy street below. 'I'm not interested in Jason.'

'Why not? He's extremely good looking and sounds quite successful. A manager, didn't you say?'

'Yes. *My* manager. It wouldn't be professional, would it? And imagine how awkward it'd be in the office if it didn't work out.' Plus, I'm married, Ally wanted to point out but knew she'd sound nuts. Luckily, she was rescued by the doorbell and she fled from the conversation to let Freya, Jared and his girlfriend into the flat.

'Isn't Jemima coming?' Ally asked once she'd ensured everyone had a drink in hand.

'She's busy. You know, homework and things,' Linda mumbled.

'You mean she had better plans?' Ally didn't really know this new Jemima very well, but she did know it was unlikely the girl was voluntarily completing her homework.

'Not *better* plans. Different plans.'

Bless Mum for trying, Ally thought as the doorbell rang again. Taking the shoes with her, just in case, she plodded down the stairs yet again. Ally could deal with the tiny kitchenette, the trickle that claimed to be a shower and the practically non-existent bedroom, but those stairs could prove to be a step too far.

'Quick, babe. Let me in before anyone sees me.' Martine took a furtive glance left and right before she slipped into the flat and closed the door behind her.

'I'm sorry. Is my flat cramping your style?'

'Mock all you like, babe.' Martine eyed the still slightly grubby carpet on the stairs before she took a tentative step. 'But this place is a shithole and yes, it is cramping my style. It should be cramping yours too. I never thought I'd see you living like *this*. It isn't too late to change your mind, you know.'

'My bank balance begs to differ.' They reached the sitting room and introductions were made. Martine's sour face brightened when she clapped eyes on Jason. She knew all about Jason through Alana's plans for HR domination, but it seemed this was the first time she'd met him. With Martine occupied, Ally shuffled around the room, making sure everyone's drinks were topped up. When the doorbell rang again, Ally's heart started to race. This time it had to be Gavin.

Grabbing the shoes, she ran down the stairs and slipped them onto her feet before swinging the door open, smile fixed in place.

'Francine! You made it.' Her smile didn't dip when she saw it was her friend on the doorstep instead of her husband, and she pulled Francine into an unreciprocated hug. 'Come in. It's a bit of a squeeze upstairs but I'm sure we'll manage. Jason's here so at least you'll know someone and I'll introduce you to the others.'

In Ally's old life, Francine would have known the others already, bar Martine, so it was strange making the introductions.

'Let me get you a drink,' Ally said after depositing Francine into Freya's capable hands. 'White wine?'

'That'd be lovely. Thank you.'

Ally inched her way through to the kitchen and poured the wine for Francine and topped up her own glass.

'Who the hell is *she*?' Martine had crept into the kitchen with such stealth that her voice caused Ally to slosh wine down her dress. She followed Martine's gaze while mopping the damp patch with a tea towel.

'That's Francine, my friend from work.'

'But she's ancient. I thought she was a friend of your mum's.'

'She isn't ancient.' Mind you, with Martine being a mere twenty-two, Francine probably *did* seem past it to her. 'You'd probably have preferred it if Kelly came. I did invite her, but she has better things to do, apparently. I forgot the two of you were friends.'

'I'm sorry, friends with who?'

'Kelly. Kelly Fox.' It suddenly occurred to Ally that Martine was supposed to be going into town with Kelly that evening. How odd. She couldn't be in two places at once.

'I'm sorry, babe, but I don't know who you're talking about. I know a Keisha Lewis. Are you thinking of her?'

So Kelly wasn't friends with Ally's Martine. There must have been two. The thought made Ally shudder.

'Never mind. Do you want another drink?'

Hope of Gavin turning up for the party began to wane as the evening wore on. Francine left after an hour and while Ally would have preferred her to stay a little longer, she was grateful that she'd showed up at all under the circumstances. Linda and Bob were next to leave, followed by Martine, who'd received a text from a mystery man. Perhaps she'd finally managed to lure you-know-who away from his poor wife.

'We're going to get off now as well. Thanks for having us over.' Where Jared would have once hugged Ally goodbye, he now gave an awkward wave. Freya left with their brother, leaving Ally alone in the flat with Jason. Most of the tea lights had given up by now, so the only light source was coming from the pillar candles on the mantelpiece.

'Can I get you another drink?'

Jason gave his bottle a shake and nodded. 'That'd be great, thanks.'

Ally grabbed a bottle from the fridge and filled a plate as best as she could from the obliterated snacks and carried them through to the sitting room. With only the sofa in there, she was forced to sit next to Jason, blushing as his thigh brushed hers.

'I never expected you to live in a place like this. I mean, it's great and everything, but I always pictured you somewhere more… pretentious.'

Ally pictured her old apartment. His picture had been pretty spot on. 'I prefer places like this. It's cosy here.'

Jason shifted slightly, his thigh pressing even more into Ally's. 'You're right about that.'

Ally sat up straighter and took a sip of wine. 'So what's your place like?'

'You know what my place is like.' Jason leant in closer and lowered his voice, despite them being on their own. 'We've had sex in every room.'

'Oh.' Ally's cheeks burned brighter than the candles. 'Yes, of course we have.'

Jason laughed. 'It was obviously fantastic sex. Memorable.' He placed his bottle on the floor and turned to Ally, his fingers sweeping her bare forearm. 'I miss you, you know.'

'You see me every day at work.'

'But it's not the same, is it? Don't you miss me?' Jason didn't wait for an answer before he leaned in, brushing Ally's jaw with his lips, tracing little kisses to her mouth. It had been so long since Ally had felt any real affection that her mind and body were clouded for a moment and she allowed Jason to kiss her, but the spell was soon broken. It didn't feel right. In her heart, she was married to Gavin and a stupid wish couldn't change that.

'Jason, I'm sorry but I can't.' Pushing him away, Ally rose to her feet and smoothed down her dress, unable to meet his eye. 'I think you should go.'

'If that's what you want.'

Ally saw Jason to the door, quickly closing and locking it behind him before rushing back up to the sitting room, switching on the light and blowing out the candles. Nothing untoward could have happened in this bright, empty room. She couldn't have just kissed Jason.

TWENTY-FIVE

Ally's life settled into a more comfortable routine after the move. She worked, had the odd night out with Martine, convincing her to frequent the local pub instead of trekking into town, and she finally became an accepted face at her parents' Sunday lunch. On Saturdays, instead of going to Sparkle – having finally convinced Martine that she really couldn't afford the weekly indulgence – she spent her mornings at The Housing Warehouse, doing her best to bump into Gavin without giving off a stalker vibe. Moving into her new flat had given her the perfect excuse to spend so much time in the shop.

'Gavin, hi.' Ally adopted a high, surprised tone, masking the fact she'd been creeping around the store in search of her husband for the last twenty minutes. She'd finally tracked him down in the kitchenware department.

'Alana.' Gavin gave a polite incline of his head.

'I'm sorry I couldn't make it to your party the other week.'

Ally gave a wave of her hand. 'Don't worry about it.' The words that came out of her mouth didn't match those thrashing around inside her brain. Why hadn't he come? What had kept him away? Wasn't he desperate to see her?

'How did the move go?'

'Perfect. Really well, thanks. But I need some more spoons.' Ally thrust her hand towards the nearby display, grabbing a fistful of teaspoons. 'You can never have too many spoons, can you?'

'I suppose not.'

You can never have too many spoons? What a buffoon! Ally mentally kicked herself, but she failed to come up with a more suitable topic of conversation. What did they usually talk about?

'Anyway, I'd better get back to work.'

'Oh. Yes. Of course.' Ally had failed to come up with a stimulating subject and now Gavin was backing away from her until it was just Ally with the spoons, standing in the middle of the store like an idiot. Dumping the spoons back into their allotted tray, Ally retreated from the shop. If she wanted to win her husband back, she'd have to do a better job than that.

'Here we have the Knightley Ottoman. It's a little pricier than the Sylvia Bedstead, but it has the storage underneath, which is very handy.'

It was a week after the spoon incident and Ally

was back at The Housing Warehouse, perched on the Knightly Ottoman bed while Gavin reeled off its pros.

'Hmm.' Ally nodded along, but storage wasn't the function that came to mind when she thought of Gavin and beds.

'It's really simple to use.' Ally hopped off the bed while Gavin popped its base up, revealing the storage beneath. 'You can store your bedding in here, or towels. Anything you want to, really.'

'Hmm.' Interesting. But how comfortable was it? Ally popped the base back down and hopped back onto the mattress, laying her head down. Oh, yes. This was more like it.

'We have a similar bed in the Oxford Supreme range, but I think this is better value for money, if I'm honest.'

'Hmm.' Ally propped herself up on her elbows and patted the empty space beside her. 'But is it as comfortable as this anyway?'

'I'm not sure about that.' Gavin pretended not to notice the invitation to join Ally on the bed. 'I could show you our Daisy range, if you'd like. They're not as practical, but they're very pretty and quite popular.'

Ally turned onto her side, resting her head on the palm of her hand in what she hoped was a sexy and inviting pose. 'I'd love to see what you've got.'

Gavin jumped back and turned on his heel, which wasn't the reaction Ally had been hoping for. She'd never been very good at flirting, having never really had the need to. 'Right then. Daisy range. It's just over here.'

Ally rolled off the bed and ambled after Gavin. She'd never noticed what a fast walker the man was.

Ally pouted her way through the Daisy range, which really was rather lovely, but if Gavin noticed her attempts to entice him, he refused to acknowledge them. He was professional and well-informed but lacked any sort of familiarity. Her plan to seduce her husband in the bedroom department was not going well at all.

'I don't know what I'm doing wrong.'

Ally and Martine were curled up on the sofa, working their way through a bottle of wine while they watched repeats of *America's Next Top Model*. Ally had confided in Martine about her attempt to seduce a man – whose identity she had kept a secret due to Martine working with Gavin – and the frustration of failing completely.

Martine covered her mouth as she started to giggle, soon putting a stop to the laughter when she caught the thunderous look from Ally. 'I'm sorry, babe, but you've never had a problem seducing *anyone*. It's quite a novelty.' The thunderous look continued. 'But obviously we need to sort this out.' Martine took a sip of wine while she pored over the limited facts. 'What were you wearing?'

Ally swept a hand down the length of her body.

'This.'

'*That*?' Martine's giggles were long gone as she took in Ally's outfit of boot cut jeans and Cookie Monster T-shirt. 'You tried to seduce a man while wearing that?' No wonder Ally hadn't been successful. There was nothing sexy about *Sesame Street*.

'What do you want me to wear? Stockings and suspenders?'

'Duh. That would be a start.'

'But I was out in public.'

'Obviously you wear something over them. Like a skirt that can accidentally ride up while you're talking.'

Ally blushed. She could never do that, not outside the bedroom. And she wasn't sure Gavin would go for that either. Their relationship had never been the stockings-and-suspender type and Ally had never had to seduce Gavin before, not seriously. They'd started out as friends, with their feelings growing from there. Ally could clearly remember the first time she realised she was falling for Gavin. She was cocooned in a bean bag on her bedroom floor, her homework propped on her knees while Gavin sat cross-legged on her bed, strumming his guitar. He'd taught himself to play the summer before and was getting pretty good.

'I learned a new song.'

'Yeah?' Ally dumped her maths book on the floor and shuffled into a more comfortable position. 'Play it for me then.'

Ally had been expecting yet another Oasis song – Gavin had nailed 'Champagne Supernova', 'Wonderwall' and 'She's Electric' so far – so was taken aback when she heard the opening of Take That's 'Everything Changes'. Ally adored Take That – she and Freya had seen them live twice – but Gavin thought they were a bunch of talentless, pretty-boy tossers.

'You can't stand Take That,' she said when Gavin had finished. 'Why did you learn to play that?'

Gavin gave a shrug of his shoulders, his eyes on the strings of his guitar. 'Because I know you love them.'

It was in that moment that Ally knew there was something special between herself and Gavin, something more than friendship developing. Gavin was her best friend, but soon it wouldn't be enough.

And there was Ally's answer.

TWENTY-SIX

The answer to the Gavin-dilemma should have been obvious. The way to Gavin's heart was not through rolling around on a shop's display bed – and definitely not through showing up in a skimpy-skirt-and-stockings get up. Ally and Gavin had fallen in love once before without any silly tactics. They'd built up their relationship from a strong friendship, and that was what Ally planned to recreate.

She started off slowly, which seemed to be working with Francine. They had now shared more than five words in one go, which was promising. Taking the same approach, Ally would give a quick wave or hello as she and Gavin happened to pass in the shop, never stopping long enough to scare the man away with her previous predatory behaviour. She pretended to shop quite a lot over the next few weeks, picking up pretty vases and crockery for the flat, though she never actually took the items home due to her budget restraints. The items were merely props in her game of cat and mouse.

'Hi, Gavin.' Ally juggled the items in her hands to give a quick wave as she passed. Gavin had always liked Ally's bum, so she was wearing a pair of skinny jeans that drew attention to the area in a subtle way.

'Hey, Alana. I keep seeing you here lately. Have you moved in?'

Yes! This was it. Conversation had been initiated – and by Gavin, which was a bonus.

'Ha, ha. I may as well move in. My flat's starting to look like a mini version of the shop.' If only. Her flat was still a shithole. 'I'm on bathroom duty today.' Ally cringed. *Bathroom duty*? Was that a new kind of sexy talk nobody else was aware of yet? She held out the chrome soap dispenser, matching toothbrush holder and fish-patterned shower curtain that would soon be back on their shelves.

'Great choices. I have the same shower curtain at home.'

See? It was meant to be. Perhaps she'd splurge on the fish-patterned shower curtain. The one she had at the flat had been up when she moved in and had several questionable stains that she did her best to ignore.

'Anyway, I'd better get going.' Ally resisted the urge to throw herself on the ground and cling to Gavin's legs as he started to back away. 'I'll see you next week.' Gavin gave a wink while Ally laughed like a maniac.

Yes! Her plan was working.

Ally managed to get chatting to Gavin on a few more occasions, their conversions stretching each time. They reminisced about school, with Ally playing along as best as she could. In her old life, Ally had hung around with Gavin, Freya and Dee, but it seemed Alana wouldn't have been seen dead with her younger sister, and she hadn't been aware of Gavin's presence at all.

'Do you fancy going for a coffee?' They'd been chatting for a few minutes and Ally could sense their time was about to come to an end. She couldn't bear the thought of leaving now, not when they were getting on so well.

Gavin flicked his wrist to consult his watch. 'I'm due a break, actually. Why not?'

Grinning like a lunatic, Ally followed Gavin to the shop's café. Butterflies quivered inside as she sat waiting at a table while Gavin ordered the drinks. This is it, she thought, taking deep breaths to calm her nerves. This was where it all started. How romantic it would be, getting to start their relationship from scratch, getting to know each other all over again. They could go on dates again and share a first kiss, falling in love a little more each time they met. She wondered how Gavin would propose this time, but it didn't really matter. Nothing could ever top that surprising bubble of pleasure at knowing Gavin wanted to spend the rest of his life with her, and the only important part was becoming Mrs Richmond again.

'Here you go. Coffee, white, no sugar.' Gavin placed the steaming cup in front of Ally and sat opposite her.

'Thanks.' It would have been nice if Gavin had automatically known how Ally took her coffee rather than needing instructions, but Ally shoved the thought to the back of her mind. They had the rest of their lives to iron out all the little details. 'So, how did you end up working here?'

Gavin shrugged his shoulders. 'I didn't know what I wanted to do when I left school. I went to college to do my A Levels, but it wasn't for me and I dropped out. My dad said I should do an apprenticeship but I didn't know what in, so I ended up taking a temporary job here while I sorted my head out. And I'm still here.' He took a sip of coffee, wincing when it scalded his tongue. 'What about you? Where did you end up?'

'I'm in HR at a coach tour company. Westerly's?' Gavin shook his head, which made Ally laugh. 'We're hardly world famous, but it's not far from here, actually.' Ally's voice took on a casual tone, though her heart was hammering. 'Do you live around here then?' When Gavin nodded, she wanted to leap up and punch the air.

'I'm over on Hill Bank Lane.'

Ally knew the street he was talking about. It was lined with large, Georgian detached properties with manicured gardens and dotted with trees filled with pink blossom. Ally had always felt the street had a fairy tale quality to it, and her chest filled with warmth as she imagined starting their new married life there instead of their grotty flat.

'Wow. You've gone all posh, haven't you?'

Gavin chuckled. 'Hardly. We inherited the house when my wife's grandmother passed away.'

The warmth drained from Ally's chest, taking her breath with it. Gavin's hands were nestled around his cup and Ally noticed the gold band entwining his finger for the first time. He was married. Gavin had married somebody else.

Why had it never occurred to Ally? Of course Gavin was married. He was a wonderfully kind and caring man – and pretty damn handsome too. Why wouldn't some lucky girl have snapped him up? How arrogant of Ally to assume he had been waiting for her to re-enter his life all these years.

'You're married?' Ally's voice was barely a squeak. Her mouth was so dry, she was forced to take a gulp of her coffee, barely noticing the sting as the hot fluid snaked down her throat.

'Yep. I have a little girl too.'

He was a father. He'd married another woman and produced a child with her. Ally attempted to mask her shallow breaths, but inside she was falling apart. Gavin had the perfect life on the beautiful Hill Bank Lane with the child he'd yearned for. A life which Ally wouldn't ever be part of.

She tuned back into Gavin, trying to keep up. He was talking about his child – a two-year-old called

Mia who, apparently, was amazing and had changed his life.

'What about you?'

Ally looked down at her bare finger, feeling the loss of her wedding band more now than ever. 'No, no husband or kids. I'm still single.' Forcing her body into motion, Ally took a final scalding sip of coffee and gathered her coat and handbag. 'I should be getting off. I'm supposed to be meeting someone soon.'

'I should be getting back to work too.' Gavin rose from his seat and accompanied Ally down to the entrance. She wanted to grab her husband by the collar and give him a good shake, to make him remember her. To remember that he loved *her* and not this other woman. She wanted to fall down at his feet and weep, to mourn her loss. She'd found Gavin, only to lose him all over again and it wasn't fair.

Somehow managing to keep it together, she turned to Gavin at the exit. 'It was lovely seeing you again.'

'You too. It was nice catching up.' Gavin reached out to push open the glass door, flashing a grin. 'I'll see you next week.'

Ally doubted that. She wouldn't be seeking Gavin out again.

TWENTY-SEVEN

She somehow managed to hold back the tears as she powerwalked towards the bus stop. They were held back as she waited for the bus and she even managed to board without blubbering. She'd been hoping to keep the tears at bay until she was safely locked away in her flat, but it wasn't to be. Sitting on the worn seat, she made the mistake of glancing out of the window and clocked a happy couple strolling along the pavement, animatedly chatting while they pushed a buggy with chubby little legs swinging from beneath a pink blanket.

Gavin was married. He was a father. He loved another woman so much that he had taken the same sacred vows he'd taken with her. His love for Ally hadn't shone through the life-altering wish as she'd hoped. Far from it. He had his own life now, a happy life it seemed, and it had nothing at all to do with her.

What now? Was she supposed to just get on with her life without him? Ignore her feelings and longings? Because Ally didn't think she could do that. She had loved Gavin since they were fifteen. For half of her life. How would she live without him?

Oh, God. Her life was turning into a Leann Rimes song.

A solitary tear wormed a hot path way down her cheek as the bus pulled away. Ally swiped at it with her sleeve, but was powerless to stop the tidal wave that followed. The tears continued to fall for the duration of her journey, much to the horror of the teenage boy sitting in front of her. Even his iPod couldn't drown out the sobs that rocked Ally's body, but she didn't care. They could come for her now. They could cart her off to a padded cell and feed her mind-numbing drugs. Not feeling anything sounded like bliss right now.

The tears were still in plentiful supply as she unlocked her front door and trudged up the stairs to the sitting room. Not bothering to remove her coat, she sagged onto the sofa and fully succumbed to her grief. She'd lost Gavin forever and it was all her own fault for making that nasty little wish. She'd taken Gavin and their life together for granted and now she would never get it back.

She needed a drink. That's what they did on TV, wasn't it? They drunk themselves stupid and threw things around, which sounded like fun. Ally grabbed a cushion and flung it across the room, narrowly missing the giant TV screen. Meh. Throwing things was overrated.

Leaving the cushion slumped on the floor, Ally moved through to the kitchenette. She was in luck as there was still plenty of alcohol left over from the housewarming party, so she poured herself a large vodka and coke, downing it swiftly before refilling her glass.

She'd never marry Gavin now, would she? She would never be Mrs Richmond. There already *was* a Mrs Richmond. What a selfish cow Ally was! She bet the new wife would never wish Gavin away. She'd appreciate him for the amazing husband that he was. She wouldn't yearn for something more. How could Ally have ever imagined there was a better life out there for her?

Ally wondered what she was like, this woman who had stolen her husband. Was she tall and striking like Kelly? Or warm with womanly curves? Did she have Gavin's tea on the table when he arrived home from work? Or did she keep him busy in the bedroom with her rampant ways. Perhaps she did both. She bet the new Mrs Richmond was kinky, into anything and everything. Horny bitch.

Pouring herself another drink, Ally imagined the Olympic effort Mrs Richmond put into their bedroom activities. Gavin would love it, the bastard. Wasn't their sex life good enough for him? Wasn't he satisfied with her? So what if she didn't dress up or have a craving to be whipped! They'd had a perfectly healthy sex life. Or so Ally thought.

Perhaps Gavin had been bored but had been too nice to say so.

Ally downed her drink and slammed her glass down on the counter. How *dare* he replace her with another woman? How dare he love her and make babies with her. Ally could never allow herself to fall in love with another man. She loved Gavin too much to even consider the notion, so *his* love obviously wasn't on the same level. She'd had the opportunity to sleep with Jason – *Jason*, a man who was so unbelievably hot it made her ache just to look at him – and she'd turned him down. Such a pity Gavin didn't have the same restraint!

How dare he?

Ally grabbed the bottle of vodka and poured a good measure into her glass before adding the last dregs from the bottle of coke. Turning towards the fridge to pull out a new bottle, she spotted the mini allotment mid-spin. The gift from Jason. She'd turned Jason down because she believed in her vows and loved her husband, but he didn't love her in return. He'd *forgotten* about her.

Ally narrowed her eyes against the brimming tears. If Gavin could forget about her so easily, she could forget about him.

Abandoning the drink – which wasn't numbing anything anyway – she took two strides into the sitting room and picked up her phone.

'Hey, Jason. Do you fancy meeting up?'

Ally needed to take her mind off Gavin and his wife

and kid, so she spent the rest of the afternoon applying a face mask, soaking in the bath and painting her toenails. Anything to keep her occupied before she could escape her dreary little flat and fill her mind with anything other than her philandering husband.

She met Jason in a bar in town that evening. Luckily, the face mask had managed to dull most of the redness from her eyes and her make-up hid the stubborn blotchiness. Jason was already there, waiting in a quiet corner and looking gorgeous in a white shirt pressed to within an inch of its life, the top two buttons left undone.

'Alana, hi.' He rose when he spotted her, pulling her towards him to peck her on the cheek. He smelled so good Ally had to pull away before she did something stupid and made a show of herself. She'd had far too much to drink that afternoon, so she had to be extra careful.

'I keep telling you to call me Ally.'

'Sorry, yes. Ally. Can I get you a drink?'

Ally realised Jason was flustered by her presence, practically flapping about the place. Was he nervous? The thought brought a smile to Ally's lips. She felt powerful and desirable, which was a welcome change after the way Gavin had made her feel earlier.

'I'll have a mojito, please.' Ally had never tried one before, but Martine was fond of them and she couldn't recall the name of the delicious yellow slush cocktails. She watched as Jason made his way to the bar, attracting appreciative glances from the female customers he passed. Ally's smile widened. This man, this *gorgeous* man, had chosen *her*. He hadn't flounced off with another woman and impregnated her at the first opportunity.

After chatting over a couple of drinks in the bar, during which Ally flexed her paltry flirting muscles, they moved on to a club. It was packed with young, stunning women so Ally upped her game. She couldn't be the old, boring Ally any more. Not with Jason. She was pretty sure he'd been attracted to Alana because of her sluttish behaviour and not her dazzling conversational skills, so Ally attempted to imitate her. Taking Jason's hand, she led him onto the dance floor and put on a performance that would have made even Martine blush. By the end of the night, Jason could have been in no doubt over her intentions, but she decided to spell it out for him anyway as they climbed into a cab.

Ally's tongue was practically lodged in Jason's ear as she leant over and purred, 'Let's go back to your place.'

TWENTY-EIGHT

Ally's first thought upon waking was that she was back home. And by home, she wasn't thinking about her lonely, miniscule flat but *home* home, the house she shared with Gavin. Ally was sprawled across a large mattress, which definitely didn't belong to her tiny single bed at the flat, with Gavin's leg draped over hers, heavy yet reassuring, the hairs tickling her smooth flesh.

Her second thought was that her eyelids had somehow been glued down during the night. She attempted to prise them open and eventually – *painfully* – the lids peeled away, only to clamp down again as the bright light burned through to her brain.

'Ow.' Groaning, Ally reached up to rub her eyes but her co-ordination was shot due to her foggy head and she poked herself in the eye instead. '*Ow.*'

'You alright?'

Ally froze, her already dry mouth gaining desert-like aridity. That was not her husband's voice.

'Oh, God.' Sod the bright light and searing pain. Ally forced her eyes fully open and yep, there he was, sitting up in bed and looking down at her with concern etched onto his handsome face.

'That bad, huh? I'll go and get you some paracetamol.' Jason slipped out of bed, thankfully wearing a T-shirt and a pair of shorts. Ally had feared Jason would be as naked as the day he was born, though she hadn't been *too* quick to avert her gaze.

What had she done? She knew technically she had nothing to feel guilty about. She wasn't married to Gavin in this life – some other woman had that pleasure – but in her heart she was still his wife and she had betrayed him.

'Here you go.' Jason returned with the paracetamol and a tall glass of water. Ally considered refusing the painkillers as punishment for last night's dirty deed, but the dull throbbing in her head really was unbearable, so she knocked them back and prayed for quick relief. The glass shook in her hand, spilling water onto the duvet. When she looked down, she realised she was still fully clothed in one of Alana's dresses, which was now in desperate need of an iron.

'Jason, did we...?' Ally blushed. She may have channelled Alana last night, but she was back to being herself this morning.

'It was obviously a memorable night then.' Jason took the glass from Ally before she gave herself a shower with it. 'No, nothing happened. Not really. We kissed, but that's it. You said that you couldn't, that you weren't a slut like Mrs Richmond.' He raised an eyebrow at Ally, but she shrugged, feigning ignorance. 'I was going to sleep on the sofa but you said you didn't want to be on your own. I kept my hands to myself though, I swear.'

'I believe you.' Ally's knickers were thankfully still very much in place. 'Thanks, Jason. I'm sorry if I led you on.'

Jason gave a shrug. 'If I'm going to be led on by a woman, I'd rather it was you.' He grinned at Ally to show there really were no hard feelings. 'Are you able to stomach breakfast? I'm starving.'

Ally spent what remained of the weekend dreading going back to work and seeing Jason again. He'd kissed her after dropping her off at the flat, a sweet little peck on the cheek that still managed to make her stomach swirl with guilt and shame. But Monday morning ignored Ally's pleas to stay away for the foreseeable future and rolled around anyway.

'Blimey, you look rough.'

It wasn't the most pleasant of greetings, but Ally accepted it with grace seeing as it came from Francine. She'd happily take any conversation from her former best friend. They'd formed a fledgling friendship since Ally's housewarming party, and while it wasn't anywhere near the closeness they'd once shared, it was better than nothing.

'I feel rough but don't waste your sympathy on me. It's all my own fault.'

'Heavy night out?' Francine reached into her desk drawer and pulled out a box of paracetamol, popping two out of the blister pack. 'Lucky you. I can't remember the last proper night out I had. It was probably before Maisie was born. Or even Emily. How depressing is that?'

Ally pounced on the opportunity, barely pausing for breath before she jumped in. 'We should go out.'

'Me and you?' Francine scrunched up her nose, imagining a rowdy night out in town involving shots, dancing around poles and sex in toilet cubicles. As a finale, they'd puke in a gutter and engage in a catfight. Not Francine's cup of tea at all.

'Why not? It'll be fun. Do you like karaoke?' Of course Ally already knew the answer. Francine adored getting up to sing. She had a lovely, rich voice and it was her one chance to shine. 'There's a karaoke night at one of the pubs near my place tomorrow. I've been thinking about getting a small group together. What do you think?'

'I don't know. It's been years since I got up to sing in front of anyone and I'm not sure Mike will be home to look after the girls.'

Ally was losing her. She had to act – and fast. 'Please, Francine. It's so lonely living in that flat on my own and I don't know any of my neighbours or anything.'

Francine closed her eyes, willing herself to say no while knowing she couldn't leave the poor girl feeling like that. She wasn't so bad now that she'd gotten to know her properly, and it *had* been a long time since she'd let her hair down. Mike would be alright with the girls and if he didn't like it, it was tough luck on his part. He was more than happy to leave her alone with the girls several nights a week while he played darts and pool at the pub.

'Fine. I'll come.'

'Yes! Fantastic. It'll be fun, I promise.' Ally scooped up the paracetamol and skipped up the stairs, the thud in her skull nowhere near enough to dampen her mood. It was only when she reached her office and spotted Jason loitering by her desk that her spirits drooped.

'Malcolm's been on at me about the training report. Can you pass it on to him as soon as possible please?'

'Sure. I'll finish it off now.' Pocketing the painkillers, Ally moved slowly towards her desk and switched on her computer, waiting for Jason's next move. She expected him to proposition her or at least mention the fact they'd almost had sex on Saturday night, but he simply gave a curt nod and strode away to his office. Maybe it had sunk in that she wasn't interested in a relationship, despite her mixed messages.

Ally completed the report and emailed it to Malcolm before starting on her toppling in-tray. Jason brought her a coffee at mid-morning and perched on the edge of her desk.

'I know I've been a bit too eager in the past, you know, about us.' He cleared his throat and shifted slightly. 'It's because I really like you. But I don't want to scare you off this time. If you want to keep it casual, that's fine by me. I won't pressure you, I swear.'

'How about we just stay friends?'

'Friends?' Jason nodded. 'If that's what we have to be, then so be it.'

'Great. Then how do you fancy coming to a karaoke night tomorrow?' She didn't imagine karaoke was Jason's kind of thing, but Ally and Francine hardly made up a group, so she was clutching at straws.

'I can't promise an X Factor performance, but yeah, okay.'

'You'll come?' Ally did a silent cheer inside her head, complete with imaginary air punch. 'Brilliant. It's at The Farthing on MacMillan Road. Do you know it?'

'I'll find it.' Jason hopped off the desk as the door swung open and Kelly wandered into the room, seemingly unaware that she was almost two hours late. As though she wasn't feeling guilty enough, yet more remorse gushed through Ally as she caught sight of her co-worker. No amount of filing and photocopying could make up for the shitty life Ally had bestowed upon her.

'Do you fancy coming to a karaoke night with us tomorrow?' Singing in front of a pissed up audience wouldn't make up for it either, but Ally had to do *something* to try to ease her conscience.

'Err, yeah right.' Kelly slung her handbag underneath her desk and jabbed at the power button on her computer.

'Come on, it'll be a laugh,' Jason said. 'And I bet you've got a killer voice.'

Kelly gave a one-shouldered shrug. 'It's not bad, actually.'

'Then prove it.'

Kelly examined her nails while she considered the challenge. Finally she let out a long sigh. 'Fine. But you're buying the drinks.'

TWENTY-NINE

Ally was the first to arrive at The Farthing, which made a change as Francine, Freya and Dee were usually at least halfway through a bottle of wine by the time Ally showed up. Her old house caught her eye from a few doors away, but Ally averted her gaze after feeling an immediate pang of loss. That life was gone and she had no choice but to move on with this one and make it the best she possibly could.

Pushing the heavy door, she made her way into the pub where Keith Barry was setting up his karaoke equipment. He was such a familiar sight from her old life that Ally felt the powerful urge to throw herself into his arms and hold onto the man, despite the patches of sweat widening by the second under the armpits of his shiny gold shirt. Resisting, Ally made her way to the bar and ordered a bottle of wine and four glasses. A lump formed in her throat as she was hit with nostalgia. She could almost hear Freya in the background, yelling something obscene to try and make Ally blush in front of the barman. Dee would be encouraging her, suggesting filthier comments to fire her way while Francine attempted to hide her face behind an empty wine bottle.

Was it a mistake trying to recreate happy moments from her old life? Perhaps tonight would only serve to remind Ally of what she had lost and make her slump into depression.

'Hey you.' Jason had arrived, looking as gorgeous as ever in a pair of jeans and a thin charcoal sweater.

'You made it.' Ally tore her eyes away from the sweater, knowing exactly how toned the stomach underneath was. Memories of their weekend had started to seep through – especially the heavy petting in the back of the taxi – but she gave them a swift elbow before they made her blush. 'I have wine but I can get you a pint if you'd prefer.'

'I'll get these.'

'Don't be daft. I invited you, so I'll get the first round. I insist.'

Jason looked as though he was about to argue but changed his mind with a shrug. 'Fair enough. I'll have a pint then, if you're sure.'

'I am.' Ally sent Jason and the wine off to secure a table while she ordered a pint and paid for the drinks. The pub was starting to fill up, but Ally spotted Jason without any trouble. How could she miss him when every single female eye was trained in his direction?

'Do you think the others will come?' She handed Jason his pint and poured herself a glass of wine.

'I don't see why not.'

'Because they both dislike me?' Ally attempted to laugh her statement off but she was fooling nobody.

'They don't know you properly, but they'll love you once they do.' Jason gave Ally's knee a squeeze under the table. She jumped, shuffling away slightly. There would be none of that, thank you very much.

'So what do you think you'll sing?'

Jason shook his head and took a sip of his pint. 'I have no idea. I've never done karaoke before.'

'Never? Not even on holiday or anything?'

'Nope. I'm a karaoke virgin.'

'It's about time we popped that cherry then, don't you think?' Ally laughed at the worried expression on Jason's face. 'Relax. You'll enjoy it, I swear. We could get up together if you wanted to. Ease you in.'

A duet was a good idea, now Ally thought about it. Otherwise she'd probably end up singing Leann Rimes' 'How Do I Live' with mascara and snot snaking down her face, which was not a good look at all.

The door opened and Francine appeared, wide and startled eyes scanning the pub for a familiar face. She visibly relaxed when she saw Ally wave her over.

'Glass of wine?'

'I'd love one, thanks.' Francine removed her jacket and looped it over the back of her chair. 'Hi, Jason. I didn't expect to see you here.'

'Ally dragged me here, kicking and screaming.' He winked at Ally while she gave him a playful nudge.

'Kelly is supposed to be coming too.'

Francine paused, glass of wine halfway to her lips. 'Kelly? As in Kelly Fox? She's coming *here*?' Francine couldn't imagine Kelly lowering herself to join them in the pub for a karaoke night. Nights out in town getting drunk beyond oblivion were more her style.

'She said she was.' Ally understood Francine's reservations, knowing Kelly wouldn't have agreed to join them had Jason not encouraged her.

As though on cue, the door opened again and Kelly breezed into the pub wearing a small and very tight red dress and ankle-shattering heels.

'Right then, ladies. Who wants to have a go with Uncle Keith first?' Keith Barry leered around the room and ran his hand up and down the shaft of his microphone, waggling his tongue above its head.

'That man is disgusting. I can't believe you brought us here.' Kelly hitched up the neckline of her dress while glaring across the table at Ally. Keith Barry had thought all his Christmases had come at once when Kelly stepped into the pub, and he'd put on quite a performance, falling to his knees and clasping his sweaty hands together.

'She's here at last. The woman of my dreams. Thank you, God!'

Kelly had been about to turn around and walk out of the pub until Ally grasped her by the hand and tugged her towards the table and the large glass of wine Jason had quickly poured. Kelly had brushed Ally off, folded her arms across her chest and shoved her nose into the air.

'Do not touch me again. Ever.' She'd then turned to Jason and the proffered wine. 'No thanks. I'll have an orange juice.' She'd then lowered herself onto a stool while Jason ran to the bar and hadn't cracked a smile since.

'He's harmless enough, I suppose.' Ally actually agreed with Kelly for once, but felt she had to jump to Keith's defence due to their shared history.

'Harmless? He's a dirty, perverted little man. I wouldn't take my chances with him.' Kelly shuddered and again, Ally found herself agreeing. Not that she'd admit that to Kelly. She'd rather cut off her own tongue with a blunt pencil than share an opinion with the girl out loud.

'Shall I get us another round of drinks?' Jason offered. His pint was long gone and the bottle of wine was rapidly being drained. 'Are you sure you don't want a proper drink, Kelly?'

Kelly rubbed her temples with a grimace. 'No thanks. I'm still feeling delicate from the weekend.'

'I'll come and give you a hand.' Ally hopped out of her seat, but her phone started to ring before they'd made it to the bar. She excused herself, promising to be back in a minute before slipping out of the pub. Keith Barry's first victim was now in session, so it would be impossible to hold a conversation inside.

'Where are you?' Martine was straight to the point, not bothering with any pleasantries.

'I'm at the pub. It's karaoke night.' Ally suddenly felt bad that she hadn't invited Martine along too. She'd been good to Ally since the switch and she could imagine Martine getting on with Kelly as they were both so similar. Either that or they'd scratch each other's eyes out, which wouldn't be *totally* unpleasant to witness. 'Why don't you join us?'

'For karaoke night?' Martine gave an incredulous yet sparkly laugh. 'I don't think so, babe. I have better things to do than listen to a bunch of low-rate X Factor wannabes.' Yep, definitely like Kelly. 'But thanks for inviting me. Better late than never, eh?'

'Yeah, sorry about that,' Ally said, but Martine had already hung up.

Jason was struggling across the room with the drinks when Ally returned.

'Sorry about that.' She relieved Jason of the bottle of wine and joined the girls, who were deep in discussion over song choices, heads bent over the song list folder.

235

'What do you think, Alana? I can't decide between "Wind Beneath My Wings" and "I Say A Little Prayer", but Kelly says they're old lady songs. What do you think?'

'I think you should call me Ally.' She *would* convince them all eventually. 'And I think you'd be amazing at "Mustang Sally".'

Francine gasped and began flicking through the folder. 'I *love* that song.'

'What about you, Kelly? What are you going to sing?'

Kelly flicked her hair over her shoulder. It was blonde again now but she'd left it at its shoulder-skimming length. '"The Edge of Glory".'

Ally topped up Francine's glass with wine before moving onto her own. 'I didn't have you down as a Lady GaGa fan.'

'There's a lot you don't know about me.'

'Mysterious.' Jason turned to Ally and rubbed his hands together. 'So what are we singing then?'

Ally grabbed the folder and perused it, pausing to applaud the girl who had just finished her song.

'Wasn't she fantastic?' Keith Barry threw his arm around the poor girl, his greasy hand clutching her bare shoulder. 'I think I'm in love. But don't tell the wife.' He winked at the crowd and patted the girl's bottom as she left the karaoke area, making way for the next target. 'What's your name, baby girl?'

The girl stepped back as Keith's microphone was thrust in her face. 'Cindy Wannamaker.'

'Cindy Wannamaker, eh?' Keith winked at the crowd again. 'Wanna make out with me?'

'I'm going to be sick.' Kelly turned to Ally, who was still scrutinising the song choices. 'Seriously, why did you bring us here? I'll break his arm if he touches me, the filthy bugger.'

'*I'll* break his arm if he touches any of you,' Jason said as Cindy opened her mouth and belted out her song.

'Aww, our knight in shining armour.' Kelly touched Jason on the arm and Ally wasn't sure if she was being genuine or sarcastic. You could never tell with that girl.

'How about "Something Stupid"?' Ally pushed the folder towards Jason, her finger on her song choice. She turned to Francine. 'I love Robbie, don't you?' They'd once gone to see him at the MEN Arena, screaming like a couple of teenagers when they spotted him on stage. It had been a brilliant night so it was a shame Francine wouldn't remember.

Jason pulled a face. 'Does that mean I have to be Nicole?'

Ally gave him a nudge. 'Don't be daft.' She picked up the stack of song request forms and filled one in for herself and Jason. 'There. It's official. We're singing "Something Stupid".'

'How apt. Because that's how I'll feel up there.' Jason grimaced as he sipped at his pint.

'You'll love it, I promise. And I'm sure Keith will keep his hands to himself.'

Jason's mouth gaped open in mock indignation. 'You mean he won't fancy me? Aren't I pretty enough?'

'Don't worry. You're a very pretty boy.' Ally gathered everybody's forms and took them over to Keith, throwing them at him before scuttling away unscathed.

The karaoke night was a roaring success. Francine wowed everybody with her rendition of 'Mustang Sally' and Kelly had a good set of lungs on her too, which was both a joy and a disappointment for Ally to listen to. A tiny part of her, a tiny part with residual resentment for the girl, had hoped she'd strip the wallpaper with a strangled-cat voice.

'We should do this again,' Francine said as they waited outside the pub for their taxi.

'How about next week?' Ally couldn't quite believe how easy this had been.

'I'm in. How about you, Kelly?'

Kelly gave a shrug of her shoulders as she examined her nails. 'Sure. Why not?'

'Jason?' Ally could tell what his answer was going to be even before she asked. Although Jason admitted it had been fun getting up to sing, he doubted he'd ever put on a repeat performance.

'I think I'll leave you girls to it if you don't mind.'

'Not at all. Thanks for coming tonight though.'

'It's been a pleasure.'

A taxi pulled up beside them and Francine and Kelly climbed inside. Ally lived a matter of streets away, so she hung back.

'I'll walk you home,' Jason said. 'Make sure you get there safely.'

'You don't have to. I'll be fine on my own.'

'I want to.' Jason shut the car door and waved at Francine and Kelly. They waited until the car was out of sight before they began the short journey to Ally's flat. Her stomach was jittery with every step, worried that Jason would get the wrong idea and try it on. A treacherous part of her brain sent a thrill through her body as it remembered being in the taxi on Saturday night.

'Do you mind if I come up while I wait for a taxi?' Jason asked, his phone already in his hand.

'Of course not.' Ally led the way, the jitters increasing. She could hear Jason ordering a taxi, but it could all be a ruse to lure her into bed. But no, it wouldn't work. It wouldn't feel right.

It would feel fantastic.

Her brain was working against her again, so Ally busied herself with filling the kettle. Jason's taxi should be there any minute but it was something to do.

'Oh, you're using the mini allotment.' Jason reached past her in the tiny kitchenette and picked up the planter. Shoots were already appearing in the soil.

'Yep. I'm growing basil, chives and parsley.'

'You're a little Miss Green Fingers on the sly, aren't you?'

Ally laughed, recalling the garden she'd tried to

create in the little yard at the back of her terraced house. She'd bought large pots and lined them up along the back wall but failed to grow anything but weeds. 'Hardly, but these are looking pretty good. I'll be cooking with my own herbs in no time.'

'And of course you'll invite me round to sample your cuisine, seeing as I bought you the kit.'

Ally laughed again. She wasn't much of a cook either. 'Maybe. We'll have to see.'

Jason grinned at her, and she felt her brain betraying her again, along with her jellied knees.

'Is that your taxi?' She crossed the room to peer out of the sitting room window at the sound of a car pulling up outside.

'I'll see you in the morning then.' Jason leant towards her and gave her a chaste peck on the cheek. 'It really has been a great night.'

Ally saw Jason to the door, waiting for the car to disappear from view before she locked up and headed back upstairs to get ready for bed. Alone.

THIRTY

With summer approaching, the weather was taking a turn for the better, so Ally and Martine decided to make the most of the warmth and met up for a pub lunch, sitting out in the beer garden to soak up the sunshine. Martine was picking at her food, refusing to meet Ally's eye or respond with anything other than dull, one-word answers.

'Look, I'm sorry, okay? I didn't think karaoke would be your thing.'

Martine threw her fork down onto her plate and finally looked Ally in the eye, her own eyes narrowed to mean little slits. It made her look quite comical, but Ally knew better than to allow herself to crack. Martine was not feeling humorous in the slightest.

'That's not it at all and we both know it. You don't need me any more because you've got new friends to play with.'

'Don't be silly.' Ally tried not to giggle as Martine pouted at her from across the table – which took amazing effort. She had never witnessed an adult acting like a toddler to this extreme before. Any minute now, Martine was going to throw herself onto the ground and thump her fists up and down on the concrete. 'We're meeting up again next week. You should come. It'll be a laugh.'

Martine gave a haughty sniff and jutted out her chin. 'Thanks, but I wouldn't attend a karaoke night if Mark Wright *begged* me to. And you know I'd do *anything* Mark Wright asked me to.'

So what was the problem?

'You don't mind if I still go, do you?' Not that Ally *wouldn't* meet up with Francine and Kelly next week. She'd finally clawed a tiny bit of her old life back, and she wasn't about to give it up without a fight.

'I suppose not. As long as you come out with me on Friday.'

'Ah, Friday.' Ally shifted in her seat and dropped her gaze. 'I have plans on Friday.'

Martine calmly picked up her fork before stabbing a tomato with frightening gusto. 'With who?'

'Jason.' He and a bunch of his friends had tickets for a comedy club, and Jason had invited her along. She owed him after the karaoke night, and if she was honest, she quite liked hanging out with him.

'*Jason*? But I thought you'd given up on the whole sexual harassment thing.'

'I have. We're just going as friends.'

Martine abandoned the forked tomato and folded her arms across her chest. 'You don't *have* male friends. You *can't* be friends with men. You always end up sleeping with them.'

'That was before.'

Martine scoffed. 'You really think you've changed? You're deluded, babe.'

'Why are you being like this? I thought we were friends.'

Martine cocked an eyebrow. It made her look demented. And it wasn't even funny this time. 'So did I.'

Ally couldn't believe how unreasonable Martine was being. Wasn't she allowed to have other friends? 'Let's not argue about this. We can go out on Saturday instead.'

Martine scraped back her chair and leapt to her feet, rattling the table as she did so. Ally clutched her glass to stop it from toppling. 'Don't do me any favours. I'll see you around sometime, I guess.'

Ally watched as Martine stalked across the beer garden, her heeled feet stomping out her anger with every step. Part of Ally wanted to call her back and appease the girl, but a stronger part was relieved that the drama was over.

Ally's friendship with Martine became strained while her friendships with Francine, Jason and even Kelly strengthened over the passing weeks. The karaoke nights at The Farthing became a regular occurrence and Ally increasingly found herself in Jason's company, first with the comedy club and then trips to the cinema and drinks in town. Nights with her new friends helped to take her mind off Gavin, but he was always there, creeping around the edges. Ally still found herself searching for him in crowds, though she had resisted stalking him in The Housing Warehouse. Knowing he was so close but out of her grasp was frustrating. She wished she could switch Gavin off at times, but she knew she would never really be able to let go.

'I hope you don't have high expectations for this meal.' Ally's mini allotment was thriving, so Jason had insisted she cook for him. She'd spent hours on the net sourcing the perfect recipes, settling on a simple tomato and basil soup for a starter, followed by grilled salmon served with buttered new potatoes with chives and parsley.

'This looks amazing. I thought you couldn't cook.' They were seated in the sitting room, plates on their laps and candles flickering from the mantelpiece.

'I can't usually.' Ally had been pleasantly surprised to find that the soup had been edible and the salmon wasn't bad either.

'You know you'll be served ready meals when you come to mine, don't you?'

'Is that an invitation?' Ally hadn't been back to Jason's place since the infamous Saturday night, and she'd made it quite clear that there wouldn't be a repeat of that. She still felt guilty that she'd almost cheated on Gavin, no matter how ridiculous that was, what with Gavin being married to another woman and everything. 'Anyway, there's nothing wrong with ready meals. How do you think I survive when I'm not trying to impress people?'

'You're trying to impress me?' Jason grinned at her, laughing as her cheeks turned pink.

'I didn't mean it like that.' Shit. Was she *flirting*?

'Yeah, keep telling yourself that. You know you want me.' Jason winked at her before tucking into his salmon.

Did she want him? Her body certainly seemed to think so at times, but it wasn't as simple as giving into her urges. Yes, she was attracted to Jason, more so now than when she'd had a silly little crush on him, but she couldn't remove her feelings for Gavin, despite knowing they were redundant.

'This is really good, you know.'

'Thanks.' Ally had barely touched her own meal, but she made the effort now, concentrating on eating rather than imagining what it would be like to actually sleep with Jason. Which was a difficult task seeing as he was sitting *right there*, their elbows almost brushing. Jason was wearing an extremely well-fitted T-shirt, which displayed every delicious contour. Imaginary fingers reached out to grasp the pesky material, tugging at the hem and revealing the delicious contours in the flesh.

'So.' Ally leapt out of her seat, grabbing Jason's half-full plate. 'Time for pudding. Would you like another drink?' Ally certainly needed one.

A couple of weeks later, Ally found herself back in Jason's flat. This time she was sober and intended to stay that way. *Friends*, she reminded herself as she stepped over the threshold. *We are friends.*

'Would you like to come through?' Jason ushered Ally along a narrow hallway to the kitchen, where the table had been laid, complete with tea lights and a centrepiece of baby pink and yellow tulips.

'Glass of wine?' Jason presented the bottle and Ally accepted. One little drink wouldn't hurt.

Ally glanced at the oven and covertly sniffed the air, but it was clear there had been no cooking taking place in this kitchen. Even the microwave sat abandoned.

'What are we having?' she asked, but was interrupted by the buzz of the intercom in the hallway. Jason left the kitchen, returning moments later with trays of delicious smelling food.

'Dinner is served.'

Ally laughed. 'You ordered takeaway? That's cheating. I actually *cooked*.'

'Believe me, it'll be better this way. Unless you wanted a side order of E. coli.'

'Hmm, tough choice, but I'll have the takeaway.'

Jason grabbed a couple of plates and dished up the meal, which they took their time over, chatting and drinking wine while soft music played in the background. Ally was slightly tipsy by the time Jason served a shop-bought tiramisu, but at least she wasn't steaming this time, giving her full control of her mind and body. After dessert, Jason made coffee, which they took through to the sitting room. The room wasn't much bigger than Ally's sitting room, but it was furnished with a plump leather corner sofa and a stuffed bookcase with matching coffee table and TV unit. It looked put together in a way that Ally's flat never would. The room overlooked a small communal garden rather than a busy main road, and the smell of garlic and grease – which turned out to be overpowering rather than appetising – didn't waft up through the floorboards.

'Who's this?' Ally had wandered over to the bookcase, plucking a framed photo of a little girl from a shelf. She was sweet-looking, with strawberry blonde pigtails and a gap between her front teeth as she grinned at the camera. Ally closed her eyes, shutting out the image. She'd done it again, hadn't she? She'd preyed on a father. At least Jason wasn't married.

'That's Kimmie, my niece. Adorable, isn't she?'

His niece! Quite why Ally was so relieved was beyond her, seeing as they were nothing more than friends, but she felt lighter as she returned the photo. 'She's very cute.'

Jason joined Ally at the bookcase, showing her another photo of Kimmie, this time as a new born with a wrinkled brow and plump, puckered lips. He seemed very close all of a sudden without the barrier of a table separating them, and Ally's heart rate picked up as he returned the photo, his arm brushing hers. She'd never been in doubt that she fancied Jason, but it was much more than that now she'd got to know him outside of work. She *liked* him. He was kind and sweet and he made her laugh, all on top of being exceptionally hot. She'd felt empty without Gavin, but Jason made her feel alive again, filling her with light and warmth.

But that didn't mean Ally had forgotten about Gavin, which made the situation all the more confusing. She still loved him, and it broke her heart whenever she thought about him with his new wife. She had to find a way to move on, for her own sanity if nothing else.

Nothing happened between Ally and Jason that evening, which was both a relief and incredibly frustrating. Jason had been a perfect gentleman, calling Ally a cab and kissing her on the cheek as they said goodbye on his doorstep. Ally began to suspect that she'd missed her opportunity, that Jason was no longer interested in her, especially when she arrived at the office on Monday morning and Jason didn't bother to get out of his seat to greet her as he usually did. But her fears were allayed when she spotted a post-it stuck to her computer monitor. She peeled the sheet off and smiled as she read the note.

Picnic @ lunchtime? X

'Well?' Jason appeared behind her, placing a hand on her shoulder.

'I'd love to.' Ally ignored the nagging voice inside her head that was reminding her of her marriage vows. She was moving on, however horrifying that thought may have been to her old self.

Jason took Ally to a local park, stopping off at a sandwich shop to pick up a pre-arranged picnic en route. The weather was behaving itself, emitting glorious sunshine while providing a cool, whispery breeze.

'You're quite the romantic on the sly, aren't you?' Ally asked as Jason poured sparkling water into plastic champagne flutes. She'd assumed Jason was a bit of a stud – the love 'em and leave 'em type – but he'd been nothing but attentive towards her.

'Only with you.'

Ally laughed it off but she felt a glow within. 'Smooth talker.'

'Hey, it's true.'

Jason unpacked the food while Ally kicked off her shoes and stretched out on the blanket they'd brought with them from the boot of Jason's car. He plucked a fat strawberry from the punnet of fresh fruit and offered it to Ally, their eyes locking as she took a bite.

The window of opportunity was still wide open.

'Are you doing anything on Friday?'

Ally selected a grape from the punnet and popped it into her mouth. 'Francine and Kelly are coming round for a girls' night in.' As the karaoke nights were going so well, Ally had decided to push her luck and had invited them round for an evening of wine, food and a tower of romantic comedy DVDs. She'd invited Martine along too, but she'd declined. Girls' nights in were for losers, apparently.

'Ooh, are you going to have pillow fights in your underwear? Can I come?'

Ally rolled her eyes. 'Sounds like you just did.' They both laughed and reached for the fruit, their hands meeting above the punnet. Ally instinctively moved her hand away but Jason was too quick for her and grasped hold, pulling her hand towards him. Ally closed her eyes as Jason's lips brushed her fingers, but she snapped them open again as Gavin's smiling face floated before her.

I am not married to Gavin, she reminded herself, but the spell was broken. She couldn't kiss Jason, not with Gavin still lingering around the edges.

THIRTY-ONE

'So what's going on with you and Jason?'

It was Friday night and Kelly and Francine were lounging on Ally's sofa with a huge bowl of popcorn between them. They'd already eaten a curry, followed by Ben & Jerry's ice cream and had now settled down to watch a film on Ally's ridiculously large television, which took up almost an entire wall in her tiny sitting room.

'Nothing's going on with me and Jason. We're friends.' Ally, wedged in a bean bag she'd claimed from Freecycle, reached behind her to grab a handful of popcorn.

'Friends? Yeah, right.' Kelly turned to Francine, her pencil-thin eyebrows raised up to her hairline. 'What do you think? Friends or lovers?'

'We are definitely *not* lovers.' Ally attempted to turn quickly but only managed to tangle herself in the bean bag.

251

'You're definitely not just friends either.'

Ally rolled off the bean bag and turned to gape at Francine while Kelly threw back her head and cackled. Ally was shocked. She thought that if anyone would be on her side on this matter, it would be Francine.

'We *are* friends. We haven't even kissed.' Unless you counted the infamous Saturday night, which, like the one-night stand at university, Ally did not.

'Yet.'

Kelly whooped and gave Francine a high-five. 'See? If Emily Bishop here thinks the two of you are up to no good, you must be.'

'Emily Bishop?' The mirth had left Francine's face and her shoulders slumped. 'Am I really that bad?'

'No, of course you're not.' Ally widened her eyes at Kelly while giving Francine's knee a squeeze.

'Okay, maybe you're not *quite* as bad as Emily Bishop,' Kelly conceded. 'But you are very straight-laced.'

'That's because I'm a mum.'

'That doesn't mean you can't have fun. Loosen up a bit.'

'Like you, you mean? No thanks.'

Ally rested her head on Francine's knee and closed her eyes. This girls' night in was not going as planned. She had to do something. And fast.

'I do fancy Jason though. A tiny bit.' A tiny bit? Yeah, right. Ally practically drooled every time she clapped eyes on the man. 'I've got to know him and he's a really nice guy too.'

Kelly gave a wave of her hand. 'Nice shmice. Jason is hot. I wouldn't blame you for sleeping with him.'

'I would if I wasn't happily married.'

Kelly stared at Francine, her jaw dropping as Francine gave a nonchalant shrug and took a sip of wine. Francine had admitted that she thought Jason was attractive in the past, but Ally hadn't realised they were anywhere near that level of closeness in this life yet.

'Go, Emily.' Kelly gave Francine another high-five. 'You're not as much of a prissy-pants as I thought you were.'

'Thanks. I think.'

'Take it as a compliment. It was meant as one.' Kelly picked up her can of coke and clinked it against Francine's glass of wine. 'And I don't give those out easily, believe me.'

Ally grabbed another handful of popcorn, Francine's words reverberating around her head. *I would if I wasn't happily married*. And Ally wasn't any more, was she?

'*Top Gear*.'

'No chance. I want to watch *A Beginner's Guide To You*.'

'But it's a repeat.'

'So is *Top Gear*.'

The one advantage of being single was having full control of the television, but Jason was currently parked on Ally's sofa, attempting to impose his own viewing preferences.

'Why don't we compromise and record *A Beginner's Guide*?'

'No way, mister. If you want to watch *Top Gear*, you have a fully functioning TV at home.'

Jason gasped and placed a hand over his heart. 'Are you chucking me out?'

'I don't recall inviting you over in the first place.'

The truth was, Ally loved being in Jason's company. He was fun to be around and they had an easy, comfortable companionship, which was what she missed most about being married. Being young, free and single could be a lonely business.

'Ooh, harsh. I'll get my coat then.'

'Don't be daft.' Ally jabbed at the remote, turning it over just in time as the opening credits of *A Beginner's Guide* were on. 'You didn't bring a coat.' She laughed as Jason turned down the corners of his mouth, dropped his head and rose from the sofa. Ally reached out to grab Jason, pulling him back down. 'I'll record *Top Gear*. Deal?'

'Deal.' But Jason still rose to his feet again. 'I'll put the kettle on.'

'There are some chocolate fingers in the cupboard.' Ally turned her attention back to the television, only looking away when Jason placed a plate of the biscuits on her lap, the fingers arranged in a heart shape.

'When did you turn so soppy?'

'What? They fell out of the box like that.'

Ally giggled as she nibbled at one of the biscuits, offering the plate to Jason.

'Look, you've broken my heart.'

Ally giggled again and went to bat Jason playfully on the arm, but he caught her hand, pushing his palm against hers and entwining their fingers. Their fingers remained entwined, resting between their bodies on the sofa as they watched the television and worked their way through the chocolate fingers. Jason managed to sit through *A Beginner's Guide* and then Ally did her best to pretend to be enthralled by all the car talk and banter of *Top Gear*.

'What now?' Jason asked once it had finished, and Ally got the feeling he wasn't talking about their TV schedule. They'd been lovers before Ally had turned cold and pushed him away, and now they were mates. But sometimes Jason got the feeling she wanted more, and he knew he certainly did.

'I'm not sure.' Ally reached for the remote, flicking through the channels and ignoring Jason's gaze, which she felt rather than saw.

'Ally.' Jason reached for the remote, gently plucking it from her fingers before resting it on the arm of the sofa. 'What now?'

'I really don't know.'

'I think you do.' Jason was so close now, his words were a whisper against her cheek. 'What now?'

Before Jason kissed her, Ally was utterly

confused about her feelings for both Gavin and Jason. After he kissed her, she was no closer to sorting out the vortex of thoughts and emotions coursing through her body, but she did know one thing. Jason was an incredible kisser and she very much wanted to further investigate this path in her new life.

THIRTY-TWO

'Well? What do you think?'

Ally stepped out of the bedroom, straight into the sitting room where Jason swivelled around on the sofa, his eyes running up and down her body.

'I think you should stay at home with me instead.'

'That's exactly the look I was going for.' Ally giggled as Jason leapt off the sofa and enveloped her in his arms, pressing their bodies close together while he kissed her. He was probably destroying her lipstick, but who cared? Ally wrapped her arms around his broad shoulders, fusing their bodies even tighter.

'Stay here with me. I'll make it worth your while.'

Ally shivered as Jason's breath rasped against her throat. 'I promised Martine I'd go. I've hardly seen her lately and I think she's feeling neglected.'

Rather than being completely obliterated by their new status, Ally and Jason's friendship had grown into a comfortable yet exciting relationship. Far from the shallow liaison they'd seemingly once shared – they hadn't even slept together yet – they enjoyed being in one another's company and were fully immersed in the honeymoon period, spending every spare minute together. Ally had abandoned her friendship with Martine far too much lately. She was already feeling pushed out by the karaoke nights, so Ally had to make the effort tonight. No matter how much she wanted to spend the evening snogging on the sofa like a teenager.

'I'll give you a lift into town then.' Butterflies took flight in Ally's stomach as Jason grabbed his car keys. Martine had invited Ally along to a work's night out to celebrate a colleague's twenty-first birthday, so there was a chance Gavin would be there. She hadn't seen him since his happy-family revelation, and she was filled with the mixed emotions of wanting to keep him and her feelings at bay and needing to see him, to remind herself that he was real. It would be torture but she couldn't seem to keep away.

'Ready?'

Ally took a calming breath and smoothed down her figure-hugging dress. 'Ready.'

Of course she wasn't really ready. How could she prepare herself to see her husband, knowing he was in love with another woman? But she followed Jason out of the flat anyway and climbed into his car, her nerves mounting the closer they inched towards the club.

'Give me a ring when you're finished and I'll come and pick you up,' Jason said as Ally unbuckled her seatbelt.

'Don't be daft. I'll get a taxi.'

'But you'll come back to mine, won't you?'

Ally wasn't sure that was a good idea. She knew what would happen if she turned up at his flat, possibly drunk, during the early hours of the morning, and she wasn't ready to go there with Jason. It was quite nice to start from scratch and build up their relationship in a way that hadn't happened since she was fifteen. Plus, it was thrilling to keep a man as hot as Jason on his toes.

'Not tonight. It'll be late.' Ally had reapplied her lipstick during the journey but didn't mind ruining it again as she kissed Jason goodbye. It was only as she pulled away that she spotted Gavin passing by. All the air was knocked out of her as she slumped back in her seat. Seeing him was every bit as tortuous as she'd imagined.

'Are you sure I can't tempt you to a sleepover? I don't mind waiting up for you.'

'I'm sure.' Ally pulled herself together, leaning over to peck Jason on the cheek before climbing out of the car. 'I'll see you tomorrow.'

Jason pulled the corners of his mouth down, which made Ally giggle. 'Tomorrow, then.'

Ally closed the car door behind her, stooping to blow Jason a kiss before turning towards the club.

Gavin was waiting on the kerb and fell into step with her as she headed towards the back of the queue. She couldn't spot Martine, but she'd probably flirted her way inside already.

'Fancy seeing you here.'

'I'm meeting Martine. She invited me.'

'Ah, yes. I forgot you're friends with Martine.' They reached the end of the queue and shuffled into place. Jason's car was still up ahead, waiting until Ally was safely inside. 'Is that your boyfriend?'

'Yes.' It felt strange referring to Jason as her boyfriend in front of Gavin. Before her stupid wish, Gavin had been her only real boyfriend, and it pained her to have moved on, but what else was she supposed to do? Gavin was well and truly out of bounds. Being married was bad enough, but the fact he had a daughter shoved an impassable wall between them. Ally wasn't like Martine. She had morals, unfortunately.

'How long have you been together?'

Ally dropped her eyes to the ground. She didn't want to discuss Jason with Gavin, but she couldn't ignore his question. 'Not long. A couple of weeks.' The queue shuffled forward and Ally took the pause in conversation to change the subject. 'So it's your work colleague's birthday?'

'Yeah, Jonathan. He's a good lad.' Gavin shook his head. 'I sometimes wish I was twenty-one again.'

'Be careful what you wish for.' If only Ally had been given that advice before her birthday.

'Sometimes it's better to stay where you are. Believe me.'

'Yeah, you're right. Actually I'm far happier now than I was back then.' Just what Ally needed shoving down her throat – Gavin's marital bliss.

'You're lucky. I don't even remember my early twenties.' In her old life, Ally had been happy, planning her wedding and setting up home with Gavin. But in this life? Who knows what happened and Ally wasn't keen to find out.

'That wild, eh?'

'Something like that.'

They continued to chat as the queue moved along until they were finally permitted inside. Flashing lights assaulted Ally's eyes instantly and it took a moment for them to adjust. When they did, she spotted Martine marching towards her.

'There you are. I thought you'd decided to hang out with your new boyfriend instead.' Martine was not impressed that Ally had settled for one guy, especially as that guy was Jason, the supposed enemy.

'Hi, Martine,' Gavin said. 'Can I get you two a drink?'

Martine flicked the corners of her mouth upwards in a vague attempt at a smile. 'No thanks. We're dancing.'

Ally wanted to protest. She would have liked a drink and she wanted to keep chatting with Gavin. She wanted to find out all about his new wife in a perverse way, but Martine was already dragging her towards the dance floor.

Ally tried to find Gavin again over the course of the evening, but Martine was always too quick and monopolised her attention in an attempt to make up for the time they'd missed recently. She introduced Ally to the birthday boy, wrangled drinks from random men and threw herself around the dance floor. Ally was exhausted and was about to sneak off in search of a seat when she spotted her sister. And it wasn't Freya.

Jemima was wearing a shiny black leather catsuit with a plunging neckline that left nothing to the imagination. Jemima was barely old enough to possess breasts, never mind have them out on display. Surrounded by men and with what Ally assumed was an alcoholic drink in her hand, Jemima threw back her head and laughed, placing a hand on one of the men's arms.

Martine grasped Ally's arm as she moved away from the dance floor. 'Where are you going?'

Ally pointed at Jemima. 'That's my sister.'

'Wow. She's a little hottie, isn't she?'

Ally snatched her arm away. 'She's too young to be a hottie.' Marching over to the group, she grabbed Jemima's arm in the same way that Martine had grabbed hers, only she didn't dig her nails in quite so much. Ally's arm was still throbbing.

'Ow, get off, you stupid bitch.' Jemima yanked her arm away and shot a dark look at Ally, but her features softened in surprise when she saw who it was. 'Alana! Come and meet these guys. They're *hilarious*.'

'Hilarious? Perverts more like.' Ally turned towards the men and raised her voice so they could all hear. 'Do you know she's only fifteen?'

Jemima's eyes widened and her mouth puckered as she glared at Ally. Her shoulders slumped as her captive audience took a step back, muttering amongst themselves before dispersing. 'I can't believe you did that. What's the matter? Are you jealous because you're past it and they'd never look twice at you? Ow, get off me, you psycho bitch.'

Ally, ensuring her grip was tight enough to remain in place despite Jemima's thrashing, marched her sister out of the club.

'What the hell are you doing in there? And dressed like that? You're *fifteen*.'

Jemima finally managed to wriggle out of Ally's clutches, but it was pointless trying to get back into the club as Ally had announced to the doormen that she was under age as they passed through.

'What's the big deal? I've been going to clubs since I was thirteen. I look older, so it's not a problem.'

Ally couldn't believe her ears. 'Not a problem? Are you crazy? You do know what those blokes were after, don't you?'

Jemima folded her arms across her chest, which had the added bonus of covering a bit of exposed flesh. 'Doesn't mean they're going to get it. I'm not a slag.'

'You're a kid, Jemima. You shouldn't be putting yourself in situations like these.'

'You did when you were my age.'

'I can assure you I did not.' Ally was outraged. She hadn't set foot in a pub or club until she was almost eighteen. But *Alana* probably had. Shit. 'But if I did, it was wrong of me and dangerous. Please don't use me as a role model, Jemima. Look how I turned out – I'm living in a shoebox, I'm up to my eyeballs in debt and I've lost the man I love.'

Jemima gasped, her eyes widening once again. 'You've been in love? With who? You always said love was for losers.'

'Never mind that.' Ally grabbed Jemima once again and tugged her towards the main road. 'My point is, you shouldn't base your actions on mine. Whatever I did, do the opposite.' Spotting a black cab, she flagged it down and pushed Jemima inside.

'Get off me. I'm not going home. It isn't even midnight, for God's sake. I'm not Cinderella.'

'But you are my sister and I'm taking you home.' Ally climbed into the cab, pinning Jemima into place with her seatbelt while she squirmed and tried to break free. Ally gave her parents' address to the driver, keeping her hand over Jemima's seatbelt buckle at all times.

'I hate you. You're so pathetic.'

Ally looked at her sister, at the girl she had

created. Jemima – *Jimmy* – had been such a sweet girl but Ally had sucked all the goodness from her with her selfish wish.

'I'm not so fond of myself, either.'

THIRTY-THREE

'Are you okay?' Jason reached across the kitchen table and took hold of Ally's hand, giving it a squeeze. She'd been in a funny mood for a few days now. Until recently, Ally had always been aloof, but this was different.

'Yeah, I'm fine.' The contact brought Ally back down to earth and she managed a small smile. 'I'm just worried about Jemima, I guess.'

Ally had told Jason all about the incident at the club, and how she'd had to drag her furious sister back into the house without disturbing their parents. But if she was honest, it wasn't only Jemima on her mind. Seeing Gavin had given her a jolt and reminded her how much she still loved and missed him.

'She's a teenager going through a rebellious stage. She'll snap out of it.'

'It took me until I was thirty.' And only because

Alana had been hoofed out and replaced by Ally.

'Do you think you should tell your parents what she's up to?'

Ally dropped her head into her hands with a groan. She didn't know what to do for the best. Her parents should know what Jemima was doing, but it would only cause them more worry. 'I don't know. I don't want to worry them, but I can't keep an eye on Jemima myself.' Her parents would be horrified if they knew Jemima was sneaking off to clubs while wearing unsuitable attire and drinking and flirting. It turned Ally's stomach to imagine what the girl got up to on the occasions when she wasn't caught out.

But perhaps they wouldn't be horrified at all. Perhaps it wouldn't even come as a shock. They'd been through all of this before, when Alana was a teenager. Maybe they'd know how to deal with Jemima.

Or maybe it would break their hearts.

'Why don't you speak to your other sister? See what she thinks?'

Ally flashed Jason her first genuine smile since the previous weekend. Talking to Freya was a great idea. Freya knew the full extent of both Alana's and Jemima's behaviour, while Ally could only take educated guesses.

'I'll speak to her at lunch tomorrow.'

'Good.' Jason gave her hand another squeeze. 'So, what do you want to do today?'

Honestly? Ally wanted to crawl back into bed,

pull the covers over her head and pretend the past few months had never happened. She wanted to wake up and realise it had all been a silly dream.

'Come on.' Jason tugged Ally to her feet and pulled her towards the hallway. 'We're going out.'

'Where are we going?'

Jason handed Ally her jacket. 'You need cheering up so we're going into town to buy you something pretty, and then we're going for a nice lunch.'

Ally was suitably cheered by the time they decided to stop for lunch. Her problems hadn't disappeared, but they had been temporarily pushed aside by a chunky beaded necklace, a wispy chiffon top and a sparkly handbag.

'How about Café Katerina?' Jason suggested, pausing outside the restaurant. Ally hesitated, one foot itching to rush inside and order their delicious lemon tart while the other wanted to run away. Café Katerina was a gorgeous blue-fronted restaurant framed with lush greenery with an impressive interior that was sophisticated yet comfortable. The waiting staff were always attentive without being intrusive, and the food was divine. It was Ally's favourite restaurant and that was the problem. Café Katerina held so many memories for Ally, from the dinner to celebrate her graduation, to her wedding breakfast and every anniversary since. Gavin had been present for every occasion and she didn't want to tarnish her precious memories.

'Ally?'

She bit her lip. She had to make a decision and fast.

'Yes.' She nodded quickly before she could change her mind. 'Let's eat here.' She couldn't live her life avoiding the places she'd been with Gavin, not if she wanted to move on with her life.

Clutching Jason's hand a little too tightly, she headed for the door but froze when she heard a yelp behind her. She turned towards the commotion and spotted a woman on her hands and knees, shopping bags scattered around her. Both Ally and Jason rushed to her aid, helping her to her feet and gathering her bags.

'Are you alright?' Ally asked as the woman brushed grit from her knees.

The woman laughed, her cheeks pink from the embarrassment of it all. 'I'm fine, thanks. Just grazed my knee a bit.' She straightened, revealing a sizeable bump.

'Oh, God. Are you sure?' Ally imagined the poor woman going into spontaneous labour, her waters gushing onto the pavement in front of her. She took a tiny step back.

'Really, I'm fine. Mortified, obviously, but I'm not hurt.'

'But what about...?' Ally indicated the bump.

'Oh, we're both fine.' The woman placed her hand on her stomach and gave it an affectionate rub. 'And my husband will be here any minute so he'll look after us. I'm meeting him here.' She nodded towards the restaurant, her hand still circling her rounded stomach.

'We were just heading inside,' Jason said. 'Why don't you sit with us? Just until your husband gets here.'

Ally swelled with pride as Jason guided the woman into the restaurant, making sure she really was fine before ordering drinks. The woman's cheeks had calmed down by the time the drinks arrived and she'd managed to tame her dishevelled hair away from her face. Ally peered at her as she sipped her tea. She hadn't noticed before but she was vaguely familiar.

'Did you go to Westbridge High?'

The woman shook her head. 'No, I didn't grow up around here. But my husband did and he went to that school.'

Ally almost sloshed her tea down her top as it dawned on Ally who the woman was. Her hand shook as she returned her cup to its saucer, her pulse pounding in her ears. It had been years since Ally had seen her, but it was definitely her. How could she have not instantly recognised her?

The woman turned as the door opened and a smile lit up her face. 'Ah, here they are.'

Gavin trooped into the restaurant, heading straight for their table. Of course her husband was Gavin. Who else could it have been when there were only billions of other men in the world for her to ensnare?

'I had a bit of a stumble outside, but these kind people helped me up,' the woman explained as Gavin reached their table. A little girl was clutching his hand, babbling away and looking adorable in a rose-printed dress, frilly white socks and tiny sandals. She had Gavin's dark hair – currently secured in high plaited pigtails – and huge chocolaty eyes that stared dotingly at her father.

'Mamma!' The little girl thrust her arms out towards the woman, her eyes sparkling as she toddled towards her.

'You fell?' Gavin completely ignored Ally as he crouched before his wife, checking her for damage.

Helena. He'd married bloody Helena. Ally had always retained a shard of jealousy towards the woman who had almost replaced her while she was away at university, but nothing compared to the searing pain slicing through her abdomen at that moment. *He'd married Helena.* Of all the women on earth, he'd married *her*.

'I'm fine, really. Stop fussing.' Helena batted Gavin away, but she had an affectionate smile on her face. The child had clambered onto her lap and Ally wanted to throw up at the sight of the three of them together.

That should have been you, a voice sang in her head. It sounded oddly like Clementine, the sort-of guardian angel and wrecker of lives.

'Are you sure? We could pop over to the hospital for a check-up.' Gavin was still fussing over Helena. Jeez, she'd tripped on the pavement, not fallen down a precipice.

The woman laughed and shook her head. 'I'm fine, Gav, really.' Gav? *Gav*? 'These two have already made sure of that.'

Gavin seemed to notice Ally and Jason for the first time. Once upon a time, his eyes would have spotted Ally immediately, no matter how crowded the room was.

'Thank you so much.' He shook Jason's hand before turning towards Ally, his eyebrows almost shooting off his face. 'Alana?'

'You know each other?' Helena asked.

'We went to school together,' Gavin explained while Ally wanted to scream *'of course we know each other! He's my husband!'*

'Really? What a coincidence.' Helena beamed at Gavin and Ally. She was still pretty, the bitch.

'Isn't it?' Ally's own smile was forced. She wondered if Clementine had anything to do with this 'coincidental' meeting, or whether Ally's new life was simply destined to suck at every opportunity. 'We also lived across the street from each other growing up.' Before we fell in love and got married, although Gavin doesn't remember that part, the scatter-brained bastard.

'Wow. How strange that we would all meet up like this. It must be fate!' Helena seemed to think this was the best thing that could have happened, grazed knee aside. 'It's my birthday today and we're having a little party tonight. Why don't you come along?'

Ally shook her head. She couldn't witness them in their home environment. It was vomit-inducing enough seeing them here in a semi-neutral setting.

But Helena hadn't spotted Ally's response. 'I'd love to say a proper thank you, and it'll give you and Gav the chance to catch up.'

'We'd love to, wouldn't we?' Jason was grinning at Ally. Was he completely blind to the horror displayed on Ally's face? Or were they all in it together to make her life as miserable as possible?

Ally glared at Jason, but he wasn't listening as he was too busy noting down Gavin and Helena's address while making silly faces at the child.

THIRTY-FOUR

'We don't have to go, you know.' Jason perched on Ally's bed while she applied her make-up. 'I thought you'd want to go, with Gavin being an old friend and everything.'

Ally screwed on the lid of her mascara and managed a small smile for Jason. 'It's fine, really. I want to go.' In a perverse way, it was true. She was desperate to see where Gavin lived and how he existed without her, but at the same time she wanted to do nothing more than curl up in a ball and pretend none of this was happening. How could she explain to Jason that the thought of seeing Gavin with his wife and child was making her feel sick? That she wasn't sure her lungs would function once she stepped inside their home?

'It's just I haven't seen him for years. We don't know each other, not really. Not any more.'

'Then we won't go.'

It was so simple for Jason. Go, stay, it was no big deal. If only the choice was as easy for Ally, because she wasn't sure she *couldn't* go now. Despite her revulsion, she was compelled to go to the party, to witness for herself Gavin's new life. It couldn't be worse than the images playing in her head, surely.

Ally picked up her raspberry lip gloss. 'No, we'll go.' She had to. She couldn't keep away.

The houses on Hill Bank Lane were far grander than Ally remembered, each with at least two cars on the driveway. Gavin's house was made of pale red brick with huge windows on either side of the shiny red door. There was a large, immaculate lawn to the front, surrounded by a low wall and a neat rectangle of lush privets, and a double garage to the side. An oak tree created a shaded seating area, with two ornate iron benches underneath, and a rope swing dangled from a sturdy branch. The swing wasn't entirely in keeping with the surroundings, but it made Ally smile. She was glad Gavin wasn't pompous enough to care.

'Are you sure about this?'

Ally and Jason had climbed out of the car and made their way to the house, but Ally had paused at the wrought iron gate to soak in Gavin's new home. She nodded and pushed open the gate.

'Yes. I'm sure.' She gave Jason the bottle of wine they'd picked up en route, afraid it would slip from her sweaty palms and shatter on the impeccable paving as they made their way to the door.

Jason pressed the elaborate doorbell and leaned in towards Ally, his voice hushed. 'Looks like they've got quite a bit of cash.'

It did indeed, but they soon discovered that the couple were down to earth as they swept Ally and Jason inside with warm hugs and handshakes. The interior of the house wasn't what Ally had been expecting. Instead of dark, period pieces and lavish wall hangings, the rooms were light, airy and modern and Ally was put at ease despite the bizarre situation.

'Gav, could you make the introductions while I organise drinks?' Helena gave Gavin's arm a squeeze before she headed for the kitchen. Ally wished she'd stop touching Gavin. She was feeling overpoweringly territorial and was afraid she was going to horribly embarrass herself by rugby-tackling Helena to the ground while snarling at her to keep her hands to herself.

Gavin led Ally and Jason through to the sitting room where the other guests were chatting. The room was large, with a grand piano taking centre-stage by the window, and was homely with worn, comfortable-looking sofas, family montages mounted on the walls and an overstuffed toy box in one corner. Ally's eyes instantly fell on Gavin's parents.

'You remember my parents, Carolyn and Doug?' Gavin led them to the nearest sofa, where the couple were entertaining their grandchild. 'Mum, Dad, you remember Alana Williams, don't you?'

A smile flickered across Carolyn's face. 'How could we forget Alana?' Ally prayed the woman wouldn't bring up her mad stalking days.

'And this is Alana's partner, Jason.'

'Pleased to meet you, Jason.' Carolyn rose out of her seat and scooped up the child, resting her on her hip. 'Come on, Mia. I think it's bedtime for you, little lady.'

'I'll do that,' Gavin said, but his mother waved him away.

'It's fine. You stay and entertain your friends.' Carolyn swept out of the room, but paused long enough to glare at Ally before she disappeared from view.

Gavin continued the introductions; everyone was a stranger to Ally. In the old days, parties at Ally and Gavin's consisted of takeaway pizza, beer and a gathering of close friends. They didn't need a room stuffed with people to have fun.

Helena returned with the drinks as Gavin was introducing them to Katie and Greg, former work colleagues of Helena's. Helena was the perfect hostess, fun and charming while hopping from one group to the next, ensuring the drinks were topped up and reminding everyone of the buffet waiting in the dining room.

'So what was Gav like at school? I bet he was a sweetie.' Helena looped her arm around her husband's waist and rested her head on his shoulder, her eyes glowing as she glanced up at him. She was obviously besotted with Gavin and the adoration in her eyes turned Ally's stomach. She'd seen enough of Gavin's life to quench her curiosity. Anything more now was pure torment.

'You're asking the wrong person that. I don't think Alana even noticed me at school.' Gavin laughed, but his words tore through Ally.

'Of course I noticed you.' How could Ally – or Alana – have missed someone as special as Gavin?

'I doubt that.' Gavin turned to Jason with a shrug of his shoulders. 'Alana was part of the popular crowd at school. I was a bit of a loser.'

'Aww, poor baby. You're not a loser.' Helena reached up on her tiptoes to kiss Gavin on the cheek. Ally wanted to projectile vomit over the pair.

'Would you excuse me?' Thrusting her drink in Jason's direction, Ally took off in search of air and found herself in the kitchen. She crossed the room, heading for the back door, but froze in front of the fridge plastered with family snaps. Gavin and Helena on their wedding day. Helena lounging on a picnic blanket, a hand rubbing her swollen stomach. Gavin holding his newborn daughter, wonder and fear filling his eyes. Mia at the beach, podgy arms working away as she dug in the sand. A scan photo.

What was she doing there? Gavin was a happily married man. He was a father. He had everything he had ever wanted. Why was she putting herself through this torment?

Backing away from the photos, she stepped out

into the garden, which was as immaculate as the front of the house. The large garden was bordered with colourful flowers and shrubs, with a summer house in one corner and a large wooden playhouse/swing/slide contraption in the other.

Gavin was happy here. This was clearly a happy house, filled with love.

'There you are.' Jason draped an arm around Ally's shoulders and dropped a kiss on the top of her head. 'Are you okay?'

Ally nodded, her eyes still on the play equipment. Would it have been so bad to have had a family? Helena didn't seem like the downtrodden wife Ally envisioned when she thought about procreating. The woman was glowing. She was content, fulfilled. She hadn't given up her life or identity.

'Do you want something to eat? Helena says there are nibbles in the dining room.'

'Sure.' Ally tore her eyes away from the playhouse and headed back into the kitchen. 'I'm just going to nip up to the loo first.'

Once inside the bathroom, Ally splashed her face with cold water. She couldn't even avoid Gavin's domesticity in there as Mia's presence was marked with bath toys and colourful flannels. She dried her face and escaped into the hallway, but even then she caught the happy squeal of the child herself, safely ensconced in her bedroom with her grandmother.

Would she have been able to do it? Raise a

child? A child that was half her and half Gavin? She would never know.

Padding away from the sound of laughter, Ally headed for the stairs, pausing when she caught sight of a familiar guitar. The door was already open, so she wasn't technically snooping. The room was lined with shelves housing row upon row of books, with a pretty daybed by the window and a desk set up to one side. The guitar was upright in a stand, a plectrum slotted between the strings.

'Do you play?'

Ally was inside the room, her hand outstretched towards the guitar, but she snatched it back when she heard Gavin's voice.

'No.' Ally backed away from the instrument, turning to face Gavin. He slid past Ally and plucked the guitar from its stand.

'I taught myself when I was a kid.' Gavin perched on a nearby stool and propped the guitar on his knee, strumming lightly. 'The only things I play these days are nursery rhymes though.'

'So you don't play any Take That?' Ally shook her head at Gavin's puzzled look. 'Never mind. I'm just a bit of a fan.'

Gavin laughed. 'Nah, they're not my thing at all.'

'I suppose you're more into Oasis.' Ally found herself wandering towards the window, sinking onto the daybed.

'In my youth, yes.' He started to play a quietened version of 'Wonderwall'.

'Do you play the piano?' Ally recalled the grand

piano downstairs, but Gavin shook his head.

'That's Helena's baby.' He looked up from the strings to smile at Ally. 'You should hear her play. She's amazing.'

Ouch. Ally clutched at her stomach, suddenly wishing she'd learned to play an instrument. Had Gavin ever described anything she'd done as amazing?

'How long have you got before the new baby arrives?' Obviously pain wasn't enough for Ally. She wanted full-on agony.

Gavin beamed at her. 'Six weeks. I can't wait.'

'You're life has turned out pretty well then.'

'Yeah. It has.'

Better than it had with Ally. She'd actually done him a favour by wishing away their marriage.

Ally forced herself off the daybed. 'I should be getting back downstairs.'

'Me too. I'm not being a very good host, am I?' Gavin hopped off the stool and placed the guitar back in its stand. He straightened as Ally passed, bumping into her and unsteadying her on her feet. 'Whoa, sorry.' He grabbed hold of Ally's elbow and righted her.

'What's going on in here?' Carolyn stood in the doorway, her gaze held fast on Ally. Her face was pinched, her chin tilted into the air.

'I was just demonstrating my guitar skills,' Gavin replied.

'I've just put Mia to bed. I don't think it's a good idea to be playing your guitar right now.'

'We've finished now anyway. We were just about to go downstairs.' As soon as Gavin left the room, Carolyn's gaze turned icy. She blocked the doorway as Ally attempted to follow, waiting until her son was out of earshot before hissing at her.

'What are you doing here?'

'Helena invited us.'

'But why did you come? Are you thinking of trying to break them up?' Ally jumped back as Carolyn stepped into the room. 'Because it won't work. They're happy.'

Like Ally needed Carolyn to break that news to her. She could see for herself and while she should have been pleased Gavin now had the life he'd always wanted, the family he'd always wanted, Ally couldn't bring herself to feel anything but regret.

'I'm not going to try to break them up. I'm with Jason.'

'Hmm.' Carolyn glanced out into the hallway as a muffled sound came from Mia's bedroom. 'Remember they have a child, with another baby on the way.'

'I told you, I'm with Jason.'

'I heard, but I also see you sniffing around my son.' Carolyn stepped into the hallway, indicating that Ally should do the same. 'Don't you think it's time you went home?'

If only she could.

THIRTY-FIVE

Ally was a wreck by the time Monday rolled around. She hadn't been able to sleep since Gavin's party, her brain a jumble of memories of her old life, happy family snaps from Gavin's new life and Carolyn's scornful face as she and Jason left the party ridiculously early. She'd attempted to shower away her maudlin mood before setting off to her parents' house for Sunday lunch, but there wasn't enough shower gel in the world to make her feel right again.

The house had been full and busy, with Jared and his girlfriend visiting as well as Freya and Ally. Ally was surprised to see Jemima gracing the family with her presence, but it wasn't long before she made her excuses and scurried out of the house. She obviously hadn't forgiven Ally for dragging her home as she refused to speak to her older sister, or even glance in her direction. Still, Ally knew she'd done the right thing and if the silent treatment kept her sister safe, she was willing to take it on the chin.

'Can I have a word?' Ally cornered Freya in the kitchen as she was putting the kettle on.

Freya heaved a sigh as she opened the cupboard to grab some mugs, thumping each one down on the counter. 'If you're after money, you're out of luck. I'm skint.'

Now it was Ally's turn to sigh. 'How many times do I have to tell you? I'm not interested in borrowing money. I'm going to pay my own way from now on.'

Freya raised her eyebrows as her lips pinched together, clearly not believing a word that was spilling out of her sister's mouth. 'So what do you want then?'

Ally pulled the lid off the tea caddy, needing to do something with her hands. She'd spent a lot of time thinking about how to broach the subject, but it still wasn't clear in her mind.

'I'm worried about Jemima.' Ally lowered her voice, just in case her parents passed by. 'I caught her in a club.'

'And?'

'And she's fifteen.' Hadn't Freya heard correctly? 'She's too young to be out in clubs and you should have seen what she was wearing. There were guys all over her. I dread to think what would have happened if I hadn't dragged her out of there.'

'You dragged her out of the club?' *Now* Freya seemed surprised. What had she expected? That Ally would have bought a round of cocktails and given Jemima a lesson in twerking?

Actually, that sounded about right for Alana.

'Yes, of course I did. I brought her home in a cab. She hates me now.'

Freya gave a hoot. 'I'm not surprised. Can you imagine how you'd have reacted at her age?'

Unfortunately, Ally could imagine exactly how her alter-ego would have reacted. It wouldn't have been pretty. 'So what should we do? Shall I tell Mum and Dad?'

'Do you think Mum and Dad don't know what she gets up to?' Freya turned towards the kettle and poured boiled water into the mugs. 'You really do live on a different planet these days, don't you?' Freya had no idea how true that was. 'Mum and Dad know exactly what Jemima gets up to. They've been through all of this before, with you. They're terrified every time she leaves the house.'

'So why don't they keep her inside?'

'Do you think they could have kept *you* inside? They tried everything with you, Alana, but nothing worked. You went completely off the rails. Sneaking into clubs is tame compared to what you got up to.'

'So we have to do something to stop Jemima going the same way.'

Freya reached for the milk from the fridge and nudged the door shut with her elbow. 'Tell us what to do and we'll do it.' She finished making the drinks, Ally silent the whole time. 'Not as easy as it sounds, is it?'

'I am sorry, you know. For the way I acted.'

'So you keep saying.' Freya grasped a couple of the mugs and stalked away, but a shift was starting to happen. Actions were beginning to speak louder than words.

Ally was clueless when it came to sorting out Jemima, so now worry about her little sister added to her misery of missing Gavin. Sleep eluded her once again, so by the time she shuffled into the office on Monday morning, she resembled a zombie.

'Bad night?' Kelly asked as Ally shrugged her jacket off her shoulders.

'Bad life, more like.' Ally was sure Kelly muttered 'join the club', but assumed she must have imagined it when Kelly beamed a smile at her.

'Shall I get us both a coffee?'

'Did someone say coffee?' Jason popped his head out of his office, cheesy grin plastered onto his face. It slipped when he caught sight of Ally. 'Hey, are you alright? You don't look well at all.'

Jason's tone was so concerned and caring it made Ally feel even more wretched. What was she doing with this wonderful man when she was still in love with Gavin? Was she *using* him? Because it didn't feel like she was. She genuinely cared about Jason, but she couldn't shake Gavin from her mind.

She loved him and her heart constantly ached for him, but they were never going to be together. Gavin was her past and Jason her future.

'I didn't sleep very well, that's all.'

'Coffee will sort you out.' Kelly sprang up from her seat like a gazelle, the polar opposite of Ally's slump. 'And failing that, I've got some really good foundation that covers up anything.'

The morning was sluggish and Ally's energy seemed to deplete with every slow second that passed, but she perked up when Francine phoned just before lunchtime.

'There's someone down in reception to see you. Gavin Richmond?'

Ally's drooping eyes popped open. Gavin was here? To see her? 'I'll be down in five minutes.' Hanging up the phone with a clatter, Ally raced across the office to Kelly's desk. 'You know that make-up you mentioned earlier? Can I borrow it? It's an emergency.'

'Be my guest.' Kelly reached into her handbag and pulled out a make-up bag. 'I can't bear to look at you like that any more.'

'Thanks. I owe you.' Ally was already halfway over the threshold as she called over her shoulder. She legged it into the ladies, where she applied a quick coat of foundation, lined her eyes with mocha eyeliner and applied a couple of coats of mascara. Kelly's fuchsia lipstick was a bit garish, but it would have to do.

'Better?' she asked as she skidded to a halt in

front of Kelly's desk and handed over the cosmetic bag.

'Hey, you look almost human again.'

That was good enough for Ally. She took a deep breath before taking off again, flinging herself down the stairs as fast as her feet would allow.

Gavin rose from the seating area and strode towards Ally as she emerged from the staircase. 'You left your cardi behind at my house the other night.' He held out a clump of cream wool. 'Martine reminded me where you worked.'

'That's very kind of you. Thank you.' Ally reached for the cardigan and her fingers brushed against Gavin's, sending a jolt throughout her whole body. Gavin *had* to have felt that too, but he gave no indication that he had.

'It's no problem, really. It's given me an excuse to come and see you actually. I thought maybe I could take you out to lunch. To say thank you for helping Helena when she tripped.'

Ally knew she should decline, that spending time with Gavin was only going to hurt her more in the long run. Gavin was her past and all that. Unfortunately, her mouth had other ideas. 'That would be lovely.'

'Great.' Gavin's face lit up as he smiled down at Ally and she knew that whatever pain lay ahead, it would be worth it.

They ended up in their old haunt, Diner 360, which was strange because it hadn't even been Ally's choice. Did Gavin somehow know that this was the café they often met at for lunch due to its convenient location between Westerly's and the garage? Or was it simply yet another infuriating coincidence?

'It's not very glamorous, is it? Sorry.' Gavin gave a sheepish grin as he shrugged off his jacket and hung it over the back of his chair.

It was perfect as far as Ally was concerned, but she gave an offhand shrug. 'It's not so bad.'

'No, I suppose it isn't.' Gavin observed the blackboard behind Ally, the menu scrawled almost illegibly upon it. 'What are we having then?'

'Spam on toast with brown sauce?'

Gavin's face lit up and Ally tried not to feel too guilty that she was cheating by choosing Gavin's favourite. 'Sounds good to me. Coffee?'

Ally nodded as she gave a happy little sigh. It felt so good – so *natural* – to be sitting here with Gavin in this slightly shabby café on the main road. This is where she should be, but she knew it wouldn't last forever, so she had to savour every single second of it.

The spam on toast with brown sauce turned into double chocolate muffins and a second cup of coffee as the two caught up, retelling their lives since they'd left Westbridge High School. Gavin had gone off to college to sit his A Levels, which he struggled through for two and a half terms before he quit and accepted a job at The Housing Warehouse, starting at the very bottom and slowly working his way up.

'It must have been fate because it's where I met Helena. She was looking for a wedding gift for her best friend. A year later, we were married ourselves.' Ally tried not to grimace. How nauseatingly romantic. 'What about you? What happened after Westbridge?'

Ally paused, taking a large gulp of her tepid coffee as she combed her brain for information. What *had* she done after Westbridge in this life? Had she gone to university? College? Had she taken on an admin role and worked her way up?

'It's all a bit of a blur, if I'm honest. I sort of went off the rails for a bit. Well, until recently, actually. I'm only just getting myself sorted.'

Gavin didn't look the least bit surprised by the revelation. 'You always were a bit wild.'

'Well, not any more. I'm boring old Ally now.'

'You'll never be boring.'

Ally felt her insides warm as Gavin caught her eye. Was he flirting with her? The thought was thrilling, yet Ally knew she must put a stop to it. 'But I *am* old? Is that what you're saying?' The mood was lightened as they both started to laugh.

'Hardly. If you're old, that means I'm old too and I'm still in my prime.' Gavin picked up his cup and drained the last of his coffee. 'We should be getting back to work. I'll walk you back.'

Ally wished they could stay in the café forever, nestled in a bubble where wishes and new wives didn't exist, but Gavin was right and so she gathered her things and fell into step with Gavin out on the street.

'It's been great catching up, Alana. You're not at all like you used to be when we were at school.'

'You mean I'm no longer a bitch?' Ally laughed as Gavin's cheeks started to turn pink. 'It's okay. I know exactly what I was like in the past and I'm disgusted with myself. But I can assure you, I'll never be like that again.'

'I believe you.'

'Glad to hear it.'

Ally's fingers itched to entwine with Gavin's as they wandered along the path towards Westerly's. It was such an alien concept not to be touching him, and she had to remind herself to keep her distance. She couldn't loop her arm through Gavin's and rest her head on his shoulder. She couldn't reach up on her tiptoes to kiss his cheek. And it made her ache.

'Thanks for lunch.' They'd reached Westerly's far too quickly and it was time to say goodbye. Ally clamped her arms by her side so that she wouldn't be tempted to throw them around Gavin and refuse to release him. Which was a high possibility.

'It was great catching up. I hope we can do it again.' Gavin stooped towards Ally, his lips brushing her cheek. Ally closed her eyes, savouring the warmth of flesh meeting flesh, but it was over all too soon. The peck on her cheek was regrettably brief and appropriate.

'Goodbye, Gavin.'

They wouldn't be meeting for lunch again, Ally knew that. Seeing Gavin and repeatedly hearing about his wonderful life with the delightful Helena and their offspring would be too much to bear.

'Who was that?' Francine asked when Ally pushed her way through the glass doors and into reception.

Ally took a moment to compose herself before she faced Francine. 'An old friend. We went to school together.'

'He's cute.'

Ally laughed and as she did so, she felt her heavy chest loosen a little. 'Hey, hands off. He's happily married. As are you.'

Francine gave a wave of her hand. 'Pesky details.'

Ally laughed again, knowing for a fact that Francine would never even consider cheating on Mike. 'I'd better get back upstairs. I'll see you later.'

'See you later, chick.'

Ally's breath caught in her throat but she somehow managed not to gasp out loud. *Chick*. It had been such a long time since Francine had used that term of endearment on her and it gave Ally fresh hope that they could regain the former glory of their friendship one day.

THIRTY-SIX

Keith Barry was wearing a tacky, metallic indigo suit over a black mesh shirt, which was straining over his gut while tufts of gingerish hair protruded through the netting. A chunky gold chain around his neck and a pair of purple shades completed the look.

'Nobody told me we were celebrating Halloween early,' Francine muttered as she and Ally carried their drinks to a table as far away from Keith as possible.

'I'll text Kelly and tell her to hurry up. She's missing a treat.' Having secured the table, Ally took out her phone and hurried Kelly along. Keith would be turning on the karaoke machine – and the 'charm' – any minute now.

'She is coming, isn't she?' Francine asked.

'She said she was when we left work earlier.' Ally dropped her phone back into her handbag and took a sip of her drink. 'Oh God, no.' She cringed as Keith fought with his jacket, squirming and attempting to pull his arms out, but the cheap material was clinging to his sweaty arms. Finally free of the garment, he tossed it to the floor and grabbed the mic, breathless from the effort.

'Hey, ladies. It's getting hot in here. So take off all your clothes.'

'Please, no.' Francine covered her eyes as Keith reached for the chunky gold buckle of his belt.

'Only kidding, ladies.' Keith gave a cheesy grin. His audience gave a collective sigh of relief. 'But maybe later.'

'If he takes off one more item, even if it's his sunglasses, I'm out of here.' Francine took a huge gulp of her drink to steady her shattered nerves.

'You'll have to fight your way to the door. There'll be a mass exodus.' Ally peeked into her handbag but Kelly hadn't replied yet. 'I think we're going to need a lot of alcohol tonight.'

'Right then, ladies. Who wants to have some fun with Keith tonight? And then do a bit of singing, if you get what I mean.' Keith guffawed into his mic while Francine gave her glass of wine a baleful look. Somehow it didn't seem enough.

'We should have bought a bottle.'

The karaoke night began – with Keith thankfully keeping his clothes on – but by their third glass of wine, Kelly had yet to show up or reply to any of Ally's messages.

'Perhaps she got a better offer,' Francine

suggested as a pretty blonde gave a tortured rendition of Katy Perry's 'Firework', with Keith acting as a strange sort of backing dancer. Or sex pest.

'Better than this?' Ally waved a hand towards the thrusting Keith. 'Surely not.' She caught Francine's eye and they both cracked up. 'We clearly need another drink.'

'Get a bottle this time.'

Every sound was like a sledgehammer to Ally's temple as she made her way to work. The bus was full to capacity and seemed to have picked up only inconsiderate pricks en route. Mobile phones blared crappy music, a couple were having a blazing row over the washing up (or lack of) and two babies and a toddler were wailing out of synch. Okay, so perhaps the babies and the toddler weren't inconsiderate pricks, but Ally's hangover was in no mood for making concessions.

It had been a fantastic night though, and Kelly would be gutted she'd missed it. Ally couldn't wait to tell her about the blonde stunner Keith Barry had tried it on with after packing up his equipment. The blonde had been leaning against the bar in a pair of skinny jeans and a leather jacket, her golden hair flowing almost to her pert bottom. Keith couldn't resist giving the pert bottom a squeeze, but he soon regretted it when the blonde turned around, revealing a goatee beard and a very manly fist. Ally winced as she recalled the crunch of fist meeting nose. She hoped that whatever had caused Kelly to miss their karaoke night, it was worth missing *that* for.

But Ally wasn't to find out what had kept Kelly away as she didn't turn up for work that day. When she'd failed to phone in by lunchtime, Ally gave her a ring, but neither her mobile nor the landline were answered. Ally began to worry when she still hadn't heard from Kelly by Wednesday. Kelly wasn't always the most reliable employee, but she should have let them know she wasn't coming into work by now at the very least.

'You know what she's like,' Francine said when Ally voiced her concern over a sneaky coffee down in reception that afternoon.

'I know, but this doesn't feel right. I'm going to try ringing her again and if she doesn't answer, I'm going over to her house tonight.'

This time Kelly's landline was answered, but the voice at the other end was male, angry and, judging by the incoherent words slung at Ally, extremely drunk. She didn't manage to gather any useful information before the phone was slammed down, but she did make the decision to investigate further.

Ally's grip tightened on her handbag as she navigated the warren of streets towards Kelly's house later that evening. She didn't even realise she was holding on so tight until the strap began to dig into her flesh, but she'd felt an immediate unease as she'd stepped onto the estate and was met by the sneers of a group of teenagers and their ferocious-looking dog that snarled at her as it strained against its lead. She supposed she should have been grateful when its owner tugged the dog back and gave it a swift boot to the gut, but, funnily enough, it didn't put her at ease in the slightest.

The last time she'd ventured to Kelly's house she'd been driving the flashy car – which she was now gobsmacked had made it off the estate in one piece – and she'd had the luxury of sat nav. Now she was relying on the dubious directions she'd downloaded from the internet that afternoon. The houses around her all looked the same, with no defining features popping out to jog her memory.

A loud rattling sound behind Ally made her jump, and she whipped around expecting to see the group of youths and the feral dog ambling after her. But it was just a little girl zipping by on a scooter. At the exact moment Ally sighed with relief, the little girl jabbed her middle finger in the air, her grubby face contorted menacingly.

Ally consulted her directions. She wanted to find Kelly and assure herself that she was well before getting the hell out of there and to the sanctuary of her flat. According to the directions, Kelly's house should be around the next corner. Ally quickened her step and was somewhat relieved to spot the familiar junkyard that was her colleague's garden. Dodging the empty cans and dog shit littering the path, she made her way to the front door and rapped on the rotting wood. When there was no answer, she tried again.

'Alright, alright. Give me a bastard chance.' Ally stepped back as the sound of footsteps thundered towards her on the other side of the door. It swung open and she was faced with the same woman she'd encountered the last time. Her unwashed hair was pulled into a lopsided ponytail and she wore a stained nightdress that was far too short to be decent.

'If you're after money, we haven't got any.'

'Who is it? Is it Five-Finger Shane? Gobshite owes me a fiver.' The new voice emerged and elbowed its way to the front. Ally took another step back. The man was tall and skeletal with long, dirty brown hair, bloodshot eyes and only half of his teeth present.

'It's one of them charity do-gooders.' The woman turned to Ally and jabbed a grubby finger at her. 'We keep telling you. We haven't got any bloody money. I can't even buy myself a pack of ciggies, so do us all a favour and bog off.'

The door loomed in front of Ally but, for some inexplicable reason, she leapt forward and stopped it from slamming shut. 'I'm not asking for money. I'm looking for Kelly Fox.'

The door was wrenched open, slamming painfully against the interior wall. 'What has our Kelly got to do with you?' It was the man who thrust himself towards Ally, bringing with him the stench of stale alcohol and cigarettes. 'Whatever it is she's supposed have done, she hasn't. Got it?'

'I work with Kelly. She hasn't turned up for a couple of days and I'm worried about her.'

'Are you her boss or something?' the woman asked.

'No. We work in the same department and —'

'Then what's it got to do with you whether she goes to work or not, you nosy bitch? Piss off and leave us alone.' The woman grabbed what Ally assumed was her husband by the collar and dragged him back inside before slamming the door shut. Ally remained standing in front of the house, staring at the closed door while she attempted to gather her thoughts.

What now?

As she turned to leave, she spotted the house next door and remembered the kind woman who'd spoken to her last time. Perhaps she'd seen Kelly over the past few days. Scurrying away from Kelly's house – and hoping she never had to return – Ally made her way to the neighbour's house and was glad when a friendly, clean face answered.

'Are you here to see Kelly?' she asked, recognising Ally from her previous visits.

'Yes. Is she here?' Ally was relieved when the woman nodded and invited her into the house. But her relief vanished when she spotted Kelly.

'Martine!' Kelly leapt up from the sofa, glaring at her neighbour. 'What have you let *her* in for?'

This was Martine? Kelly's best friend and fellow party girl? Ally had never seen a more unlikely pairing, but she couldn't dwell on that now.

'What happened to you?' She inched towards Kelly, wincing at the state of her face. Her lip had been cut, the wound now crusty and sore, and her left cheek was flushed, with a bluish hue seeping up towards her swollen eye.

'Just the usual.' The woman – *Martine* – nodded her head towards the kitchen. 'Can I get you a cup of tea, lovey?'

Kelly wrapped her arms across her chest and jutted out her chin, which Ally now noticed was bruised too. 'She's not staying.'

'Come on, Kelly. She's come all this way to see you.'

'I don't know why.' Kelly turned away to glare out of the net-curtained window.

'Because I was worried about you. You haven't been to work for the past two days and you never phoned in or anything.'

'So you've come to have a go?'

'No. Not at all. Like I said, I was worried about you.' And Ally was even more worried now. Her parents had done this to her, and they did so on a regular basis by the sounds of it. Ally recalled the bruises Kelly had attempted to cover with make-up and felt her stomach tighten with guilt. *She'd* put Kelly in this position. She'd taken over Kelly's life and left her like this.

'Well, there's no need to be. I'm fine.' Kelly threw herself back down on the sofa and picked up the remote, aiming it at the television as she flicked through the channels. 'You can go now and tell everybody about my freak show life.'

'I won't tell anybody.' Ally propped herself on the edge of the sofa but Kelly simply shuffled further away. 'But I will help you in any way I can.'

Kelly barked out a laugh. 'And why would you do that? It's not like we're *friends* or anything.' She looked up at Martine, who was still standing in the doorway. 'You can get rid of her now.'

'Kelly.' Martine sighed and moved towards the sofa. 'Don't push her away. You can't keep doing this. She wants to help you.'

'I don't want help. *I want her to go.*'

Martine shrugged her shoulders, all hope removed from her face. Ally turned to Kelly but her eyes were firmly on the television, refusing to engage further.

'I do want to help. You know where I am if you want me.' Ally rose to her feet and followed Martine out into the small hallway.

'Try not to take offence. She pushes everyone away,' Martine told her in a hushed voice. 'It's her way of protecting herself, you see.'

'Can I leave my phone number with you, just in case?'

'Of course, lovey.' Martine and Ally exchanged phone numbers before Ally braved the estate once more.

THIRTY-SEVEN

Just when Ally thought she was getting a grip on her new life, something would throw a spanner in the works, whether it was the appearance of Gavin's wife and child, or the arrival of another Martine. The new Martine didn't make sense at all to Ally, but in the end she put it to the back of her mind as it made her head hurt just thinking about it.

This time, Ally wasn't surprised when Kelly failed to show up at work the following morning. She wasn't sure what to say when Jason mentioned her extended absence, but she knew she couldn't tell him the truth. Having spent time getting to know Jason, she trusted him completely, but she'd told Kelly she would keep the information to herself and she would honour that. It was the least she could do under the circumstances.

'Are you okay?' Jason, having observed Ally

staring at the report on her screen for a full five minutes, perched on the edge of her desk and reached out to stroke her hair.

'I've just got a lot on my mind.' Ally managed a tight smile in Jason's general direction before she resumed her screen-staring.

'Like what?'

Like what? Where did she begin? Her wayward sister who was going off the rails due to her influence? Her husband shacked up with another woman? Or how about Kelly trapped in a crappy life because of her?

'I don't really want to talk about it. Sorry.' And Ally was sorry. She wanted to confide in Jason, but how could she? He'd think she was insane if she so much as hinted at alternate lives and magical angel-type things.

'How about I take your mind off it instead?'

Ally held back a sigh. 'You know I'm not ready for that.'

'I didn't mean sex, you dirty mare.' Jason gave Ally a playful nudge. 'I meant we should do something this weekend. My sister's having a barbecue.'

'I don't know, Jason. I'm not sure I'm ready to meet your family. It's a bit soon.'

'Will you relax? It's a barbecue. We'll drink, sit in the sun and eat semi-cooked food.' Ally managed a small smile. Jason kissed the top of her head before hopping off the desk. 'And my parents won't even be there. It'll be fun, I promise.'

For once, summer was being kind and the sun was emitting glorious rays, barely obstructed by the wispy clouds above. Ally dressed casually for the barbecue in a pair of pale pink denim shorts, a white vest top and strappy sandals. She'd agonised over her outfit the previous evening – Were shorts glam enough? Should she opt for a strappy, floaty dress? – until Jason told her to get a grip. It was a barbecue in his sister's tiny back yard, not a garden party at Buckingham Palace.

'Do you think this is enough?' Ally held up the two bottles of wine. 'Do you think I should have made a potato salad or something?'

'Do you even know how to make potato salad?' Jason asked and Ally shook her head. 'Stop worrying. The wine is more than enough, seriously. Shall we get going before you start attempting to knock up some sort of marinade?'

Ally bit her lip. 'Do you think I should?'

Jason laughed as he grabbed Ally's hand and pulled her towards the door. 'No. Definitely not. I hope you're not expecting too much from this barbecue. It won't be fine dining. There'll be burgers and sausages and, if we're really lucky, a bag of mixed salad from the supermarket.'

'So she's not posh then?'

Jason laughed again. They'd reached the bottom of the stairs from Ally's flat and were heading towards his car. 'God, no. Nobody in my family is posh, so will you stop worrying?'

'I suppose so.' Ally climbed into the car, resting the bottles of wine on her lap. She hadn't met a boyfriend's family in years – and then she'd already known Carolyn and Doug before she got together with Gavin. It was a strange, unsettling feeling and Ally was suddenly aware of all her shortcomings, both real and fabricated for the occasion.

Jason's sister lived in a semi-detached house on a tree-lined street, pink blossom fluttering to the pavement like confetti. Not posh, my arse, Ally thought as she climbed out of the car onto jellied legs. But Ally shouldn't have worried at all.

'You must be Alana. I'm Maddie.' Jason's sister, clad in a pair of jogging bottoms that had seen better days and a baggy T-shirt, enveloped Ally in a tight hug. She smelled of citrusy shampoo with underlying onions.

'It's Ally.' When would she ever rid herself of the name that brought with it nothing but disgrace? 'Thank you for inviting me.' She held out the bottles of wine, which were instantly pounced on.

'She's brought booze.' Maddie turned towards her brother with a nod of approval. 'This one's a keeper.' She looked down at herself and grimaced. 'Look at the state of me. I am going to get changed eventually, I promise. It's been one of those days. Kimmie!' Maddie suddenly whipped around as the sound of a disgruntled cat pierced the air. 'Put Oz down. He'll scratch you again if you're not careful.' She shot Ally an apologetic look. 'Would you like to go through to the garden? Ellie's already out there.

I'm going to nip upstairs to get changed.'

Ally and Jason headed through the kitchen to the back garden, picking up a pig-tailed toddler en route, and Ally was sure Oz the cat gave them a toothy smile of gratitude.

Jason hitched the toddler onto her hip and flicked one of her pigtails. 'This little horror here is my niece, Kimmie. And that horror over there is my baby sister, Ellie.'

'Very funny.' The 'baby' sister, who was in her mid-twenties, stuck her hand out towards Ally. 'It's nice to finally meet you. I thought somebody had to be completely cuckoo to go out with my brother, but you look pretty sane to me.'

Ally shook Ellie's hand. 'Believe me, I don't always feel sane.'

'You'll fit in with our Ellie then.' Jason laughed when Ellie stuck her tongue out. 'And Kimmie here is completely crackers.' The toddler squealed with delight, squirming down from Jason's hip as he tickled her until she reached the ground. 'Hey you, leave poor Oz alone.' Kimmie, who had one chubby foot up on the doorstep, turned to grin mischievously at her uncle before she shot into the kitchen.

Maddie joined them in the garden as a few more guests arrived, filling up the tiny garden. Jason took over the barbecue duties, sporting Maddie's floral apron, and split his time between burning meat, teasing Kimmie and checking on Ally. The barbecue was a relaxed affair and Ally found herself enjoying the afternoon, chatting with Ellie, Maddie and her friends. It was the kind of barbecue she would have enjoyed with Gavin and their friends, which made her feel a little homesick. It was late by the time everyone started to filter home, but Ally and Jason stayed behind a little longer as Jason had volunteered for bedtime duties. Ally chatted with Maddie and Ellie in the kitchen, polishing off a bottle of wine while Jason read Kimmie a story and tucked her into bed.

'See, that wasn't so bad, was it?' he asked as they climbed into the car.

'No. It was fun.' Ally dragged the seatbelt across her chest and clicked it into place. 'You're really good with Kimmie. It's sweet.'

Jason gave a shrug of his shoulders. 'She's a good kid. Maddie hasn't had it easy. Kimmie's dad walked away when Maddie was six months pregnant so I've tried to help out as much as possible.'

'You really are a big softie on the sly, aren't you?' Ally had seen the way Jason had seemed to melt around Kimmie, and they clearly adored one another. Seeing them together, tumbling around on the tiny patch of grass or brushing the mass of knots that was Kimmie's doll's hair, almost made Ally see what the fuss about children was all about. But mucking about with your niece for an afternoon was different to having a child of your own. You could hand a niece back when you were bored, and walk away from tantrums. Plus, you never had to deal with dirty nappies and snotty noses.

'Uh-oh, my secret's out.'

'Seriously, you're a natural.' Ally wasn't sure whether this fact should concern her or not. Gavin wanting children had landed her in this mess – who knows where she'd end up next time.

'It's easy when the kid isn't yours though,' Jason said. 'When you get to give them back at the end of the day. When you're not knackered from years of broken sleep and sick of reading the same book night after night.'

'So you don't want kids of your own then?'

'I do one day. But not just yet.'

And that was good enough for Ally. Perhaps it would have been good enough for Gavin too.

THIRTY-EIGHT

It was Monday before Kelly returned to work, waltzing into the HR office as though she hadn't been absent the previous week without any official notification. Her face was caked in make-up to mask the bruises, and if you didn't know about them, you wouldn't spot them.

But Ally did know about them.

'How are you feeling?' Ally approached Kelly's desk with care, as though Kelly could explode at any moment. Which she probably could.

'Fine. Why wouldn't I be?' Kelly's eyes darted towards Jason's office, where she was relieved to see he was engrossed in whatever was on his computer screen and not paying any attention to this conversation.

'You know...' Ally wasn't sure what to say. You know, your parents are foul, aggressive drunks? Perhaps not a chat to have in the office.

'No. I don't know. Now, if you don't mind, I'm incredibly busy.' Kelly began tapping ferociously at her keyboard and Ally decided against pointing out the fact that Kelly's computer had yet to be switched on.

'You know where I am if you need to talk. About anything.' Kelly ignored Ally's words, still tapping away at the dormant keyboard. Ally slipped away to her own desk but she couldn't concentrate. By lunchtime she'd made the decision to go against Kelly's wishes and stick her beak in further. She couldn't sit back and do nothing. It wasn't right, especially as it was all Ally's fault.

'Can you deal with this immediately, please?' Jason swept past Ally's desk, dropping a sheet of paper into her inbox. Ally glanced at the clock. Couldn't it wait until after lunch?

'It's urgent, Ally,' Jason called over his shoulder as he left the office. With a groan, Ally picked up the piece of paper. It was blank, apart from a lime green post-it stuck to the front.

Meet me in the basement, ASAP X

Ally groaned again. She knew exactly what occurred in the basement, and it wasn't something she was willing to participate in. Quickies against the personal files may have been acceptable to Kelly and Alana, but Ally had a little more class than that. She thought she'd made that quite clear to Jason, but obviously not.

Smoothing down her trousers and squaring her shoulders, Ally marched down to the basement, preparing to tell Jason exactly what she thought of his seedy lunchtime plans. She had a whole speech planned by the time she shoved open the basement door, but her words faded into the air as she stepped inside.

'What's this?'

Jason had laid a blanket down on the cold, stone floor, filling it with picnic goodies and a bottle of flavoured sparkling water, which had already been poured into two plastic cups pilfered from the vending machine.

'This is a secret date.' Jason patted the space next to him on the blanket. 'I even have romantic music.' He produced an iPod and, like a couple of teenagers, they shared the set of earphones. Take That's 'A Million Love Songs' started to play.

Surely this wasn't what went on down here all those times with Kelly. While Ally had assumed the worst, they were actually conducting secret mini-dates? The revelation was equally shocking and sweet, which made Ally feel even worse. Jason could have been the only shining light in Kelly's life – and Ally had taken that from her too.

'So, you're worried about our Kelly.' Ally had contacted the new Martine, arranging to meet her in a pub that evening. Martine gave a sigh. 'Me too, to tell you the truth. I hate seeing what those two do to her. I've offered her the spare room at my place, but she refuses. She comes to stay when they get too much, but I'd rather she was out of there altogether.'

'How long has this been going on for?'

Martine's shoulders rose and fell miserably. 'Who knows? For as long as I've known them. I wasn't aware of any violence when I moved in, but they certainly neglected the poor girl. She was so skinny and dirty, and the poor mite was constantly riddled with nits. I didn't want to interfere. I'd only just moved onto the estate and didn't know them, but I couldn't leave her like that. I started giving her something to eat after school, and I'd put her in the bath and wash and dry her uniform. But it was too late by then. She'd always be known as the smelly kid at school.' Martine took a sip of her drink. 'It's why she's the way she is. She's never had any friends, you see, so she keeps people at bay and pretends she doesn't care about people and friendship. It's to protect herself, really.'

'Wasn't there anybody who could have stepped in? Any family?'

'I think there was a grandmother at some point, but she'd already passed away by the time I moved in. I don't think there was anybody else. Not anybody who cared, anyway.'

'But she's an adult now. Why doesn't she move out?' Ally couldn't understand why anybody would put up with such treatment when they had the option to escape.

'I don't know, lovey. I really don't. But thank you for caring. It's good to know there's someone else looking out for Kelly.'

'I just wish there was more I could do.'

'Me too. It scares me to death whenever they start yelling.' Martine plucked a tissue from her pocket and dabbed at her eyes. 'It's always worse when they've been on a bender.'

'Can't they get help?'

Martine scrunched up the tissue and let it fall onto the table. 'Kelly's tried getting them help, but they're too selfish to change.' Martine gave a sad shake of her head. 'No, it's up to Kelly to get out of there, but she's too stubborn for her own good.'

Ally's phone started to ring from within her handbag. It was the other Martine, so she pushed the cancel button and dropped the phone back into her bag, planning to call her back later.

'Kelly came back into work this morning.' Ally zipped up the bag and nudged it under the table with her foot. 'I tried talking to her, but she pretended nothing had happened.'

The corners of Martine's lips twitched into an almost smile. 'That's our Kelly for you. She won't talk about it, not even with me, really.'

'Couldn't we go to the police or something?' Ally had to do something. She was responsible for this mess and couldn't allow Kelly to live in constant danger.

'I've tried that, lovey.' Martine closed her eyes, remembering an incident a couple of years earlier. 'I was always threatening to do it, but Kelly would beg me not to. But this one particular time, I didn't feel like I had a choice.' Martine picked up her drink and drained the glass. 'But it was no use. Kelly denied they'd ever laid a finger on her.'

'Why would she do that?'

'They're her mum and dad. She was protecting them. Despite everything, she loves them, whether they deserve it or not.' Martine slipped on her coat and hooked her handbag over her shoulder. 'I'm sorry, but I'd better get going. But keep in touch, yeah?'

'I will.' Ally watched as Martine weaved her way out of the pub. She'd never felt so powerless in her life.

'Why do I even bother phoning you when I'm the last thing on your list of priorities?' The younger Martine was not impressed in the slightest when Ally left it until the following afternoon to ring her back.

'I'm sorry. I have a lot going on at the moment.'

'Me too, actually. Callum has tickets for this awesome new club. There are going to be footballers there and everything. Just think, I could be a WAG! What should I call my perfume? Should I have just my name or something sizzling like "Erogenous"? No, "Sensual Kiss by Martine". What do you think? Are you even listening to me, babe?'

'Of course I am.' Ally wouldn't dream of missing such a scintillating conversation.

'So, will you come?'

'To what?'

Martine heaved an enormous sigh. 'To the club

opening. It's tonight. *Everyone* is going to be there.'

Ally prepared herself for an onslaught. 'I can't. It's karaoke night.' Ally was especially excited as Freya and Dee would be there. She'd been shocked when Freya suggested they all meet up when Ally had mentioned the karaoke evenings during Sunday lunch, but she'd hidden it as best as she could and passed on the details. 'Why don't you come?'

'I don't think so, babe. Like I'm going to swerve meeting celebs to hang out with you and your *new friends*.'

Ally held back a sigh. She could imagine Martine stamping her foot on the other end of the line. 'We'll do something at the weekend then. Just you and me.'

'Really?' Martine seemed brighter now, which was a relief. Ally had suspected a full-on tantrum was on the cards. 'Let's go to Sparkle. We haven't done that for *ages*. I bet you're so in need of a mani-pedi.'

Ally lifted her hand. Her nails didn't look too bad. They were a bit gnawed, but then she'd had a lot to worry about lately. 'Fine. Sparkle it is.'

'And shopping. You have to help me find a new outfit. Callum's taking me out on Saturday night. On a proper date. We're not just going back to his place to—'

'Yes, fine. Sparkle and shopping.'

'Brill. I'll book us in. Mwah, babe.'

Ally couldn't wait.

Francine was already at the pub when Ally arrived, with Freya and Dee not far behind. Ally made the introductions and felt a calming feeling of content waft over her. She would have given anything to have her old life back, but her new one was shaping out to be a close second.

'So what are we singing then?' The karaoke night was in full swing, with Freya and Dee's faces both suitably aghast at Keith Barry's antics.

'I think I'm going to go for "Mustang Sally".'

Ally smiled to herself. As if Francine would choose anything else.

'I'm going to sing the shit out of "Whole Again",' Freya said. She raised her glass and Ally, Dee and Francine clinked theirs against it.

'I can't decide between "Rolling In The Deep" and "Eternal Flame".' Dee's eyebrows knitted together over the decision. 'What do you think?'

'I think we need another drink.' Ally stood up but Freya held out a hand and rose out of her own seat.

'Let me.'

Francine leant towards Ally to stage whisper. 'She wants to go and flirt with the baby barman.'

'Hey!' Freya planted her hands on her hips but she was grinning. 'He is not a baby. He is very, *very* cute though.'

Ally scrutinised the songbook while her sister practically ran to the bar. 'I think I'll sing "Thorn In My Side".' She mused the idea before gasping. 'No, we should all sing together. What do you think?'

'I'm up for that.' Dee snatched the book. 'What shall we sing?'

'It has to be Madonna,' Ally said. '"Like a Virgin"?'

'Who's a virgin?' Freya returned to the table with Ally's drink and the barman's number.

'The barman, by the looks of it,' Francine said. 'He can't be more than twelve.'

'He's twenty-one, actually.' Freya turned to blow the barman a kiss before she settled herself down at the table. 'But seriously, what's all this virgin stuff?'

'"Like A Virgin". It's what we're all going to sing together.' Dee closed the book, decision made.

'Okay, but if that creep touches me.' She jabbed a finger at Keith Barry, who had just buried his nose in an alarmed blonde's hair, taking a deep, elaborate sniff. 'I'll chop his balls off.'

Everyone at the table agreed this was fair enough. Ally took a sip of her drink while observing her little gang. The night was perfect. They got up and sang their song and, after a warning growl from Freya, Keith Barry kept his distance.

'That was amazing.' Freya was out of breath when they returned to their seats. 'We should do this every week.'

'Deal.' Ally couldn't keep the grin off her face. The night couldn't be more perfect.

'It doesn't look like Kelly's coming again,' Francine said. Ally looked around the table at her old gang. It was how it should be, how it had always been.

But Kelly had become part of her new gang and it didn't feel right without her there.

THIRTY-NINE

'What do you want?' Kelly folded her arms across her chest and glared at Ally from the doorway. She'd left the others behind at The Farthing, promising to be back as quickly as possible.

'It's karaoke night.' Ally attempted to subtly peer around Kelly. She hoped her parents weren't around. 'We were wondering where you were. It isn't the same without you.'

Kelly rolled her eyes. 'I find that hard to believe.'

'Come on, Kelly. We're your friends.'

Kelly rolled her eyes again but her posture softened. 'Do you want to come in?' She saw the look of alarm pass across Ally's face. 'Don't worry. Mum and Dad got their benefits money today. They probably won't be back until tomorrow.'

Ally dreaded to think about the condition they'd be in when they returned. She followed Kelly inside the house, which was in as much of a state of disrepair as the garden, with torn wallpaper, grubby furniture and an odd odour about the place.

'Can I get you a cup of tea?'

'Yes please.' Ally sat down on the old, misshapen sofa while Kelly headed into the kitchen. She returned with a couple of chipped cups.

'So this is my home.' Kelly indicated the room with a grimace. 'It's a bit of a shit hole, but what can you do? Every time I clean it up, they destroy it again. I gave up ages ago.' Kelly slumped onto the sofa. 'It's a good job I don't have any friends, really. Wouldn't want them seeing this.'

'You do have friends.'

Kelly rolled her eyes. They'd roll right out of their sockets if she carried on. 'What, Martine? She's just a neighbour who feels sorry for me. I don't have any real friends.' She laughed and shook her head. 'How sad am I? I make up a social life, pretending I lead this exciting life when really I'm usually sat in front of the telly with my middle-aged neighbour. It's pathetic.'

'Francine and I are your friends. If you'll let us be.'

'I don't need your pity.'

'Good, because that's not why I'm here. Although we will help you to get out of this place. You can come and stay with me if you want. You'd have to sleep on the sofa, but it'd only be until you sorted yourself out. You can do what I did and sell your car and rent somewhere cheap.'

'I don't need to sell my car or rent anywhere cheap. I have my own house.' Ally raised her eyebrows. Kelly really wanted to stay *here*? 'No, not this crap hole. My gran left me a lovely three-bed semi. I spent most of my time there before she died. She actually gave a toss about me.' Kelly plucked a cigarette butt from down the side of the sofa and flicked it into an overflowing ashtray on the floor. 'She left me the house and some savings. I rent it out at the moment.'

'So why stay here?' Ally couldn't understand it. Why stay somewhere filthy where she was subjected to abuse? She had the perfect escape route, yet she'd never taken it.

'I can't leave them.' It was quite simple for Kelly. 'Without me here, the bills wouldn't get paid, the house would be in an even worse state than it already is, and they wouldn't eat. Plus, they'd probably kill each other.'

Ally wanted to shake some sense into Kelly. So what? They were adults. It was about time they were left to fend for themselves. Kelly's parents hadn't shown an ounce of compassion towards her when she was filthy and hungry and being bullied due to their lack of care, so why offer her help now?

'They're still my parents, Ally, whatever happens.'

Ally couldn't pretend to understand, but she reached out and touched Kelly's arm. Surprisingly,

Kelly allowed the contact. 'Whether you go or stay, Francine and I will be there for you. Even if you try to push us away.' Ally drained her cup of tea. It scalded her tongue, but she tried not to wince. The sooner she got out of that house, the better. 'Now, are you coming to karaoke or not?'

Kelly observed Ally for a moment before giving a very slight shrug. 'Go on then. I've got nothing better to do, I suppose.'

Ally found herself in the very pink Sparkle early on Saturday morning, one hand soaking in warm water while the other was being tortured with an orange wood stick.

'What colour are you going for, babe?' From across the salon, Martine waggled the fingers of one hand at Ally. 'I'm going for Paradiso Pink. Sounds well classy, doesn't it?'

It sounded well tacky. And looked it too. 'I'm going for a French manicure.'

'Again?' Martine's mouth drooped as though Ally had announced she was forgoing nail polish and was going to dip her fingertips in doggy diarrhoea instead. 'You're so boring. No wonder that married bloke wasn't interested.'

The whole room seemed to shift, its focus now entirely on Ally's flushed face. Dena, still holding onto Ally's hand, gaped at her while the other beauty therapists swivelled in their seats to take a good look at the home wrecker. It only lasted a few seconds before normal order was resumed, but it was enough to shame Ally. Time seemed to stand still from then on, but finally her treatment was over and she could leave the salon.

'I'm so sorry, babe. I didn't think everyone would hear.' Martine reached across the table to give Ally's hand a squeeze, her million bangles jangling with the movement. 'Do you forgive me?'

They were sitting in a coffee shop, a quick pit stop before their shopping trip began. Ally would never be able to set foot in the salon again. Which wasn't a great loss now that she thought about it.

'Yes, I forgive you. But only if you buy me a raspberry and white chocolate chunk muffin.' Ally may as well earn herself some cake from Martine's guilt. 'And I didn't know Gavin was married until after, you know.'

Martine's newly plucked eyebrows almost shot off her forehead. 'Of course you didn't, babe.'

'I didn't. I wouldn't go after a married man. Not any more.'

'No, I believe you. Really.' But though she said the words, Martine couldn't meet Ally's eye. 'I'll just go and get you that muffin.'

Martine sashayed across the coffee shop, revelling in the appreciative stares as she passed a table of students. They were all pretty repulsive with their greasy skin and fuzzy attempts at facial hair, but it was an ego boost nonetheless. She bought the muffin for Ally, along with a slice of cranberry upside-down cake for herself. She'd skipped breakfast and shopping would surely burn off the extra calories. She was feeling spectacular when she returned to the table after another round of appreciative stares, until she noticed Ally had put on her jacket.

'I'm sorry. I've just had a phone call from Jason. I have to go.'

'Go?' Martine couldn't believe it. She was being ditched again? And for *Jason*? Martine could have understood if she was being passed over for a footballer or a soap star – in fact, she would have actively encouraged it – but Jason was just an HR manager for a poxy coach tour company. It was insulting!

'Jason's sister was supposed to take his niece to a fundraiser at their local school, but she's ill and asked Jason to take Kimmie instead.'

'Who the hell is Kimmie?'

'The niece.'

She was being ditched for a *child*. Could this day get any worse? 'Can't Jason take the kid on his own?' Just because his day had been ruined didn't mean he had to spread the misery. Talk about selfish. 'Why do you have to go too?'

Ally slipped her handbag onto her shoulder. 'Jason thought it would be nice if we went together.'

Nice. Yep, that just about summed Jason up. *Nice*. Yuck! 'Fine. Go. Abandon me yet again for your stupid boyfriend.'

'Don't be like this, Martine.' Ally reached out to touch her arm, but Martine snatched it away, almost tossing the muffin in the air in the process. 'Come on. We did spend all morning together.'

'Jason wasn't even supposed to be your boyfriend, remember.' Martine slammed the plates down on the table before throwing her arms across her chest. 'He was supposed to be your ticket up the career ladder and now look at you. You've gone soft. The old Alana wouldn't have let Gavin slip through her fingers just because he had a wife and kid. It would have spurred you on.'

'I haven't gone soft, Martine. I've grown up. Maybe you should too.'

FORTY

Ally hadn't been sure that spending the afternoon with a kid was any more appealing than shopping with Martine, but it turned out to be quite fun. A fair had been set up at the local school with rides, prize stalls and entertainers. They ate hotdogs smothered in ketchup, had a go on the teacups and inflatable slide, and shared a bag of candyfloss. Kimmie giggled as Ally attempted to wipe her pink, sticky face with a tissue and Ally couldn't help laughing too. Kimmie now had bits of tissue stuck to her face as well as the candyfloss.

'I think we'd better get you cleaned up properly before you have your face painted.' Ally gave up trying to pluck the tiny bits of tissue from Kimmie's face. She'd be there all day.

'Aunty Ally!' Ally had been considering licking the tissue, old-fashioned-style, when a shrill voice luckily diverted her. She turned around to see a

small body hurtling towards her, arms
outstretched.

'Maisie, stop!'

Ally made an 'oof' sound as the small body
pummelled into her own, its arms wrapping tightly
around her middle.

'Maisie, I said stop. Oh.' Francine and Ally made
eye contact, confusion displayed on both of their
faces. The last place Francine expected to see her
workmate was at a school fair, and since when did
her daughter know her? Ally's heart started to
hammer its way through her ribcage. Maisie knew
her? How? She had never met Ally in this life.

'I'm so sorry. I don't know what's got into her.
She just suddenly took off and flung herself at you.'

'It's okay.' Ally peeled Maisie's arms from
around her waist and dropped to her knees so she
was eye-level with the child. 'Do you know me?'
She spoke quietly but gasped when Maisie nodded.

'You're Aunty Ally. I haven't seen you for ages
though. Are you and Mummy not friends any
more?' Ally gaped at the child, but Maisie's
attention was snapped away. 'Who's that? Did you
have a *baby*?'

Maisie was pointing at Kimmie, whose pink-
tinged mouth puckered in annoyance. 'I'm not a
baby. Am a big girl.'

'Kimmie is Jason's niece.' Ally struggled to her
feet and slipped her hand into Jason's,
unconsciously anchoring herself to her present life.

'Why are you holding his hand? He's not your

husband.'

Francine ruffled her youngest daughter's hair. 'You can be so old-fashioned sometimes.' She laughed as she reached into her handbag and pulled out a packet of wet wipes, handing them to Ally. Ally looked at the packet in her hand, confused until Francine indicated Kimmie's sticky face.

'Come on, you said you wanted a go on the bumper cars.' After returning the wet wipes to her bag once Kimmie's face was clean, Francine guided a still confused Maisie away. Ally watched her leave, wondering what she knew. Did Maisie remember Gavin? And what did that mean?

'Right then, monster.' Jason scooped up Kimmie and dropped her onto his hip. 'Let's go and get your face painted.'

Kimmie proudly sported a butterfly on her face, its glittery wings spanning across her cheeks, for the rest of the afternoon. A yellow balloon giraffe was clutched to her chest while Jason had the honour of carrying the pink teddy bear she'd won. It began to grow dark, but Kimmie wasn't finished yet.

'How about we get some hot chocolate, have one more go on the teacups and then go home?' Ally suggested, spotting the catering van ahead. There was a bench nearby too, the sight of which made Ally's feet throb. She was exhausted.

'Yeah, yeah, yeah! Hot chocolate!' Kimmie tore off towards the van, but Jason caught her within a couple of strides and scooped her into his arms.

'Not so fast, little monster. We have to join the queue.' Hoisting Kimmie onto his shoulders, the three joined the back of the long line.

Jason was so good with Kimmie and didn't appear fazed by her boundless energy, matching her vigour throughout the afternoon. Ally would never have pictured him tolerating children before the wish, assuming he was more at home charming women in bars than running around after a toddler. It was quite sweet really and, feeling a rush of affection, Ally reached up on her tiptoes, kissing Jason on the lips.

'Eww, yuck.' Kimmie stuck her tongue out, breaking the romantic spell. But, rather than finding the interruption annoying, Ally thought it was cute and gave the child an affectionate kiss on the cheek.

Once they finally had their cups of hot chocolate, Jason set Kimmie down on the ground and they wandered back towards the bench. Kimmie took two sips of her drink before demanding a go on the teacups.

'Come on then.' Ally took hold of Kimmie's hand – it seemed so natural now – and the three wandered over to the smaller rides. Ally found another bench to store their drinks, the balloon giraffe and pink teddy bear while Jason and Kimmie climbed into a lilac teacup. Kimmie was waving madly but Ally's attention had travelled to the yellow teacup behind them. Gavin was inside, giggling with his daughter. Ally looked around the outskirts of the ride and spotted a now heavily pregnant Helena. She was thinking about ducking away – that tree over there would make a good hiding place – but Helena had spotted her.

'I didn't know you and Jason had a daughter,' she said as she sidled up beside Ally.

'We don't.' Ally made room for Helena on the bench. 'That's Jason's niece, Kimmie.'

'Ah. Exhausting, aren't they?'

'God, yes.' But Ally had to admit that they were also pretty fun and she'd felt a swell of pride when she and Jason had been mistaken as Kimmie's parents throughout the afternoon.

Helena began waving suddenly. The ride had started up and was twirling Gavin and Mia towards them. Ally caught Gavin's eye and he held it until the cup spun away. 'Mia loves it here but I think we're going to have to drag her home soon. I'm not sure how much longer my back can take this.' Helena clutched the small of her back with a groan. 'Still, it's only a few weeks until this one's due and Gavin's taking me away next week. He doesn't know that I know. It's supposed to be a surprise for our anniversary, but he left the confirmation email open on the computer.' She smiled and waved as the yellow cup whirled past again. 'He's so sweet. I *really* need a break.'

Ally winced. Helena's words pounded her already bruised heart and the sight of Gavin and Mia encased in the teacup, faces alight with joy, felt like a punch to the stomach. The pride she'd felt at being mistaken for Kimmie's mum seemed silly now. What Gavin and Helena had was real and she could have had it herself, had she not rejected the very notion without giving it more than a cursory thought.

'Mummy, look at us,' Mia yelled. Ally looked up but the smile on her face drooped when she realised it was Helena she was calling out for. Of course it was Helena.

'Excuse me.' Ally stumbled away, her eyes pooling with scalding tears. Helena had everything Ally hadn't even known she wanted and there was nothing Ally could do about it. She'd always known she'd lost Gavin, but now she realised she'd lost so much more too.

Ally made her way inside the school building, following the handwritten signs to the toilets. She splashed her face with cold water while giving herself a stern talking to.

She didn't *want* children. Not yet. She wasn't ready to give up her life.

Except maybe she was. She'd been given this opportunity to spread her wings and what had she done with it? Had she lived the life of a young, free and single woman? No. Because that wasn't her, not really. The grass wasn't greener at all. It wasn't filled with fun and laughter and freedom. It was lonely and empty. Look at Helena – did she look unhappy? Did she look like she wished she could turn back the clock before she had kids? No, she didn't. As exhausted as she appeared, she was happy with everything life had given her.

And Francine. Her social life consisted of one night out a week, but would she wish her life away? Never. She wouldn't trade her children in for anything, especially not something as trivial as a few more nights out a week. Francine loved her husband and children. She loved her life. It wasn't perfect, but she wouldn't change a thing about it.

Ally glared at her reflection. What a fool she'd been. She'd had everything and she'd traded it in on a whim. Shaking her head, she dried her hands on a paper towel before leaving her temporary sanctuary.

'There you are. Everyone's looking for you.'

Ally jumped at the sound of Gavin's voice. How long had she been absent for? It couldn't have been that long, surely.

'Helena was worried. She said you looked upset.'

How very observant, Ally thought bitterly. Did the woman have to be perfect in every way? 'I'm fine, really.'

'Are you?' Gavin peered into Ally's eyes. She'd appear perfectly together to a stranger, but Gavin felt like he knew her. *Really* knew her. There was something about Ally, something he'd been feeling since the day he'd bumped into her at work. He was drawn to Ally, as though the old crush he'd had on her during their schooldays had returned. Which was ludicrous. He was a grown man now, not a horny teenage boy. A grown man who happened to be married.

He'd tried to keep his distance, but Ally was always there, and no matter how brief he kept their conversations, the need to be close to her never abated and he couldn't seem to keep away. He always seemed to find her, as though his body was seeking her out. He'd felt it keenly when she was at his house, the feeling growing to an ache until he realised he was almost pining for Ally and it had been a relief when Helena discovered the cardigan. He could have passed it onto Martine, but he needed to see Ally, to hear her voice and laughter. He wanted to touch her, knowing that her flesh would be familiar and comforting but not knowing why.

'No, I'm not fine. Not really.' Ally broke their eye contact, her eyes dropping to the ground. Gavin barely knew the woman, but he felt connected to her and it pained him to see her so distressed, which was wrong. He should leave. He should walk back outside, to his wife and daughter.

And yet he remained.

'What is it?'

Ally shook her head. She couldn't explain it to Gavin. She couldn't explain that her heart shattered on a daily basis when she woke without him, that the thought of him loving another woman crushed her.

'It's nothing really.' Ally looked up again, though she couldn't quite meet Gavin's eye this time.

333

She'd plastered a smile on her face but even a stranger could detect its insincerity.

'Is it me?' The question was out of Gavin's mouth before he could stop it. But one look at Ally's eyes told him the answer. As ridiculous as it sounded in his own head, he knew those eyes. And he knew that Ally felt the same way as he did.

FORTY-ONE

Ally's hand trembled as she reached towards her husband. He didn't flinch as her fingers brushed against the familiar roughness of his jaw, and she closed her eyes, savouring the feel of his flesh beneath her fingertips. His familiar touch and scent brought tears to her eyes as their lips met. This was what she had been denying herself, what she had been fighting against and she knew now that it was a battle she was never destined to win. She would have always found herself here, in Gavin's arms. Because they belonged together.

'Of course it's you, Gavin.' She'd been kidding herself if she thought she could ever move on – with Jason or anybody else. Ally's heart would always belong to Gavin, no matter what obstacles were put in their way.

'I know it sounds stupid, but I feel we belong together.' Gavin rested his forehead against Ally's, closing his eyes. He shouldn't have been there, shouldn't be kissing another woman and saying these words, but it was like his mind and body were no longer under his control. Everything was so messed up.

'It doesn't sound stupid.'

'No?' Gavin knew it was wrong to feel like this, to feel the spark of hope light up his heart. He was a married man. He was a *father*.

'We *do* belong together, Gavin.'

'I've never felt anything like this before.' It had been different with Helena. He'd quickly fallen in love with her, but it had never been this intense or overpowering. 'It's pretty scary, actually.'

'I know. I'm scared too.' It was terrifying. What did they do now? People were going to get hurt, no matter what happened next.

'I loved you, you know. When we were at school. I loved you so much, but you never even noticed me.' Gavin closed his eyes, as though that would block out the pain of his delicate teenage heart. He'd penned love songs for Ally back then, songs he'd scribbled down in a notebook that he kept hidden. The notebook was long gone – which was fortunate as he was sure the lyrics would be laughable now – but the feelings, it seemed, remained.

'I noticed you. I promise, I noticed you.' Ally pulled Gavin to her and everything and everyone else were forgotten. Gavin was kissing her and her heart felt like it was going to burst, only this time it was full of love rather than heartache. She had missed Gavin so much over the past few months, but she knew everything was going to be alright now, no matter what the fallout would be. As long as she had Gavin, everything would be okay.

'Ally?'

Jason was in the building, and pretty close too. His voice echoing through the corridors was like a bucket of icy water being thrown on them. The pair leapt apart, Gavin's eyes wide with shock and fear of what they had done.

'Go,' Ally hissed, pushing Gavin away before she turned and headed in the direction of Jason's voice. She found him around the corner, perilously close to where she and Gavin had kissed.

'Where've you been?' Jason's voice was laced with relief, which made Ally's gut churn. How was she supposed to explain all of this to Jason without hurting him? 'Helena said you were upset.'

'I'm fine. I went to the loo and got a bit lost. All these corridors look the same.'

'Are you sure?' She didn't look fine to him, but he wasn't sure now was the time or place to push it. 'I've left Kimmie with Helena and Mia. They're just outside. I think we should be getting her home.'

Kimmie and Mia were playing some sort of chasing game which involved an awful lot of giggling while a weary Helena rested on a bench.

'Ah, you found her. You haven't seen Gavin, have you?' Ally couldn't meet Helena's eye as she shook her head. 'He can't be far away, I suppose. Ah, here he is now.' Helena called a reluctant Mia over and heaved herself up from the bench. 'It was lovely running into you again. We should meet up with the girls sometime. Perhaps when I'm not so cumbersome.' Helena gave her bump an affectionate rub.

Jason scooped Kimmie up and rested her on his hip. 'You'd like to play with Mia again, wouldn't you?' Kimmie nodded her head. Mia was already her BFF.

'Great.' Helena rummaged in her handbag for her phone. 'Shall we swap numbers?'

'It's okay, Gavin's already got mine.' Ally, desperate to get away from Gavin's happy little family, grabbed Jason's hand and began tugging him towards the car park. 'We'll see you again sometime.'

'Bye. See you again soon.' Helena and Mia waved their goodbyes while Ally quickened her step, shooting Gavin one last look before he disappeared from view.

Kimmie's energy levels dropped suddenly once she was strapped into her car seat, and she fell asleep during the short journey home. Jason lifted her carefully from the car, managing to carry her across to the house without Kimmie stirring, but she woke up as soon as they crossed the threshold. It was as if she had some sort of in-built sensor.

'Can Uncle Jason read me a story before he

goes?' Kimmie asked as she was transferred into her mother's arms. Maddie looked weary and not in any mood for battle, so Jason threw Ally an apologetic look before settling himself on the sofa with what looked to Ally to be the thickest children's book known to man. The wait was tortuous. What happened now? Would Gavin come to the flat or would he phone her? They had so many plans to make and though ending their current relationships wouldn't be pleasant, it had to happen sooner or later. Surely it was better to get things over and done with quickly rather than prolonging the agony.

Ally checked her phone approximately every thirty seconds as Jason read the story, but there was nothing yet. Poor Gavin. He'd have to pretend everything was normal as he returned to the marital home with his family. What was he doing now? Chatting about their fun day out while keeping his emotions pushed down until it was time? Gavin hated lying, so he must have been going mad with it all.

'One more time? Please?' The book was finally finished, but Kimmie wasn't ready to let go. Was Gavin reading to Mia now? Was he getting her ready for bed? Tucking her into bed and kissing her silky hair, whispering about sweet dreams?

Ally squeezed her eyes shut. They would work everything out. They would.

'Not a chance, missy.' Maddie pushed her greying features into a smile. 'Thanks for taking her today. I really couldn't face it.'

'It's no problem,' Jason said. 'It was fun, wasn't it?'

Ally managed to nod her head.

What was she doing? She was going to destroy a family. She would be taking Gavin away from his child, an innocent little girl who had done nothing to deserve this. Yes, they would still see each other, but it would never be the same, would it? Still, it couldn't be helped. Ally and Gavin were supposed to be together.

Ally's body was on autopilot as she said goodbye to Maddie and Kimmie before following Jason out to the car.

'Shall we go back to yours or mine?'

'Would you mind if I went back to mine on my own tonight?' Ally had an awful lot of thinking to do, and she couldn't do that while somehow keeping up the pretence that everything was normal. 'Today has really tired me out and I've got a bit of a headache.'

'I knew there was something wrong earlier. You should have said. We could have left the story.'

Jason's concern only made Ally feel worse, so it was a relief when she closed the door to the flat behind her and sank onto the sofa. She was a terrible human being. Truly awful. What should she do? Her head was telling her to run as far away from Gavin as possible before it was too late, while her heart was screaming at her to cling onto him. Being a martyr wouldn't make her happy and it wouldn't eradicate the love between her and Gavin. Surely Helena deserved the truth rather than continuing a marriage based on lies.

Ally dropped her head into her hands with a whimper. Did she listen to her head, which made a lot of sense? Or her heart, which, quite frankly, was being a bit selfish? Ally needed to talk to someone who wouldn't judge her, and there was only one person she knew with worse morals than her own. Martine arrived within half an hour, a bottle of wine tucked under her arm.

'Babe, you look like shit. What's happened?'

Ally led Martine into the sitting room, grabbing a couple of glasses before joining her on the sofa.

'You know Gavin?'

The wine bottle hovered over one of the glasses as Martine paused to look at Ally. 'As in my boss Gavin? Yes, I'm vaguely aware of the man.'

Ally wrung her hands together, not quite believing she was about to confess all. 'We kissed today.'

'Oh?' Martine dumped the bottle on the coffee table and picked up her full glass before slumping back on the sofa. 'What was it like?'

Ally couldn't help the corners of her mouth stretching into a Cheshire Cat grin. 'It was the best kiss ever. It felt like when Belle and The Beast finally kiss.' The look of repulsion on Martine's face brought Ally back to reality, the smile dropping from her face. 'But he's married. He has a daughter and another baby on the way.'

341

'So what?'

Martine had forgotten to pour Ally a glass, so she poured her own extremely large measure. 'So it's wrong. I shouldn't be going around kissing married men.' She held up a hand as Martine began to speak. 'I don't do that any more. Plus, I'm seeing Jason. He really cares about me. I can't hurt him like that.'

'Do you care about Jason?'

Ally nodded. She did care about him – he was such a great guy – but she loved Gavin.

'Then you should stay away from Gavin.'

Ally's mouth gaped open at Martine's words. She'd expected Martine to tell her to forget about right and wrong, to do what *she* wanted to do. You only live once and all that. It was the main reason she'd confided in Martine and not someone like Francine.

'Avoid him at all costs. For his kids' sake if nothing else.'

'Really?' Ally had never seen this side of Martine before and, under the circumstances, she wasn't sure if she approved. 'The thing is, I'm not sure I *can* stay away.'

FORTY-TWO

Ally kept a vigil over her phone all night, willing it to ring. Surely Gavin wanted to speak to her, to discuss their next move. Waiting around in limbo was agony. What was Gavin thinking? Did he regret the kiss? Was she even going to see him again or would he carry on with his life like nothing had happened? She was sure he would have at least called her to talk about what happened by now, but her phone remained silent. She tried to take her mind off it all, but what could distract her from the possibility of getting back together with Gavin? The television spoke to itself, her bath cooled without her ever climbing inside (what if Gavin called round and she didn't hear the buzzer?) and her food congealed on a plate, untouched and unwanted.

Throughout her deliberations that night, Ally tried to keep Helena and Mia firmly to the back of her mind. She knew what she was doing was wrong, but this was *Gavin*. *Her* Gavin and, as childish as it sounded even to her own ears, he was hers first. How could she give him up? Hadn't she suffered enough because of her stupid, ill-thought-out wish?

But how much would Mia suffer? And the new baby?

Ally pushed the pair out of her mind. She couldn't think about them. If she did, she'd wake up and realise how selfish she was being. And she was afraid she'd go ahead with her pursuit of Gavin anyway.

She called in sick on Monday morning, which wasn't any great stretch of the truth. She felt awful, completely drained after a whole weekend without sleep, and there was no way she could concentrate on her work, especially with Jason there reminding her of the carnage she was about to cause. She needed to sort things out with Gavin and work out where they went from here. She still hadn't heard from him, which was odd. Wasn't he burning to see her? To finish that kiss and see where it would lead?

'You sound terrible,' Kelly said when Ally phoned the office. 'Hangover?'

'No, it isn't a hangover.' If only it were. A hangover could be solved with paracetamol and a good old lounge around on the sofa watching *This Morning*. Affairs of the heart were a much trickier beast to conquer.

'Whatever you've got, Jason probably has it too. He hasn't turned up for work either.' Kelly paused for a moment, and when she spoke again her voice was laced with suspicion. 'Wait a minute. Is he there with you? Are you two pulling a sickie so you can stay in bed all day?'

'Jason isn't in the office? Hasn't he rung in?' Now she thought about it, Ally hadn't actually heard from Jason since he'd dropped her off after the fair. His silence hadn't concerned her until now as she'd been too wrapped up in the Gavin drama.

'So he isn't with you then?'

'No. I haven't seen or heard from him since Saturday evening.'

'He's probably got what you have but is too ill to drag himself to the phone. You know what men are like. It's always worse when they have it.'

Ally doubted Jason had what she had, unless he had a husband tucked away somewhere too.

'You're probably right.' Despite her words, Ally had begun to worry. Jason wouldn't fail to contact her – and he definitely wouldn't fail to phone in sick – unless there was a good reason to. As soon as she hung up the phone, she dialled Jason's number, but it went straight through to voicemail. She should go round to his flat to check on him. And she would, later. First, she had to find out what was going on with Gavin.

Ally had never been so nervous at the thought of speaking to her husband as she dialled his number, her fingers trembling as she jabbed at the screen of her mobile. But like Jason's phone, Gavin's went straight to voicemail too.

What was it – international turn-off-your-phone day?

She would have to go and see Gavin in person.

She dressed quickly, throwing on a pair of jeans and the first T-shirt her hands came into contact with. It had been a toss-up between speediness and looking her best, and in the end her eagerness to see Gavin won. However, time was not on her side with the bus ride seeming to take forever, but finally she leapt – literally – off the bus and found herself speed-walking along Hill Bank Lane. What number was it? Ally couldn't remember. She could barely remember which side of the street they lived on. But then there it was. The house with the rope swing dangling from the tree in the front garden.

It really was a magnificent house. Would Gavin truly give all this up for her?

Ally shook her head to remove the silly doubts as she pushed open the gate. Of course he would. Ally would give up anything to be with Gavin and she was certain he felt the same.

Ally's pace slowed as she neared the front door. What would she do if Helena answered? She wasn't sure she could face the poor woman, knowing she was about to destroy her life. Helena had done nothing wrong. She didn't deserve any of this, but it couldn't be helped. Ally and Gavin belonged together.

Ally reached out to press the doorbell before she could chicken out and scurry away. Squaring her shoulders, she readied herself for whatever lay ahead. She could do this.

Only there was no answer. She tried the doorbell again and then a third time, but she remained alone on the doorstep. It was both a relief and a disappointment as she made her way back to the gate. She hadn't relished the thought of facing Helena, but she still needed answers. Reaching out for the gate, it hit Ally where Gavin would be. Of course! How silly of her to think he would be at home on a Monday morning. Gavin would be at work. Ally would go and see him at The Housing Warehouse and, one way or another, she would get her answers.

FORTY-THREE

Ally barrelled her way into The Housing Warehouse, her eyes darting left and right as she navigated the aisles. She had no idea which department Gavin would be in, but she'd work her way across the entire store if she had to. She started in the furniture department, whizzing by beautifully upholstered sofas and stunningly laid tables. Up ahead, amongst the tableware, she saw a familiar figure pretending to be busy.

'Martine!' Ally had never been so happy to see the girl. She may know which department Gavin was in, cutting down her search considerably. Martine gave a squeak as Ally pulled her to one side, buffering themselves between shelves of teapots and dinner plates.

'I'm sorry. I can explain. I didn't mean to say anything. It just sort of slipped out.' Martine's eyes were wide as the stream of words fell out of her mouth.

'What are you talking about? What did you say? And to who?'

Martine studied Ally for a moment. She didn't know? But she looked crazed, all wide-eyed and frenzied. 'Nothing. Doesn't matter. My mistake.' She tittered as she turned to scuttle away, but Ally caught her by the arm.

'Tell me. Now.'

Martine cringed. She'd known as soon as she'd said the words that they were a mistake, but she couldn't take them back. She'd done a bad thing, but Ally would forgive her, right?

'I saw Jason.' Martine didn't mention that she'd followed Jason to his flat specifically to speak to him – Ally was going to flip out enough as it was. 'And I sort of told him about you... and Gavin.'

'You what?'

'I didn't mean to, I swear.' Martine reached out for Ally, but changed her mind and whipped her hand away again. 'I was just mega pissed off with you. I'm so sick of you ditching me for those losers you work with. That club was a big deal to me. I could have really become something, you know. But you only ever think of yourself.'

Oh God. Jason knew about her and Gavin. No wonder he hadn't contacted her and wasn't answering her calls!

'Why did you tell him?' It was such a spiteful thing to do, and Ally and Martine were supposed to be friends. Yes, she may have neglected her lately, but grassing on her was surely against some sacred girls' code or something.

'Because I saw him first!' Ally blinked against Martine's sudden outburst. 'I really liked Gavin but he'd never cheat on his wife. And then you come along and he's suddenly Mr Unfaithful.'

'You like Gavin?'

'Yes, and as I work with him, I'm entitled to first dibs.' Martine stamped her foot, rattling a nearby display of side plates. 'It's so unfair. You always get the pick of the blokes and I end up with your rejects.'

'You're unbelievable.' Ally couldn't believe this creature in front of her was an adult. She was like a child, throwing tantrums and doing whatever the hell she wanted to without pausing to think of the consequences. Ally had tried to be friends with the woman but it was impossible.

'Where's Gavin?' Ally had to speak to him, to warn him that Jason knew if nothing else. Word could get out and Helena should hear the bad news from Gavin and not through bitchy gossip.

'Probably at the hospital. His wife had the baby last night.'

Ally smothered a gasp with her hand. Helena had given birth? But it was too early. She wasn't due for another month or so. Dread snaked its way through Ally's gut, gaining momentum until she feared she was about to projectile vomit over a neatly stacked pile of rose-printed dinner plates. What if this was her fault? What if Gavin had told

Helena about her and the shock had sent her into labour? Oh, God. What if something terrible happened to the baby because of her? Gavin would never forgive Ally. He'd never forgive himself.

'Where are you going?'

'As far away from you as possible.' Ally stalked past Martine with as much dignity as she could muster under the circumstances.

'You'll forgive me,' Martine called after her. 'We always forgive each other.'

Not this time, Ally thought, not bothering to look back at Martine's pleading face.

Ally stepped out of The Housing Warehouse, wrapping her coat tightly around herself as she began to shuffle back towards the main road. What did she do now? She couldn't go to the hospital to see Gavin – that really would be overstepping the mark. Did she try to locate Jason and attempt to explain her behaviour?

Before she could decide, her phone started to ring from within her handbag.

Was it Gavin? Or Jason?

Ally scrabbled inside her handbag until she located her phone, but it was neither.

'I don't know if you've managed to get hold of Jason yet, but he's just walked into the office.' Kelly's voice was hushed over the phone. 'He doesn't look ill. He looks mad. Like, proper pissed off.'

Funny that. 'Thanks for letting me know. I'm on

my way.'

'But aren't you ill?'

'Yes. Sort of. But I need to speak to Jason. Make sure he doesn't leave.' Ally dropped her phone into her handbag and quickened her step. The Housing Warehouse wasn't far from Westerly's, but she was gasping for breath by the time she made it into the building. What little energy she had left was eradicated as she threw herself up the stairs two at a time, wheezing and panting by the time she stumbled through to Jason's office.

'I thought you were ill.' Jason met her eye, folding his arms across his chest as he leant back in his chair. His dashing grin was absent from his face, which had taken on the appearance of a block of stone. The strong, brooding types may be attractive on television, but they were pretty scary up close.

'I thought you were too.' It was a stupid thing to say, but Ally's mind was suddenly blank, empty of the rehearsed speech she had perfected during the walk to Westerly's.

'I needed time to think after the little conversation I had with your good friend, Martine. I can see by the look on your face that you know what I'm talking about.'

Ally gave the tiniest nod of her head. 'It was just one kiss, I swear. I haven't been cheating on you. Not really.'

'Just one kiss? Like that means nothing? His wife is pregnant and they have a little girl. Doesn't that mean anything to you?'

'Of course it does!' Ally took a step towards Jason but retreated again when he flashed her a fierce look. Whoa, Mr Rochester had nothing on this dude.

'But not enough to stop you. Or him.' Jason shook his head and gave a humourless laugh. 'I thought he was a decent bloke.'

'He is.' Ally zipped it when the look was flashed once more.

'Really? Decent blokes cheat on their pregnant wives, do they?'

Put like that, Ally could see Jason's point. 'It's more complicated than that.'

'It always is with you, Alana. Nothing is ever straightforward. There's always something in it for you, some hidden agenda.' He shook his head again. 'I'm such a fucking idiot. I can't believe I fell for it. I can't believe I fell for *you*.'

'I'm sorry, I really am. I didn't mean to hurt you.'

Jason barked out a laugh and Ally took a further step back, colliding with the door. 'You didn't mean to hurt me? But you did mean to wreck my career, yes?'

Ally's brow furrowed. Wreck his career? 'I don't know what you're talking about.'

Jason rose from his desk and Ally instinctively reached for the door handle, but Jason simply leaned across his desk towards her. 'I'm talking about your poisonous little plan to take over my job.'

FORTY-FOUR

Ally's ashen face paled further. Martine had told him about that too? But that wasn't even *her*. She'd put a stop to it as soon as she'd realised what was going on.

'I'm talking about the utter bullshit sexual harassment complaint. Is this ringing any bells?'

'That was months ago and I dropped the complaint.'

'Oh. That's okay then.' Jason dropped back into his seat and threw up his hands. 'Silly me. It's no big deal then, is it?'

'That's not what I'm saying.'

'I don't care what you're saying any more. It's all pathetic lies and excuses. Just get out of my office.'

'Aren't you going to let me explain?' Ally didn't have a clue how she would ever attempt to do that, but she couldn't leave things like this, with Jason despising her and thinking the absolute worst. Thinking she was like Alana.

But wasn't she behaving exactly like Alana? Going after a married man. Trying to lure a father away from his children. Lying and cheating. Ally knew her actions were wrong, but she'd excused them, as though her predicament made them okay. Helena had just given birth – to a baby whose fate she didn't even know – and yet she still wanted Gavin.

What kind of woman had she become?

'There is no explanation other than you're a lying, back-stabbing little tramp.' Ally blinked against Jason's harsh words. 'Now, get out of my office.'

Ally wanted to fight her case, but what could she say? That he was right? That no matter how much she had fought it, how hard she had tried to shed the venomous image everyone had of her, she had become Alana anyway?

Ally crept from Jason's office, afraid of dislodging yet more home truths. Jason had forced her to take a damn good look at herself, and she didn't like what she had found.

'I can't believe you did that to him,' Kelly said when Ally emerged from Jason's office. So she knew too? Great.

'It's not as bad as it sounds.'

'That's good then, because it sounds like you stabbed a really nice bloke in the back. He didn't deserve that, you know?'

Ally did know but she didn't have the energy to

explain, and it was impossible to anyway.

'And to think I was beginning to trust you. Some friend you turned out to be.'

Fantastic. Another misdemeanour to add to her growing list. She was a cheating, home-wrecking, back-stabbing crappy friend. Who else knew? Who else was going to turn against her next?

Francine.

Ally flew down the spiral staircase, her feet thundering in her haste to reach her friend.

'I knew it was too good to be true.'

Too late. Of course it was too late. What had Ally been expecting? That one tiny shred of goodness could remain?

'I knew you couldn't change. You make me sick.'

'I *have* changed, I swear.' Ally could have stood at that reception desk all day – all *week* – but she knew she would never convince Francine, not again. Mud sticks and this was special extra-sticky mud she'd coated herself in. She'd managed to win Francine round once, but she wouldn't be convinced a second time.

Ally didn't want to go home to an empty flat, so she wandered to a nearby park, which was deserted at this time of day. It wasn't a particularly warm day, so she pulled her coat tighter around her body before she slumped onto a bench overlooking a small playground.

'Are you happy now, Clementine?' Ally wanted to throw her head towards the greyish sky and howl the words, but she was utterly spent and the words were barely audible. 'Because I'm not. This is not what I wanted.'

Ally looked across at the playground, at the colourful climbing frame and slide, the stilled roundabout and the toddler swings. She pictured Gavin pulling back the swing, hesitating for a moment before releasing it. The squeal of delight as the child flew through the air.

The child was not Mia. It was a nameless, faceless child. Their child. The child that would never be.

'I am not Alana.' Ally looked up at the dull sky, but the howl did not come. 'Did you hear me? I am not Alana.'

Reaching into her handbag, Ally bypassed the tissues, though they would have come in handy, and grabbed her phone. This time when she dialled Gavin's number, it was answered.

'Hey.' Gavin's voice was so familiar and full of warmth after a day of harsh, unfriendly tones that she almost burst into tears as it reached her ears.

'Hey.' She swallowed the lump in her throat and tried to add a bit of false cheer to her voice. 'I hear congratulations are in order. Is the baby okay?'

'He's great, thanks. He's a bit on the small side, being a few weeks early, but they're pleased with how he's doing.'

Silent tears ran freely down Ally's cheeks. Gavin sounded so elated, and so he should. It was further proof that she had to put an end to this, that she had to do the right thing and walk away. She would not be sucked into Alana's world.

'That's great. I'm happy for you.' And she was, deep down, past all the hurt and despair. 'So, what's he called then?'

'Finn, his name's Finn.'

Ally felt a sharp pain in her chest. 'That's lovely.' She swiped at the tears on her cheeks, the sleeve of her coat now a soggy mess.

'About the other night, Ally. At the school.'

'Yes?' Despite her convictions, despite knowing she could never be with Gavin, a tiny part of her still clung onto the hope that they were destined to be together.

'It shouldn't have happened.'

And there it was. The end of Ally and Gavin. She covered her mouth with her soggy sleeve, afraid she was about to wail down the phone. Of course it was always going to end like this. She should have known. Gavin was a good man – the greatest Ally knew – and he would never abandon his children over a quick snog in a school corridor. He wouldn't be the man Ally loved if he did.

'No.' That one word was brutal as it left Ally's mouth.

'I'd better go.'

Ally wanted to beg Gavin not to leave her. As long as he was talking to her, there was hope. Once he hung up, that would be it. They couldn't even continue to be friends now. Gavin wouldn't be in her life at all.

But she didn't beg. Gavin was happy and being without his children would destroy every last ounce of that happiness. Ally shifted on the bench, drawing her knees up to her chest and wrapping her free hand around her knees, pulling herself into a tight ball as though it could offer her some sort of protection for what was about to happen.

'Goodbye, Gavin.'

'Goodbye, Ally.'

And then Gavin was gone. For good.

FORTY-FIVE

Ally somehow made her way to her parents' house, praying her mum would be in. She needed to be held and soothed and reassured that everything would be okay, so she was relieved when the door opened. But it was Freya standing on the other side and not her mum, but, by this point, Ally wasn't fussy. Throwing herself into her sister's arms, she howled and cried, allowing everything to pour out of her; the loss and hope and devastation, the life she had given up and the life she would never have.

'What's happened?' Linda leapt out of her seat as Freya led Ally into the sitting room. She pulled Ally towards her, wrapping her in a familiar embrace, which only made Ally cry harder. Though Ally had seen her family every week, she'd missed the closeness they'd once shared. They'd all grown accustomed to Ally's presence, but it wasn't the same. Not even close. She'd been held at arm's length, skirted around as the family tried to adjust to the stranger under their roof.

'I've lost everything, Mum. Francine and Kelly hate me, Jason's dumped me and I've lost Gavin for good this time.'

'I think you'd better start from the beginning, love. Tell me everything.'

So Ally did. She told her about the false complaint about Jason, how she had tried to steal his job from under him but changed her mind, only for it to resurface and not only bite her on the arse, but completely savage her. She told her about kissing Gavin, about losing everyone and everything she had worked so hard for. The whole sorry tale poured from Ally as her mum and sister sat by her side, listening intently. Finally, drained of both energy and words, Ally slumped back on the sofa.

'I knew you couldn't change.' Freya, who had been sitting quietly and taking everything in, leapt to her feet. 'You're still the same old Alana, aren't you? You only ever think of yourself.'

'Freya, don't.' Linda shot her daughter a pleading look, but Freya was incensed. She'd let her guard down momentarily and look what had happened! She never should have trusted her sister.

'Why do you always do this, Mum? She screws up and you pick up the pieces. She isn't worth it.'

So Ally was truly back to square one then. She'd

lost Gavin, her friendship with Francine was non-existent and her family hated her. She was right back where she'd started, except now she didn't even have Martine for company. *That's* how bad things were. Marvellous.

Ally wanted to scream until she passed out. This was so bloody unfair!

'I wish I'd never made that stupid birthday wish,' she bellowed, her sudden booming voice startling both Linda and Freya.

'What is she going on about?' Freya asked. Ally was about to finally explain – a straitjacket sounded pretty comfortable right now – but her lips refused to budge. The day's events were catching up on her and she was utterly exhausted. Her head felt too heavy for her neck and lolled to one side while a woozy sensation overtook her entire body.

'What's happening to her?' Linda gasped. Ally's eyes rolled back in their sockets before she closed her lids and slumped against the sofa. 'You don't think it's the drugs again, do you?'

'Of course it's drugs again. This is Alana we're talking about, Mum. She'll be off her tits on something while we run around trying to sort her out. It happens every time. But not any more. This is it. I'm done with her.'

Ally wanted to protest but she was so sleepy. She'd have a quick nap and then she'd tell them everything.

FORTY-SIX

Ally groaned as she woke, her fists moving sluggishly to rub her eyes. She could feel the weight of some sort of blanket or duvet covering her. Her mum must have taken pity on her and thrown a cover over her. How long had she been asleep? She didn't feel very rested and her eyes were refusing to budge, so it couldn't have been for very long.

'Mum?' Ally had a lot of explaining to do. She was quite certain her family would think she was bonkers – or well and truly back on the drugs – but she had to tell them. She couldn't keep it to herself any longer. Perhaps she *was* crazy. Perhaps they'd cart her off somewhere to get help. They'd give her drugs (the prescribed variety rather than the nasty illegal stuff) and she'd feel better. Yes, she liked that idea.

'Mum?' She stretched her legs and gave a long

363

yawn. The sofa was a lot comfier than it used to be. Had her parents invested in a new one? 'Mum, are you there?' Her eyes finally opened, first a crack and then widening as she took in her surroundings.

She wasn't on the sofa. She wasn't even in her parents' house. She was home, and not in that depressing little flat. She was *home*, in the house she shared with Gavin. She was in their bed. She was staring at the beautiful four walls of her bedroom. That was her wardrobe there. Her chest of drawers. Her wicker chair stuffed with Gavin's abandoned clothes. Her husband's dirty clothes would have caused her jaw to clench in annoyance once, but today she wanted to hug them to her chest and weep with joy.

She was home!

Twisting in the bed, she was disappointed to see the vacant space beside her. But the covers were crumpled, suggesting that someone had been sleeping there recently.

'Gavin?' She hopped out of bed, enjoying the feel of her own carpet beneath her toes. She'd missed that carpet, as rough and miserably beige as it was. 'Gavin?'

She heard his chuckle before she saw the man himself. The bedroom door was nudged open and there he was, his shaggy hair in need of a good cut. He was wearing a pair of crusty old boxers that should have been thrown out years ago and a once-white-but-now-grey T-shirt. He had never looked so handsome.

'Alright, alright, Miss Impatient.' He stepped fully into the room, a breakfast tray in hand. 'Get back in bed. You can't have breakfast in bed standing in the middle of the room.'

Ally didn't take her eyes off Gavin as she shuffled across to the bed and climbed inside, afraid that he would disappear in a puff of smoke if she did. What if this was just a cruel dream and she woke up on her parents' sofa with a long queue of people waiting to yell at her again?

'Happy birthday, darling.' Gavin set the tray on Ally's lap and kissed her lips. It didn't feel like a dream, but then they never did, did they?

'It's my birthday?'

Gavin rolled his eyes. 'Yes and don't pretend it isn't. But don't worry, you haven't transformed into a wrinkly, old pensioner overnight. Turning thirty isn't the disaster you seem to think it is, you know.'

'No, I suppose it isn't.' It was her thirtieth birthday? But that had been months ago.

'I'm going to go and have a shower while you eat your breakfast. Then I'll give you your present.'

Ally gave a whimper as Gavin left the room. She was desperate to follow him, to make sure he really was there and not an illusion. Perhaps her mum had already got her help and she was drugged up to her eyeballs. This could be her happy place.

But drugged up or not, Ally didn't want to be anywhere else.

'It isn't a dream.'

Coffee splashed onto the tray as the voice startled Ally. She turned away from the bedroom door and there, standing in front of the laundry-filled wicker chair, was Clementine.

'You.' Ally glared at the girl. She had a lot to answer for, dumping her into that hell and then sodding off without another word.

Clementine smiled back serenely. 'Hello, Petal. Happy to be home?'

Ally was, more than she could ever describe. 'Is this actually real?' Ally gave a sweep of her arm, indicating not only the room but her life.

'Yes. You're back in your old life. I hope you won't take it for granted this time.'

Ally shook her head, her eyes wide. 'I won't, I swear.' Ally would never take anything for granted, ever again. 'I don't want to sound ungrateful or anything, but why bring me back now?'

'Isn't it obvious?' Clementine's eyes dropped to the floor. Ally should have been brought back a long time ago. A couple of days – a week at the most – was usually sufficient time for clients to count their blessings, but Clementine had misplaced Ally's file and forgotten all about this particular case. She was in deep shit over it, actually. But Ally didn't have to know that.

'You finally learned your lesson and considered Gavin's feelings before your own.' There, that would do it. That sounded flowery and, more importantly, plausible.

'But I tried to destroy his family.'

'But you didn't.' Jeez, did the woman want to be back or not?

'Why is it my birthday again?'

Clementine met Ally's eye again, a small smile on her lips. 'Because today is the day you made your original wish. As far as everyone else is aware, no time has passed.'

'So everything is back to normal? Gavin is a mechanic again? Francine is my best friend and my family don't hate me?'

Clementine twinkled a laugh. 'Nobody hates you. Apart from Kelly, but then she always did.'

Ally moved the breakfast tray to the bedside table and sat up straighter. 'I have a question about Kelly. Why did her life change? I thought we'd swapped lives at first, but we hadn't.'

Clementine's head tilted to one side slightly. 'Kelly's life didn't change. Only the people affected by your behaviour changed.'

'But her parents. Her childhood.'

Clementine gave a small nod of her head.

'They've always been like that?' Poor Kelly! And she'd treated the girl with such disdain all this time when she'd needed a friend, not an enemy. 'What about her neighbour?'

'Martine is still Kelly's only friend.'

'And what about the other Martine?' The cow who had betrayed her.

'That Martine isn't real, Petal. You created her. You assumed Kelly was a superficial bitch and had similar friends. You assumed she lived a superficial life of luxury. Luxury she clearly couldn't afford.'

Ally had assumed a lot about Kelly. She'd been jealous of her life. Ha! What a joke that was now.

'Enjoy your life, Ally. It's a precious thing.'

Ally opened her mouth to reply but Clementine was already gone, leaving nothing but a faint wispy cloud in her wake.

'Aren't you hungry, birthday girl?' Gavin strode into the room with nothing but a towel slung around his hips. Ally was suddenly ravenous, but not for breakfast. 'Shall I give you your present now then?'

Yes please.

Instead of pouncing on Ally, Gavin rummaged in his underwear drawer and produced a small ring-box shaped parcel. Ally quickly checked her left hand. Phew! They were still married.

'What's this?' Ally tore into the paper and opened the little black box inside. Sure enough, a ring lay inside. It was a beautiful white gold ring set with a row of tiny diamonds.

'It's an eternity ring.' Gavin perched on the bed and plucked the ring from its cushioned box.

'It's beautiful, but aren't eternity rings supposed to be given after the birth of your first child?'

Gavin took hold of Ally's hand. 'They can be, but I just wanted to show you how much I love you.'

Ally pulled her hand away as Gavin attempted to push the ring onto her finger. His face fell but Ally spoke quickly to reassure him. 'Perhaps we should keep it in the box for now. Say, for nine months?'

Gavin's brow furrowed. 'Nine months? Are you saying...?' He hesitated, not wanting to cause yet another row.

'I'm saying I want us to make a baby.'

Gavin tried – but failed – to keep the grin from his face. 'But you said you weren't ready. What about your freedom?'

Ally gave a wave of her hand. 'Freedom is overrated.' Seeing the look of adoration on Gavin's face as he held his child would easily kick freedom's arse.

'I guess we'd better put this away then.' Gavin slipped the ring back into its box and popped it into his sock drawer. 'When do you think we should start trying?'

Ally reached out for Gavin's towel and pulled it away, letting it fall to the floor. 'How about right now?'

'I'm up for that.'

'So I see.' Ally was practically salivating at the sight. It had been a long time. 'There is one condition though.' Gavin didn't care what it was. He'd grant Ally anything right now. 'We can't name the baby Mia or Finn.'

EPILOGUE

The Farthing was packed as Keith Barry set up his karaoke machine. Ally reached up to kiss her mum on the cheek, grateful that she never had to see the fear and disappointment in her eyes again. It had been almost a year since she'd returned from her nightmare alternate life, but she still counted her blessings on a daily basis.

'Is she here yet?' Linda asked, surveying the room. What on earth was the karaoke host wearing?

'Not yet but Dee says they're on their way. Let me get you a drink.' Ally fought her way to the bar, loving that so many people had turned up. She couldn't have filled a shoebox with loved ones as Alana, never mind a whole pub. She'd never stop feeling grateful to be back in her rightful place.

'Thanks, love.' Linda took the drink from her daughter and put a hand on her arm. 'You won't wear yourself out, will you?'

'I'm fine, Mum, really.' Ally spotted Francine and

Mike as they stepped into the pub and gave a wave. 'Why don't you go and find a seat before they're all taken? The karaoke will be starting soon.' Ally made as quick a dash as she could across the pub and hugged her friend. Francine was one of the many blessings she counted every day. 'Thanks for coming.'

'You know I wouldn't miss karaoke, chick.' Francine looked towards Keith Barry and pulled a face. What was he wearing? 'Is Gavin not here?'

Ally glanced around the jammed pub. 'He's… somewhere. I think he's hiding with Jared and Lovely Paul so they won't have to sing.'

'Hiding, you say?' Mike said.

Francine grabbed hold of her husband's arm and gave him a stern look. 'Don't even think about it.' She used her free hand to pat Ally's arm. 'Why don't you go and sit down for a bit? You look exhausted.'

'I'm fine, really.' Ally knew her friends and family were only looking out for her, but you'd think they'd never seen a pregnant woman before. She was only six months gone and there would be plenty of time for resting on the sofa when her maternity leave kicked in. Before then, she had lots to do. As keen as Gavin was to start a family, he wasn't so keen when it came to flat-pack baby furniture, and they hadn't even started stock-piling nappies yet. Ally had a never-ending list of things they needed to do before the baby arrived, but she had to admit that she was looking forward to the challenge that lay ahead. Who knew that one glance at a parenting magazine would unleash a tornado of maternal feelings?

'Freya will be here in a few minutes so I want to make sure everything is perfect.' Today was Freya's thirtieth birthday so Ally had organised a surprise karaoke birthday party for her.

'If you're looking for perfection, you'd better rustle up another outfit for Keith Barry then,' Francine joked. Ally groaned. Tonight, their host was wearing a lime green jump suit, unzipped to his naval. Keith Barry was one hairy beast.

'Oh, Kelly and Jason are here.' Ally grasped Francine's hand and attempted to pull her towards the pair. 'Come and say hello. Please.'

'Do I have to?' Francine couldn't understand why Ally had suddenly decided to befriend the viper-like Kelly, but the woman was persistent and had slowly worn Kelly down. They weren't exactly bosom buddies yet, but they'd called a truce on their feud and were quite friendly now. It helped that Jason's influence had softened Kelly, particularly tonight when Ally had invited them along to the party.

'Hey, Francine. Have you seen Kelly's engagement ring?'

'No.' And nor was Francine overly keen to see it.

'You haven't?' Jason turned to Kelly with mock surprise. 'You mean you've missed someone?' He turned to the others again as Kelly nudged him playfully in the ribs. 'She shows it to everyone, even strangers in the street. I can't blame her though. Any girl would shout it from the rooftops if they were about to marry me.'

Ally, Francine and Kelly all groaned, but Ally secretly agreed with Jason. Kelly was lucky to have a man like him. Their relationship had finally become official three weeks ago when Kelly turned up at the office sporting a huge rock. It turned out that not only were they engaged, they were also moving in together. Ally had never let Kelly know that she was aware of her home life – how would she explain *that*? – but the knowledge had been hard to bear, so it was a relief to know she would soon be free of her abusive family.

Ally's phone rang once before cutting off, the pre-arranged signal for Freya's arrival. 'Ssh, everyone. She's here.'

The door opened and Freya walked in to a chorus of 'surprise!', followed by a shower of party poppers. Freya was stunned as everyone surged to hug the birthday girl. Even Gavin and co came out of hiding to wish her a happy birthday.

The karaoke party was a success. Most people had a go, whether they were singing on their own or in a group, and Keith Barry was as 'charming' as ever. Freya had a turn, singing Pink's 'Get The Party Started' and the lights suddenly dimmed as she finished. Linda made her way from the pub's kitchen with a cake, complete with flickering candles, as the whole pub sang 'Happy Birthday'.

'Make a wish,' Linda urged as Freya went to

blow out the candles.

Ally gasped, leaping towards her sister, hands waving like a demented helicopter. 'No! Don't do it!'

I hope that you enjoyed reading Everything Changes But You as much as I enjoyed writing it. If you did, why not leave a review? I'd love to hear what you think and it helps other readers find books they'd enjoy too!

If you'd like to keep up to date with my new releases and book news, you can subscribe to my newsletter on my blog (jenniferjoycewrites.co.uk). I send out newsletters 4-5 times a year, with short stories, extra content, a subscriber-exclusive giveaway and more! Plus, you'll receive my ebook quick read, *Six Dates,* which is only available to subscribers, for FREE.

Printed in Great Britain
by Amazon

75070831R00227

IN THE
SHADOWS
OF
CASTLES

BOOK TWO OF THE 1066 SAGA

G.K. HOLLOWAY

SilverWood

Published in 2022 by SilverWood Books

SilverWood Books Ltd
14 Small Street, Bristol, BS1 1DE, United Kingdom
www.silverwoodbooks.co.uk

Copyright © G. K. Holloway 2022

The right of G. K. Holloway to be identified as the author of this work
has been asserted in accordance with the Copyright, Designs
and Patents Act 1988 Sections 77 and 78.

All rights reserved. No part of this publication may be reproduced,
stored in a retrieval system, or transmitted in any form or by any means,
electronic, mechanical, photocopying, recording or otherwise,
without prior permission of the copyright holder.

This is a work of fiction. Names, characters, places and incidents either
are products of the author's imagination or are used fictitiously.
Any resemblance to actual events or locales or persons,
living or dead, is entirely coincidental.

ISBN 978-1-78132-869-9 (paperback)

British Library Cataloguing in Publication Data
A CIP catalogue record for this book is
available from the British Library

Page design and typesetting by SilverWood Books

For Jack and Lucy

'I will heap disasters on them,
I will spend My arrows on them.
They shall be wasted with hunger,
Devoured by pestilence and bitter destruction;
I will also send against them the teeth of beasts,
With the poison of serpents of the dust.
The sword shall destroy outside;
There shall be terror within
For the young man and virgin,
The nursing child and the man with grey hairs.'
Deuteronomy 32: 22 to 25

'The French held the field of the dead as God granted them because of the people's sins.'
Anglo-Saxon Chronicle

List of Characters

English:	Norman:
Aethelwine, Bishop of Durham	Judith, niece of King William
Agatha, Edgar Atheling's mother	Matilda, Duchess of Normandy, Queen of England
Aldytha, Queen of England and sister to Edwin and Morcar	Odo, Bishop of Bayeux and half-brother to King William
Bondi Wynstanson, a royal housecarl	Robert, Count of Mortain, half-brother to King William
Brihtric, Worcestershire thane Norman	Robert de Comines, Norman knight
Christina, Edgar Atheling's sister	Walter Gherbod, Flemish knight
Copsig, Earl of Bernicia	William, King of England and Duke of Normandy
Edith, Dowager Queen. Wife of Edward the Confessor and sister of King Harold	William FitzOsbern, Norman knight
Eadric, the Steersman. Head of the English navy	William Malet, Norman knight
Eadric the Wild, a Shropshire thane and Queen Aldytha's lover	William Warenne, Norman
Ealdred, Archbishop of York	
Edwin, Earl of Mercia and Morcar's brother	
Edyth, handfast wife of King Harold. Mother of (Little) Gytha and Ulf	
Elfwyn, Mereswein's daughter	
Gospatric, Earl of Northumbria	

English characters continued:
Gytha, Countess of Wessex, Mother of the late King Harold and Queen Edith
Gytha, daughter of Harold and Edyth, granddaughter of Countess Gytha
Margaret, Edgar Atheling's sister
Merleswein, Shire Reeve of Lincoln
Morwenna, Merleswein's daughter
Oswulf, Earl of Bernicia
Sherilda, Morwenna's children's nurse
Siward, Earl of Gloucester
Stigand, Archbishop of Canterbury
Thurold, Thane of Lincolnshire and friend of Merleswein's
Tate, Shire Reeve Godwin's widow
Waltheof, Earl of Northampton
Whitgar, Yorkshire Thane

Other important characters:
Malcolm, King of Scotland
Osbjorn, King Swein's brother
Swein, King of Denmark
Tora, Queen of Denmark
Trygve, Danish jarl/pirate

London, Christmas Eve, 1066

Bondi Wynstanson stared enthralled as across a blood-red sky, countless black birds soared. They were everywhere, filling the heavens as though there was nowhere out of their reach. From the bedroom window of a whorehouse, Bondi followed the spectacle with fascination. He had got out of bed to close the shutter, but the natural wonder in the sky distracted him, compelling him to stare.

The birds passed above him, and he heard the rush of a million beating wings. Then they were back again. Wave upon wave of starlings, sometimes thick and black like spilt ink on parchment, sometimes a pale, delicate grey, and for a moment, a banner waving in the breeze. They flew towards a horizon lost in the mist, turned en masse as they careered around the pale winter sky. Bondi found the vision before him breathtaking. The shapes they formed enthralled him, but none so much as the final shape. In one deft movement, the birds created an enormous black crown, majestic and satanic in one, sweeping dreamlike over Lambeth marshes for just an instant, before shattering and disappearing into the trees and scrub. It was such a haunting image it took Bondi's breath away. As he looked on, a raw, sightless night obliterated the sunset.

'Come on, Bondi,' a woman said, dragging out the final syllable of his name, so it sounded like Bondee. It irritated him every time she said it. She was Hild, his companion for the afternoon.

'Close the shutters. It's getting cold in here,' she said, breaking the spell.

Bondi looked out of the window. Upriver, the lights flickered on the new fortification the Normans called a castle. He could pick out its menacing silhouette. Its construction was proceeding rapidly, as it was on the one downriver. The two fortifications mirrored each other, built to intimidate the citizens of London and constructed on artificial hills; they towered above any other building in the city. Almost finished, both housed garrisons ready to storm the town and deal with trouble in an instant.

He sighed as he closed the shutters and turned towards her. She lay in a bed wearing only a warm smile and a twinkle in her eye.

It was Christmas Eve, the night before William the Bastard's coronation, and Bondi needed a distraction. The Blue Anchor was the right place.

'Come here,' the woman said. 'I'll take your mind off things.'

Bondi had spent the last five days in taverns with women like Hild and no time in the barracks. The housecarl had failed to protect his lord at Hastings and had to deal with the shame and the guilt of living on while his king lay dead on the battlefield. Hild, and women like her, took his mind off all that.

'That's better,' the woman said as he climbed back into bed.

Bondi gazed into his cup to discover it empty.

'Would you like more?' Hild asked.

Bondi nodded in reply.

'More ale,' she called, and a maid appeared with a pitcher.

'Here you are,' the maid said, placing the pitcher by the bedside and taking the old one away.

As she opened the door, Bondi thought he could hear men's voices downstairs.

Bondi called to the maid, 'Are there Normans here?'

'Yes, but don't worry, they're not looking for you; they just want some fun,' she said.

'How many are there?'

'Three,' she answered.

The wench by Bondi's side said, 'Don't concern yourself with them, love. We've got better things to do,' and she smiled a radiant smile of perfect teeth, with a broad mouth and a dimple in her left cheek.

Bondi thought her pretty and mischievous looking. As she turned towards him, he inhaled her natural scent, delicate yet heady, and he forgot about the Normans downstairs.

'Are you going to have some more ale now, or wait until after?' she said.

'I think I'll wait until after,' he said, laughing and taking her in his arms.

After the two had spent themselves, they fell into a deep sleep, from which they awoke to find three men in the room laughing and joking.

'What do you want?' Bondi asked.

The three carried on with their laughter, gesticulating and thrusting their hips, making it obvious they wanted the Hild to grant them her favours. The biggest of the three, and they were big men, lurched toward the bed and grabbed her breasts while his friends guffawed and slapped their thighs.

'Get off me, you pig,' Hild said, smacking his head.

The Frenchman responded, slapping Hild's face and mayhem broke loose. Bondi punched the Norman in the mouth as hard as he could. The Norman's friends came to his help, yelling and flailing their fists and outnumbering him. They soon got the better of Bondi, even though he had a fierce ally in Hild, who broke a jug over the head of one of the thugs. After a few moments of brawling, the Normans threw Bondi, bruised and bloodied, out of the door, with his clothes following him. He staggered about in the frosty night air, his bare feet freezing in the oozing mud. He dressed and made off, looking for shelter on the bleak, wet winter night.

Bondi made his way down the street through the mist that rose off the river, passing a few quayside warehouses before finding the place he was searching for, a stable. He could have tried a few taverns, but he doubted anyone would want him as a guest, dishevelled and covered as he was in blood, mud, and bruises.

Bondi struggled to climb over the stable's perimeter fence and fell with a thud before getting to his feet undamaged and finding his way into the stable, surprising a few horses on the way. There he discovered a ladder leading up to the hayloft where he lay his head, warm at last. The smell of the hay and horses was a comfort, and sleep overwhelmed him. As he drifted off, he remembered it was Christmas, and there he was in a manger, just like baby Jesus, but he knew there would be no shepherds waiting to present him with gifts in the morning.

Chapter 2

Christmas morning and Westminster Abbey was crowded with guests waiting for the crowning. Half were dreading the moment; the other half were excited. One member of the guests had mixed feelings. William Malet, the half English Norman knight, had been a good friend of the late King Harold, and it troubled him that Duke William was about to be crowned only after so much bloodshed. But Malet consoled himself: the victory was God's will, making him as blameless as the next man for the slaughter. As he stood in the cold abbey watching vapour pour from the mouths of men shuffling to warm their feet, a commotion broke out. He turned, as did everyone, to see his lord entering.

William left his guard at the threshold. Uneasy in his resplendent regalia, he entered Westminster Abbey with trepidation; the atmosphere in London was tense, but he grew more at ease with every step he took. William glanced around, studying the English faces; they appeared hostile to a man. Once in the abbey, Archbishops Stigand and Ealdred flanked the man about to become their king.

'Good morning, my lord. Just a few short steps away from being King of England,' said Stigand with a conspiratorial smile. William became aware his half brothers, Robert Mortain and Bishop Odo, with their cousin, the Bishop of Coutances, had fallen in behind him. Behind them came the bishops, followed by the abbots, led by Abbot Lanfranc, invited over from Normandy by William himself.

When each man was in his place, William heard Archbishop Ealdred say, 'You may proceed now, my lord,'

William's heart pounded as he led the procession down the aisle, the English on one side and the Normans and their allies on the other. As he made his way toward the high altar, he was stunned by the glittering gold and jewellery on the archbishops' copes. William felt out of place, like an interloper rather than a participant. The majesty of Westminster surpassed anything he had ever experienced.

He took a deep breath, and the heady smell of incense filled his nostrils. At last, it was happening. But it was more than the abbey itself that awed him; it was the splendour of its English occupants. As he approached the altar, the ecclesiastics took their places, and it was then William noticed Stigand was wearing a different cope from the one he had seen him in previously. It was even more dazzling than its predecessor. Ealdred also impressed him. The Normans, by comparison, looked like country bumpkins.

William's eyes darted this way and that around the altar. The beautiful frontal stood upon it, a matchless work of art and five exquisite, jewel-encrusted, gold candlesticks, each at least three feet tall. Treasure surrounded William. There was gold, gold, gold, everywhere. Presiding over it all was a statue of the Virgin Mary, set upright on a plinth behind the altar, standing above human frailty. William began to feel dizzy and focused directly ahead. He took a few deep breaths and regained his composure.

To help legitimise his reign, William had arranged with Archbishop Ealdred the exact order of ceremony, which was to be as similar as possible to procedures devised by Saint Dunstan. The only change was that Ealdred would conduct the formalities in French and English. He hoped the ancient rituals that he had rehearsed would emphasise the continuity of rule, a natural transfer of power from earlier rulers to himself.

The elderly archbishop had been distraught when he heard of Harold's demise and was still shocked by how events were turning out, but he was sure God's will was not open to question.

After the news of Harold's death arrived in London, the Witan proclaimed Edgar AthelingKing. Ealdred had assumed that something would resolve things favourably. But there had been no such event. Ealdred thought about the star that appeared in the heavens months ago. People said it was a sign, but no one had understood what it meant until now. *But why would God send a bastard to rule over us? Perhaps God is mocking us,* he thought. Then, catching sight of Stigand, he thought it must be a punishment for the archbishop's sins. *Then again, perhaps it was all for the good, part of God's plan.* It had been fifty years since Cnut had ascended the throne and fifty years to the day since his coronation. He had been a cruel king at first, but then, after a few short years, had become one of the finest kings ever to rule England. So, like many others in the kingdom, he reassured himself, *perhaps history is repeating itself.*

As Ealdred was thinking his thoughts, William had ideas of his own. He stood and turned to face the congregation as Ealdred continued the service. 'I present unto you your undoubted king.'

William tensed as he saw the angry faces of the English glaring at him. Edgar Atheling proclaimed King of England just weeks before and now witnessing a scene where he should have the central role as the Witan had declared. There were others too, looking unhappy to be seeing the crowning of a Norman king. William wondered what would happen if they all attacked him.

Ealdred now led William to the throne, taking the oath, as directed, he proclaimed.

'In the name of the Holy Trinity, I promise to all people in my dominion true peace. I forbid robbery and all unrighteous things to all orders, and finally, I promise justice and mercy in all judgements so that the kind and merciful God may grant us all his eternal mercy, who lives and reigns. And whatever I may do unjustly, because of my might, I must give a reckoning for on Judgement Day, for all of it.'

The oath completed, Ealdred anointed William with the holy chrism. William's heartbeat raced; *No Norman duke ever experienced this. Now, I am greater than my father, his grandfather, any of his ancestors. I have reached heights of which they had only dreamed. I am touched by God, set up above the laity, superior to all around me. The unction gives me the authority of God himself,* and he felt power course through him.

Preoccupied with their dreams or nightmares, the congregation looked on as Ealdred performed the sacrament with trembling hands. William half expected the holy oil to burn him, but when he remained unscathed, he sighed, and a young cleric cried out, 'Behold, I see God!'

'Be quiet, you idiot,' Abbot Lanfranc hissed at the novice.

'I see God! I see God!' the young man cried out as he fell to the floor on his knees.

Lanfranc stepped forward, grabbed him by the scruff of the neck, and dragged him to the nearest door.

'Take him outside and don't let him back in again,' the Abbot ordered, as he hurled the novice priest towards the guards.

As Archbishop Ealdred presented William with the rod and the orb, he could not prevent himself from trembling and wondered if excitement or fear made him shake. William could not help but notice Ealdred's head nodding. Liver spots scattered amongst the wrinkles on his face gave the archbishop an elderly, venerable appearance. William wondered how much longer Ealdred had on earth and who could replace him. William then caught Edgar's eye. They stared at each other for a few moments, and for once in his life, William averted his gaze.

Next, William's eyes settled on Morcar and Edwin's blank faces and expressionless eyes. Then he caught sight of Tostig's old underling, the despised Copsig, who had, with the help of gold and silver, inveigled him into making him Earl of Northumbria. Earl Waltheof was there, too, staring at the ceiling. Amongst the once-powerful northerners was Merleswein, Shire Reeve of Lincoln. He appeared unremarkable, no taller or shorter than most men. His hair was brown and his eyes grey, but he was a royal thane and great friend of King Harold, put in charge of the north when he left York for Hastings. Soon, like it or not, all of them would swear allegiance to their new king.

William's fingers played over the hilt of Curtana, the ceremonial Sword of Mercy. A sword like many others, except the point had broken off an inch from the tip. The swordsmith had left one edge blunt, hence the name Sword of Mercy. William had always suspected King Edward impotent, and it amused him that there was no sharp tip with which to penetrate. A *little like Edward himself,* he thought. And as he eyed the slender blade, he wondered, *which edge will I need in the coming months?*

Once again, his eyes fell on Copsig and the Northumbrians. *I wouldn't trust that lot as far as I could throw them.*

Then, at last, the moment arrived. Ealdred, in English and Bishop Geoffrey, in French, demanded of all those present that they accept William as king. There was a roar as the assembly shouted its assent.

'Join with me no to sing Laudes Regiae,' Ealdred invited the guests.

The singing started well until the sound of screaming entered the church and smoke poured through the windows. Ealdred heard men shouting, but it was not until a flaming torch flew through a window that the congregation reacted. First to leave the building were the Norman nobles, scrambling to get through the doorways; the clerics stayed put, hoping to be protected by the sanctity of the house of God. The rest joined the rush for the exits. Some wanted to escape the danger, and others tried to discover the origin of the commotion and deal with it.

As the nobles left the porch, they grabbed their weapons from where they had left them. Englishmen turning left to the south, French and Normans turning right to the north. The soldiers who were guarding the church had vanished.

Edgar and the English earls raced out of the abbey to see the minster surrounded in chaos. A monk from the monastery approached them. 'My lords, help us. When the congregation began cheering, out here, the Normans set fire to the buildings.'

William, along with Ealdred and Stigand, stayed inside, while outside mayhem reigned.

'What's happening out there?' William asked the archbishops. He was white-faced and trembling.

'It's nothing,' Stigand replied. 'You'll see, it's just a few locals in high spirits. They're celebrating your coronation.'

William saw the smoke coming in through the windows and making its way to the ceiling. 'Does this kind of thing usually happen at a coronation?' he snapped.

Before Stigand could answer, the screams of a dying man echoed around the building. William, wondering if the riot might be an act of God, sat shaking in terror on his throne. The two archbishops stood on either side of him, trying to calm him while smoke continued to pour into the abbey. Outside, the disturbance spread right across the island.

King William knew he must act, and so quaking, he struggled to his feet.

'Let me help you,' said Stigand, helping his new king, quivering like an old man, out of his throne.

Chapter 3

Once on his feet, William became the warrior of old, and the mere act of walking brought him back to life. By the time he left the church, he was swaggering. It was now indisputable. He was anointed, crowned, and invested King of England. No one in his kingdom was above him. The weight of the crown on his head empowered him, invigorated him. As he strode out into the pale winter sunlight, he felt like a giant, a colossus through whose veins pure energy flowed. His coronation regalia sparkling, he knew he must be splendid to behold. Could the young priest be right? Perhaps he was God, or as close to being a god as a man could get.

'Turold, fetch my horse,' he bellowed.

A dwarf appeared with William's stallion, and as he climbed into the saddle, he caught sight of an English nobleman.

'Earl Waltheof, isn't it?'

'Yes, my lord.'

'Are there many hurt?'

'It's hard to say; the entire island's in an uproar.'

'Where are the guards?'

'They're the ones who are rioting,' Waltheof said, pointing to the nearby buildings.

William looked around him. Most of the buildings were ablaze; squealing animals and screaming people ran amok as his soldiers attacked them.

'Take your men and put the fire out. I'll take mine and deal with the rest,' William said before riding away.

Waltheof snapped commands. 'Get buckets of water. Save the houses that aren't too damaged.'

Waltheof's men found anything that would contain water and hurled it into the flames. Others beat the fire with whatever came to hand. While they were busy fighting the fire, a small group of Norman looters made off with valuables.

'Where do you think you're going?' Enraged, Waltheof snapped.

They stopped in their tracks. The leader looked the earl up and down. With contempt, he said, 'Mind your own business,' before continuing on his way, laughing and joking with his friends.

'This is my business, thief,' Waltheof said.

The Norman turned and shook a sack whose contents clanked. 'You want what's in here? Come and get it.'

Waltheof drew his sword and rushed towards the freebooters, his comrades following, weapons ready.

'Kill the bastards,' Waltheof yelled.

There was no need to encourage his men. They were incensed at the Normans and charged forward, eager to avenge the victims. Overwhelmed by superior numbers, the Normans put up a brave fight, but they all lay dead after less than a minute, and their fresh blood flowed into the ground. Waltheof stood over the bodies, his eyes staring wildly, his chest heaving as he filled his lungs with air.

'Let's see if there are any more of that scum to teach a lesson,' Waltheof said and led his men through the smoky streets looking for more thieves.

On the other side of the minster, William's half-brothers, Odo and Count Robert, took control of their riotous soldiers, who were burning, raping, and looting. Because they had received no orders from their lord, William Warenne's men had maintained discipline and stood firm throughout. They had neither joined in the pillaging nor done anything to prevent it, but everyone noticed that no sooner had King William sworn to keep the peace than a riot had broken out. Now he had appeared, looking majestic astride his horse, and restoring order. As his bodyguard formed a protective ring around him, he rode toward the sound of the disturbance.

'What on earth are you doing?' he bellowed at the rioters.

'We heard shouting and jeering,' a soldier said. And then added, 'We thought the English were starting a fight, so we came to deal with them.'

'By burning down their houses? Don't just stand there; put out the fires.'

William, barking orders at his countrymen, restored order. His men began fighting fires rather than starting them, and soon Westminster became calm, but William was anxious that Londoners, only a mile downriver, did not discover what had happened.

'Will,' the king said to his friend, William FitzOsbern. 'Gather up anyone heading for London. Bring them back here immediately. We don't want the population storming up here to help their friends.'

FitzOsbern gathered his men and headed down the strand to intercept those who had fled the bloodshed. On Thorney Island, the rioters had their hands on everything in sight. They carried their loot and piled it up on a stolen cart. Sir William Warenne caught them in the act.

'I hope you know where that lot came from because you're putting it back.'

The soldiers halted, looking dismayed. One or two of them considered challenging him, but none did.

'You heard. Put it back.'

They began moving away from the cart.

'We haven't got all day,' Warenne said.

Whether it was the authority in his voice or the way he waved his sword, they responded to his order.

Now King William had quelled the trouble on the north side of the abbey. He went to investigate the south. He found the English earls had killed several looters and forced a few more into the river. They infuriated him. He eyed the corpses and demanded an explanation.

'Earl Waltheof. What's going on here?'

'When the crowd gathered around Westminster heard the congregation cheering,' the earl said. 'They joined in the approval of your assent to the throne. Your men reacted by running riot, killing and destroying everything in sight. All this within minutes of you swearing to defend your subjects. Not an impressive start.'

William looked down from his horse and saw undisguised anger in Waltheof's face. The earl's eyes, ablaze with fury, stared into his own. 'I'll take care of any trouble in my kingdom, Earl Waltheof,' the king said. 'Is that understood?'

Waltheof cast his gaze around, surveying a scene of carnage and destruction. Bodies lay dead on the ground where they had fallen. Several were monks. A man carried the body of his infant daughter down the street while his wife wailed by his side. Smoke and flames rose from buildings where ablaze. Survivors were attending to the wounded.

Waltheof turned to confront his king. 'You'll take care of any disorder, my lord. Yes, that's clear.'

'Guard your tongue,' William said.

Waltheof made no reply but stared up at William, his hand gripping the hilt of his sword. Then, looking downriver, Waltheof saw pillars of smoke climbing from the city. Grey columns merged with a thick covering of winter clouds to stop them from falling to earth.

'You'll need to take care of more disorder soon,' Waltheof said, nodding towards London.

William turned to see a cloud of smoke above London.

'Anyone with a horse, follow me,' he ordered his men.

Soldiers rushed for their mounts and rode off after their king down the smouldering street, their eyes stinging every step of the way. They met FitzOsbern on his return journey.

'I brought back all of those who had escaped the riots at Westminster, but I'm afraid the Londoners know about the trouble,' FitzOsbern said.

'We'd best get there immediately,' William said. 'Bring your men. William Warenne can look after Westminster.'

Baynard's Castle, the colossal timber structure that now dominated the west side of London, with its high motte even overlooking St. Paul's, as well as intimidating Londoners, gave a perfect view over and along the Thames. Westminster was visible, as was the smoke pouring from its buildings. When he first saw the blaze, a guard raised the alarm. Others rushed to join him and see for themselves what the commotion was about. Amongst them was Ralph Pomeroy, a man renowned as a fierce and merciless fighter, a glory hunter who had a keen eye for loot. He deserved his reputation, of which he was proud. Pomeroy was the fourth son of an impoverished Norman knight. As a youth, he had left home after a clash with his father, afraid and unable ever to return. Not for him, a comfortable castle of his own in Normandy. Not for him, plentiful lands from which to gather tithes and rents. He would not be returning to the arms of a loving family; he had no one and nothing.

Pomeroy had been fighting in Italy when he heard William's call. Thinking of England's abundant riches, he made the journey to Normandy, taking care to avoid his old home. He was delighted to enlist in the expedition.

Crowded on the fortification with the other soldiers, it was not a disaster unfolding Pomeroy saw but an opportunity.

'We can handle this,' Pomeroy said. 'Who will join me in teaching these Londoners a lesson?'

There was a resounding cry, and Pomeroy led the charge through the gate. Within two minutes, the only Normans remaining in the garrison were the castellan and half a dozen guards. The rest had scattered in all directions, bursting into houses and halls and even St. Paul's, robbing, killing, and burning at will.

With a group of six others, Pomeroy dashed straight to Cheapside. It was the jewellers' and goldsmiths' quarter, where there would be lots of loot and little resistance. With his gang, he burst into one workshop after another. It was always the same procedure; kick the door down, storm in, grab what took their fancy and kill anyone who tried to stop them. As soon as they saw Pomeroy, shopkeepers, tradespeople, and their families ran for their lives. They could see murder in his eyes. They recognised a killer on a spree.

Pomeroy burst into a goldsmith's and stumbled across a craftsman filling a sack. He could tell by the clinking sound it contained jewellery. Shocked, the jeweller froze. Pomeroy smiled as though at an old friend, took two paces towards him, and snatched the bag. Opening it, he could see, as he suspected, jewellery. Just a few pieces; there were only three. Pomeroy emptied the contents into his hands and gasped; he felt the jeweller's eyes transfixed on him. In his hand, he held two beautiful brooches. What caught his eye was a magnificent gold ring with a blue agate stone in its centre and four deep red triangular garnet stones around it.

Pleased with his booty, he slipped his catch back into the sack. The jeweller stared at the floor, tears rolling down his face. Pomeroy stepped outside, where a cacophony of shouts and screams greeted him. Along the length of the street, buildings were on fire, soldiers running rampant, locals fleeing, bloodied, broken bodies lying here and there. A woman ran past; her skirts hitched up to run faster. With desperation written large in her eyes, she crashed against his shoulder as she passed him. A lustful Norman soldier pursued her in a scene repeated across the city. Pomeroy chuckled to himself as he returned to the castle. There was little left worth stealing, and besides, with the flames licking at every building, it was getting dangerous to stay. He had all the loot he needed, so he would rejoin his men and set about suppressing the riots.

Chapter 4

Bondi woke up in the stables, baffled as to his whereabouts. Pain seared up through his head and ribs. His lips were sore, split, and swollen. He did not know the time but judged it to be late. He wondered why no one was about until he remembered it was Christmas Day and William's coronation.

His mouth felt coated in cow pat. Dry and baked. And he was hungry. Groaning, he rose to his feet and hobbled back to the Blue Anchor and Hild. As he made his way along the street, he could smell smoke, which was not unusual at this time of the year. But it smelled much more intense than usual. He found the door of the inn open and entered.

The landlord looked him up and down and nodded. 'Ale?' he said.

'Yes, and something to eat.'

Bondi took a stool, and the landlord handed him a cup of ale, a bowl of pottage, and some bread. Bondi began spooning up his meal as fast as he could, despite it stinging his split lips.

'Had a tough night,' the landlord said.

'You could say that,' Bondi replied, his mouth full of food.

'Those Frenchies created havoc after you left.'

'What happened?' Bondi said.

'Once they'd finished with Hild, they came down here and started a brawl. They got a good kicking, though. It wasn't enough for them, and they're at it again now.'

Bondi looked around and saw nothing.

'Not in here,' the landlord said, rolling his eyes. 'They're across town. A fellow came in and told there was rioting at the abbey and then outside both castles.'

'When was this?' Bondi said.

'As far as I know, it's still going on.'

Bondi threw a coin on the counter and rushed as fast as his bruised legs would carry him along the riverbank to the nearest castle. He hoped to see for himself. He was halfway to Baynard's Castle when a couple of Normans pursued by eight or more housecarls ran across the street in front of him.

'What's going on?' Bondi asked his old comrades.

'There's been a riot at Westminster, and when they saw smoke rising, the Normans here thought they'd have some fun, too,' one of the housecarls said, gasping for breath. 'They've torched buildings, robbed, raped, and murdered. We're going to make them pay for it.'

Another housecarl who was recovering from wounds, his arm in a sling but carrying an axe in his good hand, joined them.

'I'll have that,' Bondi said, snatching the axe from the housecarl's grasp.

'Hey, wait a moment,' the man said, but it was too late. Bondi was rushing down the street with after the other housecarls.

'After them,' Bondi cried, axe held high.

Through the narrow streets, the Normans ran, pursued by the angry English pack, hoping they could get back to the safety of the castle. But burning, fallen buildings blocked their way. Trapped, the Normans turned to face their enemy.

Bondi and his friends stepped forward, flailing their axes and advancing on the Normans. The ferocity of the attack overwhelmed the defenders, who began stepping back to avoid the brutal onslaught. The Normans, caught between the housecarls and the flames, decided attack was the best defence. One of them called out in French as they advanced.

Bondi was the first to strike, his axe splintering his opponent's shield before burying its head in his chest. The soldier screamed and fell to his knees, and Bondi struck him again. When he had finished, Bondi looked to see if the other Normans had met a similar fate. The housecarls left the residents to put out the fire, and followed by the mob, made their way to Baynard's Castle. They found the garrison safe behind their fortifications when they reached it, taunting the English and shooting crossbow bolts over the moat and into the crowd.

'What do we do now?' a housecarl asked Bondi.

No answer came to Bondi. The castle walls were eight feet high with pointed posts, and to reach them, he had to cross a moat; if successful, he would have to fight his way to another eight-foot-high wall of spikes and then climb a steep mound to get to the castle proper.

'Pull back out of range of their crossbows,' Bondi said.

The housecarls looked disappointed but ordered the crowds back, and they and Bondi discussed their options when they were out of range.

While Bondi was considering his next move, King William arrived with Edgar Atheling and the other English nobles and many of his men, the clatter of the horse's hooves drowning out the shouts from the crowd. Bondi realised now that his opportunity had passed him by, William had come to the rescue. The garrison was saved, trapped inside their defences by hundreds of armed men outside baying for their blood. The housecarl looked on as William barked orders at his new subjects, surrounded by his closest comrades. He was wasting his breath; none of them spoke a word of French. He took more forceful action. Bondi braced himself for more fighting.

But Sir William Malet, reading William's thoughts, addressed the crowd. 'Calm down. The king is here to restore order.

'Those of you who still have homes, go back to them—those who do not go to the great hall and take shelter there. There's nothing we can do here tonight. Please go home, to your friends, or the great hall.'

A begrudging calm fell over the crowd and the heat dispelled.

With Malet acting as interpreter, William addressed the angry crowd. 'Loyal subjects have no fear. Today the garrison has wronged you. I assure you I will investigate this matter and bring the perpetrators to justice. The guard will commit no further transgressions. I, your king, guarantee the peace. Now, do as Sir William said, celebrate this holy day as good Christians should.'

Muttering, the crowd dispersed.

William looked down at Edgar, who was by his side on a smaller horse. 'You see, Edgar. All you need is a firm hand,' he said with a smile.

A furious expression appeared on the Atheling's face. 'Where was your firm hand earlier? Your men on Thorney Island rioted and created mayhem here in London. There is death and destruction everywhere, and the town is still burning. Where was your firm hand then?'

'I'll thank you to remember your place, Edgar. You're talking to your king. Now that I've pacified the rabble, we'll go to the other castle before returning to Westminster.'

William led his men to the East Castle, and the English dispersed. Bondi and the other housecarls, rather than return to the barracks, went to the Blue Anchor Inn, where they knew they would be sure of a warm welcome and where they could consider their options.

William had restored calm, and that night, nervous Norman troops celebrated as best they could in their newly built forts while William and his chevaliers schemed in Westminster Palace. At the combined Christmas and coronation banquet, he discussed the day's events with his half-brothers, who sat beside him at the top table.

'Odo, Robert, I know you both have the same opinions as I do about these people. You saw how unruly they were today. An insurrection is likely to break out at any time.'

'You're right,' Odo said. 'It didn't help that there were housecarls there. I saw them myself, whipping the crowd up into a frenzy. Sort them out, and you'll have no further trouble.'

'What do you think, Robert?' William said.

'I agree with Odo, Will. There are only a few English nobles left,' he said. 'The only real opposition left now is the housecarls. They're a threat we need to remove.'

'We'll need a reason for that.'

'Some terrible act that they've committed,' Odo said.

'What could they have done that's so terrible?' Robert pondered.

William thought for a while. 'What's the most terrible crime a man could commit?' he said.

William's brothers exchanged glances.

'Murder,' Robert said.

'What about treason?' Odo said. 'Couldn't that swine who fought against you at Hastings be guilty of treason against their rightful king?'

'Your thinking is faultless, Odo,' William said.

'I think it harsh,' Robert said, but as he could offer no alternative, the brothers hatched a plan.

'Are you suggesting a trial, Will?' Robert said.

'No. Not at all. It would be too public, and it might drag on.'

'Why don't we go over tonight and finish the lot off?' Odo said.

'It's a good idea,' William said. 'But we won't have time.'

'We would serve the law, so to speak, if we executed them all,' Robert chipped in. 'The only question that remains is, when?'

'What's wrong with now?' William said.

'It's still Christmas!' Odo said. 'It'll be a pleasant surprise for them. We'll visit them tomorrow.'

'Time to sharpen your swords, my friends,' William said with a wicked grin.

Chapter 5

In London's Great Hall, Whitgar Guthrumson, a young thane, looked on while his countrymen discussed their predicament. The atmosphere was tense. People who, until yesterday, had enjoyed a comfortable life were now homeless.

'We want compensation,' a butcher said.

'They killed my husband,' a woman sobbed.

Amid the chaos and confusion, Whitgar sat at the end of the table on the dais, quietly observing the commotion. This was his first visit to the city, and he wondered if this was unusual. He lived on a farmstead on the Yorkshire moors and was familiar with York, but London impressed him. Although not much bigger, it was grander, the river broader, the port busier, and the rich wealthier than anything he had previously experienced.

Whitgar was attending the coronation on behalf of his father, Guthrum, who had suffered a severe injury, losing both hands at the Battle of Stamford Bridge. It was Whitgar's darkest secret that he had caused the injuries. It was a tragedy from which both were coping in their separate ways. Three months on, Guthrum was still in pain but would survive. Adjusting to his new impairment was difficult for him. Every day he and Whitgar were together, the young thane was reminded of the accident.

They had captured a Viking, left behind on a longship to cover his comrades' retreat. To make sure he completed his task, they cut off his feet. Whitgar seized the warrior, who begged to die but pleaded with him not to disturb his long blond hair. Whitgar, having never drawn blood, volunteered to behead the lad while his father held back his golden locks. The decapitation went drastically wrong. Whitgar closed his eyes before he struck the blow and loped off his father's hands. The terror. The guilt. It relieved him to be away from home, where he could escape his agonising shame.

Calls came from the floor to those on the dais. Everyone wanted an answer; they looked to Edgar Atheling, the youth recently proclaimed king by the Witan. Now granted the title of Earl of Oxford, he was the youngest and least experienced amongst other young inexperienced earls and thanes. Whitgar eyed Edgar and wondered what it must be like to be him. He showed no leadership, so Earl Waltheof took up the reins.

'William's first day as king, and look at what's happened. We need to act and show our strength. Let him know this sort of behaviour from his troops is not acceptable,' Waltheof said, addressing the assembly. 'We should punish the guilty and William compensate for the damage.'

Merleswein, the Shire Reeve of Lincoln and a close friend of King Harold, questioned Waltheof. 'You're proposing we approach William with a full list of the dead or injured. And a note of the damages. Do you suppose he'll press charges and hold trials?'

'That's what he promised at his coronation this morning,' Waltheof said. 'This is the first day of William's reign, and it's been a disaster. I'm sure he'll listen to reason. I say we should bring him to account.'

'Earl Waltheof, you're quite right,' Edgar said. 'Tomorrow, I'll approach him and demand he take action against the transgressors.'

'Is this acceptable to everyone?' he said.

There was a lot of mumbling, which Edgar took as assent.

'In that case, I suggest we continue with the festivities,' Edgar said.

'Whitgar,' Merleswein said. 'How are you? I didn't realise you were going to be here. Are you standing in for your father?'

'Yes, I am.'

'How is he now?'

'He's recovering, better than we had hoped.'

Many knew Guthrum suffered wounds at Stamford Bridge. Few realised Whitgar caused his father's loss.

'Good,' Merleswein said. 'Tell me, what's your impression of London?'

'It's not what I'd expected. The chaos, I mean. The coronation was impressive, at least until the fighting broke out.'

'I think there'll be more trouble,' Merleswein said.

'Why?'

'It's hard to say; just a feeling I have. Look at William's soldiers.

A cheer goes up from the abbey, and their immediate response is to fire buildings and start looting.'

'But the king got his troops under control eventually,' Whitgar said.

'We'll have to see how he reacts to our demands. If he's happy to punish transgressors and compensate the victims, I'll be pleased; I'll also be surprised.'

'So, how do we respond if William doesn't act in our favour?'

'There's not much we can do. I tell you, I sense danger here.'

'You too.' Merleswein turned to see Earl Waltheof had addressed him.

'Waltheof, do you have any ideas?'

'I think William deserves the benefit of the doubt. He established himself, and I see no reason for any more unpleasantness,' Waltheof said.

Whitgar noticed the look of disbelief on Merleswein's face.

'We'll see about that,' Merleswein said. 'In the meantime, I suggest we get the opinions of the other thanes.'

'That would be interesting,' Waltheof said. 'But ultimately, it's up to Edgar what we should do.'

With that, the conversation changed to something less contentious, and the mood lifted. While the English considered what plans to make, the Normans executed theirs.

Two riders from Westminster found London's gates shut, but the sentry allowed them in. Who would refuse the king's messengers? Through the dark streets, they closed the distance between themselves and the London castles. One headed for Baynard's Castle, the other for the East Castle.

Another messenger arrived at Baynard's Castle, where the guard stopped him.

'What's your business here?'.

'I have a message for Sir Ralph Baynard from the king.'

The gates opened, and he rode across the castle keep and dismounted. Two guards escorted him to the castellan, entertaining in the hall, a timber building that looked new and raw and smelled of fresh-cut wood. Primitive but effective. Soon stone would replace wood, and the complete structure would be far more secure, safe from the city it guarded.

'What's your business?' the castellan said.

'The king orders you to have all the men you can spare ready to march at dawn tomorrow. Sir William Malet will give you further instructions when he arrives.'

In response, Baynard snapped commands, and soldiers still celebrating Christmas fell into order, their celebrations cut short. The guards opened the gates early next morning and their comrades, many of them half-drunk, headed off towards the housecarls barracks at Berkhamsted.

Astride his horse, Sir William Malet peered through the darkness and mist of early morning streets. Behind him followed one hundred mounted soldiers, all fully armed and ready for battle. Just as night fell, they reached their destination, the housecarls barracks. In search of his target, Malet caught sight of a large wooden building. His comrades from the East Castle, led by Sir William Warenne, had already arrived and waited outside. The men merged into one body and crept forward to see the silhouette of the barracks against the stars.

Malet ordered his men to light their torches, and soon a hundred or more flames lit up the night as they surrounded the barracks. Quickly and quietly, the soldiers obeyed his orders. They looked devilish in the torchlight as they moved around with barely a sound. Ralph Pomeroy led one group. He had volunteered for the task, expecting to increase his standing with the king. He saw this as his last chance for glory; once he had dealt with the housecarls, there would be no more resistance from the English.

Malet checked the men were in position; a hundred fireflies gathered in the night. When he saw they were ready, Malet commanded, 'Fire the place.'

There was a strange beauty in it, as though the stars were falling to earth. Malet's men threw torches onto the barrack roofs, while Warenne's threw pitch tar. Despite the wintry conditions, the thatch was soon ablaze, flames soaring high into the darkness.

The housecarls awoke to the sound of men shouting and screaming while fleeing from the flames. Coughing and with eyes streaming, they poured out of the burning accommodation.

'Get some water quick,' one of them said. 'Do what you can to get our friends out!' The same person yelled, looking around desperately for something to quench the fire. It was then he saw a wall of armed men surrounding the building. For a moment, he froze, and his hesitation proved fatal.

Malet threw a spear at the housecarl, which pierced the centre of his chest. Gasping for life, he fell to the ground, mortally wounded, his blood seeping into the indifferent earth.

Soon flames engulfed the barracks, and housecarls, desperate to avoid being burned to death, ran for their lives. Battling their way through scorching fire and choking smoke, they staggered out into the cold fresh air, some coughing, others screaming.

'Don't let anyone escape,' Malet commanded.

The Normans stood shoulder to shoulder, surrounding the barracks, shields in front and spears at the ready.

'Here they come, cut them down,' Warenne ordered at the top of his voice.

Malet watched as housecarls charged towards the waiting spears. One man in flames raced towards him, and the knight cut him down with one blow from his sword. Malet stepped over him and prepared for the next as men screamed in agony all around him. Some were in the wooden building, trapped or too injured to escape; they would fall victim to the flames. Others had escaped and were now trying to get past the Normans. Most of them were unarmed and easy pickings for the Normans.

The ease with which his comrades killed the housecarls sickened Malet. He had seen these men in action at Hastings, and he knew they were fine warriors. It seemed like a scene from hell to him. Flames were licking the sky, smoke billowing heavenward, beams glowing red, black silhouettes running this way and that with no chance of escape. The screams and the burning flesh. The laughter of his comrades as they massacred the Englishmen. Saddened, he turned away. There was no honour for him in this battle.

Once more, the victors of Hastings inflicted terrible punishment on their enemy, this time ensuring the complete annihilation of the defenders at little cost to themselves.

The shouts and screams shattered the night and drew locals to their doors to see the trouble. The looks and threats they received from the soldiers soon satisfied their curiosity, and it was all Malet could do to prevent the soldiers from running amok for a second time.

'Make sure there are no survivors,' Warenne ordered, yellow flames reflecting in his eyes.

Three soldiers heard Warenne's command and picked up a gravely wounded housecarl. He was staggering about, blood pouring from a wound in his shoulder, tears streaming from his eyes. He had no clear idea where he was.

'Where are you going, friend?' said one of the Norman soldiers. 'Your home's that way.' And they hurled him back into the fire.

No one escaped from the barracks alive.

'Well done, Malet,' Warenne said as he approached his comrade. 'We did a fine job. The king will be pleased.'

'Yes, he would,' Malet said with a heavy heart. The butchery he had experienced that evening did not seem like the soldiering for which he had signed up.

'You have to admit; it's been a fine evening's work,' Warenne said.

Malet surveyed the surrounding scene. His brothers in arms were searching for valuables amongst the dead. Most of the housecarls had rushed out of bed, and whatever valuables they had were likely to be in the burning barracks, leaving scant pickings for the scavengers.

'We certainly accomplished what we set out to do,' Malet said.

'Let's go to the castle. It's time for a feast and a celebration. We've earned it,' Warenne said.

When the feeble sun finally rose that morning, it cast its watery light on the still-smoking remains of the housecarls' quarters. Smoke from the ruins curled upward, mingling with that from the cooking fires of kitchens. Here and there, amongst what remained of the barracks, flames flickered, and the stench of burned flesh mingled with the smell of charred meat to hang in the chilly winter air. Charred bodies lay amongst the ruins. Those souvenirs that the Normans had not carried off lay on the ground where they had fallen. Here and there, a shield lay intact, missed by fire and looter. A few helmets lay scattered about, as did the odd sword and axe. Later that day, scavengers would collect them before the locals cleared the bodies for burial.

Once the soldiers had departed, people emerged from the huddled houses. Through the streets, rumour spread about the atrocities. Many had heard the screams in the night, but they had been afraid to investigate. Some had witnessed soldiers rushing about, slashing and stabbing their prey. Others had seen men fall to the ground and left to die.

The following evening, when Warenne and Malet reported back to King William, a wave of comfort washed over him; now, he had resolved his problems. The Royal housecarls would no longer be a force with which to be reckoned, and naturally, any property they owned he could apportion to his men. William's spirits rose as another part of England went up in flames.

Chapter 6

By mid-afternoon, everyone in London knew of the housecarls' fate. People wondered if the future held the same in store for them. One of those unaware of the slaughter was Bondi Wynstanson. At the Blue Anchor, a small group talked animatedly at the bar.

'The Normans set fire to Berkhamsted barracks,' one man said.

'What?'

'They burned down the barracks, and no one's left alive,' the man said.

'Nobody? Are you sure?'

'I am. I'd make yourself scarce,' the man said, looking at the dragon tattoos on Bondi's arms. 'Go to the great hall. Somebody might help you.'

Bondi was still coming to terms with the news as he slinked across London's back streets. The town seemed divided. One half contained the English, sullen and resentful behind their walls. The other was a Norman city, composed of two motte-and-bailey fortifications. It was as if each part of the city held the other under siege. In this atmosphere, Merleswein called the thanes together in London's great hall. Bondi arrived just as the meeting started. It was a heated affair, acrimonious and loud.

Merleswein stood up. 'Thank you all for coming,' he said. Gradually, the noise abated.

'You're all aware of what happened the other night,' Merleswein said. 'We need to decide what we are to do next. I, for one, will leave London at the earliest opportunity. If you want to come with me or join me later in Lincoln, you're welcome. If you meet any housecarls, bring them with you.'

'What of Edgar and the earls? Why aren't they here?' an old thane said.

'William is keeping them close, but don't concern yourself about them. They will have word of what's happening, and they know they can join us if they can escape.'

'So, they are prisoners, then?' the old thane said. 'What are we going to do?'

'Those who are able should go to Lincoln. William won't bother us there. He would have to send his entire army to bring us back, and he won't do that. When we've reformed up there, we'll make plans.'

'What if we can't get away? Some of us have families and work here,' someone yelled.

'All I can do for now is offer hospitality in Lincoln. Everyone is welcome,' Merleswein said.

There was a general stir as people discussed what to do.

Merleswein took his seat and turned to Waltheof. 'Do you think many of them will accept my invitation?' he said.

'No. Not unless they've lost everything. Those who still have a home or a business will stay here, hoping it won't happen again. It'll be those who have nothing to lose who follow you.'

While they were talking, Bondi made his way over to them.

'Excuse me, my lord.'

Merleswein looked down at him from the dais. 'Bondi, isn't it?'

'That's right, my lord.'

'If I were you, I'd get as far away from London as possible.'

'I've considered that, so I'm going to Ireland.'

'Why Ireland?' Merleswein said.

'I was there with King Harold when I was a boy. I heard his mother, Lady Gytha and Edyth, his wife, were going there to join his sons. My guess is they'll be coming back with an army, so I thought I'd join them.'

'And avenge your fallen comrades?'

'Yes,' Bondi said. 'Do you know what happened?'

Merleswein told Bondi what he'd heard, how William's men had fired the barracks and killed those who tried to escape. 'It was nothing short of slaughter, Bondi.'

'William really is a bastard,' Bondi snarled. 'Why, though? What was the need for it?'

'He wanted to eliminate any danger, any chance of being overthrown.

You're lucky to be here. If you don't want to meet the same fate, I suggest you leave London at the earliest opportunity,' Merleswein said. 'Some other housecarls were here earlier, and they've all left town. Why don't you come to Lincoln with me?'

'Thank you for the offer, my lord. It's kind of you, but I'll be heading for Ireland,' Bondi said.

'Good luck to you, Bondi. Although I confess, I'd hoped you'd stay with us. How will you get to Ireland?'

'I'm going to Bristol where I should be able to get a ship.'

'I'd like you to do something for me, Bondi. Would you call in at Oakley on your way? My daughters are there, and I'd like to know if they're safe,' Merleswein said. 'Morwenna, the eldest, is expecting a baby. Come to think of it; she should have had it by now.'

As Merleswein looked concerned, Bondi agreed.

'Thank you, Bondi, for this. Her husband died at Hastings, and I haven't seen her since,' Merleswein lamented.

'I'll do my best to look in on her,' Bondi said. 'I'm leaving right away.'

'That's a good idea,' Merleswein said.

'Goodbye,' Bondi said, and as he turned to go, he saw a young thane at the end of the table. *I'm sure I've seen that face somewhere,* he thought, before continuing on his way. *Ah yes, I remember Stamford Bridge.*

Outside of Westminster, survivors of the disturbance were offering prayers to the dead, laid to rest by the south transept walls. Fifty bodies, men, women and a child lay in a common grave in the sanctified grounds of an abbey consecrated only the year before. Their only crime; to have been on Thorney Island at William's coronation.

Chapter 7

It was a cold, wet, miserable dawn in late December when Bondi emerged from the edge of a wood. Having been careful to avoid Norman patrols, he had been travelling through cold winter nights for nearly a week. The Normans had not yet occupied this part of the country, so it felt safe enough to venture out in daylight. A quarter of a mile away, he could see what appeared to be a farmstead. There was a hall about fifty feet long and, to either side, some smaller buildings. Beyond the farm, a river flowed across a lane. Beyond that, he could make out a small village. Bondi hoped this was the right place.

As he studied the farm, smoke made its way skyward; someone was up and about. Bondi made his way forwards. When he was about twenty feet from the main building, a woman emerged carrying a bucket, and somehow, she still looked graceful. She stopped dead in her tracks when she saw the stranger.

'Good morning,' she said with confidence, placing the pail down beside her. She looked at the stranger impassively. Over the last few months, she had grown used to outsiders.

'Good morning. I'm Bondi Wynstanson.'

'And I'm Morwenna Merlesweinsdaughter. What do you want here?'

'I'm on my way to Bristol,' the housecarl said, quite taken aback. The woman was a vision, tall and slim and lovely. Her eyes were full of confidence, courage and pride, and she moved with a grace he would never have expected from a farm girl. He could see beauty and something more besides, something beyond simply good looks. He stood there, staring at her in wonder. She consumed him. She had the most winning smile, warm and welcoming, and a northern accent like her father.

The woman observed the gangly stranger before her; he looked pitiful, sodden, bedraggled, and cold. What also caught her attention was the hand axe he carried in his belt. He was not the sort of person she expected to come begging at her door.

'I've just come from London, and your father asked me to look in on you and your sister,' Bondi said.

'How is he?' she said, looking surprised.

'He is as well as can be expected, given the events of the last few weeks.'

'I think you'd better come in,' she said gently.

Morwenna led the way into the hall, where Bondi was glad to get out of the cold and feel the welcome warmth of the fire. He felt at home when he smelled the smoke and soot that coated the roof and rafters. Dried herbs hung from a roof beam, scenting the air. Benches lined the walls, and at one end of the hall, screened off by drapes, he could hear someone moving around. At the other end of the hall were three looms, each with a partially finished piece of work attached.

'Here, take this,' Morwenna said, handing Bondi a cup of beer.

The housecarl accepted it, glad to drink something other than water. When Bondi had finished gulping most of it down, Morwenna asked him of news of her father.

'The last time I saw him, he was well and in good spirits.' Bondi said. 'You said your name is Morwenna. Don't you have a sister, Elfwyn, who's here to help you out?

'Yes, this is my farm, and she came to help me when I gave birth to my new baby.' She paused for a moment, then in hushed tones said, 'I have a little boy, but he'll never see his father. You probably knew him, Godric, Shire Reeve of Buckingham. I named the baby after him.'

'I didn't know him, but he had a great reputation. He was quite a character by all accounts,' Bondi said. 'So, you're his wife, or rather, widow?'

'Yes, that's right,' she said, a look of sadness appearing in her eyes.

Bondi studied her for a moment. She stood tall at five feet nine inches, and her long brown hair drawn back behind her ears stressed her perfectly oval face. She had all the bearing of a high-born lady. There was also something delicate about her movements that somehow reminded him of a bird. He could not help but notice the gold ring on her finger, inscribed with her name and the lamb of God. He thought it odd that she should have a Norse rune on a pendant hanging around her neck. Feeling a little overwhelmed in the company of such a high-born lady, short of something to say, he said, 'You ought to know your father has left London and is returning to Lincoln.'

'What? Why?' Morwenna said, shocked.

'After Hastings, I went to London and helped defend the city against the Normans, but they got the better of us, and now William is king. His men massacred the housecarls, my friends and comrades in their barracks, and burned them down. None of them survived.'

Morwenna looked horrified. 'How did you survive?' she said.

'I wasn't sleeping in the barracks that night. It's the only reason I'm still alive.'

'Oh,' Morwenna said.

'William's now looking for the thanes who fought with Harold.' Bondi continued, 'Which is why your father has gone back to Lincolnshire and why I'm heading for Bristol. I'm hoping to cross the sea to Ireland.'

'So, why aren't you going to Lincoln?'

'I'm going to Ireland to see if King Harold's sons need another housecarl.'

She looked appalled. 'You can't do that.'

'Why not?'

'From what you tell me, you're needed here in England, now. You could stay here for a while. There aren't enough men, and there's lots of work to do. You'd be very welcome,' she smiled at him. 'And besides, you'd have time to think things over.'

'Perhaps for a little while,' said Bondi, looking around at the bucolic surroundings. 'So, this is your farm?'

'Yes, it is now.'

'It must be hard for you with a new baby?'

'It is.Godric has gone. But come, let's get you some food.'

'You must have known Godric's reputation?' Morwenna said. 'I think the word is colourful. He could be quite the scoundrel.'

Having brought in a tray crammed with drinks and a loaf of bread, the maid was busy serving them when Morwenna said this, and Bondi noticed the flicker of a smile on her face. After she left, Morwenna offered, 'Godric had a soft spot for her. He always said it was because she was so good at embroidering with gold.

Bondi was not sure how to respond. 'I only saw him a few times at the Witan,' he said. Images of Godric at the Witangemot flashed through Bondi's mind, quickly replaced by those from Hastings. He felt awkward and grew quiet.

Bondi rarely talked to women, let alone a lady. Unsure of what to say next, he stuck a large piece of bread in his mouth, which gave him an excuse not to speak. Morwenna, sensing his awkwardness, allowed him to chew a little while before asking how he became a housecarl.

'I'm from West Gloucestershire,' he said. 'I grew up on the banks of the River Severn. When I was a little boy, the Welsh raided my village, killed my family and left me orphaned. Earl Sweyn adopted me for a while.'

'Ah, King Harold's brother.' Morwenna nodded sagely when she remembered. She was familiar with the late earl's reputation; dreadful.

'King Edward exiled Earl Sweyn and his family. That's when I met King Harold, although he was still the Earl of Wessex then. Anyway, he took me with him to Ireland. I stayed with him when Earl Sweyn didn't come back from his pilgrimage to the Holy Land. Earl Harold trained me to be a housecarl, and here I am. He was more than a king to me, was Harold. He was like a father. Now I'll never be able to repay him,' Bondi sighed.

Morwenna knew enough about housecarls and their code of honour to know Bondi would feel shame and disgrace for not saving his lord.

'I'm sure you did all that you could,' she said.

'I wasn't with him on the battlefield. He had sent me down to Devon to gather the fyrd and lead them to Senlac. The battle was still raging, but we'd arrived too late. We killed a lot of Normans in a gully, but we couldn't get to the shieldwall on the ridge in time.'

'Would it have made a difference?' she said.

'That's the pity of it. I think it would,' Bondi said, staring at the floor. He was silent for a moment before he raised his head and looked around the hall. Against the wall stood Godric's fine oak chair, still awaiting its owner's return. From beams hung three shields, and half a dozen bows lay across a couple of supporting hooks. Bondi wondered if they were Godric's.

'What are you thinking?' Morwenna said.

'I was just wondering about the bows,' he said.

'The two big ones are Godric's; the smaller ones belong to my sister and me,' she said.

'What do you use them for?'

'My father said we should always be able to defend ourselves. We can handle spears and swords too.'

'Real shieldmaidens,' Bondi mused.

'If required,' Morwenna said, with a hint of steel in her voice.

'We could have done with you at Hastings.'

'Perhaps we'd have won.'

'Perhaps.'

'You don't think I'd be any good, do you?' she said.

'I didn't say that.'

'But you think it.'

'Well...'

Morwenna looked stern as she gazed out of the window, stood up, crossed the hall in a few paces and took the bows and quivers off their hooks.

'Let's see about that, shall we?' she said, hurling Godric's bow for Bondi to catch. 'The rain's stopped now. Come on.'

She strode outside looking for a target, seeing a thrall heading to the barn, and called to him.

'Fetch me something to shoot at, Sebbi.'

'Yes, my lady,' the man said before wandering off to find some targets.

An awkward silence fell between the two of them while both examined their bows, waiting for Sebbi. A few minutes later, he reappeared with a three-legged stool and battered skep that had seen better days. Sebbi placed the skep, a beehive resembling an upturned basket, onto the seat just before a gate post. Bondi knew he had done this before.

'We'll shoot at that,' Morwenna said.

'Do you want to go first, or should I?' she said.

'You can go first,' Bondi said, wondering if he might have made a mistake.

As he looked on, Morwenna strode thirty yards away from the target. Bondi found himself transfixed by her purposeful walk and the gentle sway of her hips. Morwenna stopped, turned, looked at the skep, and then at Bondi. She placed an arrow on the bow and drew the bowstring with expertise. In an instant, the arrow flew across the courtyard and hit the centre of the skep, driving it back into the gatepost. She smiled at Bondi mischievously.

'Show me what you can do, Bondi,' she said.

Bondi took his place by her side and prepared to shoot as he had hundreds of times before, but this time felt edgy. Bondi drew back the bowstring, aimed and shot all in one movement. His arrow landed just beside Morwenna's.

Morwenna nodded to the thrall. 'Are there any more old skeps about?' she said.

'There are a few, my lady,' Sebbi said.

'Get them and some stools,' Morwenna said.

A few minutes later, Sebbi returned laden down with three stools and as many skeps. Dutifully, he placed a skep onto a stool in front of a fence post.

Turning to Bondi, Morwenna said, 'Let's step back a few paces, shall we?'

Morwenna stepped back ten yards and shot all four skeps in a matter of moments. Turning to Bondi, she smiled mockingly, making him blush.

'Your turn now, Bondi,' Morwenna said.

Bondi shot four arrows but missed with the second.

'Three out of four isn't bad. Would you like another go?' Morwenna said.

'I'm not an archer. I told you that before,' Bondi said. His pride hurt.

'Neither am I,' Morwenna said. 'Even so, you're probably much better with an axe than I'll ever be.'

'Yes,' he said and pulled his axe from his belt. He threw it hard at the skep, splitting it in half.

'And it's one thing to shoot skeps and another to shoot men,' he said.

'You're right,' she said, sensing she had hurt his feelings. 'It's a different thing altogether. So, tell me, would you like something to eat now?'

'Thank you, my lady?'

'Then you'd better come with me,' she said, as she made for an outbuilding. 'We can have breakfast, and you can meet Elfwyn.'

Bondi collected his axe, while Sebbi collected the arrows. When Bondi and Morwenna entered the hall, they found Wulthryth, the maid, preparing breakfast.

'Wulthryth, Bondi will stay with us for a while,' Morwenna said.

Before the maid had time to reply, the curtain at the end of the hall rustled loudly. Bondi turned to see a woman appear like a vision, pulling the curtain aside. Her dress swayed as she approached him. She had fire in her eyes, just like Morwenna.

'So,' she said. 'You're Bondi Wynstanson, and you'll be staying with us for a while, I understand.'

'He'll be with us for a few days, Elfwyn,' Morwenna said.

Elfwyn looked Bondi up and down and gave him a broad smile.

Bondi said, 'Hello,' it was all he could think of to say.

He found Elfwyn beautiful too, but not so much as Morwenna, who was taller and even though they had the same good looks, Elfwyn's face was a little sharper, and she looked slightly less fierce than her sister's. She wore a gold ring in the same style, except her name was inscribed on it. He also noticed that she had a silver algiz protection rune hanging from a leather cord around her neck, identical to Morwenna's. Bondi had seen quite a few old Norse pendants, but none like these. It reminded him of a crucifix except that the arms were angled upwards rather than horizontal. On the end of each was a wolf's head, set in a fierce growl, and across the front of the algiz was an abstract pattern of lines. It fascinated him.

'Well?' Bondi heard Morwenna say. 'You are staying, aren't you?'

'Oh yes, my lady. Yes.'

Chapter 8

Far away from London, in Merleswein's hall in Lincoln, the Shire Reeve entertained his guest and newfound friend, Whitgar, who had travelled with him.

'Waltheof's wrong about William, you know. He's going to be trouble. I don't think it's a good idea to wait for Edgar to decide what we should do. We need decisive action right away. I know we've lost many good men, but there aren't many Normans. The sooner we shift them, the easier it will be,' Merleswein said. 'What do you think, Whitgar?'

Whitgar had no idea. 'First the Coronation day massacre and then the housecarls. Things seem to get worse every day. What can we do, though?'

'We have to resist. We can start in the north where we are strong and move south from there.'

'I thought William had appointed an Earl in Bernicia,' Whitgar said.

'You mean that worm, Copsig? We'll show William he can't appoint the highest bidder to whatever position he chooses. Copsig was Tostig's man and loathed in Northumbria. He has to go, Whitgar. Don't you think?'

'You're right, Merleswein. He's not the man for us.'

'Fortunately, we have a man. Oswulf Eadwulfson is the rightful Earl,' Merleswein said.

'What about Morcar?'

'Forget about that fool. After the shambles at Fulford and his failure to turn up at Hastings, he deserves everything he gets. No, Oswulf's our man. We need to get word to him that he has our support to move on Copsig. Once he's succeeded, then we'll take the rest of Northumbria. After that, Mercia will be ours. I need you to take him a message.' The expression on Merleswein's face told Whitgar this was an order, not a request.

'But I don't know where he is, and Northumbria is a big place.'

'He'll be in Hexham, waiting for you. You'll have no trouble finding it; some of my men will travel with you,' Merleswein said. 'I know you're a home bird and love your life on your farm, but you won't be away from home for long.'

A week later, Whitgar was in the high hills of the Pennines with Oswulf Eadwulfson, the former Earl of the northern part of Northumbria called Bernicia. They made their way to the frozen northeast, and now the raiding party looked across the bleak grey moor towards Newburn-on-Tyne. There, in the comfort of his hall, Oswulf's old enemy, Copsig, was feasting.

Oswulf, descended from a long line of Bamburghs, hated Copsig. Once the despised underling of Tostig Godwinson, Copsig had somehow inveigled King William into making him the new Earl of Bernicia. William had seen no need to consult Oswulf, the rightful earl. The deposed Oswulf had found no difficulty in raising a large band of loyal followers to help him in his mission to redress the natural order of the north. Whitgar's reassurances from Merleswein came as welcome news; it meant upstarts like Copsig would have no power. Northumbria differed from the south, and plenty of people wanted it to stay that way. Up here, Northumbrians did things their way; true, there might be a blood feud, but that was northern business. If outsiders interfered, the Northumbrians would forget their differences, and the squabbling northerners would band together and, like wolves, turn against them.

Copsig knew the ways of the north. When William made him earl, his first action was to send a hunting party after Oswulf. They had been searching for two months now and still no luck, but late on this cold mid-March evening, Copsig had forgotten Oswulf and was enjoying a feast in his hall overlooking the River Tyne. What could be better? A fire blazed in the hearth. The company was loud with raucous laughter, plentiful food and drink, and musicians in fine form playing a lively tune on their lyres while guests sang bawdy songs and told lewd riddles.

Copsig laughed his booming belly laugh and drank heartily from his goblet. He had returned from King William's court after a long and arduous three-hundred-mile journey. Being an earl was still a novelty. His friends considered him able and wise, but his most outstanding talent was holding an excellent feast. There had been plenty since his arrival, and this one was as enjoyable as the others.

While all the townsfolk and a few from further afield enjoyed the merrymaking, outside freezing rain-lashed buildings and wind howled through streets. It was no night for travellers. As the wind ripped across the river in the darkness, a band of twenty-five riders crossed at the ford, freezing and swift. Unheard and unseen, protected by the angry storm, the war band made their way up the north bank. Copsig's hall was not far away now. Whitgar marvelled at the efficient way Oswulf led and could not help but wonder how many times they had done this before.

Gradually, as they closed the distance, the men of darkness could hear music and laughter bursting from the unsuspecting hall. Whitgar wondered if there would be a guard. They dismounted and, in the shadows, made their way to the town gates.

'They're barred,' one of Oswulf's men said after trying the gates.

'Who's there?' A voice called from above.

Whitgar saw Oswulf look up to see a grizzled old man holding a lantern looking down at them from his elevated sentry post.

'My friend, we are a party of traders who lost our way on the moors in this vile storm,' Oswulf said. 'I beg you, as one good Christian to another, for shelter, just for the night.'

'Where are your horses? If you're traders, you'd have horses.'

'One of my men is looking after them.'

'Why didn't you ride up on them?'

'We didn't want to alarm anybody.'

'Then why are you all wearing swords?'

He might be old, but his eyesight's all right, Oswulf thought.

'In case of outlaws,' Oswulf said. 'You can't be too safe these days. The moors are crawling with them.'

'You're right there. That's why you're not coming in.'

'Ugh!' The gatekeeper groaned as a blow struck the back of his head. There was a clatter as the gate opened.

'Welcome to Newburn,' said Torsten, Oswulf's second in command, as he opened the gates. 'All are welcome here.'

Oswulf grinned as he led his men towards the hall. Like the others,

Whitgar drew his sword and stood by Oswulf as his war band surrounded the building, keeping their eyes on doors and windows alike. He could hear the merriment inside, and through the gaps in the hall's wooden sides, he could see the bright golden light of an inviting fire. Gripping his weapon firmly, he wondered if he would have to use it.

Oswulf nodded to one of his warriors, who immediately wrenched the hall door open. His men burst in, swords at the ready. For an instant, there was no reaction, and then mayhem broke loose. Six big hounds raced towards the intruders, barking and growling while the men rose from the benches. But they would offer only token resistance as the finest fighting men were out on the moors, looking for Oswulf.

Copsig shouted at the dogs to be quiet. Then, recognising Oswulf, asked, 'Oswulf, my old friend. What brings you out on a night like this?'

Oswulf brandished his sword threateningly, and one dog went for him.

'Down Ingolf! Down, you stupid mutt,' Copsig said. 'Get back here.'

'Send them outside,' Oswulf said.

'In this weather?' Copsig wanted them where they could defend him if need be.

'As long as they stay in the corner,' Oswald said.

'They'll be no trouble,' Copsig replied.

Whitgar eyed the gathering. *They're all too old, too young, or too feeble to give any trouble.* He relaxed; Oswulf appeared to know what he was doing.

The hall was much like any other, a rectangular wooden structured building sixty feet long. Crook beams supported the thatched roof, which in turn were held up by six strong oak posts running three either side. In the middle, a warm, welcoming fire blazed in the hearth. Whitgar guessed the wood must have come from the orchard because of the scent of apple-filled the air. The warmth was welcome, as was the light it provided to reveal the rosy-cheeked faces of the merrymakers who had now taken their places. The corpulent earl was standing to the left on the dais with family and local nobility. Unlike the others, he did not look merry. He wore his thinning grey hair tied back in a single plait, which looked stuck on his head like a worn-out old hat.

'Good evening,' Oswulf said, holding his sword skyward, the blade resting casually on his shoulder.

'Who do think you are bursting into my hall like this?' Copsig asked with as much authority as he could muster.

'Who do you think you are to call yourself, Earl of Bernicia? And this hall that I've burst into, it's rightfully mine, don't you agree?'

'Look Oswulf...' Copsig said, trying to sound conciliatory.

'Earl Oswulf, to you.'

While the confrontation heated up, Whitgar noticed Copsig looking fearful; sweat formed his forehead. Many armed warriors accompanied Oswulf. Copsig would find escape extremely difficult. Whitgar observed Copsig looking at his wife, her face full of dread, and then glance at his two teenage sons and daughter, who looked worried too. He reasoned Oswulf would not harm them. He also saw how Copsig kept glancing longingly at the nearest door, hoping he could get away.

'Why don't you and your men join us, Oswulf?' Copsig said. 'You've had a long and difficult journey. Warm yourselves by the fire, take a drink with us and partake in our feasting. It would be a pleasure to have your company. I'm sure we can clear up any misunderstandings in a friendly fashion.'

Copsig indicated that people make room on the benches for their guests and instructed the servants to lay more food and drink on the tables. There was a lot of shuffling as Copsig's folk made space.

'Thank you, Copsig. I'll take my usual seat,' Oswulf said.

Copsig was unharmed and so humoured his enemy.

Oswulf sheathed his sword and told his followers to do the same. Copsig's men were unarmed, so there was little chance of trouble. Casually, Oswulf walked over to Copsig, who told a servant to bring a seat for their guest. Oswulf sat down in the earl's chair and made himself comfortable. When everyone was seated, he signalled to the servants to serve. The cupbearers were already pouring wine into the newcomers' silver goblets.

A maid appeared at Oswulf's side and laid a silver goblet, dish, and a knife and spoon in front of him. The opulence on display surprised Whitgar. Copsig was a man of considerable wealth. And observing the look of avarice in Oswulf's eyes as he studied the silverware, he guessed Copsig's days were numbered.

'A toast to our visitors,' Copsig said, still on his feet with his goblet held high.

Oswulf rolled his eyes but got up, as did everyone.

'Good health and happiness.'

'Good health and happiness,' Oswulf said.

One and all drank the toast and then sat down, all except Copsig, who threw his drink in Oswulf's face with one hand and with the other grabbed a torch from its wall fitting. He then smashed his goblet over the head of the startled Oswulf before leaping over the table and hurling the torch over the fire, setting the straw at the far end of the hall ablaze. He was agile for a stocky man.

'Get him!' Oswulf bellowed, wiping wine and blood from his eyes.

Copsig ran through the hearth, kicking out embers at Whitgar and Oswulf's men, shouting, 'Kill! Kill!' to his dogs.

Before Oswulf's man by the door could react, Copsig struck him in the face with his goblet, then disappeared outside, screaming, his leggings on fire. The hall was in chaos as people struggled to put out the burning threshings, and Oswulf's warriors dealt with Copsig's vicious hounds. Oswulf, blood pouring down his face from his attack, was hot on the heels of Copsig, who had burst out into the chilly night air and was racing towards the town gates.

'Hey, you,' a voice Copsig did not recognise called out. Wanting to put as much distance as he could between himself and the mystery voice, the earl changed direction and made for the church of Saint Michael and All Angels in the hope Oswulf would respect the sanctuary of God's house. Hearing a disturbance behind him, he ran even faster as his enemies closed on him.

'Get back here if you know what's good for you,' a voice yelled in the darkness.

Copsig had a talent for knowing what was good for him, and forty days' sanctuary seemed the best option. He would have time to plan, or perhaps a rescue party might arrive. Reaching the church, he discovered the priest had left the door unlocked. Copsig entered, slamming the door behind him, his troubles over, at least for a while; he relaxed a little and then yelled as pain shot through his legs. He looked down to discover his leggings were aglow, so he rushed over to the font and dowsed them with holy water, a cool salve to ease the pain.

That's better, he said to himself.

Seeing the big wooden cross by the altar, Copsig grabbed it and groaned as he dragged it across the floor, jamming it up against the door. To give his barricade more strength, he lugged the heavy stone font. He smirked as he heard the clamour of Oswulf's hunting party, too late to catch their prey.

'Let us in, Copsig,' he heard Oswulf say.

'Earl Copsig to you, Oswulf,' he said, grinning.

Memories in the north of one of Earl Tostig's housecarls, Barcwith, were still fresh. He had chased an outlaw into St Cuthbert's Church and ordered his followers to drag him out. It had been just over a year since the reckless housecarl had chased Alden-Hemel into the church where the brigand intended to claim sanctuary. As Barcwith had screamed at his men to go in and get him, God appeared to strike him down. He fell to the ground writhing around and died horribly three days later. To the onlookers, this was undoubtedly a sign. Whitgar included. It fascinated him to see what would happen as more and more people gathered behind Oswulf. Many were secretly hoping the Almighty might strike down another offender. Dreading violence in his beautiful church, father Sabert, the local priest, came running.

Breathless, he said to Oswulf, 'You can't go in there. It's a house of God. Earl Copsig has sanctuary.'

Oswulf stared hard at the priest as if he were a madman. 'Do you really think I'm going to wait forty days?' he asked.

'Burn the place down. That'll shift him,' Oswulf ordered his men.

Whitgar was aghast. He could not believe Oswulf, or anyone else for that matter, would dare force his way into a house of God.

'No. Please, no,' begged Father Sabert.

'Get him out of here,' Oswulf said.

Father Sabert shouted abuse at Oswulf as his men dragged him away.

'What are you waiting for? Burn the church down,' Oswulf said.

As ordered, Oswulf's followers set fire to the thatched church roof, and soon the place was ablaze. Whitgar and the Merleswein's men stood by and watched; sacrilege was a crime they were unwilling to commit for an earl who was not their lord.

Coughing and spluttering, Copsig emerged from the church to find Oswulf waiting for him. The earl was wearing no chain mail for protection; only half an hour ago, he had been safe by his hearth with friends and family and had no need. Escaping from the flames of the burning church, he ran straight onto Oswulf's sword. Whitgar could only stare in shock as the doomed earl screamed his last, clutching his spilling guts as he fell to the ground. All eyes turned to Oswulf to see him struck down by God.

'Why's everybody looking at me?' Oswulf said.

No one said a word; they carried on staring at Oswulf and then at the sky, hoping a thunderbolt would crash down. The sound of a small group of people running carried towards them, and their attention turned towards the noise.

'It's Copsig's family making a run for it,' Torsten said.

Oswulf laughed. 'It must be a family trait. Leave them be; my quarrel was with Copsig, not his wife and children.'

Now the priest, having slipped away from his captors, confronted Oswulf. 'What about my church? You've burnt down a house of God.'

Remembering the huge fine Earl Tostig had to compensate for the killing of Alden-Hamel on sacred ground, Oswulf said to the priest, 'Father, have no fear. I will have your church restored to its former glory, and you'll have a new roof. I'll have all damage repaired, and I'll pay for all the craftsmen and their materials.'

Father Sabert, shaking, had no idea what to say. 'Thank you. Thank you, my lord,' was all he managed.

'Think nothing of it. Let's get back to the celebration, shall we? Once you've dealt with Copsig, of course. One of my men will help you.'

'Come on, you lot,' Torsten said. 'We're celebrating the arrival of your rightful lord, Earl Oswulf.'

Motionless, the townsfolk stood and stared.

'Come. A feast awaits us,' said Oswulf with a smile as he led his men back, and the locals followed, talking in hushed groups about what had just transpired.

Back in the hall, guests and townsfolk alike took up their places.

'Drink up! Eat up! This is a celebration. Enjoy yourselves,' Oswulf said.

As though Copsig had never existed, the feast continued quietly at first, but soon the chatter increased, and the atmosphere changed. Whitgar was pleased it had all gone so well. Tomorrow he would leave for home knowing that he had played a part in overthrowing one of William's first appointments. But first, he would travel to Lincolnshire to break the news to Merleswein. They had taken the first step on the road to William's downfall. He knew the story of Oswulf's exploit would spread through taverns and marketplaces. It was as if he had helped reclaim a bit of England, albeit in the far north. It was a victory. But where Oswulf had led, would others follow?

Chapter 9

Three months had passed since William's coronation and six since he had last been in the old Roman port of Pevensey, on the Sussex coast. Here, on a glorious spring day, he was preparing to leave for Normandy. Looking around the busy harbour that nestled beneath its new castle, he could see, after all these years, its tall stone walls still standing proud and guarding the port.

Unaware of events in the north, he was confident his kingdom was safe and secure. But security needs surety, so he took the precaution of taking hostages. William took Edgar Atheling, Earls Edwin, Morcar and Waltheof into his custody to ensure there was no focal point for English rebels to rally around. Realistically, there was no chance of uprising; two hundred king's thanes and further two thousand middle-ranking thanes had died in battle, many of them replaced by Normans. William had confiscated the land of the fallen and redistributed it to his followers. In doing so, he had been careful not to fall into the same trap as King Edward; there were no large earldoms that could become power bases to challenge his own. This policy denied the wives and sons of those who fought with Harold their inheritance. Only women who entered into marriage with the new landlords had a hope of keeping their land. He had granted compact blocks of estates for a select number of his most ardent supporters and family.

William felt deep satisfaction when he saw throngs of men preparing for the voyage, like him, heading back to their homes in Normandy and Brittany. They had performed their duty to their lord and were now free to leave with their rewards. Amongst those returning on this day was his comrade, Sir William Malet.

'It's a good day for a crossing,' said Malet. Like all of those going home, he was in good spirits.

King William looked out across the sparkling sea and felt the gentle breeze on his face.

'I agree,' he said as he surveyed the harbour and added, 'It seems an age since I arrived in England.'

Malet thought back. It seemed like a long time since William had fallen over head first when he first set foot on English soil.

'You know, it's good to see more new arrivals coming over from Normandy,' William said. 'I could have made use of them earlier. We'll need settlers now that the fighting is over.'

William, his friends, and hostages stepped aboard the Mora, the very same ship Matilda, his beloved wife, had constructed especially to carry him to England and victory. The craft had been faithfully waiting for him throughout the winter. Most of the invasion fleet lay in pieces on the seabed or the beach.

'And look at me now, fulfilling my destiny. I am a king. I bow to no man,' William said with pride.

'Did you ever bow to any man?' Malet asked.

'Only kings. But now I don't even have to do that.'

William boarded the vessel and turned to greet his fellow passengers. 'Don't you think she's wonderful? A gift from my wife, Matilda. We called her the Mora.'

William let the name sink in. Mora was an old Latin term meaning a culpable delay in fulfilling a legal obligation. Ordinarily, it would sound like an odd name for a ship, but its meaning was not lost on the English prisoners. It was a reference to a promise William claimed King Harold had made under oath. The outraged expression on his hostage's faces when he informed them amused him.

Standing on the ship's stern, William continued to survey the scene. It was one of those beautiful March days, that hint of the summer to come; clear skies, bright golden sun and a light salty breeze coming off the sea as seagulls circled in the sky – perfect. He visualised his landing just six months before in his mind's eye. He thought of his first attempt at crossing the Channel, an abysmal failure. The second attempt was a success, but when he had found himself alone at sea, his fleet lost over the horizon, he had never felt panic like it. But he had made the crossing, he had conquered, and now he was king. He congratulated himself on his magnificent accomplishment and wondered, *is there anything I can't do?*

His eyes scanned the waves, and how the light played on the silvery water fascinated him. An observer might have taken him for an old seafarer looking for a change in the weather, yet he could not tell if the tide was coming in or going out. Nevertheless, he prided himself that the spirit of the Norsemen lived on in him and, on this occasion, he looked forward to putting to sea.

'My friends, now's the time to set sail,' William said to his fellow travellers as they found somewhere to sit. Above them, on the stern, was a brightly painted carving of a child holding a horn, keeping watch over them all. It was a strange and eerie sight.

None of William's 'guests' had been to Pevensey, and the first time any had crossed the sea, including Archbishop Stigand, who had never even travelled to Rome to collect his pallium. He looked far from happy as he clambered onto the ship.

'Help the Archbishop, someone,' William said.

One of the crew stepped forward and gave Stigand a helping hand as he staggered, stumbled and swayed onto the Mora.

'It's your first sea crossing, is it not, Archbishop?' William asked.

'It is,' was all Stigand had to say.

William smiled in reply.

The king had arranged for three of the ships in the harbour to receive the treasure he intended to take home. There was loot from England's halls and churches returning as trophies. Another seven ships would sail with him, returning soldiers to Normandy. Once the tide was right, they set sail for Honfleur and then up the Seine to Rouen, where Matilda and the court awaited.

The Channel crossing, unusually calm, had buoyed the triumphant king as he led the flotilla up the Seine. People turned out to offer their lord the most tumultuous welcome he had ever received. Spectators crammed the riverbanks, old and young alike. Everyone in Normandy knew of their Duke's return, and they all wanted to join the celebrations. As word spread through the towns and villages along the river, more people came out to welcome William. Bunting decorated houses and streets, and musicians played. Everywhere was like a festival. And there was cause for celebration; change was in the air. Their Duke was now a great man and Normandy a formidable force.

Rouen was in raptures when William finally arrived. The town was bursting with spectators who had turned out to catch a glimpse of their lord and his hostages, but none so glad to meet him as Matilda, who welcomed her husband with open arms as he stepped from his ship, a happier man than he had ever been. The sunlight catching on gold threads of shot silk, he wore before his wife for the first time, the crown of England.

'Matilda, my love. It seems so long.'

He held her in his arms and kissed her, making her blush. A public demonstration of his feelings for Matilda was a rare thing, and the crowd roared its approval. His children approached their beloved father for an embrace. The five of them clamoured around him, hugging and looking up to him, their hearts bursting with love and pride. Robert, the oldest and now nearly a man, looked him almost straight in the eye.

Above the din, William smiled, turned, and said, 'Meet our guests.'

A tottering Stigand made his ungainly way off the ship and onto the quayside. It amused the crowd when his mitre slipped to one side and with it tipped at a jaunty angle, and he bowed to the Duchess.

'Welcome to Normandy, Archbishop Stigand,' Matilda said, trying hard to surpass a laugh. Feeling William shaking, she glanced to see his shoulders moving up and down. She elbowed him in the ribs, but that just seemed to make matters worse.

'Allow me to introduce you to Earl Waltheof,' William said with a slight giggle.

Meeting the earl was a shock to Matilda. He conformed to her ideal of what an Englishman should look like; tall, with long blond hair and a handsome appearance. He reminded her of Harold, and she could see in her daughter Adeliza's eyes that she thought so too.

The introductions continued, and Stigand had adjusted his appearance and looked much less rakish when they finished.

William addressed his audience from the steps of his palace, where Matilda was waiting for him, as was his sister, Adelaide, her husband Eudes, and their daughter, the beautiful Judith. He kissed them all, thrilled to see them after so long.

'Fellow Normans.' They greeted his words with a roar, which delighted William; he could feel the blood coursing through his veins, making him feel as alive as on the battlefield.

Matilda looked on proudly, admiring her magnificent husband, as did the rest of William's family.

'Fellow Normans,' he repeated once the din had settled down. 'Just six months ago, I left these shores bound on an expedition many thought would fail.' William paused for effect. 'But my companions and I were on the Pope's mission. God Almighty was with us, and our enemy was a usurper, an oath breaker! No friend of the Lord, no friend of the Church and no friend of Normandy, was he.'

There were more cheers from the crowd.

'Against all odds, and with God at our side, we won a glorious victory on the field of battle. We crushed the usurper, Harold, and his underlings within one day, and England was ours. Today, here in Normandy, the place of my birth, home of my heart, I bring you the rewards of our sacrifice. Now is the time to feast.'

The Duke of Normandy, and now King of England, mounted his horse to a mighty cheer and rode to the castle.

Apart from the dazzling treasure, William's English hostages, who, with their long blond hair and mutton-chop moustaches, were the subjects of great admiration. The crowd's opinion was that to have defeated such distinguished warriors, the Duke must be a fine fighting man himself.

Leaving Sir William Malet to organise the unloading of the ships, they made their way through crowded sunny streets to the castle, where a banquet awaited them. All thoughts of Lent and its incumbent austerity had vanished. Now was a time to celebrate.

Inside the great hall, on the dais with William and Matilda, sat the good and great of the land. The Duke and Duchess looked resplendent in their new finery, as did their entire family. William had emptied England's royal closets and more besides. As a result, Matilda now owned a dozen more gowns. The bishops and magnates from all over Normandy felt put to shame next to William's companions. Soon William would distribute the length and breadth of his dukedom, and in time, the recipients of his generosity would look magnificent, too. They were delighted to enjoy the most sumptuous banquet ever to be held in the Dukedom. But the English contingent had other things on their minds.

'What do you think of his daughter, Adeliza?' Edwin asked Waltheof.

'She's a bit young. Why do you ask?'

'Because in a few short years from now, she'll be ripe, and when the time comes, she'll make somebody a fine wife,' Edwin said. He looked across at the Conqueror's beautiful daughter and smiled. Adeliza turned away.

'She's a beauty, but I don't think she cares for me,' he said, his pale face turning pink.

'Nonsense. She's feigning disinterest to inflame your desire,' Waltheof said.

But Adeliza was doing no such thing. She had been promised to Harold and had fallen madly in love with the slain king. Still heartbroken, seeing Earl Waltheof made her pine for her lost love even more.

'What is it, my dear?' Matilda asked tenderly.

'That man father wants to marry me off too. He looks like a pig, and he smells like a pig, too. I'm not marrying him; I'd rather die in a dungeon full of rats.'

'That's a little harsh, don't you think? He may not be the most handsome man in the room, but he is one of the highest in your father's kingdom.'

'I don't care. I'm not marrying a pig. Why should I?'

'We'll discuss this later, my dear,' Matilda said.

'Don't call me, my dear.'

On Matilda's other side, William, who had overheard the conversation, whispered into her ear, 'Strong-willed and high spirited. Just like her mother.'

'William…'

'You've got your work cut out there,' William said before tucking into a shoulder of mutton with a big smile on his face.

William, his family, and guests enjoyed the most lavish banquet ever seen in Normandy. There were nine courses and entertainment that lasted for hours. Not only were the Normans at court impressed, but foreign dignitaries too, including a small delegation sent from the Vatican who were there to help William celebrate his victory over the ungodly English and to collect Rome's share of the booty.

'Abbot Gilbert,' William said. 'I have gifts for the Pope.'

The Abbot had been waiting for this moment. Smiling, he bowed and stepped forward up to the dais.

'Sir William,' the Duke asked Malet. 'Would you present the gifts on my behalf?'

As Malet stretched out his arms, two servants draped a heavy gift over them. Whatever it was, it glittered with gold. William turned to Abbot Gilbert and presented him with the Wyvern of Wessex, the enormous golden banner that had once belonged to the kings of Wessex. Two clerics stepped forward to assist the Abbot before the poor man collapsed under the weight.

'Help us, someone,' Abbot Gilbert said. Immediately, four more clerics rushed to his aid. Together they unfurled the banner William had captured from King Harold.

With eyes popping, the Abbot and clerics stared at the marvel. A pole six feet high supported a solid gold dragon head was depicted baring its teeth on its top. Attached to its neck and made with the most delicate golden thread, its snake-like body hung down to the floor. Abbot Gilbert abbot found it magnificent and terrible at the same time. The gold and the craftsmanship impressed him, but it seemed such a pagan thing, the work of the devil, something of which Satan would be proud.

'Magnificent, isn't it, Abbot?'

'Quite so,' the Abbot replied unenthusiastically.

'We have another,' William paused, 'interesting gift for the holy Father,' nodding to Sir William.

Two servants emerged with several brass rods and what looked like a rolled-up tapestry. Assembling the rods, they made a standard for what was now obviously another banner. They then rolled out the banner so that the front was visible only to those on the dais. Matilda looked shocked and amused, blushing deep red.

'Turn it around. Let everyone see,' William said.

The servants faced the court. There was an audible intake of breath. The abbot looked like he had turned to stone as his eyes fixed on King

Harold's banner. Six feet high and six feet wide, made of the finest green silk and a perfect representation of the fighting man, outlined in silver thread and waving a mighty club, stood before him. The figure had a massive erection.

Gilbert was dumbstruck. He was captivated to see around the edging, purple-coloured amethysts representing love and truth unto death, chalcedony for fortitude and chrysolite for wisdom, impressive emeralds denoting faith, hope and justice, rubies for valour, and azure sapphires to create a reflection of heaven. There was also sardonyx for lowliness, mercy, faith, and, finally, yellow topaz for justice. It was a thing of beauty and outrage at the same time. The abbot had seen nothing like before. Shocking and adorable. Vulgar, yet exquisite. As much as the Wyvern of Wessex caused the court to stir, Harold's banner struck them into silence.

'Do you think the Pope will enjoy our gifts, abbot?'

Abbot Gilbert, still dumbfounded, took a moment to compose himself. 'It's a wonderful gift and so thoughtful of you.'

'I thought you'd be appreciative,' William said. 'You can imagine the sort of man Harold was when you see that this was his idea of a banner fit for a king.'

'I can indeed. I am happy to accept these gifts on behalf of his Eminence, but I'm afraid we may have to make adjustments before the Pope can see them.'

'I understand entirely,' William said with a knowing smile.

'And may I thank you for your many gifts to God's houses across the land and indeed throughout Christendom.'

'The Church has been a good friend to me, Abbot, and as a Christian, it gives me pleasure to make donations.'

Abbot Gilbert accepted William's gifts, as did the nobles of Normandy, Brittany, France, and the Holy Roman Empire.

The banquet continued through the afternoon and early evening until William finally ended the celebrations when the guests were exhausted. The Duke and his Duchess retired to bed.

William was not content with a single celebration. He wanted to tour his Duchy, revelling in his new role as King of England while remaining Duke of Normandy. William wished to display his crown and determined this would be a time of jubilation, to be talked of for generations. He had achieved what none of his predecessors had; he had elevated himself above his father; he had become a king. Matilda was happy to share his joy.

'William, my dear, are we going to be celebrating your victory all spring?'

'Yes, and into the summer, too,' William grinned.

'Why stop there?' Matilda said with a glint in her eye.

'Yes, let's carry on until next Christmas.'

They laughed together and embraced.

'Just having you back is reason to celebrate.'

'I won't stop celebrating until you've had your coronation, and then we'll have another excuse to make merry. You'll be my queen. I can't believe it. Even after three months, I still have difficulty believing it; I am the King of England. Many people thought I was a deluded fool who would come to grief. Instead, I return a king and a wealthy one at that. What's more, I have raised the power and prestige of Normandy in the process.'

'You have, and I'm thrilled for you, William,' Matilda said with a warm broad smile.

'Or,' he said, half-joking, 'how do you like the title, King of England and Normandy? What would that young fool, Philip of France, think?'

'I'm certain he'd have something to say.'

'I won't bow to a boy,' William said. 'Not now I'm a king.'

'I'm sure you're not, but in the meantime, what do you have planned?' Matilda asked.

'A visit to Aumale to visit Adelaide.'

'I wondered when we'd be going there. You can't keep away from that sister of yours.'

'It'll be good to see Count Eudes again, too. He fought heroically at Hastings, and I haven't seen him since my coronation.'

'This is just an excuse to show off your guests and all your newly acquired treasure?'

'Perhaps,' he said with a grin before breaking out into a laugh.

And William showed off his treasure to one and all. The royal procession made its way to Aumale, with a small army of servants displaying the plunder in every village along the way. From the top of carts and carriages, they held William's booty high as crowds looked on, soldiers making sure no one came too close. When William arrived in Aumale, he made a speech before parading his hostages and loot through the crowd-lined streets up to the castle. Wearing his crown and all his royal regalia, William was a splendid sight. Few people had seen a king and felt privileged to do so. Many had travelled for miles. The vision before them took their breath away. All manner of ornaments, trinkets, and gold treasures, such as chalices and candlesticks adorned with precious stones. Never had so much wealth been on display.

Perched high on her horse by William's side, Matilda remarked, 'they're all so pleased to see you.'

'And why wouldn't they be? Haven't I been a benefactor to over a thousand churches and brought glory to Normandy?' William said in a tone that suggested he thought the adulation paid to him was something to which he was entitled.

'Have you seen the look in their eyes? When they can drag them away from the treasure, they ogle you. They adore you. You're like a god to them,' Matilda said.

Once in Aumale castle, William held court, dispensing largesse and exhibiting his trophies, including the Englishmen. He found munificence came easily to him. After all, the gifts distributed so generously amongst his subjects had only six months previously been the pride of English homes and churches. He made gifts to the Church of its property at no expense to himself. Golden candlesticks and chalices from an English church to a Norman one, not so much donated as transferred. No one complained, or at least, no one in Normandy. As for Edgar and the earls, they were becoming accustomed to being exhibited this way. Stigand, who usually stayed with the nearest cleric, had deluded himself into thinking he was on a pilgrimage.

That night at Aumale seemed like any other. William's English hostages were welcomed to the castle and shown to their rooms. William's steward brought them down to the great hall a little later. William insisted they be treated with courtesy, just as their positions demanded.

As Count Eudes introduced them all, Waltheof gazed into the eyes of a young beauty. The count introduced the young woman as his stepdaughter, Judith. Unexpectedly, Waltheof found the visit to Normandy less tedious. At this moment, William, seeing the look in Waltheof's eyes, had his idea.

'Count Eudes,' said the Duke, 'why not let my niece sit with our guest?'

'Of course,' the count agreed.

Eudes called Judith over, 'My dear, why not sit next to Earl,' he paused, searching for the Earl's name, 'the earl, and you can tell him all about our little part of the world.'

Judith blushed as she took her place by the handsome warrior. Waltheof looked on, transfixed by the young beauty.

'My lady, it's a pleasure and a privilege to meet you,' he could hardly get the words out. He wanted to say something impressive, but all he could manage was a simple greeting.

'The pleasure is mine, Earl Waltheof,' said the countess, with composure beyond her years.

Judith giggled and blushed a little. 'What do you think of Normandy so far?' she enquired.

As he answered, Waltheof found his concentration slipping. He could not help but stare into her penetrating blue eyes, which suggested she understood things about him, he did not even know himself. An intimacy hinted itself, as though she knew his deepest secrets but would never tell. He could hardly bring himself to meet her gaze, and yet he couldn't keep his eyes off her.

'I like it a lot, my lady. It's much like the south of England.'

'You feel at home, then?

'Indeed, I do. Norman hospitality is second to none.'

As Waltheof continued, Judith studied him. Her penetrating blue eyes flitted this way and that, and she found him handsome. As the evening passed, they fell into easy conversation. At first, Judith did not mention Hastings, Harold and England's defeat, but curiosity got the better of her.

'Did you fight at Hastings?'

'No. I was wounded at Fulford Gate. Another battle before Hastings.'

'Oh, I didn't know that. Was it serious?' she asked.

'My men had to carry me off the battlefield.'

'You must have quite a scar,' she said with interest, excited to be next to a wounded hero, even if he was one of the vanquished.

'It wasn't a serious wound but severe enough to prevent me fighting at Hastings.'

'Perhaps if you had fought there, my uncle might not have won,' she said, looking deep into his eyes, pulling him in.

'And then I wouldn't be here talking to you.'

She smiled a huge smile and blushed a little.

Waltheof found Judith beguiling. She seemed to have transformed from an aloof but elegant young countess to a vulnerable child, to all-knowing sage, from mischievous puppy to sultry young woman in less than a minute. He wondered which one she was.

Further along the table, William felt contentment rise as he talked with Matilda, Adelaide, and his brother-in-law, Eudes. William was glad to see them again after his adventures. He was also pleased Waltheof and Judith were getting along so well. Any alliance that would cement his relations with the English would serve him well.

The party stayed at Aumale for the best part of a week. William arranged for Waltheof to spend as much time with Judith as could be considered decent. When they sat down for their last evening feast before moving on to the next celebration in another town, William had a quiet word with his captives.

'I shall be sad to leave in the morning, Waltheof.'

'So shall I.'

'Because of Judith, you mean?'

Waltheof searched for a reply, but William asked him, 'Do you like my niece, Waltheof?'

'She's a charming young lady.'

'I've seen you together. You make a handsome couple. I think the feeling you have for her is mutual.'

'You think so?'

'Oh, yes, William replied. Then added, 'You'll be able to see for yourself when she visits England.'

'She's coming to England?'

'Definitely. I'm sure you'll meet her then.'

Waltheof was thrilled at the prospect. All his troubles and cares seemed to vanish. He was thinking of Judith and what might happen if he spent more time with her on her visit. He caught Edwin's sullen eye, and he scowled and turned to his brother, saying something Waltheof could not hear.

While William was congratulating himself, a servant approached.

'It's Sir Roger de Montfort with a message from England, my lord,' he said.

William braced himself to receive bad news.

Sir Roger entered carrying a sack, the bottom covered by a dark stain.

'What have you there?'

'Oswulf, the new self-appointed Earl of Bernicia, sent it to Westminster. It arrived just after you left,' de Montfort said, wondering if he might be the one to pay the price of the Duke's anger.

'Let me see,' William said.

Sir Roger supported the sack with his left hand while peeling back the top with his right to reveal a plait and held it tight to avoid any mishap. The roughly woven cloth fell to reveal a contorted face. Someone had been decapitated, and the evidence was before him. William looked on baffled. He recognised the head but couldn't think whose it was or why anyone would think of sending it to him. Fortunately, Sir Roger recognised William's puzzlement.

'It's Earl Copsig, my lord. It was Oswulf who beheaded him.'

'Oswulf! Who's Oswulf?' William said.

Sir Roger stepped back before answering. 'He used to be Earl of Bernicia, and now he has appointed himself to his former position.'

'Has he now? We'll see about that. Does anyone at court know about this?'

'They do,' Sir Roger replied.

'What are they doing about it?'

'There's nothing they can do about it now because Oswulf's so far north,' Sir Roger said. 'Your brothers want you to know there is no need for concern, as they have the south under control.'

'Very well. I think we've seen enough. Take it away,' William said, glancing at the head. 'It would be best if you return it to its owner for burial.'

The court was a buzz, but the Englishmen were deep in urgent conversation.

'What's going on up there?' Morcar asked.

'Things are improving,' Edwin said. 'That louse Copsig has met his end. Someone trustworthy is in control.'

Edgar's face was bright and his smile broad; he looked happier than he had looked for months. All resistance to William had proved futile, but now, at last, success. This was his first glimmer of hope. The north would not lie down because the south had submitted.

'At last, we have something to celebrate,' the Atheling said. 'A part of the kingdom is secure. If the rest of Northumbria rises, it might encourage others to join. We need to get back.'

Turning to address his king, Morcar said, 'There must be grave trouble in Northumbria. Allow me to return and restore order in my earldom.'

'Don't concern yourself on my behalf, Morcar. My men in England can deal with any situation.' He smiled meaningfully. Even so, he felt a little unsettled. 'There may be a slight problem in the north, but I have my foothold in the south, and there shall be no shifting me from there.'

William was confident his comrades would establish Norman dominance in England. Unruffled by events in Northumbria, he continued his summer of celebration, touring the length and breadth of Normandy.

Chapter 10

While William was in Normandy, back in England, Bishop Odo and Sir William FitzOsbern set about imposing Norman rule on William's new subjects. One of their helpers was Sir Ralph Pomeroy, who, on this day, was assisting the dispensation of justice in Buckingham County Sheriff's court. Sir Ralph sat with his new friends, Sir William Warenne and Sir William Malet. Ostensibly, the three were there to observe English law in action to understand the legal procedures better. They had heard such marvellous stories about the hunting in the area they could not stay away. But before they could enjoy the chase, there was work to be done.

Presiding over the court that day was the new Sheriff of Buckinghamshire, Sir Ansculf de Picquigny. He was just the sort of noble Pomeroy despised. True, as one of King William's companions at Hastings, he had distinguished himself, but it was the sense of entitlement he possessed that riled Pomeroy. Sir Ansculf sat in the late Shire Reeve Godric's chair in the Great Hall as though he was born to it. He administered the law, but not in a way Godric would have recognised. Like Sir Ansculf, Pomeroy had listened during the morning as claimants had turned up to complain about their new lords. Rape, killing and expropriation of land were the primary concerns of the plaintiffs.

The first before the sheriff was Edward Cild, watched earnestly by his wife. Father Hildefrith, the local priest, acted as a translator and explained patiently to the ill-tempered Norman why people were looking to him for redress and his function as sheriff. The cleric was brave enough to ask de Picquigny where the law codes were.

'I don't need any law codes! I just need to know whose thane he is.'

'He is a royal thane,' Father Hildefrith said.

'You mean one of Harold's men?'

'He had nothing to do with King Harold…'

'Earl Harold!' de Picquigny snapped.

'Earl Harold. He accuses Sir Ralph of taking away his land.'

'It's because he fought at Hastings,' Pomeroy said. 'I saw him with my own eyes,' he lied.

'No! No! I wasn't there,' Edward protested.

'Are you calling me a liar?' Pomeroy said.

'No, my lord must be mistaken, that's all,' was Edward's explanation.

'I don't make mistakes,' Pomeroy said, glaring at Edward.

'Take him out and hang him,' pronounced de Picquigny, indicating that the guards take Edward away.

As soon as she realised her husband was in danger, his wife pleaded for mercy. She threw herself at de Picquigny's feet, begging for mercy.

'Can't somebody shut this howling bitch up?' the new sheriff said.

'Is there any need for all this,' Malet asked.

De Picquigny looked astonished. 'What do you care for a squawking peasant?' he said.

'I think it seems most improper, that's all,' Malet said.

'You're going soft,' de Picquigny said.

Some men at arms dragged the woman from the hall, ignoring her screaming and pleading. Several townsfolk tried to rescue her, but soldiers forced them back. Once in the street, they threw her to the ground, kicking her several times. The shocked onlookers who had witnessed the proceedings stood back in fear muttering to one another.

While one group of soldiers abused Edward Cild's wife, another group was hanging her husband. He could hear her pleading as a guard placed a noose around his neck. She stood up from the ground, her clothes covered in dirt just in time to witness the futile kicking of his legs as the Normans hauled him up. As Edward swung to his death, a cry of anguish ripped through the air.

Pomeroy sat impassively while all this went on around him, but he was getting agitated; all this commotion had delayed the day's hunting. Now there was no time left.

'How much longer will this go on?' he asked FitzOsbern.

'I'm not sure. I hope not. I want to hunt,' FitzOsbern said.

'Don't we all, but it's too late, I'm afraid,' Warenne joined in.

De Picquigny, who had overheard the conversation, became

concerned. He had hoped the trial might entertain them, but they were showing signs of boredom.

'It can't be helped, I suppose. Can't you appoint a deputy?' said FitzOsbern, sitting impassively on the dais with his arms folded.

De Picquigny's brother, Sir Gilo, entered the hall, drawing everyone's attention. He was followed by two monks carrying a large wooden trunk. 'I've got something to show you,' he said. 'Look,' and Sir Gilo opened the chest to reveal it was full of scrolls. 'I just had them brought over from the church.'

Mystified, Pomeroy looked blank.

'They're records of estates and their possessions,' Sir Gilo went on.

Pomeroy and his friends were still puzzled.

'Don't you see? They have these records in every county. They tell you exactly how much the tax liability is on every hide in the shire. Who owns what land, who rents, everything you'd want to know.'

Now Sir Gilo had their attention. The men were thinking about the land they possessed and how easy it might be to discover who had to pay a forfeit for fighting with Harold.

'All you have to do is enquire with the clergy. Just promise them the church will keep possession of its property, and they'll happily reveal all. And why shouldn't they,' Sir Gilo beamed, 'after all, we have the Pope's blessing.'

'Yes. Yes. You're quite right,' said Warenne, who could not believe his luck.

Now the brothers were glad they had made the journey. So were Pomeroy, Warenne and FitzOsbern. Not only would they enjoy a few good days of sport, but they could also look forward to procuring more rewards for their services.

'Hildefrith, sort through these and let us know which of the men on here fought at Hastings,' Warenne said, indicating the trunk and its contents.

'I don't need to look at the scrolls. There's Shire Reeve Godric; he was a good friend of King, I mean, Earl Harold. He died there,' Hildefrith volunteered.

'He won't be needing any land now, will he?' Warenne said. 'Now that I think about it, it seems only appropriate that Sir Ralph takes possession of it.'

Pomeroy looked pleased with the thought of his new acquisition, and Malet looked unsettled.

'Shire Reeve Godric was the big one you killed at Hastings,' Warenne said. 'The one who got his axe stuck in somebody's head.'

'Oh, him,' Pomeroy said.

'But,' the priest protested, 'Shire Reeve Godric has a widow and children. What will they do?'

'We can be generous; we'll make her a gift of enough land to live off. Or,' said Warenne, 'find her a new husband. Ralph, why don't you take a wife? I'm sure Godric's widow will have an excellent dowry.'

'What a splendid idea,' Pomeroy said. The idea of taking a wife and the land she brought with her appealed to him. Many widows would benefit from the protection of a powerful lord, someone like himself. And of course, what harm would it do if she had plenty of land? Why, he could protect that too. This was a pattern that would repeat itself across the kingdom.

'I've planned a fine banquet for this evening,' de Picquigny said. 'There will be excellent food and festivities.'

'I'm looking forward to it,' Pomeroy said. 'But if you'll forgive me, Ansculf, I have some business I'd like to attend to first.'

De Picquigny looked puzzled for a moment until he realised what Pomeroy meant. 'Ah, Godric's farm. Yes, it's not far away. Take one of my men to be your guide.'

Pomeroy, eager to get his hands on some land, set off to find his new acquisition at Oakley. He knew Godric's widow would be there because the obliging Father Hildefrith had told him so. He wondered if she was a beauty.

Harvest time at Godric's Farm, and in the sunny summer evening, the shadows grew long. A group of five children laughed and giggled as they played in the stream that brought life to the valley. They were happily throwing sticks into the water to see whose would travel the fastest from the willow tree to the big stone on the other side of the ford. Two were

Morwenna's children, Godwin, a four-year-old boy, and Godgifu, his three-year-old sister; there were just twenty-one months between them. With the sun catching in their curly blond hair, they looked golden, like little angels. Three of their friends, Wulthryth, the maid's children, were with them. The little ones stopped and waved at the carter and his daughter as they forded the stream on their way back to the barn with yet another load of hay, tired oxen straining as they pulled the cart.

After a long dry spell, the stream the children were playing in was running low, but it still babbled just loud enough to drown out the birdsong. Dragonflies cruised along banks, and butterflies, too, were enjoying the carefree days of summer. Clouds of gnats chased each other in endless circles. Swallows dived before soaring high in the air above the hedgerows decked with flowers. As always, people helped with the harvest out in the busy fields. Occasionally, a light breeze would stir the sultry air, cooling hot skin. Not far away, apples were forming in the orchard, bringing the promise of autumn fruit; the cold, the damp, the bitter winds of distant winter long forgotten.

Out on a hillside, away from the rest of the farmstead, a sharp-eyed boy picking berries from the hedgerow had seen something approaching that would shatter the English summer idyll. The bright colours of their banners and tabards, the glint of the sunlight on metal, alerted the boy to the danger. The pit of his stomach tightened and filled with fear, and he ran as fast as his eight-year-old legs would carry him home to sound a warning. He raced down the hillside, golden barley whipping his legs as he tore through a field with his warning. 'Soldiers are coming!'

No one else had seen them; only he was alert to the danger. The boy knew that he would beat the soldiers if he were fast enough. Charging straight across the meadows that separated him from home, he raced to where he knew Morwenna and Elfwyn would be; they would know what to do. At the farm, unaware of the approaching danger, Elfwyn discussed the afternoon's tasks with the maid, and Morwenna was deep in conversation with Bondi. The housecarl, as always, listened intently to Morwenna, hanging on to her every word. From one of her neighbours, she had heard the news of rebellion in Mercia.

'They say a Shropshire thane, Edric the Wild they call him, is running around Herefordshire creating havoc,' she said.

Bondi looked blank. 'I've never heard of him,' he said.

'He's ravaged the whole of Herefordshire and burned Hereford to the ground, and the castle, too. Rumour has it a couple of Welsh princes are with him. The Normans took his land, so people say he's going to see them off back to Normandy, and then put Queen Aldytha's infant son on the throne.'

'Are Earls Edwin and Morcar behind this? It wouldn't be the first time they've conspired with their sister.'

'I don't know. All I've heard is the border counties are up in arms, the Welsh are helping them, and this Edric is with Aldytha and her son.'

Bondi looked perplexed.

The conversation ended abruptly when a desperate-looking boy ran into the yard. He reached them as the soldiers approached the nearby ford.

'Soldiers on horses, my lady. They're coming to the farm,' he gasped out his warning.

'How many?' she asked.

'Lots.'

A shiver ran down Morwenna's spine. 'Do you know exactly, Sherwyn?'

'A dozen,' he said, hoping he was right.

'Get up to the fields as fast as you can,' she said. 'And tell them I want those men with any kind of weapon down here right away. Tell the women to take the children and hide in the woods.'

The exhausted boy ran off on his errand, his legs a blur.

'What do you want me to do, my lady?' Bondi asked.

'Stay here. If they see you,' she said, looking at the dragon tattoos on his forearms, 'they'll kill you. But you never know, they might not start any trouble.'

Bondi looked doubtful. 'I'll stay hidden but be at the ready.'

'Let's see what they want first,' Morwenna said.

Morwenna made straight for the hall where she kept the weapons. Bondi headed for the woodpile, where he would be out of sight and where there was an axe. There were only a few men on the farm, and Morwenna was unsure what they could do against so many. She also feared for the safety of the women preparing the evening meal. But the children playing beneath the willow were in a world of their own. So preoccupied were they, they didn't hear the clatter of hooves as thirteen riders approached, and there was no blast of a horn to warn the villagers to expect visitors.

When Elfwyn saw the riders approaching, she felt dread descend upon her. There was something about the way they rode, an arrogance, a disdain for everything around. She called to the children. They had released their sticks and were running excitedly along the bank, down to the ford. Elfwyn's warning did not penetrate their world.

Unannounced, the Normans cantered through the stream and straight into the farmyard, scattering hens and geese everywhere. They allowed nothing to stand in their way. A farm cat ran for cover.

Bondi reached the woodpile, grabbed the axe, and peered around the corner of a barn. He could see Wulthryth, the maid, standing motionless by the well where she had gone to fetch water. Three of the Normans dismounted, approaching her with lascivious smiles on their faces; she was to be their entertainment. A fourth held the horse's reins, looking on, grinning. Pomeroy and the rest of his men rode on, four peeled off to their right, looking for trouble.

Peeping around the corner of the barn, judging by the way they approached Wulthryth, Bondi could feel the menace in the air as the Normans drew near her. Smiling at them as though she were stupid enough not to realise what was going on, as soon as she thought the distance right, she threw her bucket at their leader's face. He dodged it.

'What kind of welcome is that?'

'Get away,' Bondi heard her shout.

Incensed, Bondi ran towards Wulthryth and her assailants. Barely had he stepped out from behind the barn to go to her aid when three riders rounded the corner of the hall. They brought their horses to a sharp halt; the housecarl stopped in his tracks and looked up at them, unable to disguise the hatred he felt burning in his eyes. They looked down at him with contempt. He returned the gaze, axe in hand.

'What have we here?' their leader asked with a smirk.

'By the look of it, a peasant on his way to chop some wood,' one of his comrades said.

In response, his friends laughed the self-assured laugh of bullies who know they have a victim cornered.

Even if he had an axe, the horsemen decided to have sport with the woodsman. No chopper of trees would get the better of them. Still smiling and joking amongst themselves, they dismounted, and in this moment of vulnerability, Bondi saw his chance; with three strides, he was on the closest of them.

An ear-piercing scream split the air as Bondi's axe bit deep into the first soldier's shoulder. His cry of agony alerted his comrades before he had even hit the ground. The two horses obstructed their owners, blocking the way to the axeman. As they came forward between their mounts to attack, Bondi slipped around the back of the horses and again brought his axe down on a Norman's shoulder. The third one turned and appeared in front of Bondi, ready to defend himself. Too late did he notice the dragon tattoo on the stranger's arm as Bondi's sleeve slipped back as he raised his axe. Too late did he realise his mistake. Bondi was on him in an instant, his savage axe biting at his shield, snapping at his head. It was not just the speed of the attack but the force and accuracy of the blows that overwhelmed the Norman. All the hatred, the despair, shame, and the rage Bondi felt had now, after months on the farmstead, finally found an outlet. He could be himself again, doing what he did best, dispatching an enemy.

'Mercy! Mercy!' pleaded Bondi's victim as the axe came down. The soldier could barely hold up his shield. Bondi had broken the man's wrist under the force of his blows.

'You're going to die, you bastard. You and the rest of you scum,' spat Bondi, his jaw quivering with rage.

Defending himself as best he could, the Norman backed away from Bondi until he reached the perimeter fence. With nowhere to go, he made one last desperate attempt to deal a fatal blow to his assailant, but Bondi brought his axe in fast, striking just below his bottom rib. The wound was deep, the scream loud, and the blood plentiful. As the Norman folded groundward, doubled up in agony, Bondi's axe bit deep again, the last bite the man would ever feel.

Once Bondi had dealt with the immediate danger, he strode

purposefully around the side of the outbuilding in time to see Elfwyn climbing over the wicker fence.

She caught his eye and opened her mouth to call out, but the housecarl put his fingers to his lips to indicate silence.

In response, Elfwyn made motions imitating the drawing of a bow. Bondi nodded, and the two carried on with their missions.

Wulthryth, with her yelling, had alerted the farmworkers to the situation. With his daughter Sherilda, the carter, who had been unloading the sheaves from their cart, heard Wulthryth. The two men building a hayrick also heard Wulthryth's cries for help. Sherilda's father was the first to react.

'Sherilda, get behind the stables,' he yelled. 'Come on, lads, let's see what's happening.'

Sherilda did as ordered but peeped around the corner of the barn to see what was going on.

Casting everything aside, her father and the men rushed to the yard, where they saw three soldiers raping the maid. Four Normans charged down on them before the Saxons had time to react; defenceless, they were easy meat for the soldiers to slice through and were left screaming and writhing on the ground.

Horrified, Sherilda bolted out of the farm gate and ran for safety. The four riders, done with their deadly work, were now cheering their three comrades on, the raucous laughter of Wulthryth's assailants drowning her protests and screams. Sherilda, searching for safety, ran through the ford, hoping to put as much distance as she could between her and the Normans. She came out of her panic when she heard the screams of the infants. Two of them were wailing.

'It's all right now, little ones,' Sherilda said, trying to sound calm as she grabbed one in each arm. 'I'll look after you, but you must try to be quiet.'

She got to her feet and kissed them both, and continued her escape, trying hard not to look at the trampled bodies of the other three children as she went.

Having dealt with one small group of Normans, Bondi turned to see a soldier raping Wulthryth; judging from his groaning, Bondi guessed he was spending himself. Two comrades encouraged him while another on horseback guffawed heartily. Then finished, the leader of the little group stood back, adjusted his clothes, and walked away, looking for more mischief.

Astride his stallion, observing the chaos, Pomeroy was laughing heartily, still unaware that three of his men were dead at the hands of a housecarl.

'Get everyone out here. I'll inform them of the new arrangements,' Pomeroy said to one of his men.

The man grinned and walked his horse towards the hall.

The four soldiers, still in his company, dismounted and followed him. The murderers of the carter turned their horses to join their leader. Just then, two women emerged from the doorway, and Wulthryth's rapist thrust his hips at them lasciviously. He failed to see the bows and the quivers by their sides until it was too late.

'Now!' cried Morwenna.

She and Elfwyn took aim and shot together; simultaneously, they caught the rapist square in the chest. He died in an instant with two arrows through his heart. Before their victim hit the ground, Morwenna released a second arrow at Pomeroy, which struck him in the face, piercing flesh, gum, and sinus. Clutching at the shaft that stuck right out of his cheek, he struggled desperately to stay on his mount as blinding agony seared through his head.

Thankfully for Pomeroy, Etoile, his horse, remained calm while all around pandemonium broke out.

With no one to issue orders, the troops were slow to react. Elfwyn and Morwenna let loose more arrows, and more Normans fell to the ground.

'This way, Ralph!' a soldier yelled, galloping up, grabbing Etoile's reins, and riding out of the gate and to safety, Pomeroy crying out in pain every jolt of the way.

As Morwenna aimed, Elfwyn shot the other two Normans, killing one and wounding the other. Morwenna had Pomeroy in her sights, the arrow aimed right at the middle of his back, but she noticed Bondi in danger and changed her target to his assailant. The soldier who had held the horses for his comrades while they raped Wulthryth had his sword ready to hack down the housecarl. As he raised his weapon to lop off

Bondi's head, an arrow penetrated his side between his ribs and through a lung. He fell with a thud and a groan to the ground. Bondi turned and finished him with his axe.

The two men attacking Wulthryth, alerted by their comrade's scream to the danger, released her. One of them drew his sword and made toward the blood-drenched Bondi, a sight he found fearsome. Stepping forward bravely while his comrade grabbed Wulthryth's ankles and tipped her down the well, he approached the housecarl. The fight was short-lived; with two swings of his axe, Bondi finished the soldiers. Used to fighting spearmen or swordsmen, they were no match for an axeman. This kind of fighting was new to them, and they underestimated Bondi's reach. Their mistake proved fatal.

Turning from the well, Bondi closed in on Pomeroy. At a gallop, Pomeroy and FitzWalter raced toward the housecarl. Just in time, Bondi leapt aside. The four riders who had killed the carter and his friends were bearing down on him, too. Morwenna shot the two closest to her, and with a thud, each body fell to earth. The other two left Bondi alone and concentrated on their escape as arrows flew past their heads. Seeing a comrade and a screaming Pomeroy racing for the gate, they followed on behind. They crossed the ford, where Sherilda hid behind a hedge with the children.

'Are you all right?' Elfwyn yelled to Bondi, horrified to see him covered in blood.

'I'm all right. What about you?'

'We're unharmed,' she said, trembling from head to foot.

'Where are the children?' Morwenna asked.

'I last saw them by the stream,' Elfwyn said.

Morwenna hitched her skirts with one hand and left in an instant, running as fast as she could to where the children were.

Bondi went to the well and peered. 'Hello. Can you hear me?' he said.

There was no answer.

Taking hold of the rope, he lowered himself down to see if the maid was still alive. Elfwyn was waiting to offer help if he needed it. A minute later, out of breath, after hauling himself up, he heaved himself out of the well. He broke the news to Elfwyn. 'I'm afraid she's dead.'

'Oh, no,' Elfwyn said and burst into tears.

'Let's find Morwenna,' Bondi said.

The two ran to the stream, Elfwyn still in tears. When they arrived, Morwenna and her children, with Sherilda, were in a huddle, all crying.

'What's happened?' Bondi asked.

'The other children. They're all dead,' Morwenna said. 'All three of them. They're Wulthryth's children. The Normans just trampled them.'

'Wulthryth's dead too,' Bondi said. 'Come on. We'd better take the bodies inside. Then we'll need to get Wulthryth's body out of the well.'

Bondi's suggestion met a wail of bawling. He did not blame them; he could feel his tears welling up, too. But the job had to be done, and besides, the Normans were bound to return. They would feel compelled to take revenge.

'Come on, ladies. We have no choice, and I need your help,' he said.

Bondi walked over to the tiny bodies and picked two of them up, draping one over each shoulder. The third he carried in his arms, straining under the weight to the hall where he lay them on the ground outside. Stepping inside, Bondi returned with a drape and lay it over them. Never had he carried such a heavy burden. Morwenna, Sherilda, and the children followed behind. As they passed through the farmyard, their tears flowed anew when they saw the bodies of Sherilda's father and the others scattered around.

'I'll get Wulthryth now,' Bondi said, making his way to the well. Once there, he lowered himself down on the rope used to haul the bucket, securing it around Wulthryth's body, before climbing back up to the surface. He hauled the maid up with difficulty, and the women helped lay her limp body on the ground.

'We must give her a decent burial,' Morwenna said.

'And the children,' Elfwyn said. 'And the rest,' she added, bursting to tears again.

With urgency, Bondi said, 'We need to be quick about it. We'll have to leave; we can't stay here now.'

'Where can we go?' Elfwyn asked, pale and shaking.

'I know he's a long way from here, but what about your father in Lincoln?'

'Yes, we'll be safe there. I'll get the priest, and then we'll organise the burial,' Morwenna said before asking, 'Do you think they'll be back?'

'Oh yes. I don't doubt that,' Bondi said. 'Probably tomorrow, and there'll be more then. We have to decide what we're going to do, and we need to do it fast. Let's see who wants to come with us.'

'What will they do if they return,' Morwenna asked.

'They'll come back in large numbers and take revenge. I can't answer for the safety of anyone who stays behind,' Bondi said.

Something told Morwenna this sight was not new to him.

'We really must get a move on, my lady.'

'We'll gather everyone together.'

'And I'll fetch a priest,' he said.

Chapter 11

In Buckingham, William Malet called for a priest for Sir Ralph Pomeroy. As the sun was setting, he and his surviving followers returned to the town, creating a stir. With most of his men killed and nothing to show for all his efforts, it was a disastrous return.

Malet helped him from his horse. The arrow was still sticking out of his friend's face.

'What happened, Ralph?'

In response, Pomeroy made an unintelligible noise.

'Someone's gone to fetch the priest. We'll take you to the church.'

The rest of Pomeroy's men were busy telling the story, but. Walter had the biggest audience.

'We turned up at this farm, all friendly like, and the next thing we know, we're being shot at by a couple of archers who were hiding in this big house. Then a housecarl, by the look of him, sneaked out of an outbuilding with an axe and started chopping us up. We didn't stand a chance. Isn't that right, lads?'

There was an unconvincing murmur of agreement while the conversation continued. Somebody would ask a question, and with each answer, the story grew wilder, the archers more numerous. The axeman turned into a giant. More blood was spilt, and more fantastic was the slaughter. And as the picture became more dramatic, the call for vengeance grew louder.

While soldiers were getting excited over the skirmish, Father Hildefrith was examining Pomeroy, who was lying stretched out on a few blankets on the floor in the church.

'Can you help him?' Malet asked.

A vague look appeared in Hildefrith's eyes. 'I'll do my utmost, and with the help of God, your friend will be well again.'

'Is there anything you need?'

'No, nothing.' And having second thoughts, 'You'll have to restrain him.'

Malet instructed three men to place themselves around Pomeroy. They kneeled beside him, one on either side to pin down his shoulders and another to hold his legs.

When they looked ready, Malet said, 'Best get on with it.'

Hildefrith placed a chest on the floor by Pomeroy's makeshift bed. He opened it up to reveal three rows of small pots containing ointments, salves, and creams to treat ailments of every kind. He studied them carefully, picking out one at a time, scrutinizing it before putting it back. All the while, Pomeroy was groaning in agony.

'Ah,' Hildefrith said at last before turning, grabbing hold of the arrow and pulling it out of Pomeroy's face. He looked puzzled as he stared at the end of the shaft. Stare as hard as he might; there was no arrowhead to be seen.

'Do you have any idea what you're doing?' Malet asked with a voice so harsh it seared the air.

'No. Father Hildefrith's talents lie elsewhere,' said a woman who had appeared from nowhere.

Malet turned to see a plain-looking nun, aged about thirty, holding a wicker basket, standing in the doorway. 'Who are you?' he asked.

'I'm Sister Werburg, and I understand you have an injured soldier here.'

She had treated many a casualty and enjoyed a fine reputation as a physician. When she first started as a physic, she took care of those suffering accidents on the farms around and about, but when the call came in October, she had gone with the men to Hastings to help wounded soldiers. Later she administered to the injured at London Bridge.

Malet studied her with a penetrating gaze that seemed all-knowing. There appeared to be nothing extraordinary about her other than she looked at ease. He turned his attention to Hildefrith, who was standing watching the proceedings, still with the arrow shaft in his hand.

'Are you able to help him?' Malet asked.

'Yes.'

'It's true,' said Father Hildefrith. 'Sister Werburg is the best physician for miles.'

'Proceed,' Malet ordered.

'What should I do with this?' Father Hildefrith asked, waving the arrow shaft.

'I'm sure you'll find a place for it,' Malet hissed.

Sister Werburg knelt beside Pomeroy. He glared at her with fury in his eyes and tried to talk. He was protesting, but he could not make himself understood. Sister Werburg judged from the blood on the shaft that Hildefrith still held in his hand that it had entered Pomeroy's face to a depth of six inches. She guessed the point rested on the underside of his skull. If that were true, he had a good chance of surviving. If she could remove the arrowhead and if the wound remained uninfected.

'Let me have a close look at the arrow, Father,' sister Werburg said.

Hildefrith handed it over.

Werburg saw that whoever made it had rounded off the end to fit into the tang of an arrowhead. This was what she needed to know, and she produced a tool she had had a blacksmith make, especially for her, for this purpose. It had proved indispensable in the past and was going to be so again.

The instrument was like nothing Malet had ever seen. The tongs were ten inches long and hollow, with a threaded screw running between them. The blacksmith had filed down every edge, and there was no sharp surface anywhere. They were the same width as an arrow. Sister Werburg noticed Malet's puzzlement.

'Once I've cleaned him up, I'll slip these into the wound right into the tang of the arrowhead,' she said, holding the tongues before him. 'Then I'll turn the screw, and the tips will open, so pressing up inside the socket tight enough for me to remove it. Once that's done, we need to make sure he's clean to avoid an infection.'

'I'm impressed,' said Malet, who thought the idea masterful.

Sister Werburg cleaned the wound with white wine and applied rose honey on a stick wrapped in a linen swab while Pomeroy stifled yells and curses. Finally, she felt the iron arrowhead with the probe. Withdrawing the stick, Sister Werburg then slipped the tongues into the wound until she could feel the arrowhead again. Probing, she felt the tip of the tongues slip into the tang, and she turned the screw until she felt resistance. Pain shot through the bones of Pomeroy's skull, making him grunt and struggle, but the men held him down.

Once she was sure she had a tight enough grip, she pulled, doing her best to ignore the screams, until a sharp piece of metal appeared.

'As I thought,' she said. 'A bodkin.'

Father Hildefrith looked baffled.

'It isn't barbed, father,' Malet said. 'That's why it was easy to extract. These arrowheads are made to pierce chain mail and detach themselves from the arrow shaft when it's withdrawn.'

Then, addressing Sister Werburg, he asked, 'How do you know all this?'

'I've treated God's children before,' Sister Werburg replied while she cleaned the wound with white wine and honey.

'I'll have to treat him every two days for six weeks, and with God's help, he will survive with just a small scar.'

'What can I do?' Malet said.

'Find him somewhere quiet and cool to rest where he won't be disturbed.'

'As you wish.'

'Thank you, Sir William.'

Next morning, before dawn, in Oakley, after a night spent packing and loading carts, Elfwyn and Morwenna were organising the departure, but not all the farmworkers wanted to go. One villager was adamant.

'We have to have a lord. Everything we've ever known is here. What will become of us if we leave?' one villager asked. 'My family has lived in this valley since before anybody can remember.'

'I understand how you feel, Ricbert,' Morwenna replied. 'We wouldn't leave if we had a choice, but things have changed now. Come with us. You'll have a new lord in my father, and he'll see to it you have a place at the hearth.'

'But I farm this land, and this has always been our home,' Ricbert responded.

Bondi appreciated the urgency of the situation. 'We have to think of the future now,' he said. 'What will become of us if we stay? We can't remain here. Soon the Normans will return, seeking revenge. God help anybody who's here when they arrive.'

'Can't we get the sheriff to sort this out?' Ricbert said.

The way the others looked to him, it seemed he was their spokesman.

'The sheriff is one of them.' Morwenna replied. 'Come with me to a place of safety. A week from now, we'll be inside Lincoln's tall and sturdy walls. Who knows what will happen to those who stay?'

'Who knows what will happen to those who go?' said Ricbert.

There was a chorus of, 'aye' from those gathered around.

'We'll take our chances anyway,' Ricbert continued.

Bondi rolled his eyes in disbelief.

'If you're certain that's what you want, Ricbert,' Morwenna said, with genuine concern.

'It is, my lady.'

'Then good luck to you.'

'Good luck to you, too, my lady,' Ricbert replied, with sadness and uncertainty in his voice. He watched with trepidation as Morwenna, Elfwyn, Bondi and those who left their homes with what they could carry on a couple of carts headed for the safety of the north and Merleswein's protection.

Chapter 12

A week after leaving Oakley, Bondi arrived in Lincoln with a small band of two dozen followers who had their old life behind and had no idea what was in store for them.

They soon discovered they were not the only refugees. People from every level of society had headed north to get as far away as they could from London and the Normans. A few had sought the shelter of Lincoln. The ones staying behind were those who thought they had nothing to lose and clerics who believed they had nothing to fear.

When Lincoln came into view, the party, exhausted from their journey, felt their spirits soar. They crossed the bridge over the River Witham, where ships from all over Christendom and beyond were tied up. They passed through the first set of enormous gates in a high wall the Romans had built centuries before. Around them, artisans and traders plied their trades, and people went about their business as they had always done. It was as though the Normans had never arrived. Ahead of them, a perfectly straight street led up to another gate. Lincoln made a spectacular sight, draped like a carpet over an escarpment. Bondi and his party made their way up the entrance. If the first was impressive, this was magnificent.

Morwenna smiled and said, 'It's beautiful, but not that practical. We'll have to leave the cart behind here. Soon we'll come to the steps, which is alright for us on our horses, but the carts and wagons will never manage them.'

Some of the party stayed with the transport, and the rest continued up the hill. The South Gate looked more impressive every step of the way. A tower stood on each side of the basilica, under which there were four archways. There were two substantial central arches and a smaller arch on either side for people on foot. On top of them were the old soldiers' quarters with five arched windows. The gate was even higher than the wall. They were out of breath by the time they passed through them, and the horses needed a rest. Bondi understood why the builders chose the location; it commanded a view for miles. When they reached Merleswien's hall, their father came out to greet them.

'Morwenna. Elfwyn. What a wonderful surprise,' he said, hugging and kissing his daughters. He looked for his new grandchild.

'Ah, there we are,' he said as Sherilda approached him with the baby.

'His name is Godric,' Morwenna smiled. 'After his father.'

Sherilda pulled back the baby's blanket to expose more of his face. Merleswein smiled at his grandson. 'Good,' he said. 'Let's hope he grows up to be as big and strong as his father. Now, how are you two doing?' he asked as he grabbed young Godwin and little Godgifu, tucked them under each arm, and spun them around. The children shrieked as their grandfather danced in circles, and Merleswein laughed more like a child than either of them.

Once he had welcomed his grandchildren, Merleswein turned to Bondi and smiled. 'It's good to see you again, but I thought you were going to Ireland,' he said.

'I had a change of mind,' Bondi said.

'And you've brought my family home safe to me. You'll always be welcome here,' Merleswein said as he hugged the housecarl and slapped his back heartily.

Merleswein called to a servant, 'take care of the horses. We'll get accommodation sorted out.'

'Come with me for refreshments,' he said, leading the way. 'I've just harvested the honey. You'll love it.'

'Father's obsessed with bees and all things to do with them,' Morwenna explained. 'If he offers to show you his skeps, refuse. You'll be there forever.'

Bondi smiled in response, and he and Merleswein fell into silence, and despite the warm welcome, neither man seemed at ease. When they entered the hall, it surprised Bondi to find it laid out for a feast and full of visitors.

'What's the celebration, father?' Morwenna asked.

'Word of your return travelled fast. What kind of father would I be if I hadn't put on a feast for my daughters and grandchildren? It's so good to see you safe and sound. You and the children.'

Bondi felt honoured to be invited to the high table with Merleswein, Morwenna, and Elfwyn. A prominent Lincolnshire thane called Turgot was already seated there. He smiled broadly when he saw Bondi. Another thane at the table was Thurold. He looked in his mid-forties, and he had an odd appearance, bulging eyes, and a weak chin, which his scraggy beard failed to conceal.

'Tell us, Morwenna, what's going on in the south?' Merleswein asked.

'It was horrible, father. We were at home; most people were out in the fields, bringing in the harvest. We were getting on with things when little Selwyn came with a warning; Normans are coming. In no time, they were attacking men and women alike,' Morwenna said, her hand travelling up to her algiz talisman as she visualised the scene.

'I'm glad you had a housecarl there to help you out,' Merleswein said.

'So are we. Bondi's axe did its fair share of the work, but Elfwyn and I acquitted ourselves well with our bows.'

'So, I've got myself a pair of shieldmaidens. You would have made your mother proud. She had such spirit, did Yrsa. I suppose it was all that Viking blood she had.'

The women smiled in response at the mention of their deceased mother, and for a moment, a still quiet silence filled the air between them.

'But your daughters seem so ladylike, Merleswein,' Thurold interjected. 'It's so hard to imagine them in mortal combat.' Although he addressed Merleswein, it was Morwenna, Thurold was observing. Looking for a favourable reaction, he smiled what he thought was a seductive smile.

Morwenna offered him a weak smile in response and turned to her sister and whispered, 'Elfwyn, why is that man leering at me?'

'He's always like that,' she answered. 'After you left to marry Godric, his wife died. Since then, he's taken to visiting everyone in the neighbourhood looking for a replacement. He makes eyes at anyone wearing a skirt.'

'It's unsettling,' Morwenna said.

Merleswein, with a smile, said to Thurold, 'If there's one thing I can assure you of, both of my daughters are ladies.'

'Of that, I'm sure,' Thurold replied. Again, he smiled at Morwenna while answering Merleswein.

This time Morwenna offered no response but turned to Elfwyn and said, 'That repulsive man is leering at me?'

'Oh, don't worry about him. He's like that with everyone.'

'Well, I'm uncomfortable with it, and father seems to encourage him.'

'Well, make sure you don't,' Elfwyn replied.

The evening continued with tales of the situation in the south, Pomeroy's attack, and their uneventful journey back to Lincoln.

'But what's happening here?' Morwenna asked. 'We've heard rumours about someone called Edric the Wild. He attacked the Normans in Hereford, and he has a lot of Welshmen helping him. Is there any truth in them?'

'As far as I'm aware, there is. I'll find out in a couple of weeks when I meet with him in Chester.'

'You're meeting him?' Morwenna said.

'Yes. We must get ourselves organised. Band together.'

'Edric seems to have started on his own,' Morwenna said.

'Oh, he's not the only one. One or two other people seem to have similar ideas. Many Normans are afraid to journey outside the towns, from what I hear. It's getting too dangerous for them to travel anywhere. And that's not all. We've had word back from Normandy that Edgar and the Earls will escape at the first opportunity. We need a leader, and Edgar's our man.'

'Isn't it going to take a while for them to get back from Normandy?' Morwenna said.

'They plan to come back with the Bastard William, and then they'll get away and make their way north and start the rebellion.'

'How long will that take?' Morwenna asked.

'I can't say, but we need to be ready when the time comes.'

'With Copsig gone and Oswulf in power, we have another ally in Northumbria,' Morwenna reminded them.

'I'm afraid I've bad news. Oswulf is dead. He was travelling to Durham when robbers met him and his party. Some of his men escaped, but they killed Oswulf,' Merleswein announced. 'He was a good man, and he'll be hard to replace.'

'That's terrible,' Morwenna said. 'He was a glimmer of hope, father.'

'We thought so, too,' Merleswein said.

'So, who'll be the next earl?' Morwenna asked.

'My guess is Gospatric. He's got a strong claim, or perhaps Waltheof.'

'Don't you think it's William who will decide?' Morwenna said.

'Not if I have anything to do with it,' Thurold interrupted, trying to impress.

No one spoke, and the silence dismissed his remark.

'So, Bondi, will you join us when we go to Chester?' Merleswein asked. 'We intend to build an army, and we'd like you to play a leading part.'

'We?' Bondi said.

'There are still some thanes, and one or two earls left who are quite prepared to put up a fight,' Merleswein said. 'You've seen for yourself how the Normans have treated the south. We can expect more of the same in the rest of the kingdom. You did well at Stamford Bridge and Hastings. Your actions didn't go unnoticed.'

'I'll say,' Thurold blurted out. 'I was there at Stamford Bridge and saw you on your little boating expedition,' he said, making stabbing motions as if spearing someone above him. 'You should have seen that Berserker's face when you drove that spear home. His eyes came so far out of his head they almost ended up back in Norway,' Thurold said, laughing and slapping the table.

Merleswein gave Thurold a quizzical look before speaking. 'As I was saying,' he continued, 'You've impressed, and we'd like you to join us in Chester, where I hope we can make plans to put Edgar on the throne.'

'And what about Edwin and Morcar?' Thurold asked.

'We might need their help,' Merleswein replied.

'I think we can do without Edwin and Morcar's help,' Thurold said.

An uneasy silence fell over the group.

'I'm only saying what we're all thinking,' Thurold said. 'You can't trust those two. They let Harold down at Fulford Gate. They didn't even show up for Stamford Bridge, and they failed to arrive on time for Hastings.'

'Is this to do with what happened in Northampton?' Morwenna asked.

'Yes,' Thurold answered. 'Why would anyone expect to be trusted if they had overthrown their earl, raided their own earldom and enslaved the very folk they're there to protect? If you ask me, they're just looking for an opportunity to put their nephew on the throne.'

Elfwyn made her contribution. 'I think we need to remember that the earls are still young, and they've made a few mistakes, big ones, I'll admit, but mistakes, nevertheless. I'm sure they meant well.'

'Do you trust them?' Thurold asked.

Bondi followed the discussion carefully. His worst fears were confirmed.

Elfwyn thought for a moment. 'As I said, the earls are young.'

'Do you trust them or not?' Thurold asked, looking from one person to the next for a response.

'Thurold. Edwin and Morcar are earls and noblemen by birth, and they must be trustworthy,' Morwenna asserted.

Thurold rolled his eyes in response, then opened his mouth to speak, 'I...'

'I think you've made your point obvious, Thurold,' Merleswein said. 'Who would like more wine?'

'More wine,' Merleswein ordered.

While in the uneasy silence a servant refilled the goblets and drinking horns, Merleswein leaned towards Bondi conspiratorially and added. 'We control the north, and then we'll move on the south. Lady Gytha is organising an army in the southwest, and the counties along the River Severn will rise up too. Before they know it, we'll have the Normans trapped in London, and then we'll close in and finish them.

'Harold's sons are preparing to invade. When they do, it's our job to rise here. We might even persuade the Danes to help.'

'Who will be our leader?' Bondi asked.

For a moment, Merleswein looked a little worried, then said, 'Edgar and the earls are William's prisoners. Once they've escaped his clutches, we'll fall on him.'

'But when?'

'Come to Chester, and you'll find out as soon as the rest of us.'

Chapter 13

It was late afternoon when Bondi and Merleswein arrived in Chester, the ancient Roman walls golden in the setting sun. Queen Aldytha and Edric gave them a warm welcome, took them to the great hall, and offered them refreshments.

'Merleswein, it's so good to see you again,' Aldytha effused, approaching the shire reeve with open arms as they entered the hall. In a most unregal way, she hugged him.

'It's been so long, and so much has happened since we last met,' she said, tears forming in her eyes. She squeezed his upper arms almost as if to make sure he was really there.

Merleswein, who was a little taken aback by the warmth of the welcome, bowed, and Bondi followed suit.

'I hope your journey was pleasant,' Aldytha said before turning to Bondi. 'I don't think we've met before,' she said.

'This is Bondi Wynstanson, a Royal Housecarl, my lady,' Merleswein said. 'He fought with the king at Stamford Bridge and Hastings.'

'Ah, Bondi, I've heard so much about you,' Aldytha said with little enthusiasm.

Bondi thought her eyes said. *You should have tried harder.*

'Make yourselves comfortable,' Aldytha said, gesturing towards the benches.

'Let me introduce you to our other guests,' Edric said. 'These are our good friends from Wales, the Welsh princes, Bleddyn and Rhiwallon.' Black haired and blue-eyed, they were strikingly good looking.

'I'm so pleased to make your acquaintance,' Merleswein said.

Bondi nodded and scowled. It was their kin and countrymen who had made him an orphan.

Next to the Welsh princes sat Brihtric, a once handsome young thane from Worcestershire, who was now a bloated, red-faced old man, his hair thin and straggly, the joints of his fingers swollen with arthritis. Old forgotten rumours had emerged concerning an affair with Matilda, were now coming back into circulation. Next to him sat his old friend, Sigur, the Earl of Gloucester. He was the same age as Brihtric but looked ten years younger. He had bright green eyes and a Roman nose. He was always alert, and he had a predatory look. Bondi liked him at once.

'I'm glad we've met at last,' said Edric. 'As you know, Lady Gytha is due to be with us today, and I have received word her ship is making its way up the River Dee. She should arrive in an hour. So, while we're waiting for her, let's enjoy refreshments?'

While servants poured them drinks, they took their places on the benches. Merleswein sat next to Brihtric, an old acquaintance, and Bondi sat next to Sigur. Bondi felt ill at ease in such close company with a noble. He had been a royal housecarl, but he had only ever rubbed shoulders with other soldiers. Before Hastings, men like Sigur only ever gave men like him orders.

'So, you're the famous Bondi I've heard about?' Sigur said.

'I am, my lord,' Bondi replied.

'Your accent. Where are you from?' Sigur asked.

Bondi tensed slightly. 'Gloucestershire,' he answered.

'Like me,' Sigur said. 'Where in Gloucestershire?'

'Westbury. Westbury on Severn.'

'I know Westbury. You're Bondi Wynstanson, yes?'

'Correct,'

Sigur studied Bondi intently for a moment. 'You must be twenty-five years old,' the earl said.

'About that.'

Sigur looked Bondi in the eye and said, 'The Welsh razed Westbury to the ground in a raid, and everybody there either killed or driven off as a slave. It must have been twenty years ago.'

'Everybody but one,' Bondi said.

'My God.'

'They killed my family. It was horrible. As you say, they killed everybody or drove them off. I escaped because I was at the river attending to the salmon traps and hid.'

Sigur's eyes watered. 'So, Bondi, you must be Wynstan Athelstan's son. I have to say; you don't look a lot like him,' he said. 'You must have inherited your mother's good looks.'

'You knew them?' Bondi said, the shock showing on his face.

'Oh, yes. Your father was a distant cousin of my wife.'

'I can't recall ever having met anybody who knew them, and I can't remember much about them.'

'What happened after the Welsh left?'

'I went back to the village. I didn't know what to do, so I just stayed there. When Earl Sweyn heard what had happened, he came along and sort of adopted me. After that, I was adopted by King Harold; only then he was still an earl. He must have seen something in me because he had me trained up as a housecarl, and here I am.'

'That's quite a story, Bondi, quite a story. And it explains why you can't stand the Welsh.'

'Does it show that much?

'Don't worry; you're not the only one. But needs must, eh?'

Bondi nodded his agreement.

'So, Bondi. What's life like as a housecarl?'

Bondi told Sigur of his training and adventures, and the two discussed farming, politics, women, and every subject known to man, it seemed.

A few hours after Bondi and Merleswein's arrival, Lady Gytha entered. The doors of the great hall flew open, and before the guard could finish announcing her, she strode purposefully into the hall. Everyone rose to their feet.

'Lady Aldytha. Edric,' Gytha said, striding towards her hosts, smiling with her arms held out to embrace them, which she did heartily. Edric was surprised to find Lady Gytha so warm; he hardly knew her. Aldytha, too, was taken aback.

'How wonderful to see you both, again. I hope you weren't waiting on my account,' Gytha said as she hugged them.

'I've got a lovely surprise for you,' Gytha said. 'Meet my grandson, Godwin.'

A young man, who until that moment had gone unnoticed, stepped forward. Bondi was astonished at the resemblance he had to his father, and he heard Aldytha gasp as her eyes fell on him.

'Hello, my Lady Aldytha,' Godwin said, dipping his head in what was more of a nod than a bow. 'It's an honour to meet you,' he added in a tone that sounded more like a question than a statement.

Observing, Bondi noticed a wry look of amusement on Lady Gytha's face and defiance in Aldytha's eyes. As Edyth's usurper, he thought she should have looked uncomfortable, but she appeared calm.

'And it's a pleasure to meet you. Let's have some wine,' Aldytha said, breaking the tension.

'Yes, let's,' Gytha said.

A servant appeared and presented Gytha and Godwin with wine in beautifully decorated drinking horns.

'To everyone's health,' Gytha said, raising her horn and looking each one of them in the eye. Looking at the two Welsh princes, she turned to Godwin. 'They're the ones who tried to assassinate your father,' Bondi heard her say out of earshot of the Welshmen.

'Brihtric, Sigur. It's so good to see you again,' Gytha said. When she saw Merleswein, she looked delighted.

'Merleswein. Dear Merleswein,' she said. As she approached her late son's old friend, he got to his feet, and the two embraced, slapping each other's back. It was the first time they had met since Hastings.

'I'm so sorry.' Merleswein said before Gytha cut him short.

'There's no need. What we must do now is restore the crown to its rightful king, and you're just the man to help with that,' she said. 'I'm so glad you're here.'

Merleswein hugged her again appreciatively.

Merleswein then reached out to Godwin. 'It's good to see you again, Godwin.'

At that moment, a door opened, and a servant appeared, carrying a bundle of small blankets in her arms.

'Lady Gytha, I have someone special for you to meet. And you too, Godwin.'

The nurse handed the bundle over to Aldytha, who presented it to Gytha. 'Look, it's your grandson, Harold. He's come to see you,' she said.

All eyes focused on the two women and the baby.

Aldytha, looking in wonder at her baby, said, 'Isn't he beautiful? Doesn't he look just like his father?'

The infant peered up at Gytha from under the blankets. 'Yes, he is indeed beautiful. It has to be said; he has his father's handsome looks.'

'You can hold him for a while if you like,' Aldytha said.

'No. That won't be necessary.'

'Godwin, would you like to see your little brother?' Aldytha asked.

'I already have enough brothers, thank you,' Godwin replied, feigning boredom and keen not to show any public recognition of a potential future rival to the throne.

'Merleswein, would you care to see young Harold?' Aldytha asked.

Merleswein agreed, and when he saw the baby, he had to admit, he was the image of his old friend.

The company admired the baby and made small talk until Aldytha suggested they meet again in the evening and discuss plans while they had a feast.

On the way to their rooms, Bondi and Merleswein discussed what they had witnessed.

'What do you think of our get together so far, Bondi?' Merleswein asked.

'I think Godwin feels the same way about the Welsh I do,' Bondi said.

'Yes, he could only just conceal his contempt for them,' Merleswein replied. 'I only hope we can maintain good relations long enough to topple William,' he added.

Later that day, when the shadows were long and the sky turning salmon pink, Bondi and Merleswein sat down with their hosts, Queen Aldytha and Edric, and the other guests in Chester's great hall, the atmosphere was more formal than earlier in the day.

As those present acknowledged Aldytha as Queen of England, they accorded her due respect.

'Welcome. It's good to see you, old friends and new,' she smiled a warm smile, which raised a few eyebrows, namely Lady Gytha's and Godwin's. 'If only the circumstances were different.

'I'm sure most of us thought that William, once he became king, he'd act like his predecessors, but this is not the case. He's ridden roughshod over our rights and privileges, robbing, killing, and raping across our lovely land. That man has committed endless outrages. I doubt he'll change. I'm sure we all feel the same. The question is, what are we going to do about it? And that's why we called this meeting. The answer to the question is that no one here can do anything about it,' Aldytha paused for effect, 'on their own.

'I know William has taken the Atheling and the earls to Normandy,' she continued, 'but others here speak on their behalf. Edric and I speak for ourselves and my brothers, Edwin and Morcar. I know Merleswein speaks for Edgar Atheling and Earl Waltheof. We have our friends, Prince Bleddyn and Rhiwallon, from Wales. Earl Sigur and Brihtric from Mercia. And not forgetting Lady Gytha and Godwin, her grandson from Wessex.'

Lady Gytha's flesh crawled when Aldytha mentioned her name, and she did well to hide her feelings.

Edric spoke next. 'If we want to depose the Bastard, we have to stick together. Now is the time to settle any differences. Whatever we do, I don't care, so long as we rid ourselves of the Normans.'

Earl Sigur offered his support. 'I agree. Well said, Edric.'

The hall went quiet, and the Welsh princes exchanged meaningful glances.

Aldytha continued, 'You're right of course, Edric,' she smiled at her lover, 'Thank you.'

Brihtric interjected, 'To stick together, it'll take more than just the goodwill of the folk gathered here. If we're going to stick together, we'll need a leader.'

Aldytha continued, 'That's why William's taken Edgar and the rest of them with him to Normandy; he's left us leaderless, what we must do is plan for their return. If he keeps them there for too long, we may have to act without them before the Normans get too tight a grip on the kingdom.'

Brihtric spoke again. 'But who will lead us? We must agree on this point,' he said, looking meaningfully at Lady Gytha and Godwin. 'Mustn't we?' he added, this time focusing his attention on Aldytha and Edric.

'King Edgar will be our leader, surely,' was Merleswein's quick response.

'Of course, Edgar will be our leader,' Lady Gytha added with a cold smile.

Attention focused on Queen Aldytha and Edric.

'We had no other in mind,' Edric responded.

'Good. I'm glad that's settled,' Brihtric said. 'Do our Welsh friends have any views on the matter?' he continued.

'I think I can speak for both of us,' Bleddyn answered. 'It is of no concern to my brother and me, who is King of England once we've disposed of William. The Normans are now moving on to Wales. FitzOsbern has built a castle at Chepstow. My guess is the Normans will keep moving further west. We just want them gone.'

'I see,' Edric said.

Merleswein spoke next. 'There aren't that many Normans to worry about. Ten thousand came over with William, and after the battles and what have you, there can only be about five thousand left. They won't stand a chance if we act together, even with their castles. We already hold Northumbria and East Anglia. Most of Mercia is still free and almost all southwest Wessex. We can push them back behind their castle walls. If they don't surrender, we'll starve them out. The rest we just push and push until we drive them back into the sea.'

'That sounds simple enough,' agreed Aldytha. 'When are we going to do it?'

'Can I just say something,' Merleswein asked.

'Of course, Merleswein,' Aldytha said.

'I have a concern that leaves me feeling uneasy, and it is this. No one here is a priest. Shouldn't there be a member of the Church here to speak?' Merleswein said.

This question produced an awkward silence.

'Unfortunately,' Aldytha answered, 'the Church seems to have gone over to the Normans. We've heard nothing from Archbishop Stigand, and Archbishop Ealdred is telling anyone who'll listen that the Normans being here is an act of God. He appears to have persuaded the Church of his case.'

'But surely, my lady, we should inform the church,' Merleswein replied.

'As the Church won't fight, the Church doesn't need to know. One careless word and our whole uprising at risk.'

'Lady Aldytha is right, Merleswein,' Gytha joined in. 'There was a time the Church was firmly on our side, but now, I'm afraid, too many unreliable elements lie in its corridors, and they endanger us all.'

Merleswein thought for a moment. He was not used to women informing him of where his thinking was going wrong, but as no one else was objecting and these were the most influential women in the land, he decided he had better not push his case any longer.

'I take your point, my lady,' Merleswein conceded.

'Thank you, Merleswein.' Lady Gytha continued, 'My other grandsons, Magnus and Edmund, are organising men in Ireland. They should have enough ships to bring two thousand men over, but not until early next summer. It's quite a while, I know, but it gives us the advantage of having plenty of time to plan.

'Merleswein, how many men in the north do you think will answer the call?'

'I can raise a couple of thousand. King Edgar can raise a few hundred. We're trying to persuade King Malcolm to help. If he joins us, that'll be three thousand men he will bring down from Scotland.'

'We're hoping King Swein might join us, too,' Gytha said.

'Danes!' exclaimed Edric, startled.

'What's wrong with Danes?' asked Gytha.

'Nothing,' Edric answered swiftly when he remembered Gytha was Danish. 'It's just that I don't want to get rid of one foreign king just to find myself with another.'

'You don't need to worry about King Swein; I can vouch for him,' Gytha said.

Again, silence fell across the hall, and for a few moments, they could hear only the crackling of the fire.

'With Edric's men,' Aldytha responded. 'And, my brothers,' we should be able to raise at least eight hundred.'

'I should be able to raise around eight hundred from the southwest,' Brihtric volunteered.

'And don't forget, we can add five hundred men,' Prince Bleddyn volunteered.

'Thank you, Prince Bleddyn,' answered Aldytha.

'I can get one hundred and fifty,' offered Sigur. 'And who knows how many will join us once we start?'

'Many, I hope,' answered Aldytha. 'And that will be exactly when?'

'In Spring. Are we agreed?' asserted Lady Gytha.

'Spring might be too soon,' Brihtric said. 'What about Midsummer's Day?'

'Why Midsummer's Day?' Gytha asked.

'Because it gives us more time to get organised, and the weather can generally be relied upon,' Brihtric answered.

'It sounds like a good idea,' Merleswein said, looking delighted.

There was a general mumbling of agreement.

Aldytha said, 'So, it's agreed, we rise together on Midsummer's Day.'

Merleswein spoke again. 'What do we do if William's still in Normandy and we overthrow the Normans? We should be safe from William for a while. I'm not so sure he could raise a second fleet. But what will happen to the hostages? Are we prepared to make the sacrifice? How will we feel if William kills them? Particularly if they're family.'

They thought this over. Aldytha calculated it might mean losing two brothers. Still, after their performance the previous year, she was unsure how great a loss they would be, especially as sacrificing the hostages removed the complication of Edgar. Then there was Wulfnoth, Harold's brother. That might mean one less Godwinson to interfere. Doing her best to look sombre, Aldytha said, 'That's a risk I'm willing to take and a pain I will have to endure all my days.'

Gytha nodded sagely, 'As you know, I have a grandson in Normandy. He's been there for fifteen years, and as far as we know, no harm has come to him. I don't think William will harm them.'

'What about Edgar?' asked Merleswein. He was genuinely concerned for the Atheling.

'Don't worry, Merleswein. I'm sure no harm will come to him,' Gytha answered.

'It's not just harm befalling him,' Merleswein replied. 'If he's still alive but stuck in Normandy, how can we elect a new king when we've proclaimed Edgar king?'

Gytha replied at once. 'I'm sure we could arrange something. He could rule jointly as Harthacnut and Edward did.'

'Thank you for your comment, Lady Gytha. I agree with you wholeheartedly,' Aldytha said, with a little too much enthusiasm. As no one objected, the way was open for another to take the crown.

There was a stirring in the hall as everyone realised they had the makings of a successful plan. Only the details needed attention.

'If he is in the kingdom on Midsummer's Day, is anyone going to deal specifically with William?' Merleswein asked.

'I thought Bondi could lead a party to tackle William,' Merleswein answered. 'Would you be happy to do that, Bondi?'

'Very happy,' Bondi agreed.

'Yes, I think that's a good idea,' Queen Aldytha added. 'I think you'll be the ideal man for the job.'

'I agree,' Lady Gytha said.

'I'm honoured, my ladies.'

'Are we all in agreement?' Aldytha said.

No one objected.

'Yes, but what if something goes wrong?' Aldytha said. 'We need another option. Do you have any ideas, Brihtric?'

'I think someone needs to be in overall control, so we know what's going on. Who's doing what, where and when. That kind of thing.'

'Yes, you're right, of course,' Gytha replied. 'I think all communications should go through you. You're central, and so many traders use the River Severn, no one would notice another ship coming and going.

'I'll be in Exeter with a small force,' she continued. 'Once we have the city in our hands, my boys can take Bristol before we move on to London. Edric and Sigur, with the help of our Welsh friends,' she looked down her nose disapprovingly at the brothers, 'can seize the border counties, then move southeast. Merleswein can come down from the north and march on London.'

'Wonderful,' Brihtric said. 'The country will be up in arms, and there'll be no one at the top to tell the Normans what to do. I'll keep in touch with everyone regularly. If you have any problems you feel the rest of us should know about, contact me.'

'Does anyone have anything to add?' Aldytha asked.

The company remained silent.

'It's been a long day, Lady Aldytha, and so I'll bid you goodnight,' Gytha said.

The two women embraced, their drinking horns still in their hands. Bondi could not help but notice the shadows on the wall showed two women stabbing each other in the back, and he wondered, *an omen perhaps?*

Chapter 14

In his castle at Falaise, William waited in his chambers for a knock on the door. Exactly as expected, the door opened, and a guard announced that Stigand, Archbishop of Canterbury, was there to see him.

'Good afternoon, Archbishop. You wanted to see me.'

'Yes, my lord.'

'I hope it's important.'

'There is a conspiracy afoot in England. A rebellion is being planned right across your kingdom. The Welsh, Scots and Danes are to join forces with your English enemies and remove you from power.'

William's face paled and tensed. 'We're miles away from England, Stigand. How do you know all this?'

'I keep in touch with my people back home. Lady Gytha and her sons are behind it. None of the English nobles, who are enjoying your hospitality here, are implicated.'

'When is this uprising to take place?'

'I don't know. It's taking time to plan, and the Danes can't cross the North Sea until the Spring.'

'That's something,' William spat the words out. 'At least we can do something about it. Thank you, Stigand, you've been most helpful. I shall not forget this.'

'Oh, Archbishop. Not a word to anyone.'

'My lips are sealed.'

'Good. Thank you, that will be all,' William said.

After Stigand left the room, William felt so incensed he banged his fists on the table. *After everything I've done for them. At least I have plenty of time, and Lady Gytha and her friends have no idea I'm aware of their intentions.*

William decided to keep Stigand's information to himself for a while. He would tell Matilda of his discovery and arrange for her to rule

Normandy in his absence. Courtiers were surprised when he announced he planned to be in London for the Christmas festivities, but no one suspected his real motive. Before two weeks had passed, William was back in England; ostensibly celebrating Christmas in his kingdom, but in truth, to head off a rebellion.

A subdued Christmas had come and gone, with William still none the wiser about who exactly was involved in the plot to remove him. The day after Epiphany, once the English nobles had left for their homes, William raised the issue at court.

'I'm sure you're all aware of a plot to overthrow me.'

A shocked silence greeted the remark before calls of 'No,' and 'Impossible,' rang out. In no time, William's men were on their feet, swearing to hunt out the traitors, and it took time to calm them down.

'I'm sure no man here would plot against his king, but there are others in the kingdom whose loyalty is open to question.' William let his message sink in.

'Lady Gytha is behind this, and she and her grandsons are raising an army to attack later this year. My guess is in the spring. There will be attacks the length and breadth of the kingdom.

'Does anyone have something to say?' he snapped.

Odo was the one to speak. 'I received this from a messenger from Exeter just before the council met,' his brother, the bishop, said, holding out a sealed scroll to the king.

William glanced at it. 'What does it say, Odo?'

After unrolling it, the bishop broke the seal and said, 'I don't think we're going to have to wait until spring for trouble. I'll read the message.

'It's from Bishop Leofric in Exeter. He says, 'the people of Exeter will not swear fealty to the king, nor admit him within our wall, but will pay him tribute according to ancient custom.''

Odo looked at William for a reaction. The king was livid.

'No one here knew about the planned rebellion, and no one knows anything about this?' William said, grabbing the scroll off Odo and waving it in the air for all to see.

Every face in his company looked blank.

'So, none of you knew anything?'

Faces that were blank now appeared tense.

'The West Country is defying me, and none of you had any idea?' William hissed.

It was Stigand who spoke up. 'The conspirators are sending messages the length and breadth of the River Severn.'

'How?' William asked.

'I understand they go via Bristol, but more than that, I know nothing.'

'I think you and I need to talk, Archbishop,' William said.

Later in the king's chamber, the two men met alone to discuss the situation.

'Do sit down, Archbishop and have some wine,' said the king, and a servant sprang into action.

'I'm so glad you stayed on in your post,' the king said. 'It's vital to have someone around who I can trust, someone who understands the English.'

Stigand sat and smiled at his king, his hands held together by weaved fingers. It amazed William the Archbishop could look so sage-like.

'Tell me, Stigand. May I call you by your name?'

'Of course.'

'Tell me, since we talked in Normandy, have you learned any more about this rebellion?'

'As you know, Lady Gytha is behind it, and from what I understand, those thanes in the southwest and borders as far north as Cheshire are to rise together. The feeling is you Normans are stretched too thin on the ground to resist a large, coordinated uprising.'

A shiver ran down William's spine. What Stigand said was true.

'The people of Exeter will rise, and the other counties are to follow,' Stigand said.

'This is serious. How many are against me?'

'Let's just say; there is vehement opposition to you in many quarters; fortunately, none of it from the Church,' Stigand said.

'So, who are my enemies and who are my friends?'

'Lady Gytha has organised Exeter against you. The city is becoming a rallying point for those who want to depose you. At the same time as

Exeter rises, her sons plan to take Bristol. From Exeter, all the west will march against you to as far north as Chester. I'm only surprised they're acting now. I understood the uprising would be on Midsummer's Day.

'How do you know this?'

'Your men don't speak the language.'

'Malet does,' William said.

'Sir William may speak the language, but he is one of the enemy.'

'And you're not?'

'No. I don't take sides in such secular matters. I am a man of God, and there are many who, like me, welcome your reforms. May I remind you; the Church was the first to submit to you, and the Church will be the first amongst your loyal servants.'

William could hardly believe his ears. *He's outrageous, but you must admire his gall. It's easy to see how he rose to his position.*

'Do I have any friends, other than the Church, Stigand?'

'Eadnoth, Alderman of Bristol. He's an important man in an important city, and he has a lot of followers.'

'How do you know he can be trusted?'

'Because he is the father of Harding, Queen Edith's steward. He wouldn't do anything to harm his son's career or embarrass Queen Edith.'

'What can he do to help?'

'Defend Bristol, protect the south-west, intercept messages, and alert us to any danger. If Exeter did rise, he might make sure it remained alone, at least for a while.'

'Thank you, Stigand. I'll remember this day and how much help you have been to me.' And remember the day William did. *If Stigand can betray his countrymen so easily, how difficult would it be for him to cross me?* He asked himself.

'I think I'll pay the West Country a visit,' William said. 'It's always pleasant to have surprise visitors drop in, don't you think, Archbishop?'

'Indeed, I do,' Stigand said with a smile.

On the way to Exeter, William visited the Dowager Queen Edith to forge a better relationship. The visit enabled him to see how Harding, her steward, stood up to scrutiny. The ground was frozen hard and the icy wind merciless, as William started from London and was no easier as he approached Winchester on the first leg of his mission to quash the rebels.

After a gruelling three-day ride, King William was pleased to enjoy the hospitality of Queen Edith, who made him welcome. Upon his arrival, Harding escorted him to the great hall, where Edith was waiting for him. As he entered, she rose from her seat, a fine oak, high-backed chair, its arms and legs covered in elaborate carving.

'Welcome, King William. What a wonderful surprise to have you visit us. Can I offer you refreshment?' Edith said.

William made his way over to the fire to warm himself. Clouds of vapour rose from his damp clothes, and he breathed a quiet sigh of pleasure as he warmed up.

'Wine wouldn't go amiss, my lady. Please be seated.'

Edith smiled as she sat and indicated for Harding to serve the king.

'Excuse my bluntness,' she said. 'But do you intend to stay long? I ask because if I know your requirements, I can make sure they're met.'

'I thought I'd stay for just two nights.'

'How many men do we need to accommodate?'

'If you can feed and shelter two hundred of my companions, the rest can take care of themselves.'

'Consider it done,' Edith said, smiling.

Happy that their meeting looked as though it would be a pleasant one, the two entered into an agreeable small talk for a few minutes until William had dried out, warmed up and finished his wine, when Harding showed him to his quarters.

When William next entered the hall, just two hours later, it was as the guest of honour, and he took pride of place next to Edith on the dais. Edith's hall was full of Normans. Apart from Harding and the servants, there was not one Englishman in sight.

Edith got to her feet, and the hall fell silent.

'Welcome, my king. What an honour and privilege it is to have you here. Allow me to say on behalf of everyone,' she said, raising her goblet high. 'Long life and happiness to you.'

Edith spoke in fluent French, and it thrilled William to be greeted in such a way by a queen.

There were shouts and cheers from the hall as everyone drank the king's health before sitting down to enjoy the banquet.

Edith and her guests gathered around long tables enjoying the food, drink, and conversation, accompanied by convivial laughter and the crackling of the fire. William thought Edith appeared relaxed, she was at home, and she felt comfortable and secure, William less so. This was the first time he had sat next to a queen at her table. He found it intimidating. He could not get used to the idea of the English aristocracy not having to protect themselves behind ramparts, embankments, and moats.

'Are you happy living this way?' he asked, opening his arms and raising his eyes to the ceiling. He sounded amazed.

'What way?'

'In a hall. Aren't you bothered somebody might try to storm the building?'

'Why would they do that?' Edith asked.

'They might have designs on your land or your treasure.'

'Who's going to do that?' Edith said pointedly, but William missed the irony in what she was saying.

'What if the townsfolk turn against you or your thanes decide to make trouble?'

'There would be no point. If they have any problems, they can come and see me.'

'But what if it's an angry mob or,' he leaned forward as if for more intimacy, 'what if a baron or count decides he's going to take your lands? If you have a castle, he couldn't do that.' It was then the irony in his words suddenly struck him. From the look on her face, he could tell Edith saw it, too.

'You might have a point,' she replied.

'I'll have one built for you,' he replied as he blushed.

'You've already built one in Winchester, thank you. We managed without one in the past; I'm sure we don't need two now.'

William's mind travelled back to Normandy and the troubles he had there and wondered how long he would have lasted without a castle for protection. In some ways, he envied the English, but then again, how stupid they were; if they had proper fortifications, he doubted he would be here, now, having this conversation.

William turned his gaze to Harding, Edith's loyal servant. She had assured William that Harding's loyalty was beyond doubt. William believed her; if the rumours he heard were true, Harding had killed for her and perhaps would again.

'What do you think, Harding?'

The steward, surprised to be addressed by the king, hardly knew what to say.

'About castles?'

'Yes, Harding. Castles.'

'They make a daunting sight, especially if they are like the one you built here.'

Harding continued, 'I imagine anyone possessing a castle could control the country for miles around, knowing his home is impregnable and help from comrades not far away. It would take a large army to dislodge him.'

And with those few words, Harding revealed which way he thought the wind was blowing. His pragmatism was one reason Edith respected him so much and why William decided he could depend on their loyalty.

'And what of Exeter, Harding? It is a walled city, is it not? Built by the Romans, I believe.'

'And strengthened since.'

'Would it be easy to defend against my army?'

'You'll need more than the few hundred you have with you.'

'They're all I've got.'

'Unless you call out the fyrd,' Harding said, more in jest than sincerity.

'The fyrd?' William asked.

'A kind of militia.'

'You mean, that undisciplined rabble that fell for our tricks at Hastings?'

'Did they all fall for your tricks?'

William thought for a moment; his troops were spread a little thin, and there were none to spare. Perhaps Harding was right, he could call out the fyrd, and he would have more troops. It would also be a way of bonding with English, or at least some of them, and asserting himself with the rest. And so, he would turn a problem into an opportunity.

'Tell me, Harding. What exactly is this fyrd, and how do I call it out?'

'Thanes have to supply you with men for military service. The number of men depends on how much land they hold. Call them out, and they will be yours for forty days.

'Summon the lords of Wessex to provide troops for you, and they will do so. Tell them where and when to meet you, and they will be there,' Harding said.

'You make it sound simple. How do I know anyone will turn up?'

'They have to,' Harding replied. 'You are their king, and they owe you military service. If they refuse, you can fine them and even confiscate their land. They have horses too, and so it won't take long for them to join you, so long as you don't call in the fyrd from too far away.'

'So, you're telling me that even if they don't want to, they will have to go to war against their fellow countrymen,' William asked.

'Yes, exactly, my lord,' Harding replied.

The next day, after calling out the fyrd in the south, William continued his journey to Exeter, secure knowing that at least one part of his kingdom was safe and, as Harding had noticed, the building of enough castles would secure the rest. And he had obtained more support for his expedition. Although he wondered how much he could rely on English troops.

But still, he thought. *I'll be keeping my enemy close.*

Chapter 15

Five weeks after his first visit, William returned to Winchester to Dowager Queen Edith's hall for a second time. Harding announced the King, who entered with his closest companions, about twenty in all.

'My lord, how wonderful to see you again, especially so soon after your previous visit. It's an honour.'

'The honour is all mine,' William smiled. I have a little surprise for you.'

'Oh. I'm curious.'

William turned to his men and nodded. A gap appeared, and two young men stepped forward after a push in the back.

'I've brought with me a special guest who I think you might be particularly pleased to see.' William said.

It took a moment for Edith to recognise her nephew, Ulf. Who the other man was, she had no idea.

'Ulf,' Edith said. 'How lovely to see you.'

Before he could speak, William began boasting. 'I'm not so sure he's glad to be here. My good friend, Sir Ralph Pomeroy, caught him trying to escape from Exeter in a boat with your mother and some more of the family. He wasn't quite quick enough,' William said, turning to Ulf, 'were you boy?'

Ulf said nothing. Neither did his friend, Thorkell.

William turned his attention to Edith. 'This evening, he'll be able to keep you entertained with stories of defeat and failed escape. Make the most of it, tomorrow we leave for London.'

That evening, while the Normans gorged themselves at her expense, Edith had to listen to William's account of the Siege of Exeter.

'Of course, I knew the city would fall eventually; it was just a matter of time. Even though it's one of the best defended towns I've ever come across, it was no match for my men and me. All we had to do was undermine one of the gates and bring it crashing down. It helped that your treacherous Cornish friends opened another gate for us. All for just a few coins, too. You English really must learn to treat people better.

'Once we stormed the gates, it was all over. Your mother and her entourage ran like rats from a sinking ship. Do you have any idea where they might be, I wonder?'

'If I knew, my lord, I'd tell you,' Edith said.

'It's good to know at least one of the Godwins is loyal to their king,' William replied, casting a glance in Ulf's direction at the far end of the hall. 'Not that it matters anymore. My kingdom is secure, and your mother's little rebellion put down.'

'I'm glad to hear that, my lord,' Edith replied.

'You'll also be pleased to hear that I've left some forces behind to clear out any enclaves of rebellion. They're scouring Devon of all resistance to my rule. I may not yet control all of England, but Wessex is mine.'

Edith sat stony-faced, listening to what William had to say with no visible reaction. They made an interesting site; she slender, brittle, cultured, aesthetic graceful and refined. He, with the powerful look of someone who possesses more than his fair share of brute strength. Remarkably, they both had the same colour of strawberry blond hair.

Edith turned to face her king, 'Congratulations, my lord. Your conquest is something to be celebrated.'

'You know, that's exactly what I think, and that's why I have a favour to ask of you, my dear.'

Edith flinched at William's use of, 'my dear.'

'How can I help?'

'Your French is impeccable, my lady. So you must know what I mean by chanson de geste.'

'Of course.'

'My brother, Odo, thought having my conquest of the English a worthy subject for a chanson. Don't you agree?'

Edith's jaw tensed. 'Yes, I suppose it is, but why are you telling me this?'

'Because I'd like you to oversee its creation, from beginning to end.

I'm told embroidery is one of the many skills at which you excel.'

'That's very flattering, my lord. I'd be honoured.'

'Excellent. We can take the matter further when you come to Matilda's coronation later in the year.

Chapter 16

Pomeroy gave his bride to be a critical glance. 'Are you ready now?' he asked, even though it was apparent she was quite prepared for the brief ceremony that lay ahead.

'Yes, I'm ready,' she replied. She looked tired and resigned to her fate and thought about how her life had changed in the last two years. It seemed like a lifetime ago that her husband, Alric, kissed her goodbye and left for Hastings, never to be heard of again. She lived in hope for a while. *Perhaps he'll be home for Christmas.*

Christmas came and went, and in Alric's place came rumours. One after the other, members of the fyrd, admittedly only a few, had returned to their homes and loved ones. Stories of heroic defeat amid the savage slaughter tormented her ears, but not her husband's voice. Some returning soldiers told her they might have seen her loved one fall. *But it was dark, and they could be mistaken.* And then there was the uprising at Exeter. *Perhaps he's involved in that.* But still no word. And then the day dawned when she admitted to herself. *He's never coming home.*

After she had given up hope, Ralph Pomeroy arrived to inform her what was once Alric's was now his, a gift from the king. He had also presented her with an ultimatum; marry him or farm a small parcel of land in a far corner of her old property. She had considered an unmentioned third option: living in a nunnery, *but who will care for my boys?* So, here, now she was on the arm of a Norman soldier who had kicked in the door of her country and her life. Now here she was astride a fine horse, Pomeroy atop of Etoile, making her way from Alric's hall to the church, only a short walk away.

About twenty yards from St. Mary's, they dismounted, and like any devoted bride, she took the groom's arm as they made their way on foot for the rest of the journey.

They approached the little stone building; he dressed in his charcoal woollen tunic, trimmed with gold, red and blue silk around the sleeves and neck. A sword with an elaborate hilt and a gold pommel hung from his waist, inscribed on one side with a dragon and a wolf. On the other the name Ralph where it once said, Harold. Tate, for that was his bride's name, imagined they appeared the epitome of respectability, nobility even. Robert de Comines was the best man, prepared to protect his friend and fight off any of Tate's male relatives who might try to stop the wedding. All of Pomeroy's serfs and his dozen men, and Tate's two boys, were there to witness the event. At a later date, there could be no denying they were joined in wedlock.

The wedding was a sombre affair in the doorway of Saint Mary's with the local priest there to bless the couple, which he did before returning to his usual duties. It was a brief ceremony that lasted only a few minutes. And so it happened. Pomeroy now had a young and pretty wife, a fine woman, which was a bonus for him, and he was already looking forward to producing heirs.

'Wasn't that respectable? We even had a priest. We're officially, man and wife,' Pomeroy said to his bride.

And you have witnesses to prove it, she thought, forcing a smile and fearing her fate sealed.

Pomeroy had developed a fondness for this place. He enjoyed his new holding and gazed out over a hundred acres of woodland, ten acres of meadow and forty acres of pasture on his gently undulating land. A breeze blew in, carrying the smell of the sea. He was enjoying staying in his new home. In the coming weeks, he would take the time to get to know his forty serfs and his neighbours. He looked forward to breeding horses from Etoile, who would no doubt produce some fine colts. But before doing so, he would consummate the marriage at the earliest opportunity.

When the couple reached the door to the hall, Pomeroy picked up his bride, just as Alric had five years earlier, and carried her over the threshold. Tate's boys, Ceolwulf, the oldest aged four, and his younger brother Cuthred, aged two and their nurse, followed them in silence. Over Pomeroy's shoulder, Tate smiled at them, wondering what fate had in store for them. Pomeroy turned and grinned at them in the manner of a wolf.

Pomeroy's men cheered as they poured into the hall behind their leader and his wife. Once everybody was seated, Robert de Comines rose and proposed a toast to the bride and groom. The guests get to their feet and drink the couple's health.

'Time to feast,' Pomeroy said. There was a clatter as servants appeared with an abundance of food and wine. Tate had organised everything, and she had put in a great effort, and for a reason he could not identify, she made him feel proud.

Pomeroy reflected on similar occasions at home in Normandy, when he was a boy with the family. They were rarely joyous times. His father drank too much and offended or embarrassed the family, except his eldest brother, Roger, the favourite. He remembered the servants quaking with fear, afraid of yet another beating. Sometimes, when he was young, he would quake along with them. Occasionally, his father got roaring drunk, and no one was safe, not the servants, not him or his brothers, including Roger, and even his mother. No one was out of danger.

Pomeroy felt a dark mood descend over him and tried to think of something else. It was then he caught sight of Tate studying her new wedding ring. It was a thing of beauty, made of gold with a blue agate centre with four red agate stones around. He liked the way her hands moved so gracefully. She looked up, and their eyes met. She smiled, and he returned the smile.

Yes, Tate was attractive, and she would provide him with brave and handsome sons who would inherit his legacy. Sons of his own; her first two would have to go. All he had to do was arrange it. His gaze drifted over to where the boys sat, and as Pomeroy looked at them, their eyes met, he raised his drinking horn to them, a fleeting moment of affection, but even at their tender age, they saw murder in his eyes. In theirs, he saw fear.

Chapter 17

It was early May when Whitgar arrived at Merleswein's farmstead. His journey had been pleasant, travelling through the spring countryside enjoying the sunshine, bluebells, and blossom, but the evening was cooling rapidly, and he was glad to reach his destination. A servant took his horse to the stable while a second led him to Merleswein in the hall.

'Welcome to Lincoln,' Merleswein said.

'It's good to be back,' Whitgar replied. On the dais, he noticed two attractive women, one who looked married and the other younger woman, who had the look of a maiden. There was a man with them who he took to be the older woman's husband.

'Allow me to introduce my daughters,' Merleswein said. 'This is Morwenna, and this is my youngest, Elfwyn.'

Morwenna smiled and gave a slight nod of her head.

'Hello Whitgar,' Elfwyn said, beaming her biggest smile.

'Hello,' he said, smiling back.

'And these handsome fellows are our guests. Eadric the Steersman, and Bondi Wynstanson. Eadric, you probably know, was in charge of the navy until recently, and Bondi was one of King Harold's housecarls,' Merleswein said.

'I'm honoured to meet you both,' Whitgar said. 'Your reputations precede you.'

'Perhaps you'd like to take a place on the bench next to Bondi,' Merleswein said.

'Yes, I would,' Whitgar said and sat next to the housecarl.

'What brings you this way, Whitgar?' Merleswein asked.

'I'm going to London for Matilda's coronation.'

'You too? I have an invitation as well. Morwenna and Elfwyn don't want me to go.'

'It's a trap,' Morwenna said. 'Once you're there, you'll never get away.'

'Perhaps. Perhaps not,' Merleswein replied.

'You can't go,' Elfwyn said. 'Morwenna is right.'

'Wonderful as it is to see my girls agreeing on something, it could be an opportunity for us.'

Bondi and Whitgar looked keen to hear what he had to say next. Eadric smiled, amused by the puzzled expressions on their faces.

'William is holding Edgar and the earls' hostage,' Merleswein said. 'He calls them his guests, but we know the truth of the matter. We've planned the uprising for Mid-summer's Day, and we need to have our friends out of William's custody well before then. This invitation to Matilda's coronation might provide us with the opportunity we need.'

'How?' Morwenna asked.

'We'll have an excuse to be in London. Eadric and I have a plan to free our friends, and it was the invitation that inspired us.'

'It's reckless,' Morwenna said, yet the sisters wished they had been invited.

'You haven't even heard the plan yet,' Elfwyn said to her sister before turning to her father and asking, 'Can we come?'

'I'll give it my consideration.'

'That means no,' Elfwyn said. 'We never do anything exciting.'

'Now that's not true,' Merleswein said.

Elfwyn looked directly at Morwenna, 'When has father ever allowed us to do anything exciting?'

'Aren't you being a little harsh?' Morwenna said.

'No,' Elfwyn replied.

'It's for your own good. Remember that when you got lost in those tunnels in York?' Merleswein said.

'We were children. And it was our first time down there. Anyway, it didn't take long to find us,' Elfwyn said.

'What do you mean? "our first time down there?" Did you go again?'

Elfwyn blushed. 'Perhaps once,' she said.

Attempting to defuse the situation, Whitgar jumped in. 'When I was a boy, I used to explore the tunnels whenever I was in York.'

Merleswein gave him a scathing look, but Elfwyn smiled her appreciation.

'Anyway, I don't see what tunnels in York when we were three...'

'You were a lot older than three, young lady,' her father interrupted.

'What has something we did as little girls got to do with going to London? Why can't we come with you?'

'Because I have plans, and the two of you aren't part of them.'

'What plans?'

'Secret plans,' Merleswein replied.

'Stop teasing,' Elfwyn said. 'We could make ourselves useful.'

'Elfwyn's right,' Morwenna said.

'I'd love you to come, but it's not possible. We have to keep the party small if my plan is to work,' Merleswein said. 'Let that be an end of it.'

As Morwenna was about to reply, a steward opened the main door. 'Thurold, to see you, my lord.'

'Welcome, Thurold,' Merleswein said, getting to his feet to greet his old friend and neighbour.

Unseen by their father, Morwenna and Elfwyn exchanged a glance before rolling their eyes.

'Thank you. I'd heard your daughters were here and thought I'd come by and say hello,' Thurold said.

'You're always welcome here,' Merleswein replied.

The expressions on Morwenna's and Elfwyn's faces failed to convey the warmth of their father's welcome.

'You will stay for the night, won't you?' Merleswein said.

'Thank you.'

'Good. Take a seat next to Whitgar.'

Thurold took his place as servants served the meal, which passed in convivial conversation, with Thurold doing plenty of talking, expressing his opinions on various topics. When the evening reached a natural conclusion, Thurold gazed conspiratorially at Merleswein and eyed the door before getting up and heading outside.

'I think I'll join you,' Merleswein said. 'I'm fit to burst.'

As soon as the two were outside, Whitgar leaned over to Bondi.

'How well do you know Merleswein's daughters?'

'You mean Elfwyn?' Bondi said.

'Yes.' Whitgar asked, amazed at the housecarl's insight.

'You haven't taken your eyes off her all night.'

'Oh,' Whitgar said, blushing.

'I'll tell you this, they're proud, or at least Elfwyn is, that they're descended from King Alfred. Morwenna is more modest and sensible. She's the widow of Shire Reeve Godric, of Buckinghamshire, and she has three of his children. The Normans have stolen her lands.'

'So that's why she's here?'

'Yes. The children are with their nurse, Sherilda, in Scotland, where they'll be safe. Why do you ask?'

'I just wondered,' Whitgar replied.

Further along the dais, Morwenna was questioning Elfwyn.

'You seem quite taken with our guest. I've never seen you captivated.'

'What are you talking about?' Elfwyn said.

'You're well aware of what I'm talking about.'

'What if I do like him just a little?' Elfwyn said. 'He's just a thane from somewhere or another. I don't care for him if that's what you mean. Why are you making a fuss? And you can wipe that smile off your face as well.'

With Elfwyn's last remark, Morwenna burst into laughter.

'Be quiet. He's looking,' Elfwyn said.

While the sister's conversation concerned one man, two men were outside talking, whose discussion was about one of them. Under a star-strewn cloudless sky, Merleswein and Thurold were deep in conversation.

Thurold broke the ice. 'You must have guessed I have feelings for Morwenna, and I thought this might be an ideal time to make my feelings clear.'

'I'm not sure what you're saying, Thurold,' Merleswein said.

'I want Morwenna to be my wife, and I'd like your blessing.'

'If I said I'd be delighted to have you as a son-in-law, I'd be lying. Not because I don't think you're good enough,' *but really you're not.* 'It's because you might find Morwenna, what shall I say...'

'Headstrong?' Thurold volunteered.

'You could say that. You never met their mother, did you? She was willful, and she could be obstinate. But she had fire and beauty in excess. You always understood where you were with her, and if there were any confusion, she'd soon clear it up for you. Morwenna and Elfwyn are just the same.'

'I love a filly who has life in her,' Thurold laughed.

'She's much more than a filly,' Merleswein said. 'She can be a handful. You might want to think it over and ask me again shortly. I couldn't just marry her off. She'd have to have her say, or there'll be hell to pay.'

Thurold looked crestfallen but said, 'Very well. I'll leave things in your capable hands.'

The following day, when everyone was at breakfast, Morwenna felt unsettled. She had entered the hall with her children and Sherilda, their nurse, to find her father and Thurold deep in conversation, which ended abruptly upon her arrival. As everyone took their places at the table, Elfwyn entered and joined them.

'Good morning, everybody,' she said. A chorus of good mornings greeted her. She sat next to Morwenna, who leaned close and whispered, 'Something's afoot.'

'What?' Elfwyn asked.

'Father and Thurold? They're up to something.'

'I haven't noticed anything, but I've only just come in.'

'I suspect something's going on,' Sherilda said.

'Perhaps father's changed his mind and is going to take us to London after all,' Elfwyn said.

'We can always ask,' Morwenna said.

'Father,' Morwenna said. 'Have you reconsidered taking Elfwyn and me to London with you?'

'I'll think about it. In the meantime, Thurold, Bondi, Whitgar and Eadric, join me as I inspect my skeps?'

'Huh,' Elfwyn huffed. 'You and your bees.'

Bondi and Whitgar looked perplexed, but Eadric smiled knowingly, and they agreed to accompany Merleswein on his bee inspection. They followed him out of the hall and around to the south-facing side of an outbuilding. There, against the wall, were two shelves with ten skeps on each, basking in the sunshine. A cover ran along the top of the skeps to keep them dry, making cosy homes for Merleswein's bees.

Merleswein smiled at the skeps and said, 'Aren't they marvellous? Each one is like a city full of busy little people working away to produce something delightful.'

Eadric stood with a grin across his broad, flat face, and Bondi and Whitgar wondered where this was leading.

'I've never had much to do with bees,' Bondi said. 'How do you get to the honey without being stung?'

'That's an important skill to learn, Bondi. I'll show you,' Merleswein replied. 'I won't be long,' he said and disappeared around to the far side of the building, returning a short while later with a bundle of clothes and a strange-looking hood that had wickerwork fitted across the front to protect the wearer's face.

Merleswein put on the thick, heavy smock and the hood. 'Just as you can't tell one of the busy little bees from each other, neither can you tell one beekeeper from another,' he said, smiling at his guests.

'An important thing to remember, the best time to move them is at night,' he smiled. 'You're familiar with this, aren't you, Whitgar?'

'Father loves bees just as you do, and he's passed on some of that knowledge to me. Although I confess, he knows much more than I do,' Whitgar replied.

'He talked about nothing else whenever we met,' Merleswein said. 'Now, I can't spend all day here chewing the fat with you a lot. There's work to be done. If you like, you can watch. I'll show you how to collect the honey, but it's best if you start packing. We're leaving on the next tide to London for honey,' Merleswein said, presenting them with his most enigmatic smile.

'What do you mean?' Whitgar asked, perplexed.

'You'd best get packed.'

Four days after Merleswein had shown his friends his skeps, he, Whitgar and Bondi were sailing up the Thames. Eadric's ship, the Sea Wolf, looked majestic with a vast golden Wolf's head splashed across its red billowing sail. They were heading for Thorny Island and Westminster. Thurold had business in Lincoln and could not be with them. Bondi and Whitgar, who had never arrived in London by ship before, were surprised at how much Eadric had to snake around the river.

'The Thames is a mighty river,' the steersman said. 'It's wide, but it's so shallow in places, at low tide, it's easy to be grounded. Come to mention it; it's not too difficult at high tide to find yourself stranded on a sandbank either.'

'Yes, we wondered what you were up to,' Bondi said.

'You thought I was drunk, didn't you?' Eadric laughed.

'A little.'

When they passed William's castle, Eadric scowled, and then they reached London Bridge; Whitgar expressed surprise at how low it was. 'When I was last in London, I didn't come here. I had no idea how close it was to the water. How are ships supposed to pass under it?' he asked.

Eadric grinned at Whitgar. 'They're not,' he said. 'Not easily, anyway. It was Ethelred's idea,' Eadric explained. 'Build it low so that any vessel needing to pass had to stoop its mast. Friends could pass, but an enemy would be at the mercy of those on the bridge.'

'And because the spans are quite narrow, you can't row and have to go through with the tide or use poles to move forward,' Whitgar said. 'Ethelred wasn't so unready as I imagined.'

'Come on then, everybody. Give us a hand,' Eadric bellowed.

Gathering around and following Eadric's instructions, the crew lowered the mast, and the current took them under the wooden bridge. Once on the other side, the oarsmen rowed the last part of their journey to Westminster.

It was not Matilda's forthcoming coronation that occupied Merleswein's thoughts, but the knowledge that Mid-summer's Day was just a few weeks away. With that in mind, once he'd disembarked, he called in on his old friend, Abbot Edwin, who was also a keen beekeeper. As soon as Eadric had tied up at the wharf, Merleswein strode straight through the little gardens surrounding the abbey to find the Abbot at his skeps.

'Father Edwin,' Merleswein said, recognising one of two unusually clad men by his movements. Abbot Edwin and another monk were covered head to foot in heavy sacking, and wickerwork basket bottoms fixed into their hoods covered their faces, protecting them from the bees.

The taller of the two men turned around; he held a piece of smoking cow dung in his gloved hands.

'Merleswein. It's good to see you again,' he said.

The two men exchanged pleasantries before stepping out of the earshot of the other monk. Merleswein did most of the talking while Edwin nodded his head. Whatever the topic of conversation, Merleswein appeared pleased with the outcome.

Chapter 18

Matilda's coronation ran smoothly enough, and she was thrilled to be crowned by the Archbishop of York. William, too, had enjoyed the occasion but was unsettled for a few moments. Unwittingly, he caught the cold, piercing eyes of the dowager Queen Edith boring into him: her loathing undisguised. Now it was the morning of the following day. Lying in bed with Matilda, who was now with child, he had a flash of inspiration.

'You know I had a terrible nightmare about Harold last night?'

'Did you?'

'Yes. We were in battle, and there was a tremendous amount of bloodshed. But I've had an idea. I'm going to build an abbey on the site where he fell to commemorate the fallen.'

'It sounds as though you're honouring him.'

'Not at all.'

'Well, if it makes you feel better, my dear. Now, time to get up.'

The mid-May sun shone in through the window, casting golden light around the room, making the expectant mother look radiant.

'Was that archbishop ill?' she asked. 'His skin looked like parchment and covered in liver spots. Did you see how his hands shook? I thought he was going to drop the crown.'

William laughed, 'And his head shook so much I thought it would fall off.'

'And aren't you the little matchmaker, William?'

'What? Ah, you mean Waltheof and Judith. Everything is going according to plan there. They seem keen on each other. They'll be married before the year's out,' he said.

'I wonder if Ealdred will live long enough to perform the ceremony?' Matilda said, picturing her coronation. She found her mind wandering back to the previous day. It had seemed incredible, although the English looked less than happy. Queen Edith's cold blue eyes, fierce with resentment, burned into her. But one guest made her seethe. It was Brihtric with whom she was besotted twenty years earlier. He was the first man for whom she had fallen. He was handsome, charming and had an enchanting English accent. What's more, he appeared to delight in her company. Later, after leading her on, he spurned her advances. His words of rejection burned in her heart and now echoed around her head.

'Matilda, my dear,' he had said, with the utmost sincerity, in that delightful English accent of his. 'It's not that I don't want to marry you specifically. I have no wish to be married to anyone. It's because I've felt a calling to the cloth.'

Before the year was out, he was back in England and married to the daughter of a family friend.

But at her coronation, he looked fat and bloated. And as for the golden hair, where it had not turned silver, it had disappeared completely. Now thin and straggly, dangling to his shoulders, lank and greasy. She glowered at him while he squirmed. Their eyes had met, and attempting to charm her, he had smiled. She thought he was gloating and scowled in return. She decided then that Brihtric would pay the price for his indiscretions. William's voice brought her back to earth.

William looked into her eyes and said, 'I want you to know, I'm so thrilled you're finally my queen.'

'I'm thrilled too, William. Every girl grows up wishing she could be a queen. I never imagined it would happen to me. If I were lucky, I always thought I'd become a duchess, and when you took me for your wife, I was delighted. I had everything I'd ever dreamed of but look at us now, more than I'd ever imagined.

'The future looks good for us, William, not just you and I, but our friends at court, but as for the remaining English nobles? What do you intend to do with them?' Matilda asked.

'Ulf and his friend can stay in Normandy out of harm's way. As for the rest, apart from Waltheof, they're a bunch of n'er do wells. You know my plans for Waltheof. We'll have Judith married off to him, and then we have the beginnings of an Anglo-Norman kingdom. When Edgar gets a little older, we'll find the right match for him. As for Edwin and Morcar, I'll marry them off to someone of no importance. Why should I afflict them on a poor niece or cousin of mine?

'Gospatric is a young man with potential, and I'm sure we can find something for him. Your friend Brihtric, you can decide his fate. That Merleswein fellow, I don't know what to make of him. Ask him any question you want, and within an instant, he's talking about bees. He's just like Abbot Edwin at Westminster. Are they related?

'I'll say this for him,' Matilda replied. 'Merleswein makes marvellous honey.'

'Have you tried his mead?'

'No, I haven't,' she said.

'It's the only thing in this country worth drinking.'

William had set the day aside for business. He had so many callers who were desperate to see him. He thought it would take all day, but fortunately, Matilda was now by his side. The doors opened, and a guard stepped into the gap. 'Earl Waltheof and a thane called Gospatric are here, my lord.'

Intrigued, William said, 'Send them in.'

Two tall, handsome young men stepped into the room a few moments later.

'Good morning, Earl Waltheof. You too, Gospatric.'

'Good morning,' the two replied. Gospatric smiled a warm smile that appeared genuine. Something rare for the king to see from an Englishman.

'You have something to discuss?'

'Ah, straight to the point,' Gospatric answered. 'Yes, a vacant earldom, Northumbria to be exact. Since Oswulf departed this world, the earldom is without an earl. I could help you remedy that.'

'How?'

'I'm from a noble family. I am the great-grandson of King Ethelred,' Gospatric said.

'And I presume Earl Waltheof is here to support your claim.'

'I am, my lord,' Waltheof said.

William considered Gospatric young for such an appointment. He was inexperienced, but he knew the Northumbrians, and his inexperience might be an asset. He knew enough to take care of Northumbria for him but not enough to make a formidable opponent should he get any ideas. *All I have to do is settle on a price.*

'So, you have a valid claim, but is there anything else you have that may persuade me to appoint you?'

'I don't expect you to give away a title on a whim. I imagine; you must have gone to great expense to depose King Harold.'

'Earl Harold,' the king interrupted tersely.

'Earl Harold, how clumsy of me. My lord has spent a great deal of effort in your triumph over Harold. Might I contribute to your expenses to help relieve the burden, as it were?'

'How understanding you are, Gospatric. I'd appreciate your contribution. What, do you say, might be appropriate.'

An amiable discussion followed, and half an hour later, when the two Englishmen bade good day to King William, they both left as earls. No sooner were they gone than the steward appeared again.

'Earl Edwin is here, my lord.'

'Send him in.'

Edwin appeared, looking anxious.

'Marvellous to see you, Edwin. Tell me, what is it I can do for you?

'I thought the time might be right for another royal wedding.'

'Oh really? And why is that?'

'You promised me Adeliza's hand.'

'Dear Edwin, please don't take this hard, but marrying my daughter is no longer a possibility.'

'Have I displeased you?' Edwin said.

'Your sister is conspicuous by her absence, isn't she, Edwin?'

'Aldytha was so looking forward to meeting you, but I fear an urgent matter has kept her away.'

'That scarcely believable, Edwin. The coronation was an ideal opportunity to present her young son to his king and queen.'

'Yes, I'm sure. It's most remiss of her. I'm certain something unavoidable must have detained her. I know her child has been in ill health. Perhaps that's the explanation,' Edwin said.

'She should have brought him to court where I could have my

physicians look at him. By the way, what is his name?'

Edwin could hardly bring himself to utter it, 'Harold, my lord.'

'Harold? After her deceased husband, the Earl, who tried to usurp my kingdom. How dare she? You don't seem able to control your women, Edwin. I think you'll find Adeliza too spirited for you. I'll have to find you, someone, what shall we say, less wilful.'

'But, your daughter, you promised.'

'You'll find I made a promise to find you a bride, not marry off one of my daughters' to you.'

'If that's all you have to say on the matter?'

'It is.'

'Then I'll say goodbye to you,' said Edwin, storming out of the chambers.

Later in the day, William received a request for a private meeting from Earl Waltheof, to which he agreed at once.

Waltheof entered the king's private chamber looking sheepish.

'It's nice to see you again so soon, Waltheof. How can I help?'

'There's something I'd like to ask you.'

'Which is what?' smiled William. He had an idea what was on Waltheof's mind and was keen to hear what he had to say.

'I'm here to request Lady Judith's hand.'

'This is marvellous news, Waltheof.

'Wine! This calls for a celebration. I will have a word with her father, but he will have no objections, I am sure.'

'What did Judith say when you asked her?'

'Oh, I haven't asked her yet. I thought I'd ask your permission first.'

'Quite wise. But surely you didn't expect me to object?'

'I needed your approval.'

'You have it, Waltheof. This makes me happy. Ah, here's the wine. Let's have a toast to you and Lady Judith.'

The relationship was working out as William had hoped. It felt good to have an English earl on his side. Half the country was in arms against him, and Waltheof would make a useful ally. Things were going smoother, at last.

After meeting with William, Waltheof made his way from Westminster's great hall to the old storehouse, which provided accommodation for his friends by the river. The residence was a prison by another name. William was fond of calling the Englishmen his guests when, in reality, they were hostages.

Waltheof passed the guard and entered the building to find Edwin, Morcar, Edgar, Gospatric, Brihtric, Merleswein and Whitgar deep in discussion.

'I had a feeling this might happen,' Edwin was saying. 'William promised me his daughter's hand in marriage, and now he's gone back on his word. Worse than that, more and more of my land is disappearing from under my feet. I'm supposed to be the Earl of Mercia, but it's more like Earl of whatever's left of Mercia. It's time to start the uprising.'

'An uprising can't come soon enough for me,' Brihtric said. 'Did you notice the way Matilda looked at me during the Coronation? She wants my blood.'

'The rumours true then,' Gospatric said, grinning.

Everyone turned to Brihtric for a response.

'I don't know what you mean,' Brihtric said, to everyone's amusement, their laughter echoing off the stone walls.

When everyone calmed down, Merleswein asked Edgar what he was thinking.

'Do you think we ought to make our escape, my lord?'

'As William treats us appallingly,' Edgar said. 'I think we ought to complete plans for the uprising. William has no power in the north, so I suggest we go there. Who says, aye?'

Everyone said aye, except for Waltheof.

'You're not with us, Waltheof?' Edgar said.

'William has treated me honourably,' Waltheof replied.

Edgar said, 'William's treated Gospatric honourably, but he's still coming with us.'

'But I'm promised the hand of Judith.'

'Ah, Waltheof's in love,' Gospatric said.

'It's not that,' Waltheof said. 'William has been fair with me, and I feel I ought to give him a chance.'

'Haven't we been fair to you, Waltheof?' Edgar said.

Waltheof knew Edgar was right. His duty and his loyalty lay with them. But he thought of Judith and was torn.

'Waltheof will stay behind if that's what he wishes,' Edgar said. 'The rest of us will leave as soon as we have a plan.'

'Then we ought to leave tonight,' Merleswein said.

'How do we do that?' Edgar said, looking surprised.

'You've seen me with the bees,' Merleswein replied. 'Under the smock and hood, I could be anybody. I've moored a ship just a few yards away. We just have to put on the smocks and take a skep each onto the boat. If anybody asks, we're moving them to another abbey. As you know, the best time to move a skep is in the dark, so the bees aren't disturbed. No one will think it unusual to see a few monks wandering around Westminster with a skep now, will they?'

Edgar smiled. 'when did you think of this, Merleswein?'

'A little while ago, my lord,' Merleswein replied.

'Tell us more.'

'I'll get word to Eadric the Steersman, and he'll pick us up on the evening tide. We'll dress as beekeeper monks moving bees to another location. We take a few skeps on board, and Edric will set sail. Before you know it, you'll be back home miles away from here,' Merleswein said.

'Don't you think the guard will think it odd half a dozen monks getting on to a boat and sailing away,' Gospatric said.

'They won't see us sailing away. We'll be well out of sight, you'll see,' Merleswein said.

'I can help you with this,' Whitgar said. 'I'm of no importance to William, and I can come and go as I choose. So, if there's any way I can make myself useful, let me know.'

'I'm sure we'll find something for you to do, Whitgar,' Merleswein said.

'Will you find anything for me,' Waltheof asked.

'So, you are coming?' Edgar said.

'Yes,' Waltheof replied. 'If you'll still have me.'

The humid early summer afternoon passed slowly in a mire of anticipation. Merleswein had made himself busy with Abbot Edwin and the bees, slipping away occasionally to take smocks and hoods to his friends. By the end of the day, Merleswein had arranged everything. Eadric would tie up at the wharf and await Merleswein and the others. The sun set in a glory of colour, and after darkness fell, Merleswein emerged from the storehouse dressed in a beekeeper's smock. The guard was about to challenge him when he pointed to the hood and faceguard he carried under his arm, smiled an innocent smile, and said, 'bees.'

Now used to Merleswein's peculiar ways, the guard nodded and let him go on his way.

Merleswein turned the corner of the storehouse and paused by a barrel standing by the wall. Through a hole in the thatched roof, Morcar's head appeared.

'All's clear,' Merleswein said.

Inside, Edgar, standing on an oak beam, levered himself out and slid off the thatch and onto the barrel. In an instant, a hand holding a hood and faceguard appeared through the hole and gently threw the beekeeper's gear to the atheling. Edgar caught it with ease but then simply held it in his hand.

'Come with me,' Merleswein said. And the two men walked to the skeps.

'You'll need to put that over your head,' Merleswein said to Edgar, indicating the head covering.

'What now?'

'Yes, unless you want to be recognised. There are a few guards on duty,' Merleswein said.

Edgar did as advised and slipped the covering over his head. When he and Merleswein arrived at the skeps, Abbot Edwin was waiting for them.

'Good evening,' he said from behind his wickerwork mask. 'I have something for you.'

Abbot Edwin turned over a skep and stretched a linen cloth over the bottom, which he pegged down to keep it secure. He did this to all three skeps and then instructed Merleswein and Edgar to pick them up and follow him.

'Don't concern yourself with bees,' he said. 'They're asleep. Anyway, they can't get out. I've sealed the entrance holes with hay.'

Abbot Edwin led the way towards the waiting ship, where a grinning Eadric waited.

'Any problems?' the Steersman asked.

The three men in their beekeeper's garb stepped into the ship.

'This way,' Eadric said, leading around to the steer board side of the ship, passing three enormous barrels on their way. The barrels lay on their sides and were held in place by wedges. The three men followed and placed their skeps on a bench indicated by Eadric. It was then that they noticed the barrels had no lids.

'There you are, Edgar. Your accommodation.'

The Atheling climbed into the barrel and made himself comfortable.

Tucking Edgar's gear under his arm, Merleswein made his way back to the other hives with Abbot Edwin. Earl Morcar was waiting for them. Donning a smock and hood, he took up a skep and headed to the ship. As before, Eadric was waiting to show him the way to his quarters. The earl tore the hood off and gasped for breath.

'Here you are, my lord,' Eadric said. 'Just until we're clear of London.'

Morcar removed the smock and climbed into the enormous barrel. He looked hesitant with every movement.

'Now for the rest of our friends,' Merleswein said, returning to the outbuilding. The process was repeated several times until only Brihtric and Whitgar were left.

When Merleswein arrived at the outbuilding, no familiar head was peeping at him, but someone was groaning, and two men were arguing in subdued voices. Not wanting to make any noise himself, he looked around for a stone and soon found one and threw it through the hole. It landed with a thud, and after a few moments, Waltheof's worried-looking face appeared through the hole.

'We can't get Brihtric out,' Whitgar said.

'You'll have to get him out. He can't stay here,' Merleswein replied.

'I've had an idea, but it might take a bit of time. Just give me moment,' Whitgar said.

Merleswein stood outside listening as a series of grunts and groans and the sound of scrapping furniture emerged from the hole in the roof. After an eternity, Brihtric's head appeared, looking apprehensive. Grunting and groaning, the old thane squeezed himself through the opening and slid headfirst over the thatch. He yelled as he crashed onto the barrel and bounced off onto the ground, where he lay groaning. Merleswein, concerned Brihtric might have alerted the guard, tried to drag the old thane to his feet, but he was far heavier than he looked and besides, he made a fuss.

'Hush up,' Merleswein said.

In response, Brihtric groaned.

'Be quiet,' Merleswein said, taking anxious glances here and there. 'Let me help you,' he reached out and grabbed Brihtric's arm and dragged him to his feet.

'Put these on, Brihtric,' Merleswein said, offering the beekeeper's gear.

Brihtric steadied himself and rubbed his arm. His lack of urgency alarmed Merleswein.

'We haven't got all night,' Merleswein hissed.

'Steady on. I nearly broke my back,' Brihtric replied, stretching, rubbing the base of his spine, and wincing.

'We'll both end up with more than broken backs if the sentries catch us,' Merleswein said.

Brihtric put on the beekeeper's garb and hobbled his painful way to the skeps. When they got there, Abbot Edwin sighed.

'Where've you been,' he said.

'We had a few problems, but we sorted them out,' Merleswein answered.

'Right. Let's get on our way,' the abbot said.

The second part of Brihtric's journey proved arduous as the old man complained of pain in his back, heedless of the noise he was making. After what seemed like hours to Merleswein, they arrived on the ship.

'What's up with him?' Eadric said when he saw Brihtric lurching towards him, limping with his hand on his hip.

'He had an accident and hurt his back,' Merleswein said.

'He can have a barrel for himself then,' Eadric said. 'Bondi, show Brihtric his accommodation,' Eadric grinned.

'Do you need a hand?' Bondi said to the hobbling Brihtric.

'I can manage,' Brihtric said, following Bondi to a barrel.

'Right, just Whitgar left,' Merleswein said, heading off for the last part of his mission.

When he arrived at the hall, Whitgar was through the roof and by his side instantly. In a few moments, he dressed in beekeepers' gear.

Merleswein relaxed as he and Whitgar made their way to Edwin, and from there, they proceeded to the waiting ship with their skeps. Once on the wharf, they were surprised by a guard.

'What's going on here,' he said.

'We're moving bees to a new location,' Abbot Edwin spoke.

'And who might you be?' the guard said.

'Abbot Edwin. And these are two of my students. We're loading the skeps on that ship there. They're bound for Canterbury.'

'Let's see your faces.'

The three men placed their skeps on the ground and took off their hoods to show faces the guard recognised from other occasions. He identified none of them as one of King William's 'special guests.'

'On your way then,' the guard said.

Relieved, the three climbed aboard the ship with the others and placed the skeps on the bench. Merleswein and Whitgar climbed into a barrel alongside Waltheof, which Eadric secured behind them. They heard Abbot Edwin pick up the gear and bid farewell to Eadric, who issued orders. The Sea Wolf moved off, gently floating with the tide. There was the scraping sound of oars placed back in their oar holes and then of men rowing.

'I thought for a minute we'd had it back there,' Whitgar said in the darkness of the barrel.

'I'm glad it was you that was with us. If it had been Edwin or Morcar, we'd have been in trouble right away. We're on our way now,' Merleswein replied.

The men felt the wooden vessel pick up speed running with the tide, and with four oarsmen rowing, the craft made its way downriver towards London Bridge. In the darkness, they tried to make sense of the sounds outside.

'Do you think we've gone under the bridge yet?' Whitgar asked.

'It's hard to say,' Merleswein answered.

'What's that?' Waltheof said.

There was clattering and someone shouting.

'Get back in here,' a voice said.

'That sounded like Edwin,' Merleswein said.

'I can't stand it anymore,' Morcar said. 'I'm getting out.'

'Keep quiet. You'll get us caught,' Gospatric said.

There was a crash as the barrel's lid fell onto the deck.

'Get back in,' Edwin said.

'What should we do?' Whitgar asked Merleswein.

'Just stay here. I'm sure Gospatric and Edwin can take care of it.'

In the darkness, they listened intently as Eadric's calm voice said, 'Don't worry, Earl Morcar, we'll put the lid back up, but this time we'll leave a little space.'

'What's going on there?' a voice from ahead and above them said. The French accent sent shivers down Whitgar's spine.

'Nothing. Just a bit of trouble with loose cargo,' Eadric answered.

Merleswein, Waltheof and Whitgar listened, but the only sound was the soft glide of the boat easing through the water.

'Stop there,' a man with the French accent said.

'We can't,' Eadric replied.

In their barrel, Merleswein, Waltheof and Whitgar heard the sentry run across to the other side of the wooden bridge, calling out an alarm as he went.

'I'm going to see what's happening,' Waltheof said.

As he peered around the edge of the barrel, a sentry shouted, 'halt,' to the Englishmen. The ship continued on its way. He threw a spear at Eadric.

'Look out,' Waltheof warned, as Eadric sidestepped the shot from above. The spear flew past him and stuck hard and fast into the deck.

'Steady on,' Eadric called out to the sentry. 'We'll just pull onto the riverbank,' he added, hoping to buy a small amount of time for them.'

'Stop there,' the sentry ordered, as others joined him.

'What's happening?' Merleswein asked Waltheof.

'Problems with the sentries,' Waltheof said. 'I think we might be in trouble.' As he finished speaking, a crossbow bolt struck the deck in front of him.

'I'm going to help,' Waltheof said.

'Me too,' Whitgar said.

'About time,' Eadric said when they appeared.

Whitgar began shooting arrows at the sentries as fast as possible, forcing them to take cover and spoiling their aim while Waltheof was busy trying to find something useful to throw.

'Row you buggers,' Eadric ordered his crew, none of whom was keen to take up an oar and make a target of himself.

'Get out of your barrels, you lot,' Eadric bellowed to his passengers. 'Get something to protect my crew.'

Eadric's passengers emerged from their barrels, grabbed shields, and ran over to the rowers to protect them. Whitgar kept on shooting. Once the Sea Wolf was clear of the sentries, the men hauled up the mast and let out the sail, the gentle breeze helping them on their way. Safe in the middle of the river, they relaxed as they sailed on through the quiet of the night. They passed William's castle, a morbid, sinister sentinel, its silhouette soaring above London's townsfolk, evoking a feeling of dread. They still had to navigate the estuary, and hearing a commotion from the shore, they remembered the bend in the Thames as it made its winding way. It would be easy for men on horseback to cut them off if they knew their way through the marshes that bordered the great river.

'No need to worry,' Eadric said. 'The river is way too wide for them to be a danger downstream.'

Merleswein and the others, now on deck, listened intently in the sultry, still summer night to the thundering hooves of their enemies' horses as they rode hard to intercept them. The sounds of their pursuers softened as they faded into the distance.

To everyone's relief, Eadric said, 'That's the last we'll see of them, don't you worry.' Why would they doubt him? Eadric was the best sailor in Christendom, and he was in home waters.

The ship made its way to the sea sedately in the silvery moonlight, helped by four oarsmen and a sail filled by a gentle breeze.

'I have an important question for you, Eadric,' Gospatric said in an earnest tone.

'What's that, then?' Eadric said.

'These barrels you've got on board; do any of them contain wine?'

'I should have guessed you'd want to know that,' Eadric said as the others laughed. 'There's plenty enough in that firkin,' he said, pointing out the small barrel nestled amongst the bigger ones.

Gospatric opened the barrel and emptied half of its contents over his face and down his throat. Now free men, William's prisoners, drank to their health and happiness as they made their way downriver and up the coast to Lincoln. Those who had escaped William's clutches told their tales of their daring and Merleswein's cunning to Eadric, Bondi and the crew. Soon they passed Greenwich, where the river made a sharp turn to the north, and the wind blew a harder. Later, when they were approaching the mouth of the River Lea, at another sharp bend in the river, they heard shouting in French, and a voice called out in the night.

'You there, come here right away.' It was hard to tell in the darkness, but there looked to be thirty horsemen.

'We'll be right with you,' Eadric bellowed back before chuckling to himself.

'Will they catch us?' Edgar asked.

'I doubt it, my lord,' Eadric said. 'They don't know the river, and I do, even in the dark. There are shallows where a ship can get stuck, but I know where they are. There are places where the waters run deep where horses will prove useless. I intend to lure them until they're out of their depth. We shall soon see who shall get the better of who,' Eadric said, an enigmatic smile on his face.

As the crew rowed and Eadric steered, the passengers gathered to see what happened next. They could hear the Normans enter the water and spurring on their horses.

'They're making good time,' Gospatric remarked.

As they looked on, the Normans galloped through the shallows, and even though their pace was slow, they were gaining on Eadric's ship.

'If you have any weapons handy, this is the time to get them,' Edgar said.

'Do you have any weapons on board, Eadric?' Edgar asked.

'We've got a few spears,' Eadric answered.

'Any arrows?' Whitgar asked.

'There should be a couple of quivers up at the bow,' Eadric said.

As the Normans continued to close on them, Whitgar searched for the quivers, and Bondi gathered the spears. When they found what they were looking for, they returned to the ship's stern with the others.

'How are we doing,' Bondi asked.

'They're gaining on us,' Merleswein answered.

The Normans appeared to run into even shallower water and were at full gallop as he answered.

'Can't you make this go any faster?' Edwin asked Eadric.

'No, but don't worry, they won't catch us,' Eadric said.

They could see the Norman horses now, moving fast in the shallows, spray splashing and catching in the moonlight. When they had first entered the river, there had been a fifty-yard gap between them and their English prey. Now the distance was closer to twenty-five.

'Make a shieldwall at the stern here,' Eadric said.

Doing their best to form a shieldwall, the Englishmen crowded at the stern just as the first crossbow bolt struck, driving hard into Bondi's shield. The power of the strike shook the housecarl.

Whitgar aimed and began shooting. He missed his targets, but the Normans spread out. Two of those on the inside came to a halt as they entered deeper water. Encouraged, Whitgar let fly with as many arrows as he could, shooting over the top of the shieldwall with a ferocity his comrades found astounding and the Normans alarming. A couple of the horsemen shot crossbow bolts, but they tried to close the gap and use their spears, as they could not reload and ride simultaneously. As they came within range, it looked as though Edgar and his men might be in trouble. Eadric chuckled and turned his ship to the starboard. The Normans followed and came to a halt in the deep. There was nothing for them to do but shout abuse.

'Please don't be offended,' Eadric called back to them. 'Just because we didn't want to join you at your feast.'

The ship sailed on, and the men stored their shields and weapons for safekeeping. Gospatric picked up the small barrel of wine.

'Time for a little drink, eh, lads?' To much cheering, he took a few gulps of wine and handed around the barrel.

'What are you going to do next, Gospatric?' Merleswein asked, wiping wine off his face with his sleeve.

'If you don't mind, I'll go up to Northumbria and take up residence in my earldom.' Gospatric said. 'It'll take time to get myself established before I join the uprising.'

'Good idea,' Merleswein said. 'And the rest of you?'

'Bondi and I will come back to Lincoln with you,' Whitgar said. 'But as much as I enjoy your hospitality, I'll get back home as soon as I am able.'

'I'm going back to Worcestershire,' Brihtric said. 'Where I'll be until we join forces.'

'Morcar and Edwin, what are your intentions?'

'We will roam the woods and forests and raid the lands the Normans have stolen from us. We will gather our men together and live off the land like wild men, free from Norman shackles. Whenever we come across William's men, we'll kill them where they stand,' Morcar said.

'We'll create havoc for William and his men, and they'll regret the day they set foot on our shores,' Edwin added.

'And Waltheof, what will you do?' Merleswein asked.

'I'll go back to Northampton.'

'I wish you all the best of luck, and may God be with you,' Merleswein said

And with their futures planned, they sailed on.

Chapter 19

The next day, while having breakfast with Matilda in their chambers, William discovered Edgar, the English Earls, and thanes had vanished. It was Stigand who broke the news to him.

'Where did they get the horses?' William said.

'They left by ship.'

'Why? What are they up to? I've had news of an insurrection in the west?' William said. 'What do you know of it?'

'I knew nothing of it in advance.'

'Is this the uprising they planned?'

'I don't think so. It's possible Edric and the Northern Earls have taken matters into their own hands. I have an idea where they might be, though,' Stigand answered.

'And where's that?'

'They'll probably go to the consecration of Brihtric's new church.'

Matilda gave the conversation her full attention.

'Why would they do that?' William asked.

'He's as thick as thieves with the leaders of the rebellion. He's also a great friend of Bishop Wulfstan, who will perform the consecration in five days. And it's a wonderful opportunity to make plans. They'll be in Hanley, in Worcestershire, just across the River Severn.'

Again, Matilda listened hard. While William was having this heated conversation with Stigand, she indicated to one of her attendants, 'Find Brihtric Mau and bring him to me,' she whispered. 'You know where to find him?'

The attendant nodded and slipped away on his errand.

'You're sure of this?' William said.

'Absolutely.'

William looked at him suspiciously before saying, 'I'll get men together; we have a consecration to attend.'

Matilda calculated William needed more time to lead a large force to Hanley than a smaller, fast-moving body of her men. Brihtric might even be alone, waiting for his friends to join him. What a surprise for him when her men came calling. Brihtric was going to be her prisoner, not William's. After all, it was she he had crossed first. Besides, the less William knew of her past feelings for Brihtric and how he had treated her, the better. She would be the one to dispense retribution.

Early next morning, twenty mounted soldiers left London for Hanley. They looked like any other Norman patrol, but they were Matilda's men on a mission for their Queen. Hooves clattered when they were clear of the city, and sparks flew as the men at arms cantered over the cobbles. It took them four days to reach their destination.

On a glorious May morning, outside of the newly consecrated church of St Mary, in Hanley, Worcestershire, stood the saintly Wulfstan, Bishop of Worcester, unwittingly talking to two of the leading figures in the resistance. The old bishop, sixty now and stooping, smiled at the church's benefactor. 'I'm so pleased to be here, Brihtric. You've built such a beautiful church and a good attendance too.'

'Yes. I'm sure Edwin and Morcar would have enjoyed the ceremony. It's so unfortunate they weren't here to witness it,' Brihtric replied. He was grateful to have the Bishop there. Wulfstan always looked as though he were at prayer. Brihtric thought the bishop was, at all times, in communication with God. When he was speaking, it was as though he spoke with the voice of the heavenly Father, if not with his authority.

'I am pleased to be of help,' said Wulfstan, with a celestial tone in his voice. 'And such a privilege to have your company again, my dear Lady Aldytha. And to meet young Harold. The image of his father.'

There was so much more said in that brief statement. Wulfstan had acknowledged what had been and how things might have been for Aldytha, Harold and their son.

'Thank you,' Aldytha said. 'Let's hope he takes his rightful place in the world before too long.'

'Let's,' said Wulfstan.

'Shall we retire to the hall, where we can take the weight off our feet,' Brihtric said.

The party began making its talkative way to the hall just a short distance away. Before they were even halfway there, dogs barked, and they heard shouting. Twenty armed soldiers appeared on horseback in a flurry of squawking hens and honking geese. One of them held a spear dripping with blood.

Brihtric stepped forward. 'You're on my land. What on earth do you think you're doing?'

Their leader looked at Brihtric with contempt. 'Brihtric Mau?' He said.

'You still haven't answered my question,' Brihtric replied.

'You're under arrest,' the leader said as his soldiers strode towards the thane.

'On what charge?' Brihtric demanded to know.

'In good time,' the Norman answered.

'The king will hear of this,' Brihtric screeched as two burly soldiers manhandled him to a waiting horse.

'It's not the king you need to worry about.'

Brihtric's heart sank. He remembered the angry face and hateful looks at the queen's coronation celebration; years of bitterness and resentment had found expression.

Sifled, Brihtric's wife, ran forward. 'What do they mean?' she asked her husband.

'It's a misunderstanding, my dear. Don't worry. I'll soon get it sorted out.'

People were still milling around the church, and groups of women and children clustered here and there. As Edric had only a few men with him, as much as he sympathised with Brihtric's predicament, he had Aldytha and her infant son to consider.

'We can't sort this out now,' he said to Aldytha. 'I'll get my men together. It's a long way to Winchester. In the meantime, we need to get you and Harold away from here. If they discover who you are, you're dead.'

Distressed by how the Normans were abusing his good friend, Bishop Wulfstan stepped forward, crosier in hand.

'The king is a friend of mine. He shall hear of this,' he snapped, addressing the leader of the soldiers.

'It wouldn't surprise me. The king hears of everything,' the leader smirked.

'This is outrageous,' the Bishop yelled.

'Call it what you like. I have my orders,' the Norman said, smiling.

As Wulfstan and the Norman argued, Edric and Aldytha slipped back into the church.

'We'll just stay in here until they're gone,' Edric said. 'Once they've left, I'll get you and Harold safely on the road to Chester. Your brothers should arrive at any moment. I'll gather my men, and together, we'll give chase.'

Inside the church, Edric informed the congregation of the ongoing events outside. Everyone remained quiet, as did little Harold and his nurse, sleeping while the adults listened as events unfolded.

'Don't worry, Brihtric, we'll soon have you back with your family,' they heard the Bishop yell.

Edric peered through a window to see the stern-faced captain of the guard look at Brihtric's wife with cold eyes. 'If I were you, I'd start packing,' he said. 'You're on Queen Matilda's land now, and she won't be pleased to discover you're trespassing.'

Her jaw dropped. Shocked for a moment, into silence, but outraged by her family's treatment, she let vent her fury.

'Who do you think you are to come to our home and treat us this way? We've done nothing wrong; this is our land, and it's been in the family for generations,' she screamed.

'Not anymore. Now quieten down, or you'll be making the journey to Winchester too,' he said.

The soldiers had their swords drawn now and readied for action as local men appeared with axes, scythes and pitchforks, looking murderous. Now outnumbering the Normans, they had gathered round to block the way.

'Call your men off,' the captain snapped.

'You call your men off,' Brihtric said. 'You have no right here.'

'Call your men off, or I'll kill you where you stand.'

'You're going to kill me, anyway. You'll save me a tedious journey if you carry out your threat.'

The captain nodded to his crossbowman and, for a moment, looked at Brihtric's wife. The crossbowman aimed at her.

'If you don't call your men off, your wife won't be making any journeys anywhere. Ever again.'

Brihtric's men greeted the threat with a roar, and as one, closed in on the mounted soldiers, jabbing up at their faces. The soldiers had the advantage of height, but Brihtric's men had a long reach with their axes, pitchforks, and scythes.

Suddenly someone screamed, and all eyes turned to see what had happened. A young soldier clutched his throat while a farmhand jabbed him repeatedly.

A bolt flew through the air and tore through a farmhand's neck. His friends looked on horrified as blood sprayed and spurted over them. The victim's wife uttered a howl fit to bring down the heavens. Her wail was despairing enough to freeze a man's soul.

The second of Brihtric's men fell, mortally wounded by a Norman spear as pitchforks and axes battled the swords and shields of the horsemen.

Having no time to reload his crossbow, the soldier who had drawn first blood was now slashing with his sword at anyone and everyone he could reach.

Watching from the church with Aldytha, Edric's anger got the better of him. 'I can't stand by and watch this any longer,' he said. With his sword held high and screaming his battle cry, he ran to join Brihtric, his men following hard on his heels. Even in the commotion, he surprised everyone. Brihtric's men took heart, and the fighting became fiercer.

'Kill them. Kill the lot of them,' Edric yelled.

'Withdraw,' the captain bellowed, spurring his horse on and forcing a way through the melee with his men struggling to follow. The English, emboldened with rage, were cutting through the Normans at a fearsome pace. Four soldiers lay dead and two wounded.

Edric, responsible for at least one death, charged forward towards Brihtric, who was in the middle of the fracas.

'Come on, men, we can do it,' he bellowed and felled another Norman.

Edric closed in on the crossbowman, in view just a few feet away. The Norman had a knife and slashed at the farmhands on his right. In his enthusiasm to get to someone, he had stretched too far, exposing his left leg. Edric seized his opportunity and cut deep into the Norman's flesh. As pain seared through the man's limb, he turned to defend himself. As he did so, one farmhand swung a great scythe hard into his chest, but his byrnie saved him from death. Injured and in pain, he turned to deal with this second attack, only to expose himself to another blow from Edric, again to the leg. The crossbowman was now in a panic. Cut off from his comrades, who were doing their best to make off with Brihtric. He was isolated and vulnerable. Sensing his weakness, the crowd closed in with blood on their minds and murder in their hearts.

'Kill the bastard,' someone said.

Brihtric's men overwhelmed the crossbowman. From all sides, they hacked and slashed at him.

'Mercy,' he called out.

But no one felt merciful that day. Even though he injured a few Englishmen as he desperately fought them off, they hacked him to pieces as he cried out in search of pity. Edric was the one who struck the final killing blow.

'Brihtric. Where's Brihtric,' he asked.

Everyone turned. Heading out of the farmstead was a troop of soldiers leading Brihtric away on a horse, his wife running behind with her skirt hitched up, begging for them to release her husband. The captain issued a command, and the troop broke out into a gallop, the sooner to get away from their enemies.

'Don't worry, Sifled,' Brihtric called to his wife. 'I'll soon be back.'

Sifled stood still, dread in her expression and tears in her eyes. She looked to the heavens for help. None came.

Brihtric's men looked on, frozen in their movements, unable to think of what to do. Edric made his way over to Sifled and took her in his arms. She dropped her head on his shoulders and cried.

'He will come back, won't he, Edric?' she said.

'Let's get you away from here to somewhere safe. Come back to Chester with us where you'll be safe,' he said.

Once the Normans were out of sight, Edric gave the order to ride north, hoping to meet Aldytha's brothers. Edwin and Morcar in Chester.

Chapter 20

A few miles from Warwick, deep in the forest, Edwin and Morcar were waiting for their cousin, Earl Thorkell, the Sheriff, to arrive. They had summoned him to see if he had any news for them and discover where his loyalties lay. Thorkell, on receiving his invitation from his kinsmen, led a group of a dozen men to meet them. Vastly outnumbered, the sheriff was in no position to force them out, but he expected little trouble. The earls' scout escorted him blindfolded to their camp, and when he was finally allowed to see, he was surprised by the sight of the brothers standing before him, dressed head to foot in green.

'Welcome to our new home,' Morcar said.

Sheriff Thorkell looked around at the encampment. It was a well-chosen spot, hidden in a clearing, in a valley, amongst tall beeches. Edwin and Morcar's men disguised their tents, staining them green and brown. From a distance, they were hardly visible. What gave away the position were the fires; they were too big. Columns of smoke made their way skyward, and Thorkell guessed they were visible for miles.

'My lords, welcome to Warwickshire,' Earl Thorkell said, with all the charm he could muster. *They look like a couple of frogs.*

'Good morning. It's good of you to come out and greet us,' Edwin said.

'You're all in green,' Thorkell said. He was going to ignore their appearance but had second thoughts.

'Yes,' Morcar said with pleasure.

'We are the Wildmen,' Edwin added.

'We're like Edric the Wild. Only it will be the two of us,' Morcar said.

Thorkell glanced around the encampment and guessed there were about two hundred followers with his cousins, all dressed in green. Thorkell noted none of them looked pleased about it.

'We, and our men,' Morcar said. 'We're going to live in the woods and take on William whenever and wherever we encounter him. No Norman will dare set foot outside of his castle when we're finished.' Edwin looked on with a grin as his brother spoke.

For almost two weeks, the brothers and their followers had lived as Wildmen, or what the Normans termed Silvatici. Roaming through the woods, hills, dales, and moors of West Mercia, robbing Norman manors, and occasionally attacking a patrol. They were following in the footsteps of Edric the Wild but had done no more than make a nuisance of themselves. They had braved the elements and scorned their countrymen, who dwelt in their halls and houses, for being soft. But they had done nothing more than engage their enemy in the odd skirmish and had achieved little other than irritate William.

'It's the castles that give us so much trouble,' Edwin said. 'They're not even that big. Just a wooden fort on a pile of earth surrounded by a fence and perhaps a ditch full of water.'

Morcar agreed, 'He's right, Thorkell. They build them inside the town walls, so you have to break through those defences first. After that, cross a ditch and scale a wall of sharpened posts. Then there's a mound and a second spiked palisade, and all the time, crossbowmen will be shooting at you. It's one thing after another. So here we are, raiding and skirmishing. The Frenchies can keep their castles. We'll control the countryside.'

'You'll be able to try out your new tactics on William himself soon,' Earl Thorkell replied.

'What do you mean?' Edwin asked.

'King William is on his way. He's unhappy about your behaviour, so he's coming to pay you a personal visit,' Thorkell informed him. 'I received a messenger from him only yesterday advising me to prepare for a visit.'

Edwin and Morcar exchanged fearful glances.

'Let him come and visit if he likes,' Edwin said. 'We'll have a reception committee waiting for him.'

'That's up to you, cousins.'

'Will you stay for a drink?' Morcar said.

'As much as we'd love to, especially with kin, I have duties to perform. I'm afraid I'll have to bid you goodbye.'

Thorkell left the earls to ruminate on the news. Deep in the woods on the Warwickshire Leicestershire border, they discussed the situation. Edwin expressed his concern about William.

'I don't know about you, but I feel hemmed in.'

'You're right, Edwin. We need a plan.'

Edwin stared at his younger brother for a moment before replying, 'We've got one, Morcar, remember?'

'Oh, yes. Midsummer's Day. We're to rise up with the others.'

'Well done,' Edwin replied.

'If what Thorkell said is true, we need to leave here. William will be up here with an army soon. Let's join the others in York.'

'Right. We'll leave right away. We can call in at Nottingham on the way and top up our supplies,' Edwin said.

'Good idea,' Morcar agreed.

William and his entourage arrived at Warwick to be greeted by Sheriff Thorkell and some local dignitaries at the town gate. All mounted on their finest horses and clad in chainmail; the Normans were intimidating.

'It's such a relief to see you,' Thorkell welcomed the king.

'Sheriff Thorkell, you've been having a little trouble, I hear.'

'Edwin and Morcar have been raiding, but nothing serious,' Thorkell said.

'They're setting an example for others to follow, and I won't have it. We'll strengthen the fortifications.'

'But surely the town walls are sturdy enough.'

Still astride his fine white horse, William glanced at the walls with disdain.

'The earls haven't been a problem here in Warwick,' Thorkell added.

'We'll have to clear some space for defences.'

Thorkell looked baffled.

William cast a glance at Ralph Pomeroy. 'We're going to demolish a few houses to make way for the castle. Sir Ralph, be so kind as to organise the townsfolk?'

'Gladly.'

'Up there should be ideal,' the king said, pointing to a likely spot.

Pomeroy followed William's outstretched finger up the street to the top of a rise and guessed it was a part of the town on the bend of the river Avon. With water on three sides, it already had most of the defences it would need.

'Would you escort Sir Ralph along the street, Earl Thorkell?'

The two men walked their horses to the top of the hill, which gave them a commanding view of the surrounding countryside.

'This will make an ideal site for a castle, don't you think, Earl Thorkell?' Pomeroy said, in a tone that informed the earl he had no choice.

'You're absolutely right, Sir Ralph.'

Pomeroy surveyed the scene; just four dwellings and spread about were several outbuildings for animals, tools, and storage.

'Earl Thorkell. If you get some men and knock those buildings down, we'll get started on the construction.'

Thorkell looked at the four houses Pomeroy had indicated. It relieved him to see that none of them belonged to him.

'I'll have work started on them first thing tomorrow morning,' Thorkell answered cheerily.

'Good. Now let's join the king,' Pomeroy said with a smile.

As the two men walked their horses to the great hall, Sir Ralph reflected on his past. Choosing the site for William's castle brought the memory to the surface. That, and the way William had coerced the Sheriff into overseeing the clearing of a place for Warwick's new defences. Something about it reminded him of home, and an ironic smile appeared on his face. Home was not a cosy word for Pomeroy. Toasty fireplaces and warm welcomes were not what sprang to mind. Having said that, his mother was a kind-hearted woman. It was the rest of the family that was his problem.

He remembered his father's rages. *Anything I said was a provocation.* He did not know why. Even now, years later, humiliation crept through his bones, and he hated himself for being so weak.

His three older brothers, or to be precise, his half-brothers, lived, it seemed, to torment him. They were forever playing tricks. Geoffrey was the oldest at seventeen, and then there was Hugh, fifteen, and Stephen, fourteen. They had their father's dark, curly hair, but Ralph took after his mother. He could remember one day, in particular, an early summer day, very much like this, when builders were working on the new stable block. Pomeroy could still picture how the new stonework stood out against the older castle walls. As far as he could recall, he was about ten years old, and he was walking across the courtyard on some errand when Geoffrey called him over. *I should have known better.*

'Come and look at this, Ralph,' Geoffrey said, leaning out of the hayloft's door.

'What?'

'In here. You'll never believe it.'

He had his doubts, but his brother sounded excited.

'There's a squirrel giving birth. She's already had two babies.'

Curious, he jogged over to the stable, entering the enormous doorway. As he looked up to where he thought his brothers would be, he felt a splash of warm water over his face. The smell told him what kind of water it was; they had emptied a pot full of piss over him.

'You bastards,' he bawled.

They roared with laughter as he yelled and cried as he ran back into the castle to find his mother.

'Mother. Mother,' the young Ralph called out when he arrived. She was in the kitchen, issuing instructions to the servants. She stopped what she was doing to attend to her son.

'Ralph. What's happened to you?' she asked.

'They tricked me and poured piss all over me,' the humiliated boy replied.

It was then his father, disturbed by the commotion, appeared on the doorway, his jaw fixed and his eyes ablaze with anger. He was holding a broad leather belt.

'What lies have you been telling now?'

'I haven't...'

'Don't lie to me, boy,' he said, raising his hand, the belt hanging limply.

Pomeroy turned to run, but his father brought the belt down hard across his shoulders, and he felt the blow burn.

'Stand still and take your punishment, you coward, you little wretch,' Ralph's father bellowed.

Ralph ran and kept out of his father's way for the next few hours, hoping he would drink himself into a stupor and forget his misdemeanour. On his way out of the room, he heard a slap and his mother cry. His heart sank, and he felt sick.

The only time my father paid me any attention was when he beat me. His mother tried to make up for his father's unacceptable behaviour by being extra kind, making life worse. His brothers became even more jealous, and ever more zealous in their pursuit of his misery.

'My lord?' Thorkell said.

Pomeroy was startled to discover Thorkell had been talking to him.

'You were miles away. Missing home?' Thorkell said.

'Yes, as a matter of fact, I was,' Pomeroy said. And then he thought of Tate for an instant, and he realised with surprise, he was missing her.

Later that day, the king and his entourage, including the heavily pregnant Matilda, gathered in Warwick's great hall for a welcoming banquet. The evening was pleasant, and the king enjoyed Thorkell's hospitality. When they had finished feasting, everyone went to bed and slept untroubled by the Silvatici camped in the woods a day's march away. The following morning, after appointing Henry de Beaumont constable, William and his men, with his wife ensconced in the royal carriage, left Warwick. A party of fifty men at arms stayed behind to garrison the castle.

True to his word, Earl Thorkell supervised the demolition of the inconveniently located houses when the Normans left for Nottingham.

Chapter 21

William arrived at Nottingham, prepared for a siege, but what he encountered surprised him. From a distance of half a mile, he studied the walls, hoping to find a weak point somewhere. As he discussed a plan of action with his companions, a delegation comprising an alderman and two burgesses appeared to greet him.

William suspected a trick, but the welcoming committee arrived unarmed. He thanked them for their warm welcome and accepted twenty anxious-looking hostages. They were men of substance, as was apparent by their fine clothes.

William and his men, accompanied by their hosts, rode into town looking for a likely site for a castle.

'That gigantic rock seems the obvious choice,' Warenne said.

William had noticed the prominence as soon as Nottingham came into view. It completely dominated the city, so it would be easy to defend being in such a strategic position. He immediately issued orders for the construction of a castle.

When William left for York two days later, work on the new fortifications had progressed quickly. Like every other county town the king visited, he left behind a memento of his passing, changing the face of England as he went. Outside of York's gates, wondering if his luck would hold and the city would surrender without having to strike a blow.

'Is this an English custom?' Warenne japed while he observed a sorry-looking delegation heading his way.

'This is becoming boring,' William said. 'Spare me the tedious ramblings from grovelling Englishmen begging for their towns to be spared.'

'I wonder what they have to say?' Warenne said.

Like others before them, the delegation approached, attempting to maintain their dignity but looking fearful.

'Welcome to York,' said the leader.

'I bet the fat one has the keys to the city,' smirked Warenne.

'Why?' William said.

'He looks furtive. And I'll wager he's called Ththelwine or something ludicrous.'

On the other side of the king, Sir William Malet said, 'You might be right about his name, but he doesn't look furtive, just defeated. It's humiliation, you can see.'

Warenne shrugged by way of a reply.

The delegation's arrival ended the conversation.

'I am Arckill, thane of Northumbria. May I present my son, Wilfred and Aethelwine, Bishop of Durham.'

'Durham! I thought this was York?'

'It is, my lord. It's just that Bishop Aethelwine happened to be here.'

With much sighing and the occasional grunt, the corpulent Arckill dismounted from his mule and waddled towards his king. When he reached William, he bowed, almost overbalancing, and offered him the keys to the city.

'Told you,' said Warenne with a satisfied grin. Malet chuckled, but William kept a straight face.

'That's most kind of you, Arckill,' said William, ignoring Warenne's remark. 'Are you expecting to offer hostages?'

'Would twenty suffice, my lord?'

'Excellent.'

As in Nottingham, William looked on men of wealth. They had a lot to lose, and he could not understand why they gave in so easily.

'We accept your hostages, and now we'd like to see your splendid city,' was all he said.

William rode through the streets at the head of his column. The size of York impressed him. He entered through the grand Micklegate entrance and breathed a sigh of relief when he realised what a gruelling undertaking it would have been to storm the place had the English resisted. The walls were high and thick, and breaking through them would have been the Devil's own game. He looked to William Warenne without saying a word, who he noticed was also sizing up York's defences. When their eyes met, the king knew his friend was thinking the same thing. *We had enough trouble at Exeter. This would have been a nightmare to take.*

Making their way to the north of the city, they received a less than rapturous welcome from those townsfolk who had summoned up the courage to appear on the streets. Rumours of the Conqueror's cruelty had arrived before him, and many had fled, while most of those who remained stayed indoors. William crossed the bridge over the River Ouse, and all the men on the riverbank stopped work, removed their headgear and averted their eyes from the Conqueror. By the king's side, Sir William Warenne looked smug.

'Didn't I tell you?' Warenne said, 'If you show strength, they'll give in. There is no real will to resist. Not even the earls put up a fight. They just disappeared. Why didn't they put up a fight?'

The town, which should have been thriving, was empty. The streets were strangely quiet. Workshops were everywhere, as were traders' stalls, but no one was in attendance.

'Where is everybody?' William asked Aethelwine.

'Many people left for Scotland when they heard of your approach. I'll take you straight to Earl Edwin's Hall, shall I? It's not far now.' Aethelwine said, changing the subject.

William's party set up, and that evening, William called a council to make plans for the next move.

'I'll admit it,' William said. 'I didn't imagine York would fall so easily. I assumed we'd be putting the place under siege for at least a month.'

'The English have no stomach for a fight,' Warenne said. 'They're finished.'

'Bishop Aethelwine told us people had left for Scotland. I don't like the sound of it. Are they going as refugees looking for shelter, or are they there to recruit the help of King Malcolm? Perhaps with him behind them, they'll put up more of a fight.'

'They haven't yet put up any kind of fight,' Warenne said.

'While they're away, we'll make York secure and then march on to Durham.'

'Aethelwine. How far is it to Durham?' William asked, turning to the bishop.

'About seventy miles.'

'Where's Archbishop Ealdred? Has he gone to Scotland too?'

'No. He is visiting some of the sick. He will be with us soon.'

'Good,' William said, then turning to Warenne, 'I wish we'd known they'd surrender so readily. I could have brought Matilda with me, and the baby could be born here.'

'Perhaps it's for the best she remains in Selby and avoids travel for a while,' Warenne suggested.

'Yes, you're probably right.'

'Musicians to entertain you and your guests?' Aethelwine said.

'Thank you,' William replied.

Aethelwine nodded to a group of musicians who began playing their Lyres.

'What's this awful row? No wonder the English deserted the place,' William snapped as soon as the musicians played. 'Aethelwine. Tell those idiots to be quiet, and we'll listen to some music here instead,' William joked before bellowing out a laugh.

Warenne, who appreciated William's sense of humour, quipped, 'I would've stayed at home if I'd known I'd have to suffer that din.'

'So, would I,' William said, still laughing. 'Perhaps they're the real reason the rebels left. They went to Scotland to get a bit of peace and quiet.'

'I doubt if we can expect the rebels soon if they think they'll have to endure that racket,' Warenne added.

Some of William's musicians began playing, and the familiar songs he found less intrusive. Never keen on music, he thought, the quieter, the better. Now thoughts of his enemies came back to his mind.

'Bishop, do the rebels plan to join the Scots?'

'I was never privy to their plans.'

'We might go up to Durham and meet them closer to home, where there'll be less danger of York falling. Is Durham easily defended, do you know?'

'It is, but if you're going north, why not go further? Bamburgh is a mighty fortress by the sea.'

'Is what I've heard true?'

'It is if you heard it's an impregnable stronghold.'

'Then perhaps we'll take Bamburgh after Durham.'

'Aren't we spread a bit thin?' Warenne said.

'That's why I want an arrangement with Malcolm. We'll send Aethelwine to talk to him and Edgar. The journey will be too much for Ealdred.'

'Aethelwine?' William said to the priest. 'Pack your things. You're going to Scotland in the morning.'

'Yes,' Aethelwine replied, taken aback.

'If we take care of Malcolm, that still leaves the Danes,' William said, as much to himself as the company.

'When we go south, we'll build more castles along the way to keep any rebels and their friends penned up in the Fens,' Warenne suggested.

'Sir William,' the king said, addressing William Malet. 'I'd like you to stay on here as Sheriff. William FitzRichard and five hundred knights will stay here to support you in case of any trouble.'

'Robert,' he said to de Comines, 'I want you to be Earl of Northumbria. I should have put a Norman in the post in the first place. I'll leave you with seven hundred men to pacify your earldom. That should be enough to do the job.'

Robert remembered how easily the English had given ground in Warwick, Nottingham, and now York. To him, seven hundred sounded like six hundred and fifty too many. 'Seven hundred should do nicely. It's most generous of you,' he said.

Standing close to de Comines, his friend Sir Ralph Pomeroy whispered in his ear, 'That's a nice, simple job for you, Robert.'

'Are you jealous, Ralph? Do you think the king should honour you?'

'I could do just as well, and I've certainly done enough to deserve the title.'

'Perhaps, Ralph. But don't concern yourself now. I'm sure your turn will come.'

Before he left, William checked the building of his new castle. He was pleased with the progress, but the men of York boiled with resentment. In Coppergate, houses were demolished, the area flooded, and the river Foss dammed to make a moat. William had consulted no one. There would be no compensation.

After eight days in York, William returned to London, collecting Matilda and their new baby, Henry, on the way. This was a time for celebration. York was safe in Norman hands, and the word had spread. Lincoln, Cambridge, and Huntingdon all welcomed him, and he built castles in each town. William arrived back in London, a happy man. He had a son, an Englishman, born in his new realm. His kingdom was secure, and his enemy subdued. Subdued but not defeated.

Chapter 22

When he arrived home on a cold, bright winter day, Sir Ralph Pomeroy was surprised to find no one there except Nelda, a servant. She kept nodding her head and saying 'my lord' a lot, but other than that, everything she said was garbled. Eventually, he learned Tate was at the mill, 'and taken the baby with her.'

'She's given birth?'

'Yes, my lord,' Nelda said. 'Baby and mother are well. She's never looked better, and the baby is such a bonnie lad,' Nelda smiled, feeling safe.

'Yes, but why has she gone to the mill?'

'There was a problem that needed sorting out, so they sent for my lady.'

'What does she know about mills?' he asked, then after a moment's thought said, 'Never mind, I'll see for myself.'

Pomeroy strode out of the hall, squinting in the bright, frosty light. The cold winter air made him shiver as he walked the short distance to the mill, the frozen grass crunching under his feet. It grew chillier the closer he got to the stream. Entering the building, he heard the familiar sound of cogwheels turning and millstone grinding. Sacks of flour leaned against a wall, and voices from the floor above drew his attention.

Pomeroy climbed the stairs and entered a scene of activity. Cogged wheels rotated this way and that. The miller was dashing around, looking busy, while Tate's boys watched. Tate sat on an oak beam as though on a throne, holding the baby. As he looked at her, sunlight fell on her face, making her look radiant, bringing a smile to his lips. She returned the smile, and her face darkened as the millwheel turned, blocking the sun for a few moments. She stood up to present her husband with the new baby, and the sunlight fell on her again. Hair of fire, skin smooth as marble, the infant cradled in her arms, cherub-like, pure and innocent.

'Would you care to see your son?' Tate said, handing the bundle over to him.

He took his son, and a shadow fell over them, the light once more blocked out by the mill wheel. A coldness he had never known before crept through him. He felt his heart pound, and his thoughts turned to turmoil.

'I must go,' he said, handing the baby back. He turned and made his way down the stairs and outside, glad to be in the cold air.

Alarmed, Tate followed him, knowing something was wrong. She went outside to find her husband gulping down big breaths of fresh air. He was shaking from head to foot.

'Are you feeling unwell? What is it?' she asked as the baby cried.

In his mind's eye, an image appeared of something that occurred in Sussex before the great battle. In a watermill, just like his, with a woman and baby, just like his. He threw up on the spot.

'Ralph, what is it? You look dreadful.'

The genuine concern in her voice pierced the hardness around his heart. His head was spinning, and he was aware of the blood pumping through his veins. Dread filled him.

'It's nothing to worry about, woman; nothing at all. It must be something I ate,' he said.

'Let's get you indoors. You'll feel better. Come with me,' Tate said.

She took him by the arm and led him to the hall, her boys following in silence. When they arrived, they went straight inside, by which time Pomeroy had composed himself.

'I'm so sorry,' he said once he sat down. 'Food poisoning, I expect.'

'Would you like to see your son, now?'

She held the boy out to him, and he leaned over and gazed upon the infant's face.

Tate was disappointed he had not reached out to hold the boy but said, 'He looks like you two, don't you think, boys?'

In unison, they said, 'yes.'

Pomeroy eyed the baby and thought *he looks the same as any other baby*. Awareness of another baby, at another time, in another place, crept through his being.

'I've called him Joscelin, as you suggested,' Tate said, cradling the baby in her arms.

He looked at the boys and thought, *Now I have an heir.*

The expression in the boys' eyes betrayed their fear. It was a look he knew and had seen many times before. But in this time of dread, he remembered that there must have been a time when his eyes, too, would have shown the same emotion. And he recalled when he was their age. Turning to Tate, he said, 'He looks like his brothers.' *Perhaps I'll spare them after all. We'll see.*

'Joscelin,' Pomeroy said. 'The name suits him.'

Changing the subject, Pomeroy said, 'I was surprised to find you away from home. I thought you'd still be lying in.'

'No. I had my churching last week,' Tate said. 'You're back home, and things are back to how they should be. We could arrange for the christening as soon as possible.'

'I'll sort it out with the priest. You know I'm feeling better already. It must be the effect of being a new father.'

'Yes, it must agree with you,' she said and smiled.

'Now, you tell me all the news. What's been happening while I've been away? I'm sure you've a lot to tell me.'

'And I'm sure you've plenty to tell me.'

Chapter 23

In King Malcolm's great hall in Dunfermline, the leaders of the English resistance and the Scottish court met to discuss how to deal with the Norman threat. The exiles were discussing with their host what their next move would be. They knew William's delegation was on its way, and they had to decide that day what to do. Edgar Atheling was confident Malcolm would help him if only to win his sister's favour.

Malcolm was the widower of the beautiful Ingibiorg. He had sworn no other woman would ever take her place, but that was before Edgar arrived with his mother Agatha and his sisters, Margaret and Christina. Edgar noticed how Malcolm's eyes fixed on Margaret when he introduced them.

'Welcome to Scotland and my court, ladies,' Malcolm said, looking directly at Margaret, who blushed as the women replied, 'thank you, my lord,' in unison.

'It's a pleasure to have you with us, and you can stay as long as you like.'

'You're most kind,' Lady Agatha replied.

'Come to the dais where we'll make a place for you, and you too, Edgar. How good it is to see you again.'

The family made its way, as requested, to places at the top table.

'Here, sit next to me, Margaret,' Malcolm said with a smile.

'Thank you,' she said and sat beside the king while his eyes feasted on her.

'I don't believe you've been to Scotland before.'

'No, I haven't had that good fortune, but what I've seen of it so far is beautiful.'

'While you're here, you'll have to allow me to show you more.'

Margaret, blushing, looked Malcolm directly in the eye, but only for an instant. That was all it took. At that moment, she saw something else in the craggy face of the warrior, almost boyish and childlike. Against her better judgement, she found him, in some odd way, attractive. She ignored the coughing coming from her mother on her other side and agreed it would be a wonderful thing to be escorted around Scotland by the king himself.

Since then, Malcolm had taken every opportunity to be with Margaret and she with him. Edgar was happy. His sister was worth an army to him. But here he was today, discovering the king in a foul mood.

'What on earth is going on down there,' asked Malcolm. He was concerned about the failure resistance.

'I was told England would rise up as one and overthrow William. All I've seen is submission and surrender and no will to do anything other than hand over the keys to the town gates whenever the Normans come calling. What's happening down there?'

'Let me explain,' Edgar said. 'Brihtric, a vital part of our communications, was arrested. No one knew what was going on, and so there was no coordinated rising.'

Malcolm nodded. 'Hmmph. But why are all the towns giving up without even token resistance? From what I understand, Edwin and Morcar lived in a field for a couple of months and then ran away from the Normans when they discovered they were heading towards them. William won't be losing any sleep over your rebellion. But I can tell you something, I am.'

Edgar had no reply to Malcolm's concerns, so Waltheof stepped in. 'I can't speak for Edwin and Morcar, but I know there are many who are eager to fight to rid our kingdom of the Normans. We have the promise of help from the Welsh, which should keep William occupied in the west. Lady Gytha and her sons are going to attack the southwest. If we swoop down from the north, we'll be in York before William knows what's happening. Once we've secured Northumbria, it's on to London, with the armies converging simultaneously. William won't be able to deal with that. He hasn't got the forces for it.'

'That's if you all rebel as one,' Malcolm said.

'Yes, assuming we all rebel as one,' Waltheof replied.

Malcolm found Waltheof, with his deep husky voice, more

convincing than the pixie faced youth aspiring to be king.

'When William's delegation arrives,' Malcolm said. 'We'll tell them what they want to hear, within reason, of course. Once they've gone away, we'll prepare with haste. With a little help, you'll rid yourself of this Norman problem.'

'I would most appreciate your assistance,' came Edgar's reply. 'But won't you expect some recompense?'

Malcolm waved his hand dismissively. 'Let's not get bogged down in petty details. The important thing is we rid ourselves of that upstart as soon as possible. Have another drink, and we'll talk about organising our forces.'

The following day, Malcolm received Bishop Aethelwine. The court was keen to discover what he had to say.

'Aethelwine, I know you by reputation. It's good to meet you at last. We were expecting a Norman. You should have visited us before, but now you're here, welcome,' Malcolm said and called for wine and food as the Bishop took his place by his side. Aethelwine was pleased Edgar, Waltheof, and Merleswein were at the table, and they greeted him warmly.

'How was your journey?' Malcolm asked.

'I don't travel that much, and I'm glad to get out of the saddle,' Aethelwine said.

'Make yourself comfortable. Now tell us what you have to say.'

Aethelwine took a sip from a goblet. 'York fell to William with no resistance. He's building a castle there, and his men are moving on to Durham. Soon he'll be your neighbour.'

Malcolm's expression remained unchanging as the bishop gave his news. 'So, what are William's demands?'

'He would like your submission and for you to swear fealty and obedience to him. Oh, and just one other little thing; he would be pleased if you were to recognise him as overlord of the Kingdom of Scotland.'

'Because peace is better than war, I'll acknowledge he's King of England.'

'That's not what I meant, my lord.'

'Don't worry, Aethelwine. I know what you meant. We'll send an embassy with you to see William. They can negotiate on my behalf. In the meantime, have some more wine.'

After a servant topped up Aethelwine's drink, Malcolm asked more questions. 'So, how many of William's men are heading up to Durham?'

'Seven hundred and fifty. Once it's secure, they'll march on to Bamburgh.'

'And then the north will be in Norman hands.'

'That's what he thinks, yes.'

'With good reason,' said Malcolm, looking the bishop directly in the eye.

Aethelwine had nothing to say and simply looked awkward.

'Don't worry,' Malcolm added. 'I'll help get you out of the mess you've got yourselves into. All that remains is for us to settle a date for when we liberate the north.'

In the middle of January and the icy blasts of a northern England winter, Robert de Comines, the new Earl of Northumberland, headed north from York to Durham. Robert's troops were getting up to mischief on the journey. Breaking up into smaller bands, they would spread out across the land, attacking villages and farmsteads as they went, meeting up at an appointed place before sunset. One such group turned up at a farmstead on the Yorkshire moors. Snow fell as the raiding party approached. More concerned about sheltering from the elements, nobody in the hall was aware of the forthcoming arrival of the invaders. Why should they be? Who would travel to this remote spot in such inclement weather? Inside the great hall, enjoying the warmth of the hearth, a son tried to comfort his father while their steward threw more logs onto the fire.

'You're no trouble,' said Whitgar.

Guthrum looked at the stumps of his arms where his hands used to be. He told people he had lost them in battle at Stamford Bridge, leading them to believe an enemy had lopped them off.

'I can do nothing, not even sweep a floor,' Guthrum said to his son.

'There's your wisdom, father. We need you for that alone. Where would we be without that? Though you are right, there are indeed many things you can't do, but a lot of those things you never did, anyway. For instance, when did you last sweep a floor? When have you ever swept a floor?'

A trace of a smile appeared on Guthrum's face.

Whitgar turned to his steward, 'Have you ever seen my father sweeping a floor, Gymi?'

Gymi, a square-faced, handsome man in his early thirties, grinned. 'I can't say I have,' he said, throwing a log on the fire, sending sparks upward to the black sooty beams.

'There you are. You don't need to concern yourself,' Whitgar said to his father.

'I think I must have been feeling sorry for myself. I have a lot to be thankful for.'

The two smiled at each other, and Whitgar was about to speak when a commotion broke out outside. Chickens squawked, dogs barked, and the shouts of men and women shouting. Then an agonised scream pierced the air.

'What's going on out there?' a startled Guthrum asked his son. But he already suspected the answer to his question.

Whitgar grabbed his sword and shield. 'Run, father. Run!' he yelled.

Guthrum ran across the hall to the window. Gymi opened the wooden shutter, and the old man climbed outside into the falling snow. He heard men speaking in French to his left, so he turned right and rushed to hide around the back of an outbuilding. Gymi raced to the kitchen to find his wife.

'Get the children and come with me,' he said. She saw the panic on his face and responded immediately. She took both of her children by the hand and followed her husband and Whitgar to the door. Whitgar, once he had seen his father clamber through the window, rushed out to confront whoever was creating the disturbance. He stopped in his tracks when he realised the strength of the raiding party; there were twenty armed men on horseback. He stepped back into the hall, his heart pounding. What could he do against this enemy?

Whitgar grabbed his bow and two quivers of arrows and ran. He knew he could save nobody that day and would be lucky if he could save himself. He peered out of the doorway to see half of his father's household lay dead and scattered on the ground. Survivors fled in all directions, seeking safety.

'Over here, hurry,' Whitgar yelled, but no one needed encouragement. A dozen farmsteaders ran to the hall, soldiers on horseback charging after them. The snow was falling faster now, huge flakes descending, muffling the cries, but the white carpet covering the ground highlighted the bright red blood. As he looked on, Whitgar realised the situation was hopeless. In the few moments since he had beckoned them, most were dead after being speared in the back by horsemen. He stepped out into the open and let fly with an arrow, hitting the nearest Norman square in the chest.

'Run for it, Gymi,' Whitgar said, and the steward ran with his wife and children up the embankment and over a wall while Whitgar shot more arrows. He had caught the Normans by surprise. While their comrades carried on about their butchery, those who had encountered the archer withdrew, turning to their leader to alert him and receive orders.

Whitgar raced from the hall and up the embankment, over the wall, then alongside it, following Gymi and his family's tracks—all the time, being careful to keep the stonework between himself and the Normans. It was not long before he caught up with his steward. He stopped and peered at the farm. To his relief, he saw his father making his way to the stream that flowed past their home. Over the centuries, the beck had cut a deep gully, which provided ideal cover. Guthrum, crippled and desperate, stumbled along the snow-covered banks of the stream but slipped and fell, the poor useless stumps of his arms swimming in the slush. A Norman spear skewered him into the mud as he crawled towards safety.

Whitgar, who had witnessed the scene, stood stock still, speechless.

'We need to move,' Gymi said. 'We can't wait around here.'

Whitgar's world was disappearing before his eyes.

'My lord, we need to get away.'

Whitgar dropped behind the wall and tried to compose himself. He wanted vengeance. Nothing less than the death of every Norman on his farm would satisfy him now, but he was only one man. Gymi had his family to consider. What could one man do against many? What could one man do at all? Nothing. Nothing on his own.

'What should we do?' Gymi asked.

'Find your brother and warn him of what's happening.'

'What will you do?'

'I'll go to Durham, and with any luck, I'll get there before the Normans,' Whitgar said, still reeling from the shock of the killings. 'I am certain I'll return and take revenge. Now be off with you, and God be with you.'

Whitgar headed off to the stables where his horse was. If he were lucky, perhaps his horse would be unharmed. He took up a position behind the wall and saw no Normans anywhere. Bodies lay where they had fallen, and it made a terrible sight, but Whitgar heard laughter. The Normans must have discovered where he kept the ale, wine, and food by the sound of things. Tonight, they would feast. Tomorrow, they would burn every building to the ground. He waited a little while until they drank themselves stupid, then he would make his move.

After nightfall, Whitgar approached the farmstead to find the soldiers had quietened down. It did not take long for him to realise, in their arrogance, they had not even bothered to post a sentry. As he made his way through the snow, the sound of the coarse laughter of the intoxicated soldiers emanated from inside his father's hall. He dodged around buildings and reached the stables, happy to discover his horse, Liegitu, was still alive and well. As he saddled up, his heart pounded in his chest, but the carousing men were unaware of him. Once he had tacked up Liegitu, he peered around the stable door and saw all was clear. The snow was still falling as he led his horse out and climbed up into the saddle. Just as he thought he was going to get away, a soldier came staggering out of the hall, looking to revive himself.

'Hey, you. What are you doing?' he asked.

In response, Whitgar kicked Liegitu on.

'Hey, come back here,' the drunk shouted after him.

Whitgar continued, and the soldier disappeared into the hall to tell his comrades what had happened.

'Someone's just galloped off on a horse,' he bellowed.

'Let's get after him,' one of them screamed.

With that, all of those who were capable ran to the door and across to the stables. It didn't take long for them to saddle their mounts and gave chase, but the soft snow fouled their horses' hooves as it compacted in the snow, making the animal unsteady. Whitgar's unshod steed had no such issues and, after barely a mile, disappeared from Norman view into the snowy darkness.

After spending a sleepless night in a shepherd's hut, Whitgar made his way north, away from William's army. He knew York had fallen, but Durham was still free as far as he was aware. Whitgar looked back toward his home to see a column of smoke rising to the heavens. He had to struggle to keep his emotions buried.

Whitgar's problem now would be to make it safely through the winter landscape to Durham, some fifty miles away. He would have to move fast. With enemy troops all around and the terrible cold, he was in danger of dying if the Normans apprehended him or he found no shelter. Hunched up against the cold, Whitgar pushed Lietigu onto Thirsk. There was a Dane there called Thor, a horse trader he had done business with many times. They had always got on well and even enjoyed the occasional half-day hunting. Perhaps he would help.

It was a two-hour ride to Thirsk in ordinary conditions, but with so much snow, it would take longer. Whitgar dreaded the journey but pushed on through the bleached and hoary land, always concerned about freezing to death. His fingers and toes were numb, and his legs were stiffening up, but he was about to discover the cold was not his only worry. As he headed towards the Vale of York, he crossed the tracks of a wolf pack heading north. He judged them to be a pack of at least a dozen. The paw prints were fresh.

'Come on, we'd better make haste,' Whitgar said to his horse.

Liegitu responded and increased his pace; he too wanted to get off the high ground and out of the bitter wind. Even if it were only a breeze, it still cut deep into man and beast, and the shelter of the valley would be most welcome. They had gone less than a mile when a fearsome howl pierced the white silence of the moors. Whitgar was familiar with too many stories of people and their encounters with wolves to imagine it would be alone. Where there was one, there would be others. A surge of energy rushed through Whitgar's through his body, and he kicked his horse on. Not that he needed any encouragement. He, too, had heard the wolf.

It was a relief when, ten minutes later, he made his way off the moors and down into the relative shelter of the Vale of York, which offered some protection against the gusting breeze. From here, he would only have to travel another five miles to safety. The thought lifted his spirits, but not for long when a wolf howled again, this time much closer. Whitgar turned to see he had company, a wolf. It was big, dark but had a grey muzzle, his breath forming clouds in the air. Whitgar wondered if he was the leader introducing his pack to their next meal. Liegitu must have picked up the scent because he, too, became unsettled and jittery.

Whitgar began exercising his fingers in anticipation of using his bow; they were so cold he thought he would be lucky to string it. He had just started rubbing his hands together to get them warm when he noticed something moving in the woods to his right, another wolf and then another, fifty yards further on. He reached for his bow and strung it, no easy matter, on horseback, especially with a skittish horse tugging on the reins.

Whitgar felt Liegitu's distress as their predators closed in and wondered about how desperate his situation was. Liegitu, fast as he was, would never manage a five-mile gallop to Thirsk, and he doubted if he could outrun a pack of wolves. He would have to rely on his bow to save him.

I wonder how many there are and if I have enough arrows? he asked himself. It was then he remembered something Thor had told him a long time before about the animals, which were a common sight around Thirsk. 'They hardly ever attack humans, but if you suspect they might go for you, don't run. Hold your ground. Make yourself look bigger than you really are, make a lot of noise, and throw things at them. That should scare them away,'

'What if it doesn't?' Whitgar had asked.

'You'd better hope it's all over with quickly,' Thor said before bursting into laughter.

The wolf Whitgar had first seen moving up behind him now broke into a loping run, not fast but closing the distance between them. Another one, a little way further up the valley, appeared and ran to intercept him. Liegitu panicked and became harder to control. Three more wolves joined the pack and closed ground on them.

Whitgar did his best to keep Liegitu calm and at a walking pace, and he sent an arrow the way of the closest pursuer to see if it would scare it off. The distance between them was now twelve to fifteen yards, an easy enough shot if Liegitu remained steady. Whitgar released the reins, took aim, and shot the arrow just as Liegitu jumped forward, making him miss the target by several feet and appearing not to unsettle it.

Retaking hold of the reins, Whitgar tried to settle his horse, but Liegitu was on the verge of panic, and the wolves closed in all around them. He tried losing off another arrow, but he had the same result as the first. Liegitu began bucking and neighing, wildly shaking his head as fear got the better of him.

Whitgar decided on a change of tactic and, slipping his bow over his shoulder, drew his sword. He tried waving it around and shouting, but he seemed to frighten Liegitu more than the wolves. With Thirsk still over three miles away, Whitgar wondered how he would complete the journey when Liegitu bolted. The wolves had achieved their aim, and they raced after the horse and rider like demons, closing the gap until they were close enough to make leaps up towards Liegitu's throat. In a blind panic, he ran straight into Balk Beck, a small river Whitgar had crossed a few times on his visits to Thirsk. The horse ran straight into the middle while the wolves stayed baying on the bank. Sensing safety, Liegitu came to a halt, and he and Whitgar faced their pursuers. This was an excellent opportunity, he realised, and so he sheathed his sword, put an arrow in his bow and shot the closest wolf, which let out a sickening yelp and made off, limping and howling with the rest of the pack. Whitgar and Liegitu watched them go as Whitgar patted his horse's side.

'You're a clever fellow, Liegitu,' Whitgar said to his horse as he patted his neck. 'Fancy thinking of that. I'll remember that lesson next time wolves chase me. I'll just stand in the middle of a river.'

After an hour's more riding, Whitgar reached Thor's hall at Thirsk. It surprised the old thane to see him, and he left the comfort of the hearth to greet him outside. Thor's appearance always surprised Whitgar. The Dane had white hair, beard, and the palest skin he had ever seen and looked like a living corpse, a strange sight at any time, in the snow especially so.

'Whitgar, I haven't seen you in a while. What's brought you out in this weather?' Thor asked, knowing it must be something serious.

Whitgar opened his mouth, but only a faint rasping sound came out. His face had frozen solid.

'We'd better get you inside,' Thor said with a smile. He then called a servant to help Whitgar off his horse.

Once Whitgar was inside, he enjoyed the roaring fire blazing in the hearth. It looked as though the entire village had gathered around, all there just to keep warm.

'Get this man some wine,' Thor ordered a servant. 'When you're warm enough, you can tell us what's going on.'

Whitgar gulped the wine and shivered. Steam was rising from his cloak and leggings, and warmth was slowly returning to him.

'The Normans,' he blurted out. He had their attention now, even those who had paid him little before. 'They've killed everyone. They're roaming the countryside, destroying everything in their path. We must act.'

'There are too many for us,' Thor said.

'We can't just do nothing. Why don't we get as many people as we can and go to Durham?'

'In this weather?' someone yelled from the benches.

'If the Normans come this way,' Whitgar said, addressing Thor, 'they'll burn your homes down, and then where will you stay?'

'If the Normans come this way,' Thor repeated. 'Who's to say your place wasn't as far as they've come? Besides, they won't travel far in this weather. They're probably back in York as we speak.'

'You won't come with me then?'

'Stay here, Whitgar, by the hearth, at least while it's still snowing.'

While he was considering the offer, a servant held a bowl of steaming mutton stew in front of his face and handed him a spoon.

'Thank you,' Whitgar said and wolfed down his meal. The heat of it burst in his stomach and then spread through his body. His hands warmed, and at that moment, Thor's hall looked the cosiest place he had ever seen. 'But I have to get on. I need to get to Durham. I'll gather as many as I can along the way, and with God's grace, they'll be enough of us with the townsfolk to put up a good fight.'

'We can't have you leaving empty-handed,' Thor said. 'We'll send you on your way with plenty of food.'

Half an hour later, Whitgar left Thor's hall with enough supplies to complete his journey.

'Are you sure you won't stay for a while?' Thor asked again.

'I appreciate the offer, Thor. Are you sure you don't want to come to Durham?' Whitgar said.

'I'm certain.'

With that, the two men parted company.

'Good luck to you, Whitgar,' Thor called to him as he left.

'Thank you and good luck to you, Thor,' Whitgar replied. He turned to wave as Thor turned and stepped through the open door, returning to the comfort of his hearth.

Chapter 24

It was an arduous journey for Whitgar, struggling through the winter snow and ice, the sword-sharp wind, cutting and slashing at him every step of the way. But at least there were no wolves to contend with this time. He soon discovered the news of the Norman advance had travelled quickly, and, despite the dreadful weather, people deserted their homes and headed north to safety. He gathered men willing to put up a stand on his journey, the rest he left scattered along the highways and byways, where they would be easy victims for marauding Normans.

When Whitgar reached Durham, he had a small army with him, and it pleased him to discover the city gates were open to refugees but well-guarded against Normans.

'Who do I need to see here to organise the defence,' he asked the guards on his arrival. They were standing huddled around a brazier, warming their hands and stamping their feet.

'Bishop Aethelwine's your man,' one called out with a grin. 'You'll find him at home up the top of the hill. Straight up, there. You can't miss it.'

'I'll see you at the Bishop's House,' Whitgar said to his followers before heading up the steep hill as fast as the conditions would allow. He arrived breathless and freezing and entered Aethelwine's house to find the bishop, a crafty-looking man with a sharp-featured face, surrounded by refugees seeking shelter. Somehow, his tonsure made him look rascally.

'You'll have to wait your turn,' Aethelwine said as he caught sight of Whitgar.

'I've just come from Yorkshire,' Whitgar said.

'So have many people.'

'Yes, but I want to organise a defence of the city. I'm informed you're the man to see.'

'Do you have many men?' Aethelwine asked with interest.

'A couple of hundred who joined me on the journey north. I'm sure there'll be more willing to join us here in Durham.'

Aethelwine instructed one of his minions to take over and led Whitgar to a small room.

'It's good to see you,' Aethelwine said. 'I'm sorry, I don't know your name.'

'Whitgar Guthrumson.'

'Two hundred men, you say?'

'Or thereabouts.'

'Do you have any plans?' the bishop asked.

'I thought we could trap the Normans inside the walls. I don't want to meet them in the field, it's too cold, and snow's still falling.'

Aethelwine looked impressed. 'Tell me more,' he said.

As Whitgar and Aethelwine organised the defences, not far away, exhausted from their forays, Earl Robert de Comines and his men journeyed through the frozen landscape to Durham. The thought of finding rest and shelter from the harsh weather driving them on. If they were lucky, there might be an opportunity to do some looting and have a little sport with the locals.

Aethelwine struggled on a mule through the snow about two miles outside Durham to meet the advancing army. The Bishop was convinced Durham faced a terrible fate. Hoping their brief acquaintance in York might be enough to persuade the earl they could be friends, Aethelwine imagined he could convince Earl Robert of the error of his ways. In the howling wind, the two met on the road.

Aethelwine began the conversation, 'Earl Robert,' he bellowed above the screaming wind. 'You have caused much suffering on your journey from York, but the good people have done nothing to warrant such harsh treatment. I beg you, in the name of the Lord, stop your advance.' The Bishop's words carried away in the air.

With a smile, Robert replied, 'My dear Bishop, you're misinformed. The only encounters we've had, have been with outlaws and rebels. But as it's getting late, and it's unreasonable to expect us to camp out in this weather, perhaps the good folk of Durham might show a little hospitality and offer us shelter for the night? Wouldn't that be the Christian thing to do? They need have no fear.'

Aethelwine smiled, but even as the bitter winds cut through him, he knew events were working out just as he hoped.

'I'm happy to share my accommodation with you, Earl Robert, and as many of your men as you think could squeeze in with you. The rest will have to find lodgings where they can.'

'Thank you, Bishop Aethelwine. That is most generous of you, and I appreciate it. Now, if you'd like to lead on.'

With the Bishop huddled up in his cloak at the head of the column, the mercenary army made its way through the bone-numbing wind to Durham, grateful that at last that the snow had stopped falling. Aethelwine wondered what reception Earl Robert would meet when he arrived in Durham. The bishop left Durham when discussions between the townsfolk were still in progress. One faction wanted to allow the Normans through the gates and then kill them when they were trapped in the town; the other wanted them to freeze in the snow. Eventually, some of them stayed behind while Whitgar led men outside Durham. They planned to return once their enemy had made themselves comfortable and felt confident enough to drop their guard.

Aethelwine and de Comines arrived within sight of their destination. Earl Robert was in awe of the city. Even with the icy wind whipping at his eyes, he could see what appeared to be a citadel encircled on three sides by the River Wear, which flowed through a deep gorge. Durham struck him as impregnable, perched on a steep hill and protected by an enclosing wall. Spilling down the steep slopes between the wall and the river was a great tangled thicket of thorn bushes. De Comines edged up to Bishop Aethelwine. 'I'm impressed,' he said. 'It looks unassailable. Why are you inviting me in? In there, you could hold out for months.'

'But you're not an enemy. You are our earl, appointed by the king himself,' Aethelwine said with a smile. 'What would we have to fear from you?'

'Nothing, nothing at all, just so long as you behave yourselves,' de Comines said.

'We always behave ourselves in Durham. It's a holy place, you know.

The bones of Saint Cuthbert and the Venerable Bede lie at rest there,' Aethelwine replied, thinking somehow this would earn de Comine's respect. The earl looked unimpressed, and Aethelwine led the company alongside the River Wear. Eventually, they reached the ford, where he led them across to the road on the other side that climbed a steep gradient to the city. There were no sentries posted at the wide-open gates.

Earl Robert, smiling from ear to ear, led his men into town. As the last of the Normans crossed, Whitgar and his followers were hiding in nearby woods. The Normans were too busy thinking about food, warmth, shelter, and what fun they would have in the coming evening to notice one local man slip out of the gates. He was on his way to join five hundred armed men, a mix of townsfolk and men Whitgar had gathered on his journey, preparing for an attack.

As soon as the Normans entered the city, chaos erupted. They broke into houses to find many empty. They searched every dwelling, and if they found anything of value, they took it. They usually stole something alcoholic, so it was not long before Earl Robert's troops became intoxicated. They killed men on the spot, the women they raped and then murdered. When Aethelwine reached his quarters, havoc had broken out all over Durham. With Robert and his senior men all around him, he was a prisoner in his own home.

Earl Robert talked while warming himself by the fire. 'Bishop, take care of my men here, and those outside will take care of themselves.' As Earl Robert spoke, Aethelwine heard screaming. 'No need to concern yourself. My men are just hunting out a few opponents of the king.'

'I assure you; the king has no enemies in this city.'

'I'll be the judge of that,' Earl Robert said.

Servants brought in food and drink for the Earl and his men, who helped themselves and ate and drank heartily, while outside shouting grew louder. Soldiers were roaming the streets, killing those few who had stayed.

In the woods, the local man with news of Sir Robert's arrival searched for Whitgar. When he found him, he informed him of events.

'There are about seven or eight hundred of them. They were creating mayhem when I left. Some guards have gone to help deal with it, leaving the gates open for us as arranged.'

Whitgar bellowed above the wind. 'You all know what to do. We leave now and show them a bit of northern hospitality.' But, as he had killed no one at close quarters, he worried he might not be up to the job. The thought of combat with swords concerned him; the only blood he had ever spilt in that way was his father's. The thought of freezing at the ultimate moment troubled him greatly. He planned to use his bow whenever he could and put any thoughts of using a sword out of his mind.

A cheer went up from the men, and they were on their way. Just less than an hour later, the sound of the invading army carousing drifted down the hill, through the streets, and across the river into the ears of the Northumbrians.

Whitgar led the way across the chilly fast, flowing ford and up to the town gates, still wide open. Leading his men through the dark and eerie streets, they entered each house and made short work of any Norman they found. All proceeded quietly and efficiently until someone raided the alarm.

'English! English!' The alarm went out.

From houses and halls, soldiers emerged onto the dark streets. As Whitgar had predicted, most were drunk. The first one staggered out of a doorway just six feet in front of him, and he let fly an arrow deep into the man's chest, which took him off his feet. He was dead before he hit the ground. Two of his comrades came reeling out of the house, only to be cut down by arrows before the rest of the Normans inside realised they were safer where they were. Safer, but not safe. At least half a dozen locals pushed past Whitgar and through the doorway, followed moments later by the sounds of combat and men crying out in pain.

Whitgar took a few steps toward the house, and a man appeared. 'Come and look at this. Look what they've done here.'

Whitgar approached the man who showed him into a house. Whitgar could make out the bodies of four children by the light from the fire, all of them butchered. Looking around the room, he saw the body of a naked woman lying face up, staring at the ceiling with unseeing eyes. A Norman had cut her throat. Three Norman soldiers also lay dead where they fell. Blood had pooled all over the floor and sizzled where it ran into the hearth.

Whitgar stood and stared until alerted by a woman screaming further down the street. He fought to regain his composure and went back outside, his head feeling light and dizzy. In the narrow lane, bodies lay, and blood mixed with snowmelt flowed down to the river.

'Come on,' Whitgar said. 'We have work to do, and we need to put an end to the diabolical mischief of these Norman devils.'

Whitgar's followers poured out into the street and searched for more Normans to slay. But as the Normans died in Durham's streets and houses, Whitgar's liberating forces began making more gruesome discoveries. In home after despoiled home, the bodies of murdered children lay.

In fury and rage, it took only a matter of minutes for Whitgar's men to kill at least two hundred of de Comines. The English cut down many of them before they even knew what was going on. Those that survived the initial onslaught banded together in small groups, but they had no plan. No one knew what to do other than fight for his life. Gradually, the Normans were beaten back. It was a scene from hell; disembodied voices screaming in the darkness; rivers of blood flowing in the streets, and armed men hot from combat, releasing fogs of cloud as sweat turned to vapour in the frosty night.

'Force them back to the Bishop's House,' Whitgar ordered, smoky breath giving him a beastly appearance.

His followers forced them up the hill towards the minster as best they could. In the dark, the confusion and worse for drink, they made easy prey for the English, who gave them no quarter.

A voice bellowed, 'The Bishop's House,' and slowly, the Normans fell back to Aethelwine's, where they knew Earl Robert would be.

But there was to be no haven for Robert's men, as the fighting grew more intense all the time. The Northumbrians lost a few men but gained support with every yard they took. Whitgar and his men were making significant progress, some using weapons they found by the side of dead soldiers. Making his way through the dark, narrow streets, Whitgar had no idea of how many Normans he had killed with his arrows.

'Keep pushing forward,' he ordered, surprised by his confidence. He snapped orders, and the men followed them. *If only they knew,* he thought, his heart pounding, not just from exertion but from exhilaration. In some strange, incomprehensible way, Whitgar enjoyed the battle and the part he played.

The women of Durham had also joined the fray. Whatever they could find, they threw down from windows onto the heads of their enemies below. Within an hour of entering, Whitgar and his comrades had killed of their enemies, not enjoying the protection of the Aethelwine's home. Inside the House, the surviving Normans were desperate.

Earl Robert looked ashen-faced at Aethelwine. 'Is there a way out of here?'

'There are only the front or back doors,' Aethelwine said.

'We can hold them off, though?'

'Not for long.'

'You're enjoying this, aren't you?' Earl Robert sneered.

'I'm a man of God, and I assure you it gives me no pleasure to see good Christian souls terrified by a mob,' Aethelwine said.

'We are soldiers. We are not afraid,' Robert seethed. 'Negotiate a truce with that mob out there.'

'If you'll excuse me,' Aethelwine said.

Earl Robert nodded his assent.

Bishop Aethelwine approached the front door and opened it slightly. The moment the crowd saw movement, chanting and shouting broke out. Opening the door a little wider, the Bishop waved his crucifix through the gap. He jumped when an arrow embedded itself in the doorpost a few inches away. He persisted, and the crowd calmed down.

'What is it, Bishop?' Whitgar bellowed over the noise.

'I would like…'

'Step outside. We can't hear you,' Whitgar yelled.

The Bishop opened the door and stepped forward. Behind him, one of de Comines men followed with a sword to his neck.

'No tricks,' the soldier said.

Two archers were posted on all four corners of the Bishop's House, ready to shoot anyone who tried to escape. Two of them had a fine view of the soldier's back and shot their arrows as archers in the mob let fly at any open doors or windows.

With his sword to Aethelwine's throat, the Norman soldier fell dead with two arrows deep in his back. Two Englishmen burst out of the crowd, grabbed Aethelwine and frogmarched him to safety, where he found a grinning Whitgar.

'Oh, it's you. I thought I recognised the voice,' the Bishop said.

'Did they harm you?' Whitgar asked.

'No, not at all.'

'They did plenty of damage out here. See if you can persuade them to surrender,' Whitgar said.

Bishop Aethelwine shouted to those inside his house from a safe distance, 'Come out now without your weapons. You will be well treated.'

'I doubt it,' Earl Robert said.

'You have my word—the word of a bishop. You'll come to no harm,' Aethelwine said.

'Come out now, or we'll burn the house down, with you in it,' Whitgar added for good measure.

Earl Robert peered from a window at the mob, the bitter, angry faces glowing red in the torchlight. He fancied they all had the eyes of the devil. Dancing flames made grotesques of their features, and in the chilly night air, they all seemed to breathe smoke like some beast drawn up from the bowels of the earth. He thought better of surrendering to them.

'If you want us, come and get us,' he yelled.

Whitgar nodded to a group of men holding torches. As arrows flew towards the bishop's house, the men with torches ran forward and set fire to the thatch. Soon the roof was burning.

'Oh, no. Don't burn my house down,' Aethelwine cried.

'Too late, Bishop,' said Whitgar. 'I'm sorry, there's no other way.'

'Couldn't you have starved them out?'

'We could, but I doubt if it would be anywhere near as quick.'

'But what about my beautiful home?'

'I'm sure the Lord will provide you with another,' Whitgar said.

Now that the roof was ablaze and caving in on its occupants, soldiers made a break for safety.

'Make sure none of them escapes,' Whitgar ordered. 'Kill the lot of them.'

'That's harsh, isn't it, Whitgar?' Aethelwine said.

'You wouldn't think that if you'd seen what they've done to your parishioners, Bishop. Not one of them escaped their brutality. Not even women and children.'

No Norman got more than a few feet before being cut down with an arrow or spear.

Waiting to see if any more soldiers left the building, Whitgar asked Aethelwine what he would do next.

'Isn't that obvious, my son? We'll bury our dead; from what you tell me, there are quite a few. What happens after that depends on you. Our beloved king won't let a massacre like this go unpunished. We must have killed seven or eight hundred men tonight. That's the most he's lost in one battle since Hastings. We need to make the most of this.'

'What are you suggesting?' Whitgar asked.

'Would you and your followers fancy visiting York? It will be a challenging journey, but I'm sure the people there would be glad to see you. As for the Normans, they'll be unprepared for our visit.'

'You know, Bishop Aethelwine. I think you've had a good idea.'

Chapter 25

As they discussed business by a blazing fire at court in Dunfermline, King Malcolm and his courtiers were interrupted when a royal steward announced a messenger. Heads turned as a mud-spattered man entered the hall. Few people called in during the winter; this was someone bearing important news.

'My lord,' the messenger addressed Malcolm. 'Word from England is that the townsfolk of Durham slaughtered King William's men, all seven hundred of them. They're now heading to York to join their countrymen in an uprising.'

The announcement startled Malcolm. 'When did this happen?'

'A week ago. King William sent one of his earls to occupy Durham and build a castle there. They created havoc, but the Northumbrians organised themselves and took back the town. When they'd finished, the streets were running with blood. None of the Normans survived.'

'Whose leading them?' Edgar said.

'Bishop Aethelwine and a thane called Whitgar.'

'I think we'd better get down there, Malcolm,' Edgar said. Then he turned to the messenger, 'Have you had word from York?'

'No. Nothing.'

'Will you be joining us?' Edgar asked King Malcolm.

'Yes, but not until later. You have a smaller force to gather, but I'll be right behind you. You'd best start soon,' he said.

'Will you supply us with provisions?' Edgar said.

'See to it, our friends have the supplies they need,' Malcolm said to his Steward.

With that, the Englishmen rose to spread the news and collect their men. As word circulated, Edgar called a meeting of his war council. Outside in the frosty Scottish air, he put forward his plan to his gathered commanders.

'We must get to York as quickly as possible. It's over two hundred miles, and if the weather remains unchanged, it'll be a tough journey. We should reach it before William gets organised, and if that's the case, half of England will be in our hands before the campaign season has even begun. We should leave first thing tomorrow. Does anyone have a question?'

'When will Malcolm be joining us?' Waltheof asked.

'He'll be with us as soon as possible. In the meantime, I suggest you plan to leave in the morning,' Edgar said.

'Let's hope he's as good as his word,' Bondi said.

And with that, the meeting ended, and each man left to attend to his packing.

As Merleswein made his way with the others, his daughters approached him.

'Hello Father,' said Morwenna. 'I take it you're leaving for York?'

'Yes, but don't worry. When it's safe, I'll send word, and the two of you can come home to Lincoln, and we'll begin our lives again.'

'There's no need for that, father. Elfwyn and I are coming with you.'

'Oh, no, you're not. You're staying here, under King Malcolm's protection.'

'But he'll be with you. How can he protect us when he's not here?' Elfwyn said.

'You'll be safe here in Scotland.'

'We'll be safe in England.'

'Let me make this clear; your place is here.' Merleswein glared at his daughters. They knew he would not change his mind. 'Is that understood?'

'Yes, father,' Morwenna answered.

Merleswein turned his glare to Elfwyn.

'Yes, father.'

'Good. That's settled then. Now, I've got things to do. I'm sure you'll forgive me if I get on with them,' Merleswein said, and he continued on his way.

The sisters saw Bondi making his way to the provisions building and decided on a different tack. The two smiled and approached him.

'Hello Bondi,' Elfwyn said, fluttering her eyelashes. 'Are you going to York with the rest of them?'

'Of course,' the Housecarl said.

'I wouldn't like to be in William's shoes when you arrive.' She looked at him admiringly, a big smile on her face.

Morwenna stood silently. She had seen Elfwyn's flattery work so often on men she was glad to let her younger sister take charge.

'Tell me, Bondi, who handles the provisions?'

'Someone in the barn. Why do you ask?'

'We're coming to York with you, and father said to get supplies, but he didn't say from where.'

'You know now,' the housecarl smiled.

Elfwyn returned his smile and fluttered her eyelashes again. 'Could you get ours for us when you collect yours?'

Bondi wore a quizzical expression, but as he was about to say something Elfwyn thought she would not care for, she added, 'We'd happily do it ourselves, but we have a lot to do. You know what we ladies are like for packing.' Elwyn smiled her biggest smile.

Bondi had no idea what women were like for packing. He looked from one woman to the other as though the answer might spring from them. 'Yes,' he said.

'Thank you, Bondi. You're so kind,' Elfwyn said. Morwenna added her thanks, too.

'It's a pleasure, my Ladies,' he said before continuing on his way.

The sisters watched him go, and when he was out of earshot, Morwenna said, 'Tell me, Elfwyn, do you think men have anything between their ears?'

Elfwyn turned and smiled at her big sister. 'It's not their brains you have to appeal to.'

'Well, I must appeal to Sherilda to take care of the children while I'm gone,' Morwenna said.

'She won't mind,' Elfwyn said. 'She loves them almost as much as you do.'

'I'll see what she says. I won't be long.'

Morwenna searched for Sherilda and found her with Lady Agatha,

Margaret, and Christina in the hall. The older girls were enjoying playing mother to the young children.

'Sherilda, a word, please?' Morwenna said.

'Of course. With Lady Agatha's permission,' she said, looking for a sign from the Atheling's mother.

Lady Agatha nodded her acquiescence.

'Sherilda, I'm going to England with Edgar.'

'No. Why?'

'I can't sit around here while there's a chance we can rid England of the Normans.'

'Is it that or revenge?' Sherilda said.

'It's more than revenge. I want my country back, my land and my life as I used to live it.'

'You can't get all of it back,' Sherilda said.

'That's true. Those I've lost are lost, but I will avenge them, and one day I'll be back in Oakley,' Morwenna said. 'Please tell me you'll take care of the children.'

'You can count on me.'

The two women embraced and said their goodbyes.

'Please take care, Morwenna,' Sherilda said, with tears in her eyes.

Morwenna, her eyes welling up, strode off toward the stables.

'God be with you,' Sherilda called after her.

'And you,' Morwenna replied over her shoulder.

When she met Elfwyn back at the stables, Morwenna told her that Sherilda had agreed to look after the children.

'She's a Godsend,' Elfwyn said.

'Yes. I couldn't do without her.'

'All we have to do now is hope we don't run into Thurold when we're there,' Elfwyn said.

Later that day, after Morwenna had said goodbye to the children, she and Elfwyn slipped away with the army, taking care to avoid being seen by Merleswein.

They set off in the cold, wet, windy winter. Every soldier in the column huddled up against the bitter weather. They made good progress on windswept muddy tracks. After three days of hard travel, they arrived in Bamburgh, the wind still doing its best to tear them to shreds. Bamburgh was a spectacular sight. A gigantic wooden fortress perched on a cliff soaring into the sky, the North Sea's waves were crashing loud below, the raucous squawking of gulls above. As Edgar brought his horse to a halt outside the gates, a grinning face appeared on the battlements.

'I wondered how long you'd be,' the face said.

Edgar looked up to see Gospatric looking down at him. 'You've heard the news then?'

'Durham, you mean?'

'Yes. Well, my lord. You'd better come in out of this terrible weather. You look soaked.'

The gate opened, and Edgar entered with his army of several hundred men and two women. Elfwyn and Morwenna had remained undetected by their father since setting out three days earlier and felt confident they would remain so if they were careful until they reached York.

'I'll be glad of somewhere warm and dry to sleep tonight,' Elfwyn said to her sister.

'So will I.'

The column moved forward, and once through the gate, Gospatric's men directed them and told them where to go. The two sisters had kept themselves at the rear, carefully avoiding their father and any of his friends. Now they mingled with those who had been at the front.

'Quick. Let's get the horses to the stables,' Morwenna said.

They dismounted and walked with the horses between them and Merleswein.

'That was close,' Morwenna said as they slipped away.

They stabled the horses and made their way to the great hall, hoping to find a place on the benches well away from their father. With the hoods of their cloaks up over their heads, they blended in perfectly with the other soldiers.

Skirting around Merleswein and his friends, they heard Gospatric call their names, 'Morwenna. Elfwyn. What a pleasure.'

The sisters carried on walking.

'What's the matter? Have I offended you?' Gospatric said.

'Morwenna. Elfwyn,' Merleswein bellowed.

'He sounds quite stern. What should we say?' Elfwyn said.

'I'll just tell him it was your idea,' Morwenna answered. The sisters were still keeping their distance from their father.

'Girls,' Merleswein bellowed, even louder this time.

'We'd better see what he wants,' Morwenna said.

The two stopped in their tracks and turned to face their father.

'What are you doing here?' he demanded to know.

'We've come to help, father,' Elfwyn said, her face a picture of innocence. The cold air made her cheeks red and rosy, which showed off the white of her teeth and the blue of her eyes. As always, when about to be scolded by her father, she took on the appearance of a helpless angel. One of great delicacy and fragility to be treated with the utmost care. It was an obvious ploy everyone saw through, but it worked every time.

Merleswein sighed, 'Do you imagine we couldn't manage without you?'

Morwenna decided not to speak. Elfwyn was the favourite daughter, and if anyone could talk them out of this situation, it was her.

'Durham has fallen, and when we get there, so too will York. What harm could we come to?' Elfwyn smiled her angelic smile.

While those around him began laughing at Elfwyn's audacity, Merleswein became exasperated, and he even stamped his foot.

'You're to go back at once.'

'But York isn't far from home. We might as well stay with you now,' Elfwyn said. 'My Lord Edgar,' she continued. 'What's your opinion? Surely no harm can come to us if we're with you?'

Edgar looked startled. He had not expected to be dragged into this.

'The lady might be right. When we arrive, York will be in English hands again, and they'll come to no harm.'

That settled the argument, and a cheer went up from the men.

Merleswein rolled his eyes and approached his daughters, putting an arm around each and walking them to the great hall. They spent the rest of the day feasting and simply enjoying being dry. Those on the high table made room for them, and they sat with Gospatric, their father, and Edgar. Also, next to Morwenna was Bondi, who seemed to find himself promoted above the level of housecarl and was unsure why. He fell silent at his place at the dais, watching as others ate, drank, talked, and laughed. He studied the thralls for a minute, noticing which ones were efficient, happy to serve their lord, content with their lot and those who appeared resentful and brooding. Happy or sad, young or old, Bondi noticed they had a hungry look. Something about the evening reminded him of his childhood in Gloucestershire, and he reflected on how far he had come.

'You're miles away,' Morwenna said.

'I was,' he replied. 'I'm sorry, I didn't mean to ignore you.'

'It's been a long few days,' she said.

'And more ahead, but at the end of our journey, we'll find ourselves a comfortable place in York.'

Morwenna grinned. 'Elfwyn's convinced you?'

'It's a pleasant thought, and if it turns out to be true, that would be wonderful. Half the country would be in our hands, and in the spring, we'll march on London.'

Chapter 26

In mid-February, Edgar Atheling arrived in York, soaked to the skin and frozen to the bone. He entered the rain-lashed city at the head of his bedraggled army to discover the English in control, with not a Norman in sight. The streets deserted; anybody who could was taking shelter from the foul weather.

The army of fifteen hundred men, accompanied by a handful of women, headed for the hall. Among them were Elfwyn and Morwenna. Now that they had arrived at their destination, Whitgar greeted them, and more than one person noticed; he appeared to have grown a little taller.

'Welcome to York, my lords,' he said. 'I'm afraid you've missed most of the fun.' His heart skipped a beat when he saw Elfwyn amongst them.

'And Ladies, of course,' he added with a smile for Elfwyn. 'Please come into the hall and thaw yourselves out. You must have had an arduous journey.'

Edgar welcomed the invitation, and soon he and most of his comrades were crammed into the warm hall.

After resting for an hour, Edgar Atheling met with Bishop Aethelwine, Whitgar, Merlewein and Waltheof at the bishop's house.

'It's good to see you,' Aethelwine said.

'Likewise, Aethelwine. And it's marvellous you've rid York of the Normans,' Edgar said.

'Ah, well. We've kicked them out of town, but they're still in possession of the castle,' Aethelwine said.

'Oh, I thought they'd gone completely. How many are there?'

'Five hundred men under the command of Sir William Malet.'

'Quite a force.'

'It is,' Aethelwine said. 'But it's a lot of mouths to feed. Plus the fifteen captives.'

'Is that all I need to know?' Edgar said.

'There's the treasure. It's the loot Malet and his men have taken from the homes of people whose land they've stolen, as well as the churches they've robbed, of course.'

'Of course,' Edgar said. 'Do you have a plan for taking the castle?'

'Not yet,' Whitgar said.

Edgar looked thoughtful. 'Where's Archbishop Ealdred?' he asked.

'No one has seen him since early this morning,' Whitgar replied.

'That's a shame. I sent word I wanted a coronation here in York Minster.'

Aethelwine looked horrified. *So that's why Ealdred's disappeared,* he thought.

'You know I want him to crown me King of Northumbria,' Edgar continued. 'Then, once we've got rid of William, I'll be crowned King of England in Westminster.'

'But first, we need to deal with Malet. And then find Ealdred,' Aethelwine said.

'The sooner we get started, the better,' Edgar said.

It was at that moment Archbishop Ealdred entered.

'Archbishop, I'm so glad I found you,' Edgar greeted Ealdred warmly.

'Yes. Can I be of assistance?'

'You can. It is my intention to be crowned King of Northumbria and, naturally, I would like you to officiate.'

Ealdred's expression, one of panic, froze on his face.

'Don't you have something to say?' Edgar said.

'My lord,' Ealdred said, visibly shaking, 'as far as I am aware, there's only one king in England, and that is King William. I am not aware of any desire on his part to share the throne.'

'He has no right to be king, and it's not my intention to share the throne with anyone. For the moment, I am content to be King of Northumbria. King of England will wait until later. Now, are you going to preside over my coronation?'

'No. I cannot. Think of the turmoil such a thing will bring!' Ealdred said.

'You think there is no turmoil now?'

'I cannot do such a thing.'

'Cannot or will not?' Edgar said, spitting the words out.

Ealdred cast his glance downward, avoiding Edgar's gaze.

'I have nothing more to say,' Ealdred said.

'Ealdred. I shall remember this day,' said Edgar calmly, his eyes revealing his anger.

'So shall I, but consider this, if I were to crown you, the Normans would unleash such fury there would be countless deaths. Taking a life is a dreadful business. Think. Most of the dead will be young, and all the youthful optimism will die with them when they lose their lives. Think of the hope for the future, the promise of a world to be and the love of family and friends. Their life never to be realised. Who would do that? Who would inflict that pain on so many?'

Edgar did not know how to reply.

'William the Bastard, that's who,' Whitgar spoke up. 'You should journey north from here. Everywhere between York and Durham is laid to waste. If you think prostrating yourself before William will make for a sweet life, you're mistaken, your Grace.'

'I will prostrate myself before the Lord God Almighty, and I suggest you do the same. Have faith. Have faith.'

'You think faith alone will see us through?' Whitgar asked.

'Of course. Jesus, the good shepherd, will take care of his sheep. You're looking for a way out of these terrible difficulties; God will give you an answer. The Lord will provide.'

'We've all heard that before,' Whitgar replied.

Leaving Ealdred behind, Edgar, Whitgar, Waltheof and Aethelwine walked through the timber walkways to join Bondi, Gospatric and Merleswein in the Earl's Hall. When they arrived, plans to take the castle were well in hand. Bondi and Gospatric looked pleased with themselves.

'Please make yourselves comfortable,' Whitgar said, with a sweep of his arm indicating the dais, where the tables had been prepared fit for a king.

Edgar took his place in the centre with Whitgar by his side, and his other guests took their places. Edgar had a quick look around the hall. Its size surprised him, as it was perhaps a little bigger than the Great Hall in

Winchester and a little higher. He loved how the craftsman covered the wood with real or imaginary creatures climbing through carved vines.

Within moments of taking their places, drinks arrived, and Merleswein toasted Edgar. The food arrived and the guests, now warm and relatively dry, feasted. After a week on their winter journey, the hearth, the food, the drink, and the company seemed heavenly. To add to the good feeling, musicians struck up, and soon the hall was filled with the sound of celebration and good cheer.

After an hour, two servants entered with an enormous silver platter on which sat the most enormous pie the guests had ever seen. Protruding from the top crust was a wooden shaft with the same appearance as a flightless arrow. The locals were grinning, and elbows nudged ribs, hands covered mouths to stifle laughs. The servants placed the pie directly in front of Bondi.

'There you are. That's just for you,' Aethelwine laughed. 'But you can share some if you like,' he guffawed.

Bondi did not know what was happening as the hall filled with thunderous clapping and cheering.

An embarrassed Bondi looked to Aethelwine for an explanation.

'Spear Pie,' Aethelwine said. 'They make it every year in honour of your contribution to our victory at Stamford Bridge.'

The men were on their feet, calling for a toast. To a loud cheer, Bondi rose.

'Thank you, it's an honour for you to recognise me in such a way,' he said, smiling at the steaming pie. 'I'd like to mention I had a bit of help from one or two people. Some of you are amongst us.'

Another roar went up and a chant of, 'Eat the pie,' began.

'As you insist, I'll eat the pie,' Bondi said.

There was an ear-splitting noise as assorted objects crashed rhythmically on the tables, and Bondi shovelled a slice of pie onto his wooden trencher. On the dais, feeling mortified, Whitgar tried his best to join in, but the reminder of Bondi's heroism was also a reminder of his catastrophic ineptitude. He looked on as the pie was ceremoniously shared amongst the guests on the top table, wishing he could vanish, drowning in his discomfort while servants served up more, smaller spear pies to the others. All the aches and pains of the hard ride down from Scotland were forgotten. The only person in the hall who seemed less than happy was Edgar, and he was the only one present who did not seem to appreciate the gesture. No one noticed Whitgar's uneasiness. Any reminder of Stamford Bridge brought back terrible memories of the fate that befell him and his father. It was a relief to see the other guests, now a little merry from the drink they had consumed, laughing and joking as they tucked into their food. His blunder remained a secret.

Although he had enjoyed his moment as the centre of attention, when Bondi sat down, thoughts of Harold and his old comrades floated up from the deep recesses of his memory and images of the battle came to mind. Including one in particular. He leaned forward to talk to Whitgar, who was sitting just a few places away.

'Weren't you also at Stamford Bridge?'

'Yes, I was,' Whitgar answered, a tremor in his voice.

'I'm certain I saw you there.'

'Perhaps you did. Who knows?' Whitgar said. 'Do you like the pie?'

'It's delicious.'

Whitgar reached out with his knife to slice off another piece.

'I know,' Bondi said. 'You were on board a Viking longship on the Ouse, at Riccall. As I recall, the Norwegians left a young warrior behind. They'd cut off his feet so he couldn't escape.'

Whitgar felt tense, and his face burned. He had dreaded this moment for a long time, but he had hoped he would never meet a witness to his terrible blunder. Evidently, his luck had run out.

'I was aboard many a Viking ship that day,' Whitgar said, and as their eyes met, Whitgar could see the memory come back to Bondi, clearly and concisely as a bolt of lightning.

Bondi pictured the scene from a distance just as he remembered it. Another housecarl, Scalpi, had given him the horrific details later. He could not imagine how Whitgar must feel. He was not sure what to say, so he simply said, 'So were a lot of other men. It might have been any one of them.'

'Probably,' Whitgar agreed, relieved.

'And you've been in a few more battles since Stamford Bridge,' Bondi said. 'I hear it was you who freed Durham from Robert de Comines.'

'Yes, but like you, I had help,' Whitgar said, happy to change the subject.

Bondi smiled in response. 'Tell me,' he said, 'who's your lord?'

'By rights, Earl Morcar, but I've no idea where he is, so, I thought I'd make myself useful here.'

'It's the same for me. I was a royal housecarl, but now I have no lord,' Bondi said.

'What about the Atheling, isn't he your lord now?'

'I'm a royal housecarl, so, according to custom, the Bastard is my lord. But as I don't regard him as the rightful king, I must find someone else to follow.'

'The Atheling isn't your lord?'

'No. So, you and I are in a similar situation.'

'Who would you choose?' Whitgar asked.

Before Bondi could answer Whitgar's question, they were distracted when a group of musicians played, and cheer of appreciation went up.

It was then Bondi caught the eye of Morwenna, who was making her way back to her place. She and Elfwyn had been sitting further down the table. She gave him a huge, heartwarming smile as she passed.

While Bondi's eyes fixed on Morwenna, Whitgar found his gaze stuck to Elfwyn. She seemed to radiate something other than beauty, something he could not quite define; a vitality, vivacity, even life itself. As he stared, transfixed, Morwenna caught his eye, touched Elfwyn's arm to get her attention and, with a nod, indicated Whitgar. Elfwyn turned to see the young thane staring at her like a simpleton, a half-smile on his face. Unsure of what to do, he broadened his smile, which Elfwyn returned before blushing, giggling, and averting her gaze. She turned once more to see if he was still staring at her. He was, and he rose to his feet and made his way over to her. As he closed the distance between them, they both had their hearts in their mouths.

'Hello,' he said. 'I'm Whitgar Guthrumson, Thane of Thorkirk.'

'I know; we've met before.'

'That's right,' Whitgar said. Trying to think of something sensible to say, he said, 'Can I ask you for a dance?'

'You can if you like, but the music's stopped playing.'

Whitgar looked around to discover Elfwyn was right. No one was dancing. Mortified, he turned back to find her grinning at him and barely able to suppress a laugh.

'Perhaps we could enjoy a pleasant conversation instead?' he suggested.

'That would be lovely, but not now. I'm afraid my father has seen us, and if you value your life, you'll bid me goodbye and return to your seat.'

'Oh.'

'See me later when the women leave for the bowers,' Elfwyn said. Whitgar thought he saw a promise in her eyes.

The two returned to their places with Merleswien's eyes burning into Whitgar every step of the way. To appease him, Whitgar smiled his most charming smile. Merleswein glowered even harder in return.

Back in his place on the bench, Whitgar thought it best to keep the news that he would see Elfwyn later.

'Isn't he the one who raised Durham against the Normans and freed York?'

'I thought that was Bishop Aethelwine?'

'It was the two of them, apparently. He's quite handsome, isn't he?' Morwenna said, with mischief in her eyes.

'Who? The Bishop?'

'You know who I mean,' Morwenna said. 'Whitgar.'

'I hadn't noticed,' Elfwyn replied. But the lie did not fool Morwenna.

The lie did not fool Merleswein either, and he resolved to keep an eye on his daughters.

Oblivious to the family intrigues on the high table, friends talked, laughed, told riddles and stories, sang, and got a little drunk. Everyone enjoyed the feast, and time flew by until the moment arrived for the women to go to the bowers. As the sisters left through one door, Whitgar slipped through another, with Bondi following close behind. They met Elfwyn and Morwenna outside, and they were all relieved to discover the rain had stopped.

'Hello, I thought we'd never get out,' Whitgar said.

'Same here,' Elwyn said.

'Where would you like to go?' Whitgar asked.

'What do you have in mind?' Morwenna said.

'We could just go for a walk,' Whitgar said. 'The sky is clear, and the stars look so pretty.'

Morwenna and Elfwyn exchanged a meaningful look. 'Really?' Morwenna said.

'Yes, really,' Whitgar said.

'I have a suggestion,' Morwenna said. 'Why don't we go back to our father's? It's not far, and it will be much better than wandering around looking at the sky.'

'I didn't realise Merleswein had a house in York,' Whitgar said.

'Well, he has, and you can be our guests just as long as you promise to be on your best behaviour,' Morwenna said.

'We will,' Bondi said.

They walked the short distance to Merleswien's York home and entered, trying hard to remain unnoticed. None of them wanted to explain to Merleswein what Bondi and Whitgar were doing there. No servants were about; they were either in Lincoln, Scotland or helping in the great hall. The embers in the hearth glowed, and the house was warm. Morwenna put more logs on the fire, and Elfwyn found some mead.

'Is this where you planned to stay?'

'Yes,' said Elfwyn. 'We're staying here with father, although tonight, I suspect he'll stay in the hall with the others.'

'So, he won't be back this evening,' Whitgar said.

'He probably will,' Morwenna answered.

'No. He'll stay at the hall,' Elfwyn said.

'No,' Morwenna said. Looking sternly at her younger sister. 'He's definitely coming back.'

'Why don't we make the most of our time here?' Whitgar interrupted. 'I propose a toast to our health and good luck tomorrow when we take the castle.'

'I'll drink to that,' Bondi said, and the women raised their goblets and drank.

'I know we've just come from a feast,' Elfwyn said. 'Is anyone hungry? We've some cold meats and preserves.'

'I'm famished,' Whitgar said.

'I'll get something then. What about you, Bondi?'

'Thank you,' he said.

When Elfwyn left for the kitchen, Whitgar stood up. 'As there are no servants here, I'll give her some help,' he said. He left Bondi and Morwenna sitting at the corner of a long table, enjoying the warmth of the fire.

'It's good to see you again, Morwenna,' Bondi said.

'You saw me at the feast.'

'Yes, but it's good to talk with you.'

'Is there something you want to tell me?'

'No. I just wondered how you are,' he said.

'There's not much to say, except thanks to your help, we made it this far, and God willing, I'll be here tomorrow to witness the storming of that Norman fortress.'

'And then in the summer, we can move on London and from there, drive William into the Channel,' he said.

'Wouldn't that be a sight to behold? I'd like them to all end up in the sea, and every one of them drowned. Then people would lie safe in their beds at night. I know it wouldn't bring back Godric, but it would be something worth fighting for.'

'And then once we've rid ourselves of the Normans, we can return to where we were.'

'I don't think that's going to happen, Bondi. Not for you or me. I'll go to the farm in Oakley, but it won't be the same. You'll be a housecarl, but one of how many and who would you know? Edgar would be king.' She looked at him meaningfully.

'He's still young. He'll grow into it.' Leaning closer to her, he said, 'Morwenna…'

Morwenna read his thoughts. 'I haven't known a man since Godric. I know you must think I'm a fool, especially with his reputation, but it would feel like infidelity. Is that difficult for you to understand?'

Bondi stopped for a moment before sitting back to collect his thoughts. He concluded in a flash that Morwenna had closed the door on him. And so they talked for a while about farming, being a housecarl and what they would do after they toppled William.

In the kitchen, Whitgar had entered, took Elfwyn's hand, and gently caressing her fingers, said, 'I was hoping we'd be alone.'

'So was I,' she said. An impish grin appeared on her face.

'Your sister's quite a force to be reckoned with, isn't she?'

'Isn't she just?'

'Is Merleswein really coming home this evening?' he asked.

'Why are you so fascinated with my father?' Elwyn's smile grew bigger. 'Do you have plans of which I should be aware?'

'No. No, not at all. You've nothing to fear.' He smiled.

'Perhaps I should be afraid. You have quite a reputation, you know.'

'Do I?' *His father's mutilated arms. The bloodied sword blade. These images flew through his mind.*

'Yes. You're the one who took back Durham.'

'Of course,' Whitgar said, relieved. 'Although, I have to say, if it hadn't been for Aethelwine, I couldn't have done it.'

'Don't be so modest. You're a hero.'

'I don't feel like one.'

'Well, you are.' She reached out and touched his arm.

He took her hand, holding it in his.

'Tell me something,' he said. 'What are you doing here?'

'We heard you'd freed Durham and joined Edgar when he came south.'

'So, you thought you'd come down and help us out?'

'That's about it, yes,' she said, with a smile, Whitgar found more captivating every time he saw it.

'What are you doing here?' she asked him.

Whitgar told Elfwyn of his experience, a Norman raiding party and how they killed his father and the men, women, and children at the farmstead. How he escaped to Durham and helped deal with the Normans before coming to York with Aethelwine.

'I'm sorry to hear about your father,' she said. 'How's your mother?'

'My mother died a long time ago.'

So, he's an orphan, she thought, and her heart went out to him.

Time flew by, and they grew comfortable telling their stories, sharing their pasts. As they talked, they looked into each other's eyes, searching for a sign that gave permission, opened a door, allowed more. Gradually leaning into each other, they kissed.

'Haven't you two got that food and drink yet? What's taking you so long?' Morwenna called from the hall, and the moment was gone.

'Big sister's getting hungry. Best not to keep her waiting,' Elfwyn said.

'I wondered how long you two would be,' Morwenna said, casting a critical eye at Elfwyn when she and Whitgar returned with food and drink.

They drank a jug of mead together and toasted the battle that would come the following day.

'It's best you go now,' Morwenna said to Bondi and Whitgar. Father will be home soon.' She glanced at Whitgar and Elfwyn, transfixed in each other's gaze.

'Goodnight,' Whitgar said to Elfwyn, and sadness appeared in her eyes.

'Goodnight, Whitgar,' she said, forgetting Bondi for a moment. Perhaps we'll see each other in the morning.'

'I'd like that.'

Whitgar said, 'Goodnight,' to Elfwyn, and sadness appeared in her eyes.

'Goodnight, Whitgar,' she said, forgetting Bondi for a moment. 'Perhaps we'll see each other in the morning.'

'Yes. I'd like that.'

He was just about to follow up with more conversation when he felt a tug on his sleeve.

'Goodnight, ladies,' he heard Bondi say as his friend pulled him away. Morwenna and Elfwyn smiled at them indulgently.

Chapter 27

Early the following day, Edgar had the men gather to address them before going into battle. They waited in the pouring rain in front of the Earl's Hall. Inside, the Atheling was preparing for the assault on the Norman garrison.

'Does anyone know where Edwin and Morcar are?' he asked his leaders.

'Still no word,' Gospatric said.

'I've heard nothing either,' Whitgar added.

All eyes were on Edgar now. 'We'll carry on without them,' he said. 'Are you ready?'

'Yes, my lord,' they said, in unison.

Edgar led his comrades from the building and into the downpour to greet a man running towards him at full pelt.

'My lord, my lord. The Bastard is here, and he's brought an army. They're approaching now and fast.'

As the messenger spoke, a loud cheering went up from the castle.

'How many are there?' Edgar asked.

'Thousands.'

Alarmed, Edgar looked around him. Most men were preparing to take the castle, not to defend the city, whose gates were wide open. Unsure of what to do but knowing he had to do something, Edgar cried out, 'Withdraw,' and led his men towards the north walls and escape.

'Where should we meet?' Whitgar said as Edgar rushed away.

'Head for Haxby. We'll reform there,' Edgar said.

Even as the English were turning to run, William's men were rushing through the gates, the cavalry leading the way through the streets on the south of the Ouse. They met little resistance. The infantry was right behind, and that part of the city fell in minutes. But the Normans had to cross the river to capture the whole of York.

Whitgar peered through the rain at the groups of English soldiers making their way to the gates and disappearing through them to safety. He made out King William, leading a charge at the defenders. Without Edgar to direct them, they scattered, running through the maze of narrow streets in panic. Like others, he ran to his horse and saddled it as fast as he was able. 'Come on, Liegitu. We better get out of here.'

Whitgar ducked under the doorway; turning to see if all was clear, he saw King William's mount rearing before charging full gallop at the bridge. As he took off, the king called over his shoulder, 'Carpe Diem. What are you waiting for?'

At least a hundred the other chevaliers followed in his wake, shields up, weapons at the ready. As soon as he was in range, William threw his spear, striking an opponent in the stomach; the man fell writhing to the ground.

Whitgar saw one of William's companions laughing at the defenders, breaking ranks, and running in fear through the labyrinth of streets toward the gates in the north walls. Behind them, Ralph Pomeroy was riding as hard as his horse allowed, hoping to be seen by the king as a hero. The cavalry followed him, splitting up to cut down their scattering enemy.

The English slipped in the mud as they ran through the teeming rain. One unfortunate man tripped and fell to be trampled to death where he landed.

William, with his sword raised high, the rain lashing his blood-spattered face, charged through alleys so narrow his stirrups were catching on the wooden walls of the buildings to either side. As he burst out into a square, FitzOsbern arrived.

'Should we give chase, my lord?'

'No, don't bother. Close the gates and guard them. Be sure no one gets away and see to it anybody left who has committed treason against me is put to death,' he said.

'I will if I can catch them; we need horses just to keep up with them,' FitzOsbern said.

'You're right there. I've never seen anything move faster,' William laughed.

More Norman cavalry arrived in the square, and the infantry

poured in after them.

William addressed them. 'We have them on the run now. Go to the north wall and close the gates. When we have them trapped, we'll kill the lot of them. They'll rue the day they rebelled against us, eh, men?' And he charged, bellowing his battle cry, shield gripped firmly, sword held high. Like a raging bull after the English, he galloped, his men struggling to stay by his side.

His troops cheered as he raced off to cut off the retreat. There was a roar from the castle as Sir William Malet led his men to join the king. 'Follow me,' the king yelled as he charged along the street. 'Now it's our turn to show them what real fighting men can do.'

Amongst the English, everything was in chaos. After Edgar had given the order to pull back, those within earshot retreated to the gates. The rest saw their comrades fleeing in droves; fear had taken root in their hearts. When the garrison poured out of the castle, panic broke out. Waltheof and Bondi tried to restore order.

'Shieldwall,' Waltheof commanded.

There was no response; the rout continued.

'Bondi. Gospatric. Help me out here,' Waltheof bawled, sounding desperate.

Bondi and Gospatric stood shoulder to shoulder with their comrade. Once again, Waltheof bellowed, 'Shieldwall! Form a shieldwall!'

A few warriors stopped and formed up on either side of the three. Once that happened, more men joined. Soon they had a formidable defence blocking the way.

'Where's Edgar?' Waltheof asked.

'He left town with Whitgar. He said we're to meet up at Haxby,' Gospatric said.

'We'd better go there then,' Waltheof said.

Slowly and in an orderly fashion, the shieldwall fell back. By now, it was four men deep and bristling with spears. They had the minister on their left and a row of buildings to their right as they backed up towards the gate.

Whitgar brought Liegitu up sharply outside walls, tied him to a tree, and ran out into the road.

'Archers. Archers,' he bellowed. 'Are there any archers here?'

'Here,' someone said.

'And here,' another said, soon to be joined by more.

A column of men streamed out of the gate, and Whitgar spotted an assortment of men with bows waving to him.

'Follow me,' he called, forcing his way back through the gates and up to the stone steps to the top of the city walls, where more archers joined him. They had a marvellous view of the battle raging in below them, but the wall had been built to defend those within from those without. They were vulnerable to enemy archers.

'We can cover the retreat from here. Get ready,' Whitgar ordered.

As he stood watching the enemy advance, archers made their way past him to take their places. It came as a surprise to discover two of the archers were women he knew.

'Elfwyn. Morwenna. What are you doing here?'

'The same as you, covering the retreat,' Morwenna snapped before joining a line of fifty archers on the wall, preparing for her enemy to arrive. As she and Elfwyn took their positions, poised and ready to let fly, Morwenna complained of Whitgar's attitude.

'Who does he think he is?'

'He's the man that did so well in Durham,' Elfwyn said.

In return, Morwenna gave her sister a scathing look.

'Where's Bondi?' Elfwyn asked.

'I don't know,' Morwenna said, trying to look unconcerned.

As the sisters talked, further inside of York, Waltheof's comrades were in trouble.

'Watch out for Normans coming out of the alleys and side streets,' Waltheof warned. 'They might try to outflank us.'

Waltheof was right. The Normans were trying to outflank them, but English archers positioned along the wall above the gate were making easy work of them. But one of William's men had ideas of his own.

'Follow me, men,' it was Sir Ralph Pomeroy calling out. 'Follow me, and we'll get behind them.'

Pomeroy led a group of knights around to the south transept of the minster and charged straight through the doorway, riding his horse straight in, his men following. More Normans were following them.

Once inside, Pomeroy raced across to the north transept and out the other side. Outside, he turned sharply, his horse's hooves slipping on the cobbles. With the flat of his sword, he slapped his mount's flanks as he galloped alongside the minster wall, bursting out into the street behind Waltheof and his men.

'What are you going to do now?' Pomeroy bellowed at Waltheof.

His answer came from an unexpected direction. Over his right shoulder, an arrow flew, just missing him and burying itself in the earth. Turning, he saw fifty archers lined up along the walls as they released their arrows. Most of them fell short or flew past, but several hit his shield, one stuck in his saddle, and a couple buried themselves deep in his horse's hindquarters. The horse gave out the most terrible sound and staggered around in tight circles before collapsing and spilling Pomeroy into the dirt, trapping his leg. Protecting himself with his shield, Pomeroy struggled to free himself while arrows struck the surrounding ground.

'I'll give you a hand,' FitzWalter said.

As arrows flew around them, FitzWalter pulled on his friend's arm until he was free.

'Etoile. Etoile,' Pomeroy yelled to his horse. He found the sound of the stallion's dying gasps heartbreaking.

On the wall, Morwenna recognised the man staggering to his feet. He who had killed so many at her farm.

'Don't let him escape. Kill that man,' she yelled. 'He's the murderer who came to our farm.'

Aiming along the arrow's shaft as she pulled back the bowstring, his chest made an excellent target for Morwenna. *Now you'll get it,* and she let her arrow fly. But instead of a thud as the arrow struck its intended victim and a scream as the iron head pierced his flesh, there was a disappointing clattering as it bounced off his comrade's protective shield.

Enraged and frustrated, Morwenna shot arrow after arrow at Pomeroy.

'Don't let him get away!' she yelled.

Both sisters concentrated on Pomeroy alone, letting fly their arrows, but again they missed their target. Whitgar, who had heard Morwenna yelling for a Norman to be killed, took a shot at Pomeroy, who ordered his men back as a hailstorm of arrows flew towards him as he and his comrade ran to the shelter of the minster. They looked like hedgehogs in love as they staggered to the minster, the shields on their backs bristling with arrows.

There was panic in Pomeroy's voice as he ordered his troops back. They only had to be told once. Whitgar was organising the archers, making sure he had plenty of opportunities to unleash arrows of his own. Then he recognised a man being helped into the minster by a comrade; it was the scar that gave him away, that and the eyes. There was something of the grave about them. The man with the scar stared back at him, but only for a fleeting moment as his rescuer hauled him away. The shieldwall had now backed up to the gateway.

'You men on either end go through first,' Waltheof ordered.

Whitgar noticed a horde of Norman archers and crossbowmen charging towards him. Lined up on the wall, he and his archers made easy targets.

'Get down,' he ordered.

A few archers dropped to safety outside the city, while others scrambled to the steps, hoping to get out behind the cover of Waltheof's shieldwall. Most of the archers joined the men on the ground as they peeled off through the city gates, with Whitgar encouraging them every step of the way. When the steps were clear, and no more archers were approaching, he followed the others through the chaos at the gate. He had not noticed further along the wall from him, Morwenna and Elfwyn running in the opposite direction. The women, exposed to Norman archers and unable to escape with the others, ran for the next set of steps, hoping to evade their enemies. More concerned about driving Waltheof and his men back, the Normans ignored the sisters, at least for now.

At Bootham Bar, people were scrambling to evade capture and death. Pushing, shoving, slipping, stumbling, and sometimes falling, Whitgar struggled through the melee and made it to safety. Once through the gate, Whitgar looked back to see the shieldwall was the width of the gateway, the English gradually pulling back. The archers, who had dropped from the wall, were providing cover. Whitgar shot the last of his arrows over the defenders' heads, hoping to hit a Norman. Now that the English had recovered, the Normans were having a tough time.

'Run for it,' Waltheof ordered.

Those in the gateway or who had been lucky enough to escape ran for their lives, expecting William's men to follow them, but that did not happen.

'Close the gates,' William ordered, appearing on his big white stallion. 'Trap the seditious vermin. Those outside can run like the cowards they are. Close the gates and keep them guarded while the rest of us deal with the rebel scum.'

Norman infantry pushed the heavy oak gates to and barred them, much to the relief of those English who had escaped. They headed for Haxby as swiftly as possible, trying desperately to keep their dignity. In the crowd of fleeing Englishmen, Whitgar and Bondi met up.

'Have you seen Elfwyn or Morwenna?' Whitgar asked a breathless Bondi.

'I thought they were with you.'

'They were, but I haven't seen them since.'

'Neither have I,' Bondi said. 'We could have missed them, or they might have jumped off the wall with the others.'

'Perhaps. Have you seen Merleswein?'

'No.'

'They might with him,' Whitgar said.

'Let's find him.'

The English in York, left behind by their comrades, ran for their lives, only to discover every exit barred. Like a whirlwind, the Normans raged around the streets, killing everyone in sight. Most of the rebels ran in a panic or put up a fight with the help of others, except for two, who were hiding in the back of a pigsty; Morwenna and Elfwyn were still inside York but desperately trying to think up a plan of escape.

'What are we going to do, Morwenna?'

'Wait until it gets dark and slip out then.'

'If the Normans don't find us first,' Elfwyn said.

As Elfwyn spoke, screaming sounded; women in terror, men in agony. The two exchanged fearful looks.

'They're everywhere,' Elfwyn said.

'We need a better hiding place than this,' Morwenna said. 'What about the blacksmiths? We could hide in the hay, wait for the Normans to go to bed and sneak out then.'

'I know. The old tunnels.' Elfwyn said.

'What? The old ones we used to play in when we were girls?'

'Yes. They'll never look there. They don't even know they exist.'

'We can escape that way, too,' Morwenna said.

Elfwyn looked surprised.

'When we were little, I got out beyond the walls. I'm sure they drained the rainwater into the river,' Morwenna said.

'Which one?'

'The Foss.'

'So, if we get there, we can hide and then escape. But then how do we cross the river?' Elfwyn said.

'Let's get out of town and worry about that later.'

'All right. Which way?' Elfwyn said.

'Down Church Street and into the old stone building.'

'That's a hundred yards or more. When do you think we should go?'

'Now,' Morwenna said as she edged towards the door. Through the rain under a darkening sky, she peeped around the doorway. The street clear along its length. 'Let's go,' she said.

The two began walking at a brisk pace. Screams echoed in the gloom. In the dusk, with their shields, helmets, and weapons, they passed for soldiers.

'Let's hope we don't run into any Normans,' Elfwyn said.

They went through muddy alleys in the torrential rain, not running but walking briskly.

Halfway there and they had encountered no soldiers until ahead of them, a line of Normans crossed the street. Morwenna raised her shield and smiled as though in greeting. One soldier nodded back and said something unintelligible, but without a break in their step, they continued, the rain driving into the ground like spears all around them.

Chapter 28

While the sisters searched for the tunnels in York, those fortunate enough to have escaped the city assembled not far away in Haxby. As Edgar approached the great hall, the door opened.

'Welcome, my lord,' said a young woman. 'I am Alvina Ivarsdaughter. My father is the thane of most importance here. He asked me to greet you. Would you care for some refreshment?'

'Thank you.'

'Make yourselves comfortable in the hall. Your men can camp wherever they choose. The servants will provide them with refreshments,' she said. 'Follow me to your places.'

'Bondi. Whitgar,' Edgar said when he saw them, 'there you are. I'm pleased to see you're safe and well.'

The two got to their feet. 'My lord,' they said in unison.

'Sit down. I'll join you in a drink,' he said.

Edgar joined them on the bench and began discussing the day's events. Merleswein and Gospatric arrived as they did so, striding into the hall. Merleswein's eyes darted this way and that; he seemed puzzled and concerned.

'Aren't Morwenna and Elfwyn with you?' he asked.

'We thought they were with you,' Whitgar said.

'We thought they were with you,' Merleswein said.

'The last time I saw them, they were in York,' Whitgar said.

'The same here,' Bondi added.

'I think we'd better search the camp,' Merleswein said, concern showing on his face.

Leaving the hall, the four comrades separated and began searching. An hour later and they were back together with no news.

'No one has seen them here, but there are a few who last saw them fighting inside the walls,' Merleswein said. 'We must find them.'

Edgar, who had overheard the conversation, interrupted. 'I strictly forbid anybody to go looking for them,' he said.

'But they're my daughters,' Merleswein pleaded.

'And daughters of whom to be proud, but I can't risk a rescue attempt, especially when it's doomed to failure.'

'But...'

'No,' Edgar said. 'Search the camp again. For all we know, they're both here somewhere.'

'With your permission,' Merleswein said, 'we'll start right away.'

Once outside the hall, Merleswein, Bondi, Gospatric and Whitgar engaged in a heated conversation.

'I hope and pray they can find a way out,' an anxious Merleswein said.

'You're not thinking of leaving them there?' Bondi said. 'Let's get them out.'

'How are we going to do that, Bondi?' Merleswein asked.

'What about the about the old tunnels?' Whitgar said. 'I used to play them as a child. With any luck, the Normans won't know about them, but the ladies do. What do you say, Merleswein?'

'They played in them when they were girls.'

A light of hope shone in Whitgar's eyes. 'If they hide there, there's a chance they can stay hidden.' he said.

'Yes, and we're able to get in so that we might find them,' Bondi said.

'How?' Merleswein said.

'It's best if Bondi and me go. The more of us go in, the more likely we are to be seen. I could go in with Bondi.'

'I'll come with you,' Merleswein said.

'No. You'd better stay. Edgar's more likely to miss you.' Whitgar said.

'You'd better leave now.'

As Bondi and Whitgar raced to York, Morwenna and Elfwyn arrived at the old Roman baths and entered, stepping over two bodies in the doorway as they did so.

'Can you remember where the tunnel entrance is?' Elfwyn asked.

Before Morwenna could answer, screams pierced the air outside, and a woman begged, 'No, don't! Please don't!'

Silence followed by laughter before silence fell again. Rape was commonplace now.

'It's dark in here. I wonder if we can find a torch,' Morwenna said.

After a couple of minutes scrabbling about in the dark, they found what they were looking for in a bracket secured to a wall. In no time, the flame provided enough light for them to see. They searched around the building, finding nothing but confusion in the dancing shadows. And then, 'What's that?' said Morwenna, standing stock still.

'What?' Elfwyn said.

'Running water. Listen.'

Elwyn listened hard. 'It's coming from over there,' she said, pointing to a corner of the room.

The two women approached the corner, and the sound grew a little louder. Elfwyn shivered. 'It's cold in here,' she said.

'Yes. There's a draught over the floor,' Morwenna said.

'What's this?' Elfwyn said. She followed the source of the cold air until she found a pile of old wicker baskets. She pulled them aside to discover stone steps leading down to an underground stream. Immediately, the sound of running water grew louder.

'It's smaller than I remember,' Elfwyn said, with a hint of dread in her voice.

'No,' Morwenna replied. 'We're bigger.'

'Do you think we'll still fit?' Elfwyn asked.

More screams pierced the silence.

'We'd better,' Morwenna answered.

'What about rats?' Elfwyn said. 'Weren't there rats down here?'

'No,' Morwenna lied.

'But I remember them clearly.'

'No. You're mistaken,' Morwenna said, trying her best to reassure her sister.

The two women looked at each other in silence for a moment.

'You'd better go first,' Morwenna said.

'Why not you?' Elfwyn asked.

'Because you're the smallest.'

'We'll have to leave these behind,' Morwenna, indicating the shields. They slipped them off and put them aside.

'Should we take our bows?' Elfwyn asked.

'If they'll fit. We might need them when we get out on the other side.'

Both women took off their bows and quivers, and Elfwyn eased her way down the entrance hole and into the tunnel.

'What's it like in there?'

'Just as I remember. Cold, wet and smelly.'

Morwenna handed the torch to Elfwyn, who wedged it into the wall. Morwenna then handed down the bows and quivers and wriggled in after her sister and followed her. They splashed their way along the tunnel to safety, their feet freezing in the cold water.

'My feet are going numb,' Elfwyn said.

'At least there aren't any rats,' said Morwenna.

At first, the drain was tight and constricting, but they came out to a bigger tunnel after a few yards, enabling them to stand almost upright, but the stream still flowed around their ankles, numbing their feet. Every so often, beams of light penetrated the pitch darkness, shining through the old stone drain covers, making the water sparkle. If it had not have been for their predicament, it might have been a sight they would have enjoyed.

'God, it stinks down here,' Elfwyn said, her words bouncing off the walls.

Just at that moment, they heard voices above them. The women stopped dead in their tracks and remained motionless while the talking continued, but neither could make any sense of it.

Elfwyn felt a hand on her shoulder. 'Come on,' Morwenna whispered. 'No time to waste.'

Elfwyn moved on, with Morwenna following close behind. They walked stooped over with their backs catching on the stonework roof, which was uncomfortable and unpleasant for them. The smell and ice-cold water made matters worse. *Even so,* they told themselves, *we're making good progress. It can't be far now.*

'What's that?' Elfwyn said.

'What?'

'There.'

'I can't see a thing,' Morwenna said. 'Nothing to worry about down here.'

'It's a rat, I'm sure. I can't go on with rats everywhere.'

'It was nothing. Let's press on.'

'There it is,' Elfwyn said, pointing in the flickering light to a shadow swimming in the water.

'No. It's just a piece of wood,' Morwenna said, sounding convincing.

'It's a rat. I can see it clearly,' Elfwyn insisted.

'It's only a small one. If you don't bother it, it won't harm you. Come on. We have to get out of here,' Morwenna said.

Elfwyn took a breath and forced herself forward. When they passed under the next drain cover, their problems worsened. As Elfwyn was about to go under it, she gasped as two spearheads appeared right in front of her eyes, jabbing up and down.

Elfwyn heard laughing and shouting as she jumped back, bumping into Morwenna, who she caught off-balance, sending them both crashing into the water.

More laughter came from above, echoing around them.

'What should we do?' Elfwyn said.

'We'd at least better get up.'

The two struggled to their feet, the laughter and goading in a foreign tongue echoing all around them, water dripping from their clothes.

'Their voices sound so close,' Morwenna said.

'A spear's length away,' Elfwyn said.

'Give me the torch,' said Morwenna. Elfwyn handed it over. The spears continued jabbing.

Morwenna took the torch, holding it in front of her as far as possible. The thrusting of the spears grew furious, and she pulled back. Heckles and calls came down from the street above.

'Hold the torch,' she said, handing it to Elfwyn.

The spearmen seemed to have calmed down a little now, and they were talking among themselves. While Elfwyn held the torch high, Morwenna pressed her back against the tunnel wall and side-stepped past the cover above to the safety of the other side. She breathed a sigh of relief. *But how to get Elfwyn to safety?*

Morwenna looked up at the place where the two spears came thrusting through and had an idea.

'Elfwyn. I'm going to shoot an arrow up through the drain cover,' she whispered. 'And I want you to slip across immediately after. Cross the way I did, with your back close to the wall.'

'What about the torch? Won't it give me away?' Elfwyn said.

'Get down on your knees and pass it to me, holding it as low as you can. I'll take it from you and prop it up against a wall. Then I'll lie down and shoot a couple of arrows.'

From the tone of her voice, Elfwyn knew Morwenna was not looking forward to being drenched in freezing water for a second time that day.

'Do as I say,' Morwenna said. 'I'll keep them back long enough for you to pass. After that, we'll get out as fast as we can.'

'How?'

'Hand me the torch,' said Morwenna, disguising her uncertainty. 'I'll let them have an arrow or two, and while they're dodging them, step across. Now, give me the torch.'

Elfwyn squatted down and handed Morwenna the torch as quickly as she could. As she did so, the spears again started jabbing furiously, but she came to no harm.

Morwenna placed the torch to one side, picked up her bow, and took two arrows from her quiver. She made ready, sat in the cold, dirty water, leaned back, pulling the bowstring as she went and shot an arrow through a hole in the drain cover. A commotion broke out above her, and she let fly her second arrow. There was an almighty scream, and she knew she had hit her target. Elfwyn took her chance and leapt across and through the beams of weak winter light. Morwenna was on her feet instantly, and the sisters dashed off.

'Quick. We'd better get a move on,' Morwenna said. 'This water seems to be getting deeper.'

Elfwyn, who was scurrying along the tunnel, needed no instruction.

The women had covered quite a distance when they heard scraping and scratching ahead of them.

'What's that?' Elfwyn asked as she stopped dead.

'I don't know. It sounds like someone's dragging something heavy.'

In the street above Morwenna and Elfwyn, the soldiers were hatching a plan.

'What about these slabs? Try and lift them,' one of them said.

'Run towards the river and see if there are any more. If you find any, lift them. Then we'll have them,' said a soldier who seemed to have authority.

'You two,' he said, addressing another couple of soldiers. 'Find out where they got in and go after them.'

With mischief and murder in their hearts, Normans ran down the street towards the city wall. They found a cover and, with their spears, scraped years of dirt, grit, and grime from around it, but it was hopeless. Try as they might, they could not lift it. It was heavy and too difficult to raise at three feet by three feet and nine inches deep.

The other two soldiers who headed in the opposite direction had better luck. Running up the street, they came to an old stone building. They went in through the same entrance the women had used. It did not take long for them to find the tunnel and head underground towards Elfwyn and Morwenna.

Chapter 29

Outside of York's walls, two men appeared on horseback on the east bank of the Foss. They had two spare horses with them, which they tied to a tree. They dismounted to the sound of screaming in York. Across the river, silhouettes of a group of drunken sentries appeared on the wall.

'This might be easier than we imagined,' Whitgar said.

'Where's the fisherman's place?' Bondi asked.

'Back there,' Whitgar answered, pointing to a stand of reeds.

'I can't see anything.'

'Follow me,' Whitgar said.

Whitgar led the way, and Bondi followed.

'How do you know anyone's here?' Bondi asked.

'There's been a fisherman here ever since I can remember. He's always on the river in a coracle.'

Whitgar led the way to the hut and knocked on the door; after a brief wait, it opened, and an old man's head appeared. He had a broken tooth and a leathery face.

'Who is it, and what do you want?' he said, his darting eyes full of suspicion.

'We need help.'

'You must be desperate if you've come to me,' the man replied with a broken tooth smile.

'We're here to rescue two ladies who are trapped in York,' Whitgar said.

'How can I help?' The door opened, and the leathery faced man appeared, beaming at them.

'We were wondering, can we borrow your coracle?' Whitgar said.

The old man stared at the strangers. 'It's a good un, that is. But it'll only hold two. So, how are you going to bring the ladies back?'

'I've no idea.'

'Why don't you take both of 'em?'

'You've got more than one?'

'Perhaps,' Leatherface replied. 'What if you get caught?'

'We'll tell them we stole them.'

'Go on then.'

'You'll be handsomely rewarded,' Whitgar said.

'I don't need no payment. I hate the Normans, and if you can get one over them, that alone will be worth it. Are you going up the tunnels?'

'You know about the tunnels?'

'Everybody knows about the tunnels,' the old man said, looking at them as though he thought them idiots.

Bondi, Whitgar, and exchanged troubled glances.

'Everybody?' Bondi asked.

'Everybody who lives there. I doubt if the Normans do. Still, you'll soon find out if they do, eh?' He chuckled, a big grin on his face.

'I suppose you want the coracles now?' Leatherface said.

'Yes. They'd be useful,' Bondi said.

'Follow me,' Leatherface said, leading them into his hut.

'Here you go,' Leatherface said, showing them two coracles propped up against the back wall.

Whitgar took the one closest and prized it apart from the second.

'Give me a hand,' he said to Leatherface, who helped him manoeuvre the little vessel outside. Bondi was also experiencing difficulties extracting the other coracle but managed on his own.

Once outside, Whitgar grabbed the strap attached to the bench board seat and hauled it up onto his back before making his way to the riverbank. Bondi watched him, memories of his childhood on the banks of the Severn returned. He copied Whitgar and joined him by the river.

Leatherface followed on behind, chuckling to himself.

'Can you paddle these things, Whitgar?' Bondi asked.

'Yes. It's easy when you have the knack.'

'I haven't been in one since I was a boy.'

'What about a washtub?'

'That was different. I used a spear.'

'Watch me then.'

Whitgar approached the riverbank where Leatherface had dug out a little harbour for the little boat. He placed his coracle in the water, and he stepped in gingerly and sat down.

'I suppose you'll be wanting to borrow this,' said Leatherface, waving a paddle.

'Thank you,' Whitgar said, relieved it was dark enough to hide his blushes.

Leatherface was slapping his thighs. 'I'm so glad you three came along to liven up my day,' he said, guffawing at Whitgar, who was frantically paddling his coracle and going nowhere.

'Use the paddle to shove yourself off,' Leatherface said.

Whitgar did as instructed, and he was away from the bank and afloat in a few moments.

'It's easy,' Whitgar yelled to Bondi. 'Just do what I did.'

Leatherface chuckled at Whitgar's comment, and Bondi looked alarmed.

'Get in quick and smooth, and you'll have no problems. Not until you're on the water, anyway,' Leatherface laughed, handing him a paddle.

Bondi placed his coracle in the river and stepped in.

'Push off and paddle. Hold the top of it in your left hand and grip it halfway down with your right. Then you go like this,' Leatherface said, moving his arms as though stirring a stew.

Bondi followed the instructions and was surprised to find himself heading out across the water. Turning to Whitgar, he said, 'It's easy. Just do what I do.'

Whitgar paddled but went around in circles.

'Copy me, and you won't go wrong,' Bondi said, grinning.

Once again, Whitgar was glad of the darkness to conceal his blushes.

Leatherface was slapping his thighs. 'I'm so glad you two came along to liven up my day,' he said.

But Whitgar copied Bondi's actions and was soon crossing the river.

'It looks like you're going to be all right,' Leatherface said.

Bondi and Whitgar paddled their coracles, Whitgar giving directions. As they reached the far riverbank, the shouting and laughing, screaming and pleading grew louder.

'We'd better hurry,' Bondi said, with a mix of fear and urgency in his voice. 'I thought you could paddle one of these things?' he added.

'I can, but it's been a long time. Head left a bit, aim towards that clump of bushes. The tunnels come out there.'

Bondi peered through the darkness and made out the bushes. Paddling hard, he reached them first. The coracle bobbed up as he stepped out. Once on the riverbank, he grabbed a bush and pulled it toward him, tying the coracle to a branch.

'That was easy,' he said to Whitgar. 'It's easier than you think.'

Encouraged by Bondi, Whitgar made his way to the riverbank. Standing up, he overbalanced and fell backwards into the chilly water. Bondi would have laughed, but Whitgar made so much noise he feared he must have alerted the sentries. But there was no need to worry; they were drunk or otherwise preoccupied.

Whitgar crawled out of the river, dragging his coracle with him while Bondi stood grinning at him. 'Thank heaven you know how to use these things, Whitgar. Imagine the mess if you didn't,' he said.

'Let's get on with it,' Whitgar said, squeezing water out of his clothes.

A soaking wet Whitgar led Bondi to the entrance. It was five feet above the level of the river and obscured by undergrowth.

'I'd better leave my bow here; it'll only get in the way,' Whitgar said, lying his weapon in the grass.

'I'll leave my axe, too,' Bondi said.

After hiding their weapons, Whitgar pulled aside the willow tree branches that grew at the foot of the wall.

'Here we are,' he said as he exposed an entrance. 'Follow me.'

Whitgar heaved himself into the tunnel, and Bondi followed.

'Listen. Look,' Whitgar said as soon as Bondi had entered.

It sounded like two men shouting in French, and flames flickered from a torch.

'Normans,' Whitgar said. 'Do you think they're down here looking for the women?'

'They must be. What else would they be doing?'

'It must be them. Come on, let's give them a hand.'

Slowly, they made their way further into the tunnel.

'How far does this go?' Bondi asked.

'Right across the city. And smaller tunnels lead off.'

'I wonder where the women are?'

'Anywhere. We'll have to be patient.'

Further up the tunnel, Morwenna and Elfwyn were fighting for their lives. Above them, the soldiers had raided a blacksmith and found a couple of iron rods with hooked ends. They had used them to pull up one of the stone drain covers, and three of them were in the drains. Their lascivious calls echoed through the darkness growing louder as they closed in on the sisters. Demons danced in the torchlight along the walls as their pursuers neared them.

'What are we going to do now?' Elfwyn said, realising they had soldiers in front and behind them.

'Teach them a lesson,' Morwenna said.

In the pitch black, Morwenna placed an arrow in her bow, which she turned at an angle because the roof was so low. She began shooting in rapid succession. Elfwyn did the same in the other direction, and the sound of arrows striking shields echoed through the dark.

Morwenna shot more arrows, losing sight of them as they vanished into the blackness. On her third arrow, a man cried out in pain. She had found her first target. She shot the fourth arrow without pausing, and another scream echoed off the walls. The animal sounds distorted as they bounced around the tunnel. Whoever the wounded man was, he must have been carrying a torch because suddenly darkness fell.

'I got a couple of them,' she said to Elfwyn.

'I don't think I had any luck,' Elfwyn replied, drawing more arrows from her quiver as she spoke. Morwenna was ready too and once more shot into the darkness. But this time, a soldier from Elfwyn's side let out a scream. Despite the casualties, the Normans came on. The splashing of feet running in water intensified. And the sound of soldiers panting and straining grew louder.

'They'll be on us any moment,' she said to Elfwyn.

'Let's get up a side tunnel. It's our only hope,' Elfwyn replied.

'Come on, then.'

Morwenna turned and ran behind her sister, feeling the wall as she went. They hadn't gone far when they found the tunnel for which they'd been looking.

'In here,' Elfwyn said, slipping into the smaller side tunnel, Morwenna following, hoping they would not be discovered.

'Where does it lead?' Morwenna asked.

'I don't know,' Elfwyn said.

'Let's hope it comes up somewhere safe.'

Elfwyn was scurrying into the darkness. Into cold, wet, oblivion.

'Stop,' Morwenna said. 'If we make no noise, they might not find us.'

Elfwyn slowed to a walk, her hands in front of her, feeling her way. They were making good progress when Elfwyn grunted.

'What is it?'

'The tunnel's blocked,' Elfwyn answered.

Something caught their eye, and the women turned to see the flickering of a torchlight.

'Are they coming this way?' Morwenna whispered.

'I can't tell,' Elfwyn answered.

Elfwyn heard Morwenna draw her seax in the dark, and she did the same. Against men armed with swords, she doubted the chances of their success. It was a surprise for both women to hear arrows striking shields, followed by shouting in French and English.

When Bondi and Whitgar first entered the tunnel, a man screamed from deep inside.

'Quick. They're in trouble,' Bondi said, barging past Whitgar.

The two men ran towards the sound of fighting.

The nearest group of three Normans had run into difficulties. One of them had been shot twice, first in the leg and then in the shoulder. Blood spurted from an artery, and he realised he was in grave danger. His two comrades left him propped up and were now closing on the women. Further up the tunnel, one of the two men who had followed Morwenna and Elfwyn through the old baths lay dead, an arrow in his throat. His friend, not so long ago looking for mischief, was now looking for revenge.

The women in the side tunnel could make out three silhouettes approaching them in the darkness, like fiends in the night, coming their way.

'Morwenna. Elfwyn,' Bondi called.

'Here,' the women answered.

'What's this?' Bondi said as he clattered into something. He groped about and found something he realised from the shape he had discovered a few Norman shields left behind because they were too big to be of any use in the smaller side tunnel. The soldiers who had dropped them there were now aware they had enemies in front and behind.

'Quick! Someone is behind us. Forget the women. We'll take on whoever it is and deal with them later,' said one Norman to the other.

The two men turned around and charged, one behind the other in the cramped space, moving forward as fast as possible while bent double.

'Die you bastard,' Bondi screamed as he drove his spear as deep into the man's chest. The impact of the blow took the Noman off his feet, leaving him winded. But the soldier's mail and padding had saved him from the worst damage the spear might inflict. He flailed about on the floor, hoping to dodge the spear's sharp blade.

A few feet away, Morwenna crept upon another soldier from behind and thrust her seax hard and upward, driving it right up the man's rectum. The soldier reared up as he screamed, and he smashed his head against the top of the stone tunnel, not enough to injure him but enough to give him a shock. With a searing pain in his innards and a dizzy head, he was in no position to defend himself when Morwenna struck again with her seax, this time plunging the blade deep into his right buttock. Yelling in agony, the man felt the weight of the seax and the force of the blow as Morwenna hacked at him. But this time, his mail protected him, but he lost his balance and fell onto his back. He clung to the torch as Morwenna slashed at his wrist, severing his hand from his arm. The torch fell into the icy water, extinguishing it, leaving the combatants blind to each other.

The Norman who had fallen victim to Morwenna's seax knew his time was not long. Determined to take his assailant with him, he reached for his sword, wrapped his fingers around the hilt, and began swinging it around, hoping to do damage his assailant. He was too late; Elfwyn, hearing him gasping, stabbed at the noise and buried her spear in his throat. In the confined space, his gurgled screaming was ear-splitting.

His comrade had never felt so alone as he did now, lost in a subterranean battlefield, surrounded by people who wanted him dead. In the darkness, panic washed through him. He struck out at an enemy hidden by darkness and hoped blind luck would save him. Bondi was jabbing his spear, attempting to finish him, but he only injured the wounded soldier a second time.

'Have you got them both?' Whitgar asked.

'I'm not sure. I'm still trying to finish the first one.'

'His friend is dying,' Morwenna said, her voice echoing in the dark.

Bondi continued thrusting his spear to where he thought his enemy lay struggling. With his comrade thrashing in the water and two Englishmen above him, the soldier's days were over. A spearhead pierced his eye and brain.

'Quick. Let's get out of here,' Bondi yelled above the ear-piercing screaming.

Morwenna and Elfwyn staggered past the dying Normans and crashed into Bondi.

'Let's go,' Bondi said.

The party reached the main drain and turned right for the outlet. The four ran forward, bent double, faster now they were in a bigger tunnel but still catching their backs on the stonework. In the chaos and confusion, they had lost the torches, and they struggled to find their way.

'Stop. What's that?' Whitgar said.

They heard shouting in front of them but saw no torch. Weak light fell from above.

'What's going on, Whitgar?'

'It sounds like they've lifted a drain cover. What do we do now?' Whitgar said.

'Have you got a bow, Whitgar?' Morwenna asked.

'No. I thought it would be useless in here.'

'Here, use mine,' she said, passing her bow forward. 'Take the arrows too,' she said, handing them up the line.

'Let's keep quiet and shoot them when we get close. By the time they've realised what's happening, it'll be too late,' Morwenna said.

In silence, the four stepped through the water, their soaking wet feet numb. They were closing in on the beam of light and the shouting.

'They're coming through an entrance hole,' Whitgar whispered.

As he spoke, one of the Normans handed a torch to his comrade. The flame lit up his part of the tunnel a few yards away from Whitgar, who had his bow ready and continued stepping forward. The Norman yelled, 'Qui est la?'

'Mon ami,' Whitgar answered, in the best accent he could muster, two of the few French words he knew.

The soldier was puzzled, but not for long; an arrow struck him deep in the throat. He clutched at the shaft, made the most horrible gurgling noise, dropped to his knees, and fell into the water.

Above, the Normans were curious about what was happening below but were unsure what to do.

'Geoffrey. Geoffrey.' One of them called out. He fell screaming to the ground when an arrow struck him in the face. His companions stepped back as more flew up at them. Their quarry had escaped them by the time they had recovered, scuttling off along the drain. They turned as one when a nobleman addressed them.

'What's happening here?' asked the man with an ugly scar on his cheek.

'There are English in the tunnel.'

'What tunnel?'

'There are tunnels under the city, and the rebels are escaping through them. They got in over there,' the soldier said, pointing to the old bathhouse, 'and they're heading towards the wall.'

Pomeroy thought for a moment. 'It must come out somewhere,' he said. 'Follow it. See if you can catch them when they get out at the end.' He looked at the smallest men. 'You three, get after them. The rest of you, follow me.'

Three soldiers made their way down the hole to discover their dead friend. Angered, they began pursuing the English. In the street, Pomeroy ran towards the wall with the men charging on behind him. 'If we get to the wall before they do, we can catch them when they come out,' he barked to them.

While the Normans raced along the surface, Bondi, Elfwyn,

Morwenna, and Whitgar dashed through the labyrinth. The sound of soldiers splashing feet behind them. 'Hurry,' Elfwyn said, 'they're catching up with us.'

Whitgar, in the lead, rushed toward the dim light. Even as he hurried forward, his heart filled with dread. In the short time he had been in the tunnel, he had grown to hate it; now, with the Normans above and behind them, escape was something he desired more than ever. Even if there were a welcoming party waiting for them at the end of the old drain, at least he would be outside away from the smell, the wet, the discomfort and the haunting echoes of disembodied voices. And there it was. The tunnel entrance grew slowly as he closed the distance to the end. On the surface, Pomeroy was making good progress. Charging down a street looking for a drain cover, he caught sight of one in the middle of the road. He ran over to it, and as he got there, flames flashed by beneath him.

'Outside quick. They're escaping. Follow me,' Pomeroy said as he charged out of the building, looking for a way onto the wall. He caught sight of a flight of steps and took them three at a time as he raced to the parapet. He peered over the parapet and spotted the English on the riverbank trying to launch the coracles.

'Come on. You don't have all day. Use your spears on them,' he bellowed.

'On to the wall,' he cried out, forcing his men aside as he stormed past.

'Archers. Archers,' he bellowed out as the small party of three Norman soldiers he had sent after his quarry burst out of the tunnel. The first one instantly fell victim to an arrow in the chest.

Turning to his men, Pomeroy yelled, 'What are you standing there for? Use your spears.' And he again called for archers as the English below struggled to drag something out of the bushes.

On the banks of the Fosse, Whitgar and Elfwyn had climbed into his coracle. Bondi and Morwenna in the other. As Bondi heaved the paddle against the bank, three Normans burst out of the yawning mouth of the sewer, charging down towards them.

'Look out,' he called to Morwenna, but she had seen them and felled one with an arrow.

Bondi stepped back onto the riverbank, dodging a spear thrown from the city wall above. As he did so, a Norman who had followed them through the tunnel charged at him, ready to bring his sword down on the housecarl. Too late, he noticed the axe, and in an instant, Bondi split him in half. There was a thud, and Bondi saw another Norman fall to the ground, killed by Morwenna, who was unleashing arrow after arrow at the soldiers on the wall.

'It's him, Bondi. He's the one who came to the farm. He's the one I wounded.' Morwenna said, looking up at the scarred face peering down from the top of the wall.

Bondi glanced over his shoulder but did not recognise anyone.

Out of range of the spears, Morwenna placed her bow across her thighs, 'Thank God we're safe now, Bondi.' And she sighed. But on the wall, crossbowmen appeared and let fly their crossbow bolts. She screamed as one passed close to her head.

'Quick, Bondi. Paddle,' she said.

'What do you think I'm doing?'

'Paddle harder,' she said as two more bolts tore into the water beside them.

But the crossbowmen were wasting their time. Their prey, just in range as they began shooting, had now reached safety. On the wall, Pomeroy was furious. He suspected the identities of Bondi and Morwenna and was keen to apprehend them.

'You numbskulls,' he bellowed at his men. 'Where were you? Don't just stand there. Get them.'

Pomeroy rushed down the steps, his spurs clattering on the stone. 'Follow me.'

His men, afraid of the consequences if they did not, followed.

Whitgar had already arrived at the far bank and was helping Elfwyn out of the coracle. Once on solid ground, she was relieved to find Bondi and her sister behind them, safe and sound.

'Thank heaven you're both safe,' she said.

Bondi grinned, 'We're not out of the woods yet.'

The coracle crashed into the riverbank, and Leatherface helped him and Morwenna out.

'Thank you. Thank you so much. We couldn't have escaped without you,' Morwenna said, throwing her arms around Bondi.

Bondi felt happier than he had ever done.

'And you too, Whitgar,' she added, stepping across to Whitgar to hug him while Bondi's heart sank.

'Thank you for your help.' Bondi said to Leatherface. 'I don't know your name.'

'Good. You won't be able to tell anyone,' Leatherface answered, glancing at the city walls. 'You'd best be on your way.'

The party mounted the horses and were long gone when Pomeroy and his men arrived at Leatherface's cottage. They were too far away to hear the screams or to come to their new friend's help. And too far away to give him the Christian burial he deserved.

Chapter 30

In the Great Hall in Roskilde, before the Danish court, the English visitors bowed before Swein, King of Denmark, who sat high on his carved ivory throne. Beside him sat Tora, his austere looking queen. She was the widow of Harald Sigurdsson, and she fixed an icy stare on Lady Gytha, the woman whose son was responsible for the death of her late husband.

'Welcome, Lady Gytha. How's my favourite aunt?' Swein said as he rose to his feet and strode over to her as well as he was able with his limp. He was a tall, muscular man, and he gave her a hug she thought might crush her.

'And welcome to you too, Godwin and Edmund,' giving each of the brothers a backslap. 'Who's this young lady?' Swein said, looking lustfully towards Edyth's daughter, Gytha, now a nubile young woman.

Lady Gytha introduced her daughter-in-law and granddaughter.

'Wonderful. It's always good to see my English kin. I'd like to say just how sorry we were to hear of Harold's death. It's a great loss for us all.'

Tora remained silent, still seated on her throne in a state of contained rage.

'Thank you, my lord,' Edyth said.

'That's kind of you, Swein,' Lady Gytha answered. The instant he referred to her family as kin, she knew she could count on his support for her plans.

'Tora, won't you welcome our guests?' Swein said in a manner that made it plain he was not asking a question but issuing an instruction.

Tora stood and greeted her guests with a perfunctory, 'Welcome.' There was no accompanying smile.

After the usual exchange of pleasantries, everyone made themselves comfortable, and a conversation sprang up between Lady Gytha and Swein.

'It's so good to be back home,' she said. 'Back in a country where each subject loves their king. And queen, of course.'

'I hear things are different now, in England,' Swein said.

'Nobody cares for King William. Most loathe him,' Gytha said. 'He's busy robbing everybody, and the only people who can match him for greed are his fellow Normans. Englishmen, the length and breadth of the kingdom are preparing to fight if they're not fighting already.'

'Is that so? This sounds interesting. Tell me more.'

'If England were to be attacked by another country, it would collapse in no time.'

'I can't imagine anyone attacking England after what happened at Stamford Bridge,' Swein said, oblivious to the glare Tora was giving him. 'It certainly wouldn't be Norway. And every other country near enough to mount an invasion has too many concerns of their own,' Swein said.

'Do you have troubles, Swein?'

Swein beamed a knowing smile. 'What are you trying to tell me?'

'Your kingdom is safe, and your people love you. Isn't this a perfect time to expand?'

'It had not occurred to me.'

Lady Gytha smiled at his audacity.

'You'd never thought of it?' she said. 'If you were to invade, you could count on the support of all England? We're sick of that bastard tyrant William, and I'm not the only one with friends and relatives across the North Sea.'

'But he's not an easy man to shift?'

'Any warrior king worth his salt could overthrow him. At least give it your consideration. I'm sure we could come to an arrangement.'

'Your son didn't manage to shift him, did he?' Tora said. 'Was he worth his salt?'

The hall fell into silence.

'Harold had recently fought and won a great battle just before his encounter with the duke. Otherwise, he would have slaughtered him.' Gytha replied.

'We only have your word for that,' Tora said.

'Enough ladies. Enough.' Swein said.

The two women fell silent and glared at each other.

'You were saying Gytha. Something about an arrangement?'

'One that's worth your while, Swein.'

Swein returned to his throne and sat back, thoughtful for a moment, before leaning forward and looking Lady Gytha in the eye.

'Be honest with me, Gytha. Who do you represent here today? Do you speak for all of the English or just one faction? I need to know because I want to understand what I would let myself in for should I choose to come to your aid.

'I am well aware of the animosity between the Godwins and the House of Leofric. Queen Aldytha, as the widow of the last ruling king and as the mother of that king's son, surely expects her boy to be named heir. That can't be your plan. You have other grandsons you'd rather see crowned, and so would I. After all, they're my kin. But why should I drive out one king just to replace him with another? Why shouldn't I wear the crown of England as Cnut did before me?'

It was Lady Gytha's turn to look thoughtful. 'William has to go. Are we agreed?'

'As far as you're concerned, he does. He's no problem for me.'

'Very well. If you help us overthrow the Bastard, the throne will be yours. All I ask is that our lands and titles are returned, and that applies to the other Englishmen, too.'

'What about Edwin, Morcar, and Aldytha? Won't they want their lands and titles reinstated?'

Lady Gytha shifted in her seat. 'Don't worry about them. They are quite ineffectual. They've put up minimal resistance against William. Their men are deserting in droves. They're powerless and unpopular. As for Aldytha, she's won the affections, as women like her do, of an inconsequential thane. You needn't trouble yourself about her. She has even less support than her brothers.'

'So, the door is open for me?' Swein said.

'It is.'

'What about Edgar? Won't he have something to say? And King Malcolm too. Hasn't he set his eyes on Edgar's sister, Margaret?'

He's better informed than I thought, she realised.

'Edgar is a minor complication,' Lady Gytha said. 'He's a good, intelligent and brave lad. And therein lies the problem, he's a boy, and England needs a man.'

'He won't always be a boy, though, will he?' Swein said.

'He'll never make a good king, let alone a great one. For you, things are different. Cnut's blood flows through your veins, which is one of the reasons you're suited to kingship. Think of it, England and Denmark united. Perhaps Norway might fall to you, and you would become Emperor of the North.'

Emperor of the North, Swein liked the sound of that. *England is rich, perhaps not as rich as before the Bastard got his hands on it, but still wealthy.* Swein considered the taxes he could collect in the years ahead, and the power of England and Denmark joined together. A weakened Norway with Olaf, the boy king, might easily be his.

'If I help you, Gytha, I have to make it worthwhile for those who follow me. If I were to reinstate your family to its previous position, there's not so much land left to go around. To keep my followers happy, I would have to reduce my share. Is there something else you can offer me?'

'I'm glad you asked, Swein. As the family has had to leave England, finding the right suiters for my granddaughter is proving difficult. I wonder if you're able to help,' Lady Gytha answered.

'I'd be delighted,' Swein said. *Young Gytha is just as beautiful as her mother. It won't be difficult to marry her off and get myself an ally into the bargain. Someone to guard my back while I'm away in England.*

'Good. I'm glad we have that settled,' Gytha said.

'I suggest a toast to the future,' Swein said, and servants refilled their goblets.

The following day, Swein sent out to friendly neighbouring countries for soldiers to help him invade England, just as William had done a few years earlier. One messenger was on his way east with a proposition for a prince.

Chapter 31

The weather had changed for the worst, and rain was falling hard. Clouds obscured the moon and stars, and for the four fugitives, progress was sluggish. Through the pitch-black darkness, they travelled at snail's pace.

'I can just make out something over there,' Whitgar said, pointing into the darkness.

'I can't see a thing,' Bondi said, peering into the rain.

'It's a farm,' Whitgar said.

'Let's take a closer look,' Bondi said.

As they approached, the outline of a building grew slowly more apparent, but it was eerie. No dogs barked, no geese honked. All they could hear was the sound of the falling rain as it spattered on the ground. Whitgar and Bondi dismounted, leaving their horses with the ladies. With swords drawn, they entered the hall. The fire was reduced to glowing embers, but they could still feel its warmth. Something was burning in a pot suspended over the hearth.

'Hello,' Bondi said, but there was no reply.

'Hello,' he yelled, louder this time, his voice echoing in the darkness, but there was still no reply.

'Let's see if we can find a candle or something,' he said to Whitgar.

The two gazed into the gloom, searching for anything that would cast light.

Whitgar returned with a lantern, and Bondi called the others inside.

They lit some torches and candles to discover the hall deserted.

'There's no one here,' Whitgar said.

'It looks as though whoever was here just left and, in a hurry, too,' Bondi said, looking all around.

'I'll check the stables,' Whitgar said. He was gone for only a few minutes before he returned. 'There's nothing in the stables except our horses. There are a few servants' huts out there. They're all new too, from what I can tell.'

'Whoever lived here panicked when they discovered the Normans were back,' Morwenna said.

'Most likely,' Bondi said. 'Let's find something to eat.'

Whitgar sampled the stew in the pot.

'This is ruined,' he said.

Elfwyn had got the fire going, providing more light and warmth.

'This hall was recently built,' Bondi said. 'Everything is so clean.'

'And you can even smell the wood,' Elfwyn said. She looked up at the roof. 'The thatch has hardly any soot on it.'

'The tapestries,' Morwenna said, pointing to the hangings on the walls. 'They're beautiful. Whoever left here must have been terrified to have left this behind.'

Each one stood in wonder, looking around the hall.

Morwenna broke the silence. 'I'll see if I can find the pantry,' she said.

Elfwyn offered to help her, and the two searched for food and soon found a storeroom brimming with delights. They also found a large washtub.

'This is a Godsend,' Morwenna said. 'We can have a bath and wash our clothes.'

'There are some cauldrons and cooking pots here too,' Elfwyn said. 'And I've found some towels.'

'I'm surprised they left these behind; they're beautiful,' Morwenna said, examining the towels, which had gold thread running through them. 'If this is what they left behind, I wonder what they took with them.'

The women called the Bondi and Whitgar through, and soon they had cauldrons filled with water heating over the fire. Morwenna organised the men before she and Elfwyn washed their clothes and had a bath. Wrapped in towels, they returned to the hall to find the meal was almost ready.

'We'll take over now if you'd like to get cleaned up,' Morwenna said.

'It's all right. We'll wash later,' Whitgar aid.

'No, it's not all right,' Morwenna said. 'You're filthy. You two need to get yourselves and your clothes cleaned up. Heaven only knows what's on them after you've been in those tunnels.'

'Come on,' Bondi said to Whitgar. 'Let's get ourselves clean.'

Once the men had washed and dried, and everyone's clothes were drying by the fire, steam slowly climbing to the rafters, they tucked into their meal, which was simple, hearty fayre served on wooden trenchers; the residents had taken the silverware with them. Nevertheless, sitting by the blazing fire simply enjoying being warm and dry was a pleasure, a luxury even.

'This food's good,' Morwenna said.

'You did most of the cooking,' Bondi said.

'Well, you did your share,' Morwenna said. 'You know, we haven't thanked you for coming to our rescue.'

'You seemed to do well enough without us,' Bondi said.

'No. They would have caught us. Even if we'd escaped from the tunnels, we would never have crossed the river. They were right behind us.

'Thank you. You probably saved our lives,' Morwenna said.

Even the light-hearted Elfwyn became serious. 'Morwenna's right; we owe you our lives,' she said. Bondi and Whitgar blushed.

Bondi was the first to speak. 'Somebody had to get you out of there,' he said. Whitgar followed quickly, 'Let's have another drink, and I'll raise a toast to our health and good fortune.'

'I'll drink to that,' Bondi said, and after Elfwyn topped up their cups, drank their toast.

Whitgar had found some mulberry wine, which turned out to be excellent. In no time, the four were in high spirits, discussing their afternoon adventure. The women explained how they were cut off from Edgar's men and then remembered the old Roman drains when they hid in a pigsty.

'Hid in a pigsty?' Whitgar said. 'That explains a lot.'

'Are you saying we smell?'

'How do you think we found you in those tunnels?' Whitgar said.

'Really?'

'Only a little,' Whitgar said.

'Well, we're clean now, and that's the main thing. Our clothes should be dry in the morning, and we can continue on our way,' Morwenna said.

They talked for a short while, and Whitgar went to get some more wine. On his way, he opened the wrong door and discovered a stairway. Climbing silently upwards, he finally reached a landing, off which were three doors. He opened the first one to discover a bedroom. He then tried the other two doors and found another two bedrooms. *This might not turn out to be such a bad day after all.*

Whitgar reappeared with the wine, a smile on his face and a plan in his head. He poured everyone another drink. Everyone felt cosy, warm and dry with full stomachs while the rain thrashed against the walls and roof.

'I wonder who this hall belongs to.' he said.

'I've no idea,' Elfwyn said. 'Don't you know? You live in Yorkshire.'

'It's someone rich and powerful probably, but I really can't say.'

'I wonder if he'll mind us using his place and helping ourselves to food and drink?' Morwenna said.

'Whoever he is, he'll be grateful when we rid the kingdom of William.'

With the last remark, silence fell over the company.

'Do you think we can do it?' Elfwyn asked the question in everyone's mind.

'Of course,' Bondi said. 'We just need to get reorganised, and we'll soon see the back of him.'

'Good riddance to William,' Whitgar said, raising his cup.

The others drank with him, and Whitgar poured them some more wine.

'I'm tired now,' he said. 'I'm going to turn in. Before you bid me goodnight, I'd just like to say I've discovered three bedrooms upstairs.'

'What's upstairs?' Bondi asked.

'I found three bedrooms when I was getting more wine.'

'Why didn't you tell us before?' Morwenna asked.

'What difference it would it have made? Would you like to see them?'

'What a good idea,' Elfwyn said.

Morwenna sighed as the others got to their feet. Whitgar led the way, hand in hand with Elfwyn, both a little unsteady on their feet.

Whitgar opened the door to what everyone had mistaken for a cupboard and began climbing the stairs. When they were all gathered on the landing, he said, 'There, what did I tell you.' He opened the door to the first room and stepped inside with his lantern lighting the way.

'Let's have a look at the others,' Morwenna said.

They looked in the other rooms, and they too had been left as though the owner intended to return.

'You don't suppose they are likely to come back, do you?' Morwenna said.

'Not now. Not tonight. It looks as whoever was here just bolted. Perhaps one day they'll come back,' Bondi said.

'In that case,' Elfwyn said. 'I'll have the first room. Goodnight, everyone,' she said, casting a glance at Whitgar.

A little taken aback, Morwenna said, 'If no one has any objections, I'll take the next room.'

Bondi and Whitgar looked at each other for a silence laden moment before Whitgar said, 'I'll sleep downstairs.'

'It's a gigantic bed, Whitgar. Easily big enough for the two of us,' Bondi said.

'So I see, but I'm tired, and I'll sleep better by the fire. I also snore very loudly.'

'As you wish,' Bondi said. 'I'll have a comfortable bed for myself.'

Everyone said goodnight, and Whitgar made a noisy journey downstairs to the hall below while Morwenna and Bondi retired to their respective rooms.

At the bottom of the stairs, Whitgar stopped and waited until everyone seemed settled down before journeying back upstairs soundlessly. Once on the landing, he groped his way around in the dark. He was surprised when he put his hand on something soft.

'Elfwyn?' He whispered.

'Not quite,' Morwenna's voice answered in the dark. 'You seem to have lost your way, Whitgar. You're sleeping downstairs, or had you forgotten?'

For a moment, Whitgar froze.

'Oh, it's you, Morwenna.'

'Yes. Were you expecting someone else?'

'No. No. Of course not.'

'Goodnight, Whitgar,' Morwenna said, with a hint of steel in her voice.

Although Whitgar could not see Morwenna's face, he knew the expression it held even in the dark. 'Goodnight, Morwenna,' he said.

In her room, Elfwyn heard the exchange and the sound of footsteps as Whitgar made his way downstairs. After a short while, she heard Morwenna making her way to her room. Elfwyn was stealthier by far than her sister or Whitgar. Once Morwenna had retired, she waited a few minutes and crept down the stairs. She made out Whitgar by the light of the fire.

'Whitgar,' she whispered.

'Elfwyn?'

She made her way over to him, being careful not to trip in the dark. Finally, she reached him and sat beside him.

'I thought we'd never get a moment together,' she said.

'So did I.'

'I'm so grateful to you for saving our lives,' she said, putting her arms around him.

'You seemed to manage very well on your own.'

'Be serious for once. You didn't have to, but you put yourself at such great risk for me.'

'Oh, I didn't do it for you. I thought somebody else was stuck down there,' he said, followed by a sudden, 'ouch,' as Elfwyn's elbowed him in the ribs.

Their eyes had grown used to the darkness now, and in the firelight, they made out each other's laughing faces in the gloom. The dancing light of the fire caught in their eyes. The fire crackled as if a sign for them to begin what they had intended. They leaned into each other and kissed, coyly, gently at first, and then more passionately.

'Not now, not here,' she whispered. 'Morwenna's bound to hear us.'

'We can't go to your room, but there are servants' quarters just outside,' Whitgar said.

Elfwyn remained silent, and Whitgar stood up, holding his hand out for her. She looked up, and for a few moments, their eyes met, and they gazed into each other. She took his hand and got to her feet. Whitgar led the way to the servant's quarters and opened the door.

'Here,' he said, guiding her to the bed.

The night was silent except for the sound of gently falling rain and their breathing. Whitgar turned toward her. They embraced and kissed and began losing themselves in each other. They were living in the moment, the intense immediacy of the here and now. Nothing else existed. Their hands seemed to have wills of their own and, in the darkness, pulled each other's towels off. Neither could work quickly enough, and momentum built up in their passion, driving them on, pushing them further with an insistence impossible to ignore.

There was a freedom Elfwyn experienced now she was naked with her lover. It was all new to her and so exciting. She felt as though she were flying. Apart from a few fumbles with one of two local boys, she had little idea of what was about to happen. Her body spoke a language of its own that she barely understood.

'You will be careful, won't you?' she said.

'Of course,' Whitgar whispered.

Under the blanket, she submitted to him gladly and as he entered her, pain seared through her that soon gave way to pleasure. His every movement shot waves of rapture through her right to her core. Intensifying the euphoria for them both, she thrust her hips as he pushed into her. Pleasure overwhelmed her as her instincts took over. She unleashed a creature with cravings of its own, unrestrained in its desire to find fulfilment. They became more vigorous until she exploded at the height of pleasure in an ecstatic frenzy.

Whitgar had experienced nothing like the intimacy he shared with Elfwyn, and as they lay in an embrace, both knew their lives would never be the same. Entwined in each other's limbs, they lay together, her head on his chest as he stroked her hair and kissed her forehead.

'You're beautiful,' Whitgar murmured.

He felt her movement as she smiled, and he kissed her again. They lay in each other's arms, talking until the sky began to brighten.

'It's getting light,' Elfyn said. 'I think we'd better get back.'

The two, wrapped in their towels, made their way hand in hand, back to the hall. At the bottom of the stairs, they kissed and said goodnight.

Morwenna was the first to wake in the morning, and within minutes, she had everyone on their feet and downstairs.

'Come on, everybody, get up,' Morwenna said, clapping her hands. 'It's not far to Haxby. If we leave now, we can be there in a few hours.'

Bondi, Whitgar, and Elfwyn reached the bottom of the stairs, Whitgar and Elfwyn a little worse for wear.

'Good morning. If you're all ready now, we'll be on our way,' Morwenna said.

Bondi, who was at the back of the three when they came downstairs, gave Morwenna a meaningful look as he walked towards the door. Whitgar and Elfwyn acted as though there was nothing between them, but neither could meet Morwenna's suspicious gaze.

It was the way they looked at each other that gave them away. Morwenna found it impossible not to notice their eyes fixed on each other. Even Bondi noticed. As her sister and Whitgar followed behind Bondi to the door, Morwenna said, 'Elfwyn, can I have a quick word, please.'

Elfwyn stopped, turned, and stared challengingly at her sister.

'I know what you've been doing,' Morwenna said.

'I don't know what you mean,' Elfwyn said, a picture of innocence.

'Don't take me for a fool.'

'What about you and Bondi? Don't tell me nothing happened there,' Elfwyn said.

'Nothing did. I'm only thinking of you. You need to be careful, Elfwyn.'

'You're not my mother,' Elfwyn replied, with fire in her eyes.

'What do you think father will say when he finds out?' Morwenna said.

'Not as much as he will when he finds out what's going on between you and Bondi. He might admire him as a housecarl, but he wouldn't want his precious daughter becoming involved with a common soldier,' Elfwyn said, ending the conversation.

Silence fell as they stared out of the window at the dales beyond.

Chapter 32

Pomeroy returned to York in a foul temper; his horse had cuts from his spurs to prove it. Not only had he not caught the English rebels, but he had also extracted no information from Leatherface, who now lay dead and charred in his burned-out home. It was sunset and too late to give chase to the rebels. As he passed through the city gates, he ran a finger across the scar on his face, and his sergeant spoke.

'Where are we going to stable the horses, my lord?'

'In the minster where they'll be warm and dry.'

'The minster?'

'Are you deaf? Yes, the minster.'

The horsemen led their mounts up to the church to find their path blocked by Archbishop Ealdred and a few other churchmen standing in the doorway.

'Make way, old man,' Pomeroy said.

'Do you know who I am?'

'Yes, now get out of the way.'

'This is a house of God, not a stable.'

Sir Ralph dug his spurs into his horse, which stepped forward, pushing the Archbishop aside. Regardless of whether he meant to push him over, the Archbishop fell to the ground, his legs waving in the air.

'Hey, look, granddad's had too much to drink,' Pomeroy laughed, his men laughing with him.

'This is an outrage, which I cannot bear,' Archbishop Ealdred said, getting to his feet and attempting to regain some composure.

'Take my advice, pray for guidance,' Pomeroy called over his shoulder as his horse trotted into the minster. He arrived to discover plenty of others were using it as a stable. There must have been at least a hundred horses already there.

So, what was the fuss about? Pomeroy thought to himself.

Outside, a distraught Ealdred was up on his feet talking to himself, his eyes blank. 'Where is my England?' The Archbishop turned his gaze skyward. 'Father, why are you doing this to us? What sin have we committed to deserve this? Not only do they despoil my country, but they also desecrate your house.' The breeze blew away his whispered words. His friends escorted him back to his home, where they hoped he might find respite from his ordeal.

Later that evening, at a celebratory banquet in York's Great Hall, King William had made a decision.

'Sir William,' he said to his old friend William Malet. 'I have an offer for you to consider. We need another castle here in York, and I'd like you to oversee its construction and be the castellan. What do you say?'

'It would be an honour, and I thank you,' Malet replied.

'Good, because you'll begin construction tomorrow,' William said with a smile. Now if you would pass me the lampreys, we'll enjoy the entertainment.

William nodded, and two itinerate jugglers entered the hall and began their act.

True to his word, Malet started work on the new castle first thing the next day. It was to be a perfect replica of the one on the south of town, on the other side of the River Ouse. A week later, the fortification was completed. William came to inspect it before leaving for Winchester and the Easter Court.

At dawn, on the palisade on top of the motte, William surveyed the scene. Before him lay the bailey surrounded by an eight-foot-deep ditch and a wall of sharpened posts, which protected the barracks, stables, workshops, and hall. Beyond there, the great city of York and the other older castle.

'Well done, William,' the king congratulated Malet.

As he stood there complimenting his comrade, William's gaze strayed along a road where someone familiar walked towards him. An English nobleman by the look of him. He walked with effortless, loose-limbed strides, his long golden hair trailing onto his shoulders. William was convinced he knew him but could not place him.

For a moment, the man faced him and, at first glance, appeared handsome, but then William noticed; an eye was missing. Shock ran through him to his core. He stared in disbelief. Just yards away, Harold as large as life. He even flashed a wicked smile.

'My lord,' William heard with a start.

He looked around to see Malet staring at him with concern.

'Are you all right?'

'Who's that man?' William asked, pointing down the empty road.

'No one, my lord. No one.' Malet replied, stunned by his king's outburst.

A shiver ran up William's spine. *I could have sworn I saw him.*

Chapter 33

In the scorching August sun, on the banks of the River Humber, the Danish fleet's two hundred and forty ships made an impressive sight. They had arrived at first light, and an army of Vikings had spilt from their decks. The Atheling was waiting to greet them with his followers and Archbishop Ealdred.

'We're here to answer your call for help,' said their leader. 'I am Osbjorn, King Swein's brother, and I have bought my nephews, Harald and Cnut.'

'We're pleased to welcome you,' Edgar said, wondering why Swein wasn't with them. 'I'm sorry your father's not here. My understanding was he would lead the army.'

Osbjorn was having trouble taking Edgar seriously. He seemed too young. Other men had been king at his age, but he lacked authority. Osbjorn said the words he had rehearsed with his brother. 'King Swein is keen to avenge the death of his housecarls who died at Hastings and, of course, his cousin King Harold.'

'But he's not here to share the glory.' Edgar said.

'My lord has sent me to speak on his behalf,' Osbjorn said.

Waltheof and Gospatric also wondered why Swein had not come in person.

A frail Archbishop Ealdred was present and pleased to meet Christian, Bishop of Aarhus.

Perhaps the Danes are civilised after all, Ealdred thought, as Osbjorn introduced Bishop Christian. *With his help, I might persuade them of the folly of taking on William.*

Ealdred said, 'If we resist, it will only make matters worse. God protect us from the fury of the Normans.'

Miles away from York, at Saint Briavels, in the Forest of Dean, King

William was heading home after a successful morning's hunting. He was in conversation with Sir William FitzOsbern when riders approached at speed. Both raced to get their messages to their lord before the other. The winner brought his horse to a halt, leapt from it, and bowed before his king while the other was still twenty yards away.

'My lord, the Danes are raiding along the east coast and are making their way to York.'

'Is there any danger of York falling?'

'It's impossible to say, my lord.'

'Very well, find a fresh horse and take this message to Sir William Malet. Tell him I can be up there in a week or so if he requires assistance.'

The second messenger then presented himself.

'What is it now?'

'News from Flanders. Count Baldwin has died. His son Arnulf succeeds him, but his brother, Robert, claims the title and is gathering forces.'

'And Arnulf is requesting my help?' *As if we haven't got enough problems with the rebels and the Danes.* 'Tell Ranulf he can expect aid from us just as soon as we've dealt with this minor rebellion. It shouldn't take long.'

In York, William Malet was preparing defences against the rebels. He was in the street outside of his castle discussing plans with Gilbert de Ghent, newly appointed castellan of York's second castle. The conversation halted when a messenger appeared. He dismounted and approached the two men.

'My lords,' the king says, 'should you require assistance, he can be here with an army in one to two weeks.'

'I don't think we need to worry about a few rebels,' a confident William Malet replied.

'It's more than just a few English rebels. The whole Danish army has joined them,' the messenger said.

'How do you know?'

'I saw them myself. There are hundreds of ships and thousands of warriors.'

Sir Gilbert looked alarmed, and William Malet's face paled when he heard this news. 'We'd better prepare for a full-on assault. We'll forget defending the town. Our men will be spread too thinly along the walls, but the castles we can hold.'

Malet addressed the messenger, 'Go back to the king. Tell him of our situation, but let him know we are secure enough to last a year in our castles.

'No. Wait a minute. Get one of the other messengers to find the king. You've done your share over the last few days. But make sure he tells the King the Danes are here.'

'Yes, my lord.' And with that, the tired messenger went in search of a colleague to run his errand.

'Get back to your castle and prepare for an onslaught, Gilbert,' Malet said to his comrade.

Without hesitation, Sir Gilbert hurried to his castle.

Deep in thought, Sir William surveyed the defences, trying to anticipate the enemy's next move. Then the idea struck him. If the rebels demolished the surrounding buildings and filled the moat with debris, they could overrun the garrison. Malet had a cure for this.

'Burn the buildings,' he ordered his captain. 'Just those around the castle. If the rebels get past the city walls, they might demolish the houses and use the debris to fill the moat. Then we'll be in trouble.'

Half an hour later, a sergeant left the castle with forty armed men; ten had torches. They were barging their way into properties and setting fire to homes and businesses. The occupants fled with what they could grab.

Malet watched with a smile of satisfaction on his face. He felt pleased with his idea and execution, but his expression changed. The wind, which had been nothing more than a gentle breeze, gusted. Soon sparks flew, and flames licked neighbouring buildings.

'Guard! Guard!' Malet bellowed, trying not to sound panicked. 'Take as many men as you can and put out the fire.'

The sergeant, who had started the fire only a short time ago, was now leading two hundred men to put it out.

'I wish he'd make up his mind. First, he says, start a fire. Now he says, put it out,' he muttered to himself as he made his way through the smoke-filled streets.

While the Normans ran towards the fire, ships' crews were racing to the quays to save their vessels. The more fortunate ones still had their cargo on board and left to find another market.

The sailors were joined in a race for the river by rats. Streams of them poured out of warehouses, making for safety; a moving carpet of vermin. Birds took flight. A cacophony of destruction as the thatch on a roof burst into flames, and the crash of falling timber beams sent domestic animals fleeing in terror.

Out of sight, a few miles downriver, English rebels and Danish and Scottish warriors watched bewildered as more and more smoke climbed up into the early autumn sky.

'Do you think this is a trick?' Osbjorn said.

'It might be. But then again, it might not,' Whitgar said.

'Do you think that's helpful?'

'It's hard to tell just yet. Why not wait before we make a decision?' Whitgar said.

Osbjorn looked surprised that Whitgar had had a good idea.

'Send the scouts up to take a closer look,' he said.

As ordered, scouts went out, and when they returned three hours later, they had a lot to report.

'The entire town is going up in flames,' they said. 'Everywhere, people are putting out fires.'

A pall of smoke hung over the town below in which great yellow, red, and orange flames licked the buildings. Even at that distance, the rebel army could smell the fire and hear the shouting of panic-stricken inhabitants. Two days passed while the rebels watched as York burned to the ground.

'Edgar, you know the town well. How are we going to storm it?' Osbjorn asked.

'Why not undermine part of the town walls the way the Normans did at Exeter.'

'Ah, you were at Exeter?'

'No, but I heard about it. Once we breach the walls, we can storm the gap, open the gates, and the rest of the army can pour in,' Edgar said.

'It's a good plan, but my men don't care to dig,' Osbjorn said.

Osbjorn saw the mighty town walls, solid and formidable. Yet, he also perceived weakness. The Ouse flowed through the middle of York, and two bridges connected one side of the town with the other. Inside the walls, the Normans had built two castles, one on either side of the river. Each perched on a man-made hill thirty feet high. From inside a keep, a soldier could see for miles around.

'Tell me about the bridges?'

'There's a couple of them. The wooden one, which the Vikings built and then upstream from that, the old Roman Bridge,' Edgar said.

Osbjorn considered the options. 'I say we wait until they're exhausted from fighting the fire and then sail upriver to the bridge and then attack both the castles at once.' Looking pleased, he asked, 'Who agrees?'

'It sounds like a good idea to me,' Edgar said.

'What do you say, Waltheof?'

'Why not enter while York still burns? The town's gates are open to allow people to flee. If we surround the town and attack before dawn, charge through the gates and overrun them before they'd even got out of bed.'

Merleswein said, 'That's a good idea.'

The Danish princes thought so too, and they agreed upon the plan.

'We'll wait until the moment looks right, and then we'll strike,' Edgar said, and the meeting dispersed. As he turned to walk back to his tent, Merleswein approached him.

'There's something I have to say,' Merleswein said.

'What's that, Merleswein?'

'Ealdred is a great family friend. He has been for many years. As the gates of the city are open, I'd like to take a small party and see if he's safe,' Merleswein said. 'The Normans are preoccupied putting out the fire. They'll be too busy to notice a few more Englishmen in town.'

Edgar thought the matter over. 'Very well,' he said. 'But no heroics. Just find out if he's safe and if he's not, persuade him to leave.'

'Thank you, my lord. You won't regret this,' Merleswein said.

Within minutes, Merleswein, Bondi and Whitgar were riding towards York and an enormous fire.

While Edgar and his allies were deciding on their plan, back in

York, mayhem had broken out. Sir William Malet was trying hard to get the blaze under control. Locals and occupying troops were caught up in the confusion as fights broke out over which fires to put out, and Malet tried in vain to enforce discipline.

'Forget those buildings,' bellowed to a group of his men. 'Form a line in front of the fire and stop it spreading.'

Luckily, the moat, fed from the River Foss, supplied plenty of water.

Malet and his men had little experience of dealing with fires. They tried their hardest to extinguish the blaze but to little effect. Soldiers ran in every direction, desperate to find buckets or any kind of large container, ransacking homes and workshops alike. Despite the chaos, the soldiers formed a line and passed buckets full of water from one to the other, right up to the fires.

'It's hopeless. The fire is spreading everywhere,' a soldier cried, having thrown a whole bucket of water onto the thatched roof, only to watch as sparks ignited a neighbouring building. Another man was trying to beat out flames with his cloak. Malet found it impossible to work out whose struggle was the more futile.

Sir William was trying to think of something encouraging to say when he was horrified to see the fire had spread to the south side of the Ouse, and houses there were burning. With the whole of York now under threat, Malet felt his stomach tie into a knot when he realised he had lost control, but he must try to save the city, or at least that part still standing.

He looked around for a solution as the townsfolk ran for the gates with their belongings.

'Forget those houses, pull back to Coppergate, and soak the buildings there. If we can make them wet enough, they might not catch fire. Pull back! Pull back!'

As ordered, the men pulled back and formed a chain. Soldiers at the end began throwing buckets of water on the houses, but as most of these small wooden dwellings with their thatch roofs were only a few feet apart, Malet's men knew they were losing the battle against the flames. The raging fire leapt across the tops of two or three buildings at a time and set upon a fresh one. On the two-storey warehouses packed with goods, people climbed with ladders, throwing water over the thatch, while friends and family emptied as many of the valuables as they could and took them to safety.

The flames roared, and the heat from the inferno forced the firefighters back. Even with two hundred and fifty pairs of Norman hands there to help, the job was impossible. They were overwhelmed; there was nothing to be done.

'Get back to the castle,' Malet ordered, coughing because of the smoke, his eyes stinging and streaming. But as much as he feared the fire, the Danes concerned him more as every minute passed.

The troops retreated to the castle, leaving York to burn as ordered.

The black and grimy faced soldiers found a route through the flaming streets to the safety of the castle, where they took rest, collapsing onto the ground, calling for help and treatment for burns and assorted injuries.

Malet realised he could not save York. He now paid attention to the rebel army camped outside York's walls. He made his weary way up the steps of the keep, reaching the highest point, out of breath. He could taste smoke and burned wood in his mouth.

It was a sorry sight that greeted him from the topmost point of his castle. Most of York's buildings were on fire. Coppergate was on fire, taking most of the city's produce with it, and beyond Coppergate, the minster had just become engulfed in flames. The king's palace was threatened and, beyond that, the Earl's Hall. Thank heavens he had ordered the valuables removed from there and taken to the castle. It was then he remembered the Royal Mint and its gold and hoped he had not lost it.

Malet yelled to his sergeant. 'Take half a dozen men and find out what state the Royal Mint is in.'

'Yes, my lord,' the sergeant answered before rushing off.

As Malet surveyed the scene, the stables behind the blacksmith burst into flames. The tang of burning buildings filled the air. He saw a couple and their two children on the city wall escape the fire by leaping to the riverbank, twenty feet below.

The sound of screaming filled the air. Screams of women frightened for their children. Cries from men, suffering agony, mothers were calling to children, young calling for their mothers. It was becoming too much for him to bear.

Malet looked across the Ouse to discover Gilbert de Ghent glaring at him from the other castle. He knew, even at two hundred yards, it was a glare. He shrugged and raised his arms by way of an explanation.

Malet turned his attention back to the fire and wondered, *how long will the fire last at this rate?* He made a rough calculation. *This time tomorrow and the entire city will have gone up in smoke.*

He gazed to the southeast, where he could pick out the rebel army. Thousands of Englishmen, with hate-filled hearts and thousands more Danes, ready to kill every soldier in the garrison, were camped within view. Fear ran through him from head to foot, not for himself; he was a courageous man, but for his wife and children. *Heaven only knows what will happen to them if that lot get their hands on them.* Malet knew it was not an English or Danish custom to take hostages. Kill prisoners or take slaves, yes. Hostages, no.

'Time to concentrate on preparing for the attack,' Malet bellowed to his men. 'We'll be safe from the rebels while the fire's raging.'

None of his exhausted men appeared cheered by the thought.

'Let's thank heaven for small mercies,' Malet bellowed.

A few hours later, on the other side of the town, Merleswein, Bondi, and Whitgar entered the city to discover an inferno and stared in astonishment at the scene before them as flames raged through the minster.

'My God, what a sight,' Merleswein said.

The three stared in disbelief as flames and sparks roared up towards the heavens through the night. Most of the roof had gone up in flames, and smouldering beams were all that remained of the timbers. Away from danger, gathered in a group staring at the inferno, were the clerics and Archbishop Ealdred, tears running down his face. Merleswein ran over to him.

'Father. Are you all right?'

'Merleswein, it's you. God bless you. Look what they've done to my beloved house of God. Look, it's like the apocalypse,' Ealdred said.

Merleswein scrabbled for words to comfort him; they were difficult to find.

'We'll make them pay for this, father. When we've seen them off, we will rebuild and restore your minster to its former glory,' Merleswein said.

Ealdred shook as he peered into the conflagration, trying to pick out the altar. There before him, nailed on the cross, enveloped in flames, was a helpless Jesus. Ealdred knew the minister was doomed to destruction; holy relics, beautiful frescoes lovingly painted onto the walls, consumed by fire.

Ealdred's despair was bottomless. The minster was gone, and the city was going up in smoke. It was as though God had abandoned them, destroying the world he loved, before forsaking him.

'Ealdred, you ought to come away. Come with us to safety,' Merleswein said.

Ealdred gasped and stared, stumbled forward and grabbed hold of his old friend's arms. He gasped, put a hand to his heart and dropped to his knees.

'Ealdred. Ealdred,' Merleswein said, reaching to support his friend.

Weakened with age, the old man's heart gave out, and he collapsed.

Brother Brice rushed forward to help. 'What is it?' he asked. But by the time he reached him, the Archbishop was lying flat out, the tears still wet on his face, Merleswein on his knees leaning over him.

'The Lord has taken him,' the monk said, after listening for a heartbeat in the old man's chest. 'We should prepare him for his last resting place,' He said, crossing himself.

'Of course,' Merleswein said.

The monk gave Merleswein, Bondi and Whitgar a studied look before saying, 'Thank you for coming, my lords, but our archbishop is with Our Lord now. You should return to your men, who I suspect are somewhere outside of the city.'

'Yes, you're right,' Merleswein said. 'We'll be back soon and put this right.'

'The world is full of men putting things right. That's why it's in such a mess,' the monk replied.

'God be with you, my Lord Merleswein, and your friends.'

An hour later, they talked to Edgar, Malcolm and Osbjorn of Ealdred's demise. They informed them York was for the taking, 'Micklegate is wide open. If we're quick, we can pass through it.'

'Are you sure?' Edgar said.

'Yes. Come quickly,' Merleswein said.

Edgar, Malcolm and Osbjorn signalled their men, who followed Merleswein silently toward York, over which columns of smoke were still climbing into the morning sky.

As they got close, Osbjorn said, 'Merleswein's right. It's wide open.'

The rebel army made their way through refugees camped in the fields, hurrying through the half-light to Micklegate.

'I'll take the castle on this side of the river,' Osbjorn said. 'Edgar, if you take the bridge, there's nothing to stop you from catching them asleep in the other castle.'

Osbjorn led the Danes while the English and Scots followed Edgar and Malcolm at a run.

While fires smouldered, the rebels arrived to find the only stone buildings still stood, and those were shells. The wooden castles, protected by their garrisons and moats, were unharmed.

Shouts from a sentry broke the early morning silence at the new castle, and the garrison sallied out to confront the enemy.

'Close those gates,' a voice cried out.

Gilbert de Ghent led his men out of his castle towards Micklegate and the rebel army. It was too late. The rebels were streaming through the gates, and Edgar's forces were racing across the bridge. The Danes charged towards the new castle, making quick work of the group sent out to close the gate.

Asleep in his quarters, the shouting woke Sir William Malet. Even before anyone had time to warn him, he was dressing for battle.

His wife looked startled. 'What are you going to do, Will?'

'Stay here and keep the children safe, Helise,' he said.

Scared, she pulled her boys towards her.

'Father, let me come with you,' Robert, the elder son, pleaded as he helped his father with his chain mail. Once dressed for battle, Robert handed him his sword and shield. 'Please, let me come.'

'I need you here to look after your mother and brother,' Malet said.

'Be careful,' Helise said to her husband.

'This won't take long,' he said. 'I'll see you later.'

William Malet emerged into the early morning light to discover the rebels slaughtering the soldiers from the other garrison. The English and Danish armies had cut off the two castles, and they trapped his comrades. Malet regretted sending word to the king that he could hold out for a year. He knew he would be lucky to withstand a siege for a matter of days.

'Open the gates. We're going out to meet them,' Malet commanded.

Malet led his men through the castle gateway, relieved to see Gilbert de Ghent had had the same idea, and he, too, was going to meet the enemy.

'Charge,' he roared.

Outside the castle walls, the English waited to greet the Normans.

'Shieldwall.' Edgar commanded, but his order only caused confusion.

'Do the best you can in each street,' Waltheof shouted out.

The men formed up along the debris lined streets, and the two opposing sides charged their enemy between burned-out buildings with charred beams and debris, from which smoke was rising.

There was a thunderous crash of shield on shield. The sound of battle cries filled the air, and sword and spear battering at an opponent while all around blood-chilling screams of the wounded. The glistening blood of the fallen spattering amongst the black battlefield skeleton buildings, filling with the dead; a vision of hell. This was good territory for the archers. Unable to fight in the burning buildings, infantry flanks were vulnerable to archers' arrows, which hissed as they flew towards their target. A scream sounded when they found their mark.

'Watch your flanks,' Waltheof ordered, aware that his men too were in danger from archers, but there was no need for the order. Those on the sides of the attacking forces soon had their shields up for protection.

It was rage that fuelled the rebels and fear that fired the Normans; for many, this was the first time they had fought without cavalry to support them, and it played to the English strength.

Bondi glanced over his shoulder and was heartened to see the Danes form their shieldwall and begin battering their foe on the south side of the Ouse. Turning to face his enemy, he was confronted by men exhausted by days of firefighting.

'Charge,' he yelled, and as one, his men charged forward with him, past charred buildings, streets and into a square. Both armies now faced each other, but two days of trying to put out a fire meant the Normans were exhausted. Now they had to take on three armies of fresh soldiers. Men on both sides stood shoulder to shoulder. Bondi recognised a Norman issuing orders.

'Hold steady, men. Hold steady,' Malet barked out.

While the men stood firm, Malet noticed a man leading an English charge he recognised from King Harold's court. It was Bondi, and he was a terrifying sight to behold. Drenched in blood, the English housecarl swung his axe at shoulder height, slicing off two Norman heads in one swoop. He was an inspiration to his men and a fiend to his enemies.

'Hold fast men,' Malet ordered. 'You can hold them back,' but he knew he lied even as he spoke the words. It was just a matter of time; de Ghent's men were already falling back, cowering under the Danish storm.

Whitgar and Elfwyn, with the other archers, were moving forward behind the foot soldiers, shooting over their heads, picking off any enemy careless enough to let his guard drop. Morwenna was fighting in the shieldwall close to Bondi, she with a sword, he with his axe.

As the morning progressed, the odds swung further and further in the rebels' favour. As they pushed forward, they tripped over the Norman dead.

Everywhere Bondi looked, Malet's men were being cut down or forced back, and the English were rapidly moving forward. Waltheof possessed limitless strength and energy. Every time Bondi caught sight of him, a Norman fell victim to the Englishman's axe. Edgar, too, was putting on an impressive display. As each minute passed, English spirits rose, and Norman morale fell. Falling back towards the castle, Malet was panicking. He hoped and prayed the king would come and save the day. Hugh, his Flemish sergeant, said, 'Victory is beyond us. Shall we surrender?'

'Do you think we'll be shown mercy?' Sir William said.

'I doubt it. So, we'll put up a damn good fight, and no one can say we're cowards.'

'That's the spirit,' Malet said.

Hugh charged back into the fray with renewed vigour. He still had something to fight for, his honour. After killing two Englishmen, he ran up against a tall, blond, rangy housecarl and carried an axe. Hugh thought it the weapon of a savage.

As Hugh closed in on Bondi, their eyes met, and they understood one of them would be dead within a few minutes, each convinced victory would be his.

They sized each other up for an instant, and Bondi noted Hugh was not too eager to make the first move. Bondi struck the first blow, and Hugh countered.

'Come on then, Frenchie. Let's see what you can do,' Bondi said before bringing his axe down hard. Bondi saw the force of the first blow came as an almighty shock to his opponent, even though he had seen it coming. Hugh had raised his shield and braced himself for the impact, screaming in agony as pain seared through his forearm. In an instant, he knew it was broken. Bondi knew it too.

With Hugh shaken, Bondi aimed a second blow, this time to his head. Just in time, the Fleming protected himself. Again, pain seared through his arm, this time even worse than before, but another feeling was harder to bear. He knew the end had come, and he suspected the housecarl knew it too.

Bondi brought the axe down, hoping to finish him, but Hugh stepped back to avoid another blow. The housecarl cursed as the axe sailed past Hugh's head, but this was only a momentary break from the onslaught, and he continued his attack. Stepping forward, this time, the axe came to Hugh's right, and it took clever footwork and agility to dodge the blow, but Bondi was relentless, and his eyes blazed as he swung his axe hard towards Hugh's neck.

Hugh put up a clumsy defence. Although he protected himself from the full force of the heavy blade, his shield smashed into his head, splitting his ear and dazing him. As he backed away from the onslaught, an aching took hold of the Fleming's heart; his dreams of glory, fame and fortune were ending. Fear welled up inside him. For the first time in years, he felt helpless and then he stumbled over the body of a fallen comrade, lost his balance, and fell to the ground amongst the corpses. Above him in the September sky shone the sun, golden and warm, giving light, giving life. A sparrow flew across his line of vision before he saw the grey blur of an iron head fly to greet him with one last cold kiss from a thin-lipped axe to bid him farewell to this troubled world.

That's one more out of the way, Bondi thought, as his opponent breathed his last.

It was now becoming difficult for the rebels to find anyone left to fight. Nine-tenths of the garrison lay dead or wounded and only a few English casualties. The housecarl looked around for more opponents to see Waltheof putting an enemy out of his misery. The Atheling, too, was impressive, dazzling with his sword. He saw Morwenna, giving a remarkable account of herself. Beyond them, Bondi could see William Malet, ashen-faced. The Norman knew he was soon to be overwhelmed. He did his best to rally around his troops on his fine bay horse, but it was to no effect.

'Don't give up the fight, lads. Hold them back,' the castellan roared.

'We're just fighting to stay alive,' a Norman soldier yelled to his lord. 'You'd best save your family. Malet swallowed hard, his mouth bone dry. This was his first defeat. He wondered if it would be his last.

Malet spurred his horse on into the keep, where the gates were closed behind him by half a dozen guards left on duty in the castle. He felt safe now since he had escaped the fray and found security behind the protection of the fortification.

Chapter 34

While the fighting in York was at its fiercest, not far from the village of St Briavels in the Forest of Dean, King William and his hunting party had come to a halt. William was admiring the splendour of the early autumn colours.

'Beautiful, isn't it?' William FitzOsbern said, as much to himself as the king.

'It is, Will. What a wonderful part of the world you've found for yourself. I'm glad you're settling in here. You appear to be happy in your new castle at Chepstow?'

'I am. The locals can be troublesome, but it's nothing to worry about.'

FitzOsbern turned at the sound of horses approaching at a gallop. 'Speaking of trouble, this looks like news of more.'

It was the messenger Sir William Malet had sent. Dismounting, he approached the king, an earnest expression on his face.

'My lord, word from Sir William Malet.'

'Are you going to tell me he needs help?'

'Yes, he does. There's a large rebel English army, and the Danes have landed.'

'Danes?' asked William.

'And Scots, too.'

William paled. 'But he assured me he could hold out for a year.'

'That was before the fire. The grain stores burned down, as did most of the city.'

'And the fortifications?'

'They were still standing when I left, five days ago.'

William turned to FitzOsbern and said, 'We'd better get back to Chepstow.'

'Is there anything else I ought to know?' William asked the messenger.

'Yes. There are uprisings all over the country. On my way here, I encountered trouble.'

'Tell me about it on the way back.'

And on the short ride back, the messenger told the king what he had seen on his journey south.

'The roads were empty until I reached Derby when I heard the first rumours of insurrection. The news was that Stafford and Shrewsbury were under siege by the one they call Edric the Wild. Earls' Morcar and Edwin are creating a nuisance of themselves, raiding and pillaging manor houses before razing them to the ground. Outlaws are robbing and murdering travellers. No one is safe, even in their own home. The only place folk feel secure is in a castle. Bodies of the dead litter the countryside. I met people fleeing Stafford, and they told me there had been more trouble. Most of northwest Mercia is in turmoil.'

When William arrived in Chepstow feeling shocked, the news grew worse. Three more messengers were waiting for him.

'Give me your message and don't spare me any unpleasantness,' William said to the first messenger.

'I've just come up from the south-west, my lord. Englishmen from Somerset and Dorset are attacking Montacute Castle. When I left, the castellan was certain he could stand firm for months.'

'Was he as confident as Sir William Malet?' William snapped.

'Pardon my lord.'

'Never mind. Is that all?'

'There is more. Harold Godwinson's sons are in the Bristol Channel with a fleet of up to two hundred ships.'

'An invasion?'

'Yes, my lord.'

'Very well. What do you have to say?' William said, addressing the second messenger.

'The men of Devon and Cornwall are besieging Exeter,' the messenger said.

'How strong are their forces?'

'I don't know exactly, but I'd say about five or six hundred. I don't think there's any danger of Exeter falling to them, my lord.'

'But these uprisings could encourage others to join in the rebellion. That's what this is, a rebellion,' William said. 'I've been dreading this.'

'No doubt you have awful news for me,' William said to the third messenger.

'I'm afraid Shrewsbury Castle is under attack from Edric the Wild and an army of Welshmen.'

'Welshmen? So, the Welsh are in this too?'

'Yes, my lord,' the messenger replied.

'Sir William, we need to discuss this urgently,' the king said to FitzOsbern.

'May I suggest we confer in the hall this evening? We can gather everyone together and decide what to do then. It's too late in the day to do anything now but make plans,' FitzOsbern proposed.

'Yes. Good idea.'

In the evening, King William's war council met over a banquet. More bad news poured in during the early evening. In a tense atmosphere, William addressed his comrades.

'Friends, I've given some thought to the matter of the English and their allies, Scottish, Welsh and Danish. I can't put down these uprisings myself, so I'd appreciate a little help.'

'You can count on every man here,' FitzOsbern offered. There were calls of agreement all around.

'Thank you, men. It's appreciated. Tell me if you agree. At dawn tomorrow, my brother Robert will head to Montacute and deal with the rebels there. With luck, it won't take long. Once he's dealt with them, he'll go north and meet me. I'll leave for Stafford in the morning and quash the rebellion there before going on to York.'

'It'll be my pleasure,' Robert said.

'Count Brian and Sir William, be so kind as to quash the uprisings in Shrewsbury and then Exeter. Are there any questions?

'Robert, you look as though you're about to say something. Does anyone have a question?' William asked.

'No, none. I just can't wait to get started,' Robert replied to the laughter of his friends.

'Very well. We'll leave for our various destinations in the morning and show these rebels our mettle. I'll also add; we've been far too soft on the English. They need to understand there is a price to pay for disloyalty to their king. They must pay in full for their crimes,' William said. 'Show them no mercy.'

Chuckles rippled through his companions for a moment. When had they ever shown mercy?

Chapter 35

In York, Sir William Malet entered his private quarters to find his wife, Helise, and his sons, Robert and Gilbert, waiting for him. They had been watching events unfold from a window, and now they all rushed up to greet him.

'William, thank God you're safe,' Helise said, but the look in her eye said something different. Malet knew she was worried about the boys.

'We're all going to be all right,' Malet said, pulling his family into a close embrace. 'You'll see. We might fall hostage for a short time, but before long, the king will pay our ransoms, and we'll be free again. No harm will come to us. Have no fear. He's on his way to us now, I'm sure.'

Helise looked unconvinced.

'My dear, we're worth far more as hostages,' Malet reassured her.

Outside, the sound of battle grew louder. Malet suspected most of the screams came from his comrades. More and more of the voices were English. His enemies were forcing their way into the keep, cutting down, escaping Frenchmen who had nowhere to flee.

Outside, in the milieu, he could see an Englishman and woman pulling arrows out of Norman corpses. He looked down to discover them looking up and then, like so many others, walk towards him in his lofty tower.

Whitgar and Elfwyn, having run out of arrows, pulled them from their victims to reuse. They soon had a fine collection and joined their comrades in slaying their enemies once more.

'Push them back,' Whitgar called out to the spearmen in front.

'We're pushing,' Bondi shouted back.

The rebels pursued the remaining Normans, forcing them across the drawbridge and through the main gate. In the shieldwall, the men were sweating, grunting, and groaning as they strained behind their shields to push the Normans back. There were so few of them left to fight that the English soon forced them back before they could close the gates. In the bailey, the defenders were outflanked and outnumbered twenty to one. Those Normans still on their feet ran for their lives towards the keep and what they hoped would be safety.

The Normans had built an excellent defence that would have held out against the English under normal circumstances, but so high was English confidence and so depleted were the defenders that they had no chance.

Now they had more arrows; Whitgar and Elfwyn were shooting at will, any enemy in sight.

'Have you seen Morwenna?' Elfwyn asked Whitgar.

'She's there, behind Bondi,' he said.

Elfwyn looked and could make out her sister amongst the English, pushing the Normans back.

'You'll soon be able to join her,' Whitgar said. 'We've got them on the run. Look, they're panicking.'

As Whitgar spoke, the Normans ran for the gates that led to the steps connected to the keep. They could see their comrades cutting off their only chance of escape. They would have to turn and fight a battle they could never win.

There was a brief pause in the fighting while the Normans lined up with their backs to the palisade while the English formed up in front of them.

'Forward,' Whitgar heard Edgar order. He was pleased to see the Atheling in the thick of it in the attack's van.

Edgar's men advanced toward their enemy, driving them back, where they stood little chance. English axe, sword, arrow, and spear were making short work of them, finding their way through an iron defence. Under a hail of blows and screams, the Normans fell one by one to the ground until none were left standing. Edgar's men finished the wounded where they lay. Now those few Normans who had survived were safe behind the inner barrier for the time being. The English attack came to a halt as soldiers gathered to get their breath back and for Edgar to decide on the next course of action.

'You know, fighting on is futile. Give up now, and we'll spare you your lives,' Edgar called up to the castle keep.

'You surrender, and we'll be the ones sparing your lives,' Malet shouted back. 'You've done the easy part. Getting up here will be much harder. How many men are you prepared to lose Edgar?'

'You know as well as I do, Sir William; it's just a matter of time, and you're done for,' Waltheof answered.

'That's all right, Earl Waltheof. We have all the time in the world,' Malet yelled. 'The king is on his way. What will you do then, eh? What will you do then?'

'What are we going to do now?' Edgar asked Waltheof.

'We can ram the gates and force them open. If that doesn't work, we'll burn them down.'

'Bondi, see if you can find something to build a ram,' Edgar said.

Straight away, Bondi organised a group of men who returned with a beam from one of the barrack huts. They had some rope and soon had an excellent battering ram to smash open the gates. The sixteen men rammed the gates with ropes looped around their shoulders and strapped around the beam.

The Englishmen ran full pelt, and there was a loud crash as the beam smashed into the gates. The men took heart as they felt them give on the first attack.

'Try again,' Edgar commanded.

Bondi ordered the men back. Once in position, he gave the command, 'Charge.'

The result was the same, but they burst open after a few minutes of battering at the gates. Those carrying the beam stopped in their tracks when they discovered a wall of shields bristling with spears. Bondi and his men were out of the way in a few brief moments, and Edgar, Waltheof and Gospatric charged and crashed into the Norman defence. The Normans resisted bravely at first, but soon fatigue and fear got the better of them, and they were overwhelmed, speared where they fell or cut up, trying to get back on their feet.

'What do we do now?' asked a breathless and bloodied Edgar.

Waltheof turned and looked up the steps that led up the steep scarp to the keep. Walls of sharpened wooden posts six feet high flanked both sides. Straight ahead lay another gate, beyond which the castle keep stood.

'No doubt there'll be a welcome party to greet us up there,' Waltheof said.

'Can't we just batter the gates down?' Gospatric suggested.

'We'll burn them down,' Edgar said. 'Get firewood and anything that will catch fire.'

Men ran into the stable and barracks, returning with bails of straw, beds, tables, benches, and stools until they had more than enough material to build an impressive bonfire.

Men ran up the steps with their shields held high and formed a protective tunnel.

In their rush to build a fire, men were crashing into each other the length and breadth of the steps. Gospatric stayed by the gates where the men piled up the kindling.

'Come on, men, more wood and bring some straw too,' he bellowed.

The men piled furniture and any pieces of wood they could find against the gates. Somebody had been clever enough to find a torch and light it. Gospatric set fire to a dozen sheaths of straw that he had rammed in amongst the wood, and soon, the lot was ablaze.

'There. Let them roast their chestnuts on that,' he laughed as he stepped back from the fire.

The flames roared skyward, and the men stood back to watch the fire burn. If any Norman tried to throw a bucket of water on it, a hailstorm of arrows would greet him. Soon the gates were on fire, and the English hurled more wood into the flames.

At last, the burning gates fell, the signal for the English to charge. Up the steps, they raced; through the flames, they leapt, swords and shields at the ready. Waltheof, leading the charge, made quick work of his enemies. His axe was bold in its business, and head after head fell to the ground, dismembered and decapitated bodies lay all around. Then a silence fell upon them all. Waltheof, Gospatric and Edgar exchanged glances and then looked around at the gruesome sight before them. They had destroyed their enemy.

'It's over,' Waltheof said.

'How many's that you've killed?' Bondi asked.

'I can't say.'

'I'd have thought at least a hundred.'

'No wonder I could do with a drink,' Waltheof joked. 'I tell you what, let's get up to the top there and see if Malet's got any.'

In their quarters, Sir William and his boys were listening for clues as to what was happening outside. On bended knees, his wife was praying. Closer and closer came the footsteps and voices until they stopped right outside. Malet raised his sword to defend his family. He tensed at the sound of a forceful rap on the door.

'What is it?' he said.

'It's me, Sir William. Edgar Atheling. Don't be afraid. We will not harm your family if you surrender. We intend to hold you hostage. You'll be well cared for, I promise.'

'Do I have your word?'

'You do, and that of my men,' Edgar said.

Warily, Malet opened the door. Outside, Edgar was waiting with Waltheof by his side.

'You can keep your sword; if you give your word, it'll stay in its scabbard,' Edgar said.

'Thank you, Edgar,' Malet said.

It was then Waltheof noticed Lady Malet across the other side of the room, hugging her children protectively.

'Lady Malet, don't be afraid. You're perfectly safe with us. We'll find accommodation for you outside of the city walls. It seems someone was careless and burned the town down,' Waltheof said with a smile. 'You'll be in good company; Gilbert de Ghent and his family will stay with you. I'm sure you'll have plenty to talk about.'

The family gathered a few things together and made for the door.

'Do you have any wine?' Waltheof asked Sir William as he was on his way out.

'Help yourself,' he replied.

Some soldiers led Malet, his family, and two servants outside the city wall to Haxby Hall.

Osbjorn appeared in the doorway with a big grin on his face. 'Those

Normans are nowhere near as tough as they think. They only lasted a couple of hours,' he said, before looking around and adding, 'There's no shelter and no food. What do we do now?' He was no longer smiling.

'At least Sir William was good enough to keep some wine and look after the treasure for us.'

Later, Edgar, Waltheof, Merleswein and Bondi gathered in Malet's quarters in the wooden castle, the smell of burned wood in the air.

'I've been thinking about what Osbjorn said,' Edgar said. 'We've taken York, but all we have are the perimeter walls and a lot of ashes. Ordinarily, we would celebrate capturing a city and defeating an enemy, but there's not so much as a barrel of beer to be found anywhere.

'And I'd love to know what's going on in the rest of the kingdom. None of the messengers I sent out calling the fyrd has yet returned,' Edgar said. 'But the kingdom should be up in arms now.'

'So, can we expect reinforcements?' Waltheof wondered out loud.

'I don't know about that, but William should have his work cut out for him dealing with uprisings here, there and everywhere. '

'I hope you don't mean Morcar and Edwin?' Gospatric said. 'I've heard nothing from them or about them for months.'

'No, not Edwin and Morcar, Edric the Wild, Sigur and Harold's sons. In the meantime, we rebuild as soon as possible,' Edgar said.

Osbjorn looked decidedly irritable. 'I didn't bring an army here to capture ruins and build houses,' he snapped.

'The city might be a burned-out hulk, but we've at least got the treasure,' Edgar reminded Osbjorn.

'Treasure is always welcome, but we still need a roof over our heads,' came Osbjorn's swift reply.

'Then first we have to rebuild,' Edgar said, as though to a child.

'You'll have to be quick. You might end up with a roof over your heads, but there's not one over ours and soon, no food in our bellies. It looks like your friend Sir William Malet wasn't so stupid after all,' Osbjorn replied.

'We'll build something to get us over the winter, then make a good start in the spring. We'll put roofs on the bigger buildings first; that way, we can provide shelter to more of the men,' Edgar said.

Osbjorn looked as though he had his doubts. 'Why don't we just move south to Lincoln?' he said.

'We're waiting for reinforcements,' Edgar replied.

'It's not a bad idea,' Waltheof said. 'William won't be expecting us to move.'

'I agree,' said Merleswein. 'There's not much in the way of food here. If we went to Lincoln, at least the barns would be full.'

'And after Lincoln, why not march on London? If all the kingdom is up in arms, let's march on London. What's keeping us here?' Waltheof said.

'I'm not so sure,' Edgar said. 'I'll see you all first thing in the morning, and we can make plans.'

'Good night.'

'Good night.'

The men bid their farewells, and the Danes left for their ships. The English stayed behind to discuss matters amongst themselves.

'What do you think, Edgar?' Waltheof asked.

'I understand why they're disappointed with York. They expected to spend the winter in the jewel of Northumbria, and the way things are going, they'll be sleeping under the stars. What do you think about moving to Lincoln?' Edgar said.

'Let's go. The sooner, the better,' Waltheof said.

'I think we need to rebuild York,' Gospatric said. 'Securing Northumbria will encourage men to our sides and give them the confidence to join us. Then, in the summer, we can march south to London.'

'What about striking right away while we have them on the run? I think the Danes have the right idea. Let's move on London,' Waltheof said.

'We need to know what's happening in the rest of the country first. William could be under siege in one of his castles down south,' Edgar said, 'for all we know.'

'Or he could be fighting for his life on a battlefield,' Waltheof said.

Gospatric looked thoughtful, 'Let's decide when we hear from the messengers,' he said. 'In the meantime, I suggest we make ourselves comfortable for the night and resume the discussion first thing tomorrow when we might know a little more.'

'I agree,' Edgar said. 'We'll discuss matters in the morning.'

'They'll be more of us to discuss matter than you think,' Waltheof said, looking out of a window to the city walls. 'King Malcolm is approaching with his army.'

'More mouths to feed,' Gospatric said.

'But more forces to help us put down William,' Edgar said on a cheerful note.

'Let's go out and welcome them,' Waltheof said.

The next day, in Malet's castle, the commanders met to discuss final plans. No one was happy with any of the options open to them. The destruction of York was the cause, and King Malcolm objected to every idea put forward.

'I'll not spend the winter here. I didn't bargain for this, Edgar. Sitting around in a burned-out ruin. Don't worry though, I'll be back next spring, and then we'll march on London.'

'Why not now?' Waltheof said.

'It's too late in the year to go tramping all that way. If we get held up somewhere, we'll be worse off than here.'

'What about going to Lincoln?' Waltheof said.

'I've come far enough south, and there's nothing here. What if everywhere else gets burned down? No, Scotland is where I'm bound,' Malcolm said.

'But what if William comes here?' Edgar said.

'Don't worry about him. Just keep the gates closed, and he'll never prize you out,' the Scottish king said. 'Besides, you've got the Danes to help you. You'll have no use for my men and me. We'll only get in your way. And anyway, I have business at home to attend to.'

Edgar knew full well what business it was Malcolm alluded to, and the thought of him alone with his sister, while he hung on in York had no appeal for him.

'We'll see you next spring,' was all Edgar said.

Osbjorn, who had said nothing, looked alarmed. 'So, we'll have no Scottish army here?'

'No, you won't,' Malcolm said. 'And that's lucky for you because

I very much doubt if York can support itself, an English army, and a Danish army. Let alone a Scottish army as well.'

What Malcolm said was glaringly true and evident to all.

'I can see by your expressions, you all agree. Good luck over the winter, and I look forward to seeing you next spring,' Malcolm said.

With that, farewells were said, and the Scottish army left for home and mischief along the way.

No one said a word, but now all eyes were on Edgar. 'We'll manage perfectly well without our Scottish friends. What we need to do now is to concentrate on rebuilding York and putting up defences along the River Aire.'

After a brief silence, a babble built up in the hall as people made plans and gave orders. Edgar relaxed and looked at Waltheof, who smiled and nodded in response.

For three weeks, the re-building of York continued, and gradually the city became more habitable. Edgar had defences constructed on the River Aire, Humber, and the West Riding. One day, just after dawn, as the city was waking, there was a warning blast on a horn. Waltheof was the first outside into the chilly morning air, stepping out to meet a messenger galloping at full speed towards the great hall. Approaching Waltheof, he stopped his horse, dropping its haunches and sliding across the flagstones, sparks flying from its shoes. He dismounted and gave the earl his message.

'You'd better come with me,' Waltheof said, leading the way to Edgar's quarters.

The breathless messenger followed on behind as Waltheof strode through the main hall to Edgar's door, where he knocked and walked in to find Edgar curled up with a young woman.

'This better be important,' Edgar said.

'It is, my lord, we have a problem, which the messenger will explain.'

'What's your message?' Edgar said.

'The Danes have gone.'

'What? Why would they do that?'

'Perhaps because they discovered King William is only thirty miles from here with an army,' the messenger said.

'How big an army?' Edgar asked.

'Thousands.'

Edgar paled. The tide was turning yet again.

Chapter 36

At Pontefract, twenty-six miles from York, King William was outraged to discover his garrison in the great northern city had been annihilated. Vital, the scout, had brought him the news.

'What? All of them put to the sword?' William demanded to know.

'As far as we can tell,' Vital answered. 'The English murdered the lot of them, everyone; killed and their bodies thrown into the Ouse. They didn't even have a Christian burial.'

The horror of it struck hard. William's valiant, undefeatable army of occupation butchered and fed to the fish, dumped into the river with the rubbish to be swept away and forgotten.

'This is appalling,' William raged. 'The English are nothing but barbarians. Savages. Murdering scum. They'll pay for this. I'll take revenge for every man I lost. The rebels will rue the day they did this.'

Word of the terrible fate that had befallen their comrades soon spread around the Norman camp. Every man amongst William's troops was eager to spill English blood. In no time, William and his men were marching through the winter sleet to York, seeking vengeance. Three days later, on the city's outskirts, William waited with his brother, Robert of Mortain, for scouts to return to the camp. They were chatting by the warmth of an open fire when Vital appeared.

'It's as you thought. The Danes have gone, but the English are still there. The entire town's burned to the ground,' Vital said.

'And the Scots?' William asked.

'It looks as though they're going back to Scotland.'

'I understand the rebels are two thousand strong,' William said.

'About that, my lord.'

'Tonight, we'll stay here. Tomorrow we go to York.'

The next day, William's army prepared itself for the attack. There was fire in the heart of every one of William's soldiers. They wanted revenge for the killing of their comrades and craved Englishmen's blood. It was as though their hatred, bloodlust and steel resolve went ahead of them and found its way into York. In the great hall, there was uproar. Upon the dais, Edgar called for order.

'One at a time.' he bawled out to the men gathered there.

'How can we hold them off without the Danes and the Scots?' an elderly man called out to a roar of approval.

'We'll keep the gates closed and post a guard,' Edgar said.

'And how long do you think we'll last?' the same man asked. 'There aren't any buildings fit to live in, and we have our food sent in from outside.'

'Don't worry, we can hold them off forever,' Edgar said.

'That's what Malet said, and look what happened to him,' a man in the crowd yelled. 'I doubt King William will be as merciful to us. You can stay, my lord. But I'm off.'

Someone else called out, 'We're not scared of a fight, we think we can win, but there's no hope for any of us who stay here,' before making his way to the door.

'Wait,' Edgar shouted.

Even as he spoke, men on horseback were galloping towards the gates.

As his army evaporated before his eyes, Edgar was at a loss as to what to do.

'We need to leave now,' Waltheof said.

'What are we going to do with the hostages?' Gospatric said.

'He's right,' Merleswein said. 'Perhaps we could use them to bargain with.'

'We need to send someone to take a message to William,' Gospatric said. 'To see if we can persuade him to spare the townsfolk in exchange for us freeing Malet and the others.'

'It's a good idea,' Edgar agreed. 'But who's going to do it?'

'I'll do it,' Whitgar said. 'I don't think he'd harm a messenger.'

'Very well,' Edgar said. 'May God go with you.'

'I'll see you here later,' Whitgar said.

Every building in the hulk of a town was in a state of ruin. The rebels had repaired the fire damage, but the stables were far from complete.

Whitgar had tied his horse to a glorified set of hitching rails with a roof made up of old scorched wooden shingles. As he saddled Liegitu, he heard footsteps from behind approaching. He turned to see who it could be.

'Don't go, Whitgar,' Elfwyn said, wrapping her arms around him.

'I must,' he said, returning her embrace.

'Why you?'

'Somebody has to.'

'Then I'm coming with you.'

'No. No, you're not.'

'Don't tell me what to do,' Elfwyn snapped, brushing his arms off her.

'That's not what I meant. It's just best if I go alone.'

'Why?'

'There's no point in two of us going,' Whitgar said.

'No point in both of us getting killed, you mean.'

'No. Not at all. William might be a bastard, but he doesn't kill messengers. They're about the only ones who are safe. Stay with the others until I return. I won't be long,' he said, taking her in his arms again.

They embraced and kissed before Whitgar climbed into the saddle.

'I'll be here waiting for you,' she said and watched as he rode off toward the Norman camp.

As William and his army approached the city gates, he could hear the panicking inhabitants, even half a mile away.

'Oh, they know I'm coming,' William said, amused. 'Presumably, they'll meet us with their usual fire. In which case, we'll be tasting the finest that York has to offer well before sunset.'

William's brother Robert smiled, 'You say that with such confidence, Will.'

'Mark my words; this will be an easy victory.'

'We'll soon see,' Robert said. 'That looks like a messenger heading this way.'

From the direction of the city, a rider was approaching with caution. He stopped before William and introduced himself.

'My lord, I am Whitgar Guthrumson. I have a message from the Atheling.'

'What is it?'

'My lord, Edgar wants you to know no harm will come to the castellans, Sir William Malet and his family and Sir Gilbert de Ghent if you guarantee the safety of the people of York.'

William was relieved to discover the English had not killed all of his men, but he was not in the mood to bargain.

'Why would I do that?' he asked.

'So that the hostages come to no harm.'

'Tell Edgar I'll pay no ransom, and if he hasn't opened the city for me in an hour, I'll take it by storm.'

'But...'

'You'd better be on your way.'

Whitgar made a swift journey back to York and, entering through the gates, found Edgar standing with his courtiers in the street. They had the furtive look of men with an eye for an escape. Whitgar relayed William's reply to Edgar.

'He says he'll not pay a ransom for the hostages, and he'll not make any other agreements.'

Edgar turned to see. Already the defenders were dwindling, slipping away when they thought no one was looking. He surveyed the scene. Attempts to rebuild had little effect, and there were few supplies. York was in ruins, a damaged empty vessel.

'We'll leave the hostages and put as much distance between William and ourselves as possible,' Edgar said.

'Where will we go?' Waltheof asked.

'My farm is only half a day's ride away. We can go there,' Whitgar said. 'At least for the time being.'

'Very well. Return the hostages to William and have them deliver this message; tell him they are unharmed and in return, we expect free passage,' Edgar said.

'Bondi, collect them for me and bring them over to Saint Peter's?'

'Of course,' Bondi said, setting off for Malet's castle to get the castellans and their families. As he passed Whitgar, he asked him to fetch his axe and a whetstone and meet him at the minster.

It took Bondi just a few minutes to reach the castle, and he entered

Malet's quarters to find the two families waiting apprehensively.

'This must be your lucky day,' he said. 'Edgar Atheling wants to see you.'

The families exchanged anxious glances.

'Jump to it,' Bondi ordered.

The hostages got warily to their feet and stepped outside into the dreary grey day.

'Down the steps,' Bondi said, prodding Malet in the back with his sword.

The hostages made their way out of the timber castle and through the charred streets, which still smelled of burned wood.

'Head for the minster,' Bondi said, and they did as instructed. After a few minutes, they arrived in a square surrounded by the charcoal remains of timber homes and the stone skeleton of Saint Peter's. Malet saw Rebels gathered around and people heading for the city gates. His heart skipped a beat when he saw a menacing looking man staring at them. He held a two-handed axe in one hand and a whetstone in the other. Fear struck the hostages as they realised Bondi and the man with the axe knew one another.

'Form a line,' Bondi ordered his captives.

Reluctantly, they obeyed.

'Whitgar,' Bondi said to his friend, holding out his hand expectantly.

Whitgar handed Bondi his axe and his whetstone.

'Right, you lot, on your knees,' Bondi said to the hostages.

'No, surely not,' Malet protested.

'You heard,' Bondi said, looking menacing.

'And the children?' Lady Malet said.

'Them too.'

'This is outrageous,' Malet said.

'Have you seen the state of this once fine city?' Bondi said. 'And you have the nerve to say what I intend to do is outrageous. Have you given a thought to the dead you and your friends leave in your wake? I saw what you did in Ninfield and other places. Then there's your treachery. You called yourself a friend of our king, and then you helped bring him down. Shut your mouth and get on your knees.'

The children were now in tears; even young Robert Malet, who was a brave little boy, was blabbing.

Bondi nodded to a group of soldiers who came over and menaced the prisoners with their spears. The men did their best to calm their women, and the women tried to ease the suffering of their children. The hostages sank to their knees.

Bondi began sharpening his axe with a whetstone. His eyes met Malet's, and he grinned.

'You're a barbarian,' Malet said. 'A savage, and nothing more.'

Edgar Atheling appeared before Bondi could reply and asked, 'What's going on here?'

'Why does everybody think the worst of me?' Bondi asked Malet.

'What are they doing on their knees?' Edgar said, eyeing Bondi's axe.

'Showing contrition,' Bondi said, a wicked glint in his eyes.

'Then why are you making a show of sharpening your axe?' Edgar said.

'I'm just sharpening it, that's all,' he said, looking as innocent as a baby.

'I'm pleased to hear it, Bondi.'

Bondi turned to the hostages. 'You thought I'd do it, didn't you, Malet? Is that because in my place, it's what you'd do?'

There was a moment's silence.

'I think we both know the answer to that question, don't we?'

'Stay here. Don't move. Pray to God for forgiveness,' Bondi said. 'And when that bastard king of yours turns up, tell him you're unharmed in exchange for safe passage.'

'I will,' Malet said.

Gilbert de Ghent scowled.

Bondi left them to re-join his friends and began the journey north with the rest of the army. As he walked away, he gave Lady Malet a mischievous smile and a wink. She looked back at him with an icy stare. Bondi returned a grin.

Chapter 37

With the rebel leaders already outside the city gates and heading to the country, William met brief resistance when entering York. Those rebels who had stayed behind, thinking they had free passage, were unprepared for the onslaught. William ordered them all killed.

William brought his horse to a halt outside of the great hall and studied the city's ruins all around him.

'We'll stay here tonight,' William said to his brother and then noticed the hopeless expression on his face.

Robert said nothing.

'The men will have to make do with what accommodation they can find. I'll stay in Malet's Castle. The English made much headway rebuilding. Tomorrow we continue the work, and I'll send for my crown.'

'Your crown, Will?' Robert said, looking startled.

'Yes, my crown. We'll celebrate Christmas and my third anniversary as king. We'll show them who they're dealing with. Now, where are the hostages the English captured?'

'They're on their way, now,' Robert said, nodding toward the ruins of the minster. The two families were making their way on foot towards their king.

William watched as the shamefaced group approached. When they arrived, they bowed before him.

'Come to my quarters, Sir William. You can tell me everything. The rest of you can go with Sir Gilbert to the other castle.'

King William, on his horse, made his way to the castle north of the River with Sir William Malet by his side, feeling foolish on foot. Once in his old quarters, Malet was surprised by the king's mood.

'What happened?' William asked Malet.

'The English turned up, and I thought I'd be able to deal with them, but then the Danes arrived, and the Scots, too. I knew we'd never hold the city, but we could defend the castles. I feared they might demolish the surrounding houses and use the debris to block the moat, so I ordered them burned down. All went well at first, then the wind got up, changed direction, and you can see the result,' Malet said.

'Bad luck, old friend. Let's find somewhere a little quieter for you. How does East Anglia sound?'

'It would be an honour,' my lord, Malet said, feeling relieved.

'Good. That's settled then. Now perhaps you'd like to join your family.'

'Thank you,' said Malet as he left, astounded he had got off so lightly. He had half expected a public flogging.

After Malet left, William called a guard and asked him to fetch his brother, Robert, over. A short while later, Robert arrived, looking flustered.

'You asked to see me, Will,' Robert said.

'Yes. Are you all right?'

'The men were disappointed when they arrived at this ruin. If they'd done battle, they would have suffered casualties, but there'd be food and shelter at the end of it all. But here, what is there? They feel there's nothing for them either now or in the future except disappointment.'

'Very well. We'll stay here tonight and start rebuilding the city first thing in the morning. Once we've got this place sorted out, we'll sort out the English.

'You have a question, Robert?'

'How are we going to survive here until Christmas?' Robert looked genuinely concerned.

'Tomorrow, we're going on a hunting expedition,' William said with a wicked smile.

Robert looked perplexed.

'Don't worry, Robert. We'll keep ourselves and the garrison fed. It'll be the English and their Danish friends who'll go hungry.'

'Do you really think so, Will? The winter is ahead of us. A few years ago, we arrived with eight thousand men. We lost half at Hastings, and although it was a substantial loss, I assumed the fighting over. I imagined after your coronation that would be the end, but now the English keep on rebelling.'

'The south is ours. Our hold is firm there.'

'Only in the south-east. The southwest is up in arms, as is a vast swathe of Mercia. Trouble keeps flaring up like forest fires. Something goes up here, it's dealt with, and that appears to be the end of it. Then the next thing you know, whoosh; trouble flares up somewhere else,' Robert said.

'Yes, but these little fires are soon extinguished, and once put out, they stay out.'

'Do they?'

'They do if you smother them with castles,' William said, his eyes a twinkle. 'How long will it take, Robert, until the fire's gone out of the English altogether? We don't have forever. We lost four thousand at Hastings. Seven-hundred and fifty at Durham. And now another three hundred in York. They've killed almost the same number of men as I had when we first arrived. I know more men join us from Normandy, Britany, Flanders, Anjou, and beyond. But my fear is Robert, if the men under my command keep dying at this rate, who's going to want to come and join me. The Pope isn't offering absolution to new arrivals, and if they think they've got more chance of getting killed than winning land, men might look elsewhere for rewards.'

'And there are those who are losing heart and returning home to Normandy,' Robert said.

'Not that many, though.'

Robert thought how best to put it. 'You know morale is low, Will. Like you, many imagined this would be a brief campaign, one that at most would last just a few months, and there would be rewards aplenty.'

'They've had their rewards,' snapped William.

'Yes, but no time to enjoy them, and what's more, many haven't seen their families in a while and those who have, only briefly. There are many more who are longing for home.'

'What do you suggest, Robert? What do you suggest?'

'You must deal the opposition a fatal blow. Crush them once and for all.'

'My thoughts entirely.'

'Rid ourselves of the leaders of the resistance, and their followers will go home to a comfortable life.'

'I've considered that too, but we need to go further. We must wipe out all resistance and teach the English a lesson they'll remember for generations, for all eternity. Instil fear into them so deep they will never again dare challenge my rule.'

'What about the Danes, Will? They must be dealt with, too.'

'Always assuming they haven't gone home. See if you can find them. Send out scouts and when you find out where they are, arrange a meeting.'

Robert gave his brother a quizzical look.

'They came here looking for treasure, Robert.'

'Treasure or the crown?'

'You might be right. But now they've discovered getting their hands on the crown isn't going to be as easy as they imagined. They might be happy with a few baubles.'

'For a while, perhaps.'

We only need a while. If we can keep them out of the way while we deal with the English, they'll be isolated and much easier to handle.'

The following day, Count Robert led his men out along the south bank of the Humber, and he found the Danes on Axholm Island, where he arranged a meeting between Osbjorn and William. It took a considerable amount of work on Robert's part as each party was suspicious of the other. Still, eventually, Osbjorn and William met in boats on the water separating the Isle of Axholm from the mainland. Dark low cloud hung low, and the day was cold and grey. A chilly breeze rustled the reeds, and a croak of waterfowl pierced the air. William's boat drew alongside the Danes.

'Prince Osbjorn, at last, we meet,' William said.

'Greetings, King William,' Osbjorn said, with a slight nod of his head.

'It seems we have a problem to solve.'

'Indeed,' Osbjorn said, waiting for William to make his move.

'I understand you've gone to a lot of trouble to come to the aid of your brother's friends, and until now, you've been successful. But isn't it time to cut your losses?'

'Cut my losses?' asked Osbjorn, puzzled.

'Yes. York is in ruins, so you can't spend the winter there. You can't go North; there's nothing there. The south is blocked, but to the east lies Denmark and home.'

'Most of what you say is true, but I'm afraid travelling east is out of the question.'

'Why's that?' said William, a little irritated.

'Winter storms. It's too dangerous now to cross the North Sea until spring.'

'So, like it or not, you'll spend the winter in England?'

'We have no choice,' Osbjorn said.

'But you'll have a choice when the spring comes.'

'We will,' Osbjorn answered.

'So, when spring arrives, you'll go home?' William said.

'That would depend, my lord.'

'On what, Prince Osbjorn?'

'Imagine, if I returned to Denmark empty-handed, what would my brother say?'

'Ah, I see your difficulty. Perhaps I can help. After all, aren't we kinsmen?'

'You mean, aren't we all Northmen?'

'Yes. Kin, if you like,' William said.

'In that case, I have kin in York too.'

William thought hard on this reply.

'Let me make you a proposition, Prince Osbjorn. Spending the winter in the marshes of East Anglia might be much easier if you had the freedom to hunt whatever and wherever you like, south of the Humber and north of the Orwell. With whatever the English can provide you, you and your men should survive the winter in comfort. When spring arrives, you shall be able to return to your homeland with treasure, which I will provide for you, therefore avoiding any embarrassment on your return.'

'That's generous of you, King William, but what do you expect from me in return?'

'Nothing.'

'Nothing? Surely, you must want something?'

'Nothing. I simply require that you spend the winter quietly and go home once the spring arrives. No more. No less, William said.'

'And what do I tell Edgar?' Osbjorn asked.

'Oh, don't worry about him. He won't be in any position to do anything for you when spring arrives.'

Osbjorn studied William. With York burned to the ground, he thought the English would retreat to the north to survive the winter. William would take York, and they would be back where they started. Anyway, he could always come back at another time, perhaps with more men and a better plan.

'I can accept your kind offer once we've sorted out the details.'

'Good. You won't regret it, Prince Osbjorn.'

Chapter 38

Whitgar arrived with his companions to find his farm repaired and functioning. Waiting to greet them outside the great hall were Gymi and his family.

'Welcome home,' Gymi said, pleased to see Whitgar again.

'It's good to be here, Gymi.'

'You've taken good care of everything while I've been away, Gymi.'

'Thank you. We did what we could. It's not as it was, but serviceable.'

Whitgar noticed the new roofs on the buildings, new timbers here and there, repairs to fences and the well moved.

'The place may not look as magnificent as it once did, but at least the barns are full, and we've replaced most of the livestock. '

'You've done a marvellous job, Gymi.'

'Thank you, my lord.'

'Show our guests inside and prepare a meal.'

'Yes, my lord,' Gymi said and indicated the entrance in a flurry of self-importance.

Whitgar led his guests inside and was pleased to see the hall, almost as he remembered it. The thatch was new, so the roof was an improvement. The oak beams were original, cleaned up, but still charred. Most of the floor was new.

'You've done a good job in here, too, Gymi.'

'I'll organise refreshments for you and your guests,' Gymi said.

'Thank you.'

The guests settled into places around the hall. Edgar had pride of place at the head of the dais with Whitgar by his side.

'Tonight, we feast,' Whitgar said.

'What is there to celebrate?' Edgar asked.

'We're alive, and we can fight another day. Reorganise. Make a plan.'

'For pity's sake, man. We've just lost York, or had you forgotten?' Edgar snapped.

'We'll have to get it back again,' Waltheof said. 'What can they do with it? The place is just a shell. It will be as difficult for them to maintain as it would have been for us. Perhaps this is a blessing in disguise. Let them make the repairs, and then we'll take it back. There's no food for them, so they might just leave and go back to London.'

'That's a good point,' Gospatric said.

'I can't see that happening now,' said Edgar with a sigh.

It was at this moment Morwenna began a coughing fit. 'Excuse me,' she said. 'I've not been feeling too well.' She stood up and made her way to the door. 'I'll just get some fresh air.'

Elfwyn left to join her outside and found her huddled up in her cloak, shivering.

'You don't look well, Morwenna. Are you sure you're all right?'

'I'm fine,' Morwenna said. 'Just a cold. I need time away from the men. They'll talk endlessly about the Scots and the Danes, but it won't solve our problem now. I just want to see Sherilda and the children again.'

'You will. We'll be back in Scotland deciding on a summer campaign in a few weeks.'

'It's cold out here. Let's bet back inside by the fire,' Elfwyn said.

Once back inside, it was as Morwenna had said; the men were talking about their allies.

'You might think that the Bastard won't be going back to London, but you can't know it. We need to find the Danes and work something out with them,' Waltheof said.

'The Danes. The bloody Danes,' Edgar snapped. 'You can't trust them as far as you can throw them. Where are they now? Who knows? They were supposed to stay and fight with us. As soon as William and his friends turned up, they disappeared.'

Gospatric said, 'Perhaps Waltheof's right. It can't do any harm to talk to them.'

'Who's going to find them, even if they're still in the kingdom?' Edgar said.

'I know the country around here best,' Whitgar said.

'Then I suggest you look for them,' Edgar replied. 'See if you can find them and ask what they intend to do. While you're away, we'll make plans for any eventuality.'

'That's settled,' said Whitgar. 'Now it's time to eat.'

That evening, the party went to bed warm, dry, well-fed and sheltered from the elements. Many other soldiers in the English army were not so fortunate. Edgar's troops were scattered to the winds making their way northward with FitzOsbern's forces nipping at their heels all the way.

In the early morning mist, Whitgar left to find the Danes at the coast. He disappeared into the grey like a phantom, while in the hall, the others made plans. As they discussed their options, in an idle moment, Bondi glanced out of the window and what he saw shocked him. Heading straight towards them came thirty horsemen.

'Normans!' Bondi yelled. 'They're coming up the valley.'

'How many?' Edgar asked.

'More than we can cope with,' Bondi answered.

There was mayhem as everyone ran from the hall to the stables and saddled their horses. In moments, they were ready to go. As each one was ready, its rider mounted and made off, but with no time to grab supplies. FitzOsbern and his men were only half a mile away when Edgar galloped out of the stable, Waltheof and Gospatric right behind him, with Merleswein, his daughters, and then Bondi. The Normans were bearing down on them fast.

'Split up,' Edgar commanded, but no one obeyed. When they galloped through the gates, they turned north for the moors.

Taking charge, Waltheof bellowed, 'We'd best separate. Bondi, take the ladies and head west, then turn for Durham.'

'I'll go with them, Merleswein replied.'

'No. Edgar will need you.'

Edgar, Waltheof, Merleswein, Gospatric and the others continued northward. It filled Merleswein with reluctance to leave his girls.

'Don't worry, I'll take care of them,' Bondi yelled. 'Follow me,' Bondi bawled to Morwenna and Elfwyn.

They rode their horses at full gallop while crossing the moors.

Looking back, they could see the Normans split into two groups—a smaller group of ten following them. Thirty followed Edgar's party.

They were a mile from Whitgar's farm when Elfwyn's horse stumbled, and she fell, winding herself as she landed. Struggling to breathe, she saw her horse galloping after Bondi and Morwenna. She would ride nowhere, but she had to get away. The group of Norman horsemen were closing on her fast. *Did they see me fall?* she wondered.

Soaking wet and bruised, she crawled as fast as she was able through the sodden clumps of grass and heard a babbling stream. It was the only place she could find any cover. She lay motionless, listening for the Normans; the sound of thundering hooves grew louder. They could not be far away now. She crawled forward and made her way to where the beck had cut deep and jagged into the land, a place offering concealment. She felt safe; although her heart was pounding so hard, she feared it might burst. If the soldiers were looking for her, they would be upon her at any moment.

She looked around and discovered the gully at this point was eight feet deep and had lots of bushes, brambles and rocks amongst which to hide. The thundering hooves were much closer now and even slowing as if coming to a halt. *They're coming for me,* she thought. She fingered the algiz that hung around her neck. Her heart was pounding so much now she thought they would hear it. It was then she noticed, a few feet away in the side of the deep gully, what appeared to be a small cave, an alcove really, just above the level of the beck. It could serve as a hiding place. Elfwyn squeezed herself in just as she heard the horse above her. She listened to a few men's voices speaking French and then, for a few moments, silence. She became motionless, trying to stay silent, afraid they might hear her breathing. She stared into the water below, hoping she might see a reflection to let her know what was going on just above her head, but the stream flowed too fast for that; she had the unnerving feeling someone was watching her. She started when she saw there amongst the rocks, smooth and grey and speckled with lichen, looking just like the stones surrounding it, was a skull, its eyeless sockets staring at her. The dark eye sockets seemed to fix on her, unseeing yet all-comprehending and the manic grin, the merciless blank stare that saw everything but spoke of nothing, silent while the brook babbled senselessly. The skull lay staring with blind, frosty eyes straight back at her.

A horse neighing focused her attention on events above her head.

The Normans are still there, she thought. She heard something that sounded as though it might be an order, and she breathed a sigh of relief when the horses galloped away.

Elfwyn waited until sunset, when cold, wet, and tired, she ventured out of the gulley.

Where do I go? she asked herself. She did not know how to get to Durham, and the Normans were chasing after Edgar.

Lincoln, I'll head back to Lincoln, where I have friends who'll shelter me. Perhaps I'll run into Whitgar on the way.

Heading south, she began her walk to Lincoln, home and safety.

Further up the valley, as Bondi and Morwenna galloped towards the safety of the moors, Morwenna, in the corner of her eye, noticed Elfwyn's horse coming up alongside her. She turned to greet her sister, but she was nowhere in sight.

'Bondi,' she cried before coughing hard.

Bondi's heart sank. He looked round to see Elfwyn's horse alongside them, but no rider. A quarter of a mile away, a group of Norman horsemen pursued them. Even at that distance, he could see murder in their eyes. If they captured them, a grizzly fate would be in store for them.

'We can't stop!' he yelled.

These were the words Morwenna did not want to hear. She glanced behind her, saw the riders in pursuit, and felt fear run through her veins. But then slight relief; Elfwyn was nowhere in sight, and her pursuers appeared unaware of her. She knew they had to ride on. They were in no position to help. It was all they could do to hang on, let alone go looking for Elfwyn. Perhaps the Normans neither knew nor cared about what had happened to Elfwyn. They were heading straight for her and Bondi.

Morwenna kicked her horse on, and with tears in her eyes, prayed for her sister while they rode westwards, clinging to their mounts for dear life. With no equipment or supplies to weigh them down, they left behind their pursuers. After half an hour, they came to a river and halted.

'Which way now, Bondi?' Morwenna said.

'We'd best ride up the valley and into the hills. If the Normans are still following us, they'll back off. They'll keep out of the hills, and they won't want to be out after dark in a hostile country.'

Morwenna would rather not be there after dark, either, but it seemed better than an encounter with their pursuers.

Riding on the riverbank heading upstream, Morwenna asked, 'Did you see what happened to Elfwyn?'

'No. I had no idea she might be in trouble until her horse came alongside us,' Bondi said.

'Do you think she'll be alright?' It was a stupid question, she knew, but she needed reassurance. She also felt unwell. A little feverish and a constant cough made matters worse.

'If she's got any sense, she'll go somewhere where she knows people. Lincoln is my best guess.'

'What river is this?' she asked, changing the subject.

'I don't know. But if we travel up it far enough, we're bound to come across a farm or village.'

Bondi was right. They had travelled for only a couple of hours when Morwenna spotted the silhouettes of buildings in the distance. It was just as well; rain teemed down, and her horse was going lame.

'Look, what's that over there?' she said.

'It could be a farm. Let's see,' Bondi replied.

'I'm going to dismount. My horse is lame.'

Bondi dismounted too and walked by her side, both shivering in the chilly evening.

'I can't see any lights or any sign of life,' Bondi said.

'Neither can I,' Morwenna said before coughing again.

Bondi took hold of Morwenna's horse and led it to the stable with his own. He emerged from the building with a torch and, crossing the rain lashed yard, opened the door to the hall, which he discovered was a paltry affair, thirty feet by fifteen. Bondi walked over to the hearth and held his hand out.

'You can still feel the heat from the fire,' he said.

'Whoever lived here must have left in a hurry.'

'That's what I thought,' said Bondi.

'I wonder if the Normans have been here?' Morwenna said.

'No. Nothing has been destroyed.'

'I'll see if they've left any food behind,' Morwenna said.

'I'll get a fire going. With that cough of yours, you'll need to keep warm. I'll get a good blaze going, and we can at least dry our clothes.'

Sometime later, the two were eating stale bread and cheese beside a warm fire. They chewed on their food while steam rose from their wet clothes; the fire crackled, and rain hammered the building.

'Let's stay here tonight, where we're warm and dry,' Bondi said. 'We'll press on in the morning.'

Morwenna had another coughing fit before she spoke. 'What about Elfwyn? What are we going to do? We can't just leave her.'

'What else can we do?' he said.

'We must do something.'

'Morwenna, I know it's difficult for you, but we don't even know where she is. She must have fallen off her horse when we were making our escape. The Normans weren't interested in her, or they'd have gone after her. She's a resourceful woman, and she'll make her way to somewhere she knows she'll be safe. She'll get word to us, and we'll see her again.'

'That's all right for you to say. She's not your sister.'

'Sister or not, we'd be foolish to look for her with Normans rampaging around the hills and dales,' Bondi said.

Morwenna knew he was right; she just did not want to give up. 'If we...'

'No,' the housecarl interrupted. He thought the chances of finding Elfwyn remote, even if the country had not been swarming with Normans. They did not know where it was, and Bondi became more concerned about Morwenna. She was pale, feverish and her cough worsened by the minute.

Looking downcast, Morwenna got on with eating, staring into space while steam rose from her clothes and the heat of the fire warmed her legs. Still, the coughing persisted and sounded worse than the morning. When she had dried out, she announced she was going to bed.

'I've found a jug of beer,' he said, prising a plug out of the neck.

'Oh, that's wonderful, Bondi. We've nothing to worry about now.'

'Well,' he said with a smile. 'Not until we run out.'

She looked at him in mock disapproval and then laughed.

'We need to rest, Bondi. We have a journey tomorrow.'

Bondi did not know what to say. His head was spinning, and he felt intoxicated by her. When he looked at her, she stared straight back at him. Now their eyes met again. Words deserted him. He stepped forward, but she stepped back.

'Bondi, I need my sleep. I'm feeling unwell.'

'Your cough?' he said,

'I think I have the beginnings of a fever. Of all things, at a time like now.'

'Get into bed, then. I'll put more wood on the fire.'

She curled up in the corner on the bed, shivering, and he placed his cloak over her trembling body. He found a spot by the hearth to sleep.

The next day, they rose to discover the weather had changed for the better. It was a crisp, clear, dry morning, and the sun shone brightly. Neither had slept well because of Morwenna's constant coughing.

'How do you feel?' the Bondi asked.

'Not too bad,' she replied.

Bondi was not so sure. Approaching her, he held out his hand and reached out to touch her head, but she had a coughing fit. When she finished, he felt her brow.

'You're boiling. You have quite a fever, and we ought to stay here until you've recovered.'

'But I'm fine,' she protested.

'No. We don't want you to be out in the open in this weather. A couple of days' rest will do you a world of good.'

'What about the Normans?'

'They won't come this far. Go back to sleep, and I'll get us something to eat.'

Morwenna rested her head on the make do pillow. In moments, she was asleep, and Bondi scoured the farmstead. Eventually, he had enough preserves and flour to last them a few days. After his search, he spent most of his time keeping the fire going, watching out for Norman patrols, and preparing meals for himself. During this time, Morwenna's fever raged until she awoke feeling recovered on the morning of the third day.

'Good morning, my lady.'

'Good morning, Bondi. How long have we been here?'

'Three nights.'

'Good heavens,' Morwenna said, stretching. She attempted to get to her feet, but the fever had drained her strength.

'Stay where you are and have this,' Bondi said, handing her a bowl of broth. 'It'll build up your strength.'

She took a sip from the bowl.

'What's this?'

'I'm not an expert cook,' he said.

'I can see that. What's that you're eating?'

'It's stale bread,' he said, sounding hurt.

'We must leave right away,' she said, to Bondi's surprise.

'Get up and try walking.'

Morwenna rose to her feet. 'There', she said cheerily before grabbing onto a post to steady herself.

'Another day's rest for you, my lady.

'While you've been ill, I gathered up as much wood as I could find. The woodpile was well stocked, so that didn't take long. Food wasn't the problem I thought it would be. When they left, they couldn't take everything with them.

'We'll be safe enough here for another day, at least. The Normans have probably gone north. They'll be chasing Edgar back to Scotland as we speak.'

'Do you think they'll go to Scotland?' she asked.

'If you're worried about the children, don't,' Bondi said. 'I can't imagine William invading Scotland at this time of the year, and besides, King Malcolm would have something to say.'

'And what about Elfwyn?'

'There's nothing we can do now but hope and pray. She's resourceful, and she knows the country. She'll be with Whitgar in your father's hall in Lincoln by now, is my guess.'

'Do you really think so?'

Bondi did not know. 'Yes,' he said. 'I'm certain.'

Morwenna fell in and out of sleep throughout the day, but they spent most of the time chatting when she was awake.

'I don't know why I thought it was a good idea to go to York with the army. I have slipped back into my old ways. That was when I was carefree, when I could do anything, go anywhere, do whatever I liked. Look at me now. I'm losing my fire. Ever since I became a mother, especially after losing Godric, I think I must be there for the children. I've told no one else, Bondi. Not even Elfwyn.

'It's different for you. You spent your life training to be a Housecarl. I'm not a warrior. As much as my father likes to think of me as his shield maiden, I'm a mother and a woman who enjoys life on a farmstead. And it might surprise you to hear this, but I enjoy the pursuits of a lady.'

Bondi looked surprised.

'It's true. I love the life of an English country lady. There's more to me than meets the eye, Bondi.'

'There's more to me than meets the eye, too, Morwenna. I wasn't brought up to be a housecarl but lived in a village by the River Severn in Gloucestershire. What you don't know is that I was a thrall. You're the first person I've ever told, only you know. Although there might be one man who suspects I'm not all I pretend to be.'

'Tell me, Bondi.'

'Everything I've told you is true, where I lived and the raid and the Welsh killing my parents. They drove off everyone in the village who was still alive and looked like they could do a good day's work. All of them were forced into slavery. But I was the lucky one. I escaped. I survived. When Earl Sweyn arrived, he was as mad as hell with the Welsh and happy to see a survivor.'

'What happened then?'

'He asked me who I was, and I told him, but I forgot to mention my family were thralls. I ended up in Bristol, and Earl Harold took me under his wing. I would have worked on a farm or something, but I got into a few scraps, and he thought I might make a good housecarl.'

'Did you forget to tell him you were a thrall as well?' Morwenna asked.

'Yes, I must admit it slipped my mind.'

'Well, you're not a thrall now, are you?' she said.

'I had to escape the drudgery, the humiliation and the hopelessness of it. Can you understand that?' he said.

'Of course. Anyone could. I've never met anyone who longed to be a thrall. But who suspects you of making up your past?' Morwenna asked.

'Earl Sigur. He asked me some awkward questions, but then again, it's been a long time, and details can slip a man's mind.'

'Let's hope so. He'll have his secrets, too, Bondi. Everyone does.'

For a moment, Bondi thought of Whitgar and his hidden shame; how it was he who was responsible for his father's horrific injuries.

'Everyone?' Bondi asked.

'Yes, everyone,' Morwenna said. She then gave out an enormous sigh. 'You know what, Bondi? Suddenly I feel a lot better.'

'I'm glad to hear it.'

Morwenna asked, 'Tell me, Bondi, when you became a housecarl, did you get to know King Harold personally?'

'Yes,' Bondi said, as a matter of pride. 'I could have ended up as a ploughboy or something, but he saw something in me.'

'I've heard stories. The Hero of Stamford Bridge and a place called the Malfosse. You're a legend, you know.'

'So they tell me.'

'Then what is it?'

'What?'

'Something's bothering you. Is it Hastings?'

Bondi said nothing.

'From what I understand, you did what you could. I heard you turned up with five-hundred men and saw off a lot of Norman cavalry.'

'But it was too late.'

'You did what you could, Bondi. You could do no more. And ever since, you've been trying to make amends.'

'You could say that. I'll get more firewood,' he said and left to get wood.

When he returned a short while later with a bundle of firewood in his arms, Morwenna sat on a stool by the hearth. He noticed she had changed the bedclothes.

'Feeling better,' Bondi asked.

'A little,' she said with a smile.

Sparks shot upward as Bondi put more fresh logs on the fire. Soon they were ablaze, flames licking at the bark.

'Bondi,' Morwenna said. 'You've been so kind to me. Taking care of me while I've been ill.'

'It's just what you'd do for someone you love,' he said.

And there it was, out in the open, how he felt about her. The instant the words left his mouth, Bondi wanted to vanish. His face reddened, and he had to avert his gaze away from Morwenna. It truly mortified him. Staring at the floor, he was unaware of her approaching him until she was directly in front of him, her arms held out, ready to embrace him.

'It's all right to love me,' she said as she took him in her arms.

Bondi had longed for this moment for a long time. He held her tight, kissed her neck, smelled her hair and felt her surrender to him enthusiastically. They broke away for a second and looked into each other's eyes, and bridged the gulf between common soldier and lady. Just for an instant, and no more, Morwenna cast a glance toward her newly made bed. Bondi needed no second invitation. He picked her up, walked her over to the bed, and dropped her on it. Even before she had landed, he was undressing, and so was she. They fumbled at their clothes, which they could not remove fast enough. And then, at last, both were naked, and Bondi lay beside her, holding her close, powerful and yet gentle. As his fingers ran over her, knowing their destination and purpose, made her groan with pleasure. Bondi knew precisely what he was doing, how it made her feel and how it thrilled her. It was the most sensual assault she had ever known. Her body had taken over, now relentless in its seeking of pleasure, and she wanted more; she ached for more. She was not disappointed.

Bondi moved his body over hers, and she felt him enter her, slow and rhythmic at first, becoming gradually harder and faster. He couldn't get enough of her, and he wanted to get deep into her. Further and further until there came the point when they felt they were one, luxuriating in warm wet skin. On and on, they went, consuming each other. Bondi moved her legs over his shoulders, penetrating her depths.

'Oh, God. Oh, God,' Morwenna said as immeasurable waves of pleasure surged through her.

In response, Bondi thrust harder, and the feeling became more intense. He felt his heart might burst. Both were giving in to forces that were beyond their control, forces that had been around for millennia. Like the sea, the tide was rising, and no one could stop it. Waves of longing broke over them. Rapture flooded through them.

Morwenna threw back her head and groaned as she was about to come.

'Nearly there,' she moaned. Their excitement mounted harder and harder, faster and faster. He could hardly hold back anymore. She reached her climax, and so did he, feeling spasms of ecstasy tear through their beings to the core. One after another, after another.

Exhausted, they fell back and lay entwined together in the bed, Morwenna's head on Bondi's chest. They held each other in post-coital bliss until Bondi spoke.

'Well,' he said. 'I wasn't expecting that when I bought in the firewood.'

'You'll just have to do it more often,' Morwenna said.

The next day, Bondi and Morwenna woke up after a deep sleep, and neither of them wanted to get up to end what had begun in the night. They made love again, and as they once more lay in each other's arms, the reality of their situation came back to them. As Morwenna felt much better, the two continued their journey to Durham.

'We ought to take whatever we can carry in the way of provisions,' Bondi said, once they had dressed.

Now they were up and about; he no longer felt so masterful as he did when they were together in bed, and he was vaguely aware of having a feeling of not wanting to disappoint her in little ways. He was a housecarl, not a thane or an earl, the equal of any lady in the land. As he gathered provisions in the storeroom, he began giving matters consideration.

How would Merleswein react if he knew? He wondered. *It's one thing to have a dalliance with a willing wench or a maid of easy virtue. It's another to get involved with someone the like of Morwenna.*

As Bondi considered his position, Morwenna came in to inform him the horses were ready.

'You look miles away, Bondi,' she said, smiling warmly.

Bondi was unsure of what to say and just mumbled.

Morwenna took him in her arms and kissed him lightly on the cheek.

'Come on. We need to get a move on.'

They mounted their horses and began making their way up the valley. At first, the journey was uneventful and quite pleasant, considering the frequent downpours. They talked until mid-way through the afternoon when Morwenna said, 'There's something wrong with my horse. He's gone lame.'

'Ride on, and I'll look at him.'

Morwenna did as Bondi said, and after a few paces, he told her to stop.

'It's her left foreleg. You'd better get up behind me.'

She climbed up behind him and held on to him.

'Let's hope we can find someone who can help,' Bondi said. 'We've been riding for a while. Something should turn up.'

They made slow progress with both of them on Bondi's horse and Morwenna's horse on a lead. After an hour and covering only a couple of miles at most, Bondi sniffed the air.

'What is it?' Morwenna asked.

'Someone has a fire burning.'

They continued following the river until they came to where a beck joined it. Here they discovered the source of the wood smoke. In the half-light, they could make out a farmstead on the other side of the river. They forded the river and approached with caution. A door opened, throwing light out in front of the building.

'Good evening,' Bondi called.

'Good evening,' the silhouette in the doorway replied.

'I'm Bondi Wynstanson, one of Earl Waltheof's housecarls.'

'I'm Sigulf Oswicson.' Sigulf looked at the horses and noticed their condition. His eyes flicked over Bondi's scabbard, then onto Morwenna, who he noticed wore fine clothes.

'We can put your lame horse right. You look as though you might have left somewhere in a hurry.'

'We did, Sigulf Oswicson. King William's men drove us off a friend's farm. We had to make a quick getaway.'

Bondi noticed the change of expression on Sigulf's face. The farmer began looking right and left. 'Don't worry, no one followed us here.'

'Thank God.'

'The horses are tired and hungry, and so are we. If we could have something to eat and a bed for the night, then move on in the morning.'

'You'll be here for a couple of days until your lame horse recovers. Let me take them to the stable.'

Two young children emerged from the cottage to see what was happening.

'Stable these horses, will you?' Sigulf said. Then addressing Bondi and Morwenna, 'This way,' he said, leading them into the warmth of his home.

'Cynwise,' he said to a round, warm-hearted looking woman they took to be his wife, 'Meet Bondi Wynstanson. And, I'm sorry, my lady, I didn't catch your name.'

'I'm Lady Morwenna Merlesweinsdaughter.'

The farmer and his wife did not know who she was, but they guessed she must be important.

The farmstead was not much more than a collection of huts. Bondi took the largest of them to be the hall, but it was small with no more room than enough to seat twenty people at the most.

People were gathered around the hearth, talking amiably. Bondi and Morwenna, feeling the warmth of the fire, immediately felt grateful. Pottage was cooking in a pot, and both felt their mouths water.

All eyes turned to Morwenna. It was rare to have a visit from a lady, especially one unknown to them and one so obviously wealthier than anyone ever to have visited them. Most were transfixed. As she made her way to her place, Bondi looked at her, too. It was as she hitched her skirts up to step over a sleeping dog that suddenly her beauty caught his attention. His heart skipped a beat as he remembered the previous night. It seemed unreal now, a dream.

When Morwenna took her place by Bondi, he became acutely aware of her presence, and her fragrance enveloped him. Try as he might, he could not resist the urge to turn and look at her, just to see her. Self-consciousness flooded over him as he realised eyes were shifting from Morwenna and back to him, and he wondered what thoughts were crossing their minds.

As Bondi and Morwenna ate their meal, they told tales to eager listeners of their adventures in York and what was happening in the countryside. They explained how they needed to keep watch in case the Normans ventured out.

'Is it likely they'll come here?' someone called Oslac Hean asked.

'I can't say. They'll probably go back to York for Christmas, then with any luck, leave a small party behind and go back down south,' Bondi said, to everyone's relief.

'But you don't know for certain what they'll do, do you?' Oslac said.

Bondi looked at the man, a miserable-looking fellow in his early forties, with thinning hair and a wrinkled face. Instinctively, he knew, whatever he said, it would never be satisfactory. He was about to say something when Sigulf interjected.

'I've got a question for you,' Sigulf said. 'I bet your horse needs a couple of days to recover.'

'You could say that,' Bondi said, glad to start an easier conversation.

'You can't go much further. Stay for a few days,' Sigulf offered.

'That seems a good idea.'

'Whose food is he going to eat?' Oslac asked.

'Don't worry about that, Oslac. We'll make sure you get your share,' Sigulf said.

'See that you do,' came the reply.

It was then the door opened, and one of the local people entered.

'You'd better hear this,' he said to Sigulf in particular and the room in general.

'Come inside and get warm,' the local said to someone out of view as he ushered a small family into the hall.

The father looked to Sigulf. 'Won't you help us? Frenchies have driven us out of our home,' he said, to a gasp from his audience.

The stranger had Bondi's attention immediately. He was a man of importance in his blue cloak with its delicate, ornate clasp and distinctive red silk trim, which matched that on his tunic. His family was well dressed, and his wife had a fastening on her cloak that matched his.

'Frenchies?' Bondi asked, while in his mind's eye he pictured Sussex villages in 1066 when he had been making his way to Senlac.

'Yes. On horses, and they spoke a strange language I've never heard. They turned up in our village, Ramskirk, and the slaughter began. If it breathed, it died at the hands of these devils. They even killed children,' he said, the anger burning in his eyes. 'Even the animals suffered, either driven away or killed on the spot and burned.'

'Once the killing stopped,' the stranger continued, 'they began destroying everything, and I mean everything. We only escaped because we lived on the edge of the village and hid in a nearby forest. We watched as they burned everything to the ground; houses, barns, carts, pigsties, ploughs, hoes they destroyed could get their hands on.

'After they left, we went back, but nothing remained,' the stranger said. 'We had to leave. There is nothing for us there anymore. Our families have lived there for generations. Even the Vikings weren't as bad as this.'

'Where will you go now?' Morwenna asked.

'We have no idea. We just want to get as far away as possible.'

'Come and get something to eat,' Cynwise said, guiding them into the hall. 'You haven't told us your names yet.'

'I'm so sorry,' the stranger said. 'My name is Alfstan Elwynson, and this is my wife, Elfgyfu and my daughters, Elfreda and Elfryth,' he said, introducing a refined-looking blonde and two pretty girls aged ten and twelve.

'And we also have a son,' he said with delight. Alfstan's wife pulled back her cloak to reveal a baby of six months suckling her breast. There was a unanimous, ah, from those in the hall.

'His name is Alfred. It's so kind of you to offer us shelter. Thank you so much.'

'You're most welcome,' Cynwise said. 'Make yourselves comfortable,' she added with a smile, showing them a place on a bench.

'Are there any more out there?' Oslac asked.

'Anymore what?' Sigulf asked.

'Any more scroungers looking for a free meal,' Oslac said.

Cynwise gave him a cutting look, and Sigulf said, 'Don't worry yourself, Oslac. There's enough to go around. Let's hear from our guests. They'll have something interesting to say, I'm sure.'

Sitting at the hearth, the family munching on bread or shovelling down stew, at Sigulf's invitation, Alfstan gave further details of the family's ordeal. It was a tale of murder, rape, robbery, and destruction.

'Did you see which way they headed after they left your village?' Bondi asked.

'Back to York.'

'To celebrate Christmas. Let's hope they go back to the south afterwards,' Bondi said.

Sigulf looked worried; he wondered if more people would turn up seeking help. Then he asked himself if his village was too far away from York for the Normans to bother themselves. In bed that night, Sigulf and Cynwise discussed their fate.

In the flickering candlelight, Cynwise looked into Sigulf's eyes, 'We'll be all right here, won't we?'

'There's nothing to worry about, Cyn. Ramskirk is a long way off, and they'll never come here. York is even further away, so they won't bother us?'

'Do you think so?' Cynwise asked.

'Yes. I know Alfstan seems a pleasant enough fellow, but you wonder what the people of his village got up to bring the Frenchies down on them like that.'

'That's true enough. And we've only his word for it,' Cynwise said.

'He's probably exaggerating. I don't think we've got any reason to worry, Cyn.'

With that, they kissed goodnight. It took them a while to fall asleep, and when they woke up the following day, there was an atmosphere of dread all around the farmstead.

In the hall, Alfstan and his family were ready to leave. They, too, had had a fitful night's sleep. The little family said their goodbyes to the villagers and Bondi and Morwenna.

'Thank you for your kindness, all of you,' Alfstan said. 'We're going to head north, hoping to find shelter. We shall throw ourselves on the Christian generosity of the church.'

The whole farmstead wished them good luck and wondered if the day would soon come when they would be the ones looking to the church for refuge. But they managed a smile and a wave as they parted company, the father's loping walk making his cloak sway, the early morning sun catching on the silk trim. A silence fell over the group as they watched their visitors leave, and slowly, they parted to get on with their tasks. When Cynwise returned to the hall, she discovered a silver coin on the table in the kitchen. Alfstan's generosity touched her, and she regretted not showing more herself.

Two days later, when Morwenna's horse had rested and the horse doctor had worked on it, it no longer limped. Bondi's horse had recovered well, and it was time for them to leave for Durham. Sigulf and Cynwise were there to say goodbye. Cynwise was wearing her best clothes for the occasion and, in her way, looked quite resplendent in a pale blue woollen ankle-length gown with ornate wrist clasps.

'Have a safe journey, you two,' Sigulf said.

Cynwise smiled and waved goodbye but had a sad look in her eyes.

When Bondi and Morwenna were out of earshot, Cynwise said to Sigulf, 'Do you think we'll be safer now they've gone?'

'Why should we be any safer?'

'You don't think the Frenchies are looking for them?' Cynwise asked.

'Nobody's been around here asking questions, and we've seen no strangers since Alfstan arrived. We'll be all right. Anyway, what could one housecarl do against so many? If you ask me, it was all those lords and ladies that got us into trouble in the first place. If they hadn't kicked up a fuss, I doubt the Frenchies would bother folk.'

'Perhaps you're right. Are you going to post sentries tonight?'

'We've got the geese. They're better than any sentries.' Sigulf said, but he did not think Cynwise looked reassured.

'And if you like, I'll dig a nice hole and hide our valuables in it.'

Cynwise responded with a smile.

Sigulf added. 'If the Frenchies come, we can always take refuge in the church. We're bound to be safe there.'

After Bondi and Morwenna left the farmstead, feelings were mixed amongst those they left behind. Some feared the Normans would turn up at any moment and murder them. Others thought the stories they had heard were just traveller's tales made up to make the teller look impressive. But when darkness fell, there was a lot of activity as people dug holes to hide their valuables. Oslac dug deeper than most. It was a precaution in case the worst happened. He hoped Frenchies would not come his way. And then again, he thought, even if they did, they would probably do no harm.

Bondi and Morwenna climbed out of the valley and up to the sunlit moor. Bringing their horses to a halt, they inspected the countryside for movement. There was nothing to be seen for miles, just rolling hills and scrubland. Feeling safe, they journeyed on and saw no one. It was when darkness fell they grew concerned. They had hoped to find shelter for the night, but on the moors, there seemed to be no habitation of any kind, not even a shepherd's hut.

'What will we do now?' Morwenna said, deferring to Bondi.

'Keep going. There must be something somewhere.'

The sun set over bleak moorland hills, and Bondi and Morwenna scanned the horizon. There was no sign of life, but they could just make out in the failing light, in a fold in the moors, a cluster of buildings.

'It's quiet there, Bondi.'

Bondi agreed. He could see no movement.

'Keep your eyes peeled,' he said as they grew closer.

Nothing moved, nothing stirred, not a sound as the two approached, except for the wailing of the wind. Cautiously, they made their way along the track that led to the village, and other than the lack of signs of life, nothing seemed unusual. The first sign of a Norman visit was a body they discovered sprawled across the track. And then there were more scattered here and there, alone and in groups.

Now that they were close, they could pick out the charred remains of buildings. Black silhouettes against the pale blue winter sky were all that remained of what so recently had been a thriving village.

'They have burned down the buildings, Bondi. And I can't see any animals,' Morwenna said.

Everywhere was silent. Not even a dog barked. Two more bodies lay on the ground by the entrance to the hall.

Bondi went to the well and pulled on the rope. When the bucket appeared, he dipped his finger in and tasted the water, before quickly spitting it out.

'This well's ruined. The water's undrinkable,' he said.

'I think we're all right for tonight,' Morwenna said. 'Finding somewhere to sleep is our problem for now.'

'What about that church?' Bondi said, nodding towards the black outline of a large stone building.

'Let's take a closer look,' Morwenna said.

The two approached the church cautiously but could not hear a sound. Dismounting, Bondi drew his sword and entered to find a priest staring at him in terror. The priest fell to his knees, clasping his hands together.

'For the love of God, please spare me,' he begged.

'Don't worry, father, I'm English.'

'Oh, thank the Lord,' the priest said, getting to his feet. 'It was the king himself who did this,' he added, between sobs.

'Do you think they'll come back?' Bondi asked.

'No. They rode off in a hurry. They had more of the devil's work to do while there was still daylight.'

'Morwenna, it's safe. You can come in,' Bondi called out. The turning to the priest asked, 'Where are we?'

'You're in Lastingham, and I am Father Raedwald. I don't know why they didn't destroy the church. They razed everything else to the ground.'

'When were they here?' Bondi asked.

'They came early this morning, killing and burning. It was unspeakable. My flock came to me for protection, but it did them no good. The Normans dragged them outside and murdered them.

I pleaded with them to have mercy, but they showed none, not even to the children.'

Bondi only nodded in response; he could find nothing to say regarding the massacre. So instead, he said, 'I'll start a fire. It's almost dark, and there's not much we can do now. Do you have anything to eat?'

'I'll get you something,' Raedwald said.

Bondi soon had a fire burning in the church while Morwenna shivered under the priest's blankets. They sat down to eat bread and cheese while they stared into the flames produced by the remnants of people's homes burning before them. Bondi and Morwenna remained silent while Father Raedwald rambled on about the church's history, the abbey, Danish raids, and so forth. When they had finished eating, they turned in for the night, sleeping close to the fire, glad to get away from his incessant chatter.

After a fitful night's sleep, Bondi and Morwenna left first thing in the morning.

'Won't you help me bury the dead?' Father Raedwald asked them when they told him they were leaving.

'We need to make good progress, Father. The sooner we join up with our comrades, the better. We have to get to Durham as soon as we can.'

'Who are your comrades?'

Bondi explained who he and Morwenna were and their part in the uprising.

'Why don't you go to the Tees Valley then?' Father Raedwald asked.

'Why would we go there?'

'Because that's where the Atheling and his men are,' Raedwald replied as if stating the obvious.

'Why didn't you tell us this before?' said Bondi.

'You didn't ask.'

Bondi rolled his eyes in frustration, but Morwenna was calm. 'Thank you, Father Raedwald,' she said. 'That's so useful. Tell me, do you know whereabouts in the Tees Valley we might find them?'

'As far as I could gather, they'll be near the coast somewhere.'

'How do you know this?' Bondi asked.

'Because some of Edgar's men were here, and they talked about it. They left the stores there.'

'I know the place. Thank you, Father Raedwald,' Bondi said. 'With any luck, we'll be there this evening.'

Despite the inclement weather their spirits raised, Bondi and Morwenna made off in the direction of the mouth of the River Tees, feeling happier than they had for a week. Climbing up onto the moors, the full force of the wind hit them. Dark, angry clouds scudded across the sky from the east, promising rain or worse. The two were even more eager to move on and re-join their friends and comrades. Onward they pushed the horses, but soon enough, the clouds caught up with them and unleashed a torrent of hailstones on them, lashing their faces and stinging any exposed skin. They could barely keep open their eyes. They had covered a good five miles when they spotted horsemen in the distance. Peering through the raging wind and hail, they found it difficult to make out who they were, but they looked like soldiers. Even in the atrocious conditions, there was something in the way they rode that gave them away as Normans.

'I wonder what they want?' Bondi bellowed above the wind. But whoever the riders were, they had no interest in the couple on a distant ridge. They were heading for York, shelter, a warm fire and a hot meal. Nothing would distract them.

For the rest of the day, Bondi and Morwenna made the arduous journey across moors and then to the marginally more sheltered lowlands. By evening, they were approaching the place on the banks of the Tees where they hoped their friends would be. They were on a peninsular that thrust out into the North Sea like a sword. The land here was uninviting, a windswept scrappy looking place, a scrubland littered with bogs. Peering through the greyness, the two could see no signs of life. And then, through the hail, four armed riders emerged. Bondi and Morwenna hoped they were Edgar's men and not just local outlaws.

'Who are you, and what are you doing here?' asked one man. He was about thirty, portly, and pompous.

'I am Bondi Wynstanson, and this is Morwenna Merlesweins daughter. We're looking for the Atheling.'

'I thought I recognised you. You've come to the right place. One of my men will take you to his camp.'

Bondi and Morwenna followed the man through the bog infested scrubland until they came upon Edgar's encampment, which comprised a hastily constructed hall, a glorified cabin, a few outbuildings and lots of tents. Bondi's heart sank. No one seemed happy to be there. A disturbance broke out as Merleswein appeared from the hall and ran to greet his daughter.

'Morwenna, you're safe,' he said. As she dismounted, her father grabbed her in a bear hug and spun her around as he laughed heartily and kissed her repeatedly.

'It's so good to see you, Morwenna. I thought we might have lost you forever.'

'You needn't have worried. Bondi was there to take care of me,' she answered.

Merleswein gave Bondi a suspicious look and a begrudging nod before leading Morwenna to the hall. Edgar, Waltheof, Gospatric and others had gathered at the entrance to see for themselves if it was true Bondi and Morwenna had returned safely.

'Is there any news of Elfwyn, father?'

The smile disappeared from Merleswein's face in an instant. 'I'm afraid we've heard no word of her and nothing from Whitgar either.'

'Oh, no,' Morwenna said. 'I thought she'd be safe in Lincoln by now.'

'She might be safe, but word hasn't got through yet,' Merleswein said.

Gospatric stepped forward, 'But at least you're here now, and that alone is worthy of a celebration,' he said, lifting the mood. 'Come in, and you too, Bondi.'

They entered the warmth of the hall and made for the dais.

'I'm glad you turned up today, Bondi. I'm going north to see King Malcolm in the morning. He and his men are getting up to mischief in Cumbria, so I need to sort them out. Between you and me, nothing will happen here before next summer. You'll be spending Christmas and Easter here, so, if you'd prefer, why not come with me? You don't have to let me know now; take a little time to consider it. You might prefer coming with me to kicking your heels here.'

'I'll think it over,' Bondi said.

On the other side of the hall, Merleswein was breaking news to his daughter.

'Ah, Morwenna, there you are,' Merleswein said.

'Father.'

'You must know why I've sent for you.'

'No, I don't.'

'I'm concerned about your future,' he said.

'I'm concerned about all of our futures, especially Elfwyn's,' Morwenna replied.

'That's why I'm involved in discussions. I don't want you disappearing like Elfwyn. You need someone to take care of you.'

'First, what do you mean by 'involved in discussions,' and second, I don't need anybody to take care of me.'

'I've been discussing your future with Thurold…'

'What's my future got to do with him?' Morwenna interrupted, and then she realised what her father meant. 'Have you been making wedding plans for me?'

'You need a husband.'

'No, I don't.'

'You do. If we can't get rid of William, we'll be landless. You and the children will be in a perilous position,' Merleswein insisted. 'Thurold will take care of you.'

'How do you know? He might lose his land as well. Everyone else has.'

'William doesn't know of his involvement with the rebels, so he's safe,' Merleswein countered.

Morwenna glared at her father, who seemed intent on having his way. As she eyed him, she knew he had made his mind up, and this might well turn out to be a conversation they would both regret.

'What if there's someone else?' she said.

'You think Thurold might be interested in another woman?'

'Don't be ridiculous. For all you know, I have plans of my own, father.'

'So, there's another interested party. Is it that housecarl?' Merleswein asked.

'Why do you say it like that? You know his name, and you know it well.'

'Yes, I know his name. He's a great housecarl, a wonderful housecarl, but that's all he is, just a housecarl.'

'Was he just a housecarl at Stamford Bridge or in York when he saved my life?' Morwenna snapped.

'He was doing his duty. You don't have to marry him for doing that.'

'It's more than that.'

'Jesus Christ. You're not pregnant?'

'No, I'm not,' she said. *At least, I don't think so.*

'Just as well. He can't look after you and the children the way Thurold can. You could have a future with him, a thane of great standing in the county.'

'There might not be a future with William on the throne, at least not for the likes of us.'

'But whatever your future, it has more promise for you with Thurold than with a common soldier,' Merleswein said, frustration showing in his voice.

'That's not fair, father.'

'Very well then, Bondi is a hero. We know that. But the thing is, you need more than a hero. You need security, and Thurold can provide that in a way Bondi can't. It would mean so much to me, Morwenna, to know you were cared for and safe. Thurold cares for you, you know. And he is from quite a good family himself. He's not an earl, but he has an ancestry of which he can be proud.'

'And what if I were miserable in this marriage you're arranging for me? Have you given that any thought?'

Merleswein looked shocked.

'Why would you be miserable?' he asked.

'Because I wouldn't be with Bondi.'

Anger showed on Merleswein's face before he said calmly, 'Couldn't you keep him on as a guard or something?'

'What are you saying?'

'Well, I just thought…'

'I know what you thought, and it's a horrible idea.'

'No. No. You've got the wrong end of the stick.'

'I don't care what you think. I'm not marrying that pig-faced lecher. He makes my skin crawl. You couldn't have found anybody less suitable if you tried,' Morwenna yelled, turned on her heel and stormed off.

Merleswein was taken aback. He had seen her temper a few times over the years but never had he seen her so angry, determined, or defiant as he had that day. He hoped no one had heard their argument.

An hour or two after Morwenna and Merleswein had had their exchange, Bondi sat amongst friends in the hall. Flattered and surprised by the Gospatric's offer, he preferred to stay with Edgar. Still harbouring hope of a future with Morwenna, he considered his options. Looking over to where she was listening intently to something her father had to say, Merleswein was smiling. Her face looked like stone. Bondi recognised a man, a wealthy thane by his look, who at first Bondi could not place, but then it came to him, it was Thurold. Somehow, he must have made his way up from Lincolnshire. Thurold's bulgy eyes shifted gaze from Morwenna to Merleswein and back again, a look of deep concentration on his face. Everyone seemed dissatisfied with the outcome. Although when the conversation ended, Morwenna smiled, she seemed less than pleased with her father and his friend.

Merleswein noticed Bondi's had fixed his attention on his little group.

'Isn't it great news, Bondi?' Merleswein said with a broad grin. 'Morwenna and Thurold are considering marriage.'

'What?'

'She'll have a husband to look after her and take care of her. With Normans roaming the length and breadth of the land, she needs to be safe.'

'I thought she felt safe, despite the Normans,' Bondi said, his face ashen.

'Oh no, she keeps her feelings well hidden,' Merleswein said. 'She needs a man. Thurold is the ideal choice. What's more, he's wealthy enough to support her,' Merleswein said, looking meaningfully at Bondi.

'You don't look pleased, Bondi,' Merleswein added.

'Has she agreed to this proposition?' Bondi asked. He was in shock. Of all the things he had imagined when he re-joined his friends and comrades, this was not one of them.

'Not yet. Not completely. Details to sort out, you know. Thurold's a clever man. He'll win her over.'

'You must be delighted.'

'Oh, I am Bondi. I am,' Merleswein said, a smile of satisfaction on his face. 'You'll attend the wedding, of course?'

'Yes, of course.'

'Good.'

With that, Merleswein went off to break the news to the Atheling and prepare a feast for the announcement. Bondi went looking for Earl Gospatric.

'I've decided I'd like to take you up on your offer and go with you to Cumbria if you don't mind?'

'That's good news, Bondi. It will be good to have you with us,' Gospatric said.

'Thank you.'

'You've heard Thurold's proposed to Morwenna?' Gospatric said.

'Yes.'

'I think Cumbria might hold more interest for you. We might be stuck here for months.'

'I think you're right.'

There was a commotion as a boat sailed onto the beach. A man climbed out and began making his way to the hall. It soon became clear it was Whitgar. Bondi went to meet him.

'Hello Bondi, it's good to see you. Where's Elfwyn?' Whitgar said.

'It's good to see you, too, Whitgar. We don't know where Elfwyn is. We were hoping she might be with you. After you left, a Norman patrol arrived, and she fell from her horse in a hurry to get away. We don't think she's injured, and we're fairly sure the Norman patrol didn't capture her.'

Whitgar stopped in his tracks. 'So, you don't know where she is?'

'No. We're hoping she might have gone to Lincoln. You need to get over to the hall. The Atheling will want to see you,' Bondi said. 'What's happening in York?'

'It's bad news, I'm afraid. After I left you, I made my way to the south of the Humber, and it didn't take long to find the Danes. The locals are treating them like long-lost family. I arranged a meeting with Osbjorn. He's agreed with William for the Danes to go home in the spring, and in return, William leaves them alone.'

'The bastards.'

'That's the arrangement, anyway. I'm not sure if Osbjorn will honour it, though. I had the feeling he was in a tight spot, and, given half a chance, he'd be by our side again. Don't forget it's not his expedition; it's his brother's.'

Arriving at the hall, Bondi said, 'Edgar won't like this.'

'You're right there,' Whitgar said. 'Tell me, Bondi, if I went in search of Elfwyn, would you come with me?'

Before he could answer, Whitgar said, 'Think it over while I talk to Edgar.'

Bondi and Whitgar were correct in thinking Edgar would not like the news. When Whitgar told him, the Atheling looked alarmed.

'Do you think Swein will claim the crown?' Edgar asked the question his friends were thinking.

'Who knows?' Whitgar answered and then, looking at Edgar meaningfully, said, 'I've seen terrible things. William is slaughtering every living thing for miles.'

Edgar nodded sagely and said, 'I've heard similar tales from Bondi and refugees heading north. When we get the army back together, we'll wait until William has marched south and then we'll march on York, and from there to London.'

'So, you won't need me here anymore, will you, my lord?' Whitgar said.

'Why do you ask?'

'I want to search for Elfwyn.'

'I can't allow that. We need every man we can get, and besides, Elfwyn could be anywhere.'

'That's why I need to look for her. She's most probably in Lincoln.'

'If she's in Lincoln, she'll get word to us, Whitgar, and when she does, you need to be here. Now, let's have no more talk of rescue missions. You went on one before, and it was successful, but it's asking too much this time.'

While Edgar and Whitgar talked, ninety miles away in Lincolnshire, Elfwyn was enjoying the shelter of Saint Mary's church in Stow, close to Lincoln. But she had had an exhausting journey and had not slept well. With ten miles to go, she was confident she would arrive home before sunset. Elfwyn's primary concern was what had happened to her sister, lover, father, and friends. Since falling from her horse, she had spent the time trudging to her father's hall in Lincoln and hiding from Norman patrols.

She was saying farewell to Father Larcwide, who had been kind enough to offer her a place to stay for the night. They were at the altar when armed men burst into the church. She froze in fear until one of them spoke. She relaxed when she realised they were Danes and not Normans. It was good to be back amongst allies again.

The leader of the Danes stepped forward. 'I am Trygve Roarson,' he said.

Father Larcwide introduced himself and Elfwyn to his new congregation.

'Are you Elfwyn Merlesweinsdaughter?' Trygve asked.

'I am,' she said. 'I became separated from my father and friends, so I'm going home to Lincoln.'

'Don't you know Lincoln is full of Normans? They've built a strong fortification. You'll be in danger there. Come to Axholm with us. We can keep you safe from the Normans, and once we find Prince Osbjorn, he'll reunite you with your father.'

'Do you know Prince Osbjorn?'

'Yes, I do. Why do you ask?'

'Do you know if Whitgar, one of Edgar Atheling's companions, is with him?' Elfwyn asked.

'No, I don't, but come with us, and you'll be able to see for yourself.'

'That's kind of you.'

'Oh, it's no trouble. We just need to find a little food. We're on a foraging expedition.'

'Oh, I'm sure we can find you something,' Father Larcwith said. 'Follow me.'

Trygve ordered one of his followers, an older man than you might expect in such company.

The old man grunted, and Trygve and his men followed Father Larcwith out of the church. Elfwyn stayed and waited for them to return. Her elderly companion, bored and with nothing else to do, began scratching on the stone wall of the chancel. He seemed completely immersed in his task, and gradually Elfwyn could make out the image of a longship. The men were gone long enough for him to have completed his carving before they returned without Father Larcwith.

'We'd best be quick. A Norman patrol is on its way,' Trygve said, his head appearing around the doorway. 'We've got food and found a horse for you.' He smiled at Elfwyn.

'But I must say goodbye to Father Larcwith after he showed me such kindness,' Elfwyn said.

'He's busy, my lady,' Trygve replied. 'He's preparing for visitors,' he said with an unsettling look.

'Come on. No time to waste,' he said, taking her by the arm and leading her outside.

Within moments, she was astride a horse and galloping east with her new Danish friends. Father Larcwith wanted to bid farewell to Elfwyn, too, but he lay dying in the barn. Before long, the party headed north on the old Roman road.

'Straight up here now, my lady,' Trygve said. 'Let's hope we don't meet any Norman patrols. They shouldn't be any trouble, but you never know.'

They were in luck. During the entire journey of thirty miles, they encountered not one patrol. By the time they reached their destination, the sun was sinking in the west, and the air was growing cold. They arrived on the south bank of the River Humber, where a dragon ship lay in wait for returning foraging parties. Elfwyn thought it made a fearsome sight. Long and sleek with a tall mast made it look stealthy, but what caught her eye was the dragon's head prow, which struck fear into her. It was breath-taking with its golden scaly skin, green eyes, a long bright red tongue, pure white teeth, and great fangs that could strike fear into a man's heart. At the other end of the ship, its tail curled skyward and coiled at the tip.

'Here we are,' Trygve said. 'See, the Valkyrie is waiting for us.' Trygve noted the expression on Elfwyn's face and smiled. 'Isn't she beautiful?'

Two of Trygve's men escorted Elfwyn on board. She looked around to see the crew going about their business, but there seemed no one who was their leader, although everyone appeared to look up to Trygve.

'Which one is Osbjorn?' she asked.

'We thought he'd be here, didn't we, lads?' Trygve answered. 'He must be downstream. We'll find him now. Why don't you make yourself comfortable?' he said, nodding to a sea chest on which she could sit. Trygve then issued orders, and there was much activity as the crew cast off and hoisted a white sail on which was emblazoned the head of a fierce-looking Valkyrie. The ship made its way into the mysterious darkness of the Humber estuary, and as the sky grew black, stars appeared to guide them on their way.

Elfwyn had expected to disembark and ride downstream, but she now found herself sailing along in the middle of a great river. She thought they were going to meet up with the Danish prince downstream. The prospect excited her. Elfwyn had never been aboard a real seafaring ship before, and this certainly was a mighty one. The sail unfurled, caught the wind, and moved the vessel forward with effortless speed and grace. It was a distinct feeling from her experience in the coracle with Whitgar. With that thought, the memory of the young thane came back to haunt her. Feelings of joy remembering the precious moments of fun, love and laughter now mixed with concern for him. Did he escape the Normans and find Prince Osbjorn? Perhaps he was with him now, and they would meet again soon. And then there were Morwenna and Bondi and the rest of them. *Maybe I'll find him with Prince Osbjorn,* she told herself. *And perhaps Osbjorn will have word of the others.* But the ship seemed to make for the open sea.

'Where are we going?' she asked Trygve.

'Don't worry your pretty little head about that.'

'I've a right to know. You told me we were going to see Prince Osbjorn.'

'You'll see him soon enough,' Trygve smiled a lascivious grin.

'Put me ashore now!' Elwyn snapped.

Trygve's responded by laughing in her face.

Livid, she threw herself at him, trying to smash his face with her fists. The Dane grabbed her wrists and carried on laughing.

'Do you know who I am? Don't you know who my father is?'

'Your father may have been something once, but these days he's just another outlaw, and I don't think he'll be bothering me.'

Trygve ordered one of his men to take Elfwyn to his quarters. A huge burly man grabbed hold of Elfwyn, and as the crew laughed, he carried her to Trygve's quarters, which turned out to be something resembling a tent in the middle of the ship. Elfwyn found herself thrown onto a fur and ordered to shut up and stay put. The crewman who had thrown her into Trygve's quarters stood right outside on deck, baring her way. Feeling hopeless and miserable, Elfwyn cried and, as she often did in moments of danger, reached for her algiz pendant, only to discover it had gone. Tears ran down her face, and even as she sobbed, she could not decide whether she was crying in self-pity or anger. But Elfwyn promised herself that Trygve would pay for his actions.

Sometime later, after nightfall, Elfwyn noticed a change in the ship's motion, which at first, she thought was because they had sailed out on the open sea. It seemed to travel faster and writhe through the water. Outside, she could hear raised voices; they appeared to be arguing. Peering through the gap in the tent doors, she saw her guard had gone. She looked around to notice the men busy pulling on ropes or disappearing entirely. She presumed they were under canvas, taking shelter. At the stern, Trygve was in animated conversation with the helmsman.

'It's either ride the storm or starve, but the decision isn't ours to make. We can't turn in this; we must run before the wind.'

'I still say we should have stayed.'

'It's too late now, old friend.'

The helmsman said nothing but carried on, his hands struggling to keep a grip on the juddering tiller as he fought against the sea in his battle to keep them on course.

'Elfwyn,' Trygve called when he spotted her. 'How are you enjoying the Valkyrie? Isn't she marvellous?' he said, his eyes ablaze, a manic grin on his face.

Strangely, Elfwyn had to agree. The dragon ship made a spectacular sight, sliding over waves, appearing to twist as it did so. The swell thudding against her sides, spray drenched, and with full sail, she raced through the black tempest toward home.

'Come here. Stand by me,' Trygve bellowed above the storm. 'You'll be safe.'

Elfwyn did as requested because for a reason she could not explain, she believed Trygve. She scrambled out of the shelter and made her way towards him, staggering as the ship pitched and rolled. A gust of wind caught her hair, whipping her face as she made her way across the deck. Trygve called out to her, but the gale carried his words away.

Staggering around on the deck, she finally reached him. He held her by the arm to steady her, and she felt reassured by his firm grip.

'Have you ever been to sea in a storm?' he yelled.

'I've never even been at sea,' she answered.

'You'll love it,' he said, laughing. 'It's always like this.'

Elfwyn looked around her in disbelief. A green-faced man vomited over the side as wave after wave crashed over the decks. The wind roared, and mountainous seas gathered around the Valkyrie, towering above her. They appeared out of the darkness from nowhere. The sea seemed a wild, angry beast raging against their ship, trying to throw them to their deaths, but the dragon ship fought back, mortal enemies in a fight to the end. Elfwyn had never felt so small, so helpless, her life entirely in the hands of others. The ship juddered as another colossal wave-battered its side, and terror entered her heart when she realised the green-faced man had disappeared—swept away by the sea.

'A man has fallen overboard,' she cried above the wind.

Trygve stared at the space the man had occupied just moments earlier, and for the first time since Elfwyn had met him, the smile disappeared from his face.

'Hold on tight to something,' he said.

Elfwyn noticed he was holding on to a rope, and he held her firmly around her waist. She looked at the steersman and two other sailors struggling with the tiller for all they were worth. Around the deck, the grim-faced crew continued their battle with the storm. The Valkyrie fought her way through the wild, wild sea. Up and down, she rose and fell over wave after wave, the wind roaring like a monster all around, while she slithered across the mountainous waves.

'She's a great ship,' Trygve said to reassure Elfwyn. 'She's practically unsinkable.'

Just then, a wave crashed viciously into the side of the hull, rising and tipping the ship to a dangerous angle. Elfwyn thought they would capsize, but at the last moment, the Valkyrie righted herself and sped on through the raging night.

Trygve turned to the helmsman, 'We should have made her out of one of your turds, then she would never sink.'

The helmsman looked unimpressed and carried on with his struggle against the raging elements.

When dawn broke, the storm subsided as if calmed by the sun. The sea, though still rough, had exhausted itself and managed only a few occasional gusts. Elfwyn was soaked through and spent, as were the crew. Trygve looked at her and smiled. 'Didn't I tell you everything would be all right?' he grinned.

Elfwyn smiled back at him, relieved that her ordeal was now over, and then the thought struck her. *It's only the storm that's finished. This is just the beginning of my troubles.*

'Tomorrow we land in Denmark, and you will see what the future holds for you,' Trygve said.

Elfwyn's stomach churned. It was apparent what Trygve had in mind. She did not know how she would get herself out of this situation, but she resolved to keep her eye open for any opportunity to escape.

While Trygve was talking to Elfwyn, miles away, Bondi was in Waltheof's tent in conversation with Waltheof and Whitgar.

'Why did Edgar make camp here? There's nothing for miles, and it's not an easy place to get away from,' Bondi said.

'William will never look for us here,' Waltheof answered.

'I'm not surprised to hear that. How long do you intend to stay?' Whitgar asked.

'The plan is to wait until William has gone south and then reoccupy York. When summer is here, we'll march on London.'

Bondi and Whitgar exchanged glances.

'Do you think we can rely on the Danes and the Scots?' Whitgar asked.

By way of a reply, Waltheof shrugged his shoulders.

'So, what if it's just us with no outside help? And what's going on in the rest of the kingdom, do you know?' Bondi asked.

'Can we do it on our own? If you look out there,' Waltheof said, pointing to that part of the English army that stayed with the Atheling, 'No. There's not enough of us. If we can persuade the entire kingdom to rise as one, then we just might succeed.'

Neither Bondi nor Whitgar looked hopeful.

'What if it's just us, and what if the Bastard comes looking for us?'

'If it's just us, it would be a struggle. And don't worry about the Bastard coming this way. We're too far off the beaten track, and besides, we can always escape by ship if we have to.' Waltheof said.

Bondi looked to the shore, where a dozen longships were hauled up onto the beach.

'There'll never be enough ships to get you away if you have to leave at once,' he said.

Waltheof gave Bondi a quizzical look. 'What do you mean, 'never enough to get you off?" he said. 'Aren't you going to come with us?'

'No. I'm leaving with Gospatric as soon as he's ready,' Bondi replied. 'Malcolm is raiding Cumbria, and Gospatric intends to have a word with him.'

'I wish I could come with you, but I'm needed here,' Waltheof said. 'We'll miss you, Bondi. Try to get back for the summer; we might have work for you.'

'I will.'

Chapter 39

The day after Epiphany, King William strode across the great hall and out into the dazzling sunshine to address his gathered men. Out in the open, Turold the midget was waiting with his horse. William climbed into the saddle and addressed his men.

'Now that Christmas is over, it is time for us to drive the rebels from our kingdom. We will show no mercy to them or the misguided unfortunates who sheltered them. Now is the time to force them off the land. Every one of them.

'We will teach the English a lesson they'll never forget, a lesson that will forever instil fear and respect into their hearts. There will be no more uprisings after we've finished with them. Today, we begin a new campaign. We are going to destroy all opposition from here to the Scottish border. All opposition.'

William signalled his men and led them out of York, north and west. As they had done before Christmas, they were to eradicate every sign of life. Once again, William and his men would murder innocent villagers, destroy their property, and ruin their land.

'All the way to Scotland, my friends. Don't leave a thing, even for the rats. We must destroy everything,' he said, finishing his brief address.

William was happy now that Christmas was over; it had been a strange affair. First, the celebrations in a burned-out minster were a subdued affair. The crown that William had sent for arrived only just in time for the festivity, and the guests comprised no Englishmen of any import, even though it was England's king, who, for the first time, was spending Christmas in York. There had been few women present. Queen Matilda celebrated in London, as did Queen Edith, who Matilda had especially invited to Westminster for the occasion. Those few women who had been in York for the crown-wearing were the wives of local Norman nobles, William Malet, Gilbert de Ghent, and the like. Snow had fallen through the partially repaired roof of the great hall, but at least there had been plenty to eat. William's men had driven animals from farms far and wide to make a banquet fit for the king.

William was happy to be on campaign again, but many men lived in tents and had had enough of York and the North. But William wanted to deliver one last assault on the Northerners, one final blow to render them vanquished once and for all. There would be no more rebels emerging from the moors and forests once he had departed for the south. Christmas was over. He had worn his crown in York, and now he would assert his authority for all to see.

William had only just passed through the city gates when a rider approached at full gallop. Once again, it was Vital, the scout with important news. He stopped so suddenly his horse had to drop onto its hindquarters to stop in time. He slid to a halt right beside his king.

'You're in a hurry, Vital. What is it?' William asked.

'The rebels. There's a party of eighty down at Holderness, on the coast. If we hasten, we'll have them trapped,' the scout replied.

'How far away is Holderness?' William asked.

'Two day's ride. I don't think they'll be going anywhere. It looks as though they've settled in for the winter,' Vital answered.

'Comrades, we need to ride hard. Follow me,' William ordered.

In a moment, William led his cavalry towards the peninsular on the north bank of the Humber. The infantry continued, as ordered, north towards Durham.

After two days and two nights, William rose at dawn in his camp just a few miles away from the English encampment on Spurn Head. Quietly, they mounted their horses.

'We should catch them in the open. They won't stand a chance,' William said to his men. 'We'll approach slowly and quietly. Follow me.'

With Vital at his side, William led his men across the misty lowland of the marshy Humber estuary towards the English camp. The men formed their horses into a column five wide, any wider, and there was a danger their mounts would get caught in a bog. Walking through the misty murk, the horses and men seemed to make a tremendous din; saddles creaked, shields banged against byrnies, every hoof clattered stones, and the horses neighed. But there was no sign the English had heard a sound.

As William rode forward, he suspected a trap. He could not understand why they had remained undetected. *Why has no sentry sounded the alarm?* He had the dreadful feeling they might be falling into a trap.

On his signal, the cavalry moved forward at a slow canter. They spurred their horses on when they reached the harder ground around the encampment. There was still no response from the English. Soon, realisation dawned on him. He was too late. The English had gone.

'There they are,' William heard someone call out.

William looked round to see someone pointing out to sea. There on the iron-grey waters, he could see three ships full of Englishmen sailing away to safety. They were shouting insults, but in the wind, and at that distance, William could not make them out.

Astride his horse, for a moment, the anger boiled within him. Although frustrated in his attempt to capture leading rebels, at least he could continue his mission to destroy their support, and he would inflict maximum damage in his search for them.

'We will comb every forest and even the most remote of mountains. Every hill, every dale, every hall, every hut, every cave. Anywhere that can offer shelter to the barbarians, and when we find them, we will put them to the sword.'

William's army split into factions, and they searched for their prey, spreading across the land like a plague. One after another, William destroyed villages and farmsteads and individual dwellings. The story everywhere was always the same. A group of soldiers would arrive, and killing, raping, and destruction would follow. The children met with the same fate as adults. No one was too young or too old to escape William's wrath. His troops slaughtered all the animals, and those they did not eat, they burned with the buildings and chattels.

No mercy was shown to those who hid in the church. Soldiers dragged out members of the congregation and killed them or set fire to the church with its occupants still inside. Those who fled met their maker with the thrust of a spear or the slash of a sword. All the time, the cold winter wind blew in from the east, bringing with it snow, sleet or hail.

Soon word of the Norman atrocities spread, and people left their homes with what they could carry, most of them heading north to Scotland, the Normans following on behind. The slaughter continued until William reached the River Tees, where he learned the whereabouts of Edgar the Atheling. It was Sir Ralph Pomeroy who made the discovery.

Leading a small raiding party of half a dozen along the riverbank, Pomeroy caught sight of a small party of three men and investigated. When they saw him, the men tried to escape, but on foot, they stood little chance against men on horseback.

'After them,' Pomeroy ordered, digging his spurs into his horse's flanks.

Charging forward, the knights soon caught up with the three men and surrounded them in no time.

'What are you doing here?' Pomeroy demanded to know.

'Nothing. Just a bit of hunting,' one man replied.

Pomeroy could see they looked like hunters by their equipment; snares, bows, arrows, and gunny sacks.

'Had any luck?' Pomeroy enquired.

The man relaxed a little. 'No. The hunting doesn't isn't good today.'

'Is it usually good here?'

The man hesitated before saying it was excellent.

'How do you know?'

'What do you mean?' the man asked.

'You're not from around here, are you?' Pomeroy said.

'We are, my lord.'

'Where do you live?' Pomeroy asked.

'Just over there,' the man said, waving his arm about at nowhere in particular.

'How many are you hunting for?'

'Just our families.'

The men were looking uncomfortable now. Pomeroy wondered if it was just through fear or if they had something to hide.

'You're with the rebel army, are you not?'

'No, my lord,' the man answered, backing away from danger but only succeeding in closing the gap between himself and the knight behind him.

'Just tell us where they are, your friends, and we'll show our gratitude,' Pomeroy smiled.

'I'm sure I don't know what you mean,' the peasant answered.

Pomeroy looked at one of his men. One who with a crossbow. He nodded, and his comrade shot a bolt straight into the chest of the Englishman, who fell to the ground, dead before he hit the earth. His friends turned and ran for their lives.

'Stop them, but keep them alive,' Pomeroy barked.

In an instant, the knights were upon them. A spear jabbed into the shoulder of one brought him to the ground, and his friend got a kick in the back. Both men went sprawling.

'Why are you in such a hurry to leave? We were just having such an interesting conversation with your friend,' Pomeroy said. 'Is there anything you'd like to tell us?'

Neither of the men said a word.

Pomeroy looked at his comrade with the crossbow. The man had a bolt ready.

'The leg should do,' Pomeroy said.

There was a piercing scream as one man received a crossbow bolt deep in his thigh.

Pomeroy dismounted and was on him in moments. Grabbing the man by the hair, he pulled his head back, exposed his white throat, held his knife against it, and demanded to know where the Atheling was, but the Englishman refused to speak.

'Hold him down,' Pomeroy commanded.

Some men dismounted and held him down while Pomeroy set about his business. Ten minutes later, he had the answers to his questions, and the hunters were dead. Leaving the bodies where they lay, Pomeroy re-joined the king with his friends. He approached William, bowed, and said, 'We need to go further downstream. It seems Edgar and some of his followers have made camp on the coast for the winter. My informant told me there are only a couple of hundred at most.'

William smiled. 'Good. Well done, Sir Ralph. I think we ought to visit them. They must be feeling lonely out in the middle of nowhere,' he said.

It did not take long for William to organise his men. Vital and Wadard found out where the rebels were encamped and the exact lie of the land. They met William on their return with the news that Edgar was only a few miles away.

'The terrain is terrible. It's a flat, windswept place, and it looks marshy,' Vital said. 'They're right up at the end of a point. They have a few ships with which to make their escape. They're almost bound to see us coming from miles away, and the path they use for coming and going is only a few feet wide. It's the perfect place for them to go into hiding.'

'Do they have any horses?' William asked.

'One or two but not enough to go around.'

'So, if we're fast enough, we might capture them?'

'Yes. If we're fast enough, my lord.'

'We'll get as close to them as we can before nightfall and then, first thing in the morning, give them a pleasant surprise,' William said with a wicked grin.

Before dawn the following morning, William led his men, all of whom were on foot, through the maze of tracks that wove their way through the forest of gorse that covered the peninsular. The cavalry waited in the rear. No neighing horse would spoil the surprise. About five hundred Normans were advancing on the English camp through the grey dawn. They could hear nothing above the wind whistling through the black spiky undergrowth. The Normans moved forward unseen by their enemy, who lay sleeping in the false comfort of their beds.

Fifty yards away from the encampment, the gorse gave way to rough, scrappy grass, which gave them a clear view of the hideaway, but it would also mean the English could observe anyone approaching.

'On my signal, we'll rush them,' William said.

When he guessed everyone was ready to attack, William bellowed his war cry, and dozens of men burst into the clearing.

'Normans!' The cry went out from the sentries. In an instant, tent flaps opened, and half-dressed, half-asleep Englishmen appeared. Edgar Atheling was one of them.

'Make for the boats,' he yelled.

With the Normans bearing down on them, the English made for

the ships on the beach, Whitgar and Bondi amongst them.

'Where's Morwenna?' Bondi asked his friend as they raced across the beach to the nearest boat.

'I don't know. I haven't seen her,' Whitgar answered.

The two men ran towards the boats, just like most of the others.

'She's there,' Whitgar told Bondi, waving his arm toward a cluster of English thanes. Whitgar was correct; Morwenna was there amongst the dozen thanes, running for the ships. The band was backing away from the Normans and towards safety as fast as possible, but twenty horsemen were closing in on them. Armed with spears and crossbows, they would make quick work of the English caught out in the open.

'Morwenna, come with me. I'll get you to safety,' Thurold said, grabbing her forearm.

'We must all go together, or they'll just pick us off,' Morwenna answered.

'Go with him,' she heard her father say. 'Get back to the ships.'

Thurold was still tugging on one arm as she brandished her sword with the other.

'Go,' she heard Merleswein say over the din of clashing swords and shields.

Falling back, still being pulled by Thurold, Morwenna saw horsemen closing down on them. She saw one of them raise a crossbow and the blur of a bolt as it seared through the air towards them. Before she could move, her father blocked her view, and there was a scream as he took the full force of the crossbow bolt in his chest.

'Run,' Thurold yelled at Morwenna.

An old thane grabbed her and dragged her towards the ships, which the crews were pushing out to sea as Thurold knelt beside Merleswein, whose blood flowed from his chest.

'Help me, Thurold. Help me.'

'It's too late for you, old friend,' Thurold said, looking up to see soldiers fighting all around him. 'Too late.'

Thurold got to his feet, Merleswein's words, 'Don't leave me here to die,' echoing in his head. He raced to the nearest ship, leaving his comrades behind him, his feet splashing in the water; the deeper it became, the slower he ran. He had almost reached it when the crew hauled up the sail, and the wind filled it and moved the vessel forward. Throwing his sword and shield away, he made one last spurt to safety. Hands reached out and grabbed him, dragging him on board. Thorold collapsed, breathless, on deck at Morwenna's feet. As their eyes met, he saw the unasked question.

'No. He died in my arms,' Thurold said.

Morwenna wailed, and Thurold got to his feet and held her tightly in his arms.

From their ship, the Sea Wolf, Bondi and Whitgar had looked on. They had watched as Morwenna ran for safety, and they had seen Merleswein fall and Thurold kneel beside him for a second before rising and fleeing the scene. After Thurold ran for cover, they saw Merleswein roll onto his side and struggle to his feet. They looked on as Waltheof fought his way to his comrade's side to help him, but he had no arm free to support him because he was using his axe. Waltheof fought off the enemy while Merleswein staggered on until a horseman galloped by and smashed his skull in with a mace, killing him on the spot. He fell to the ground just as Morwenna reached safety. His last sight of her was her climbing aboard to safety.

Bondi and Whitgar watched the rest of the scene unfold. Waltheof and half a dozen of his companions fought off a much larger group of Normans, cutting cut them off from the ships.

'We must help them,' Whitgar said.

'We can't. It's hopeless,' Bondi said. 'There would be more of us dead or captured.'

Aboard their crowded vessel, the crew began pulling on their oars. Soon the sail filled with wind, and their ship lumbered out into the estuary, away from danger.

'Bondi, can you still see Waltheof?' Whitgar asked.

Bondi looked back to shore and saw a group of Normans surrounding a lone Englishman. He knew right away it was Waltheof and his heart sank.

'He's still on the beach. The Normans have him,' Bondi said.

'Never,' Bondi said. Bondi knew Whitgar was right; a crowd of Norman soldiers had gathered around Waltheof, and he looked as though he might surrender.

'Head upriver. We're too full,' Bondi heard the Steersman say. 'We'll have to lose some weight.'

Bondi and Whitgar, as the last aboard, knew they would be amongst the first to get off.

'We'll be all right as long as we don't go out to sea. Take us to the north shore,' Bondi said to the steersman.

'Very well, my lord.'

'Eadric. Eadric the Steersman. I didn't realise it was you,' Bondi said, suddenly aware of what ship he was on. He turned to see if Edgar was there and saw him hanging on to the mast.

'If that's all right with you, my lord?'

Edgar nodded his approval.

'At least Morwenna's all right,' Whitgar said.

'Let's go back and get Waltheof,' Bondi said.

'No. We'd only be wasting our time. Besides, there's the safety of the Atheling to consider,' Whitgar said. 'And you'll notice, the other ships aren't going back for him, including Gospatric's. We should press on to the far shore, and we'll drop off some men there.'

Bondi looked at the other ships, and Whitgar was correct; none was going back. He could also see Morwenna in the arms of Thurold. She seemed to cry while the old thane comforted her. As Bondi looked on, Thurold caught his eye and beamed a smug smile, which grew broader when he saw the anger in Bondi's eyes.

'When we land on the far shore,' Bondi said, 'to drop off some men. We'll get off with them and then make our way to York to see what we can do there. It's where they're sure to take Waltheof. Perhaps later, we can look for Elfwyn.'

'Good idea, Bondi,' Whitgar said.

The Sea Wolf, sailing low in the water, proceeded slowly across the estuary. All heads turned to the south, watching the developments on the shore. It seemed Waltheof was alive but a prisoner of the Normans.

Waltheof was indeed a prisoner of the Normans. There were not enough ships to take all the men, and he had stayed behind as leader of the rear guard, enabling the Atheling to make his escape. Now he was paying the price, as had Merleswein. Surrounded, he prepared to die, fighting for his cause. But then William appeared, looking invincible on his fine black stallion. A gap appeared amongst the men who formed a human wall around Waltheof.

'Earl Waltheof,' William said. 'It seems your friends have left without you. Did you upset them?'

Waltheof said nothing.

'You'll not get anywhere waving that axe around, and I think you know that as well as I do. You're too clever to die for nothing. Why don't you surrender, and we'll see if we can arrive at an accommodation? You've put up a heroic defence of your leader, Edgar the pretender, and you should feel proud. But now is the time to see sense. Now is the time to recognise you're beaten. Accept your fate, which might be rosier than you think.'

Waltheof surveyed the surrounding faces. He didn't doubt for a moment any of them would have taken pleasure in ending his life. True, he would take a few with him, and his name would live on in legends for generations, and then he rethought his situation. The English now, he knew, were defeated. Edgar would be on his way to Scotland, and in Waltheof's mind, it was doubtful if he would ever return.

Waltheof sighed. 'Can I keep my axe?' he asked William.

'Of course, you can. As long as you promise not to use it,' William said, smiling.

Waltheof lowered his axe, much to the disappointment of those around him looking forward to some action. A scowling Ralph Pomeroy was one of those disappointed not to be the one who dealt the fatal blow to the infamous rebel.

'Good,' William said. 'You've made the right choice.'

'Now, come with me, and we'll see if we can find a horse for you,' William said. And Waltheof felt humiliation in every fibre of his being.

Looking beyond his enemies, he could see his comrades making their way to the other side of the river in overloaded ships. *They'll be heading to Scotland; I'll be bound.* It was then he realised the rebellion was finished. William would probably follow the rebels up to the Scottish border and build more castles. There would be no shifting him then.

*

Edgar's ship approached the shore on the north bank of the River Tees to drop off some passengers. Amongst the two dozen to disembark were Bondi and Whitgar.

Once on shore, the men all looked to Bondi for leadership.

'It's up to you what to do,' Bondi said. 'Most of you are Edgar's men, so I would expect you to make for Scotland. I will head west hoping to meet up with William and rescue Earl Waltheof.'

The men looked shocked.

'Rescuing Waltheof would be suicidal,' one of them said. 'Besides, they'll only keep him as a hostage for a while. He's an earl, and they'll look after him.'

'I'll not be going to Scotland,' and even as he said it, Bondi knew he was avoiding Scotland because the thought of seeing Morwenna and Thurold together would be more than he could stand.

'Neither will I,' Whitgar added.

'We'll miss you, Bondi, and you too, Whitgar, but we're off to Scotland. Good luck to you.'

'Good luck to you, too. All of you,' Bondi said.

With that, the men parted company.

'We'd better get some horses,' Bondi said.

'Yes. I don't fancy walking either,' Whitgar replied.

Once a mount had been found for Waltheof, William led his men west, heading for Yarm, where they would cross the river and head north to create more mayhem. They broke into groups when they crossed the Tees before heading up quiet wintry hills and dales. Snow flurries swirled around, and cavalrymen hunched upon horses. Infantry stooped as they marched on the ice-cold ground against the icy wind. The northern winter was a beast they could not tame. Much harder than their homelands, it bit them with sharp, cold teeth that seared through their thighs. Fingers and toes turned to ice. And the weather looked set to continue. Columns of men snaked across Yorkshire, heading towards Scotland, leaving a trail of destruction in their path.

When they first started on their expedition, the villages close to York were unoccupied, but after a few days, the Normans reached points where people had been foolish enough to believe they were out of the Conqueror's reach. All of them died, and the Normans would leave the village razed to the ground in the morning. The ploughshare and anything that would burn, thrown to the flames. They would slaughter the animals for food or, more often, just leave them to rot. They left nothing alive. Then it would be the turn of the next farm, village, or hamlet. Nothing and no one would escape the Conqueror's wrath.

Chapter 40

When Bondi and Whitgar parted company with Edgar's men, they both had the strangest feeling of foreboding.

'Are you really thinking of rescuing Waltheof?' Whitgar asked.

Bondi thought for a moment. 'You know, I didn't want to go to Scotland,' he said.

'Neither did I. Do you have a plan?'

'No, but we could go to East Anglia. As far as I'm aware, there are no Normans there.'

'Do you fancy going by way of Lincoln?'

'So we can look for Elfwyn, you mean?'

'While we're there, yes.'

'Very well,' Bondi said. 'Just one thing.'

'What's that?'

'Shouldn't we find some horses?'

'I was thinking the same thing. Where do you think we'll get some?'

'We'll just have to take our chances,' Bondi answered. 'If we carry on upriver, we might find some. If not, we'll probably bump into the Normans somewhere, and we can steal theirs. We also need to find a crossing place.'

'We'd best get a move on then.' Whitgar said.

The two began their trek west along the marshy estuary. In the vast expanse of the river mouth, the freezing wind soon found its way through every gap in the clothes.

'This is a grim country,' Bondi observed.

'That's County Durham for you,' Whitgar replied.

Bondi gazed around him and across the slate grey river to Yorkshire on the far side. The view was the same, flat marshy and woebegone.

'I can't tell the difference between land and sea. Everything's grey,' the housecarl said.

'That's because you've spent too much time in the south,' Whitgar replied as the two struggled on through the cutting wind. They were glad after a few miles when a stone tower came into view.

'Have you seen the church?' Whitgar asked.

'Yes. There must be a village. We'll ask for directions there. They might even have some horses.'

They had not been walking for long when they met a man pollarding trees.

'Hello. Do you know anywhere where we can get some horses?' Bondi asked.

The man nearly fell off his ladder.

'I can't say I do,' he said.

'What about crossing the river?' Whitgar enquired.

'Just keep going until you arrive at St. Cuthbert's church. Ask anybody in the village for Wilburh. He runs the ferry.'

With the news lifting their spirits, they pressed on to St Cuthbert's, and half an hour later, they were enjoying the shelter of the church and talking to Osgar, the priest, who was suspicious of the two armed men.

'We need to cross the river, and we were told someone called Wilburh can help.'

'Yes, Wilburh's your man. I'll send for him. You're not from around here, are you?'

'No, we're Edgar Atheling's men,' Whitgar replied.

Father Osgar looked perplexed.

'You're probably wondering why we're here. It's because the Normans forced us from York, and now Edgar is heading for Scotland and the court of King Malcolm for the winter.'

'You do know, Scotland's this side of the river, to the north? If you cross it, you'll be going south. That's the wrong way.'

'It's complicated,' Whitgar said.

Just then, a man appeared at the church door. 'Somebody looking for me?' he asked.

'If you're Wilburh, yes. We need to cross the river,' Whitgar said.

'If you're quick, we can go now before the tide turns.'

'We'll be right with you,' Whitgar said.

Half an hour later, Bondi and Whitgar landed on the south bank of the Tees. As they clambered up the riverbank, they said their goodbyes to Wilburh and continued their journey. The ferryman headed for home. It was then they heard the unmistakable sound of an army marching across the land, hundreds of hooves striking the ground, the creak of leather saddles, and the neighing of horses that gave them away. And then it came into view, there on the horizon not more than a quarter of a mile from them, the approaching Norman cavalry with William riding proudly at its head.

'Quick, let's hide,' Bondi said as he ducked and began crawling to a nearby reed bed, with Whitgar following close behind. Bondi parted the reeds and slipped in, disappearing in moments. Whitgar followed, and the two were invisible to the soldiers proceeding along the riverbank.

'Can you see Earl Waltheof anywhere?' Bondi asked.

'Yes, he's up at the front with the Bastard himself.'

'He doesn't appear to have come to any harm,' Bondi said.

'That's the nobility for you; they always take care of their own.'

'Do you think we should rescue him?'

'There are hundreds of them, Bondi. I don't think even a hero like you could get him free.'

Bondi had the pained look like a man trying to think up a plan far beyond his capability. He said nothing.

Changing the subject, Whitgar said, 'How long do you think we'll have to say here? I'm up to my knees in mud and water.'

'Same here,' Bondi replied. 'Don't worry. They'll be gone soon.'

The two watched undetected as the column passed on its way to make more mischief. When William and his men had passed by, Bondi turned to Whitgar. 'Let's follow them.'

'What for?'

'They've got horses, and if we go about it the right way, two of them will soon be ours.'

Whitgar felt a sense of alarm sweep through his body. 'I'm sure we could find some somewhere else?' he said.

'Don't be soft. Who else would have a horse? Let's go after them.'

They heaved their feet free of the mud and staggered out of the reed bed and onto firmer ground. The Norman column disappeared into the distance.

'Come on, Whitgar,' he said. 'There's no time to waste.'

They followed the soldiers along the riverbank for the rest of the day. Cold and wet, their feet numb. Until eventually, as the grey skies turned to black, at Yarm, William made camp. There was a flurry of activity while soldiers butchered the local men and sorted out the young and attractive women from the older, less desirable ones. Young children were done away with on the spot and animals slaughtered for the evening meal. Their usual entry into an English town completed, the Normans sought out their accommodation, which meant commandeering someone's home or pitching a tent. Bondi and Whitgar hid behind a wall at the edge of the town while in the darkness, the sounds of hell broke out all around them. Screams of the townsfolk of all ages and sexes, and those of their domesticated beasts, pierced the chilly night air while an impassive moon and indifferent stars looked down on them.

'I can't stand this any longer,' Bondi said, rising to his feet and drawing his sword.

'No,' Whitgar said, grabbing Bondi's arm. 'You can't. You'll just get yourself killed.'

'I've got to do something.'

'Yes, but not now,' Whitgar said. 'Do something later when it will make a difference, and you won't be adding your name to those of the dead.'

The two friends took a long look into each other's eyes; Whitgar recognised the rage in Bondi's. Bondi could perceive the wisdom in Whitgar's, and they took up their positions behind the wall.

Once William and his men had settled down, Bondi and Whitgar approached the town cautiously. They knew the horses would be liveried anywhere that offered shelter, including the church and any outlying buildings. It was to one of these Bondi and Whitgar were heading. They had watched as the Normans entered the village and found their places for the night. Bondi and Whitgar could just make out Waltheof entering a great hall with at least thirty Normans, and there were plenty more outside.

'We need help,' Whitgar said. 'We can't rescue Waltheof on our own.'

Bondi had to agree. 'Have you seen them?' he said, nodding towards a small group of five soldiers who were staying in what looked like a barn. They had hitched their horses to a tree just ten feet from the doors. From the sounds emanating from inside, they had taken a woman back for entertainment. The laughter had increased until reaching a crescendo, the merriment had subsided, and now they could hear only snoring coming from the barn.

'Time to get some horses, Whitgar.'

'What about saddles?'

'They'll be inside,' Bondi replied.

'So are the soldiers,' Whitgar said.

'We'll sneak in and deal with them; then we'll take their tack.'

Other than the snoring, the night was eerily quiet as they crept up to the barn, finding their way easily in the bright moonlight. Only Norman animals were left alive; they had killed the rest. Bondi and Whitgar checked the horses and decided which the two they would take.

Bondi drew his seax and made towards the Barn door.

'Why don't you use your sword?' Whitgar asked.

'Because we might be cramped in there, and a sword won't be so much use.'

'Oh, right,' Whitgar said, sliding his sword back in its scabbard and pulling out his seax.

They opened the creaky barn door with seaxes drawn. Bondi slipped into the building, lit by a single flickering torch. In the light from the dancing flame, he let his eyes adjust to the darkness. There, sprawled about in the hay, were the five Norman soldiers, and tethered to a post was a naked girl bruised and bleeding, tears running down her swollen face. She looked terrified when she saw Bondi and Whitgar. Luckily, she was too frightened to make a sound.

Once more, Bondi's anger bubbled up and, with two purposeful strides, fell on the first of the Normans lying asleep in the hay. He pushed hard on the man's mouth with his left hand and drove his seax through his heart with his right. When he withdrew his weapon, fountains of blood spurted upwards, horrifying the young woman, who began screaming at the top of her voice. Whitgar was already standing over his first victim, so he dealt him a fatal blow in the chest. By this time, the other three soldiers were waking, one to receive a fierce kick in the head from Bondi, which stunned him.

They turned their attention to the two soldiers coming out of their sleep. Bondi and Whitgar closed the gap between them before they could get to their feet. Bondi's victim tried to defend himself by kicking, but Bondi slashed his legs before falling on him. The last thing he saw was the face of the young woman he had abused less than an hour before. She was hysterical and desperately struggling with her bonds to get free.

Whitgar closed in on the remaining Norman, who had retrieved his sword and used it to keep the Englishman at bay. To his credit, the Norman succeeded, at least until a hand axe thrown by Bondi struck him square in the forehead, putting an immediate end to his resistance.

'I told you we should have used swords,' Whitgar said.

'Get a saddle,' Bondi told Whitgar.

The two men grabbed a saddle each and raced through the door with the tack. In no time, the men had the horses ready.

'We need to get the girl out of there,' Bondi said.

Whitgar looked reluctant to go back. 'Why?' he asked.

'Because we can't leave her.'

Bondi walked off, disappearing into the barn. He approached the woman and cut her bonds while she cowered against the wall. Once free, she curled up into a ball, quivering and whimpering. Bondi threw one of the soldier's blankets over her.

'Give me your hand,' he said, holding out his. 'We have to leave now. Soon, others will be here.'

She was reluctant at first, but after some coaxing, she held out her hand. With the blanket draped around her, she let Bondi lead her outside. On the way, he picked up the torch and threw it onto the hay.

Once outside, he mounted his horse and helped the woman up behind him, and she held on for dear life. The alarm sounded as they rode off, but no one followed them. When they were about two miles away from Yarm, they came to a halt.

'What are you going to do now?' Bondi asked the woman.

She said nothing. She seemed lost in a private world of her own, one that was not a pleasant place to be.

'What's your name?' Whitgar asked her.

'Wynflaed,' she said.

'You can't go home, Wynflaed; you have no home to go back to.'

'Can't she come with us?' Whitgar said.

Bondi looked alarmed at the prospect.

'We can't leave her on her own,' Whitgar said. 'Let's just take her to York, where she'll be safe now the Normans have gone.'

The woman looked from one to the other. There was a silent plea in her eyes.

'Let's ride on to the next village. We might find some shelter for the night,' Bondi said.

They rode through the cold moonlight and arrived in the village of Osmotherley, where they headed for the shelter of the Church. It was here they spent the night. After a restless sleep, the three awoke surprised to find a tall, gangly priest standing over them with drinks and something to eat; a jug of beer and a loaf of bread, together with half a wheel of cheese.

'It's not much,' he said. 'But it is something. I'm Father Godric. I suppose you're keeping out of the way of the Normans,' he said.

The three exchanged glances. Bondi and Whitgar were surprised. Terrified, the woman curled up into a ball beneath her blanket.

Bondi spoke first. 'Thank you, Father Godric. Yes, you're right. We are keeping out of the way of the Normans. 'I am Bondi Wynstanson. This is Whitgar Guthrumson. The wench is Wynflaed; we found her last night.'

The priest understood at once and responded with a knowing nod.

'We've had a few refugees coming this way. By the grace of God, we remain free of a visit from the Normans. They have the most fearsome reputation. There is an abbey not far away, and I'm sure the nuns will take good care of her.'

'That's kind of you, Father,' Whitgar said. 'This bread and cheese are good too. Thank you.'

As they ate, they told him something of their adventures, and later, after leaving Wynflaed behind, they continued their journey to York.

'We can go back the way I came out with Morwenna,' Bondi said. 'I know the way, and I think, for most of the journey at least, we won't meet any Normans.'

'That sounds all right to me,' Whitgar said. 'Are you thinking we'd call in at my father's farm on the way?'

'I was.'

'I'm looking forward to it.'

The two rode on through the frozen countryside, Norman blankets over their coats to give them a little extra warmth. Soon they were upon the windswept moors where it was even colder, but where they thought there would be much less chance of meeting any Norman patrols. By the end of an uneventful day, they were entering Lastingham, where Bondi was hoping to find Father Raedwald, shelter for the night and, with any luck, something hot to eat.

'Something's wrong,' Bondi said, bringing his horse to a halt.

'What?'

'Something's not right,' Bondi repeated as he scanned the village. It was a collection of ruins, pretty much as he had left it. Then he realised; the church was in ruins too.

'They've burned down the church, Whitgar. It was untouched when we left,' Bondi said.

They dismounted at the edge of the village and led their horses towards the church, whose missing roof and charred beams laid testimony to a fire. There was nothing but ghostly quiet; not a thing stirred. All the men could hear was the wind.

Entering the church, Bondi discovered debris littered the floor and there, staring down with unseeing eyes, bound to a cross, was the body of Father Raedwald. They had stripped him naked, stabbed him in the side, and made him wear a crown of thorns. Father Raedwald's face expressed profound anguish.

Whitgar entered the church and stopped dead in his tracks, wondering what had caught Bondi's attention. He followed his friend's gaze to the atrocity the Normans had committed.

'It looks like the Normans returned,' Whitgar said. 'We'd better get him down.'

They struggled as they lowered the cross, but they got him to the floor with as much dignity as was possible in the circumstance. They cut him free and stood looking at him for a time before Whitgar suggested they cover him.

'With what?' Bondi said. 'There's nothing here.'

'What are we going to do then?'

'We'll have to bury him.'

'The ground's too hard. What would we dig with?'

'Let's take him to the graveyard and cover him with stones. It's not much, but it's the best we can do.'

In the failing light, they carried Father Raedwald's body outside, and once they found an appropriate place, covered him with stones they pulled out of the dry-stone wall that surrounded the church. Once they had finished covering Raedwald' s body, they looked sheepishly at each other, barely picking out each other's faces in the darkness.

'Aren't you going to say anything?' Whitgar asked.

'Aren't you?'

'I don't know what to say. I didn't know him.'

Bondi felt he had no choice but to say a few words, but he did not know what to say.

'Dear lord,' he said and was relieved it sounded like a good start. 'Here lies Father Raedwald, who you'll know, as he's one of yours. Amen.'

'Is that it?'

'I told you, I didn't know him.'

'He deserves a bit more than that, don't you think?'

'The Father was a good man, as I'm sure you'll know, and he was good to Morwenna and me when we were here.' Bondi looked at Whitgar to see if he thought he had said enough. Whitgar looked like he was expecting more. 'And he was a wonderful priest to his parishioners. It was a pleasure knowing him. Amen,' Bondi said with finality.

He looked up to meet Whitgar's gaze. 'It's getting cold. Let's find some firewood,' he said.

Once they found firewood, they started a fire in the ruins of the church. 'At least the walls will keep the wind off,' Bondi said when they started the fire.

After another terrible night's sleep, they continued their journey. They had only gone a few yards when Whitgar turned to Bondi and said, 'I'm concerned about food.'

'I've got enough for a couple of days.'

'Same here, but I'm not sure where we'll get any more. If all the places between here and York are wasted, they'll be nothing anywhere.'

'What do you suggest?'

'I have friends in Thirsk who'll be happy to help us out,' Whitgar said.

'It's out of our way, though,' Bondi said.

'It's out of the Normans' way, too. I think it's far enough to the west to be safe. If we get a move on, we could be there before it gets dark,' Whitgar said.

'Come on then, let's go.'

With the thought of hot food, a warm hearth, and a cosy bed in mind, the two set off with purpose and in good spirits to Thirsk. They left Lastingham, the ice-capped puddles cracking under hooves, the branches blown from black, naked trees lay scattered on rock hard ground, and mist hung in the air.

They climbed onto the moors to where the air was clear and breezy. The winter wind cut in from the east and stabbed them with icy fingers, but at least they could be grateful it was at their backs. It was a struggle. They rode through the day, glad in the afternoon to come off the hills and down into the Vale of York. Here it was more sheltered and slightly warmer than the moors. As sundown approached, the two friends were pleased when the silhouette of a town came into view.

'Not long now, Bondi. We should be there well before dark,' Whitgar said.

The two men kicked their horses, keen to close the distance, eager to enjoy the comforts of Thor's hall in Thirsk. But a feeling of foreboding came over the travellers as they approached the town.

'Something isn't right,' Whitgar said.

'I have the same feeling, too,' Bondi agreed.

The two stopped their horses and observed the scene in front of them.

A glorious pink sun was setting in an ice blue sky, the black skeletons of trees and bushes scatted across the countryside made for a beautiful scene, but the only sign of life was a bird struggling in the wind as it looked for somewhere to perch.

'There's nothing alive here,' Bondi said.

All the familiar sounds of the town were missing. No dogs barked, no horses neighed, no donkeys brayed, no sheep bleated. There was nothing but the sound of the breeze in the trees and the babbling of a brook.

'Let's get a bit closer,' Whitgar said.

The two moved cautiously toward the town, but there was still nothing but silence.

'There,' Whitgar said.

There were hoofprints in the snow covering a large area in front of them.

'Normans,' Bondi said, confirming Whitgar's worst fears.

'Do you think they've gone?'

'Yes. It's too quiet. We'd better be careful, just in case they left somebody behind. There's no sign of life?' Bondi said.

They continued on their way, keeping a watch over the town as they went. Soon there were more tracks in the snow. There had been a lot of riders, and then the first of the corpses they were to find lay spread-eagled in the snow. By the look of him, he had been there for a week.

The black carcasses of the burned-out building told the familiar story, the Normans had arrived, created mayhem, and destroyed all around them to leave behind lifeless ruins.

'Let's go to the hall and see if there's anyone left alive,' Whitgar said.

Bondi followed his friend through the streets, where more bodies lay scattered all around. Young and old, men and women, boys and girls: individuals and groups whose lives had so brutally come to an end. Whitgar was passing one little group by a fishpond. In the frost, the pond had glazed over, a hard, cold eye bearing witness to nothing. Bondi pulled his horse up short.

'Stop a moment,' he said.

He looked down from the saddle at a small family. Something

caught his eye, something that glittered even in the failing light. What he saw next made his heart skip a beat; it was the sight of the silk braid on the dead man's cloak. He recognised it immediately as Alfstan Elwynson's. By his side lay the bodies of his two daughters, Elfreda and Elfryth, draped over their mother, Elfgyfu. There was no sign of little Alfred, but Bondi guessed where he might be. Dismounting, Bondi strode over to the bodies and pulled back Elfgyfu's cloak; the baby was dead on his mother's breast. Bondi covered the bodies. It was then he noticed Elfgyfu's beautiful clasp was missing. He turned to Alfstan and noticed his was missing too.

'What is it?' Whitgar asked.

'They're a family I know, used to know. They've been killed and robbed. We have to bury them.'

'Do you want to do that now?' Whitgar said.

'No. We'll come back later.'

Whitgar nodded and continued towards the great hall, with Bondi following. Along the way were more bodies. People who must have died together as they were all covered in the same amount of snow, and, from what they could see, they were all equally decomposed. Carrion made off as the two approached. Finally, they arrived at Thor's great hall. The place was a charred ruin, just like every other building in the town. The man himself lay on the ground, dead. He made an odd sight, with his white hair and beard blending into the snow.

'Is he someone you know?' Bondi asked.

'Thor. This is his hall, or what's left of it. He was a great friend and a wonderful man.' Whitgar attempted to conceal his emotions as he visualised Thor, his big smile, humour, generosity, and kindness. He knew his old friend would have put up a tremendous fight to save his family and friends.

'We'll bury him later as well,' he heard Bondi say.

God, is that all we do now? Bury our friends?

The two men stared at the ground in contemplation, trying to understand the enormity of the situation. Whitgar was the first to speak.

'Do you think it's like this all over everywhere?' he asked, dreading the answer.

Chapter 41

William left Yarm, none the wiser about Bondi and Whitgar's escapade of the previous night. He thought some drunks had knocked over a torch and burned themselves to death. No one paid much attention to the incident.

'Today, Earl Waltheof, we are to continue with our expedition to Durham, another of your towns that needs to be taught a lesson.'

'Why?'

'Why? They murdered Robert de Comines and his men, that's what. They probably think they can act with impunity because they live so far north in a godforsaken wilderness. I'm here to teach them they can't, not under my rule.'

'Let's make haste; we have a lot of work to do.'

But William had less to do than he could ever imagine. News of Norman atrocities had travelled fast. Everywhere he went, towns, villages, farmsteads were deserted, abandoned by their owners who had taken what they could carry to Scotland.Even so, the Normans wasted everything they came across. Northumbria was a ghost land, white and frozen with not a soul in sight. And still, the Normans burned down villages and farms. And still, they poisoned the wells. And still, they salted the fields. Until eventually, William and his army arrived at Durham, the scene of the massacre just a few years before. An unnatural silence greeted the king.

'No one appears to be here to welcome us,' William said to his brother Robert.

'Perhaps it's a trap,' Robert replied, nodding towards the wide-open gates.

No sound emanated from the other side of the city walls, no pedlars cries, no sentries' alarms, no children's laughter, no warnings from barking dogs. Nothing.

'I'll wager there's not a soul to be found on the other side of that wall. We'll send someone to investigate.

'Sir Ralph,' William called to Pomeroy.

Pomeroy drew alongside his king and waited for orders.

'See what's happening.'

Pomeroy led his men across the river and up the steep hill into Durham. What he found there surprised him. Everywhere the streets were deserted, with no sign of life anywhere, except for the birds of the air.

They made their way to the Bishop's House, expecting at least somebody to be at home, but the story was the same. All the movables had gone.

'Search the church and the bigger houses,' Pomeroy ordered, but even as he spoke, he knew they would find nothing.

After a quarter of an hour, his men returned all with the same observation to report. The English had abandoned their city.

Pomeroy went back to his king and informed him of what he had found.

'We'll rest here for the night, and tomorrow go further north and see what we what's happening there. Lead me to the Bishop's House. I'll stay there tonight, and the rest of you can find your accommodation.'

As William made his way up the ghostly streets, he wondered where the townsfolk could be hiding. In truth, the last of them had left that morning.

While William had been travelling north, Bishop Aethelwine had been told more and more stories of Norman atrocities and expected more of the same in Durham. As refugees flooded into the town, he had no difficulty persuading the townsfolk to leave and continue heading north. They were now scattered along the road to Scotland, and the Bishop was hiding on the holy island of Lindisfarne, discussing the future with the Atheling in the ancient stone priory.

'I'm going to spend the winter with Malcolm in Scotland,' Edgar said to Aethelwine.

'Malcolm's in Cumbria, fighting against Gospatric,' Aethelwine replied. 'You'll need to ask your sister Margaret if you can take refuge. I doubt she'll say no, and I'm sure Malcolm won't mind. He has designs on her, so I hear.'

'So I understand,' Edgar said.

'You don't seem to have as many companions as the last time we met, Edgar?' Aethelwine remarked.

'No, I'm afraid not,' Edgar replied. 'The Normans killed Merleswein and captured Waltheof. Bondi and Whitgar are on a rescue mission to get Waltheof back, but don't worry; he'll come to no harm. The last anyone saw of him; he was being led away under guard, but he didn't seem to be in any danger.'

'That's something, I suppose,' Aethelwine said.

'I'm hoping to build up an army in Scotland and march south in the summer. Won't you join us, Aethelwine?'

'It would be an honour.'

'Good. What will you do in the meantime?'

First, I'll see my people are safe and then 'I'll follow you up to Scotland.'

'Good. I'll be leaving on the first tide tomorrow. I'll look forward to seeing you at Malcolm's court. In the meantime, I'm going to find Eadric. He's discovered a few problems with the ships, any problems with the ships.'

'Goodbye, my lord.'

As Edgar left, Aethelwine noticed Morwenna sitting on a bench with a man. She looked distraught, and he walked over to her, hoping he might help.

'Hello Morwenna,' he asked, 'How are you?'

'Haven't you heard?' she answered.

'About your father? It's such a terrible loss to us all. He'll be missed by so many. You have my heartfelt condolences, Morwenna.'

'I need to talk to you privately,' Morwenna said in such a way Aethelwine understood she needed to get away from the man by her side.

'Come with me,' he said.

Aethelwine gestured for her to follow him and nodded to Thurold as if to say, 'this won't take long. I know you'll understand.'

They walked down the passageway in silence and entered his room, where Morwenna burst into tears.

'My father is dead. Elfwyn is missing, and Bondi and Whitgar have gone off somewhere, and I don't know what to do, and I might have to marry that horrible man.'

Aethelwine took her in his arms and held her while she cried on his shoulder.

'All this time, I've been fighting to rid the kingdom of a tyrant, and now I'm to be saddled with a leering monster.'

'Do you have to?' Aethelwine asked.

'It was my father's dying wish,' Morwenna said, her eyes welling up.

'That he expressed to you personally?'

'No. But he told Thurold just before he died.'

'On the battlefield?'

'Yes.'

Aethelwine thought for a moment before asking, 'Are there any witnesses to this?'

'Not that I know of.'

'Did you agree to any of this? Have there been any exchange of gifts?'

'No.'

'Then your conscience is clear.'

'Is it? My father saved my life. He put himself between me and a crossbow bolt so I wouldn't get hit. It was his dying wish I marry Thurold.'

'I'm not saying Thurold is untruthful, but we only have his word for it. So, you must do what you think is right, not what others say has been promised to them. What will you do, my dear?'

'I'm don't know. I miss the children desperately, but at least they are in good hands. Thurold is going to Scotland, which is where they are. If I go to Scotland, he'll be there.'

'Would that be so difficult? At least you'll be with your children and amongst friends,' Aethelwine said.

'Not my dearest friends, though,' Morwenna said. 'But you're right.'

As Edgar departed Lindisfarne the next day, William led his men out of Durham, flanked by Robert and Earl Waltheof. No sooner had they forded the river than an elderly monk appeared before them, barring the way. Dressed head to foot in the filthiest habit William had ever seen, and his scalp, where he had tonsured, was covered in cuts. More creature than man, he had a hint of the supernatural about him.

'Which of you is King William?' the monk asked, holding his staff in the air with one hand and waving a wooden crucifix with the other.

'I am your king,' William answered. 'Get out of my way.'

The monk took a few steps forward until he was at William's side, not in the least intimidated by the man high on his horse.

'The land on which you tread is holy. You are in the lands of Saint Cuthbert, and you bring only violence. You are the devil incarnate,' the monk said. 'The demonic deeds you do will deliver you nothing but your destruction. You are Satan, and the Lord will strike you down.'

'On the contrary,' William said. 'I am your lord, and I will strike you down.'

With that, William kicked the monk hard in the chest and sent him flying backwards into the roadside ditch.

William and his men laughed as the monk cried out and struggled to get to his feet. As they rode by, the monk began cursing them all.

'A curse on you, bastard king. Saint Cuthbert will send you to hell.'

A scream followed as one of William's knights lopped off the monk's head with his sword. Without pausing, the column moved on.

'I want you to pay special attention today, Waltheof,' William said. 'What you are about to witness is the wrath you have brought upon your countrymen. They will pay the price for their misdeeds, just like that wretch back there, for their support of you rebels; their treason. You are about to discover the full cost as I take reprisals for the actions of you reckless few.'

'Aren't we going back to York?' Waltheof asked, puzzled.

'No. We're to continue on our mission.'

'Haven't you done enough?'

'I've hardly got started,' William said. 'We're going as far north as Scotland, and when we've cleared up there, only then will we return to York.'

William then kicked his horse into a canter, and his followers followed suit. Once outside the city gates, they split up into two groups, one to harry the eastern side of the county and the other to harry the central areas on their way north. After three days filled with destruction, they arrived outside of Jarrow. Waltheof, with William's party, met up with Robert of Mortain.

'It was such a shame,' William said to his brother. 'Everywhere, villages were abandoned, deserted by one and all. They even took their animals with them.'

'It was the same for us, too. No sign of life anywhere. They all took to the hills.'

'I hope you destroyed everything just the same,' William said.

'Of course,' Robert replied.

'Good. Jarrow's waiting for us to pay a visit. Let's get going before sunset. There doesn't seem to be any daylight in this God-forsaken land.'

William's army made its way into Jarrow to discover the town deserted, just like all the other towns they had visited over the previous few days. The monastery was in ruins, as was its church, so William and his men made the best of what the little was on offer. William made himself comfortable in the hall in the middle of the deserted town. Soon, his cooks were scurrying about preparing the meal for the evening. As they waited for their meal, William and Waltheof talked.

'You English, you make so much of your Venerable Bede, but you let his church fall into disrepair. Why?'

'We didn't let it fall into disrepair. It was the Danes that did the damage, but even though they were pagans, the destruction they inflicted pales into insignificance compared to the devastation wreaked by your men upon my country.'

'My kingdom, you mean, Waltheof.'

'What use is a kingdom if it is in ruins?'

'It won't always be like this. Eventually, these lands will be farmed again, perhaps by new settlers. They will have to make new farming tools, ploughs, and they'll have to build up herds and flocks from nothing. When they do this, they can reflect on why they have the opportunity. One thing is certain; they will have respect for their king, which will run deep. You may think my actions drastic, but they are necessary. Tomorrow we travel to the Tyne Valley and persuade more people of the futility of resistance to my rule.'

There was a clatter as servants entered the hall with trays of piping hot food.

'Ah, here's our supper. Enjoy your meal Waltheof; you deserve it. You've had a hard day.'

William was as good as his word. The next day, he again split his forces, one travelling along the north of the Tyne and the other along the south. Sir Ralph Pomeroy was a part of those forces that roamed south of the river. For three days, they wasted the land, travelling up hills and down dales, destroying everything in their path. Each day the wind blew fiercer, and the weather grew colder until every bone in everybody felt chilled. They slept in halls, stables, grain stores, and outbuildings each night. Their tents, more than adequate for summer campaigns, were in tatters. Some soldiers were so desperate to keep warm they even slept in pig styes. The freezing conditions were taking their toll. William's party was relieved when the troops woke up to discover the sun had appeared on the fourth day of their expedition.

'At last, something like a pleasant day,' William said. 'We'll be in Hexham by nightfall. Saddle up, and we'll be on our way.'

William and his men made their way across the moor with morale rising. Noticing a ridge that ran south to north, William ordered Pomeroy to see the far side.

'Sir Ralph, look and see what's on the other side of that ridge, will you? Someone might live down there, and we wouldn't want to disappoint anybody. How would they feel if they discovered their king had passed them by without stopping to say hello?'

Pomeroy smiled at William's little joke and turned his horse up to the top of the ridge. As he neared the top, fear struck his heart in a way it had never done before; revealed before him was a cloud-filled valley. As he rose high over the ridge, a giant appeared on the cloud, but worse still, emanating from the giant's head was a halo of rings that were all the colours of the rainbow. Pomeroy halted, and his horse, sensing his master's fear, reared up.

'No need to worry. Stay calm,' Pomeroy stammered to his horse before casting a glance at the giant, who seemed to turn away.

'Let's rejoin the king, shall we?'

William watched perplexed as Pomeroy made his return journey. As the white-faced knight approached him, William knew he would not be the recipient of good news. He walked his horse forward to be out of hearing distance from his men.

'What is it?' he asked Pomeroy when he brought his horse to a halt.

'I've seen nothing like it,' Pomeroy said quietly. 'There's a giant in the clouds on the other side of the valley. It has rainbows surrounding its head.'

If it had been another knight telling such a story, William might have thought him mad.

'Show me,' he said.

Pomeroy led William towards the top of the ridge, and William, not being much of a horseman, dismounted. If his horse were going to rear up, he would prefer not to end up flat on his back in front of his men.

While Pomeroy stayed with the horses, William cautiously approached the top of the ridge, his breath forming clouds in the chilly morning air. As he reached the top, he noticed a gigantic figure appear on the clouds opposite. Just as Pomeroy had said, a multicoloured halo emanated from its head. William stared in wonder and dread at the deathly silent figure and wondered if it might be an angel. He knew no one could kill him in battle, but would he meet his end at the hands of an apparition? He had no idea. And then he thought about the monk who had cursed him before being beheaded. Was this something to do with him?

Backing away from the ridge, he made his way to Pomeroy, 'Say nothing to the men,' he said. 'I don't want to alarm them. We'll go to Hexham, and once we've rested, carry on north.'

The order was perfectly acceptable to Pomeroy, and once William had mounted his horse, the two rejoined the column.

'Carry on, men. Nothing there of any interest,' William said.

The column moved forward and reached Hexham by the end of the day, where they were to stay for a few days of rest and recovery. The cold, harsh weather of the north was taking its toll on men more used to the milder climate of the south. Life, too, was difficult for the northerners who had to leave their homes. They were heading north to Scotland or had taken to the hills or woods. The lucky ones found a roof over their heads. Most were making do with whatever shelter they could assemble or find, a cave, a shepherd's hut. They took whatever supplies they could, including as many of their animals as they could. They prepared to hide until the storm was over, and then, when the skies were clear again, they would step out into the sunshine. All of them had made the same mistake. They all thought there would be something to go back to once the Normans had gone.

At the end of the second day at Hexham, night fell early, as it always did in the north. The sky was clear star-studded and beautiful to behold. It was gone midnight when the demons appeared, if that is what they were. They started quietly at first, barely audible crackling and green like, like a snake wriggling its way across the sky, alarming the sentries. Gradually the sound grew louder, and the snake turned to beams, which in turn formed curtains that moved this way and that across the sky until they filled the whole of a man's field of vision. By this time, the alarm had gone out, and every man was on his feet out in the open weapon in hand, staring skyward. William, his brother Robert and Earl Waltheof were amongst them.

'Do you know what this is?' William asked the earl.

Waltheof did not know the nature of the light in the sky, but he had seen displays like these on rare occasions. As far as he was aware, the stories told about them were old wives tales.

'They are the curse of Saint Cuthbert,' Waltheof lied. 'There is trouble ahead.'

'What do you mean, 'Curse of Saint Cuthbert?''

'It's said that Saint Cuthbert shows the gates of hell to anyone who incurs his wrath. But you need not worry; only if you offend him a second time does he take you beyond the gates and into hell itself.'

'Rubbish,' William said.

Waltheof held his gaze, staring him out.

William turned his attention to the lights that were now flaring red and green but harming no one.

For a quarter of an hour, the Normans looked up into the heavens, fearfully watching the dazzling display until the lights faded away. In the morning, William led his men south to York. Once again, leaving a trail of death and destruction behind them, William's army spent a week descending on village after village, leaving desolation and ruin in their wake.

Once, while travelling, William watched as Waltheof observed a crow pecking at the eyes of a corpse. It made a gruesome sight, but it was the nauseating smell of the dead that was something he would never forget. Naturally, he had seen bodies before, and some of them had suffered dreadful wounds, but they were newly dead. Some bodies here had been lying around for quite a while, and animals and birds had eaten some.

'Can't we at least stop and bury them?'

'No. They are there as a warning.'

'A warning to who? There's no one left alive.'

'In the future, people will come to these lands, and they will take heed of what happened here.'

'But these people weren't soldiers. What harm had they done?'

'They sheltered rebels. They supported a pretender to the throne and the acts of atrocity committed by him and his men. We will leave the bodies here as a reminder to those who contemplate resisting me; the same fate awaits them.'

William eyed the scene. 'So, Earl Waltheof, what do you think of your chances of putting Edgar on the throne now?'

Waltheof cast a glance around him. In an instant, he knew there was no future for Edgar as King of England. The price to be paid in blood would be way too high, even if he were successful. He turned to William to find the king looking knowingly into his eyes.

William answered for him, 'There is no chance, is there? These bodies you see strewn about here are testaments to my resolve. I will meet any move against the crown with such force my enemies will think themselves in Armageddon.'

Waltheof could see William meant every word.

'Never underestimate the power of violence,' the king continued. 'It's something everybody respects. The message is unequivocal. You English need to know your place. I'm not interested in you loving me. I don't even need your respect. I just need you to know your place. A cowering animal will never give you trouble. It's simply grateful not to take a beating. People are the same, make them cringe, and they'll give you no trouble. If you have trouble, teach them respect with a sharp steel blade. You may think me cruel, but do I have any choice? Do you imagine kingship to be so easy? Do you think a king simply does what he wants whenever he chooses? My friend, kingship is a gilded cage made with a golden crown. Even if I had wings, I couldn't fly. The burden of responsibility weighs me down. I always have my subjects to consider.'

Waltheof was aghast.

'Everyone makes demands, the Pope, not least amongst them. Then I have my barons, who I must reward for services rendered. And as if that isn't enough, I have the Danes breathing down my neck, the Scots and Welsh raiding across the border wherever the fancy takes them. And on top of all that, you, Edgar and all your friends rise against me at every opportunity.'

Exasperated, William came to a halt.

'It's all very well leading an uprising against your king, but unless you're successful, you'll find there is a price to pay for treason.'

'But these people had nothing to do with any of that. This is a slaughter of the innocents, and they deserve a Christian burial. You could at least grant them that.'

'How can you be so self-righteous with me? You dare to take the moral high ground when you and your men butchered the garrison in York to a man. You spared just two castellans, and that was only because you thought they'd be worth a pretty penny. Could you spare me the sermon and hear the lesson? Any more uprisings, and I will treat the rebels the same as those here. I don't care if I have to kill every Englishman, woman, and child. I am and will be the King of England to my dying days.

'I will hear no more of your judgements.'

It was another two days before the two spoke to each other again.

Chapter 42

Bondi and Whitgar had another dreadful night at Thirsk and buried Alfstan, his family, and Thor in the churchyard in the morning. It was a solemn affair. They had no shrouds to cover the bodies, but they made sure they laid them to rest facing west to east. Both said words over the graves of the people they knew before continuing their journey. Their destination for the day was Sigulf's farmstead.

'You'll like Sigulf and his wife too,' Bondi said.

'I hope they haven't had a visit from the Normans yet,' Whitgar replied.

'They should be all right where they are. They're off the beaten track.'

They picked their way through the town with feelings of trepidation, regret, and revulsion. They were dreading what might be ahead of them, regretting not having buried the dead in Thirsk and horrified by the sight of so many bodies killed while they fled.

Wrapped up to keep out the cold, they made good time through the frozen haunted landscape where only carrion stirred. By the end of the day, they spotted Sigulf's Farmstead, where the beck flowed into the river and Bondi was relieved to see a little column of smoke rising from the village. As they got closer, the whiff of roasting meat greeted their nostrils.

'Smells like someone's cooking,' Bondi said.

'Yes. I smelled it too,' Whitgar said. 'A hot meal, wouldn't that be nice?'

Bondi smiled, but he had the strangest feeling something was wrong. So did Whitgar.

'I know it's dark, Bondi, but there seems to be no other sign of life. There's not the usual commotion when you approach a farm. It's too quiet.'

Whitgar was right. The place was as silent as the grave. On the alert for anything unusual, the two made their way forward until they could pick out the silhouettes of derelict buildings.

'They've been here then,' Whitgar said. He did not have to say who. 'But it looks as though somebody's survived.'

Bondi surveyed a scene, which was becoming familiar north of the River Ouse. Everywhere was in ruins. When they reached the first charred outbuilding, they dismounted and tethered their horses.

'Let's look around,' Bondi said.

The fire-blackened door had fallen off its hinges and lay flat on the ground. Looking through the doorway, Bondi and Whitgar could pick out three severely burned corpses sprawled across the floor. They exchanged glances. 'Let's get over to the hall,' Bondi said.

They crept over to the ruin of a hall with swords drawn. As they approached the charred husk of a building, they noticed the rough attempt at repair; a poor effort at re-thatching part of the roof and window shutters rehung, as was the firmly closed door. Someone had patched up the walls with the remains of other buildings in the farmstead.

'I don't think it's Normans in there. There are no horses around here, and I can't hear anyone talking,' Bondi whispered.

'Perhaps there's just a sole survivor,' Whitgar replied.

'There's only one way to find out,' Bondi said, pulling up the latch on the door and opening it to see Oslac Hean roasting a haunch of meat by the fire.

'Hello, Oslac,' Bondi said.

Oslac looked at his uninvited guest with suspicion. When Whitgar appeared in the doorway, his eyes fixed on him.

'Who are you?' he said.

'I'm Bondi Wynstanson. I stayed here a while ago,' he said, sheathing his sword. Whitgar followed Bondi's lead.

'I remember. Who's your friend?'

'Whitgar Guthrumson.'

'Where's your fine lady?' Oslac asked.

The question surprised and stung Bondi.

'She is not my fine lady; she is a lady I was escorting to the Atheling.'

'So, what are you doing back here?'

'We're on our way to Lincoln. What happened here? Are you the only one left alive?' Bondi said.

'I think you'd better come in and shut the door. The Frenchies visited, killed every living thing, and burned the place down. I'm the only one who survived. Those animals they didn't kill, they drove off. It was terrible.'

'We've seen the bodies. Why haven't you buried them?' Bondi said.

'I've only got one pair of hands,' Oslac said. 'And the ground's frozen solid.'

'What happened to Sigulf and Cynwise?'

'Killed with the rest. They'd have killed me too, but I saw them coming and hid.'

Bondi could hear the fat sizzling and smell the meat roasting, and his mouth watered. Oslac gave him a contemptuous look. 'I suppose you want something to eat?' he said.

'We have a wild boar strapped to a horse. We're happy to share.'

The offer appeared to interest Oslac because the scowl disappeared from his face. Bondi despised the man and considered relieving him of his cooking task. He could never stand up to a housecarl. Oslac read his mind.

'Thank you,' he said. 'I'd ask you to take a seat, but there aren't any to sit on. I'd fetch your horses and boar in now if I were you. If you don't, the wolves will have them.'

'Whitgar, would you bring in the horses?' Bondi said.

As he stepped out of the door, he could hear howling in the woods.

'The sooner he brings the horses in, the happier I'll be,' Bondi said.

'I don't doubt it,' Oslac replied.

Whitgar returned, led the horses inside, and tied them up at the far end of the hall. With the thought of a juicy roast in mind, he made his way back towards Bondi and Oslac, who were by the fire, with his and Bondi's wooden trenchers in his hands.

'Give us your plates, then,' Oslac said.

Whitgar handed them over, and Oslac cut a few pieces off the joint for them.

'I'm sorry, I can only offer you spring water to drink. The Normans poisoned the well; heaven only knows what's in the river. I'm lucky to

361

have the spring.' Oslac said. 'I don't know where I'd be without it.'

'You're right there. Did anybody else escape?' Bondi asked.

'No, just me.'

'What happened to Sigulf and Cynwise?' Bondi said.

'They were amongst the first to go, killed outside the hall there,' Oslac said, nodding towards the door. 'I've taken care of some of the dead, though. No need to worry about that.' He smiled reassuringly, his eyes sparkling brightly.

Bondi noticed a big, two-handled adze leaning against the side of the hall. The handle looked to be made of green wood but judging by the in-ground dirt and grease, he had used it a lot.'

'I had to make a new handle for that,' Oslac said. 'The bastards burned everything,' Oslac said, spooning meat and juice into his mouth as fast as he could. 'I fished the metal part out of the ashes.'

Bondi noticed a couple of sacks by the adze and wondered what could be in them. Oslac followed his gaze. 'You're lucky you found me here. I'm leaving first thing in the morning,' he said.

Having wolfed down his meal, Bondi asked where he intended to go.

'I'm going west, where it will most likely be safe. Chester seemed the best choice.'

Bondi nodded in agreement. Whitgar was still too busy eating to pay attention to the conversation.

'How are you going to get there?' Bondi asked.

'I thought I'd walk,' Oslac said.

'It's a long way. Do you have any provisions?'

'Oh, yes. I've got a nice piece of wild boar,' Oslac said, smiling and nodding at Whitgar and Bondi's catch.

'What were you going to survive on before we came along?' Bondi asked.

'Oh, I've got a few other bits and pieces that should be enough to get me there.'

Bondi's gaze flicked across to the sacks by the adze, and Oslac tensed.

'What's in the sacks?' Bondi asked.

'Like I said, just a few bits and pieces to get me by.'

'What bits and pieces?'

'You're inquisitive for a guest in someone else's home, but if you insist on knowing, I'll tell you. In my sacks, I have all my worldly possessions, which I intend to take with me when I leave in the morning.'

Bondi's eyes moved back to the adze, and he wondered if all of Oslac's digging had been for burials.

Whitgar, who had finished his meal, was now paying attention.

'What are you staring at?' Oslac demanded to know.

'Is anything for sale?' Whitgar asked. 'You might have something we like, and we could give you a good price.'

Oslac was wrongfooted by this question and wasn't sure what to say.

'Let's see, Oslac,' Bondi said. 'As Whitgar says, we can give you a good price and think how useful it would be to have a few coins hidden from outlaws, rather than bulky eye-catching sacks full of valuables.'

The suggestion made sense, but Oslac appeared reluctant to take up the offer, but after some thought, he agreed.

He picked up a sack and spilt the contents onto the makeshift table. Before their eyes, Bondi and Whitgar could see pendants, brooches, wrist bands, amulets, and a pair of drinking horns with silver fittings. What stood out to Bondi was a pair of pewter wrist clasps that looked familiar.

'That's an awful lot of bits and pieces, Oslac,' Bondi said. 'How did you come by them?'

'They've been in the family for years.'

'Whose family?' Bondi asked.

'I...'

'Those are Cynwise's wrist clasps,' Bondi said.

'What if they are? She's got no further use for them,' Oslac snapped.

'You took them off the bodies. What else did you steal?'

Bondi was uncomfortable with the look Oslac gave him. 'What else?' he asked again.

Oslac laughed, and Whitgar walked across the hall and picked up the other sack. Oslac grabbed it too, and the pair struggled with it until Bondi intervened, twisting Oslac's arm behind his back.

Whitgar emptied the sack on the tabletop to reveal more valuables and a joint of roast meat.

'That's odd,' Whitgar said, 'There's a tattoo on it.'

Oslac grinned manically.

'It's the same one as Sigulf had,' Bondi said.

Bondi and Whitgar exchanged a glance, and Oslac giggled.

Whitgar's head turned to look at the meat on the spit, then at the tattooed joint on the table and then at Oslac. The horror of what had happened struck him hard, and he vomited over the floor. Bondi was heaving with him. Both men were violently sick.

Bondi was the first to recover. Still doubled up, he stared hatefully at Oslac. 'You despicable shit. How could you?' he said.

'They don't need their trinkets now, and they won't be missing them. You might as well put them to good use. You could say the same about the leg,' Oslac replied. 'I don't know what the fuss is about. Sigulf was never any use for anything. The only thing good about him is he tasted delicious, better than fish or pork.'

There was a roar, and the two men turned to see Whitgar, with sword raised, crossing the room. He brought his blade down hard into Oslac's shoulder, cutting down to his chest. Oslac fell open-mouthed, landing face-first into the fire.

Whitgar continued screaming as he hacked and hacked at Oslac's body.

'You need to stop now,' Bondi said. Whitgar did not hear a word.

'I said stop,' Bondi bellowed. 'Now!'

Whitgar froze and turned to his friend, his eyes ablaze with indignation. 'Can you believe it?' he said.

Bondi wretched again at the thought of what they had done.

'What do we do now?' Whitgar asked when his friend had finished.

'We can't stay here,' Bondi said.

'We can't leave,' Whitgar said. 'It's too cold and dangerous out there. Let's clear up and leave in the morning.'

They dragged Oslac's body out of the fire by his legs and left it outside for the wolves.

Once they were back into the hall, Whitgar asked, 'What will we do with those?' nodding towards Sigulf's remains.

'Bury them,' Bondi said.

'We can't bury them now. The ground's too hard, and besides, it's too dark. We'll have to do it first thing in the morning.'

'What should we do with the valuables?'

'Bury them with Sigulf's remains. I never want to see them again,' Bondi replied.

'I know how you feel,' Whitgar said.

Holding his head in his hands, 'I don't believe this. I've never known anything so evil, heart-breaking, so monstrous. I thought I'd seen it all, but this, this…'

Bondi stopped talking. He could find no words to explain how he felt.

'We'd better put what's left of your friend in a sack with the rest of the things,' Whitgar said.

'Put them in the corner at the other end of the hall, away from the horses, and we'll turn in for the night.'

'Why should I do it? He was your friend.' Whitgar said.

'Yes, he was my friend. Which is why I think you ought to do it.'

Whitgar saw the pleading looking Bondi's eyes and had to admit to himself; it was not something he would want to do with someone close to him.

'All right,' he said.

Once he had performed his task, Whitgar and Bondi turned in for the night. Both had a fitful sleep riddled with bad dreams and dread. It was not just the last few hours' events that plagued them. Bondi dreamed of Morwenna, and Whitgar fretted about Elfwyn. When they awoke before dawn the following day, they were both preoccupied with thoughts of their loved ones. Nevertheless, they had to get on with things, and they wanted nothing more than to put a lot of miles between themselves and the farmstead.

The next day, when it was light enough, they buried Sigulf's remains after digging a hole with Oslac's adze. They continued to Lincoln with the untouched boar strapped onto their saddles. Hunger gnawed at them later, but they could not eat.

Chapter 43

When William finally reached York, he breathed a sigh of satisfaction. The city was partially rebuilt, enough to offer a good deal of his men shelter. His troops could recover from the ravages of the northern winter before making the journey south and the comfort of their homes and dwelling places.

'Comrades, here we shall rest before pushing on to Winchester,' William addressed his soldiers from horseback while they were gathered in the square. He told them how proud he was of what they had achieved and their victory over the English.

'I'm sure you'll be glad to get away from this place. But now, for the next few days, I want you to enjoy yourselves.'

To a cheer, he left his men and made his way to the great hall, where he discovered a messenger waiting for him.

'What is it?' William asked, his instincts telling him, whatever it was, this news would not be good.

'A request for help from Earl Roger. An army, led by Edric the Wild, has descended on Shrewsbury and taken the town but not the castle. Stafford was also in rebel hands when I left, but the garrison was still holding out.

'Rebels are also launching attacks in Cheshire. They can't capture any castles but are creating havoc, ravaging the countryside and its Norman settlers. Our men are confined to their garrisons and cannot mount a concerted attack. We need your help to crush them.'

William listened while the message was relayed to him. His face grew tense and turned redder and then white. He was a perfect picture of contained explosive rage. His thoughts flew back over the past few weeks; the trekking over the bitter frozen wilderness seemed to have been for nothing. He felt as though he were dealing with wildfires. *I extinguish one, and another bursts out immediately afterwards.*

I'll lead the men to Chester and Stafford, but they want to go home. They've had enough. I've had enough. We've all had enough. But there was nothing else for it. He would have to put off going to Winchester.

William decided his troops needed to recover before facing the ordeal of another expedition through the freezing wastelands of the frozen north. He would break the news right away but give them two days' rest in York to recuperate from their ordeals. At a war council, he told his Lieutenants, 'Comrades, I know it was Winchester to which we were going to travel, but because of attacks by the rebels, we will make a diversion into Cheshire, to visit our English friends on the way.'

The hall remained silent. No one showed any enthusiasm for the task. The 'diversion' would involve crossing the backbone of England. The Pennines.

'I expect you to be ready first thing the day after tomorrow. Prepare your men and enjoy what remains of your time here before we leave.'

William had strengthened his position. The Northumbrians had suffered a terrible blow, killed, or chased off their lands. What remained was now part of the royal demesne and supported the sheriffs William had appointed over the area. Parts of Mercia were going to suffer the same treatment. And so, the king led his begrudging comrades out of York, but with no one familiar with the territory, they set off in the wrong direction. Two days later and the troops were complaining. Another week, after a repeat of their earlier expedition inflicting murder and misery upon the people of the north, dissent grew in the ranks. They nominated Robert of Mortain to approach the king.

'The men want to talk to you, Will.'

'About what, Robert?'

'They feel you have led them into something to which they had not agreed?'

William's face turned white. A quiet rage boiled up in him. 'All of them or just a few loudmouths?'

'About fifty. But many remain silent.'

'Are you telling me mutiny is brewing?'

'I'm saying we have a problem that needs addressing. For those who've been with you from the start, we joined the cause to remove a usurper from the throne. We did this a long while ago.'

'Continue,' William said, with a stern look in his eye.

'This was to be a short affair which most of us thought would be over after your coronation. By now, we imagined we'd either be back home or reaping the rewards of the conquest and enjoying the fruits of our new lands. We wouldn't mind the additional time we've spent on campaign, but we're from Normandy, Anjou, Brittany, and Maine. This place, this frozen hell, it's too much to endure. Every day, men and horses are dying. They ask, most respectfully, you release them from the terms they accepted when given their fiefs.'

'Have I asked them to do anything I haven't done myself? Am I from the far north of Norway and blessed with a constitution that allows me to feel no cold and never a deprivation? No. I am a man just like them. I suffer the same ordeals as them, and I carry the burden of command with me as I do so.

'I won't release them from their terms, but I will reward them for their efforts. There'll be no bargaining. They'll settle down for the night, and in the morning, we shall continue on our mission and on to Chester, where food, warmth and rest await us.'

Robert looked unsure.

'What are you waiting for?' William snapped.

Robert had no answer. Slowly, he turned and left. When he explained what William had to say to the men, he added, 'We have to make the journey, anyway. At least we're heading in the right direction now.'

He impressed no one. But what else was there to do? Robert was right. So the army trudged on through dales, snowdrifts, and harsh, biting winds. William, always to be seen at the chief of his troops, led them on under a pitiless sky and through merciless snow while a callous Jack Frost cruelly nipped at any exposed skin.

Events took the same course. Soldiers proceeded up a valley or across a moor, looking for a farm, a village, anywhere there was mischief to be had. They robbed and burned even the smallest churches, leaving nowhere to pray to God for help. It was as though the Devil himself paid a visit and delivered them into a hell of a sort they had never imagined. No fire, no brimstone, no embers to melt the flesh, but he appeared first as men, every bit as devilish as he. Death by torture, murder, and unimagined brutality for those the Normans caught. Those who escaped the cold blades were cast into frozen oblivion. Sword and spear carried most away, and slavery took the rest. They left the carcases to rot.

Soon, word of the approach of the Normans reached the ears of those in Chester, a town crammed with those fortunate enough to have escaped King William's wrath. In the Great Hall, Aldytha and Edric were deep in conversation. Edric was pleading with Aldytha to take her son to the safety of Ireland.

'You need to leave the country, my love. At least for a while. He's in danger here,' he said.

'What about you? Aren't you coming with us?' Aldytha answered.

'No. I'll stay here and salvage what I can. This doesn't have to be the end of the rebellion. We find more men, but you must get Harold to safety. King Lochlain is expecting you. I'll send for you when it's safe.'

'But Edric,' she said. And before she could finish her sentence, a servant appeared in the doorway. 'We're ready to set sail,' he said.

Edric held her arms in his hands. 'I'll hear no more. Go now,' he said, leading her towards the doors.

They stepped out into the warm winter sunlight to find Harold and his nurse waiting with the manservant. They climbed aboard a wagon, which proceeded through the crowds on Watergate Street and the quays, where a ship was ready to leave for Ireland.

'It won't be long before we're together again, my love,' Edric said. 'I just need to take care of a few things before I join you.'

Turning to the little boy in his nurse's arms, he said, 'Look after your mother for me, won't you?'

Harold looked confused, and Edric laughed. 'Time to climb aboard,' he said.

Aldytha and her servant and nurse climbed into a fearsome-looking longship and at once recognised her wooden chests stowed on the deck. The crew cast off, and Harold waved goodbye to the only father he had ever known. Edric returned the wave, and the tide carried his lover and her son away.

'Farewell and have a good journey. I'll see you in Ireland in a few weeks,' Edric said, with a quiver in his voice and tears in his eyes.

Aboard the ship, Aldytha paled but still smiled and waved as the longship spirited them towards the Irish Sea.

Chapter 44

Bondi and Whitgar had kept well clear of York as they headed southward. Time after time, they came across ruined buildings, churches, farms, homes, and mills. The perishing cold had given way to a thaw, wholly welcome at first, but then the snow had turned to water revealing the gruesome winter crop, the bitter harvest of the north, there, lying on the ground, robbed of life, respect, and dignity. The two men were glad to leave Yorkshire behind them and finally arrive in Lincolnshire, where there had been no wasting, and the countryside looked strangely normal.

'Do you think they'll be many patrols here, Bondi?' Whitgar asked his friend.

'I'm not sure, but we'd best keep off the main roads,' he said.

For two days, they travelled until they reached Lincoln. The sight that greeted them was shocking and becoming more commonplace. They passed through the city gates and made their way through the busy streets up to Merleswein's Hall, arriving to discover the building vanished and a castle in its place. They stopped in their tracks.

'What do you make of this?' Bondi said.

'What do we do now?' Whitgar asked.

'Stable the horses and find someone to help us.'

Later, Bondi and Whitgar took a walk around town. Bondi caught sight of someone he recognised. A servant of Merleswein's.

'What's happened to Merleswein's Hall?' Whitgar asked.

'The Normans flattened it to make way for the castle.'

'Where did everybody go?' Bondi asked.

'Scattered to the winds. Most of them have joined Edgar; the rest have mostly left for the Fens or the forests, but I hear Lord Thurold's back in Spalding with his new wife.'

Bondi felt the shock wave course through his system as the news registered.

'What's he doing there?' Whitgar asked.

'I've no idea. He comes and goes as he likes. I'd get away from here if I was you. It's not a good place to be. The Frenchies are everywhere, and they're not nice. They run the place now, from their fortress,' he said, nodding towards the castle.

Bondi looked up the street to the stronghold, which was constructed of timber but had a look of permanence. Stonemasons were working on the formidable-looking entrance. He wondered if the entire fortification would one day be made of stone. Once again, his heart sank.

'Let's go to Spalding,' Whitgar said, hoping he might hear word of Elfwyn.

'Yes,' said Bondi, hoping to talk to Morwenna.

'Thanks for your help. We'll take your advice,' Whitgar said.

They left Lincoln behind them and travelled along the byways where the Normans dare not set foot. At the end of the second day's hard riding, they arrived at Thurold's Hall outside Spalding. They entered the thane's home to find him with Morwenna seated by the fire, enjoying its warmth.

'Welcome,' Thurold said. He smiled, but his bulging eyes remained expressionless. 'Dry yourselves off by the hearth,' he said before calling for servants to bring drink. Morwenna, looking so gaunt, came as a shock to Bondi. Usually, in good colour, she was pale now and even though it had not been long since they had last seen her, she seemed to have lost weight and aged a little. When they greeted her, she smiled at the two but said nothing, and Bondi had to fight the desire to take her in his arms.

When they had made themselves comfortable, Thurold asked, 'How can I help you?'

'We'd just like a roof over our head for a few nights,' Whitgar said, doing the talking while Bondi wrestled with his emotions.

'Of course, you may stay here and rest awhile. Where is it you're heading?'

'We're not sure. We went south when we had to leave our ship, as there were too many Normans up north. We thought Merleswein's Hall would be a safe place, but when we got to Lincoln, we discovered the Normans had built a castle on top of it. We heard you gone to Spalding.'

'I realised I'd best serve the Atheling here,' Thurold said. 'Come the summer, he'll return, and he needs a friendly port in which to land. Why don't you stay until he arrives, and you can join him then?'

'That's a truly kind offer, and we'll be glad to accept,' Whitgar said. He then addressed Morwenna, 'Have you any news of Elfwyn?' he asked.

'Not a word from anyone,' Morwenna said. 'We've made enquiries, but no one's seen her since she fell from her horse. We thought she'd go to our father's hall, but no one in Lincoln has seen hide nor hair of her. I can't think where she can be. She's completely disappeared.'

Whitgar was crestfallen by the news, and it showed in his expression.

'I wish I could tell you more, Whitgar. I really do,' Morwenna said, wiping a tear from her eye.

A door opened, and a nanny appeared with three children, who left her side and ran to their mother.

'Thank you, Sherilda,' Morwenna said, taking the children in her arms. She held them close, her face full of joy, and Bondi saw the woman he knew. He had to force himself to look away from her, to find a distraction.

'Sherilda,' Bondi said. 'Don't you remember me?'

The nurse looked at him for a second before she recognised the grimy-looking man standing before her.

'Bondi,' she said, as a smile burst out across her handsome face. She stepped forward and hugged him before blushing and stepping back as she wiped imaginary hair from her face.

'It's good to see you too, Sherilda,' the housecarl said, smiling.

'It's wonderful to see you three again as well,' Bondi said to the children, who didn't recognise him and were unconvinced as to his identity. They just stared at him with suspicion.

'How did you like Scotland?' Bondi asked. The children said nothing.

'They loved it but missed me,' Morwenna said. 'So, I brought them here to their new home where we'll be together.'

'And soon there may be more of us,' Thurold said with a leer everyone present found nauseating, Bondi especially. When Morwenna had addressed him for those few moments, he felt a thrill, as though they had connected on another level. And as their eyes met, he saw something he had never seen in them; pleading.

'Ah, here's our meal,' Thurold said as servants entered with trays of piping hot food, the smell of freshly roasted meat filling the air making every mouth water.

Plates were filled, drinks poured, and the company settled down to eat.

'Is it wise to stay here, Thurold?' Bondi said. 'I'm thinking of the danger. Scotland is safe. Here you could get a visit from the Normans.'

'They don't worry me,' Thurold replied. I can take care of any visiting Normans.

'If you'd seen what Whitgar and I saw in the north, you wouldn't be so keen on staying here, especially with the ladies and the children.'

'Are you questioning my judgement, Bondi?'

'I'm just expressing my concern.'

'There's no need for that. I can keep us safe enough. I have twenty good men and a well-defended farmstead. If you think you're in danger, you're free to leave,' Thurold said before taking a deep gulp of wine from a fine glass beaker. 'Now, if you'll excuse me for just a little while,' he said, getting to his feet and making his way outside.

The instant Thurold disappeared through the door, Bondi leaned over to Morwenna and said, 'I can't stand it here. Tell me what's going on?' Bondi said. 'Why are you with him? Come away with me.'

'What about the children?'

'Bring them too, and Sherilda. You can bring half of Lincolnshire with you. I don't care. I just can't go on seeing you with Thurold.'

'But my marrying Thurold was my father's dying wish. He so wanted us to be married.'

'Rubbish,' Bondi said. 'While your father was breathing his last, Thurold was running for his life.'

Shock appeared on Morwenna's face.

'It's true,' Whitgar said. 'I saw it myself.'

Silence fell on the table as Thurold, looking relieved, entered the hall. He could tell straight away Morwenna was seething and the rest of the company looked livid.

'Is there a problem?' Thurold asked?

'Is it true?' Morwenna demanded.

'Is what true?' Thurold answered, a picture of innocence.

'My father never asked you to marry me, 'with his dying breath?"' Morwenna said, spitting out the words.

'My dear, it was your father's wish that we marry,' Thurold said.

'Not his dying wish, though?'

'It would have been if he had had the opportunity to speak,' Thurold asserted. 'On the morning of his final day, it was the last time he spoke to me. He told me there was nothing he wanted more than for us to be man and wife. If he did, he could go to his grave a happy man. I imagine him looking down on us now, joyful in his knowledge that you are in the safe hands of a man of substance,' Thurold said, his eyes turned heavenward.

'You make me sick, you toad,' Morwenna said, standing to face him. 'How can you have the temerity to lie to me?'

Thurold reached to touch her, but Morwenna pulled her arm away.

'Don't lay a hand on me, you wretched man.'

Morwenna stormed out of the hall to their chambers, where, in the dark, she smashed her shin on the bedframe. She cried out in pain and then in misery as she sat on the bed with her head in her hands.

Back in the hall, Thurold excused himself and bade goodnight to his guests. He entered the chamber with a candle to light his way, and he found Morwenna crying as she lay curled up on the bed.

'Don't upset yourself, my love,' he said. 'It's true, in essence. You know your father wanted us married, and here we are. Soon you'll come to love me as I love you. We'll make a family together, and you'll be happy, you'll see.'

The idea filled Morwenna with dread.

'We'll talk about this in the morning when everything will seem much clearer, and you'll understand it's for the best,' Thurold said.

He got up, went around to his side of the bed, undressed, and climbed in before blowing out the candle. While his wife lay beside him sobbing fitfully, Thurold fell asleep. Eventually, Morwenna also fell asleep, and there they slept in the darkness, oblivious to the world and the man who entered their chamber.

Bondi crept into the pitch-black room, silent as a ghost and stopped in the doorway, waiting until his eyes had adjusted to the dark. When ready, slowly and quietly, he crossed the bedroom where they slept, Thurold snoring gently. It was a shame he lay on his side; it would make things more complicated but not impossible.

Bondi positioned the pillow at the correct angle, leaned forward with stiffened arms and forced it onto Thurold's face. Thurold's muffled protest failed to wake Morwenna. Bondi kneeled onto the struggling man's chest, pinning his arms down but failing to control his legs which flailed violently. The old thane was putting up a heroic fight, but his strength was no match for Bondi's. Soon his protests had subsided, and he lay still. It was then Morwenna awoke.

'What are you doing?'

'I think he's had a seizure. Claimed by God in his sleep.'

Morwenna peered through the darkness at her husband's body husband beside her in bed, an expression of horror on her face. Her eyes moved to the pillow in Bondi's hands.

'What else could I have done?' he said.

'But this is murder,' she whispered.

'No. He just died.'

'You killed him,' she said.

'Shh. You'll wake everybody up.'

'What are we going to do?'

'Nothing,' he said. 'Just get up first thing, act sad, cry a little, and tell everybody he passed away peacefully. Play the part of the grief-stricken widow for a while, and then it'll be forgotten.'

'We'll never get away with it.'

'Why not? The world is in turmoil. The Normans are butchering people the length and breadth of the kingdom. Do you imagine someone passing away in their bed in the night is going to raise questions? People have too many other worries.

'You're free now, Morwenna. You've escaped a loveless marriage based on a lie.'

'Are you saying you killed him for me? Am I supposed to feel grateful?'

'It was partly for you, partly for me. I'd die for you; I'd kill for you. We can be together now. Isn't that what you want?'

'Yes, but not like this,' she answered.

'I don't think there was any other way. Stay here till morning and then rush into the hall distressed.'

'Don't you think people will work out what happened when they see us together?' she said.

'Not if we wait a while. Anyway, what's the alternative. If we tell everybody I murdered him in his sleep, how do you think they'd react?'

Morwenna had no answer.

'Stay in here until daybreak and then make your announcement,' he said.

'Very well.'

'I'll see you at dawn.'

Bondi held her tightly, and they kissed.

'Everything will be all right,' he said as he left.

Morwenna lay on the floor as far away from Thurold's dead body as she could.

Bondi made his way back to his room, failing to notice Sherilda peeping through the crack of her open door.

Chapter 45

After an arduous journey, William and his men approached Chester and gazed across the River Dee at the imposing high stone walls of a Roman city before them. It was a citadel capable of withstanding a siege for weeks or months, perhaps even years. Along the tops of the walls lined up shoulder to shoulder, looking down on him was every citizen in the town. On the other side of the river, side by side on their horses and in their armour, were knights, Sir Walter Gherbod and Sir Ralph Pomeroy. The two friends talked as William's army continued its slow march onwards.

'I hope we're not going to have another bloodbath,' Sir Walter said.

'Does that bother you, Walter?' Pomeroy asked.

'It's not the spilling of blood I mind. It's the spilling of peasants' blood. There's no honour in it. Chasing around the streets on a horse, spearing carpenters, millers, smiths, and the like, it's not for me. It's not soldiering. It's slaughtering.'

'I understand what you mean, Walter. The Battle of Hastings was one thing, but what we're doing up here is another. But you must know, the king is right. We must teach these people a lesson,' Pomeroy said. 'And if destroying everything they possess is the only way to do it, then so be it.'

'But how do you feel about killing women and children?' Sir Walter asked.

'I'll admit it's not so easy.'

'Quite,' Sir Walter said.

As Sir Walter spoke, the city gates opened wide and out strode a wealthy-looking man with a bunch of keys in his hands. A few other important-looking men followed him.

'It looks, Ralph, as though we might have a peaceful day of it,' Gherbod said, looking pleased.

Someone else who looked pleased was the king. 'I wasn't expecting this,' he said to his brother, Robert.

'Neither was I,' Robert said. 'Things might be getting back to normal.'

William brought his horse to a halt just outside the city gates, where a small reception party of local dignitaries stood. One man crossed the bridge across the river and approached William.

'Greetings, King William. Chester welcomes you,' the shire reeve said, ashen-faced and visibly shaking.

News of the slaughter and destruction unleashed by William's army had reached Chester, and the word spread by the refugees had induced nightmares amongst the townsfolk. Many had taken their belongings and departed, leaving empty homes behind them rather than staying and submitting to the hardship and suffering William offered them. Others thought staying was a risk worth taking and were willing to do whatever it took to ensure their beautiful and prosperous city did not share the same fate as York and the other places William had destroyed.

Chester's townsfolk had hoped William might journey south and spare them a visit. Many had prayed for this. Their prayers went unanswered. Now they were wondering if their nightmares might come true.

'Who are you?' William asked the shire reeve.

'Winebald the Reeve, my lord,' the trembling man replied.

'Have you come to offer me the keys to the city?'

'That I have.'

'Where are they?'

'Here. Welcome to Chester,' Winebald said, handing over the keys.

'You've already said that. Now lead us into your wretched town,' William ordered.

The Reeve complied and led the mounted column back across the wooden bridge, through the gates and into the town.

'Will you be staying long?' Winebald was imprudent enough to enquire.

'I'll stay as long as I choose and in the best place in town.'

'Of course. That'll be the great hall, my lord,'

'Will I find an earl there or that Edric fellow?' William asked.

'No, my lord. We haven't seen the earls in years, and Edric left yesterday for Rhuddlan, in Wales,' Winebald replied.

'Show me the delights of your town, and while you're doing that, have someone prepare a feast to celebrate the liberation.'

Winebald snapped orders in an authoritative tone, and the men jumped into action and ran off towards the great hall.

'Where would you like to go first, my lord?'

'Take me for a walk around these impressive-looking walls that offer such a formidable defence.

'Robert,' William called to his brother. 'Come and join me.'

William turned his attention to Winebald. 'I imagine you could hold an army off for months behind these fortifications,' he said, nodding towards the high stone walls.

'Without any trouble,' Winebald replied, a proud smile on his face.

'Then why didn't you?'

In response, Winebald's mouth fell open.

They reached the set of steps that led up to the top of the wall. William and Robert dismounted. 'Lead on, Winebald,' William said.

The Reeve climbed the steps, and when they reached the top, William and Robert admired the view. It was easy to understand why the Romans had built their town and why the Saxons had revived it. Chester commanded an excellent position on the bend of the River Dee with views for miles around. William had an idea.

'Gherbod,' he called to one of his companions below. 'Come up here.'

Walter de Gherbod dismounted and, with a pounding heart, strode over to the foot of the steps. He was unsure whether he ought to feel honoured or wary, but he took the steps two at a time toward his king.

'Yes. What can I do?' the Fleming said, a little out of breath.

'You see that place there between the old wall and the newer one, just there?' William gestured with a sweep of his arm.

Walter looked down to see, apart from thatched roofs and a few wooden shingled roofs, a network of streets running between dwellings and a few workshops, pigsties, and fruit trees dotted about the place. This was a mainly residential part of the town.

'Yes,' Gherbod answered.

'Be a good man and build a castle there. Big as you can manage,' William said.

Gherbod looked shocked but soon recovered his composure. 'When should I start?'

'First thing, tomorrow. And by the way, before you start, go to that minster over there,' William said with a rare warm smile. 'This time tomorrow, you'll be Walter de Gherbod, the Earl of Chester. How does that sound?'

Gherbod, taken by surprise and at first did not know what to say, but he quickly recovered, 'That sounds wonderful,' but his eyes told a different story.

'Go on, Walter. Better rejoin your comrades,' William said, still smiling.

'Lead on Winebald,' William said. Winebald obeyed.

The shire reeve pointed out places of interest as they walked. William and Robert listened and occasionally passed comment.

'There is the wonderful Minster of Saint Werburgh's,' Winebald said, pointing out the minster that, along with its outbuildings, took up about a quarter of the town. 'There are the royal mints,' Winebald said, pointing to buildings indistinguishable from many of the others around and about.

William and Robert gazed about the town from on high. Apart from the Saint Werburgh's, they were just about at rooftop level with every building in Chester. It was quiet for a town of three thousand adults. It was as though the place was holding its breath. After the initial welcome, every inhabitant stayed indoors, hoping to remain unseen.

On the way, William and Robert's attention had turned back to the countryside around the town. The broad river flowed on its way to the sea not far away. Robert noticed an island where someone had erected a cross. He was about to ask Winebald what it was when William asked the reeve, 'What's going on down there?' he snapped, pointing to the wharves.

Winebald looked to where William pointed and saw nothing unusual. 'They're just the wharves. Ships are being loaded or unloaded,' he said.

'What about those people over there? What's happening to them?' William asked, pointing to the far end of the line of ships.

Winebald looked puzzled as he studied the waterfront. The only group of people he could see were a bunch of slaves being herded onto a ship at the far end of the quaysides.

'Do you mean that lot down there climbing onto the knarr?' Winebald asked.

'Yes, I do.'

'They'll be going to Dublin Market,' Winebald said.

'Dublin Market? The slave market, you mean?' William barked.

'Yes,' Winebald said innocently, before adding, 'They'll probably fetch a good price too, by the look of them.'

Enraged, William screamed at his host, 'Get me down there now.'

Startled, Winebald immediately led William and Robert to the steps that took them to the waterfront. On the way, William ordered a few of his men to join them. When William arrived at the slave ship, he demanded to see the captain.

A huge, bearded man stepped forward. 'I am the captain,' he said.

'What's going on here? Are you taking these people for slaves?' William demanded to know.

'What if I am?' the captain replied. 'I've done nothing wrong. I've paid my dues, fair and square, and I'm doing nothing illegal. If you don't believe me, ask the Port Reeve.'

'Do you know who I am?' William said, with malice in his voice.

'No, I don't. Do you know who I am?'

William's men appeared on the quayside and made their way towards him. The burly captain noticed them, but their presence did not affect his attitude.

'I am the King of England,' William informed the captain, who was unimpressed.

'You're not my king, though, are you? Diarmiat Mac Mael na mBo is my lord, as he is to the rest of my men.'

The captain turned his head to indicate the crews of at least eight of the ships tied up at the waterside. There were about fifty armed men there, and they followed the conversation intently.

Sir Ralph Pomeroy, who had arrived on the quays to support his king, though he would turn the odds in the Normans' favour. Slipping quietly away, he returned with a stream of soldiers following behind him, Walter de Gherbod at their head. They crammed onto the wharves and made a menacing sight to the seamen.

'Let me relieve you of your burden, Captain,' William said.

'What burden?'

'The slaves. I'll have no slavery in my kingdom.'

'They're not in your kingdom. They're on my ship,' the captain replied with a grin.

Robert of Mortain said, 'Perhaps we can come to an arrangement with the captain, whereby no one is out of pocket. If he should return them to the trader who sold them and the trader were to reimburse him his money, wouldn't that solve the problem?'

'What say you to that, captain? Who are you?' Robert asked.

'I'm Gluniairn,' the man said. 'Son of Diarmiat.'

Robert paled when he heard the name. He realised he was talking to a prince, the son of the Irish King.

'And I am Robert Count of Mortain. So, what do you say, Gluniairn?' Robert said with his most charming smile.

Gluniairn considered his options. Comply with Robert's request and look weak. Start a battle he could never win, or try to make a profit and make the Normans look foolish and return home with a tale to tell. With an eye on his reputation, he looked Robert in the eye and said, 'Pay me what they're worth, and you've got a deal.'

'I'm not paying you a penny,' William interrupted.

'Who sold them to you?' Robert asked.

'Alric Alwineson,' Gluniairn answered.

'Bring him to me,' Robert ordered one of the men. Within a few tense minutes, Alric Alwineson was standing at the quayside. He was the most devious looking man Robert had ever seen.

'Alric, return Gluniairn's money to him, and you can have the slaves,' Robert said.

'I don't want the slaves,' Alric said, his eyes darting this way and that.

'They're your slaves. Take them back, and we'll say no more about it,' Robert said. He was looking menacing now, and Alric thought perhaps, as the count had many friends, he had best do as ordered.

'I'll accept the slaves,' Alric said.

'There you are, Gluniairn. Are you happy with the arrangement?' Robert said.

'You haven't said how much he's going to pay me yet?'

'I'll pay you what you paid me,' Alric said.

'How is that fair?' Gluniairn asked.

'I sold them to you for sixteen shillings each, and that's what I'll pay you now.'

'Ah, but they're worth more now,' Gluniairn said, grinning from ear to ear.

'How do you work that out?' Alric asked.

'If I sell them at Dublin market, I'll get at least shilling a head more than you're offering.'

'No, you won't.'

'We'll see, shall we?' Gluniairn said with a grin.

'I'll not give you a penny more than you gave me,' Alric replied.

The haggling bored William and Robert, and Pomeroy saw an opportunity to make his mark. He approached Alric and said to Robert, 'Might I be of help.'

Before Robert could answer, he turned his gaze to Alric, took two steps towards him, so they were just a few inches apart, and said calmly and with a leer on his face, 'Give him his money.' All the while, his eyes bored into Alric's.

Alric protested, but Pomeroy grinned and slowly moved his hand to his dagger without taking his eyes off the trader.

Alric returned the gaze, but only for an instant. He had seen the devel, with a scar on his cheek and death in his eyes. 'Very well,' he said, pulling a pouch from inside his tunic. He was about to count out money when Pomeroy grabbed it from him and threw it to Gluniairn.

'There, now you have your money,' Pomeroy said. He glanced at William, looking for a reaction, and William saw a boy looking for approval. Pomeroy saw a father standing in judgement. The king nodded and smiled at his subject, making his heart swell with pride.

Gluniairn caught the pouch and counted out the money. It was less than he had asked for, but it was more than he had paid out only a few hours before. He beamed a huge smile and grinned at his men. 'Fair pay for a fair day's work,' he laughed, and his men laughed with him.

Turning to his crew, Gluniairn said, 'Release them. They're free to go.'

Released from their chains, the slaves made their way to the quay, where they stood around aimlessly. Alric was about to lay claim to them but thought better of it when he saw the look on William's face. As he made to leave, William approached him. 'How can you treat people this way?' An accusation that raised a few eyebrows, even amongst his men.

For the devious looking Alric, this was one humiliation too many. 'Me, treat people that way? They've only offered themselves up for slavery because you drove them off their lands. Who was it who burned down their homes, killed their animals, ruined their crops, destroyed their farming tools, and poisoned their wells? These are the lucky ones, the ones you didn't kill. What else could I do with them? And you dare to judge me?'

The remark stunned William into silence and inaction, and Alric slipped away into hiding while he still had eyes in his head.

William departed for Winchester a week later, leaving the new Earl of Chester, Walter de Gherbod, in charge. William left the city, not as he found it, but with a good part demolished to make way for the new castle, which now stood tall and proud on its mound, casting half of Chester in its shadow. His men destroyed houses and workshops while newly destitute families looked on, their few possessions gathered around them. William had wrecked their livelihoods along with their homes. It would take years for the city to recover. Most of the slaves freed by William gave themselves up, either to Alric Alwineson or Gluniairn, to be sold in Dublin Market or bought by the few locals who could afford them. When William built the castle, the people made destitute joined those to be sold as slaves. None of them had a future in England. The Normans' arrival had shattered their lives for good.

But not everyone was unhappy. Edric the Wild, after receiving a promise of safe passage from William, had submitted. Gospatric had done the same but had been prudent enough to stay in Cumbria. William was satisfied now the North was under his control. Nothing much of it remained, but it would recover eventually, and the lessons learned would last the northerners for decades to come. But first, he had to journey to Stafford, razing every town and village on the way, after which, he would put down another insurrection and build yet another castle before heading south for Winchester, the Easter court and Matilda.

After Stafford, the wasting stopped, and the journey continued to Salisbury, just twenty-five miles short of William's final destination, Winchester. He brought his army to a halt to disband it. With the kingdom finally subdued, his men could go back to their new homes for a much-needed rest.

When they arrived in Salisbury, William had his men gather in the town square to address them.

'Congratulations, men. I thank you for your hard work. We have finally pacified the kingdom. Thanks to your efforts, there will be no more trouble from the English. As I promised, you will be well rewarded for your efforts,' and here he paused, before adding, 'including those who challenged me in Yorkshire when the going was hard.

'You, too, shall leave with your rewards, but only after you have completed another forty days service.' He gave the men one of his icy stares as if to challenge them to dare to oppose him. The square remained silent. No one made a sound.

'I'm glad we understand one another,' William said. 'Dismissed.'

William disappeared into the great hall and left the men to mill about in the square. They had plenty to say to each other.

'What will you do now, Walter?' Pomeroy asked his friend.

'I'm going home to Ada and the children. I've had enough of this country, which is why I've renounced my earldom.'

Pomeroy did not conceal his surprise at Walter's announcement.

'I think there's too much innocent blood on my hands in this kingdom,' Gherbod said.

'Have you told the king yet?'

'Yes. He was surprised. But at least he knew I meant no offence and appeared to understand my thinking. It made things easier for me, my not being the only one to renounce titles and land, but it's unsettled him. Quite a few of us are thinking of becoming monks by way of atonement.'

Again, Pomeroy could not hide his surprise.

'Will you be joining them, Walter?'

'Not yet. Perhaps one day. For the moment, I just want to get back to Flanders and see my family.'

'It's been good knowing you, Walter. I wish you a speedy journey, and I wish you good fortune.'

'And the same to you, Ralph. You've done well here. Long may it continue.'

The two men hugged and parted company, each heading for home. On his journey back to Berie, Pomeroy reflected on his friend's words. He found Gherbod's feelings for his family touching, and he soon thought of his younger days back in Normandy with his hateful brothers and his drunken father. He thought of the last time he was with them. The memory was not a pleasant one.

It was one of those evenings that occur more often at this time of the year. It was early spring, and the campaign season had ended. His father grew more restless every day and more drunk every evening until one evening, the storm raged. The old man had drunk copious amounts of wine and grown more irritated as the evening wore on.

As he returned to his place after throwing a few logs on the fire, he tripped on a flagstone as he passed Ralph.

'You tripped me, you little swine,' he snarled at Ralph.

'I wouldn't dream of such a thing, father,' the young man replied.

'He did, father, he did. I saw him,' Geoffrey, the eldest and favourite son, said.

'So did I,' said Hugh.

'And me too,' Stephen, youngest of the three, said.

His father lurched towards him, but little Ralph was too quick for the old drunk, although not too fast for his brothers. Although he was off the bench instantly, Geoffrey grabbed his arm, and the other two soon had him in their grip.

'Got him, father. Got him,' Geoffrey said. Geoffrey was a good seven years older than Ralph and now a man. It took little effort to overpower him.

'I'll have you now, you little bastard,' his father said, the irony of the insult lost on him.

His father drove his fist hard into his son's face as his brothers held him, and Ralph screamed in pain. Laughing, the brothers let go of him and kicked his backside as he made for the door. Pomeroy never forgot the pain and the humiliation.

He remembered hearing his father call after his mother, 'Where are you going? Don't you dare go after him. Come here, you bitch.'

The sound of his father charging after his mother and his brother's laughter as they followed. He ran one way, his mother another. He heard her cry in pain when his father caught her and beat her, shouting and cursing with every blow.

Terrified, Ralph made himself comfortable in the stable. After a while, the beating and crying stopped, and he fell asleep once he was warm. When he awoke with no idea of the time but a ravenous hunger, he went to the kitchen to get something to eat.

As stealthily as possible, Ralph made his way towards the kitchen, keeping close to the castle walls. He doubted if anyone inside could hear him, but there were sentries to consider. When partway there, he heard a peculiar noise but continued on his way. Getting closer, he realised it was a woman struggling.

Ralph quickened his pace and burst into the gloomy kitchen, which was illuminated by the light of a single candle. In the gloom, he discovered his father trying to rape the maid. He felt the anger surge through every part of his being, and although his ear was still ringing and his lips still swelling from his beating, he was determined to do something.

'What are you doing here, you little turd?' his father said, still trying to rip off the maid's clothes with one hand while covering her mouth with the other.

'I could ask you the same question,' Ralph said, eyeing the maid.

'A man needs entertainment. Your frigid mother provides none, and as the wench here was asking for it, I thought I'd oblige her.' His father grinned like a daemon.

It was then Ralph sprang at his father, striking with the first thing that came to hand. In just a few moments, Ralph's father fell back against the kitchen wall, groaning and clutching his stomach.

'Thank you, master,' the maid said, looking at him as if for permission. She grabbed a skillet and struck Ralph's father hard across the head with all the force she could muster. There was a clang as metal clashed with bone and her assailant became her victim. She kicked Ralph's father hard, again and again, until Ralph dragged her away. He looked at his father lying helpless and, for the first time, felt free from his temper. It surprised him to discover violence so liberating.

'Stay here,' he told the maid. 'And don't move.'

Ralph went to his parents' chamber and ransacked the place for anything of value, waking his mother.

'Ralph, what are you doing?' she said.

'I'm leaving. I can't stay here. I've just attacked father, and he's badly hurt.'

'What have you done? Oh my God, where is he?'

'He's in the kitchen. He was trying to rape a maid, so I taught him a lesson,' Ralph said, filling a sack with anything that looked of value.

'I must go to him,' his mother said.

'No. Leave him.'

'I must.'

'Well, don't wake my brothers and don't call the guards. I have to get out of here. You can't protect me, and I can't protect myself here, where I have no friends. I'm leaving, and I'm going to make my fortune.'

'I'll talk to you later,' she said, making off for the kitchen.

While his mother rushed to see her husband, Ralph collected his armour, his sword, and some more valuables. He crossed the courtyard and, in the darkness, saddled up two horses, which he led back to the kitchen and tied to a post. He entered the kitchen to find his mother on her knees by his father's side. She was dabbing something on his head whilst embroiled in a heated conversation with the maid, who was describing what had happened. His father lay motionless where he had left him, blood pooling on the floor.

'Ralph, what have you done?' his mother said, her voice laden with anguish, her eyes filled with horror.

'I've saved your honour,' Ralph replied.

'You've almost killed your father,' she said.

'He deserved it. Not just for the way he treats me, but also for how he treats you. I've had enough. If he comes around, he'll kill me. I'm leaving now,' Ralph said.

'Get the priest,' his mother said.

'No. I'm going,' Ralph said. 'Are you coming with me?' he asked the maid.

'I've nowhere to go,' she answered.

'Do you think it wise to stay here?' Ralph said. He looked over at his parents as if to say, 'What do you think will happen when he comes round, and my brothers wake up?'

The maid said nothing.

'I'm leaving now. Are you coming with me?'

'Yes,' she said, getting to her feet.

'Ralph, you can't go,' his mother said.

'I certainly can't stay.'

His mother got to her feet, but Ralph and the maid were gone instantly. When she reached the kitchen door, she stopped and peered into the half-light of a moonlit courtyard, where she made out the silhouettes of riders making their way to the castle gate. She heard Ralph's voice over the clatter of the hooves when he ordered the sentries to open the gates.

'But it's not yet dawn, my lord.'

'I don't care. Open the gate.'

There was a creak as a sentry opened the gates, and Ralph passed through and was gone. By the time anybody else discovered what had happened, he was miles away.

But that was the nightmare side of my life.

That was in the past. Now he could look forward to a bright future. He thought about Tate and the children and made his mind up there and then. He would never be like his father. And his sons, even his stepsons, would never experience a father like the one he had had. *There'll be no drunken beatings, no molested servants. I'll find another way of ruling the roost. Perhaps then I'll be free of this guilt and anger.*

He sighed and enjoyed the warm spring sun on his face. Soon he would be home. The very word made him feel good. Tate would be waiting. She always seemed happy to meet him when he returned. He offered a silent prayer of thanks for his luck.

He felt the excitement rise as he thought of what lay ahead. When he arrived home, he was not disappointed. As soon as he arrived, Tate came out to meet him. It warmed his heart to see her. She was a vision. A servant took his horse, and the instant he had dismounted, she attempted to hug him. They both laughed as her new size presented an obstacle.

'Ralph, it's so good to have you back,' Tate said and kissed him.

He smiled and looked at her belly. 'How long now?' he asked.

'Not long,' she said. 'Six or eight weeks.'

'You will be here when he's born, won't you?'

'There's nowhere else I'd rather be,' he answered.

Arm in arm, they made their way to the hall, and when they entered, the boys were there with their nurse. Tate smiled at them and said, 'Look boys, your father's home.'

As one, they looked at him and one after another and said, 'Hello.'

Pomeroy studied them and smiled. Joscelin smiled back broadly, Ceolwulf and Cuthred too, but not so enthusiastically. The Norman was pleased to note the fear had left their eyes.

I'm home, he thought. *Where I belong.*

Chapter 46

Easter and the early morning April sun shone brightly on the ancient city of Winchester, even as rain showers fell. Gathered inside Winchester's Roman walls were the clerics of the Papal Legate who had travelled from Rome and dignitaries and ecclesiastics from England. They were there for William's second coronation, this time to be performed for the benefit of the Pope. Before the coronation formalities began, William called Archbishop Stigand into the castle's great hall. In the corridor outside, Stigand approached, wondering why the king had summoned him. *Perhaps he wants me to officiate,* he thought, although it seemed unlikely.

A guard opened a door. 'Archbishop Stigand, my lord,' he said.

'Send him in,' William replied.

Stigand entered in all his finery.

'Ah, Archbishop, there you are,' William greeted Stigand with a smile.

Stigand took a few paces into the hall before stopping at a respectful distance from his king, conscious that the guards, who would usually have stayed outside, had followed him in.

'You asked to see me,' the Archbishop said and shivered. The stone building seemed to have retained the cold of winter.

'Yes, I did. It's a question of irregularities,' William said.

'What do you mean?' Stigand asked, sounding surprised.

'You know too well, Stigand. Let me put it another way; you're a rich man, are you not? If I'm correct, after the king and the Godwinsons', you were the wealthiest man in the kingdom at the time of my arrival in England. And from what I understand, you've been getting richer ever since.'

'Oh,' Stigand said, beaming his vacuous smile, 'there's been a terrible misunderstanding. I'm nowhere near being one of the richest men in the country.'

'Not anymore, you're not. Your lands, goods and possessions are now the property of the crown.'

'What?'

'Don't worry, Stigand, I'm not persecuting you. Your brother, Bishop Ethelmer, has met with the same fate, as have a few more of your, what shall we call them, colleagues, associates, or accomplices?

'Take him away,' William said to the guards. 'He can have Brihtric's old residence, as he has no further need of it.'

The guards took an arm each and frog marched the Archbishop away. Within a few minutes of his last audience with the king, Stigand was a captive in a roughly constructed cell, in a crudely built fortification, from which there appeared to be no escape. Now in his early seventies, the Archbishop wondered if he would end his days as a prisoner, rotting away in captivity, like Brihtric, or if there might be the hope of salvation. While Stigand was in his new home pondering his future, William discussed the vacancy in Canterbury with Lanfranc.

'Ah, here you are. It's so good to see you again, old friend,' William said. He was genuinely pleased to see the Abbot. William's use of the term old friend put Lanfranc on his guard at once.

'It's good to see you, too,' the Abbot replied.

'I wanted to talk to you right away because I have an important offer to make you,' William said.

Lanfranc felt even more uncomfortable.

'I'm intrigued and excited. What is this offer? Do tell me,' the Abbot said.

'I need someone of great integrity. A man who stands above all others, especially in matter ecclesiastical,' William answered.

Oh, bugger. He's going to offer me the Archbishopric, Lanfranc thought. 'Ah, well, if you're asking me to recommend...'

'No, no, no, my friend,' William interrupted. 'You're too modest. Let me get to the point. Stigand has, shall we say, vacated his position.'

'I'm so sorry to hear that. I hope the Archbishop makes a speedy recovery and resumes his duties as soon as he is able.'

William looked perplexed. 'Why are you sorry to hear that, Lanfranc? You loathe the man. You told me yourself.'

'I think that recently he has had an epiphany,' Lanfranc smiled his gap-toothed grin. 'And you've said yourself; he's been extremely useful to you.'

'His time has passed, and I want you to replace him,' William said.

'I'm honoured,' Lanfranc said. 'But as much as I'd love to, I'm afraid my duties in Normandy require my presence.'

'Oh, don't worry about that. I'll take care of everything.'

Lanfranc said nothing, but he did look a little nauseous.

'Are you feeling unwell, Abbot?'

'I've not been feeling well for a while. My strength is failing me, and besides, I am unworthy of such a position.'

'Nonsense. I'm sure you're fit for the office or any other.'

'Please don't ask me to do this. I hate England and the English. Even the best of them are barbarians. Besides, I can't understand a word they say,' Lanfranc pleaded.

'Which is why you must accept my offer,' William replied. 'I need a strong man with conviction to put this unruly rabble in to order. Thomas of Bayeux will be Archbishop of York, so you'll have a little help.'

'Please, I beg you. Don't ask this of me. Ask anything else, and I'll gladly do your bidding, but please, not this.'

'Arrangements have been made with the Pope himself. Don't disappoint us, old friend,' William said.

'If I am not to disappoint you, there is something you must do,' Lanfranc replied. 'And that is, see to it, Canterbury holds primacy over York. You really can't consider Odo's protégée, Thomas, to be my equal.'

This sounded more like an order than a request to William, but still, he knew Lanfranc was right. One head was better than two when it came to leading.

'As you wish,' William said. 'Pope Alexander is looking forward to his old teacher becoming Archbishop.'

Realising there was nothing more to be said, Lanfranc made a shallow bow to his king. 'Thank you, my lord. The honour is mine.'

William smiled as if to say, yes, it is. 'You may go now,' he said.

In the Royal Chapel, clerics gathered from across the land and a few from further afar. Amongst them was Erminfrid of Sion, the only cardinal to speak in defence of King Harold at his hearing in the Vatican some years before. Other members of the Papal Legate included Peter and John Minutus. William would hold the council first, after which he would have his coronation.

Stigand's dismissal and the appointments of Lanfranc and Thomas of Bayeux were announced to the gathering of clergy, and so were other removals from office and nominations. By the time the Council finished its business, just an hour after convening, only the aged Bishop Siward of Rochester and the saintly Bishop Wulfstan of Worcester survived the purge of the English higher churchmen. Bishop Wulfstan, a firm advocate of manumission, hoped his new foreign king, no believer in slavery, would support him in his mission to free every thrall in the kingdom. For Wulfstan, a difficult road lay ahead.

Chapter 47

The day after William had worked through the dismissals of most of the remaining English clergy, the Papal coronation began. Those few English clerics still holding office remained as Norman nobles streamed into the minster. Some of those present would become the most powerful in Christendom. Some were subjugated nobles or regal hostages taken during on campaign.

Matilda was there with the children to watch the grand occasion; having missed William's first crowning, they were delighted to see him as the centre of attention, the most important man in the land, fawned on by everyone.

Also in attendance were the Dowager, Queen Edith, looking pale and cool as marble and just as cold. Harding, her steward, was, as ever, by her side. To his mind, this second coronation was another nail in the kingdom's coffin. He looked at the surrounding faces and recognised few from five years before. As he had suspected for a while but now knew, resistance to the new regime was futile. William was here to stay, and nothing the English could do would shift him.

Close to Edith sat her nephew, Ulf, and his friend Thorkell. William had held them hostage since their capture in Exeter, wheeled out at court for the amusement of guests. Both had vowed that someday, somewhere, somehow, they would avenge Harold, no matter how long it took.

Waltheof and Judith, William's niece and newly betrothed, were standing where William had placed them with his family. Edric the Wild was with them, but Gospatric was still busy squabbling with King Malcolm in the North. It shocked the English to learn that they were to have two new archbishops, and neither of them would be fellow countrymen.

Erminfrid presided over the coronation, with due formality and solely in Latin. Once the ceremony was over, the king and his guests made their way to the Great Hall for a banquet. The expected crowds jostling for glimpses of their king failed to appear, and the Normans present in the gathering were the only ones to raise a cheer.

William's banquet was a lavish affair with course after course of steaming hot dishes, and the Normans had a wonderful time. But the English counted the hours. Once the food had stopped coming, Erminfrid, the guest of honour, leaned over to William on the high table. 'May we have a word?' he said.

'Of course,' William replied.

Cardinal Erminfrid, a tall, thin, ascetic looking man with a long face and prominent forehead, did the talking while the other two cardinals, John and Peter, sat in silent observation. Erminfrid had the presence of a man of courage, integrity and, oddly, innocence. He had in his possession a sealed parchment, which he presented to William.

'No need to read it now,' he said. 'It's about your penance and that of your army, of course. Pope Alexander has instructed me to inform you; you must complete atonement for the sins of the Conquest of England. Namely, homicide, adultery, rape, fornication, and violation of church property. You must repair any damage and restore to their owners all their goods.' Erminfrid gave William a damning look.

The king was dumbfounded and stared at Erminfrid, a quiet rage, his face turning a deeper red.

Erminfrid continued, 'You'll find there are differing amounts of time to be spent serving penance depending on where the sinful acts were performed. You'll see it's all in here,' Erminfrid said, handing the scroll over to William.

'There is penance for those who sinned at the Battle of Hastings. Penance for those who sinned between Hastings and your coronation on Christmas day. For those who sinned after your coronation, there will also be a special penance.' Erminfrid said with the most solemn expression.

'It's all there. Everything you need to know,' Erminfrid added.

Without looking at it, William put the scroll down on the table.

'Is that it?' William asked, his anger showing.

'We will talk about the promises you made to the Pope in return for his support,' Erminfrid added. His smile left his face as he looked accusingly at William. 'A lot of good Christians died so you could wear the crown of England.'

'I'm aware of that, your eminence,' William replied. 'But I know nothing of any promises made to Pope Alexander. Besides, haven't I already sent him enough gifts?'

'You've sent him many little gifts, and for all of them, he is profoundly grateful,' Erminfrid replied. 'But the question is, without his help, would you have enjoyed your victory?'

'It's heart-warming to hear the Pope is grateful for my little gifts, and I'm grateful for his support in my rightful claim to the crown,' William hissed. 'You might also remember the English Church was in a dire state and drifting towards the views of the Greeks. Married priests, celebrating mass in English, and the bible too, available in English. Well, we're curing all of that. Soon my kingdom will be in line with Rome, something our beloved Pope failed to achieve. And you come here waving a scroll around and telling me my men and I have to atone for our sins.'

'I can see this is a subject for another day,' Erminfrid said.

'Or not at all. Good day, your eminence.'

'Good day, my lord.'

William sat seething on his throne with Matilda by his side. She had remained silent through all the proceedings, maintaining a quiet dignity befitting a queen. Now they were alone together, she became a different creature.

'Who does he think he is?' Matilda snapped, unable to conceal her fury. 'How dare he talk to you like that?'

'He's a cardinal on an errand for the Pope. When he talks to me, it is the Pope who is speaking.'

'Send him packing to Rome then, at once. The stupid man. And as for the Pope, didn't he know people would get killed in battle? He gave you his blessing. Now he orders you to make atonement. It's outrageous. I'm speechless,' Matilda said before calming down and recomposing herself.

'He needs putting in his place,' she said, still agitated.

'Don't concern yourself with the cardinal, my dear. I'll soon have him off my back, and anyway, if all I have to do is give the Pope a few more trinkets, I can easily arrange it.'

'If you say so, Will,' she said.

'England is now mine. After all this time, it's mine. From the English Channel to the Scottish border and from the Irish sea to the North Sea.'

'I'm so happy for you, Will,' said Matilda. 'As I imagine, we all are.'

'Not all. Some of the English are far from happy.'

'But our men are content?'

'They aren't restless. Put it that way just so long as I keep their respect. There were times when I thought I would lose that, and between you and me, respect is something no king can do without. Now we have subdued the north, things will settle down right across the land. I have more to give, but not too much to any one man, or they might think they don't need me. Neither can I hold back, or they'll end up hating me and perhaps rebel. The trick is to give each man just enough, so he thinks he's doing well and is content with that.

'And so many of them do extremely well, my dear. There's no reason to fear the English, and our men are content. Rebellious malcontents can cause trouble, but nothing too serious.'

'You don't fear a grab for the crown?'

'Why would I?'

'You have two half-brothers and so many cousins, Will.'

'That's true, but they're all on my mother's side of the family,' William replied with a knowing smile. 'They have no legitimate claim to the throne.'

That night in bed, Matilda lay awake, mulling things over in her mind. The conversation came up, and she started, as she realised that deep down, William knew all along, his claim to the throne through his great aunt Emma was fallacious.She thought of the blood William had spilt over the years. What had it all been for? Her husband's avarice?

William woke with a start. His hand moved towards the dagger under his pillow. Once again, something had awoken him, but he couldn't imagine what. In the predawn half-light, everything was still. He raised his head and looked in the direction where he thought he had seen his former rival to the crown. There was nothing to be seen. A cock crowed and supposed that was what had disturbed him. Satisfied there was nothing there, he withdrew his hand from beneath his pillow and closed his eyes. But it was growing light, and the dawn chorus had started; William always had difficulty sleeping once the sun was up.

He turned his back to the window and curled up next to Matilda, who stirred a little. He slipped his arms around her and immediately relaxed, and, feeling safe, once more, he fell asleep. William was looking forward to the coming year and a time of peace and prosperity. *How different things are from this time last year. I've put down the uprising, and the English are well and truly subjugated. The Church is under Norman control, and my men are enjoying the fruits of their labour.* With those reassuring thoughts in his head, William fell into a deep and pleasurable sleep.

Chapter 48

Lady Gytha arrived at the quays in Roskilde to supervise the loading of her baggage onto King Swein's longship before embarking on her journey back to England. She would sail with the Danish Fleet, which was on its way to free the kingdom of its tyrant. Edyth, her granddaughter Gytha, and Father Edmund, an old family friend, were there to say goodbye. Eadric the Steersman would sail in the Sea Wolf alongside her to Ely.

The quays were busy as thousands of men embarked on hundreds of ships. Gytha talked to one of the crew when a burly sailor pushed past her.

'You. Watch where you're going?' she called after him. The man turned and faced her. By his expression, he was about to say something offensive when he realised who Lady Gytha was.

'I'm so sorry,' he said, sounding sincere. 'I didn't see you there, my lady. The fault was entirely mine.' He beamed a huge smile at her. It would not do to make an enemy of King Swein's aunt.

Gytha nodded her acceptance graciously, and the man went on his way, climbing aboard the ship next but one to King Swein's. She watched him go. There was something about him that caught her eye; his boyish good looks reminded her of the young men she knew in her youth. And she had noticed the unusual algiz pendant on a leather cord around his neck.

Once the ships were laden with soldiers and supplies, King Swein appeared, boarded his longship, and prepared to lead his fleet to England. After Swein barked out a few orders, the crew set sail, and sixty oarsmen pulled hard to make time. The rest of the fleet followed, and they were soon clear of the harbour.

Gytha watched the quays of Roskilde disappear as the fleet made its way across the fjord. She looked on from King Swein's ship as he sailed towards England. Unbeknown to her, Trygve Roarson was sailing with them, leaving his new concubine, Elfwyn Merlesweinsdaughter, behind in his village. Fat bellied with Whitgar's baby and broken-hearted, the disconsolate Englishwoman prayed every day someone would rescue her and every day, her prayers went unanswered.

Edyth, Lady Gytha's daughter-in-law, waved from the shore with Father Edmund. During their time in Denmark, they had enjoyed the generous hospitality of King Swein. Now Gytha was sailing west with him to meet up with the rest of his army in East Anglia. She had hoped her grandsons, Edmund, and Godwin, would bring support from Ireland, but their failure to win a battle and a lack of funds meant they were stuck in Ireland for the time being. They planned to join the fray later in the year. Also in Ireland were Aldytha and Harold, her infant son, Edmund, and Godwin's half-brother. The brothers were unaware of Aldytha and Harold's presence; she kept out well of their way. But none of this, for the moment, was Gytha's concern. It was what was happening in England now that interested her. In one part of the country, things were about to change dramatically.

In the morning, at Thurold's Hall, a cry for help pierced the dawn chorus, silencing every bird for miles around.

'Help. Help. Thurold is dead,' Morwenna yelled.

Whitgar, Bondi, Sherilda and others rushed to Morwenna's bedroom.

Bondi made a cursory examination of the body, 'I'm afraid Morwenna's right. Thurold has passed away. God rest his soul.'

Bondi saw the shock written on the faces of those around him, all except Sherilda, who he thought was looking at him accusingly. As his eyes met hers, she looked away.

'But how did he die?' Whitgar asked.

'He must just have died of apoplexy or something. Perhaps he choked,' Bondi suggested.

'Better find a priest,' Whitgar said. 'There's nothing we can do.'

'Best get dressed and come to the hall,' Sherilda said to Morwenna.

While they were in the hall waiting for the priest, a messenger arrived from Lady Gytha. Bondi invited him in.

'Lady Gytha sent me with a message for Shire Reeve Merleswein, but I understand he's passed away.'

On hearing this, Morwenna sobbed.

'She is Morwenna Merlesweinsdaughter, and her husband has just died in his sleep,' Bondi explained.

'I'm sorry to hear that,' the messenger answered, unsure of what to do next.

'Perhaps you could give us Lady Gytha's message,' Bondi said.

'Yes. The Danes should arrive at Ely soon. Lady Gytha wanted Merleswein to gather as many supporters as possible and meet her there. Edgar Atheling, Earls Edwin, Morcar, Gospatric and Sigur should answer the call. We shall have an army powerful enough to dislodge William and send him packing.'

'What will happen now?' the messenger said.

'Tell Lady Gytha, Bondi Wynstanson promises he will arrange everything as she hoped. I'll get word to Merleswein's men, and we'll meet her at Ely.'

'Very well. With your permission, I'll leave for Ely and convey your message to Lady Gytha.'

'Aren't you going to stay for something to eat?'

'No, thank you.' the messenger said.

'God be with you,' Morwenna said as the messenger left.

'Whitgar and I will leave shortly for Ely. Will you be coming with us?' Bondi said.

'Yes, I'll arrange for Sherilda to take the children to Scotland first, and we need to put Thurold in his grave.'

'Good. Let's make preparations.'

Morwenna arranged for the priest to collect the body, and before sunset, Thurold's corpse was waiting in St. Dunstan's, and his grave was dug, ready for burial the next day. Morwenna had explained the urgency of the situation to the priest. 'Speed is of the essence,' she said. 'The Normans might be here soon, so we need to go to Ely to join the Danes. I know it must appear unseemly, but we have no choice. And Thurold was such a wonderful husband too.'

'I'm sure he'd understand, my lady. These are difficult times,' the priest had said.

Morwenna organised a ship for Sherilda and the children to travel to Scotland the following day, immediately after Thurold's funeral. After some haggling and an exorbitant fee, a local trader agreed to take passengers up to Edinburgh. They were to meet on the quay at noon.

The day proved a busy one. There was the funeral and then the goodbyes at the quayside. After which, Sherilda and the children departed, heartbroken for Scotland.

'You have Sherilda to look after you,' Morwenna said to the children. 'And Sebbi, to take care of you. Remember, in just a few days, you'll be safe in King Malcolm's court.'

Morwenna, Bondi, and Whitgar watched them leave.

'I hate doing this, Bondi,' Morwenna said. 'I'm sick of saying goodbye to them, and I'm not sure which one suffers most. Godric's only three, and he doesn't know what's happening. Godwin seems only too aware and Godgifu even more so. Those extra few years at their age seem to make all the difference.'

'Just concentrate on getting through the next few months, and then you'll see them again,' Bondi said.

'I won't be doing this again, Bondi. I've said too many goodbyes to them.'

'Come on then,' Whitgar said. 'Time to go.'

The three mounted their horses and set off for Ely. Travelling through the flat countryside in the early May sunshine was a pleasure. Bondi and Whitgar thought back to their journey earlier in the year, which had been so different. Blossom had replaced the snow, and a cool breeze blew instead of an icy wind, and the horses made easy going of the terrain. They had pack horses too, which meant there was no shortage of provisions, and a couple of tents guaranteed shelter for the night wherever they were.

After two overnight stays, the three arrived at Belsars Hill, where they could find a ferryboat over to the Isle of Ely. They enjoyed a short quarter of an hour's journey and reached their destination to discover others there on the same mission. They were in great spirits as they made camp close to Ely's minster. Morwenna started a cooking fire while Bondi and Whitgar put up the tents. Soon they were sitting around the campfire eating freshly cooked wildfowl.

'This food smells appetising. Better than the swamp or whatever you call it,' Bondi said, remarking on the smell of the Fens, which smelled of rotten eggs.

They tucked into their meals and discussed the situation, taking generous swigs of the local cider as they did so.

'It feels like a new start,' Bondi said. 'The summer's here, and the Danes should soon be arriving. More and more of our men are turning up all the time. We'll show the Normans a thing or two.'

'I'm looking forward to our first encounter already,' Morwenna replied.

'And this entire island is a fortress,' Bondi said. 'They'll never be able to reach us here.'

'It's big enough to support an army, too,' Morwenna said.

Whitgar thought, although it was a joy to see them together as a couple, it was also a constant reminder that Elfwyn was somewhere else. While he was deep in thought, Morwenna caught his eye.

'You look far away,' Whitgar. 'And sad. Are you thinking of Elfwyn?'

'Yes, and I think she's still alive,' he said.

'So do I.'

Bondi was not so sure and so held his tongue.

'It's been a long time,' Whitgar said.

'It certainly seems like it.'

'Six or seven months,' Whitgar said. 'It seems like years.'

'I'm convinced, wherever she is, as soon as she's able, she'll send word,' Bondi said, hoping to bring the conversation to an end. 'Let's have one last drink of cider before we go to bed.'

Bondi, Morwenna, and Whitgar sat by the shore, watching with excitement as the Danish fleet arrived at Ely.

'What a wonderful sight these longships make,' Bondi said as they came into view.

Whitgar and Morwenna could not agree more. In full sail and with colourful shields lined up along the sides of every ship, making a glorious spectacle with the golden May sunshine picking out the colours perfectly. Built in the same long sleek fashion, each one with an individual figurehead on its prow, all of them fearsome, designed to strike terror into the hearts of enemies. Dragons and mythical stared out at mere mortals, inducing fear in the timid and brave alike. All were brightly coloured and imaginatively carved. Some had inlaid gold decorations to provoke jealousy in an onlooker and make them tempted to steal. None did.

'Is that King Swein's ship?' Morwenna asked.

'Yes. It must be,' she heard a familiar voice say. She turned to discover Edwin and Morcar had joined them. They were still dressed all in green.

They politely exchanged greetings.

'We've been here a couple of days,' Edwin said. 'We've come to join the final push and get William out for good.'

'I thought you were Green Men of the woods,' Bondi said.

'We weren't having much luck with that,' Edwin said.

'Perhaps that will change now,' Bondi said.

The group looked out over the water to see a colossal longship ship at the head of the flotilla. It made an imposing sight with a black raven on a red and gold sail. Its prow, a golden-headed dragon with sharp white teeth in a snarling red-lipped mouth, was as fearsome as any monster could be. As the longship drew closer, they could make out a man who they knew must be King Swein and beside him a tall woman with a long grey plait that hung down to her waist.

'Is that Lady Gytha,' Morwenna said.

'You're right. It is. Let's meet her.'

At the mention of Gytha's name, Edwin and Morcar became alarmed. They had always found Lady Gytha intimidating but followed Morwenna, Bondi and Whitgar to the shore, where Swein drove his longship onto a sandy beach. He leapt ashore and waited for Lady Gytha to be lowered down by his side. As they walked up to the assembled dignitaries waiting to greet them, Swein noticed two men dressed head to foot in green.

'I'll introduce you to the kingdom's favourite earls,' Lady Gytha said.

'How wonderful to see you again, Edwin, and you too, Morcar,' she said. 'This is my nephew, King Swein of Denmark.'

'It's good to meet you. I've heard so much about you,' said Swein, crushing both men with a hug.

'What have you been doing since last we met?' Lady Gytha asked. 'Anything?'

'We have become the wild men,' Edwin said, beaming with pride and pleased with himself.

'And what are the wild men when they're about?' Gytha asked.

'We are the wild men who make William's life a misery,' Edwin replied.

'Wild men,' Gytha said wistfully. 'I wouldn't have described you as either.'

Edwin and Morcar looked crestfallen.

'Green,' Gytha said, looking Edwin and Morcar up and down. 'That's not my favourite colour.' Gytha leaned forward and whispered in the manner of someone offering advice, 'don't stand still for too long; you'll have birds nesting in your hair.'

She moved on and introduced Morwenna. 'This is Morwenna Merlesweinsdaughter,' Gytha said. 'Merleswein was a great friend of Harold's.'

Morwenna bowed.

'Is your father here somewhere?' Swein enquired.

'No, he's not. The Normans killed him.'

'I'm sure he is a great loss. Are you here to avenge him?'

'I'll do my best,' she said.

Swein smiled and nodded sagely.

'I'd like you to meet a former housecarl of Harold's,' Gytha said, introducing him to Bondi.

'Bondi,' Swein said. 'Aren't you the one whose exploits at Stamford Bridge are legend all over the north?'

'It seems so, my lord,' Bondi said, surprised to hear the word had travelled as far as the ear of a king.

'It's a privilege to meet you, Bondi. I hope you and your friends can feast with me tonight.'

'The privilege is mine,' Bondi said.

The introductions continued, and when they were over, people went about their business, filling in time until the evening.

At the end of a glorious May day, those lucky enough to be invited to Ely's Great Hall made their way to the feast, especially held by the shire reeve to Honour King Swein. Bondi, Morwenna and Whitgar were surprised to find themselves shown to the Dais and seated next to Gytha. As Morwenna took her place, her pendant swung free, and it caught Gytha's attention.

'How extraordinary,' Gytha said. 'I'd never seen a pendant like it until a few days ago, and now I see another that's the same.'

Morwenna's heart skipped a beat, and Whitgar listened to the conversation in case of news of Elfwyn. He was acutely aware of the pounding in his chest.

'Really,' she said. 'Do you remember where?'

'Oh, yes. Clearly. It was in Denmark around a sailor's neck. Why do you ask?'

'There is another just like this one, and it belongs to my sister, who we haven't seen for months.'

'And you think the man who I saw might know something?'

'Yes. I have to go to Denmark to find out,' Morwenna said.

'No need for that, my dear. He's here.'

'Could you point him out?'

'He's not here in the hall, but he came over with King Swein. He's one of Trygve's men. If you like,' Gytha said. 'I'll have a word with King Swein, and perhaps he'll make some enquiries.'

'I'd be so grateful,' Morwenna said.

'It's the least I can do.'

Morwenna turned to Whitgar. 'Did you hear that? Lady Gytha saw a Dane wearing an algiz the same as this,' she said, holding her pendant before him. 'And he's here in Ely. She's going to persuade King Swein to find out what the sailor's doing with it.'

'That's wonderful news,' Whitgar said. He could hardly contain himself. At last, there might be news of Elfwyn.

The next day they were sitting around a campfire when a Dane approached them. By his dress and demeanour, he was important.

'Hello,' the man said, addressing Morwenna. 'I am Trygve Roarson. I understand you wanted to know how one of my men got hold of this?' he said, holding out an algiz pendant.

'Oh, you've found it. Look, this is its twin,' Morwenna said, showing hers to Trygve.

'I'm indebted to you. One of my men found it and kept it for himself. Elfwyn will be delighted to have it returned.'

'So, you are Morwenna. Elfwyn has often spoken about you,' Trygve said.

Morwenna looked shocked.

'You know Elfwyn?' Morwenna said. 'Is she well? Where is she? What happened to her?'

'Wait,' Trygve smiled, holding up his hands. 'I can't answer all of your questions at once. What do you want to know first?'

'How is she?'

'She's in excellent health.'

Morwenna gave an enormous sigh and then asked, 'Where is she?'

'She's in Denmark. She would be here with me now, but she is safe at home.'

'Oh, that is good news,' Morwenna said. 'I'm surprised she didn't want to come with you.'

'Oh, she did.'

'I don't understand,' Morwenna asked.

'It's just that we thought it best that in her condition, she didn't travel.'

'What condition?' Morwenna asked, sounding alarmed.

'Of course, you don't know. She's expecting our baby any day now.'

'How did this happen?'

'We met in Lincolnshire when she tried to get back to her father's home. The Normans were everywhere, but I got her aboard my ship and to safety. I offered to drop her off, but she insisted she come to Denmark with me. How could I say no? We were madly in love. We would have invited you to the wedding, but travel across the sea is not easy in the winter.'

An angry Whitgar was about to get to his feet, but Bondi held him back.

Morwenna was speechless.

'I suppose this makes us kin,' said Trygve with a smile. 'You must come and visit whenever you like.'

'Yes, I will,' Morwenna said, still shocked and unable to think of anything else to say.

'I have to go now, but I'm sure our paths will cross again,' he said and disappeared.

'Do you think any of what he said is true?' Whitgar said.

'He has her pendant, and he knows something about her, so they must have met,' Morwenna said.

'But married and expecting a baby. It can't be true,' Whitgar said.

'He probably made the last bit up,' Bondi said.

'What if he didn't?' Whitgar said.

Morwenna joined in, 'When did you and Elfwyn…?'

'About nine months ago,' Whitgar answered.

'So, there might be two people we have to rescue,' Morwenna said. 'And the sooner, the better.'

'At least we know where she is,' Bondi said.

'But what can we do about it?' Whitgar said. 'How are we going to get there? We haven't got a ship.'

'No, we haven't,' Bondi said, looking out across the water to the Sea Wolf. 'But Eadric has.'

'That's a great idea, Bondi. But will he be up for it?' Whitgar asked.

'I'm certain. We just need to ask.'

'I'm sure he'd agree,' Morwenna said. 'We could have her home in a few days.'

'What do you mean, 'we,'' Bondi said.

Anger flashed in Morwenna's eyes. 'Elfwyn is my sister, in case you'd forgotten,' she said. 'And besides, people will be less suspicious of you if you're with a woman.'

Realising Morwenna had put him in his place, Bondi agreed. 'Yes, you're right, of course,' he answered.

'What are you grinning about?' he snapped at Whitgar.

'Nothing,' Whitgar said.

'Good,' Bondi answered. 'I think it's time we made plans.

Chapter 49

The North Sea had been as flat as a tabletop, and the crossing had been pleasant. Cutting through the milky grey water, the Sea Wolf carried Bondi, Morwenna and Whitgar past the Jutland peninsula, across the Kattegat and into the Roskilde Fjord. Now their destination was coming into view, Roskilde itself – high on a hill overlooking the harbour.

Morwenna slipped her hand into her tunic to check King Swein's letter was still there. It had been five days since they had left England, and she had made sure she had it in her possession every hour or so. With luck, it would bring an end to Elfwyn's incarceration. It was Lady Gytha who had made their mission possible. Morwenna had approached Lady Gytha in Ely. 'We think Trygve has abducted my sister Elfwyn. From what we understand, she's pregnant with Whitgar's baby, but Trygve thinks it's his. It should be born any day now. Elfwyn might already have given birth.'

For good measure, Morwenna added, 'It's outrageous that someone would drag away an English lady to be a slave in a far off country. Especially in her condition.'

Gytha studied the woman before her. She had first met Morwenna when she was a little girl. Merleswein had brought her to court with Elfwyn. The sisters were daughters of one of her son's best friends and probably his only true friend in the north. Merleswein had always shown the House of Godwin unswerving loyalty. Now was the time for that loyalty to be rewarded.

'Are you sure of this, Morwenna?

'Absolutely.'

'Well, we'll just have to get Elfwyn back then, won't we?' Gytha said.

'That would be wonderful.'

'I'll have a word with my nephew. I'm sure he won't be pleased to hear one of his men has carried off the daughter of one of his kinsman's best friends.'

'Thank you so much, my lady.'

A few hours after Morwenna had met with Lady Gytha, one of Swein's servants approached her. 'My King instructed me to give this to you,' the servant said, handing over a sealed scroll. 'You're to take it to Queen Tora, and she will help you with your sister's release. You are to sail with Eadric and his crew, and you must leave on the next tide.'

It seemed an age ago now and how easy it all seemed. Now they had arrived at their destination and soon could go home with Elfwyn. Within two hours of setting foot in Denmark, they stood before the formidable Queen Tora, sitting regally on her throne. At forty-five, she exercised her seniority with ease.

'We have a letter from King Swein, my lady,' Morwenna said, presenting the queen with the scroll.

Queen Tora took the letter, studied the seal as if she doubted its authenticity, opened it and read it, an enigmatic expression on her face.

'So, you've come in search of your sister?' She said when she looked up, her cold grey eyes looking directly into Morwenna's.

'That's correct, my lady,' Morwenna replied, holding her gaze.

'Bondi. You were one of King Harold's housecarls, weren't you?'

'Yes.'

'Aren't you the one who skewered a berserker on Stamford Bridge?'

'Yes,' he replied.

'He was a fine man. A great warrior, as was my first husband, King Harald. Our daughter, Maria, died of a broken heart when she heard the news of his death.'

'I'm sorry to hear about your daughter. The berserker and King Harald were noble warriors, but I am merely a soldier, and I serve my king without question.'

'And which king do you serve in these times, Bondi Wynstanson?'

'I serve the Atheling, Edgar.'

'Not King William?' she said, looking down her nose at him.

'No, my lady.'

She looked at him with barely disguised contempt.

'No matter. I will comply with King Swein's instructions, and you shall have Elfwyn returned. Jarl Trygve lives some way from here. I will have her brought to you. In the meantime, someone will show you to your quarters. Is there anything else I can do for you?'

'Would it be possible to see Lady Edyth?'

'I'm afraid she's not here at the moment. She's in Nakskov. It's quite a way from here.'

'Would it be possible to visit her?'

'No. It wouldn't. Is there anything else?'

As they were leaving, Tora called for a servant and whispered in his ear. The man left in a hurry.

A week passed, and there was no sign of Elfwyn. Although the English were guests at court, Tora did not place them on the high table but close to the door. The queen paid them no attention for the duration of their stay. If they made enquiries with any of the courtiers, they were always given the same answer. 'Queen Tora is dealing with the matter, and you shall see your sister in good time.'

And the days passed slowly, and with each sunset, a little hope died, only to be rekindled with each new dawn at the end of a sleepless night.

On the sixth day, Morwenna left the bowers and walked over to the great hall, where she met Bondi and Whitgar sitting talking on their usual bench by the door.

'Good morning.'

'Is it?'

'Get out of the wrong side of the bed?'

'It's been almost a week and no sign of Elfwyn,' Morwenna said.

'So that's it,' Bondi answered.

'What's taking so long?'

Bondi shrugged.

'Something is wrong,' Morwenna said. 'Let's ask Tora what's happening. I'm sick of being led a goose chase by this lot,' indicting the courtiers.

'What do you think, Bondi?' Whitgar said. 'I'm going mad sitting around here waiting and having no word of anything.'

'We'll insist on an audience with the Queen herself,' Bondi said. 'Come on. Let's strike while the iron's hot.'

'Where is she?'

'In her quarters, I think. Let's go.'

Morwenna and Whitgar followed Bondi to the queen's quarters. Outside the door stood two big, burly, armed guards.

'Queen Tora's English guests to see her,' Bondi said.

'She's not receiving any callers today,' the taller of the two said.

'Then we'll wait.'

'You'll be here a long time.'

'We haven't anything else to do.'

'Please yourself.'

The three prepared for a long wait and made small talk. After half an hour, the queen called a guard, who spent only a few seconds in her company before returning.

'The queen will see you now.'

The three entered the queen's quarters, where Tora appeared more austere than ever.

'You wanted to see me?'

'We were hoping to have heard news of Elfwyn by now, my lady,' Morwenna said.

'We too were hoping to have your sister with us by now, but she was too far into her confinement to move. I understand she is to give birth any day soon. Perhaps once the child is born, she'll be here.'

'Would it be possible to visit her? I'd love to be there for the birth. The baby would be my first nephew.'

'I'll arrange for someone to find you a boat to take you out there. It might take some time. Everyone has left for England, so there is a shortage of ships.'

'We could go in the Sea Wolf,' Morwenna suggested.

'Very well. There are many isles and inlets along the coast, and there are sandbanks everywhere, so it's difficult to find your way. I'll provide you with a guide.'

'That's very kind of you, my lady.'

'You may go now,' the queen said.

When they stepped outside, Bondi said, 'We'd better let Eadric know so he can prepare.'

The three began the walk down the busy street to the harbour when a woman's voice called out, 'Bondi. Bondi, is that you?'

Startled, Bondi searched the sea of faces. He knew the voice, but he couldn't place it.

'It is you.' They heard the voice again.

Bondi found himself face to face with Edyth Magnusdaughter, widow of the late King Harold.

'My lady,' he stammered. 'What are you doing here?'

Edyth laughed. 'I could ask you the same thing.'

'We're on our way to the harbour. We're going to let Eadric know we're going to see Elfwyn Merlesweinsdaughter. We'll be on our way to Nakskov as soon as the guide arrives.'

'Why are you going to Nakskov?'

'That's where she's staying, at Jarl Trygve's hall.'

'But Trygve lives in Aalborg,' Edyth said.

'What?' Morwenna said.

Edyth turned to her in surprise.

'I'm Morwenna, Elfwyn's sister.'

'Morwenna. I know your father. He was a great friend of Harold's,' Edyth said and noticed the change in Morwenna's expression. 'What is it?' Edyth asked, her eyes darting this way and that.

'Father is no longer with us. William's men killed him.'

'I'm so sorry to hear that. Harold held him in high regard.'

'Thank you. And now we want my sister back, and Tora's playing games with us.'

'She hates the English because of Stamford Bridge.'

'We thought as much. We also thought you'd gone away.'

'I had, but I had to come back to collect a few things'

'It's lucky for us you did.'

'Aalborg isn't too far from here and is easy to find. It's also on your way back to England. All you have to do is sail out of the bay and up Roskilde Fjord. When you've done that, carry on up Isefjord and when you leave it, head northwest. Then, when you get to the coast of Jutland, keep going north until you come to the mouth of the Limfjord. Head up there, and you can't miss Aalborg.

'When you leave Aalborg, if you keep going west, you come out onto the North Sea, but it's easy to get lost because of all the islands and fjords. You'd be better off returning to the Kattegat and getting to the North Sea that way.'

'Thank you so much,' Morwenna said.

'As much as I'd like to spend time with you, I'll have to go now,' Edyth said, glancing up and down the street. 'I've slipped away from my guards, and it won't be long before they find me.'

'Are you a prisoner here? Would you like to come back to England with us?' Morwenna offered.

'No, I'm not a prisoner. Tora just wanted to keep us apart. I'm going to Kyiv with my daughters, so England no longer has a part to play in my life. I couldn't face going back there anyway, not with William on the throne.'

'He won't be ruling for much longer,' Bondi said. 'Not if we have anything to do with it.'

'When you have an Englishman on the throne, I'll return.'

Bondi was about to say something when Edyth said, 'Here comes my escort. Good luck, and God be with you.' With this, accompanied by a chorus of goodbyes, she disappeared into the crowd. A few moments later, three armed men passed them by, looking for somebody.

'Let's get down to the Sea Wolf,' Bondi said.

Arriving at the busy harbour, it did not take long to find Eadric. They told him they had met Edyth and what she had to say.

'So the queen lied about where Elfwyn is?'

'That's right,' Bondi said.

'Let's leave then.'

'Wait for the guide. We don't want to alert Tora what we're up to,' Bondi said.

'I'll organize supplies and get the crew together,' Eadric said.

As they were talking, a man approached. 'Which one of you is Eadric?' he said.

'I am,' Eadric said.

'The queen has sent me. I am to be your guide.'

On the tide, with the Sea Wolf provisioned and the crew in their places, Elfwyn's rescuers sailed out of Roskilde harbour. The wind was gentle and progress slow until they reached Kattegat.

'You need to turn to the east now,' the Danish guide said.

'You don't say,' Eadric replied.

'Yes. You head east from here.'

'Shall I tell you where we're heading?' Eadric said.

The guide looked puzzled.

'I'm turning west, and you're going for a swim,' Eadric said, and before the guide could react, Eadric threw him overboard.

'I hope you can find your way home,' Eadric laughed. 'You seem a bit confused about directions.'

'I can't swim.'

'Well, now's the time to learn.'

Eadric set course for Aalborg, and the wind caught the sail, pushing them on until, during a glorious sunset, they reached the mouth of the Limfjord, where they drove up onto the beach and made camp for the night.

'We leave at dawn for Aalborg,' Eadric said.

No one disagreed.

Also heading for Aalborg were Trygve and his followers; one hundred and forty men in all. Queen Tora's servant had made good time on his errand to inform the jarl of the English visitors and their intention to rescue Elfwyn. Trygve was furious when he was told, and he and his men were on the Valkyrie within an hour of hearing the news.

Trygve had had a frustrating crossing, which only served to fuel his bad temper. Winds either blew in the wrong direction or were not strong enough for him. But as day dawned on the morning of the Sea Wolf's arrival in Aalborg, the Valkyrie was fast approaching the Danish coast.

'Have you noticed?' Bondi asked Whitgar.

'There are no fighting men to be seen. They're probably all in England with Trygve.'

'That's what I thought.'

As Aalborg did not have a harbour, Eadric drove up onto the beach. Bondi Whitgar and Morwenna were the first ashore, and the townsfolk looked alarmed as the crew poured off the ship, all armed to the teeth.

They approached an old man, who stood his ground, while the rest slipped away. Whitgar arrived first.

'Have you seen an English woman?' he asked.

The man feigned innocence.

'Where's the English woman?' Whitgar demanded to know, the tip of his sword at the man's throat.

The Dane was rigid with fear, the point of the sword pressing under his jaw. He mumbled something unintelligible and pointed up a street to a large wooden building Whitgar took to be Trygve's hall.

'If she's not there, we'll be back,' Whitgar said.

Whitgar led the men through the streets while women and old men looked on. They arrived at Trygve's hall to find two guards at the door.

'Out of the way,' Whitgar commanded as he approached.

The sentries exchanged a glance.

'There's a hundred of us and two of you. What are you going to do?'

The men opened the doors and let Whitgar pass.

Whitgar entered the hall to discover it looked little different from many others; built of timber, roof beams exposed, smoke from the central fire curling up through the thatched roof. Whitgar looked to his left and right and detected movement behind a heavy woollen curtain.

'Elfwyn,' he called.

A hand appeared and pulled the curtain aside to reveal Elfwyn, pale and wan, with a newborn baby in her arms.

Whitgar dropped his sword and shield, walked over to her, and held her in his arms.

'I thought I'd never see you again,' she said.

'I thought the same.'

The tears flowed down her cheeks, and Whitgar held her close.

'I've come to take you home.'

She took her head off his chest for a moment and turned her attention to her baby for an instant.

'Me and your son,' she said, looking into his eyes.

'My son?'

'Yes, he's yours. It was the first time.'

'Gather your things.'

'I'll help,' Elfwyn heard a woman's voice.

'Morwenna. You're here, too.'

'Of course.'

'And Bondi,' Elfwyn said on seeing the housecarl.

'What did you expect?'

There was an exchange of hugs and kisses and more tears and sighs of relief before Morwenna said, 'Let's get your things.'

Hurriedly, Elfwyn packed while Morwenna cradled her nephew. Soon, she had packed, and they were on their way.

'What shall I tell my master?' a servant asked.

'Tell your master, if I ever see him, I'll cut off his cock and ram it down his throat. After I've done that, I'll split him up the middle and feed his guts to the pigs. Then use his skull for a piss pot.'

'Very well, my lord,' the servant said, judging Whitgar to be a man not to tangle with.

The crowd that had gathered outside of Trygve's hall parted as the English left. They were agog at the audacity of their visitors, but no one raised a hand to stop them. Once Elfwyn, her baby, and Morwenna were aboard, the crew pushed off and made sail for England. Elfwyn and her baby made their way to the stern with Whitgar, and they sat down side by side. Elfwyn felt the ship's movement on the water, and relief washed over her.

'It's been horrible here,' she said and began crying. That bastard Trygve tricked me into getting on his boat. I met him in a church in Lincolnshire, and he offered to take me to meet Prince Osbjorn and instead, he brought me to Denmark. I've been a prisoner ever since.

'He says he loves me, and he thinks the baby is his.'

Elfwyn looked at Whitgar meaningfully, 'Not because I let him,' she said.

'He wants to call him Beorn,' she continued. But I can't stand the idea. He's not the father anyway. You are.'

'What would you like to call him?'

'I thought Guthrum, after your father.'

'Guthrum it is then,' Whitgar said, studying the tiny pink face of his son.

The journey was straightforward at first. Eadric followed the fjord along its course, but the route became more difficult as the banks fell away and islands appeared before them on either side.

'Do you know which side of these islands we have to pass?' Eadric asked.

Elfwyn said, 'I have no idea. It's been months since I was here. These waters lead out to the North Sea, though, I'm sure of that.'

'I've been to Denmark before, but I've never taken this route,' Eadric said. 'We'll just have to do our best. There are bound to be fishermen and traders about to ask the way. In the meantime, I'll take the channel directly ahead and hope we take the right direction.

The channel was wide now, at least ten miles wide, but narrowed between the island on their right and the mainland on their left. They sailed on, and after twenty-five miles, the channel narrowed again to about a mile wide. Onward they sailed, and again, the waters opened wide.

'I can't see a way through,' Eadric said as the land ahead seemed to close up.

Let's keep going until we get a better view,' Elfwyn said. 'I seem to remember coming through a very narrow straight that looked a lot like this.'

'Very well.'

They sailed on until the early evening, and Eadric ordered a man up to mast.

'There's a gap we can pass through,' he said when he came down. 'It looks like the North Sea on the other side.'

A cheer went up from the crew.

'Another hour, and we'll be in the open sea,' Whitgar said to Elfwyn. 'What do you think, Eadric?'

'We'll see when we get there.'

There were three miles to go to the straights when a ship passed through from the other side. Eadric fixed his gaze on the approaching vessel.

'That ship looks familiar. Look at the sail,' Eadric said.

Bondi, Morwenna, and Whitgar followed Eadric's gaze. The ship seemed to head straight for them. It was a warrior's ship; shields lined its sides. Its stripped sail emblazoned with the head of a fierce-looking Valkyrie.

'It's Trygve,' Elfwyn said. 'I'd know that sail anywhere. Do you think they'll recognise us?'

'I don't see why they should,' Eadric said. 'We sailed together from Denmark only a few weeks ago, but we were one ship amongst many.'

The crew of the Sea Wolf looked on at the Valkyrie, soon they would pass within a few yards of each other.

'Look.' Bondi said. 'There's that servant who was with the queen when we went to see her. Remember. She whispered something in his ear, and he slinked off.'

The servant was standing next to Trygve in the prow, staring hard at the Sea Wolf, suddenly changed expression and pointed. Trygve leaned into the servant for a few moments listening intently. He looked to where the servant pointed, and his eyes fixed on Morwenna.

'Elfwyn,' he bellowed. 'Elfwyn. Beorn.'

The ships passed each other, cutting through the water.

'Hide your faces,' Eadric ordered.

Everyone busied themselves, pretending to be getting on with something important.

'Too late. They're turning this way,' Bondi said.

Elfwyn stared in dread as the Valkyrie changed course.

Morwenna read the expression on her sister's face. 'Don't worry, he won't get his hands on you.'

Eadric leaned hard on the helm. 'Let's see if we can lose them amongst those islands,' he said, turning his ship towards another fjord. 'Man the oars.'

As the Sea Wolf made its escape, the Valkyrie turned to catch them.

'To your oars men,' Trygve ordered.

'They've kidnapped my woman and my son. I'll skin them alive when I get them.'

While Trygve ranted, the Sea Wolf sailed through a narrow channel between two islands. The Valkyrie had changed course and was now three-quarters of a mile behind them. When they had passed the island to their left, they sailed past a point on the island to the right. What they did now would be decisive.

A few islands were scattered in the sound. 'We could be anywhere,' Eadric said. This country seems full of fjords and the sea full of islands.'

As he spoke, the ship jarred over to one side and slowed suddenly before continuing on its way.

'What was that?' Bondi asked.

'It was a sandbank,' one of the crew chirped up.

'Get up the prow and keep an eye out for them,' Eadric replied.

Eadric leaned hard on the helm and headed to port.

'There's a gap down there we can get through before the Valkyrie gets here. They won't know where we've gone.'

'Where are you going?' Bondi asked.

'Along that channel. The Valkyrie is faster than the Sea Wolf but not so easy to manoeuvre.'

They continued up a channel that snaked to the left and right.

'Hard starboard,' the crewman in the prow called out, and Eadric responded. They sailed by a sandbank, which would have grounded them had they not changed direction.

'I think there's a way out ahead.'

'Get up the mast and see.'

'There might be a way out ahead. He turned his head and said, 'I think we've shaken off the Danes.'

'No, it's a spit of land. I can't see a way through.'

What had initially looked like sandbars from two islands turned was an isthmus connecting a peninsula. The land at either end of the isthmus was heavily wooded with silver birches. In the middle was scrubland, rising just a few feet above sea level and only five hundred yards across.

'What are we going to do now, Eadric? Any ideas?' Bondi said.

Eadric eyed the spit of land that barred their way.

'Move in closer to shore,' Eadric said, indicating a spot where the beach sloped gently to the water. 'But don't get too close.'

Eadric climbed out of the ship and waded a few yards onto inland.

He clambered up the sandy beach until he reached the scrubland.

'This spit looks to be a quarter of a mile wide at the most. As far as I can tell, beyond it lies the open sea.' He turned to his crew. 'Get your axes. Time to chop wood.'

A mass disembarking followed, and the men split up to chop down trees. Bondi and Whitgar stayed with Eadric, and the men brought back tree trunks cut to length. While some men made a cradle for the Sea Wolf, others laid a track for the ship to slide over.

Bondi, Whitgar and Morwenna helped with menial tasks but marvelled at how Eadric and his crew carried out their duties. After a couple of hours, the Sea Wolf was hauled into the cradle and secured with ropes. Now ready to be moved across the land, everyone pulled on the four lines attached to the cradle, and slowly it moved forward.

'Heave,' Eadric bellowed, and the Sea Wolf inched forward. Little by little, the men dragged the ship up the incline until they had hauled it up the slope, which now levelled out.

'Now you've enjoyed a rest; it's time to start work again,' Eadric said.

This time hauling, although challenging, was not as demanding as heaving the vessel up the bank. They made good time, and each man got on with his task, whether pulling the Sea Wolf, pulling up the birch trunks from behind the ship and placing them down in front, or cutting more timber. Each performed to his best. It was important the Danes did not catch them on land like a beached whale. If Trygve and his men caught them here in the open, it would be the end of their days.

Through the night, they laboured, until as the sun rose, they had only fifty yards to go. It was then Whitgar spotted a small fishing boat making its way across his line of vision. As it was within hailing distance of the shore, he ran out onto the beach and called out to them. The two men on board, father and son, by the look of them, looked astonished to see eighty men hauling a ship across the land. When Whitgar arrived at the shoreline, he thought the North sea looked suspiciously calm.

'Hello,' he called. 'Is this the North Sea?'

'No,' the older man answered.

'What is it then?'

'This is Nissum Bredning. The North Sea is that way. There is a narrow channel you have to pass through. Just sail in line with the beach here and when it falls away, just keep going in a straight line. You can't miss it.'

'Thanks, and good luck with your fishing.'

'Good luck with your fishing, too. Although I doubt if you'll catch anything there,' the fisherman said, nodding toward the Sea Wolf. 'Have you thought of casting your nets into the sea? You'll stand a better chance of catching something there.' The two men guffawed wildly and went on their way.

When Trygve had spotted the Sea Wolf, he had a feeling he had seen the ship before but could not remember where. When Tora's servant told him the Sea Wolf was the one Elfwyn's sister, and friends were using, he realised the ship had sailed with him from Roskilde with King Swein carrying Lady Gytha. *So she's behind this. I wonder how much Swein knows?*

Trygve had given the order to turn about and give chase, and although the Valkyrie had manoeuvred quickly, the Sea Wolf had slipped away. By the time he had passed the islands into a broader part of the fjord, the English had vanished. There were several directions they could have taken, and the odds of picking the right one were not favourable. But Trygve had expert knowledge of the waters and knew there would be no escape for the English. From where they were in the fjord, if they wanted to get out into the open sea, they would have to go through the Oddesund, the only channel that led to the Nissum Bredning, which in turn led to the Thyboron, beyond which was the North Sea. He would sail to Oddesund and wait there for his love and the baby. It would be impossible for the English to pass through the narrow channel without him seeing them, but if by some strange occurrence they did, he would catch them at the Thyboron Channel. There would be no escape.

The Valkyrie arrived at Oddesund just after dark and waited with two men on watch the entire night. They saw nothing. Trygve guessed the English would appear soon. It was just a matter of time.

As he and his crew waited for the Sea Wolf, a fishing boat approached, its two-man crew heading for the Oddesund to try the fishing on the other side.

'Good morning,' the older man greeted the crew of the Valkyrie. One or two of them called back in response.

'Are you looking for the Englishmen?' the fisherman called out.

'What do you know about any Englishmen?' Trygve yelled.

'They are dragging their ship across the spit between Helingso Drag and Lyngs Drag. If you hurry, you might catch them.'

Trygve's face paled with rage.

'Up anchor. Hoist the sail. Man the oars,' he roared.

The crew jumped to their places, and soon the Valkyrie was on its way.

'Those English and their tricks,' Trygve addressed the crew. 'They're scared to fight us, and now they're running away like cowards. But we'll catch them.'

The Valkyrie was gliding across the water at full speed, the wind in its sails and the men at the oars. The Sea Wolf was still on dry land, two hours' sailing time away.

'Heave. Heave,' Eadric called to men who had been pulling on ropes and carrying tree trunks all night.

They responded but feebly.

'Come on. Just a few feet to go, and we're on the bank. It'll be easy from there. Come on, heave.'

The men heaved and heaved again until the ship slipped down the gentle bank and its bow splashed into the water before settling.

Eadric and Bondi climbed aboard and untied the cradle from the ship. Once that was done, the crew pushed hard, and the sea wolf floated free of its support, and everyone climbed aboard, Morwenna helping Elfwyn with the baby.

'All we have to do now is steep the mast, and we can be on our way,' Eadric said.

The crew were already at their places and began raising the mast. Exhausted from their night's work, they made hard going of it. Once the mast was upright and secured, it was time to hoist the sail.

'Oh Christ,' Whitgar said. 'We've got company.'

All heads turned to see what they had all dreaded; the Valkyrie was bearing down on them fast.

'Hoist that sail,' Eadric ordered. But the crew did not need telling. Half a dozen men were already pulling hard on the halyard and raising the sail. The tide was already taking them out to sea.

'To your places and row,' he instructed the rest of his men. They were already on their way.

Elfwyn sat right at the back with the baby. Whitgar Bondi and Morwenna were with her. They were relieved when the sail was hoisted and caught the wind. The men rowed, and the Sea Wolf set off briskly toward the Thyboron Channel and the North Sea. With the current behind them, they were making good time. But so was the Valkyrie.

The race was on, but both crews were exhausted—the Valkyries from rowing for two hours and the Sea Wolf's from their all-night labours.

'She's gaining on us,' Bondi told Eadric.

Eadric looked to see Trygve at the prow of the ship glaring at him from two hundred years away.

'He'll never catch us on the open sea; we can dodge him all day. But here,' Eadric looked around with a hopeless expression on his face. 'I don't know,' he said. 'And there's only one way out.'

'We'd better get a move on then,' Bondi said.

With its tired crew, the Valkyrie was still gaining on the Sea Wolf. As each minute passed, the Danes grew closer, and the features of Trygve's face grew clear. Soon they would be within arrow range if the crew's strength held out.

The Sea Wolf caught a sandbar, and it jolted the crew about, but with a struggle, they managed to push themselves off.

'You, get up to the prow,' Eadric said, ordering the man who had the duty the previous day. 'And you,' he called to another man, get up the mast and keep your eyes open for sandbanks.'

The Sea Wolf was underway again, but the Valkyrie was gaining, although she lost a little distance turning to avoid the sandbank. With the space between the two ships closing, the first arrows struck the Sea Wolf.

'Row harder,' Eadric ordered. But the crew were exhausted and could summon no more extra energy.

'Come on, men. I can see the North Sea beckoning,' Eadric said, eyeing the white water of the Thyboron Channel.

'Starboard,' the man at the prow shouted. At the helm, Eadric responded.

'We're all right now,' the crewman called.

Eadric adjusted his course, making straight for the gap between the two headlands and the North Sea beyond. Bondi and Morwenna used their shields to protect him from the Danish arrows flying uncomfortably close as he hung onto the helm.

On the Valkyrie, Trygve could sense the English were going to escape. The contorted expression on his oarsman's faces as they rowed belied their exhaustion. But the archers were in range, and all that was needed was one final push, and Elfwyn would be his.

'Row! Row!' Trygve bellowed, and he even jumped up and down as he issued his orders, so desperate was he to capture his prey. But recklessness had got the better of caution, and there was a crashing sound as the Valkyrie struck a sandbank. The archers all lost their balance, and three of them fell overboard. Oarsmen slipped from their places, and Trygve fell to his knees.

'Everybody get overboard; we'll float her off,' Trygve said, with no concern for his crew.

'Quick. Now.'

With no enthusiasm, the crew climbed out of their ship. After two-and-a-half hours rowing they were exhausted. They were not keen to renew the chase by freeing the Valkyrie. Half-heartedly, while Trygve ranted and raved, they attempted to re-float their ship. But the tide was against them. It would be hours before they would be free and too late to intercept the Sea Wolf.

Stranded on the sandbank, Trygve watched as the Sea Wolf sailed, some of its crew looking back at him.

'You might have escaped today, but there will be other days, and you will not be so lucky then. I will have my wife and child back, and the rest of you will die.' Trygve's words were carried away on the wind. From the Sea Wolf, no words could be heard, but the tragic lonely figure of an angry Viking could be seen gesturing on the deck of his ship.

At the end of the fourth day, with the sun setting over England, the Sea Wolf approached the English coast, storks flew overhead, heading for home, disappearing into the sunset. At first, there were just a few and more and more, hundreds and then thousands. Over the gentle wind, Bondi could hear their wings beat and their calls. Soon they would join them in England and discover what fate had in store.

Lightning Source UK Ltd.
Milton Keynes UK
UKHW010727170622
404574UK00001B/140

9 781781 328699